The Science Fiction Century, Volume Two

By David G. Hartwell from Tom Doherty Associates

NONFICTION

Age of Wonders: Exploring the World of Science Fiction

EDITOR

Bodies of the Dead
Centaurus
The Ascent of Wonder (with Kathryn Cramer)
Spirits of Christmas (with Kathryn Cramer)
The Hard SF Renaissance (with Kathryn Cramer)
Christmas Forever
Christmas Magic
Christmas Stars
The Dark Descent
Foundations of Fear
Northern Stars (with Glenn Grant)
Northern Suns (with Glenn Grant)
The Science Fiction Century
The Screaming Skull
Visions of Wonder (with Milton T. Wolf)

Edited by **DAVID G. HARTWELL**

The Science Fiction Century, Volume Two

A Tom Doherty Associates Book

New York

The stories collected in *The Science Fiction Century, Volume Two*, and the previously published *The Science Fiction Century, Volume One*, were published together in hardcover as a single volume under the title *The Science Fiction Century* in November 1997.

THE SCIENCE FICTION CENTURY, VOLUME TWO

Copyright © 1997 by David G. Hartwell

Introduction copyright © 2003 by David G. Hartwell

Book design by Fritz Metsch

An Orb Book
Published by Tom Doherty Associates, LLC
175 Fifth Avenue
New York, NY 10010

www.tor.com

ISBN-13: 978-0-765-31492-5
ISBN-10: 0-765-31492-4

First Trade Paperback Edition: October 2006

Printed in the United States of America

0 9 8 7 6 5 4 3 2 1

Copyright Acknowledgments

Acknowledgments

*To Maron Waxman, Susan Ann Protter, Les Pockell, and
Kathryn Cramer, without whom this book would never
have been completed.*

I would like to acknowledge the significant presence of John W. Campbell, Isaac
Asimov, Robert A. Heinlein, and Arthur C. Clarke, and all the other science
fiction writers who are not reprinted in this book. I used their work to support
my argument for the consideration of science fiction as a worthwhile literature
in *The World Treasury of Science Fiction*. I used many of them again to illuminate and uphold the value of the hard SF tradition in *The Ascent of Wonder*. In
this book, I chose the work of other major writers, some of them less familiar,
some of them equally famous, so as not to allow my argument to get lost in the
particular aesthetic of SF that is so dominant in their work. But their presence
is here anyway, anyhow, even in the absence of representative examples of their
work.

Contents

Rooted as they are in the facts of contemporary life, the phantasies of even a second-rate writer of modern Science Fiction are incomparably richer, bolder, and stranger than the Utopian or Millennial imaginings of the past.

—ALDOUS HUXLEY

Science fiction is no more written for scientists than ghost stories are written for ghosts. Most frequently, the scientific dressing clothes fantasy. As fantasies are as meaningful as science, the phantasms of technology now fittingly embody our hopes and anxieties.

—BRIAN W. ALDISS

Introduction

Science fiction is a literature for people who value knowledge and who desire to understand how things work in the world and in the universe. In science fiction, knowledge is power and power is technology and technology is good and useful in improving the human condition. It is, by extension, a literature of empowerment. The lesson of the genre megatext—that body of genre literature that in aggregate embodies the standard plots, tropes, images, specialized diction, and clichés—is that one can solve problems through the application of knowledge of science and technology. By further extension, the SF megatext is an allegory of faith in science. Everyone knows there are science fiction addicts—I am one—and this is why: it expresses, represents, and confirms faith in science and reason.

The literary history of the twentieth century in the U.S. is significantly different to that of the U.K. in regard to science fiction. The tradition of H. G. Wells remained stronger, for longer, in the U.K., and although many of the works in the Wells tradition (the Scientific Romance tradition delineated by Brian Stableford in his fine book, *Scientific Romance in Britain, 1890–1950*) prior to 1950 are remembered today only by literary historians, it was not until the late 1940s, after the Second World War, that American SF became the primary model for the genre outside its own national boundaries. And as many critics have noted, there were and remained characteristic differences between American Science Fiction and British Scientific Romance even into and during the decades of international American dominance of the genre.

This has meant, among other things that the British tradition, while not acceptable to the Modernists from the beginning, was still a literary tradition that might aspire to high art, although it usually had other intentions.

This is clear in the resolution of the famous literary argument between H. G. Wells and Henry James at the start of the twentieth century. James, who was often referred to as Master by the Modernist writers of the day, carried the literary high ground and Wells declared that he was not an artist but a journalist. Wells did not so much desire to dominate literature as to dominate reality, so he ceded the territory of literary art to James and the Modernists.

At the time of the first edition of *The Science Fiction Century*, I thought everybody knew about this and I was wrong. Brian Aldiss and John Clute remarked at a conference shortly after the original publication that there was no apparent evidence for my assertion that SF was generally anti-Modernist. I promised them both that I would get around to writing up some of the evidence, and this revised introduction is my first attempt to do so. On the face of it, I never intended my statement to hold entirely for British SF, which has a different, although still strained, relationship with Modernism than the U.S. branch of the genre. And of course the New Wave of the 1960s stood for the injection of Modernist literary techniques and the abandonment of genre attitudes. The influence of the New Wave has been dominant in the U.K. ever since, as it has not in the U.S.

The idea that Modernist poetry is nonsense goes back a long way in SF. As early as the 1920s, at the very beginning of the fashion for Modernism in the United States, H. P. Lovecraft, a virulent anti-Modernist whose influence on SF writers in the 1930s and beyond is unquestionable, wrote a long parody of T. S. Eliot's *The Waste Land,* called "Waste Paper," and never reconciled himself to the new attitudes of fashionable literature. This response extends at least into the 1980s—Lester del Rey and I had more than one discussion in which he maintained stoutly that contemporary poetry had died in the 1930s, with the triumph of Modernist free verse. Del Rey remained an anti-Modernist to the end. So was John W. Campbell. So was Isaac Asimov. So is Orson Scott Card.

And from the 1920s to the late 1940s, one of the main voices raised outside the SF field in America against Modernism was that of the editor of the important little magazine, *Wings,* Stanton A. Coblentz, a minor poet and, coincidentally, a significant SF writer of the period. He is now more often remembered by graduate students and literary historians of twentieth-century American literature as the loser who led the vocal opposition than he is remembered as an SF writer or by SF readers. Coblentz was still mentioned in American literature graduate school courses at Columbia University in the late 1960s when I studied there.

Some of the attitudes of the field toward Modernism in the 1950s are apparent in the fiction. For example in the fantasy story "Stickney and the Critics" by Mildred Clingerman (*F&SF,* Feb. 1953), the dead poet Stickney (and it is not unlikely that Clingerman is alluding to the modernist poet Trumbull Stickney) has critics that interpret deep metaphors into his poetry, when in fact it is has literal correspondences. While of course this is an attack on Modernist criticism, not necessarily the writing itself, the clear implication is that the writing would be nonsense if it didn't have those literal referents. So I see the story, which was anthologized by Judith Merril, among others, as clearly anti-Modernist.

However, there have been notable defenders of Modernism in the American SF field, Alfred Bester and James Blish it seems to me were among the most prominent from the 1940s until the 1960s' advent of the New Wave. Bester left college in the late 1930s and famously bored some of the New York SF writers of the early 1940s with talk of the virtues of James Joyce. James Blish was an authentic Joyce scholar (he gave papers at academic conferences) but there is no noticeable influence of this in his science fiction or fantasy until perhaps, arguably, his late novel, *The Day After Judgment.* Bester got a job outside SF for almost a decade in the early 1940s and again for nearly fifteen years in the late 1950s, and James Blish moved to England in the mid-'60s. This would have been more comfortable for these writers because the American SF scene was not in general hospitable to Modernism or Modernist techniques until the 1970s.

The Milford Writing Workshops of the 1950s were an early injection of Modernist ideas about writing into SF, and in my opinion were the seeds that germinated to form the American New Wave. In any case, by the middle of the 1960s the idea that an individual style was of value in SF, as well as in mainstream writing, had caught hold, and since Modernism had lost most of its force and authority in high literary circles, over the next decade Modernism became merely a repository of techniques and attitudes that might be appropriated piecemeal by a science fiction writer. In particular the Modernist idea that fiction is properly about the inner life of a character in relatively ordinary circumstances took hold for the first time in SF, and by the 1980s had become a common mode in the field, though certainly not universal.

However, a substantial body of SF even today is not devoted to the illumination of character but to the external circumstances of the story. Much SF is about what actions a character takes and what happens in strange and unusual circumstances, not primarily about how someone feels about it.

Nevertheless, the genre has been strengthened and enriched immeasurably in my opinion by the proliferation of possibilities in literary treatment, and by the aesthetic conflicts and arguments that have ensued. For instance, the Humanist versus Cyberpunk arguments of the middle 1980s (see Michael Swanwick's essay, "A User's Guide to the Postmoderns" for coverage of that in medias res.).

Gregory Benford, a writer who has prominently appropriated chunks of Modernist technique and attitude in the service of his SF, wrote in response,

> I believe you're fundamentally right about classical SF opposing modernism, but with the caution that one must not mistake fuddy-duddy reactionism for theoretical difference. Many, like Lester del Rey, opposed modernism because they opposed the entire literary culture, or didn't know any better. Their critiques were not profound, but visceral.
>
> Further, the customary choice of "plain writing" because the landscapes of SF are already strange enough works only in a limited sense. The reaction of real people in such stories can have all the signatures of modernist modes, particularly in the rejection of a consensus epistemology. In Bester's narrative gyres we are swept along by people who themselves find their worlds wrenching. Conveying this requires more than the flat, clear prose of a Clarke or Niven—who nonetheless are stylists, too.

I quite agree with the second of Benford's paragraphs, but wish to say that although Del Rey's critique could be mistaken for shallowness, I believe it was not. Lester del Rey was an articulate and intelligent polemicist who hung out with contemporary poets in New York City in the 1930s and '40s, (in somewhat the same circles as Theodore Sturgeon did) and did know about Modernism, although his particular critique was generally and globally antiliterary in later years, a part I believe of his decision circa 1970 to become a marketer to the nonliterary popular culture of the mass market. His Del Rey Books period is not continuous with his earlier personality or intellectual stance.

Orson Scott Card went through a graduate school program in English Literature and has chosen to reject Modernism and its high art/low art distinctions by name, yet does not reject the entire literary culture—only that portion of it that maintains that SF is inherently second-rate, if I understand him correctly.

Furthermore, a large portion of the discourse about Modernism has been encoded in the SF versus the mainstream arguments that have persisted since the late 1930s, in which Modernism has rarely been mentioned by name.

Having now written at some length about this subject, I return to the object of this anthology, and these stories that show much of what was present in the fiction from the beginning to the end of the century just gone. I would like to point out that *The Science Fiction Century* was conceived as a companion volume to an earlier large anthology, *The World Treasury of Science Fiction*, and the two were originally to be sold together. The writers and stories in the *World Treasury* were a kind of penumbra to this book, in which the selection of writers and stories was, in addition to other purposes, meant to complement the earlier compilation. This is why there is so little overlap in writers between the two huge books. Together, they form a representative selection of world SF in the twentieth century. Since the *World Treasury* is now out of print, and *The Science*

Fiction Century is being republished as two mammoth volumes by Tor, I tell you this to explain why some obvious representative stories by masters of SF are not in evidence here. You hold in your hands only one part of a much larger possible selection formed in the mind of this editor; a selection from a glorious and terrible century, filled with wonder for those with eyes to see.

DAVID G. HARTWELL,
Pleasantville, N.Y.

The Science Fiction Century, Volume Two

Cordwainer Smith

Cordwainer Smith was the pseudonym of Paul M. A. Linebarger (1913–66), who wrote the first text on psychological warfare and was involved in sensitive government work while a professor of Asiatic politics from 1946 to 1966 in Washington, D.C. His pseudonym was kept a close secret during his lifetime. He went to college with L. Ron Hubbard, the famous pulp SF writer who invented Dianetics (later Scientology), and they published in the same literary magazine. There was apparently some real competitiveness in Linebarger, for he wrote an entire book manuscript (never published) in the late 1940s, at the same time his first SF story was published, on the science of mental health.

His science fiction was nearly all published between 1959 and 1963, and first collected in paperback between 1963 and 1968, then reassembled in 1975 and reissued, at which time serious interest in Smith began to grow. He is now considered a major figure in science fiction. Nearly all of Smith's science fiction takes place in a consistent future history, The Instrumentality of Mankind, comprising many stories (*The Rediscovery of Man* [1993] collects his complete short fiction) and one novel, *Norstrilia* (1975). The series chronicles events in the millennia-long struggle between the human Instrumentality and the Underpeople, intelligent animals biologically transformed into humanlike forms. A devout Christian, Smith built complex levels of religious allegory into his series.

The title of "Drunkboat" is an allusion to Arthur Rimbaud. It is a work that shows Cordwainer Smith's distinctive and unusual voice in science fiction.

DRUNKBOAT

Perhaps it is the saddest, maddest, wildest story in the whole long history of space. It is true that no one else had ever done anything like it before, to travel at such a distance, and at such speeds, and by such means. The hero looked like such an ordinary man—when people looked at him for the first time. The second time, ah! that was different.

And the heroine. Small she was, and ash-blonde, intelligent, perky, and hurt. Hurt—yes, that's the right word. She looked as though she needed comforting or helping, even when she was perfectly all right. Men felt more like men when she was near. Her name was Elizabeth.

Who would have thought that her name would ring loud and clear in the wild vomiting nothing which made up space$_3$?

He took an old, old rocket, of an ancient design. With it he outflew, outfled, outjumped all the machines which had ever existed before. You might almost think that he went so fast that he shocked the great vaults of the sky, so that the ancient poem might have been written for him alone. "All the stars threw down their spears and watered heaven with their tears."

Go he did, so fast, so far that people simply did not believe it at first. They thought it was a joke told by men, a farce spun forth by rumor, a wild story to while away the summer afternoon.

We know his name now.

And our children and their children will know it for always.

Rambo. Artyr Rambo of Earth Four.

But he followed his Elizabeth where no space was. He went where men could not go, had not been, did not dare, would not think.

He did all this of his own free will.

Of course people thought it was a joke at first, and got to making up silly songs about the reported trip.

"Dig me a hole for that reeling feeling . . . !" sang one.

"Push me the call for the umber number . . . !" sang another.

"Where is the ship of the ochre joker . . . ?" sang a third.

Then people everywhere found it was true. Some stood stock still and got gooseflesh. Others turned quickly to everyday things. Space$_3$ had been found, and it had been pierced. Their world would never be the same again. The solid rock had become an open door.

Space itself, so clean, so empty, so tidy, now looked like a million million light-years of tapioca pudding—gummy, mushy, sticky, not fit to breathe, not fit to swim in.

How did it happen?

Everybody took the credit, each in his own different way.

"He came for me," said Elizabeth. "I died and he came for me because the machines were making a mess of my life when they tried to heal my terrible, useless death."

"I went myself," said Rambo. "They tricked me and lied to me and fooled me, but I took the boat and I became the boat and I got there. Nobody made me do it. I was angry, but I went. And I came back, didn't I?"

He too was right, even when he twisted and whined on the green grass of earth, his ship lost in a space so terribly far and strange that it might have been beneath his living hand, or might have been half a galaxy away.

How can anybody tell, with space$_3$?

It was Rambo who got back, looking for his Elizabeth. He loved her. So the trip was his, and the credit his.

But the Lord Crudelta said, many years later, when he spoke in a soft voice and talked confidentially among friends, "The experiment was mine. I designed it, I picked Rambo. I drove the selectors mad, trying to find a man who would meet those specifications. And I had that rocket built to the old, old plans. It was the sort of thing which human beings first used when they jumped out of the air a little bit, leaping like flying fish from one wave to the next and already thinking that they were eagles. If I had used one of the regular planoform ships, it would have disappeared with a sort of reverse gurgle, leaving space milky for a little bit while it faded into nastiness and obliteration. But I did not risk that. I put the rocket on a launching pad. *And the launching pad itself was an interstellar ship!* Since we were using an ancient rocket, we did it up right, with the old, old writing, mysterious letters printed all over the machine. We even had the name of our Organization—I and O and M—for 'the Instrumentality of Mankind' written on it good and sharp.

"How would I know," went on the Lord Crudelta, "that we would succeed more than we wanted to succeed, that Rambo would tear space itself loose from its hinges and leave that ship behind, just because he loved Elizabeth so sharply much, so fiercely much?"

Crudelta sighed.

"I know it and I don't know it. I'm like that ancient man who tried to take a water boat the wrong way around the planet Earth and found a new world instead. Columbus, he was called. And the land, that was Australia or America or something like that. That's what I did. I sent Rambo out in that ancient rocket and he found a way through space₃. Now none of us will ever know who might come bulking through the floor or take shape out of the air in front of us."

Crudelta added, almost wistfully: "What's the use of telling the story? Everybody knows it, anyhow. My part in it isn't very glorious. Now the end of it, that's pretty. The bungalow by the waterfall and all the wonderful children that other people gave to them, you could write a poem about that. But the next to the end, how he showed up at the hospital helpless and insane, looking for his own Elizabeth. That was sad and eerie, that was frightening. I'm glad it all came to the happy ending with the bungalow by the waterfall, but it took a crashing long time to get there. And there are parts of it that we will never quite understand, the naked skin against naked space, the eyeballs riding something much faster than light ever was. Do you know what an *aoudad* is? It's an ancient sheep that used to live on Old Earth, and here we are, thousands of years later, with a children's nonsense rhyme about it. The animals are gone but the rhyme remains. It'll be like that with Rambo someday. Everybody will know his name and all about his drunkboat, but they will forget the scientific milestone that he crossed, hunting for Elizabeth in an ancient rocket that couldn't fly from peetle to pootle. . . . Oh, the rhyme? Don't you know that? It's a silly thing. It goes,

> " '*Point your gun at a murky lurky.*
> (Now you're talking ham or turkey!)
> *Shoot a shot at a dying aoudad.*
> (Don't ask the lady why or how, dad!)'

"Don't ask me what 'ham' and 'turkey' are. Probably parts of ancient animals, like beefsteak or sirloin. But the children still say the words. They'll do that with Rambo and his drunken boat some day. They may even tell the story of Elizabeth. But they will never tell the part about how he got to the hospital. That part is too terrible, too real, too sad and wonderful at the end. They found him on the grass. Mind you, naked on the grass, and nobody knew where he had come from!"

They found him naked on the grass and nobody knew where he had come from. They did not even know about the ancient rocket which the Lord Crudelta had sent beyond the end of nowhere with the letters I, O and M written on it. They did not know that this was Rambo, who had gone through space₃. The robots noticed him first and brought him in, photographing everything that they did.

They had been programmed that way, to make sure that anything unusual was kept in the records.

Then the nurses found him in an outside room.

They assumed that he was alive, since he was not dead, but they could not prove that he was alive, either.

That heightened the pubzzle.

The doctors were called in. Real doctors, not machines. They were very important men. Citizen Doctor Timofeyev, Citizen Doctor Grosbeck and the director himself, Sir and Doctor Vomact. They took the case.

(*Over on the other side of the hospital Elizabeth waited, unconscious, and nobody knew it at all. Elizabeth, for whom he had jumped space, and pierced the stars, but nobody knew it yet!*)

The young man could not speak. When they ran eye-prints and fingerprints through the Population Machine, they found that he had been bred on Earth itself, but had been shipped out as a frozen and unborn baby to Earth Four. At tremendous cost, they queried Earth Four with an "instant message," only to discover that the young man who lay before them in the hospital had been lost from an experimental ship on an intergalactic trip.

Lost.

No ship and no sign of ship.

And here he was.

They stood at the edge of space, and did not know what they were looking at. They were doctors and it was their business to repair or rebuild people, not to ship them around. How should such men know about space₃ when they did not even know about space₂, except for the fact that people got on the planoform ships and made trips through it? They were looking for sickness when their eyes saw engineering. They treated him when he was well.

All he needed was time, to get over the shock of the most tremendous trip ever made by a human being, but the doctors did not know that and they tried to rush his recovery.

When they put clothes on him, he moved from coma to a kind of mechanical spasm and tore the clothing off. Once again stripped, he lay himself roughly on the floor and refused food or speech.

They fed him with needles while the whole energy of space, had they only known it, was radiating out of his body in new forms.

They put him all by himself in a locked room and watched him through the peephole.

He was a nice-looking young man, even though his mind was blank and his body was rigid and unconscious. His hair was very fair and his eyes were light blue but his face showed character—a square chin; a handsome, resolute sullen mouth; old lines in the face which looked as though, when conscious, he must have lived many days or months on the edge of rage.

When they studied him the third day in the hospital, their patient had not changed at all.

He had torn off his pajamas again and lay naked, face down, on the floor.

His body was as immobile and tense as it had been on the day before.

(*One year later, this room was going to be a museum with a bronze sign reading, "Here lay Rambo after he left the Old Rocket for space₃," but the doctors still had no idea of what they were dealing with.*)

His face was turned so sharply to the left that the neck muscles showed. His right arm stuck out straight from the body. The left arm formed an exact right angle from the body, with the left forearm and hand pointing rigidly upward at 90° from the upper arm. The legs were in the grotesque parody of a running position.

Doctor Grosbeck said, "It looks to me like he's swimming. Let's drop him in a tank of water and see if he moves." Grosbeck sometimes went in for drastic solutions to problems.

Timofeyev took his place at the peephole. "Spasm, still," he murmured. "I hope the poor fellow is not feeling pain when his cortical defenses are down. How can a man fight pain if he does not even know what he is experiencing?"

"And you, sir and doctor," said Grosbeck to Vomact, "what do you see?"

Vomact did not need to look. He had come early and had looked long and quietly at the patient through the peephole before the other doctors arrived. Vomact was a wise man, with good insight and rich intuitions. He could guess in an hour more than a machine could diagnose in a year; he was already beginning to understand that this was a sickness which no man had ever had before. Still, there were remedies waiting.

The three doctors tried them.

They tried hypnosis, electrotherapy, massage, subsonics, atropine, surgital, a whole family of the digitalinids, and some quasi-narcotic viruses which had been grown in orbit where they mutated fast. They got the beginning of a response when they tried gas hypnosis combined with an electronically amplied telepath; this showed that something still went on inside the patient's mind. Otherwise the brain might have seemed to be mere fatty tissue, without a nerve in it. The other attempts had shown nothing. The gas showed a faint stirring away from fear and pain. The telepath reported glimpses of unknown skies. (The doctors turned the telepath over to the Space Police promptly, so they could try to code the star patterns which he had seen in a patient's mind, but the patterns did not fit. The telepath, though a keen-witted man, could not remember them in enough detail for them to be scanned against the samples of piloting sheets.)

The doctors went back to their drugs and tried ancient, simple remedies— morphine and caffeine to counteract each other, and a rough massage to make him dream again, so that the telepath could pick it up.

There was no further result that day, or the next.

Meanwhile the Earth authorities were getting restless. They thought, quite rightly, that the hospital had done a good job of proving that the patient had not been on Earth until a few moments before the robots found him on the grass. How had he gotten on the grass?

The airspace of Earth reported no intrusion at all, no vehicle marking a blazing arc of air incandescing against metal, no whisper of the great forces which drove a planoform ship through space$_2$.

(*Crudelta, using faster-than-light ships, was creeping slow as a snail back toward Earth, racing his best to see if Rambo had gotten there first.*)

On the fifth day, there was the beginning of a breakthrough.

Elizabeth had passed.

This was found out only much later, by a careful check of the hospital records.

The doctors only knew this much: Patients had been moved down the corridor, sheet-covered figures immobile on wheeled beds.

Suddenly the beds stopped rolling.

A nurse screamed.

The heavy steel-and-plastic wall was bending inward. Some slow, silent force was pushing the wall into the corridor itself.

The wall ripped.

A human hand emerged.

One of the quick-witted nurses screamed, "*Push* those beds! *Push* them out of the way."

The nurses and robots obeyed.

The beds rocked like a group of boats crossing a wave when they came to the place where the floor, bonded to the wall, had bent upward to meet the wall as it tore inward. The peace-colored glow of the lights flicked. Robots appeared.

A second human hand came through the wall. Pushing in opposite directions, the hands tore the wall as though it had been wet paper.

The patient from the grass put his head through.

He looked blindly up and down the corridor, his eyes not quite focusing, his skin glowing a strange red-brown from the burns of open space.

"No," he said. Just that one word.

But that "No" was heard. Though the volume was not loud, it carried throughout the hospital. The internal telecommunications system relayed it. Every switch in the place went negative. Frantic nurses and robots, with even the doctors helping them, rushed to turn all the machines back on—the pumps, the ventilators, the artificial kidneys, the brain re-recorders, even the simple air engines which kept the atmosphere clean.

Far overhead an aircraft spun giddily. Its "off" switch, surrounded by triple safeguards, had suddenly been thrown into the negative position. Fortunately the robot-pilot got it going again before crashing into Earth.

The patient did not seem to know that his word had this effect.

(*Later the world knew that this was part of the "drunkboat effect." The man himself had developed the capacity for using his neurophysical system as a machine control.*)

In the corridor, the machine robot who served as policeman arrived. He wore sterile, padded velvet gloves with a grip of sixty metric tons inside his hands. He approached the patient. The robot had been carefully trained to recognize all kinds of danger from delirious or psychotic humans; later he reported that he had an input of "danger, extreme" on every band of sensation. He had been expecting to seize the prisoner with irreversible firmness and to return him to his bed, but with this kind of danger sizzling in the air, the robot took no chances. His wrist itself contained a hypodermic pistol which operated on compressed argon.

He reached out toward the unknown, naked man who stood in the big torn gap of the wall. The wrist-weapon hissed and a sizeable injection of condamine, the most powerful narcotic in the known universe, spat its way through the skin of Rambo's neck. The patient collapsed.

The robot picked him up gently and tenderly, lifted him through the torn wall, pushed the door open with a kick which broke the lock and put the patient back on his bed. The robot could hear doctors coming, so he used his enormous hands to pat the steel wall back into its proper shape. Work-robots or under-people could finish the job later, but meanwhile it looked better to have that part of the building set at right angles again.

Doctor Vomact arrived, followed closely by Grosbeck.

"What happened?" he yelled, shaken out of a lifelong calm. The robot pointed at the ripped wall.

"He tore it open. I put it back," said the robot.

The doctors turned to look at the patient. He had crawled off his bed again and was on the floor, but his breathing was light and natural.

"What did you give him?" cried Vomact to the robot.

"Condamine," said the robot, "according to rule 47-B. The drug is not to be mentioned outside the hospital."

"I know that," said Vomact absentmindedly and a little crossly. "You can go along now. Thank you."

"It is not usual to thank robots," said the robot, "but you can read a commendation into my record if you want to."

"Get the blazes out of here!" shouted Vomact at the officious robot.

The robot blinked. "There are no blazes but I have the impression you mean me. I shall leave, with your permission." He jumped with odd gracefulness around the two doctors, fingered the broken doorlock absentmindedly, as though he might have wished to repair it; and then, seeing Vomact glare at him, left the room completely.

A moment later soft muted thuds began. Both doctors listened a moment and then gave up. The robot was out in the corridor, gently patting the steel floor back into shape. He was a tidy robot, probably animated by an amplified chicken-brain, and when he got tidy he became obstinate.

"Two questions, Grosbeck," said the sir and doctor Vomact.

"Your service, sir!"

"Where was the patient standing when he pushed the wall into the corridor, and how did he get the leverage to do it?"

Grosbeck narrowed his eyes in puzzlement. "Now that you mention it, I have no idea of how he did it. In fact, he could not have done it. But he has. And the other question?"

"What do you think of condamine?"

"Dangerous, of course, as always. Addiction can—"

"Can you have addiction with no cortical activity?" interrupted Vomact.

"Of course," said Grosbeck promptly. "Tissue addiction."

"Look for it, then," said Vomact.

Grosbeck knelt beside the patient and felt with his fingertips for the muscle endings. He felt where they knotted themselves into the base of the skull, the tips of the shoulders, the striped area of the back.

When he stood up there was a look of puzzlement on his face. "I never felt a human body like this one before. I am not even sure that it *is* human any longer."

Vomact said nothing. The two doctors confronted one another. Grosbeck fidgeted under the calm stare of the senior man. Finally he blurted out,

"Sir and doctor, I know what we *could* do."

"And that," said Vomact levelly, without the faintest hint of encouragement or of warning, "is what?"

"It wouldn't be the first time that it's been done in a hospital."

"What?" said Vomact, his eyes—those dreaded eyes!—making Grosbeck say what he did not want to say.

Grosbeck flushed. He leaned toward Vomact so as to whisper, even though there was no one standing near them. His words, when they came, had the hasty indecency of a lover's improper suggestion:

"Kill the patient, sir and doctor. Kill him. We have plenty of records of him. We can get a cadaver out of the basement and make it into a good simulacrum. Who knows what we will turn loose among mankind if we let him get well?"

"Who knows?" said Vomact without tone or quality to his voice. "But citizen and doctor, what is the twelfth duty of a physician?"

" 'Not to take the law into his own hands, keeping healing for the healers and giving to the state or the Instrumentality whatever properly belongs to the state or the Instrumentality.' " Grosbeck sighed as he retracted his own suggestion. "Sir and doctor, I take it back. It wasn't medicine which I was talking about. It was government and politics which were really in my mind."

"And now . . . ?" asked Vomact.

"Heal him, or let him be until he heals himself."

"And which would you do?"

"I'd try to heal him."

"How?" said Vomact.

"Sir and doctor," cried Grosbeck, "do not ride my weaknesses in this case! I know that you like me because I am a bold, confident sort of man. Do not ask me to be myself when we do not even know where this body came from. If I were bold as usual, I would give him typhoid and condamine, stationing telepaths nearby. But this is something new in the history of man. We are people and perhaps he is not a person any more. Perhaps he represents the combination of people with some kind of a new force. How did he get here from the far side of nowhere? How many million times has he been enlarged or reduced? We do not know what he is or what has happened to him. How can we treat a man when we are treating the cold of space, the heat of suns, the frigidity of distance? We know what to do with flesh, but this is not quite flesh any more. Feel him yourself, sir and doctor! You will touch something which nobody has ever touched before."

"I have," Vomact declared, "already felt him. You are right. We will try typhoid and condamine for half a day. Twelve hours from now let us meet each other at this place. I will tell the nurses and the robots what to do in the interim."

They both gave the red-tanned spread-eagled figure on the floor a parting glance. Grosbeck looked at the body with something like distaste mingled with fear; Vomact was expressionless, save for a wry wan smile of pity.

At the door the head nurse awaited them. Grosbeck was surprised at his chief's orders.

"Ma'am and nurse, do you have a weapon-proof vault in this hospital?"

"Yes, sir," she said. "We used to keep our records in it until we telemetered all our records into Computer Orbit. Now it is dirty and empty."

"Clean it out. Run a ventilator tube into it. Who is your military protector?"

"My what?" she cried, in surprise.

"Everyone on Earth has military protection. Where are the forces, the soldiers, who protect this hospital of yours?"

"My sir and doctor!" she called out. "My sir and doctor! I'm an old woman and I have been allowed to work here for three hundred years, but I never thought of that idea before. Why would I need soldiers?"

"Find who they are and ask them to stand by. They are specialists too, with a different kind of art from ours. Let them stand by. They may be needed before this day is out. Give my name as authority to their lieutenant or sergeant. Now here is the medication which I want you to apply to this patient."

Her eyes widened as he went on talking, but she was a disciplined woman and she nodded as she heard him out, point by point. Her eyes looked very sad and weary at the end but she was a trained expert herself and she had enormous respect for the skill and wisdom of the Sir and Doctor Vomact. She also had a warm, feminine pity for the motionless young male figure on the floor, swimming forever on the heavy floor, swimming between archipelagoes of which no man living had ever dreamed before.

Crisis came that night.

The patient had worn handprints into the inner wall of the vault, but he had not escaped.

The soldiers, looking oddly alert with their weapons gleaming in the bright corridor of the hospital, were really very bored, as soldiers always become when they are on duty with no action.

Their lieutenant was keyed up. The wirepoint in his hand buzzed like a dangerous insect. Sir and Doctor Vomact, who knew more about weapons than the soldiers thought he knew, saw that the wirepoint was set to HIGH, with a capacity of paralyzing people five stories up, five stories down or a kilometer sideways. He said nothing. He merely thanked the lieutenant and entered the vault, closely followed by Grosbeck and Timofeyev.

The patient swam here too.

He had changed to an arm-over-arm motion, kicking his legs against the floor. It was as though he had swum on the other floor with the sole purpose of staying afloat, and had now discovered some direction in which to go, albeit very slowly. His motions were deliberate, tense, rigid, and so reduced in time that it seemed as though he hardly moved at all. The ripped pajamas lay on the floor beside him.

Vomact glanced around, wondering what forces the man could have used to make those handprints on the steel wall. He remembered Grosbeck's warning that the patient should die, rather than subject all mankind to new and unthought risks, but though he shared the feeling, he could not condone the recommendation.

Almost irritably, the great doctor thought to himself—where could the man be going?

(To Elizabeth, the truth was, to Elizabeth, now only sixty meters away. Not till much later did people understand what Rambo had been trying to do—crossing sixty mere meters to reach his Elizabeth when he had already jumped an un-count of light-years to return to her. To his own, his dear, his well-beloved who needed him!)

The condamine did not leave its characteristic mark of deep lassitude and glowing skin: perhaps the typhoid was successfully contradicting it. Rambo did seem more lively than before. The name had come through on the regular message system, but it still did not mean anything to the Sir and Doctor Vomact. It would. It would.

Meanwhile the other two doctors, briefed ahead of time, got busy with the apparatus which the robots and the nurses had installed.

Vomact murmured to the others, "I think he's better off. Looser all around. I'll try shouting."

So busy were they that they just nodded.

Vomact screamed at the patient, "Who are you? What are you? Where do you come from?"

The sad blue eyes of the man on the floor glanced at him with a surprisingly quick glance, but there was no other real sign of communication. The limbs kept up their swim against the rough concrete floor of the vault. Two of the bandages which the hospital staff had put on him had worn off again. The right knee, scraped and bruised, deposited a sixty-centimeter trail of blood—some old and black and coagulated, some fresh, new and liquid—on the floor as it moved back and forth.

Vomact stood up and spoke to Grosbeck and Timofeyev. "Now," he said, "let us see what happens when we apply the pain."

The two stepped back without being told to do so.

Timofeyev waved his hand at a small white-enameled orderly-robot who stood in the doorway.

The pain net, a fragile cage of wires, dropped down from the ceiling.

It was Vomact's duty, as senior doctor, to take the greatest risk. The patient was wholly encased by the net of wires, but Vomact dropped to his hands and knees, lifted the net at one corner with his right hand, thrust his own head into it next to the head of the patient. Doctor Vomact's robe trailed on the clean concrete, touching the black old stains of blood left from the patient's "swim" throughout the night.

Now Vomact's mouth was centimeters from the patient's ear.

Said Vomact, "Oh."

The net hummed.

The patient stopped his slow motion, arched his back, looked steadfastly at the doctor.

Doctors Grosbeck and Timofeyev could see Vomact's face go white with the impact of the pain machine, but Vomact kept his voice under control and said evenly and loudly to the patient, "*Who—are—you?*"

The patient said flatly, "Elizabeth."

The answer was foolish but the tone was rational.

Vomact pulled his head out from under the net, shouting again at the patient, "*Who—are—you?*"

The naked man replied, speaking very clearly:

> "*Chwinkle, chwinkle, little chweeble*
> *I am feeling very feeble!*"

Vomact frowned and murmured to the robot, "More pain. Turn it up to pain ultimate."

The body threshed under the net, trying to resume its swim on the concrete.

A loud wild braying cry came from the victim under the net. It sounded like a screamed distortion of the name Elizabeth, echoing out from endless remoteness.

It did not make sense.

Vomact screamed back, "*Who—are—you?*"

With unexpected clarity and resonance, the voice came back to the three doctors from the twisting body under the net of pain:

"I'm the shipped man, the ripped man, the gypped man, the dipped man, the hipped man, the tripped man, the tipped man, the slipped man, the flipped man, the nipped man, the ripped man, the clipped man—aah!" His voice choked off with a cry and he went back to swimming on the floor, despite the intensity of the pain net immediately above him.

The doctor lifted his hand. The pain net stopped buzzing and lifted high into the air.

He felt the patient's pulse. It was quick. He lifted an eyelid. The reactions were much closer to normal.

"Stand back," he said to the others.

"Pain on both of us," he said to the robot.

The net came down on the two of them.

"*Who are you?*" shrieked Vomact, right into the patient's ear, holding the man halfway off the floor and not quite knowing whether the body which tore steel walls might not, somehow, tear both of them apart as they stood.

The man babbled back at him: "I'm the most man, the post man, the host man, the ghost man, the coast man, the boast man, the dosed man, the grossed man, the toast man, the roast man, no! no! no!"

He struggled in Vomact's arms. Grosbeck and Timofeyev stepped forward to rescue their chief when the patient added, very calmly and clearly:

"Your procedure is all right, doctor, whoever you are. More fever, please. More pain, please. Some of that dope to fight the pain. You're pulling me back. I know I am on Earth. Elizabeth is near. For the love of God, get me Elizabeth! But don't rush me. I need days and days to get well."

The rationality was so startling that Grosbeck, without waiting for orders from Vomact, as chief doctor, ordered the pain net lifted.

The patient began babbling again: "I'm the three man, the he man, the tree man, the me man, the three man, the three man. . . ." His voice faded and he slumped unconscious.

Vomact walked out of the vault. He was a little unsteady.

His colleagues took him by the elbows.

He smiled wanly at them: "I wish it were lawful. . . . I could use some of that condamine myself. No wonder the pain nets wake the patients up and even make dead people do twitches! Get me some liquor. My heart is old."

Grosbeck sat him down while Timofeyev ran down the corridor in search of medicinal liquor.

Vomact murmured, "How are we going to find *his* Elizabeth? There must be millions of them. And he's from Earth Four too."

"Sir and doctor, you have worked wonders," said Grosbeck. "To go under the net. To take those chances. To bring him to speech. I will never see anything like it again. It's enough for any one lifetime, to have seen this day."

"But what do we do next?" asked Vomact wearily, almost in confusion.

That particular question needed no answer.

The Lord Crudelta had reached Earth.

His pilot landed the craft and fainted at the controls with sheer exhaustion.

Of the escort cats, who had ridden alongside the space craft in the miniature spaceships, three were dead, one was comatose and the fifth was spitting and raving.

When the port authorities tried to slow the Lord Crudelta down to ascertain his authority, he invoked Top Emergency, took over the command of troops in the name of the Instrumentality, arrested everyone in sight but the troop commander, and requisitioned the troop commander to take him to the hospital. The computers at the port had told him that one Rambo, "sans origine," had arrived mysteriously on the grass of a designated hospital.

Outside the hospital, the Lord Crudelta invoked Top Emergency again, placed all armed men under his own command, ordered a recording monitor to cover all his actions if he should later be channeled into a court-martial, and arrested everyone in sight.

The tramp of heavily armed men, marching in combat order, overtook Timofeyev as he hurried back to Vomact with a drink. The men were jogging along on the double. All of them had live helmets and their wirepoints were buzzing.

Nurses ran forward to drive the intruders out, ran backward when the sting of the stun-rays brushed cruelly over them. The whole hospital was in an uproar.

The Lord Crudelta later admitted that he had made a serious mistake.

The Two Minutes' War broke out immediately.

You have to understand the pattern of the Instrumentality to see how it happened. The Instrumentality was a self-perpetuating body of men with enormous powers and a strict code. Each was a plenum of the low, the middle and the high justice. Each could do anything he found necessary or proper to maintain the Instrumentality and to keep the peace between the worlds. But if he made a mistake or committed a wrong—ah, then, it was suddenly different. Any Lord could put another Lord to death in an emergency, but he was assured of death and disgrace himself if he assumed this responsibility. The only difference between ratification and repudiation came in the fact that Lords who killed in an emergency and were proved wrong were marked down on a very shameful list, while those who killed other Lords rightly (as later examination might prove) were listed on a very honorable list, but still killed.

With three Lords, the situation was different. Three Lords made an emergency court; if they acted together, acted in good faith, and reported to the computers of the Instrumentality, they were exempt from punishment, though not from blame or even reduction to citizen status. Seven Lords, or all the Lords on a given planet at a given moment, were beyond any criticism except that of a dignified reversal of their actions should a later ruling prove them wrong.

This was all the business of the Instrumentality. The Instrumentality had the perpetual slogan: "Watch, but do not govern; stop war, but do not wage it; protect, but do not control; and first, survive!"

The Lord Crudelta had seized the troops—not his troops, but the light regular troops of Manhome Government—because he feared that the greatest danger in the history of man might come from the person whom he himself had sent through space₃.

He never expected that the troops would be plucked out from his command—an overriding power reinforced by robotic telepathy and the incomparable communications net, both open and secret, reinforced by thousands of years in trickery, defeat, secrecy, victory, and sheer experience, which the Instrumentality had perfected since it emerged from the Ancient Wars.

Overriding, overridden!

These were the commands which the Instrumentality had used before recorded time began. Sometimes they suspended their antagonists on points of law, sometimes by the deft and deadly insertion of weapons, most often by cutting in on other peoples' mechanical and social controls and doing their will, only to drop the controls as suddenly as they had taken them.

But not Crudelta's hastily called troops.

The war broke out with a change of pace.

Two squads of men were moving into that part of the hospital where Elizabeth lay, waiting the endless returns to the jelly baths which would rebuild her poor ruined body.

The squads changed pace.

The survivors could not account for what happened.

They all admitted to great mental confusion—afterward.

At the time it seemed that they had received a clear, logical command to turn and to defend the women's section by counterattacking their own main battalion right in their rear.

The hospital was a very strong building. Otherwise it would have melted to the ground or shot up in flame.

The leading soldiers suddenly turned around, dropped for cover and blazed their wirepoints at the comrades who followed them. The wirepoints were cued to organic material, though fairly harmless to inorganic. They were powered by the power relays which every soldier wore on his back.

In the first ten seconds of the turnaround, twenty-seven soldiers, two nurses, three patients and one orderly were killed. One hundred and nine other people were wounded in that first exchange of fire.

The troop commander had never seen battle, but he had been well trained. He immediately deployed his reserves around the external exits of the building and sent his favorite squad, commanded by a Sergeant Lansdale whom he trusted well, down into the basement, so that it could rise vertically from the basement into the women's quarters and find out who the enemy was.

As yet, he had no idea that it was his own leading troops turning and fighting their comrades.

He testified later, at the trial, that he personally had no sensations of eerie interference with his own mind. He merely knew that his men had unexpectedly come upon armed resistance from antagonists—identity unknown!—who had weapons identical with theirs. Since the Lord Crudelta had brought them along in case there might be a fight with unspecified antagonists, he felt right in assuming that a Lord of the Instrumentality knew what he was doing. This was the enemy all right.

In less than a minute, the two sides had balanced out. The line of fire had moved right into his own force. The lead men, some of whom were wounded, simply turned around and began defending themselves against the men immediately behind them. It was as though an invisible line, moving rapidly, had parted the two sections of the military force.

The oily black smoke of dissolving bodies began to glut the ventilators.

Patients were screaming, doctors cursing, robots stamping around and nurses trying to call each other.

The war ended when the troop commander saw Sergeant Lansdale, whom he himself had sent upstairs, leading a charge out of the women's quarters—directly at his own commander!

The officer kept his head.

He dropped to the floor and rolled sidewise as the air chittered at him, the emanations of Lansdale's wirepoint killing all the tiny bacteria in the air. On his helmet phone he pushed the manual controls to TOP VOLUME and to NONCOMS ONLY, and he commanded, with a sudden flash of brilliant mother-wit, "Good job, Lansdale!"

Lansdale's voice came back as weak as if it had been off-planet, "We'll keep them out of this section yet, sir!"

The troop commander called back very loudly but calmly, not letting on that he thought his sergeant was psychotic.

"Easy now. Hold on. I'll be with you."

He changed to the other channel and said to his nearby men, "Cease fire. Take cover and wait."

A wild scream came to him from the phones.

It was Lansdale. "Sir! Sir! I'm fighting *you*, sir. I just caught on. It's getting me again. Watch out."

The buzz and burr of the weapons suddenly stopped.

The wild human uproar of the hospital continued.

A tall doctor, with the insignia of high seniority, came gently to the troop commander and said, "You can stand up and take your soldiers out now, young fellow. The fight was a mistake."

"I'm not under your orders," snapped the young officer. "I'm under the Lord Crudelta. He requisitioned this force from the Manhome Government. Who are you?"

"You may salute me, captain," said the doctor, "I am Colonel General Vomact of the Earth Medical Reserve. But you had better not wait for the Lord Crudelta."

"But *where* is he?"

"In my bed," said Vomact.

"Your *bed?*" cried the young officer in complete amazement.

"In bed. Doped to the teeth. I fixed him up. He was excited. Take your men out. We'll treat the wounded on the lawn. You can see the dead in the refrigerators downstairs in a few minutes, except for the ones that went smoky from direct hits."

"But the fight . . . ?"

"A mistake, young man, or else—"

"Or else what?" shouted the young officer, horrified at the utter mess of his own combat experience.

"Or else a weapon no man has ever seen before. Your troops fought each other. Your command was intercepted."

"I could see that," snapped the officer, "as soon as I saw Lansdale coming at me."

"But do you know what took him over?" said Vomact gently, while taking the officer by the arm and beginning to lead him out of the hospital. The captain went willingly, not noticing where he was going, so eagerly did he watch for the other man's words.

"I think I know," said Vomact. "Another man's dreams. Dreams which have learned how to turn themselves into electricity or plastic or stone. Or anything else. Dreams coming to us out of space₃."

The young officer nodded dumbly. This was too much. "Space₃?" he murmured. It was like being told that the really alien invaders, whom men had been expecting for thirteen thousand years and had never met, were waiting for him on the grass. Until now space₃ had been a mathematical idea, a romancer's daydream, but not a fact.

The sir and doctor Vomact did not even ask the young officer. He brushed the young man gently at the nape of the neck and shot him through with tranquilizer. Vomact then led him out to the grass. The young captain stood alone and whistled happily at the stars in the sky. Behind him, his sergeants and corporals were sorting out the survivors and getting treatment for the wounded.

The Two Minutes' War was over.

Rambo had stopped dreaming that his Elizabeth was in danger. He had recognized, even in his deep sick sleep, that the tramping in the corridor was the movement of armed men. His mind had set up defenses to protect Elizabeth. He took over command of the forward troops and set them to stopping the main body. The powers which space₃ had worked into him made this easy for him to do, even though he did not know that he was doing it.

"How many dead?" said Vomact to Grosbeck and Timofeyev.

"About two hundred."

"And how many irrecoverable dead?"

"The ones that got turned into smoke. A dozen, maybe fourteen. The other dead can be fixed up, but most of them will have to get new personality prints."

"Do you know what happened?" asked Vomact.

"No, sir and doctor," they both chorused.

"I do. I think I do. No, I *know* I do. It's the wildest story in the history of man. Our patient did it—Rambo. He took over the troops and set them against each other. That Lord of the Instrumentality who came charging in—Crudelta. I've known him for a long long time. He's behind this case. He thought that troops would help, not sensing that troops would invite attack upon themselves. And there is something else."

"Yes?" they said, in unison.

"Rambo's woman—the one he's looking for. She must be here."

"Why?" said Timofeyev.

"Because *he's* here."

"You're assuming that he came here because of his own will, sir and doctor."

Vomact smiled the wise crafty smile of his family; it was almost a trademark of the Vomact house.

"I am assuming all the things which I cannot otherwise prove.

"First, I assume that he came here naked out of space itself, driven by some kind of force of which we cannot even guess.

"Second, I assume he came *here* because he wanted something. A woman named Elizabeth, who must already be here. In a moment we can go inventory all our Elizabeths.

"Third, I assume that the Lord Crudelta knew something about it. He has led troops into the building. He began raving when he saw me. I know hysterical fatigue, as do you, my brothers, so I condamined him for a night's sleep.

"Fourth, let's leave our man alone. There'll be hearings and trials enough, Space knows, when all these events get scrambled out."

Vomact was right.

He usually was.

Trials did follow.

It was lucky that Old Earth no longer permitted newspapers or television news. The population would have been frothed up to riot and terror if they had ever found out what happened at the Old Main Hospital just to the west of Meeya Meefla.

Twenty-one days later, Vomact, Timofeyev and Grosbeck were summoned to the trial of the Lord Crudelta. A full panel of seven Lords of the Instrumentality were there to give Crudelta an ample hearing and, if required, a sudden death.

The doctors were present both as doctors for Elizabeth and Rambo and as witnesses for the Investigating Lord.

Elizabeth, fresh up from being dead, was as beautiful as a newborn baby in exquisite, adult feminine form. Rambo could not take his eyes off her, but a look of bewilderment went over his face every time she gave him a friendly, calm remote little smile. (She had been told that she was his girl, and she was prepared to believe it, but she had no memory of him or of anything else more than sixty hours back, when speech had been reinstalled in her mind; and he, for his part, was still thick of speech and subject to strains which the doctors could not quite figure out.)

The Investigating Lord was a man named Starmount.

He asked the panel to rise.

They did so.

He faced the Lord Crudelta with great solemnity. "You are obliged, my Lord Crudelta, to speak quickly and clearly to this court."

"Yes, my Lord," he answered.

"We have the summary power."

"You have the summary power. I recognize it."

"You will tell the truth or else you will lie."

"I shall tell the truth or I will lie."

"You may lie, if you wish, about matters of fact and opinion, but you will in no case lie about human relationships. If you do lie, nevertheless, you will ask that your name be entered in the Roster of Dishonor."

"I understand the panel and the rights of this panel. I will lie if I wish—though I don't think I will need to do so"—and here Crudelta flashed a weary intelligent smile at all of them—"but I will not lie about matters of relationship. If I do, I will ask for dishonor."

"You have yourself been well trained as a Lord of the Instrumentality?"

"I have been so trained and I love the Instrumentality well. In fact, I am myself the Instrumentality, as are you, and as are the honorable Lords beside you. I shall behave well, for as long as I live this afternoon."

"Do you credit him, my Lords?" asked Starmount.

The members of the panel nodded their mitered heads. They had dressed ceremonially for the occasion.

"Do you have a relationship to the woman Elizabeth?"

The members of the trial panel caught their breath as they saw Crudelta turn white: "My Lords!" he cried, and answered no further.

"It is the custom," said Starmount firmly, "that you answer promptly or that you die."

The Lord Crudelta got control of himself. "I am answering. I did not know who she was, except for the fact that Rambo loved her. I sent her to Earth from Earth Four, where I then was. Then I told Rambo that she had been murdered and hung desperately at the edge of death, wanting only his help to return to the green fields of life."

Said Starmount: "Was that the truth?"

"My Lord and Lords, it was a lie."

"Why did you tell it?"

"To induce rage in Rambo and to give him an overriding reason for wanting to come to Earth faster than any man has ever come before."

"A-a-ah! A-a-ah!" Two wild cries came from Rambo, more like the call of an animal than like the sound of a man.

Vomact looked at his patient, felt himself beginning to growl with a deep internal rage. Rambo's powers, generated in the depths of space$_3$, had begun to operate again. Vomact made a sign. The robot behind Rambo had been coded to keep Rambo calm. Though the robot had been enameled to look like a white gleaming hospital orderly, he was actually a police robot of high powers, built up with an electronic cortex based on the frozen midbrain of an old wolf. (A wolf was a rare animal, something like a dog.) The robot touched Rambo, who dropped off to sleep. Doctor Vomact felt the anger in his own mind fade away. He lifted his hand gently; the robot caught the signal and stopped applying the narcoleptic radiation. Rambo slept normally; Elizabeth looked worriedly at the man whom she had been told was her own.

The Lords turned back from the glances at Rambo.

Said Starmount, icily: "And why did you do that?"

"Because I wanted him to travel through space."

"Why?"

"To show it could be done."

"And do you, my Lord Crudelta, affirm that this man has in fact traveled through space$_3$?"

"I do."

"Are you lying?"

"I have the right to lie, but I have no wish to do so. In the name of the Instrumentality itself, I tell you that this is the truth."

The panel members gasped. Now there was no way out. Either the Lord Crudelta was telling the truth, *which meant that all former times had come to an end and that a new age had begun for all the kinds of mankind,* or else he was lying in the face of the most powerful form of affirmation which any of them knew.

Even Starmount himself took a different tone. His teasing, restless, intelligent voice took on a new timbre of kindness.

"You do therefore assert that this man has come back from outside our galaxy with nothing more than his own natural skin to cover him? No instruments? No power?"

"I did not say that," said Crudelta. "Other people have begun to pretend I used such words. I tell you, my Lords, that I planoformed for twelve consecutive Earth days and nights. Some of you may remember where Outpost Baiter Gator is. Well, I had a good Go-captain, and he took me four long jumps beyond there, out into intergalactic space. I left this man there. When I reached Earth, he had been here twelve days, more or less. I have assumed, therefore, that his trip was more or less instantaneous. I was on my way back to Baiter Gator, counting by Earth time, when the doctor here found this man on the grass outside the hospital."

Vomact raised his hand. The Lord Starmount gave him the right to speak. "My sirs and Lords, we did not find this man on the grass. The robots did, and made a record. But even the robots did not see or photograph his arrival."

"We know that," said Starmount angrily, "and we know that we have been told that nothing came to Earth by any means whatever, in that particular quarter hour. Go on, my Lord Crudelta. What relation are you to Rambo?"

"He is my victim."

"Explain yourself!"

"I computed him out. I asked the machines where I would be most apt to find a man with a tremendous lot of rage in him, and was informed that on Earth Four the rage level had been left high because that particular planet had a considerable need for explorers and adventurers, in whom rage was a strong survival trait. When I got to Earth Four, I commanded the authorities to find out which border cases had exceeded the limits of allowable rage. They gave me four men. One was much too large. Two were old. This man was the only candidate for my excitement. I chose him."

"What did you tell him?"

"Tell him? I told him his sweetheart was dead or dying."

"No, no," said Starmount. "Not at the moment of crisis. What did you tell him to make him cooperate in the first place?"

"I told him," said the Lord Crudelta evenly, "that I was myself a Lord of the Instrumentality and that I would kill him myself if he did not obey, and obey promptly."

"And under what custom or law did you act?"

"Reserved material," said the Lord Crudelta promptly. "There are telepaths here who are not a part of the Instrumentality. I beg leave to defer until we have a shielded place."

Several members of the panel nodded and Starmount agreed with them. He changed the line of questioning.

"You forced this man, therefore, to do something which he did not wish to do?"

"That is right," said the Lord Crudelta.

"Why didn't you go yourself, if it is that dangerous?"

"My Lords and honorables, it was the nature of the experiment that the experimenter himself should not be expended in the first try. Artyr Rambo has indeed traveled through space$_3$. I shall follow him myself, in due course." (How the Lord Crudelta did do so is another tale, told about another time.) "If I had gone and if I had been lost, that would have been the end of the space$_3$ trials. At least for our time."

"Tell us the exact circumstances under which you last saw Artyr Rambo before you met after the battle in the Old Main Hospital."

"We had put him in a rocket of the most ancient style. We also wrote writing on the outside of it, just the way the Ancients did when they first ventured into space. Ah, that was a beautiful piece of engineering and archaeology! We copied everything right down to the correct models of fourteen thousand years ago, when the Paroskii and Murkins were racing each other into space. The rocket was white, with a red and white gantry beside it. The letters IOM were on the rocket, not that the words mattered. The rocket has gone into nowhere, but the passenger sits here. It rose on a stool of fire. The stool became a column. Then the landing field disappeared."

"And the landing field," said Starmount quietly, "what was that?"

"A modified planoform ship. We have had ships go milky in space because they faded molecule by molecule. We have had others disappear utterly. The engineers had changed this around. We took out all the machinery needed for circumnavigation, for survival or for comfort. The landing field was to last three or four seconds, no more. Instead, we put in fourteen planoform devices, all operating in tandem, so that the ship would do what other ships do when they planoform—namely, drop one of our familiar dimensions and pick up a new dimension from some unknown category of space—but do it with such force as to get out of what people call space$_2$ and move over into space$_3$."

"And space$_3$, what did you expect of that?"

"I thought that it was universal and instantaneous, in relation to our universe.

That everything was equally distant from everything else. That Rambo, wanting
to see his girl again, would move in a thousandth of a second from the empty
space beyond Outpost Baiter Gator into the hospital where she was."

"And, my Lord Crudelta, what made you think so?"

"A hunch, my Lord, for which you are welcome to kill me."

Starmount turned to the panel. "I suspect, my Lords, that you are more likely
to doom him to long life, great responsibility, immense rewards, and the fatigue
of being his own difficult and complicated self."

The miters moved gently and the members of the panel rose.

"You, my Lord Crudelta, will sleep till the trial is finished."

A robot stroked him and he fell asleep.

"Next witness," said the Lord Starmount, "in five minutes."

Vomact tried to keep Rambo from being heard as a witness. He argued fiercely
with the Lord Starmount in the intermission. "You Lords have shot up my
hospital, abducted two of my patients, and now you are going to torment both
Rambo and Elizabeth. Can't you leave them alone? Rambo is in no condition
to give coherent answers and Elizabeth may be damaged if she sees him suffer."

The Lord Starmount said to him, "You have your rules, doctor, and we have
ours. This trial is being recorded, inch by inch and moment by moment. Nothing
is going to be done to Rambo unless we find that he has planet-killing powers.
If that is true, of course, we will ask you to take him back to the hospital and
to put him to death very pleasantly. But I don't think it will happen. We want
his story so that we can judge my colleague Crudelta. Do you think that the
Instrumentality would survive if it did not have fierce internal discipline?"

Vomact nodded sadly; he went back to Grosbeck and Timofeyev, murmuring
sadly to them, "Rambo's in for it. There's nothing we could do."

The panel reassembled. They put on their judicial miters. The lights of the
room darkened and the weird blue light of justice was turned on.

The robot orderly helped Rambo to the witness chair.

"You are obliged," said Starmount, "to speak quickly and clearly to this court."

"You're not Elizabeth," said Rambo.

"I am the Lord Starmount," said the investigating Lord, quickly deciding to
dispense with the formalities. "Do you know me?"

"No," said Rambo.

"Do you know where you are?"

"Earth," said Rambo.

"Do you wish to lie or to tell the truth?"

"A lie," said Rambo, "is the only truth which men can share with each other,
so I will tell you lies, the way we always do."

"Can you report your trip?"

"No."

"Why not, citizen Rambo?"

"Words won't describe it."

"Do you remember your trip?"

"Do you remember your pulse of two minutes ago?" countered Rambo.

"I am not playing with you," said Starmount. "We think you have been in
space₃ and we want you to testify about the Lord Crudelta."

"Oh!" said Rambo. "I don't like him. I never did like him."

"Will you nevertheless try to tell us what happened to you?"

"Should I, Elizabeth?" asked Rambo of the girl, who sat in the audience.

She did not stammer. "Yes," she said, in a clear voice which rang through the big room. "Tell them, so that we can find our lives again."

"I will tell you," said Rambo.

"When did you last see the Lord Crudelta?"

"When I was stripped and fitted to the rocket, four jumps out beyond Outpost Baiter Gator. He was on the ground. He waved good-bye to me."

"And then what happened?"

"The rocket rose. It felt very strange, like no craft I had ever been in before. I weighed many, many gravities."

"And then?"

"The engines went on. I was thrown out of space itself."

"What did it seem like?"

"Behind me I left the working ships, the cloth and the food which goes through space. I went down rivers which did not exist. I felt people around me though I could not see them, red people shooting arrows at live bodies."

"*Where* were you?" asked a panel member.

"In the wintertime where there is no summer. In an emptiness like a child's mind. In peninsulas which had torn loose from the land. And I *was* the ship."

"You were what?" asked the same panel member.

"The rocket nose. The cone. The boat. I was drunk. It was drunk. I was the drunkboat myself," said Rambo.

"And where did you go?" resumed Starmount.

"Where crazy lanterns stared with idiot eyes. Where the waves washed back and forth with the dead of all the ages. Where the stars became a pool, and I swam in it. Where blue turns to liquor, stronger than alcohol, wilder than music, fermented with the *red red reds* of love. I saw all the things that men have ever thought they saw, but it was me who really saw them. I've heard phosphorescence singing and tides that seemed like crazy cattle clawing their way out of the ocean, their hooves beating the reefs. You will not believe me, but I found Floridas wilder than this, where the flowers had human skins and eyes like big cats."

"What are you talking about?" asked the Lord Starmount.

"What I found in space₃," snapped Artyr Rambo. "Believe it or not. This is what I now remember. Maybe it's a dream, but it's all I have. It was years and years and it was the blink of an eye. I dreamed green nights. I felt places where the whole horizon became one big waterfall. The boat that was me met children and I showed them El Dorado, where the gold men live. The people drowned in space washed gently past me. I was a boat where all the lost spaceships lay drowned and still. Seahorses which were not real ran beside me. The summer month came and hammered down the sun. I went past archipelagoes of stars, where the delirious skies opened up for wanderers. I cried for me. I wept for man. I wanted to be the drunkboat sinking. I sank. I fell. It seemed to me that the grass was a lake, where a sad child, on hands and knees, sailed a toy boat as fragile as a butterfly in spring. I can't forget the pride of unremembered flags, the arrogance of prisons which I suspected, the swimming of the businessmen! Then I was on the grass."

"This may have scientific value," said the Lord Starmount, "but it is not of judicial importance. Do you have any comment on what you did during the battle in the hospital?"

Rambo was quick and looked sane: "What I did, I did not do. What I did not do, I cannot tell. Let me go, because I am tired of you and space, big men and big things. Let me sleep and let me get well."

Starmount lifted his hand for silence.

The panel members stared at him.

Only the few telepaths present knew that they had all said, "Aye. *Let the man go. Let the girl go. Let the doctors go.* But bring back the Lord Crudelta later on. He has many troubles ahead of him, and we wish to add to them."

Between the Instrumentality, the Manhome Government and the authorities at the Old Main Hospital, everyone wished to give Rambo and Elizabeth happiness.

As Rambo got well, much of his Earth Four memory returned. The trip faded from his mind.

When he came to know Elizabeth, he hated the girl.

This was not his girl—his bold, saucy, Elizabeth of the markets and the valleys, of the snowy hills and the long boat rides. This was somebody meek, sweet, sad and hopelessly loving.

Vomact cured that.

He sent Rambo to the Pleasure City of the Herperides, where bold and talkative women pursued him because he was rich and famous.

In a few weeks—a very few indeed—he wanted *his* Elizabeth, this strange shy girl who had been cooked back from the dead while he rode space with his own fragile bones.

"Tell the truth, darling." He spoke to her once gravely and seriously. "The Lord Crudelta did not arrange the accident which killed you?"

"They say he wasn't there," said Elizabeth. "They say it was an actual accident. I don't know. I will never know."

"It doesn't matter now," said Rambo. "Crudelta's off among the stars, looking for trouble and finding it. We have our bungalow, and our waterfall, and each other."

"Yes, my darling," she said, "each other. And no fantastic Floridas for us."

He blinked at this reference to the past, but he said nothing. A man who has been through space$_3$ needs very little in life, outside of *not* going back to space$_3$. Sometimes he dreamed he was the rocket again, the old rocket taking off on an impossible trip. Let other men follow! he thought. Let other men go! I have Elizabeth and I am here.

J. H. Rosny *aîné*
Translated by Damon Knight

J. H. Rosny *aîné* was the pseudonym of the important French (Belgian) writer Joseph-Henri Boëx (1856–1940). He was the author of 107 novels, essays, plays, memoirs, etc., a friend of Alphonse Daudet, and a President of the Académie Goncourt. He wrote a small number of SF works, including prehistoric romances such as *The Giant Cat* (1918; translated 1924) and *The Quest for Fire* (1901; translated 1967), from which the film *Quest for Fire* (1981) was made. Only three of his important SF stories have been translated into English, but he is the most important French SF writer between Jules Verne and the contemporary period. This story has only appeared once before in English, in an early 1960s anthology. So his influence on the evolution of the genre in English has thus far been indirect.

Damon Knight, the well-known SF critic and the translator of this piece, said that while only a few of Rosny's works were science fiction, "those few were precedent-making, germinal works. Rosny, not Verne, is considered the father of French science fiction." Knight goes on to say, "I love this story for its human warmth, and for what it has to tell us, not only about one superman, but about the adolescence of all gifted, 'different' human beings. I admire it for many reasons, but chiefly for the absolute, circumstantial conviction with which it describes an imaginary order of living creatures. Few writers have even attempted this most difficult kind of fictional invention; fewer still have succeeded so brilliantly."

This is both a unique "fourth dimension" story and a superman story, set in a small village in France where the events have no impact on the outside world. It is the earliest story in this anthology, published the same year as Wells's *The Time Machine*, 1895. It is every bit as powerfully imaginative as Wells, and gives evidence of the substantial trend in literature in the 1890s toward the themes and ideas of science fiction in works that later coalesced into the founding documents of the genre in a work by an early Modern writer.

ANOTHER WORLD

I

I was born in Gelderland, where our family holdings had dwindled to a few acres of heath and yellow water. Along the boundary grew pine trees that rustled with a metallic sound. The farmhouse had only a few habitable rooms left and was falling apart stone by stone in the solitude. Ours was an old family of herdsmen, once numerous, now reduced to my parents, my sister and myself.

My fate, dismal enough at the beginning, became the happiest I could imagine: I met the one who understands me; he will teach those things that formerly I alone knew among men. But for many years I suffered and despaired, a prey to doubt and the loneliness of the soul, which nearly ended by eating away my absolute faith.

I came into the world with a unique constitution, and from the very beginning I was the object of wonder. Not that I seemed ill-formed; I was, I am told, more shapely in face and body than is customary in newborn infants. But my color was most unusual, a sort of pale violet—very pale, but quite distinct. By lamplight, especially by the light of oil lamps, this tint grew paler still, turned to a curious whiteness, like that of a lily submerged in water. That, at least, was how I appeared to others (for I saw myself differently, as I saw everything in the world differently). To this first peculiarity others were added which only revealed themselves later.

Though born with a healthy appearance, I developed poorly. I was thin, and I cried incessantly; at the age of eight months, I had never been seen to smile. Soon my life was despaired of. The doctor from Zwartendam declared I was suffering from congenital weakness; he could think of no remedy but a strict regimen. Nonetheless I continued to waste away; the family expected me to disappear altogether from one day to the next. My father, I think, was resigned to it, his pride—the Hollander's pride in regularity and order—little soothed by the grotesque appearance of his child. My mother, on the contrary, loved me all the more for my strangeness, having made up her mind that the color of my skin was pleasing.

So matters stood, when a very simple thing came to my rescue. Since everything concerning me must be out of the ordinary, this event was the cause of scandal and apprehension.

A servant having left us, her place was given to a vigorous girl from Friesland, honest and willing, but inclined to drink. I was placed in her care. Seeing me so feeble, she took it into her head to give me secretly a little beer and water mixed with Schiedam—remedies, according to her, sovereign against all ills.

The curious thing was that I began immediately to regain my strength and from then on showed a remarkable predilection for alcohol. The good girl rejoiced in secret, not without drawing some pleasure from the bafflement of my parents and the doctor. At last, driven into a corner, she revealed the secret. My father flew into a violent passion; the doctor inveighed against superstition and ignorance. Strict orders were given to the servants; I was taken out of the Frieslander's care.

I began to grow thin again, to waste away, until my mother, forgetting everything but her fondness for me, put me back on a diet of beer and Schiedam. I promptly grew strong and lively again. The experiment was conclusive: alcohol was seen to be necessary to my health. My father was humiliated. The doctor got out of the affair by prescribing medicinal wines; and from that time on my health was excellent—but no one hesitated to prophesy a life of drunkenness and debauch for me.

Shortly after this incident, a new oddity grew apparent to the household. My eyes, which had seemed normal at the beginning, grew strangely opaque, took on a horny appearance, like the wing cases of certain beetles. The doctor concluded from this that I was losing my sight, but he confessed that the ailment was absolutely strange to him, of such a nature that he had never had the opportunity to study a like case. Shortly the pupils of my eyes so fused into the irises that it was impossible to tell one from the other. It was remarked, more-over, that I could stare at the sun without showing any discomfort. In truth, I was not blind in the least, and in the end they had to admit that I saw very well.

So I arrived at the age of three. I was then, in the opinion of the neighborhood, a little monster. The violet color of my skin had undergone little change. My eyes were completely opaque. I spoke awkwardly, and with incredible swiftness. I was dextrous with my hands, and well formed for all activities which called for more quickness than strength. It was not denied that I might have been graceful and handsome if my coloring had been normal and my pupils transparent. I showed some intelligence, but with deficiencies which my family did not fully appreciate, since, except for my mother and the Frieslander, they did not care much for me. I was an object of curiosity to strangers, and to my father a continual mortification.

If, moreover, he had clung to any hope of seeing me become like other people, time took ample pains to disabuse him of it. I grew more and more strange, in my tastes, habits and aptitudes. At the age of six I lived almost entirely on alcohol. Only very seldom did I take a few bites of vegetables or fruit. I grew with prodigious swiftness; I became incredibly thin and light. I mean "light" even in its specific sense, which is just the opposite of thinness. Thus, I swam without the slightest difficulty; I floated like a plank of poplar. My head hardly sank deeper than the rest of my body.

I was nimble in proportion to that lightness. I ran like a deer; I easily leaped over ditches and barriers which no man would even have attempted. Quick as a wink, I could be in the crown of a beech tree; or, what caused even more aston-ishment, I could leap over the roof of our farmhouse. In compensation, the slightest burden was too much for me.

All these things added together were nothing but phenomena indicative of a special nature, which by themselves would have done no more than single me out and make me unwelcome; no one would have classified me outside human-ity. No doubt I was a monster, but certainly not to the same degree as those who were born with the ears or horns of animals; a head like a calf's or horse's; fins; no eyes or an extra one; four arms; four legs; or without arms and legs. My skin, in spite of its startling color, was little different from a sun-tanned skin; there was nothing repugnant about my eyes, opaque as they were. My extreme agility was a gift, my need for alcohol might pass for a mere vice, an inheritance of drunkenness; however, the rustics, like our Frieslander servant, viewed it as no more than a confirmation of their ideas about the "strength" of Schiedam, a rather lively demonstration of the excellence of their tastes.

As for the swiftness and volubility of my speech, which made it impossible to follow, this seemed to be confounded with the defects of pronunciation—stam-mering, lisping, stuttering—common to so many small children. Thus, properly speaking, I had none of the marked characteristics of monstrosity, however ex-traordinary my general effect might be. The fact was that the most curious aspect of my nature escaped my family's notice, for no one realized that my vision was strangely different from ordinary vision.

If I saw certain things less well than others did, I could see a great many things that no one else could see at all. This difference showed itself especially in relation to colors. All that was termed red, orange, yellow, green, blue or indigo appeared to me as a more or less blackish gray, whereas I could perceive violet, and a series of colors beyond it—colors which were nothing but blackness to normal men. Later I realized that I could distinguish in this way among some fifteen colors as dissimilar as, for instance, yellow and green—with, of course, an infinite range of gradations in between.

In the second place, my eye does not perceive transparency in the ordinary way. I see poorly through glass or water; glass is highly colored for me, water perceptibly so, even at a slight depth. Many crystals said to be clear are more or less opaque, while, on the other hand, a very great number of bodies called opaque do not interfere with my vision. In general, I see through objects much more frequently than you do; and translucence, clouded transparency, occurs so often that I might say it is for my eye the rule of nature, while complete opacity is the exception. In this way I can make out objects through wood, paper, the petals of flowers, magnetized iron, coal, etc. Nevertheless, at variable thicknesses these substances create an obstacle—as a big tree, a meter's depth of water, a thick block of coal or quartz. Gold, platinum and mercury are black and opaque; ice is grayish black. Air and water vapor are transparent and yet tinted, as are certain specimens of steel, certain very pure clays. Clouds do not hinder me from seeing the sun or the stars. On the other hand, I can clearly see these same clouds hanging in the air.

As I have said, this difference between my vision and that of others was very little remarked by those around me. My color perception was thought to be poor, that was all; the infirmity is too common to attract much attention. It had no importance in the small daily acts of my life, for I saw the shapes of objects in the same manner as most people, and perhaps even more accurately. Designating an object by its color, when it was necessary to distinguish it from another of the same shape, troubled me only when the two objects were new. If someone called one waistcoat blue and another red, it made little difference in what colors these waistcoats really appeared to me; blue and red became purely mnemonic terms.

From this you might conclude that there was a system of correspondence between my colors and those of other people, and therefore that it came to the same thing as if I had seen their colors. But, as I have already written, red, green, yellow, blue, etc., *when they are pure*, as the colors of a prism are pure, appear to me as a more or less blackish gray; they are not colors to me at all. In nature, where no color is simple, it is not the same thing. A given substance termed green, for instance, is for me of a certain mixed color;* but another substance called green, which to you is identically the same shade as the first, is not at all the same color to me. You see, therefore, that my range of colors has no correspondence with yours: when I agree to call both brass and gold yellow, it is a little as if you should agree to call both a cornflower and a corn poppy blue.

II

Were this the extent of the difference between my vision and normal vision, certainly it would appear extraordinary enough. Nevertheless, it is but little com-

---

*And this mixture naturally does not include green, since green, for me, belongs to the realm of darkness.

pared with that which I have yet to tell you. The differently colored world, differently transparent and opaque, the ability to see through clouds, to perceive the stars on the most overcast nights, to see through a wooden wall what is happening in the next room or on the outside of a house—what is all this, compared with the perception of a *living world*, a world of animate Beings, moving around and beside man without man's being aware of them, without his being warned by any sort of immediate contact?

What is all this, compared with the revelation that there exists on this earth another fauna than our fauna, and one without any resemblance to our own in form, or in organization, or in habits, or in manner of growth, birth and death? A fauna which lives beside and in the midst of ours, influences the elements which surround us, and is influenced, vivified, by these elements, without our suspecting its presence. A fauna which, as I have demonstrated, is as unaware of us as we of it, and which has evolved in ignorance of us, as we in ignorance of it. A living world as varied as ours, as puissant as ours—perhaps more so—in its effect on the face of the planet! A kingdom, in short, moving upon the water, in the atmosphere, on the earth, modifying that water, that atmosphere and that earth entirely otherwise than we, but certainly with formidable strength, and in that way acting indirectly upon us and our destiny, as we indirectly act upon it!

Nevertheless, this is what I have seen, what I alone among men and animals still see; this is what I have *studied* ardently for five years, after having spent my childhood and adolescence merely *observing* it.

III

Observing it! As far back as I can remember, I instinctively felt the seductiveness of that creation so foreign to ours. In the beginning, I confounded it with other living things. Seeing that no one took any notice of its presence, that everyone, on the contrary, appeared indifferent to it, I hardly felt the need to point out its peculiarities. At six, I understood perfectly its difference from the plants of the fields, the animals of the farmyard and the stable; but I confused it somewhat with such nonliving phenomena as rays of light, the movement of water, and clouds. That was because these creatures were intangible: when they touched me I felt no sensation of contact. Their shapes, otherwise widely variant, nevertheless had this singularity, that they were so thin, in one of their three dimensions, that they might be compared to drawings, to surfaces, geometric lines that moved. They passed through all organic bodies; on the other hand, they sometimes appeared to be halted, entangled by invisible obstacles.

But I shall describe them later. At present I only wish to draw attention to them, to affirm their variety of contours and lines, their quasi-absence of thickness, their *impalpability*, combined with the autonomy of their movements.

At about my eighth year, I became perfectly sure that they were as distinct from atmospheric phenomena as from the members of our animal kingdom. In the delight this discovery afforded me, I tried to communicate it to others. I never succeeded in doing so. Aside from the fact that my speech was almost entirely incomprehensible, as I have said, the extraordinary nature of my vision rendered it suspect. No one thought of pausing to unravel my gestures and my phrases, any more than to admit that I could see through wooden walls, even though I had given proof of this on many occasions. Between me and the others there was an almost insurmountable barrier.

I fell into discouragement and daydreams; I became a sort of little recluse; I caused uneasiness, and felt it myself, among children of my own age. I was not exactly an underdog, for my swiftness put me beyond the reach of childish tricks and gave me the means of avenging myself easily. At the slightest threat, I was off at a distance—I mocked all pursuit. No matter how many of them there were, children never succeeded in surrounding me, much less in holding me prisoner. It was not worthwhile even to try to seize me by a trick. Weak as I might be at carrying burdens, my leaps were irresistible and freed me at once. I could return at will, overcome my adversary, even more than one, with swift, sure blows. Accordingly I was left in peace. I was looked on as innocent and at the same time a bit magical; but it was a feeble magic, which they scorned.

By degrees I made a life for myself outdoors, wild, meditative, not without its pleasures. Only the affection of my mother humanized me, even though, busy all day long, she found little time for caresses.

IV

I shall try to describe briefly a few scenes from my tenth year, in order to give substance to the explanations which have gone before.

It is morning. A bright glow illumines the kitchen—a pale yellow glow to my parents and the servants, richly various to me. The first breakfast is being served: bread and tea. But I do not take tea. I have been given a glass of Schiedam with a raw egg. My mother is hovering over me tenderly; my father questions me. I try to answer him, I slow down my speech; he understands only a syllable here and there. He shrugs. "He'll never learn to talk!"

My mother looks at me with compassion, convinced that I am a bit simple. The servants and laborers no longer even feel any curiosity about the little violet monster; the Frieslander has long ago gone back to her country. As for my sister, who is two years old, she is playing near me, and I feel a deep affection for her.

Breakfast over, my father goes off to the fields with the laborers; my mother begins to busy herself with her daily tasks. I follow her into the farmyard. The animals come up to her. I watch them with interest; I like them. But, all around, the other Kingdom is in motion, and it attracts me still more; it is the mysterious domain which only I know.

On the brown earth a few shapes are sprawled out; they move, they pause, they palpitate on the surface of the ground. They belong to several species, different in contours, in movement, and above all in the arrangement, design and shadings of the lines which run through them. Taken together, these lines constitute the essential part of their being, and, child though I am, I know it very well. Whereas the mass of their bodies is dull, grayish, the lines are almost always brilliant. They form highly complicated networks, radiating from centers, spreading out until they fade and lose their identity. Their tints and curves are innumerable. These colors vary within a single line, as the form does also, but to a lesser extent. The creature as a whole is distinguished by a rather irregular but very distinct outline; by the radiant centers; by the multicolored lines which intermingle freely. When it moves, the lines tremble, oscillate; the centers contract and dilate, while the outline changes little.

All this I see very well already, though I may be unable to define it; a delightful spell falls over me when I watch the *Moedigen.** One of them, a colossus ten meters long and almost as wide, passes slowly across the farmyard and disappears. This one, with some bands the size of cables, and centers as big as eagles' wings, greatly interests and almost frightens me. I pause for a moment, about to follow it, but then others attract my attention. They are of all sizes: some are no larger than our tiniest insects, while I have seen others more than thirty meters long. They advance on the ground itself, as if attached to solid surfaces. When they meet a material obstacle—a wall, or a house—they cross it by molding themselves to its surface, always without any significant change in their outlines. But when the obstacle is of living or once-living matter, they pass directly through it; thus I have seen them appear thousands of times out of trees and beneath the feet of animals and men. They can pass through water also, but prefer to remain on the surface.

These land *Moedigen* are not the only intangible creatures. There is an aerial population of a marvelous splendor, of an incomparable subtlety, variety and brilliance, beside which the most beautiful birds are dull, slow and heavy. Here again there are internal lines and an outline. But the background is not grayish, it is strangely luminous; it sparkles like sunlight, and the lines stand out from it in trembling veins; the centers palpitate violently. The *Vuren*, as I call them, are of a more irregular form than the land *Moedigen* and commonly propel themselves by means of rhythmic dispositions, intertwinings and untwinings which, in my ignorance, I cannot make out and which baffle my imagination.

Meanwhile I am making my way across a recently mowed meadow; the battle of a *Moedig* with another one has drawn my attention. These battles are frequent, and they excite me tremendously. Sometimes the battles are equal; more often an attack is made by the stronger upon the weaker. (The weaker is not necessarily the smaller.) In the present case, the weaker one, after a short defense, takes to flight, hotly pursued by the aggressor. Despite the swiftness of their motions, I follow them and succeed in keeping them in view until the struggle begins again. They fling themselves on each other—firmly, even rigidly, solid to each other. At the shock, their lines phosphoresce, moving toward the point of contact; their centers grow smaller and paler.

At first the struggle remains more or less equal; the weaker puts forth a more intense energy and even succeeds in gaining a truce from its adversary. It profits by this to flee once more, but is rapidly overtaken, strongly attacked and at last seized—that is to say, held fast in a hollow in the outline of the other. This is exactly what it has been trying to avoid, as it counters the stronger one's buffets with blows that are weaker but swifter. Now I see all its lines shudder, its centers throb desperately; and the lines gradually thin out, grow pale; the centers blur. After a few minutes, it is set free: it withdraws slowly, dull, debilitated. Its antagonist, on the contrary, glows more brightly; its lines are more vivid, its centers clearer and livelier.

This fight has moved me profoundly. I think about it and compare it with

---

*This is the name which I gave them spontaneously in my childhood and which I have retained, though it corresponds to no quality or form of these creatures.

the fights I sometimes see between *our* animals. I realize confusedly that the *Moedigen*, as a group, do not kill, or rarely kill, that the victor contents itself with *increasing its strength* at the expense of the vanquished.

The morning wears on; it is nearly eight o'clock; the Zwartendam school is about to open. I gain the house in one leap, seize my books, and here I am among my fellows, where no one guesses what profound mysteries palpitate around him, where no one has the least idea of the living things through which all humanity passes and which pass through humanity, leaving no mark of that mutual penetration.

I am a very poor scholar. My writing is nothing but a hasty scrawl, unformed, illegible; my speech remains uncomprehended; my absence of mind is manifest. The master calls out continually, "Karel Ondereet, have you done with watching the flies?"

Alas, my dear master! It is true that I watch the flies in the air, but how much more does my mind accompany the mysterious *Vuren* that pass through the room! And what strange feelings obsess my childish mind, to note everyone's blindness and above all your own, grave shepherd of intellects!

V

The most painful period of my life was that which ran from my twelfth to my eighteenth year.

To begin with, my parents tried to send me to the academy. I knew nothing there but misery and frustration. At the price of exhausting struggles, I succeeded in expressing the most ordinary things in a partially comprehensible manner: slowing my syllables with great effort, I uttered them awkwardly and with the intonations of the deaf. But as soon as I had to do with anything complicated, my speech regained its fatal swiftness; no one could follow me any longer. Therefore I could not register my progress orally. Moreover, my writing was atrocious, my letters piled up one on the other, and in my impatience I forgot whole syllables and words; it was a monstrous hodgepodge. Besides, writing was a torment to me, perhaps even more intolerable than speech—of an asphyxiating slowness, heaviness! If occasionally, by taking much pain and sweating great drops, I succeeded in beginning an exercise, at once I was at the end of my energy and patience; I felt about to faint. Accordingly I preferred the masters' remonstrances, the anger of my father, punishments, privations, scorn, to this horrible labor.

Thus I was almost totally deprived of the means of expression. Already an object of ridicule for my thinness and my strange color, my odd eyes, once more I passed for a kind of idiot. It was necessary for my parents to withdraw me from school and resign themselves to making a peasant of me.

The day my father decided to give up all hope, he said to me with unaccustomed gentleness, "My poor boy, you see I have done my duty—my whole duty. Never reproach me for your fate."

I was strongly moved. I shed warm tears; never had I felt more bitterly my isolation in the midst of men. I dared to embrace my father tenderly; I muttered, "Just the same, it's not true that I'm a halfwit!" And, in fact, I felt myself superior to those who had been my fellow pupils. Some time ago my intelligence had undergone a remarkable development. I read, I understood, I divined; and I had enormous matter for reflection, beyond that of other men, in that universe visible to me alone.

My father could not make out my words, but he softened to my embrace. "Poor boy!" he said.

I looked at him; I was in terrible distress, knowing too well that the gap between us would never be bridged. My mother, through love's intuition, saw in that moment that I was not inferior to the other boys of my age. She gazed at me tenderly, she spoke artless love words that came from the depths of her being. Nonetheless, I was condemned to give up my studies.

Because of my lack of muscular strength, I was given the care of the horses and the cattle. In this I acquitted myself admirably; I needed no dog to guard the herds, in which no colt or stallion was as agile as I.

Thus, from my fourteenth to my seventeenth year I lived the solitary life of the herdsman. It suited me better than any other. Given over to observation and contemplation, together with some reading, my mind never stopped growing. Incessantly I compared the two orders of creation which lay before my eyes; I drew from them ideas about the constitution of the universe; vaguely I sketched out hypotheses and systems. If it be true that in that period my thoughts were not perfectly ordered, did not make a lucid synthesis—for they were adolescent thoughts, uncoordinated, impatient, enthusiastic—nevertheless they were original, and fruitful. That their value may have depended above all upon my unique constitution, I would be the last to deny. But they did not draw all their strength from that source. I think I may say without pride that in subtlety as in logic they notably surpassed those of ordinary young men.

They alone brought consolation to my melancholy half-pariah's life, without companions, without any real communication with the rest of my household, even my adorable mother.

At the age of seventeen, life became definitely unsupportable to me. I was weary of dreaming, weary of vegetating on a desert island of thought. I fell into languor and boredom. I rested immobile for long hours, indifferent to the whole world, inattentive to anything that happened in my family. What mattered it that I knew of more marvelous things than other men, since in any case this knowledge must die with me? What was the mystery of living things to me, or even the duality of the two living systems crossing through each other without awareness of each other? These things might have intoxicated me, filled me with enthusiasm and ardor, if I could have taught them or shared them in any way. But what would you! Vain and sterile, absurd and miserable, they contributed rather to my perpetual psychic quarantine.

Many times I dreamed of setting down, recording, in spite of everything, by dint of continuous effort, some of my observations. But since leaving school I had completely abandoned the pen, and, already so wretched a scribbler, it was all I could do, with the utmost application, to trace the twenty-six letters of the alphabet. If I had still entertained any hope, perhaps I should have persisted. But who would have taken my miserable lucubrations seriously? Where was the reader who would not think me mad? Where the sage who would not show me the door with irony or disdain?

To what end, therefore, should I consecrate myself to that vain task, that exasperating torment, almost comparable to the requirement, for an ordinary man, to grave his thoughts upon tablets of marble with a huge chisel and a

Cyclopean hammer? My penmanship would have had to be stenographic—and yet more: of a superswift stenography! Thus I had no courage at all to write, and at the same time I fervently hoped for I know not what unforeseen event, what happy and singular destiny. It seemed to me that there must exist, in some corner of the earth, impartial minds, lucid, searching, qualified to study me, to understand me, to extract my great secret from me and communicate it to others. But where were these men? What hope had I of ever meeting them?

And I fell once more into a vast melancholy, into the desire for immobility and extinction. During one whole autumn, I despaired of the universe. I languished in a vegetative state, from which I emerged only to give way to long groans, followed by painful rebellions of conscience.

I grew thinner still, thin to a fantastic degree. The villagers called me, ironically, *"den Heyligen Gheest,"* the Holy Ghost. My silhouette was tremulous as that of the young poplars, faint as a shadow; and with all this, I grew to a giant's stature.

Slowly, a project was born. Since my life had been thrown into the discard, since my days were without joy and all was darkness and bitterness to me, why wallow in sloth? Supposing that no mind existed which could respond to my own—at least it would be worth the effort to convince myself of that fact. At least it would be worthwhile to leave this gloomy countryside, to go and search for scientists and philosophers in the great cities. Was I not in myself an object of curiosity? Before calling attention to my extrahuman knowledge, could I not arouse a desire to study my person? Were not the mere physical aspects of my being worthy of analysis—and my sight, and the extreme swiftness of my movements, and the peculiarity of my diet?

The more I thought of it, the more it seemed reasonable to me to hope, and the more my resolution hardened. The day came when it was unshakable, when I confided it to my parents. Neither one nor the other understood much of it, but in the end both gave in to repeated entreaties: I obtained permission to go to Amsterdam, free to return if fortune should not favor me.

One morning, I left.

VI

From Zwartendam to Amsterdam is a matter of a hundred kilometers or thereabouts. I covered that distance easily in two hours, without any other adventure than the extreme surprise of those going and coming to see me run so swiftly, and a few crowds at the edges of the villages and towns I skirted. To make sure of my direction, I spoke two or three times to solitary old people. My sense of orientation, which is excellent, did the rest.

It was about nine o'clock when I reached Amsterdam. I entered the great city resolutely and walked along its beautiful, dreaming canals, where quiet merchant fleets dwell. I did not attract as much attention as I had feared. I walked quickly, among busy people, enduring here and there the gibes of some young street Arabs. Nevertheless, I did not decide to stop. I wandered here and there through the city, until at last I resolved to enter a tavern on one of the quays of the Heerengracht. It was a peaceful spot; the magnificent canal stretched, full of life, between cool rows of trees; and among the *Moedigen* which I saw moving about on its banks it seemed to me that I perceived a new species. After some hesitation, I crossed the sill of the tavern, and addressing myself to the publican as slowly as I could, I begged him to be kind enough to direct me to a hospital.

The landlord looked at me with amazement, suspicion and curiosity; took his huge pipe out of his mouth, put it back in after several attempts, and at last said, "You're from the colonies, I suppose?"

Since it was perfectly useless to contradict him, I answered, "Just so!"

He seemed delighted at his own shrewdness. He asked me another question: "Maybe you come from that part of Borneo where no one has ever been?"

"Exactly right!"

I had spoken too swiftly: his eyes grew round.

"Exactly right," I repeated more slowly.

The landlord smiled with satisfaction. "You can hardly speak Dutch, can you? So, it's a hospital you want. No doubt you're sick?"

"Yes."

Patrons were gathering around. It was whispered already that I was an anthropophagus from Borneo; nevertheless, they looked at me with much more curiosity than aversion. People were running in from the street. I became nervous and uneasy. I kept my composure nonetheless and said, coughing, "I am very sick!"

"Just like the monkeys from that country," said a very fat man benevolently. "The Netherlands kills them!"

"What a funny skin!" added another.

"And how does he see?" asked a third, pointing to my eyes.

The ring moved closer, encircling me with a hundred curious stares, and still newcomers were crowding into the room.

"How tall he is!"

In truth, I was a full head taller than the biggest of them.

"And thin!"

"This anthropophagy doesn't seem to nourish them very well!"

Not all the voices were spiteful. A few sympathetic persons protected me:

"Don't crowd so—he's sick!"

"Come, friend, courage!" said the fat man, remarking my nervousness. "I'll lead you to a hospital myself."

He took me by the arm and set about elbowing the crowd aside, calling, "Way for an invalid!"

Dutch crowds are not very fierce. They let us pass, but they went with us. We walked along the canal, followed by a compact multitude, and people cried out, "It's a cannibal from Borneo!"

At length we reached a hospital. It was the visiting hour. I was taken to an intern, a young man with blue spectacles, who greeted me peevishly. My companion said to him, "He's a savage from the colonies."

"What, a savage!" cried the other.

He took off his spectacles to look at me. Surprise held him motionless for a moment. He asked me brusquely, "Can you see?"

"I see very well."

I had spoken too swiftly.

"It's his accent," said the fat man proudly. "Once more, friend."

I repeated it and made myself understood.

"Those aren't human eyes," murmured the student. "And the color! Is that the color of your race?"

Then I said, with a terrible effort to slow myself down, "I have come to show myself to a scientist."

"Then you're not ill?"

"No."

"And you come from Borneo?"

"No."

"Where are you from, then?"

"From Zwartendam, near Duisburg."

"Why, then, does this man claim you're from Borneo?"

"I didn't want to contradict him."

"And you wish to see a scientist?"

"Yes."

"Why?"

"To be studied."

"So as to earn money?"

"No, for nothing."

"You're not a pauper? A beggar?"

"No!"

"What makes you want to be studied?"

"My constitution—"

But again, in spite of my efforts, I had spoken too swiftly. I had to repeat myself.

"Are you sure you can see me?" he asked, staring at me. "Your eyes are like horn."

"I see very well."

And, moving to left and right, I snatched things up, put them down, threw them in the air and caught them again.

"Extraordinary!" said the young man.

His softened voice, almost friendly, filled me with hope. "See here," he said at last, "I really think Dr. van den Heuvel might be interested in your case. I'll go and inform him. Wait in the next room. And, by the way—I forgot—you're not ill, after all?"

"Not in the least."

"Good. Wait—go in there. The doctor won't be long."

I found myself seated among monsters preserved in alcohol: fetuses, infants with bestial shapes, colossal batrachians, vaguely anthropomorphic saurians.

This is well chosen for my waiting room, I thought. Am I not a candidate for one of these brandy-filled sepulchers?

VII

When Dr. van den Heuvel appeared, emotion overcame me. I had the thrill of the Promised Land—the joy of reaching it, the dread of being banished. The doctor, with his great bald forehead, the analyst's penetrating look, the mouth soft and yet stubborn, examined me in silence. As always, my excessive thinness, my great stature, my horny eyes, my violet color, caused him astonishment.

"You say you wish to be studied?" he asked at length.

I answered forcefully, almost violently, "Yes!"

He smiled with an approving air and asked me the usual question: "Do you see all right, with those eyes?"

"Very well. I can even see through wood, clouds—"

But I had spoken too fast. He glanced at me uneasily. I began again, sweating great drops: "I can even see through wood, clouds—"

"Really! That would be extraordinary. Well, then! What do you see through the door there?" He pointed to a closed door.

"A big library with windows . . . a carved table . . ."

"Really!" he repeated, stunned.

My breast swelled; a deep stillness entered my soul.

The scientist remained silent for a few seconds. Then: "You speak with some difficulty."

"Otherwise I should speak too rapidly! I cannot speak slowly."

"Well, then, speak a little as you do naturally."

Accordingly I told him the story of my entry into Amsterdam. He listened to me with an extreme attention, an air of intelligent observation, which I had never before encountered among my fellows. He understood nothing of what I said, but he showed the keenness of his intellect.

"If I am not mistaken, you speak fifteen to twenty syllables a second, that is to say three or four times more than the human ear can distinguish. Your voice, in addition, is much higher than anything I have ever heard in the way of human voices. Your excessively rapid gestures are well suited to your speech. Your whole constitution is probably more rapid than ours."

"I run," I said, "faster than a greyhound. I write—"

"Ah!" he interrupted. "Let us see your writing."

I scrawled some words on a tablet which he offered me, the first few fairly legible, the rest more and more scrambled, abbreviated.

"Perfect!" he said, and a certain pleasure was mingled with his surprise. "I really think I must congratulate myself on this meeting. Certainly it should be very interesting to study you."

"It is my dearest, my only, desire!"

"And mine, naturally. Science . . ."

He seemed preoccupied, musing. He finished by saying, "If only we could find an easy way of communication."

He walked back and forth, his brows knotted. Suddenly: "What a dolt I am! You must learn shorthand, of course! Hm! . . . Hm!" A cheerful expression spread over his face. "And I've forgotten the phonograph—the perfect confidant! All that's needed is to revolve it more slowly in the reproduction than in the recording. It's agreed: you shall stay with me while you are in Amsterdam!"

The joy of a fulfilled vocation, the delight of ceasing to spend vain and sterile days! Aware of the intelligent personality of the doctor, against this scientific background, I felt a delicious well-being; the melancholy of my spiritual solitude, the sorrow for my lost talents, the pariah's long misery that had weighed me down for so many years, all vanished, evaporated in the sensation of a new life, a real life, a saved destiny!

VIII

Beginning the following day, the doctor made all the necessary arrangements. He wrote to my parents; he sent me to a professor of stenography and obtained some phonographs. As he was quite rich and entirely devoted to science, there was no experiment which he could not undertake, and my vision, my hearing, my musculature, the color of my skin, were submitted to scrupulous investigations, from which he drew more and more enthusiasm, crying, "This verges on the miraculous!"

I very well understood, after the first few days, how important it was to go about things methodically—from the simple to the complex, from the slightly abnormal to the wonderfully abnormal. Thus I had recourse to a little legerdemain, of which I made no secret to the doctor: that is, I revealed my abilities to him only one at a time.

The quickness of my perceptions and movements drew his attention first. He was able to convince himself that the subtlety of my hearing was in proportion to the swiftness of my speech. Graduated trials of the most fugitive sounds, which I imitated with ease, and the words of ten or fifteen persons all talking at once, which I distinguished perfectly, demonstrated this point beyond question. My vision proved no less swift; comparative tests between my ability to resolve the movement of a galloping horse, or an insect in flight, and the same ability of an apparatus for taking instantaneous photographs, proved all in favor of my eye.

As for perceptions of ordinary things, simultaneous movements of a group of people, of children playing, the motion of machines, bits of rubble thrown in the air or little balls tossed into an alley, to be counted in flight—they amazed the doctor's family and friends.

My running in the big garden, my twenty-meter jumps, my instantaneous swiftness to pick up objects or put them back, were admired still more, not by the doctor, but by those around him. And it was an ever renewed pleasure for the wife and children of my host, while walking in the fields, to see me outstrip a horseman at full gallop or follow the flight of any swallow; in truth, there was no thoroughbred but I could give it a start of two-thirds the distance, whatever it might be, nor any bird I could not easily overtake.

As for the doctor, more and more satisfied with the results of his experiments, he described me thus: "A human being, endowed in all his movements with a swiftness incomparably superior, not merely to that of other humans, but also to that of all known animals. This swiftness, found in the most minute constituents of his body as well as in the whole organism, makes him an entity so distinct from the remainder of creation that he merits a special place in the animal kingdom for himself alone. As for the curious structure of his eyes, as well as the skin's violet color, these must be considered simply the earmarks of this special condition."

Tests being made of my muscular system, it proved in no way remarkable, unless for its excessive leanness. Neither did my ears yield any particular information; nor, for that matter, did my skin—except, of course, for its pigmentation. As for my dark hair, a purplish black in color, it was fine as spiderweb, and the doctor made a minute examination of it.

"One would need to dissect you!" he often told me, laughing.

Thus time passed easily. I had quickly learned to write in shorthand, thanks to my intense desire and to the natural aptitude I showed for this method of rapid transcription, into which, by the way, I introduced several new abbreviations. I began to make notes, which my stenographer transcribed; for the rest, we had phonographs built, according to the doctor's special design, which proved perfectly suited to reproduce my voice at a lower speed.

At length my host's confidence in me became complete. During the first few weeks he had not been able to avoid the suspicion—a very natural one—that my peculiar abilities might be accompanied by some mental abnormality, some cerebral derangement. This anxiety once put aside, our relations became perfectly cordial, and I think, as fascinating for one as for the other.

We made analytic tests of my ability to see through a great number of "opaque" substances; and of the dark coloration which water, glass or quartz takes on for me at certain thicknesses. It will be recalled that I can see clearly through wood, leaves, clouds and many other substances; that I can barely make out the bottom of a pool of water half a meter deep; and that a window, though transparent, is less so to me than to the average person and has a rather dark color. A thick piece of glass appears blackish to me. The doctor convinced himself at leisure of all these singularities—astonished above all to see me make out the stars on cloudy nights.

Only then did I begin to tell him that colors too present themselves differently to me. Experience established beyond doubt that red, orange, yellow, green, blue and indigo are perfectly invisible to me, like infrared or ultraviolet to a normal eye. On the other hand, I was able to show that I perceive violet, and beyond violet a range of colors—a spectrum at least double that which extends from the red to the violet.*

This amazed the doctor more than all the rest. His study of it was long and painstaking; it was conducted, besides, with enormous cunning. In this accomplished experimenter's hands, it became the source of subtle discoveries in the order of sciences as they are ranked by humanity; it gave him the key to far-ranging phenomena of magnetism, of chemical affinities, of induction; it guided him toward new conceptions of physiology. To know that a given metal shows a series of unknown tints, variable according to the pressure, the temperature, the electric charge, that the most rarefied gases have distinct colors, even at small depths; to learn of the infinite tonal richness of objects which appear more or less black, whereas they present a more magnificent spectrum in the ultraviolet than that of all known colors; to know, finally, the possible variations in unknown hues of an electric circuit, the bark of a tree, the skin of a man, in a day, an hour, a minute—the use that an ingenious scientist might make of such ideas can readily be imagined.

We worked patiently for a whole year without my mentioning the *Moedigen.* I wished to convince my host absolutely, give him countless proofs of my visual faculties, before daring the supreme confidence. At length, the time came when I felt I could reveal everything.

---

*Quartz gives me a spectrum of about eight colors: the longest violet and the seven succeeding colors in the ultraviolet. But there remain about eight more colors which are not refracted by quartz, and which are refracted more or less by other substances.

IX

It happened in a mild autumn full of clouds, which rolled across the vault of the sky for a week without shedding a drop of rain. One morning van den Heuvel and I were walking in the garden. The doctor was silent, completely absorbed in his speculations, of which I was the principal subject. At the far end, he began to speak:

"It's a nice thing to dream about, anyhow: to see through clouds, pierce through to the ether, whereas we, blind as we are . . ."

"If the sky were all I saw!" I answered.

"Oh, yes—the whole world, so different . . ."

"Much more different even than I've told you!"

"How's that?" he cried with an avid curiosity. "Have you been hiding something from me?"

"The most important thing!"

He stood facing me, staring at me fixedly, in real distress, in which some element of the mystical seemed to be blended.

"Yes, the most important thing!"

We had come near the house, and I dashed in to ask for a phonograph. The instrument that was brought to me was an advanced model, highly perfected by my friend, and could record a long speech; the servant put it down on the stone table where the doctor and his family took coffee on mild summer evenings. A miracle of exact, fine construction, the device lent itself admirably to recording casual talks. Our dialogue went on, therefore, almost like an ordinary conversation.

"Yes, I've hidden the main thing from you, because I wanted your complete confidence first—and even now, after all the discoveries you've made about my organism, I am afraid you won't find it easy to believe me, at least to begin with."

I stopped to let the machine repeat this sentence. I saw the doctor grow pale, with the pallor of a great scientist in the presence of a new aspect of matter. His hands were trembling.

"I shall believe you!" he said, with a certain solemnity.

"Even if I try to tell you that our order of creation—I mean our animal and vegetable world—isn't the only life on earth, that there is another, as vast, as numerous, as varied, invisible to your eyes?"

He scented occultism and could not refrain from saying, "The world of the fourth state of matter—departed souls, the phantoms of the spiritualists."

"No, no, nothing like that. A world of living creatures, doomed like us to a short life, to organic needs—birth, growth, struggle. A world as weak and ephemeral as ours, a world governed by laws equally rigid, if not identical, a world equally imprisoned by the earth, equally vulnerable to accident, but otherwise completely different from ours, without any influence on ours, as we have no influence on it—except through the changes it makes in our common ground, the earth, or through the parallel changes that we create in the same ground."

I do not know if van den Heuvel believed me, but certainly he was in the grip of strong emotion. "They are fluid, in short?" he asked.

"That's what I don't know how to answer, for their properties are too contradictory to fit into our ideas of matter. The earth is as resistant to them as to us, and the same with most minerals, although they can penetrate a little way into a humus. Also, they are totally impermeable and solid with respect to each other.

But they can pass through plants, animals, organic tissues, although sometimes with a certain difficulty; and we ourselves pass through them the same way. If one of them could be aware of us, we should perhaps seem fluid with respect to them, as they seem fluid with respect to us; but probably he could no more *decide* about it than I can—he would be struck by similar contradictions. There is one peculiarity about their shape: they have hardly any thickness. They are of all sizes. I've known some to reach a hundred meters in length, and others are as tiny as our smallest insects. Some of them feed on earth and air, others on air and on their own kind—without killing as we do, however, because it's enough for the stronger to draw strength from the weaker, and because this strength can be extracted without draining the springs of life."

The doctor said brusquely, "Have you seen them ever since childhood?"

I guessed that he was imagining some more or less recent disorder in my body. "Since childhood," I answered vigorously. "I'll give you all the proofs you like."

"Do you see them now?"

"I see them. There are a great many in the garden."

"Where?"

"On the path, the lawns, on the walls, in the air. For there are terrestrial and aerial ones—and aquatic ones too, but those hardly ever leave the surface of the water."

"Are they numerous everywhere?"

"Yes, and hardly less so in town than in the country, in houses than in the street. Those that like the indoors are smaller, though, no doubt because of the difficulty of getting in and out, even though they find a wooden door no obstacle."

"And iron . . . glass . . . brick?"

"All impermeable to them."

"Will you describe one of them, a fairly large one?"

"I see one near that tree. Its shape is extremely elongated, and rather irregular. It is convex toward the right, concave toward the left, with swellings and hollows: it looks something like an enlarged photograph of a big, fat larva. But its structure is not typical of the Kingdom, because structure varies a great deal from one species (if I may use that word) to another. Its extreme thinness, on the other hand, is a common characteristic: it can hardly be more than a tenth of a millimeter in thickness, whereas it's one hundred and fifty centimeters long and forty centimeters across at its widest.

"What distinguishes this, and the whole Kingdom, above all are the lines that cross it in nearly every direction, ending in networks that fan out between two systems of lines. Each system has a center, a kind of spot that is slightly raised above the mass of the body, or occasionally hollowed out. These centers have no fixed form; sometimes they are almost circular or elliptical, sometimes twisted or helical, sometimes divided by many narrow throats. They are astonishingly mobile, and their size varies from hour to hour. Their borders palpitate strongly, in a sort of transverse undulation. In general, the lines that emerge from them are big, although there are also very fine ones; they diverge, and end in an infinity of delicate traceries which gradually fade away. However, certain lines, much paler than the others, are not produced by the centers; they stay isolated in the system and grow without changing their color. These lines have the faculty of moving within the body, and of varying their curves, while the centers and their connected lines remain stable.

"As for the colors of my *Moedig*, I must forego any attempt to describe them to you; none of them falls within the spectrum perceptible to your eye, and none has a name in your vocabulary. They are extremely brilliant in the networks, weaker in the centers, very much faded in the independent lines, which, however, have a very high brilliance—an ultraviolet metallic effect, so to speak. . . . I have some observations on the habits, the diet and the range of the *Moedigen*, but I don't wish to submit them to you just now."

I fell silent. The doctor listened twice to the words recorded by our faultless interpreter; then for a long time he was silent. Never had I seen him in such a state: his face was rigid, stony, his eyes glassy and cataleptic; a heavy film of sweat covered his temples and dampened his hair. He tried to speak and failed. Trembling, he walked all around the garden; and when he reappeared, his eyes and mouth expressed a violent passion, fervent, religious; he seemed more like the disciple of some new faith than like a peaceful investigator.

At last he muttered, "I'm overwhelmed! Everything you have just said seems terribly lucid—and have I the right to doubt, considering all the wonders you've already shown me?"

"Doubt!" I said warmly. "Doubt as hard as you can! Your experiments will be all the more fruitful for it."

"Ah," he said in a dreaming voice, "it's the pure stuff of wonder, and so magnificently superior to the pointless marvels of fairy tales! My poor human intelligence is so tiny before such knowledge! I feel an enormous enthusiasm. Yet something in me doubts . . ."

"Let's work to dispel your doubt—our efforts will pay for themselves ten times over!" .

X

We worked; and it took the doctor only a few weeks to clear up all his uncertainties. Several ingenious experiments, together with the undeniable consistency of all the statements I had made, and two or three lucky discoveries about the *Moedigen*'s influence on atmospheric phenomena, left no question in his mind. When we were joined by the doctor's elder son, a young man of great scientific aptitude, the fruitfulness of our work and the conclusiveness of our findings were again increased.

Thanks to my companions' methodical habits of mind, and their experience in study and classification—qualities which I was absorbing little by little— whatever was uncoordinated or confused in my knowledge of the *Moedigen* rapidly became transformed. Our discoveries multiplied; rigorous experiments gave firm results, in circumstances which in ancient times and even up to the last century would have suggested at most a few trifling diversions.

It is now five years since we began our researches. They are far, very far from completion. Even a preliminary report of our work can hardly appear in the near future. In any case, we have made it a rule to do nothing in haste; our discoveries are too immanent a kind not to be set forth in the most minute detail, with the most sovereign patience and the finest precision. We have no other investigator to forestall, no patent to take out or ambition to satisfy. We stand at a height where vanity and pride fade away. How can there be any comparison between the joys of our work and the wretched lure of human fame? Besides, do not all these things flow from the single accident of my physical organization? What a petty thing it would be, then, for us to boast about them!

No; we live excitedly, always on the verge of wonders, and yet we live in immutable serenity.

I have had an adventure which adds to the interest of my life, and which fills me with infinite joy during my leisure hours. You know how ugly I am; my bizarre appearance is fit only to horrify young women. All the same, I have found a companion who not only can put up with my show of affection, but even takes pleasure in it.

She is a poor girl, hysterical and nervous, whom we met one day in a hospital in Amsterdam. Others find her wretched-looking, plaster-white, hollow-cheeked, with wild eyes. But to me her appearance is pleasant, her company charming. From the very beginning my presence, far from alarming her like all the rest, seemed to please and comfort her. I was touched; I wanted to see her again.

It was quickly discovered that I had a beneficial influence on her health and well-being. On examination, it appeared that I influenced her by animal magnetism: my nearness, and above all the touch of my hands, gave her a really curative gaiety, serenity, and calmness of spirit. In turn, I took pleasure in being near her. Her face seemed lovely to me; her pallor and slenderness were no more than signs of delicacy; for me her eyes, able to perceive the glow of magnets, like those of many hyperesthesiacs, had none at all of the distracted quality that others criticized.

In short, I felt an attraction for her, and she returned it with passion. From that time, I resolved to marry her. I gained my end readily, thanks to the good will of my friends.

This union has been a happy one. My wife's health was re-established, although she remained extremely sensitive and frail. I tasted the joy of being like other men in the essential part of life. But my happiness was crowned six months ago: a child was born to us, and in this child are combined all the faculties of my constitution. Color, vision, hearing, extreme rapidity of movement, diet—he promises to be an exact copy of my physiology.

The doctor watches him grow with delight. A wonderful hope has come to us—that the study of the *Moedig* World, of the Kingdom parallel to our own, this study which demands so much time and patience, will not end when I cease to be. My son will pursue it, undoubtedly, in his turn. Why may he not find collaborators of genius, able to raise it to a new power? Why may he also not give life to seers of the invisible world?

As for myself, may I not look forward to other children, may I not hope that my dear wife may give birth to other sons of my flesh, like unto their father? As I think of it, my heart trembles, I am filled with an infinite beatitude; and I know myself blessed among men.

Gordon Eklund & Gregory Benford

Gregory Benford (1941–   ) and Gordon Eklund (1945–   ) were sometime collaborators in the 1970s. At the start, Eklund was "the writer," producing many other stories and novels on his own, and Benford was "the scientist," a full-time physicist who occasionally published science fiction. But by the end of the decade, Benford had become one of the leading younger writers, producing two significant works, *In the Ocean of Night* (1977) and *The Stars in Shroud* (1978) and then the classic *Timescape* (1980), and Eklund, who had published many short stories and nine novels by 1976—*If the Stars Are Gods* (1977) was his tenth—stopped writing for long periods of time after 1979. Of all their works, this one (1975), later developed into the novel of the same title, is the best. It was to a large extent written by Eklund and revised by Benford.

Benford in his later works is the first among the hard SF writers to have mastered and integrated Modernist techniques of characterization and use of metaphor, and some of this may have been assimilated through his early collaboration with Eklund. The tension between the daily work of science and the avocation of writing in Benford's life has led him to write some of the finest science fiction of recent decades. Brian W. Aldiss says: "If he takes the close and narrow view of his characters—an all-too-human view, of illness, work and marital problems—his vision of the universe in which such frail beings exist is one of vast perspectives, rather in the tradition of Stapledon and Clarke."

"If the Stars Are Gods" is an intrusion of the metaphysical into the ordinary world of science fiction. It is very much in the tradition of Clarke, in the mode of *2001: A Space Odyssey*.

IF THE STARS ARE GODS

A dog cannot be a hypocrite, but neither can he be sincere.
—Ludwig Wittgenstein

It was deceptively huge and massive, this alien starship, and somehow seemed as if it belonged almost anywhere else in the universe but here.

Reynolds stepped carefully down the narrow corridor of the ship, still replaying in his mind's eye the approach to the air lock, the act of being swallowed. The ceilings were high, the light poor, the walls made of some dull, burnished metal.

These aspects and others flitted through his mind as he walked. Reynolds was a man who appreciated the fine interlacing pleasures of careful thought, but more than that, thinking so closely of these things kept his mind occupied and drove away the smell. It was an odd thick odor, and something about it upset his careful equilibrium. It clung to him like Pacific fog. Vintage manure, Reynolds had decided the moment he passed through the air lock. Turning, he had glared at Kelly firmly encased inside her suit. He told her about the smell. "Everybody stinks," she had said, evenly, perhaps joking, perhaps not, and pushed him away in the light centrifugal gravity. Away, into a maze of tight passages that would lead him eventually to look the first certified intelligent alien beings straight in the eye. If they happened to have eyes, that is.

It amused him that this privilege should be his. More rightly, the honor should have gone to another, someone younger whose tiny paragraph in the future histories of the human race had not already been enacted. At fifty-eight, Reynolds had long since lived a full and intricate lifetime. Too full, he sometimes thought, for any one man. So then, what about this day now? What about today? It did nothing really, only succeeded in forcing the fullness of his lifetime past the point of all reasonableness into a realm of positive absurdity.

The corridor branched again. He wondered precisely where he was inside the sculpted and twisted skin of the ship. He had tried to memorize everything he saw but there was nothing, absolutely nothing but metal with thin seams, places where he had to stoop or crawl, and the same awful smell. He realized now what it was about the ship that had bothered him the first time he had seen it, through a telescope from the moon. It reminded him, both in size and shape, of a building where he had once lived not so many years ago, during the brief term of his most recent retirement, 1987 and '88, in São Paulo, Brazil: a huge ultramodern lifting apartment complex of a distinctly radical design. There was nothing like it on Earth, the advertising posters had proclaimed; and seeing it, hating it instantly, he had agreed. Now here was something else truly like it, but not on Earth.

The building had certainly not resembled a starship, but then, neither did this thing. At one end was an intricately designed portion, a cylinder with interesting modifications. Then came a long, plain tube and at the end of that something truly absurd: a cone, opening outward away from the rest of the ship and absolutely empty. Absurd, until you realized what it was.

The starship's propulsion source was, literally, hydrogen bombs. The central tube evidently held a vast number of fusion devices. One by one the bombs were released, drifted to the mouth of the cone and were detonated. The cone was a huge shock absorber; the kick from the bomb pushed the ship forward. A Rube Goldberg star drive—

Directly ahead of him, the corridor neatly stopped and split, like the twin prongs of a roasting fork. It jogged his memory: roasting fork, yes, from the days when he still ate meat. Turning left, he followed the proper prong. His directions had been quite clear.

He still felt very ill at ease. Maybe it was the way he was dressed that made everything seem so totally wrong. It didn't seem quite right, walking through an alien maze in his shirtsleeves and plain trousers. Pedestrian.

But the air was breathable, as promised. Did they breathe this particular oxygen-nitrogen balance, too? And like the smell?

Ahead, the corridor parted, branching once more. The odor was horribly powerful at this spot, and he ducked his head low, almost choking, and dashed through a round opening.

This was a big room. Like the corridor, the ceiling was a good seven meters above the floor, but the walls were subdued pastel shades of red, orange and yellow. The colors were mixed on all the walls in random, patternless designs.

It was very pretty, Reynolds thought, and not at all strange. Also, standing neatly balanced near the back wall, there were two aliens.

When he saw the creatures, Reynolds stopped and stood tall. Raising his eyes, he stretched to reach the level of their eyes. While he did this, he also reacted. His first reaction was shock. This gave way to the tickling sensation of surprise. Then pleasure and relief. He liked the looks of these two creatures. They were certainly far kinder toward the eyes than what he had expected to find.

Stepping forward, Reynolds stood before both aliens, shifting his gaze from one to the other. Which was the leader? Or were both leaders? Or neither? He decided to wait. But neither alien made a sound or a move. So Reynolds kept waiting.

What had he expected to find? Men? Something like a man, that is, with two arms and two legs and a properly positioned head, with a nose, two eyes and a pair of floppy ears? This was what Kelly had expected him to find—she would be disappointed now—but Reynolds had never believed it for a moment. Kelly thought anything that spoke English had to be a man, but Reynolds was more imaginative. He knew better; he had not expected to find a man, not even a man with four arms and three legs and fourteen fingers or five ears. What he had expected to find was something truly alien. A blob, if worst came to worst, but at best something more like a shark or snake or wolf than a man. As soon as Kelly had told him that the aliens wanted to meet him—"Your man who best knows your star"—he had known this.

Now he said, "I am the man you wished to see. The one who knows the stars."

As he spoke, he carefully shared his gaze with both aliens, still searching for a leader, favoring neither over the other. One—the smaller one—twitched a nostril when Reynolds said, ". . . the stars"; the other remained motionless.

There was one Earth animal that did resemble these creatures, and this was why Reynolds felt happy and relieved. The aliens were sufficiently alien, yes. And they were surely not men. But neither did they resemble blobs or wolves or sharks or snakes. They were giraffes. Nice, kind, friendly, pleasant, smiling, silent giraffes. There were some differences, of course. The aliens' skin was a rainbow collage of pastel purples, greens, reds and yellows, similar in its random design to the colorfully painted walls. Their trunks stood higher off the ground, their necks were stouter than that of a normal giraffe. They did not have tails. Nor hooves. Instead, at the bottom of each of their four legs, they had five blunt short fingers and a single wide thick off-setting thumb.

"My name is Bradley Reynolds," he said. "I know the stars." Despite himself, their continued silence made him nervous. "Is something wrong?" he asked.

The shorter alien bowed its neck toward him. Then, in a shrill high-pitched voice that reminded him of a child, it said, "No." An excited nervous child. "That is no," it said.

"This?" Reynolds lifted his hand, having almost forgotten what was in it. Kelly had ordered him to carry the tape recorder, but now he could truthfully say, "I haven't activated it yet."

"Break it, please," the alien said.

Reynolds did not protest or argue. He let the machine fall to the floor. Then he jumped, landing on the tape recorder with both feet. The light aluminum case split wide open like the hide of a squashed apple. Once more, Reynolds jumped. Then, standing calmly, he kicked the broken bits of glass and metal toward an unoccupied corner of the room. "All right?" he asked.

Now for the first time the second alien moved. Its nostrils twitched daintily, then its legs shifted, lifting and falling. "Welcome," it said, abruptly, stopping all motion. "My name is Jonathon."

"Your name?" asked Reynolds.

"And this is Richard."

"Oh," said Reynolds, not contradicting. He understood now. Having learned the language of man, these creatures had learned his names as well.

"We wish to know your star," Jonathon said respectfully. His voice was a duplicate of the other's. Did the fact that he had not spoken until after the destruction of the tape recorder indicate that he was the leader of the two? Reynolds almost laughed, listening to the words of his own thoughts. Not *he*, he reminded himself: *it*.

"I am willing to tell you whatever you wish to know," Reynolds said.

"You are a . . . priest . . . a reverend of the sun?"

"An astronomer," Reynolds corrected.

"We would like to know everything you know. And then we would like to visit and converse with your star."

"Of course. I will gladly help you in any way I can." Kelly had cautioned him in advance that the aliens were interested in the sun, so none of this came as any surprise to him. But nobody knew what it was in particular that they wanted to know, or why, and Kelly hoped that he might be able to find out. At the moment he could think of only two possible conversational avenues to take; both were questions. He tried the first. "What is it you wish to know? Is our star greatly different from others of its type? If it is, we are unaware of this fact."

"No two stars are the same," the alien said. This was Jonathon again. Its voice began to rise in excitement. "What is it? Do you not wish to speak here? Is our craft an unsatisfactory place?"

"No, this is fine," Reynolds said, wondering if it was wise to continue concealing his puzzlement. "I will tell you what I know. Later, I can bring books."

"No!" The alien did not shout, but from the way its legs quivered and nostrils trembled, Reynolds gathered he had said something very improper indeed.

"I will tell you," he said. "In my own words."

Jonathon stood quietly rigid. "Fine."

Now it was time for Reynolds to ask his second question. He let it fall within the long silence which had followed Jonathon's last statement. "Why do you wish to know about our star?"

"It is the reason why we have come here. On our travels, we have visited many stars. But it is yours we have sought the longest. It is so powerful. And benevolent. A rare combination, as you must know."

"Very rare," Reynolds said, thinking that this wasn't making any sense. But then, why should it? At least he had learned something of the nature of the aliens' mission, and that alone was more than anyone else had managed to learn during the months the aliens had slowly approached the moon, exploding their hydrogen bombs to decelerate.

A sudden burst of confidence surprised Reynolds. He had not felt this sure of himself in years, and just like before, there was no logical reason for his certainty. "Would you be willing to answer some questions for me? About *your* star?"

"Certainly, Bradley Reynolds."

"Can you tell me our name for your star? Its coordinates?"

"No," Jonathon said, dipping its neck. "I cannot." It blinked its right eye in a furious fashion. "Our galaxy is not this one. It is a galaxy too distant for your instruments."

"I see," said Reynolds, because he could not very well call the alien a liar, even if it was. But Jonathon's hesitancy to reveal the location of its homeworld was not unexpected; Reynolds would have acted the same in similar circumstances.

Richard spoke. "May I pay obeisance?"

Jonathon, turning to Richard, spoke in a series of shrill chirping noises. Then Richard replied in kind.

Turning back to Reynolds, Richard again asked, "May I pay obeisance?"

Reynolds could only say, "Yes." Why not?

Richard acted immediately. Its legs abruptly shot out from beneath its trunk at an angle no giraffe could have managed. Richard sat on its belly, legs spread, and its neck came down, the snout gently scraping the floor.

"Thank you," Reynolds said, bowing slightly at the waist. "But there is much we can learn from you, too." He spoke to hide his embarrassment, directing his words at Jonathon while hoping that they might serve to bring Richard back to its feet as well. When this failed to work, Reynolds launched into the speech he had been sent here to deliver. Knowing what he had to say, he ran through the words as hurriedly as possible. "We are a backward people. Compared to you, we are children in the universe. Our travels have carried us no farther than our sister planets, while you have seen stars whose light takes years to reach your home. We realize you have much to teach us, and we approach you as pupils before a grand philosopher. We are gratified at the chance to share our meager knowledge with you and wish only to be granted the privilege of listening to you in return."

"You wish to know deeply of our star?" Jonathon asked.

"Of many things," Reynolds said. "Your spacecraft for instance. It is far beyond our meager knowledge."

Jonathon began to blink its right eye furiously. As it spoke, the speed of the blinking increased. "You wish to know that?"

"Yes, if you are willing to share your knowledge. We, too, would like to visit the stars."

Its eye moved faster than ever now. It said, "Sadly, there is nothing we can tell you of this ship. Unfortunately, we know nothing ourselves."

"Nothing?"

"The ship was a gift."

"You mean that you did not make it yourself. No. But you must have mechanics, individuals capable of repairing the craft in the event of some emergency."

"But that has never happened. I do not think the ship could fail."

"Would you explain?"

"Our race, our world, was once visited by another race of creatures. It was they who presented us with this ship. They had come to us from a distant star in order to make this gift. In return, we have used the ship only to increase the wisdom of our people."

"What can you tell me about this other race?" Reynolds asked.

"Very little, I am afraid. They came from a most ancient star near the true center of the universe."

"And were they like you? Physically?"

"No, more like you. Like people. But—please—may we be excused to converse about that which is essential? Our time is short."

Reynolds nodded, and the moment he did, Jonathon ceased to blink. Reynolds gathered that it had grown tired of lying, which wasn't surprising; Jonathon was a poor liar. Not only were the lies incredible in themselves, but every time it told a lie it blinked like a madman with an ash in his eye.

"If I tell you about our star," Jonathon said, "will you consent to tell of yours in return?" The alien tilted its head forward, long neck swaying gently from side to side. It was plain that Jonathon attached great significance to Reynolds' reply.

So Reynolds said, "Yes, gladly," though he found he could not conceive of any information about the sun which might come as a surprise to these creatures. Still, he had been sent here to discover as much about the aliens as possible without revealing anything important about mankind. This sharing of information about stars seemed a safe enough course to pursue.

"I will begin," Jonathon said, "and you must excuse my impreciseness of expression. My knowledge of your language is limited. I imagine you have a special vocabulary for the subject."

"A technical vocabulary, yes."

The alien said, "Our star is a brother to yours. Or would it be sister? During periods of the most intense communion, his wisdom—or hers?—is faultless. At times he is angry—unlike your star—but these moments are not frequent. Nor do they last for longer than a few fleeting moments. Twice he has prophesied the termination of our civilization during times of great personal anger, but never has he felt it necessary to carry out his prediction. I would say that he is more kind than raging, more gentle than brutal. I believe he loves our people most truly and fully. Among the stars of the universe, his place is not great, but as our home star, we must revere him. And, of course, we do."

"Would you go on?" Reynolds asked.

Jonathon went on. Reynolds listened. The alien spoke of its personal relationship with the star, how the star had helped it during times of individual darkness. Once, the star had assisted it in choosing a proper mate; the choice proved not only perfect but divine. Throughout, Jonathon spoke of the star as a reverent Jewish tribesman might have spoken of the Old Testament God. For the first time, Reynolds regretted having had to dispose of the tape recorder. When he tried to tell Kelly about this conversation, she would never believe a word of it. As it spoke, the alien did not blink, not once, even briefly, for Reynolds watched carefully.

At last the alien was done. It said, "But this is only a beginning. We have so much to share, Bradley Reynolds. Once I am conversant with your technical vocabulary. Communication between separate entities—the great barriers of language . . ."

"I understand," said Reynolds.

"We knew you would. But now—it is your turn. Tell me about your star."

"We call it the sun," Reynolds said. Saying, this, he felt more than mildly foolish—but what else? How could he tell Jonathon what it wished to know when he did not know himself? All he knew about the sun was facts. He knew how hot it was and how old it was and he knew its size and mass and magnitude. He knew about sunspots and solar winds and solar atmosphere. But that was all he knew. Was the sun a benevolent star? Was it constantly enraged? Did all mankind revere it with the proper quantity of love and dedication? "That is its common name. More properly, in an ancient language adopted by science, it is Sol. It lies approximately eight—"

"Oh," said Jonathon. "All of this, yes, we know. But its demeanor. Its attitudes, both normal and abnormal. You play with us, Bradley Reynolds. You joke. We understand your amusement—but, please, we are simple souls and have traveled far. We must know these other things before daring to make our personal approach to the star. Can you tell us in what fashion it has most often affected your individual life? This would help us immensely."

Although his room was totally dark, Reynolds, entering, did not bother with the light. He knew every inch of this room, knew it as well in the dark as the light. For the past four years, he had spent an average of twelve hours a day here. He knew the four walls, the desk, the bed, the bookshelves and the books, knew them more intimately than he had ever known another person. Reaching the cot without once stubbing his toe or tripping over an open book or stumbling across an unfurled map, he sat down and covered his face with his hands, feeling the wrinkles on his forehead like great wide welts. Alone, he played a game with the wrinkles, pretending that each one represented some event or facet of his life. This one here—the big one above his left eyebrow—that was Mars. And this other one—way over here almost by his right ear—that was a girl named Melissa whom he had known back in the 1970s. But he wasn't in the proper mood for the game now. He lowered his hands. He knew the wrinkles for exactly what they really were: age, purely and simply and honestly age. Each one meant nothing without the others. They represented impersonal and unavoidable erosion. On the outside, they reflected the death that was occurring on the inside.

Still, he was happy to be back here in this room. He never realized how important these familiar surroundings were to his state of mind until he was forcefully deprived of them for a length of time. Inside the alien starship, it hadn't been so bad. The time had passed quickly then; he hadn't been allowed to get homesick. It was afterward when it had got bad. With Kelly and the others in her dank, ugly impersonal hole of an office. Those had been the unbearable hours.

But now he was home, and he would not have to leave again until they told him. He had been appointed official emissary to the aliens, though this did not fool him for a moment. He had been given the appointment only because Jonathon had refused to see anyone else. It wasn't because anyone liked him or respected him or thought him competent enough to handle the mission. He was different from them, and that made all the difference. When they were still kids, they had seen his face on the old TV networks every night of the week. Kelly wanted someone like herself to handle the aliens. Someone who knew how to take orders, someone ultimately competent, some computer facsimile of a human being. Like herself. Someone who, when given a job, performed it in the most efficient manner in the least possible time.

Kelly was the director of the moon base. She had come here two years ago, replacing Bill Newton, a contemporary of Reynolds', a friend of his. Kelly was the protégé of some U.S. Senator, some powerful idiot from the Midwest, a leader of the anti-NASA faction in the Congress. Kelly's appointment had been part of a wild attempt to subdue the senator with favors and special attention. It had worked after a fashion. There were still Americans on the moon. Even the Russians had left two years ago.

Leaving the alien starship, he had met Kelly the instant he reached the air lock. He had managed to slip past her and pull on his suit before she could question him. He had known she wouldn't dare try to converse over the radio; too great a chance of being overheard. She would never trust him to say only the right things.

But that little game had done nothing except delay matters a few minutes. The tug had returned to the moon base and then everyone had gone straight to Kelly's office. Then the interrogation had begun. Reynolds had sat near the back of the room while the rest of them flocked around Kelly like pet sheep.

Kelly asked the first question. "What do they want?" He knew her well enough to understand exactly what she meant: What do they want from us in return for what we want from them?

Reynolds told her: They wanted to know about the sun.

"We gathered that much," Kelly said. "But what kind of information do they want? Specifically, what are they after?"

With great difficulty, he tried to explain this too.

Kelly interrupted him quickly. "And what did you tell them?"

"Nothing," he said.

"Why?"

"Because I didn't know what to tell them."

"Didn't you ever happen to think the best thing to tell them might have been whatever it was they wished to hear?"

"I couldn't do that either," he said, "because I didn't know. You tell me: Is the sun benevolent? How does it inspire your daily life? does it constantly rage? I don't know, and you don't know either, and it's not a thing we can risk lying about, because they may very well know themselves. To them, a star is a living entity. It's a god, but more than our gods, because they can see a star and feel its heat and never doubt that it's always there."

"Will they want you back?" she asked.

"I think so. They liked me. Or he liked me. It. I only talked to one of them."

"I thought you told us two."

So he went over the whole story for her once more, from beginning to end, hoping this time she might realize that alien beings are not human beings and should not be expected to respond in familiar ways. When he came to the part about the presence of the two aliens, he said, "Look. There are six men in this room right now besides us. But they are here only for show. The whole time, none of them will say a word or think a thought or decide a point. The other alien was in the room with Jonathon and me the whole time. But if it had not been there, nothing would have been changed. I don't know why it was there and I don't expect I ever will. But neither do I understand why you feel you have to have all these men here with you."

She utterly ignored the point. "Then that is all they are interested in? They're pilgrims and they think the sun is Mecca?"

"More or less," he said, with the emphasis on "less."

"Then they won't want to talk to me—or any of us. You're the one who knows the sun. Is that correct?" She jotted a note on a pad, shaking her elbow briskly.

"That is correct."

"Reynolds," she said, looking up from her pad, "I sure as hell hope you know what you're doing."

He said, "Why?"

She did not bother to attempt to disguise her contempt. Few of them did any more and especially not Kelly. It was her opinion that Reynolds should not be here at all. Put him in a rest home back on Earth, she would say. The other astronauts—they were considerate enough to retire when life got too complicated for them. What makes this one man, Bradley Reynolds, why is he so special? All right—she would admit—ten years, twenty years ago, he was a great brave man struggling to conquer the unknown. When I was sixteen years old, I couldn't walk a dozen feet without tripping over his name or face. But what about now? What is he? I'll tell you what he is: a broken-down, wrinkled relic of an old man. So what if he's an astronomer as well as an astronaut? So what if he's the best possible man for the Lunar observatory? I still say he's more trouble than he's worth. He walks around the moon base like a dog having a dream. Nobody can communicate with him. He hasn't attended a single psychological expansion session since he's been here, and that goes back well before my time. He's a morale problem; nobody can stand the sight of him any more. And, as far as doing his job goes, he does it, yes—but that's all. His heart isn't in it. Look, he didn't even know about the aliens being in orbit until I called him in and told him they wanted to see him.

That last part was not true, of course. Reynolds, like everyone, had known about the aliens, but he did not have to admit that their approach had not overly concerned him. He had not shared the hysteria which had gripped the whole of the Earth when the announcement was made that an alien starship had entered the system. The authorities had known about it for months before ever releasing the news. By the time anything was said publicly, it had been clearly determined that the aliens offered Earth no clear or present danger. But that was about all anyone had learned. Then the starship had gone into orbit around the moon, an action intended to confirm their lack of harmful intent toward Earth, and the entire problem had landed with a thud in Kelly's lap. The aliens said they wanted to meet a man who knew something about the sun, and that had turned out to be Reynolds. Then—and only then—had he had a real reason to become interested in the aliens. That day, for the first time in a half-dozen years, he had actually listened to the daily news broadcasts from Earth. He discovered—and it didn't particularly surprise him—that everyone else had long since got over their initial interest in the aliens. He gathered that war was brewing again. In Africa this time, which was a change in place if not in substance. The aliens were mentioned once, about halfway through the program, but Reynolds could tell they were no longer considered real news. A meeting between a representative of the American moon base and the aliens was being arranged, the newscaster said. It would take place aboard the aliens' ship in orbit around the moon, he added. The name Bradley Reynolds was not mentioned. I wonder if they remember me, he had thought.

"It seems to me that you could get more out of them than some babble about stars being gods," Kelly said, getting up and pacing around the room, one hand on hip. She shook her head in mock disbelief and the brown curls swirled downward, flowing like dark honey in the light gravity.

"Oh, I did," he said casually.

"What?" There was a rustling of interest in the room.

"A few facts about their planet. Some bits of detail I think fit together. It may even explain their theology."

"Explain theology with astronomy?" Kelly said sharply. "There's no mystery to sun worship. It was one of our primitive religions." A man next to her nodded.

"Not quite. Our star is relatively mild-mannered, as Jonathon would say. And our planet has a nice, comfortable orbit, nearly circular."

"Theirs doesn't?"

"No. The planet has a pronounced axial inclination, too, nothing ordinary like Earth's twenty-three degrees. Their world must be tilted at forty degrees or so to give the effects Jonathon mentioned."

"Hot summers?" one of the men he didn't know said, and Reynolds looked up in mild surprise. So the underlings were not just spear-carriers, as he had thought. Well enough.

"Right. The axial tilt causes each hemisphere to alternately slant toward and then away from their star. They have colder winters and hotter summers than we do. But there's something more, as far as I can figure it out. Jonathon says its world 'does not move in the perfect path' and that ours, on the other hand, very nearly does."

"Perfect path?" Kelly said, frowning. "An eight-fold way? The path of enlightenment?"

"More theology," said the man who had spoken.

"Not quite," Reynolds said. "Pythagoras believed the circle was a perfect form, the most beautiful of all figures. I don't see why Jonathon shouldn't."

"Astronomical bodies look like circles. Pythagoras could see the moon," Kelly said.

"And the sun," Reynolds said. "I don't know whether Jonathon's world has a moon or not. But they can see their star, and in profile it's a circle."

"So a circular orbit is a perfect orbit."

"Q.E.D. Jonathon says its planet doesn't have one, though."

"It's an ellipse."

"A very eccentric ellipse. That's my guess, anyway. Jonathon used the terms 'path-summer' and 'pole-summer,' so they do distinguish between the two effects."

"I don't get it," the man said.

"An ellipse alone gives alternate summers and winters, but in both hemispheres at the same time," Kelly said brusquely, her mouth turning slightly downward. "A 'pole-summer' must be the kind Earth has."

"Oh," the man said weakly.

"You left out the 'great-summer,' my dear," Reynolds said with a thin smile.

"What's that?" Kelly said carefully.

"When the 'pole-summer' coincides with the 'path-summer'—which it will, every so often. I wouldn't want to be around when that happens. Evidently neither do the members of Jonathon's race."

"How do they get away?" Kelly said intently.

"Migrate. One hemisphere is having a barely tolerable summer while the other is being fried alive, so they go there. The whole race."

"Nomads," Kelly said. "An entire culture born with a pack on its back," she said distantly. Reynolds raised an eyebrow. It was the first time he had ever heard her say anything that wasn't crisp, efficient and uninteresting.

"I think that's why they're grazing animals, to make it easy—even necessary—to keep on the move. A 'great-summer' wilts all the vegetation; a 'great-winter'—they must have those, too—freezes a continent solid."

"God," Kelly said quietly.

"Jonathon mentioned huge storms, winds that knocked it down, sand that buried it overnight in dunes. The drastic changes in the climate must stir up hurricanes and tornadoes."

"Which they have to migrate through," Kelly said. Reynolds noticed that the room was strangely quiet.

"Jonathon seems to have been born on one of the Treks. They don't have much shelter because of the winds and the winters that erode away the rock. It must be hard to build up any sort of technology in an environment like that. I suppose it's pretty inevitable that they turned out to believe in astrology."

"What?" Kelly said, surprised.

"Of course." Reynolds looked at her, completely deadpan. "What else should I call it? With such a premium on reading the stars correctly, so that they know the precise time of year and when the next 'great-summer' is coming—what else would they believe in? Astrology would be the obvious, unchallengeable religion—because it worked!" Reynolds smiled to himself, imagining a flock of atheist giraffes vainly fighting their way through a sandstorm.

"I see," Kelly said, clearly at a loss. The men stood around them awkwardly, not knowing quite what to say to such a barrage of unlikely ideas. Reynolds felt a surge of joy. Some lost capacity of his youth had returned: to see himself as the center of things, as the only actor onstage who moved of his own volition, spoke his own unscripted lines. *This is the way the world feels when you are winning,* he thought. This was what he had lost, what Mars had taken from him during the long trip back in utter deep silence and loneliness. He had tested himself there and found some inner core, had come to think he did not need people and the fine edge of competition with them. Work and cramped rooms had warped him.

"I think that's why they are technologically retarded, despite their age. They don't really have the feel of machines, they've never gotten used to them. When they needed a starship for their religion, they built the most awkward one imaginable that would work." Reynolds paused, feeling lightheaded. "They live inside that machine, but they don't like it. They stink it up and make it feel like a corral. They mistrusted that tape recorder of mine. They must want to know the stars very badly, to depart so much from their nature just to reach them."

Kelly's lip stiffened and her eyes narrowed. Her face, Reynolds thought, was returning to its usual expression. "This is all very well, Dr. Reynolds," she said, and it was the old Kelly, the one he knew; the Kelly who always came out on top. "But it is speculation. We need facts. Their starship is crude, but it *works.* They must have data and photographs of stars. They know things we don't. There are innumerable details we could only find by making the trip ourselves, and even using their ship, that will take centuries—Houston tells me that bomb-thrower of theirs can't go above one percent of light velocity. I want—"

"I'll try," he said. "But I'm afraid it won't be easy. Whenever I try to approach a subject it does not want to discuss, the alien begins telling me the most fantastic lies."

"Oh?" Kelly said suspiciously, and he was sorry he had mentioned that, because it had taken him another quarter hour of explaining before she had allowed him to escape the confines of her office.

Now he was back home again—in his room. Rolling over, he lay flat on his back in the bed, eyes wide open and staring straight ahead at the emptiness of the darkness. He would have liked to go out and visit the observatory, but Kelly had said he was excused from all duties until the alien situation was resolved. He gathered she meant that as an order. She must have. One thing about Kelly: she seldom said a word unless it was meant as an order.

.   .   .

They came and woke him up. He had not intended to sleep. His room was still pitch-black, and far away there was a fist pounding furiously upon a door. Getting up, taking his time, he went and let the man inside. Then he turned on the light.

"Hurry and see the director," the man said breathlessly.

"What does she want now?" Reynolds asked.

"How should I know?"

Reynolds shrugged and turned to go. He knew what she wanted anyway. It had to be the aliens; Jonathon was ready to see him again. Well, that was fine, he thought, entering Kelly's office. From the turn of her expression, he saw that he had guessed correctly. And I know exactly what I'm going to tell them, he thought.

Somewhere in his sleep, Reynolds had made an important decision. He had decided he was going to tell Jonathon the truth.

Approaching the alien starship, Reynolds discovered he was no longer so strongly reminded of his old home in São Paulo. Now that he had actually been inside the ship and had met the creatures who resided there, his feelings had changed. This time he was struck by how remarkably this strange twisted chunk of metal resembled what a real starship ought to look like.

The tug banged against the side of the ship. Without having to be told, Reynolds removed his suit and went to the air lock. Kelly jumped out of her seat and dashed after him. She grabbed the camera off the deck and forced it into his hands. She wanted him to photograph the aliens. He had to admit her logic was quite impeccable. If the aliens were as unfearsome as Reynolds claimed, then a clear and honest photograph could only reassure the population of Earth; hysteria was still a worry to many politicians back home. Many people still claimed that a spaceship full of green monsters was up here orbiting the moon only a few hours' flight from New York and Moscow. One click of the camera and this fear would be ended.

Reynolds had told her Jonathon would never permit a photograph to be taken, but Kelly had remained adamant. "Who cares?" he'd asked her.

"Everyone cares," she'd insisted.

"Oh, really? I listened to the news yesterday and the aliens weren't even mentioned. Is that hysteria?"

"That's because of Africa. Wait till the war's over, then listen."

He hadn't argued with her then and he didn't intend to argue with her now. He accepted the camera without a word, her voice burning his ears with last-minute instructions, and plunged ahead.

The smell assaulted him immediately. As he entered the spaceship, the odor seemed to rise up from nowhere and surround him. He made himself push forward. Last time, the odor had been a problem only for a short time. He was sure he could overcome it again this time.

It was cold in the ship. He wore only light pants and a light shirt without underwear, because last time it had been rather warm. Had Jonathon, noticing his discomfort, lowered the ship's temperature accordingly?

He turned the first corner and glanced briefly at the distant ceiling. He called out, "Hello!" but there was only a slight echo. He spoke again and the echo was the same, flat and hard.

Another turn. He was moving much faster than before. The tight passages no longer caused him to pause and think. He simply plunged ahead, trusting his own knowledge. At Kelly's urging he was wearing a radio attached to his belt. He noticed that it was beeping furiously at him. Apparently Kelly had neglected some important last-minute direction. He didn't mind. He already had enough orders to ignore; one less would make little difference.

Here was the place. Pausing in the doorway, he removed the radio, turning it off. Then he placed the camera on the floor beside it, and stepped into the room.

Despite the chill in the air, the room was not otherwise different from before. There were two aliens standing against the farthest wall. Reynolds went straight toward them, holding his hands over his head in greeting. One was taller than the other. Reynolds spoke to it. "Are you Jonathon?"

"Yes," Jonathon said, in its child's piping voice. "And this is Richard."

"May I pay obeisance?" Richard asked eagerly.

Reynolds nodded. "If you wish."

Jonathon waited until Richard had regained its feet, then said, "We wish to discuss your star now."

"All right," Reynolds said. "But there's something I have to tell you first." Saying this, for the first time since he made his decision, he wasn't sure. Was the truth really the best solution in this situation? Kelly wanted him to lie: tell them whatever they wanted to hear, making certain he didn't tell them quite everything. Kelly was afraid the aliens might go sailing off to the sun once they had learned what they had come here to learn. She wanted a chance to get engineers and scientists inside their ship before the aliens left. And wasn't this a real possibility? What if Kelly was right and the aliens went away? Then what would he say?

"You want to tell us that your sun is not a conscious being," Jonathon said. "Am I correct?"

The problem was instantly solved. Reynolds felt no more compulsion to lie. He said, "Yes."

"I am afraid that you are wrong," said Jonathon.

"We live here, don't we? Wouldn't we know? You asked for me because I know our sun, and I do. But there are other men on our homeworld who know far more than I do. But no one has ever discovered the last shred of evidence to support your theory."

"A theory is a guess," Jonathon said. "We do not guess; we know."

"Then," Reynolds said, "explain it to me. Because I don't know." He watched the alien's eyes carefully, waiting for the first indication of a blinking fit.

But Jonathon's gaze remained steady and certain. "Would you like to hear of our journey?" it asked.

"Yes."

"We left our homeworld a great many of your years ago. I cannot tell you exactly when, for reasons I'm certain you can understand, but I will reveal that it was more than a century ago. In that time we have visited nine stars. The ones we would visit were chosen for us beforehand. Our priests—our leaders—determined the stars that were within our reach and also able to help in our quest. You see, we have journeyed here in order to ask certain questions."

"Questions of the stars?"

"Yes, of course. The questions we have are questions only a star may answer."

"And what are they?" Reynolds asked.

"We have discovered the existence of other universes parallel with our own.

Certain creatures—devils and demons—have come from these universes in order to attack and capture our stars. We feel we must—"

"Oh, yes," Reynolds said. "I understand. We've run across several of these creatures recently." And he blinked, matching the twitching of Jonathon's eye. "They are awfully fearsome, aren't they?" When Jonathon stopped, he stopped too. He said, "You don't have to tell me everything. But can you tell me this: these other stars you have visited, have they been able to answer any of your questions?"

"Oh, yes. We have learned much from them. These stars were very great—very different from our own."

"But they weren't able to answer all your questions?"

"If they had, we would not be here now."

"And you believe our star may be able to help you?"

"All may help, but the one we seek is the one that can save us."

"When do you plan to go to the sun?"

"At once," Jonathon said. "As soon as you leave. I am afraid there is little else you can tell us."

"I'd like to ask you to stay," Reynolds said. And he forced himself to go ahead. He knew he could not convince Jonathon without revealing everything, yet, by doing so, he might also be putting an end to all his hopes. Still, he told the alien about Kelly and, more generally, he told it what the attitude of man was toward their visit. He told it what man wished to know from them, and why.

Jonathon seemed amazed. It moved about the floor as Reynolds spoke, its feet clanking dully. Then it stopped and stood, its feet only a few inches apart, a position that impressed Reynolds as one of incredulous amazement. "Your people wish to travel farther into space? You want to visit the stars? But why, Reynolds? Your people do not believe. Why?"

Reynolds smiled. Each time Jonathon said something to him, he felt he knew these people—and how they thought and reacted—a little better than he had before. There was another question he would very much have liked to ask Jonathon. How long have your people possessed the means of visiting the stars? A very long time, he imagined. Perhaps a longer time than the whole life-span of the human race. And why hadn't they gone before now? Reynolds thought he knew: because, until now, they had had no reason for going.

Now Reynolds tried to answer Jonathon's question. If anyone could, it should be he. "We wish to go to the stars because we are a dissatisfied people. Because we do not live a very long time as individuals, we feel we must place an important part of our lives into the human race as a whole. In a sense, we surrender a portion of our individual person in return for a sense of greater immortality. What is an accomplishment for man as a race is also an accomplishment for each individual man. And what are these accomplishments? Basically this: anything a man does that no other man has done before—whether it is good or evil or neither one or both—is considered by us to be a great accomplishment."

And—to add emphasis to the point—he blinked once.

Then, holding his eyes steady, he said, "I want you to teach me to talk to the stars. I want you to stay here around the moon long enough to do that."

Instantly Jonathon said, "No."

There was an added force to the way it said it, an emphasis its voice had not previously possessed. Then Reynolds realized what that was: at the same moment Jonathon had spoken, Richard too had said, "No."

"Then you may be doomed to fail," Reynolds said. "Didn't I tell you? I know our star better than any man available to you. Teach me to talk to the stars and I may be able to help you with this one. Or would you prefer to continue wandering the galaxy forever, failing to find what you seek wherever you go?"

"You are a sensible man, Reynolds. You may be correct. We will ask our home star and see."

"Do that. And if it says yes and I promise to do what you wish, then I must ask you to promise me something in return. I want you to allow a team of our scientists and technicians to enter and inspect your ship. You will answer their questions to the best of your ability. And that means truthfully."

"We always tell the truth," Jonathon said, blinking savagely.

The moon had made one full circuit of the Earth since Reynolds' initial meeting with the aliens, and he was quite satisfied with the progress he had made up to now, especially during the past ten days after Kelly had stopped accompanying him in his daily shuttles to and from the orbiting starship. As a matter of fact, in all that time, he had not had a single face-to-face meeting with her and they had talked on the phone only once. And she wasn't here now either, which was strange, since it was noon and she always ate here with the others.

Reynolds had a table to himself in the cafeteria. The food was poor, but it always was, and he was used to that by now. What did bother him, now that he was thinking about it, was Kelly's absence. Most days he skipped lunch himself. He tried to remember the last time he had come here. It was more than a week ago, he remembered—more than ten days ago. He didn't like the sound of that answer.

Leaning over, he attracted the attention of a girl at an adjoining table. He knew her vaguely. Her father had been an important wheel in NASA when Reynolds was still a star astronaut. He couldn't remember the man's name. His daughter had a tiny cute face and a billowing body about two sizes too big for the head. Also, she had a brain that was much too limited for much of anything. She worked in the administrative section, which meant she slept with most of the men on the base at one time or another.

"Have you seen Kelly?" he asked her.

"Must be in her office."

"No, I mean when was the last time you saw her here?"

"In here? Oh—" The girl thought for a moment. "Doesn't she eat with the other chiefs?"

Kelly never ate with the other chiefs. She always ate in the cafeteria—for morale purposes—and the fact that the girl did not remember having seen her meant that it had been several days at least since Kelly had last put in an appearance. Leaving his lunch where it lay, Reynolds got up, nodded politely at the girl, who stared at him as if he were a freak, and hurried away.

It wasn't a long walk, but he ran. He had no intention of going to see Kelly. He knew that would prove useless. Instead, he was going to see John Sims. At fifty-two, Sims was the second oldest man in the base. Like Reynolds, he was a former astronaut. In 1987, when Reynolds, then a famous man, was living in São Paulo, Sims had commanded the first (and only) truly successful Mars expedition. During those few months, the world had heard his name, but people forgot quickly, and Sims was one of the things they forgot. He had never done more than what he was expected to do; the threat of death had never come near Sims' expedition. Reynolds, on the other hand, had failed. On Mars with him, three men had died. Yet it was he—Reynolds, the failure—who had been the hero, not Sims.

And maybe I'm a hero again, he thought, as he knocked evenly on the door to Sims' office. Maybe down there the world is once more reading about me daily. He hadn't listened to a news broadcast since the night before his first trip to the ship. Had the story been released to the public yet? He couldn't see any reason why it should be suppressed, but that seldom was important. He would ask Sims. Sims would know.

The door opened and Reynolds went inside. Sims was a huge man who wore his black hair in a crewcut. The style had been out of fashion for thirty or forty years; Reynolds doubted there was another crewcut man in the universe. But he could not imagine Sims any other way.

"What's wrong?" Sims asked, guessing accurately the first time. He led Reynolds to a chair and sat him down. The office was big but empty. A local phone sat upon the desk along with a couple of daily status reports. Sims was assistant administrative chief, whatever that meant. Reynolds had never understood the functions of the position, if any. But there was one thing that was clear: Sims knew more about the inner workings of the moon base than any other man. And that included the director as well.

"I want to know about Vonda," Reynolds said. With Sims, everything stood on a first-name basis. Vonda was Vonda Kelly. The name tasted strangely upon Reynolds' lips. "Why isn't she eating at the cafeteria?"

Sims answered unhesitant. "Because she's afraid to leave her desk."

"It has something to do with the aliens?"

"It does, but I shouldn't tell you what. She doesn't want you to know."

"Tell me. Please." His desperation cleared the smile from Sims' lips. And he had almost added: for old times' sake. He was glad he had controlled himself.

"The main reason is the war," Sims said. "If it starts, she wants to know at once."

"Will it?"

Sims shook his head. "I'm smart but I'm not God. As usual, I imagine everything will work out as long as no one makes a stupid mistake. The worst will be a small local war lasting maybe a month. But how long can you depend upon politicians to act intelligently? It goes against the grain with them."

"But what about the aliens?"

"Well, as I said, that's part of it too." Sims stuck his pipe in his mouth. Reynolds had never seen it lit, never seen him smoking it, but the pipe was invariably there between his teeth. "A group of men are coming here from Washington, arriving tomorrow. They want to talk with your pets. It seems nobody—least of all Vonda—is very happy with your progress."

"I am."

Sims shrugged, as if to say: that is of no significance.

"The aliens will never agree to see them," Reynolds said.

"How are they going to stop them? Withdraw the welcome mat? Turn out the lights? That won't work."

"But that will ruin everything. All my work up until now."

"What work?" Sims got up and walked around his desk until he stood hovering above Reynolds. "As far as anybody can see, you haven't accomplished a damn thing since you went up there. People want results, Bradley, not a lot of noise. All you've given anyone is the noise. This isn't a private game of yours. This is one of the most significant events in the history of the human race. If anyone ought to know that, it's you. Christ." And he wandered back to his chair again, jiggling his pipe.

"What is it they want from me?" Reynolds said. "Look—I got them what they asked for. The aliens have agreed to let a team of scientists study their ship."

"We want more than that now. Among other things, we want an alien to come down and visit Washington. Think of the propaganda value of that, and right now is a time when we damn well need something like that. Here we are, the only country with sense enough to stay on the moon. And being here has finally paid off in a way the politicians can understand. They've given you a month in which to play around—after all, you're a hero and the publicity is good—but how much longer do you expect them to wait? No, they want action and I'm afraid they want it now."

Reynolds was ready to go. He had found out as much as he was apt to find here. And he already knew what he was going to have to do. He would go and find Kelly and tell her she had to keep the men from Earth away from the aliens. If she wouldn't agree, then he would go up and tell the aliens and they would leave for the sun. But what if Kelly wouldn't let him go? He had to consider that. He knew; he would tell her this: If you don't let me see them, if you try to keep me away, they'll know something is wrong and they'll leave without a backward glance. Maybe he could tell her the aliens were telepaths; he doubted she would know any better.

He had the plan all worked out so that it could not fail.

He had his hand on the doorknob when Sims called him back. "There's another thing I better tell you, Bradley."

"All right. What's that?"

"Vonda. She's on your side. She told them to stay away, but it wasn't enough. She's been relieved of duty. A replacement is coming with the others."

"Oh," said Reynolds.

Properly suited, Reynolds sat in the cockpit of the shuttle tug, watching the pilot beside him going through the ritual of a final inspection prior to takeoff. The dead desolate surface of the moon stretched briefly away from where the tug sat, the horizon so near that it almost looked touchable. Reynolds liked the moon. If he had not, he would never have elected to return here to stay. It was the Earth he hated. Better than the moon was space itself, the dark endless void beyond the reach of man's ugly grasping hands. That was where Reynolds was going now. Up. Out. Into the void. He was impatient to leave.

The pilot's voice came to him softly through the suit radio, a low murmur, not loud enough for him to understand what the man was saying. The pilot was talking to himself as he worked, using the rumble of his own voice as a way of patterning his mind so that it would not lose concentration. The pilot was a young man in his middle twenties, probably on loan from the Air Force, a lieutenant or, at most, a junior Air Force captain. He was barely old enough to remember when space had really been a frontier. Mankind had decided to go out, and Reynolds had been one of the men chosen to take the giant steps, but now it was late—the giant steps of twenty years ago were mere tentative contusions in the dust of the centuries—and man was coming back. From where he sat, looking out, Reynolds could see exactly 50 percent of the present American space program: the protruding bubble of the moon base. The other half was the orbiting space lab that circled the Earth itself, a battered relic of the expansive seventies. Well beyond the nearby horizon—maybe a hundred miles away—there had once been another bubble, but it was gone now. The brave men who had lived and worked and struggled and died and survived there— they were all gone too. Where? The Russians still maintained an orbiting space station, so some of their former moon colonists were undoubtedly there, but where were the rest? In Siberia? Working there? Hadn't the Russians decided that Siberia—the old barless prison state of the czars and early Communists— was a more practical frontier than the moon?

And weren't they maybe right? Reynolds did not like to think so, for he had poured his life into this—into the moon and the void beyond. But at times, like now, peering through the artificial window of his suit, seeing the bare bubble of the base clinging to the edge of this dead world like a wart on an old woman's face, starkly vulnerable, he found it hard to see the point of it. He was an old enough man to recall the first time he had ever been moved by the spirit of conquest. As a schoolboy, he remembered the first time men conquered Mount Everest—it was around 1956 or '57—and he had religiously followed the news- paper reports. Afterward, a movie had been made, and watching that film, seeing the shadows of pale mountaineers clinging to the edge of that white god, he had decided that was what he wanted to be. And he had never been taught otherwise; only by the time he was old enough to act, all the mountains had long since been conquered. And he had ended up as an astronomer, able if nothing else to gaze outward at the distant shining peaks of the void, and from there he had been pointed toward space. So he had gone to Mars and become famous, but fame had turned him inward, so that now, without the brilliance of his past, he would have been nobody but another of those anonymous old men who dot the cities of the world, inhabiting identically bleak book-lined rooms, eating daily in bad restaurants, their minds always a billion miles away from the dead shells of their bodies.

"We can go now, Dr. Reynolds," the pilot was saying.

Reynolds grunted in reply, his mind several miles distant from his waiting body. He was thinking that there was something, after all. How could he think in terms of pointlessness and futility when he alone had actually seen them with his own eyes? Creatures, intelligent beings, born far away, light-years from the insignificant world of man? Didn't that in itself prove something? Yes. He was sure that it did. But what?

The tug lifted with a murmur from the surface of the moon. Crouched deeply within his seat, Reynolds thought that it wouldn't be long now.

And they found us, he thought, we did not find them. And when had they gone into space? Late. Very late. At a moment in their history comparable to man a hundred thousand years from now. They had avoided space until a press- ing reason had come for venturing out, and then they had gone. He remembered that he had been unable to explain to Jonathon why man wanted to visit the stars when he did not believe in the divinity of the suns. Was there a reason? And, if so, did it make sense?

The journey was not long.

It didn't smell. The air ran clean and sharp and sweet through the corridors, and if there was any odor to it, the odor was one of purity and freshness, almost pine needles or mint. The air was good for his spirits. As soon as Reynolds came aboard the starship, his depression and melancholy were forgotten. Perhaps he was only letting the apparent grimness of the situation get the better of him. It had been too long a time since he'd last had to fight. Jonathon would know what to do. The alien was more than three hundred years old, a product of a civilization and culture that had reached its maturity at a time when man was not yet man, when he was barely a skinny undersized ape, a carrion eater upon the hot plains of Africa.

When Reynolds reached the meeting room, he saw that Jonathon and Richard were not alone this time. The third alien—Reynolds sensed it was someone important—was introduced as Vergnan. No adopted Earth name for it.

"This is ours who best knows the stars," Jonathon said. "It has spoken with yours and hopes it may be able to assist you."

Reynolds had almost forgotten that part. The sudden pressures of the past few hours had driven everything else from his mind. His training. His unsuccessful attempts to speak to the stars. He had failed. Jonathon had been unable to teach him, but he thought that was probably because he simply did not believe.

"Now we shall leave you," Jonathon said.

"But—" said Reynolds.

"We are not permitted to stay."

"But there's something I must tell you."

It was too late. Jonathon and Richard headed for the corridor, walking with surprising gracefulness. Their long necks bobbed, their skinny legs shook, but they still managed to move as swiftly and sleekly as any cat, almost rippling as they went.

Reynolds turned toward Vergnan. Should he tell this one about the visitors from Earth? He did not think so. Vergnan was old, his skin much paler than the others', almost totally hairless. His eyes were wrinkled and one ear was torn.

Vergnan's eyes were closed.

Remembering his lessons, Reynolds too closed his eyes.

And kept them closed. In the dark, time passed more quickly than it seemed, but he was positive that five minutes went by.

Then the alien began to speak. No—he did not speak; he simply sang, his voice trilling with the high searching notes of a well-tuned violin, dashing up and down the scale, a pleasant sound, soothing, cool. Reynolds tried desperately to concentrate upon the song, ignoring the existence of all other sensations, recognizing nothing and no one but Vergnan. Reynolds ignored the taste and smell of the air and the distant throbbing of the ship's machinery. The alien sang deeper and clearer, his voice rising higher and higher, directed now at the stars. Jonathon, too, had sung, but never like this. When Jonathon sang, its voice had dashed away in a frightened search, shifting and darting wildly about, seeking vainly a place to land. Vergnan sang without doubt. It—*he*—was certain. Reynolds sensed the overwhelming maleness of this being, his patriarchal strength and dignity. His voice and song never struggled or wavered. He knew always exactly where he was going.

Had he felt something? Reynolds did not know. If so, then what? No, no, he thought, and concentrated more fully upon the voice, too intently to allow for the logic of thought. Within, he felt strong, alive, renewed, resurrected. *I am a new man. Reynolds is dead. He is another.* These thoughts came to him like the whispering words of another. *Go, Reynolds. Fly. Leave. Fly.*

Then he realized that he was singing too. He could not imitate Vergnan, for his voice was too alien, but he tried and heard his own voice coming frighteningly near, almost fading into and being lost within the constant tones of the other. The two voices suddenly became one—mingling indiscriminately—merging—and that one voice rose higher, floating, then higher again, rising, farther, going farther out—farther and deeper.

Then he felt it. Reynolds. And he knew it for what it was.

The Sun.

More ancient than the whole of the Earth itself. A greater, vaster being, more powerful and knowing. Divinity as a ball of heat and energy.

Reynolds spoke to the stars.

And, knowing this, balking at the concept, he drew back instinctively in fear, his voice faltering, dwindling, collapsing. Reynolds scurried back, seeking the Earth, but, grasping, pulling, Vergnan drew him on. Beyond the shallow exterior light of the sun, he witnessed the totality of that which lay hidden within. The core. The impenetrable darkness within. Fear gripped him once more. He begged to be allowed to flee. Tears streaking his face with the heat of fire, he pleaded. Vergnan benignly drew him on. *Come forward—come—see—know.* Forces coiled to a point.

And he saw.

Could he describe it as evil? Thought was an absurdity. Not thinking, instead sensing and feeling, he experienced the wholeness of this entity—a star—the sun—and saw that it was not evil. He sensed the sheer totality of its opening nothingness. Sensation was absent. Colder than cold, more terrifying than hate, more sordid than fear, blacker than evil. The vast inner whole nothingness of everything that was anything, of all.

I have seen enough. No!

Yes, cried Vergnan, agreeing.

To stay a moment longer would mean never returning again. Vergnan knew this too, and he released Reynolds, allowed him to go.

And still he sang. The song was different from before. Struggling within himself, Reynolds sang too, trying to match his voice to that of the alien. It was easier this time. The two voices merged, mingled, became one.

And then Reynolds awoke.

He was lying on the floor in the starship, the rainbow walls swirling brightly around him.

Vergnan stepped over him. He saw the alien's protruding belly as he passed. He did not look down or back, but continued onward, out the door, gone, as quick and cold as the inner soul of the sun itself. For a brief moment, he hated Vergnan more deeply than he had ever hated anything in his life. Then he sat up, gripping himself, forcing a return to sanity. I am all right now, he insisted. I am back. I am alive. The walls ceased spinning. At his back the floor shed its clinging coat of roughness. The shadows in the corners of his eyes dispersed.

Jonathon entered the room alone. "Now you have been," it said, crossing the room and assuming its usual place beside the wall.

"Yes," said Reynolds, not attempting to stand.

"And now you know why we search. For centuries our star was kind to us, loving, but now it too—like yours—is changed."

"You are looking for a new home?"

"True."

"And?"

"And we find nothing. All are alike. We have seen nine, visiting all. They are nothing."

"Then you leave here too?"

"We must, but first we will approach your star. Not until we have drawn so close that we have seen everything, not until then can we dare admit our failure. This time we thought we had succeeded. When we met you, this is what we thought, for you are unlike your star. We felt that the star could not produce you—or your race—without the presence of benevolence. But it is gone now. We meet only the blackness. We struggle to penetrate to a deeper core. And fail."

"I am not typical of my race," Reynolds said.

"We shall see."

He remained with Jonathon until he felt strong enough to stand. The floor hummed. Feeling it with moist palms, he planted a kiss upon the creased cold metal. A wind swept through the room, carrying a hint of returned life. Jonathon faded, rippled, returned to a sharp outline of crisp reality. Reynolds was suddenly hungry and the oily taste of meat swirled up through his nostrils. The cords in his neck stood out with the strain until, gradually, the tension passed from him.

He left and went to the tug. During the great fall to the silver moon he said not a word, thought not a thought. The trip was long.

Reynolds lay on his back in the dark room, staring upward at the faint shadow of a ceiling, refusing to see.

Hypnosis? Or a more powerful alien equivalent of the same? Wasn't that, as an explanation, more likely than admitting that he had indeed communicated with the sun, discovering a force greater than evil, blacker than black. Or—here was another theory: wasn't it possible that these aliens, because of the conditions on their own world, so thoroughly accepted the consciousness of the stars that they could make him believe as well? Similar things had happened on Earth. Religious miracles, the curing of diseases through faith, men who claimed to have spoken with God. What about flying saucers and little green men and all the other incidents of mass hysteria? Wasn't that the answer here? Hysteria? Hypnosis? Perhaps even a drug of some sort: a drug released into the air. Reynolds had plenty of possible solutions—he could choose one or all—but he decided that he did not really care.

He had gone into this thing knowing exactly what he was doing and now that it had happened he did not regret the experience. He had found a way of fulfilling his required mission while at the same time experiencing something personal that no other man would ever know. Whether he had actually seen the sun was immaterial; the experience, as such, was still his own. Nobody could ever take that away from him.

It was some time after this when he realized that a fist was pounding on the door. He decided he might as well ignore that, because sometimes when you ignored things, they went away. But the knocking did not go away—it only got louder. Finally Reynolds got up. He opened the door.

Kelly glared at his nakedness and said, "Did I wake you?"

"No."

"May I come in?"

"No."

"I've got something to tell you." She forced her way past him, sliding into the room. Then Reynolds saw that she wasn't alone. A big, red-faced beefy man followed, forcing his way into the room too.

Reynolds shut the door, cutting off the corridor light, but the big man went over and turned on the overhead light. "All right," he said, as though it were an order.

"Who the hell are you?" Reynolds said.

"Forget him," Kelly said. "I'll talk."

"Talk," said Reynolds.

"The committee is here. The men from Washington. They arrived an hour ago and I've kept them busy since. You may not believe this, but I'm on your side."

"Sims told me."

"He told me he told you."

"I knew he would. Mind telling me why? He didn't know."

"Because I'm not an idiot," Kelly said. "I've known enough petty bureaucrats in my life. Those things up there are alien beings. You can't send these fools up there to go stomping all over their toes."

Reynolds gathered this would not be over soon. He put on his pants.

"This is George O'Hara," Kelly said. "He's the new director."

"I want to offer my resignation," Reynolds said casually, fixing the snaps of his shirt.

"You have to accompany us to the starship," O'Hara said.

"I want you to," Kelly said. "You owe this to someone. If not me, then the aliens. If you had told me the truth, this might never have happened. If anyone is to blame for this mess, it's you, Reynolds. Why won't you tell me what's been going on up there the last month? It has to be something."

"It is," Reynolds said. "Don't laugh, but I was trying to talk to the sun. I told you that's why the aliens came here. They're taking a cruise of the galaxy, pausing here and there to chat with the stars."

"Don't be frivolous. And, yes, you told me all that."

"I have to be frivolous. Otherwise, it sounds too ridiculous. I made an agreement with them. I wanted to learn to talk to the sun. I told them, since I lived here, I could find out what they wanted to know better than they could. I could tell they were doubtful, but they let me go ahead. In return for my favor, when I was done, whether I succeeded or failed, they would give us what we wanted. A team of men could go and freely examine their ship. They would describe their voyage to us—where they had been, what they had found. They promised cooperation in return for my chat with the sun."

"So, then nothing happened?"

"I didn't say that. I talked with the sun today. And saw it. And now I'm not going to do anything except sit on my hands. You can take it from here."

"What are you talking about?"

He knew he could not answer that. "I failed," he said. "I didn't find out anything they didn't know."

"Well, will you go with us or not? That's all I want to know right now." She was losing her patience, but there was also more than a minor note of pleading in her voice. He knew he ought to feel satisfied hearing that, but he didn't.

"Oh, hell," Reynolds said. "Yes—all right—I will go. But don't ask me why. Just give me an hour to get ready."

"Good man," O'Hara said, beaming happily.

Ignoring him, Reynolds opened his closets and began tossing clothes and other belonging into various boxes and crates.

"What do you think you'll need all that for?" Kelly asked him.

"I don't think I'm coming back," Reynolds said.

"They won't hurt you," she said.

"No. I won't be coming back because I won't be wanting to come back."

"You can't do that," O'Hara said.

"Sure I can," said Reynolds.

It took the base's entire fleet of seven shuttle tugs to ferry the delegation from Washington up to the starship. At that, a good quarter of the group had to be left behind for lack of room. ooReynolds had requested and received permission to call the starship prior to departure, so the aliens were aware of what was coming up to meet them. They had not protested, but Reynolds knew they wouldn't, at least not over the radio. Like almost all mechanical or electronic gadgets, a radio was a fearsome object to them.

Kelly and Reynolds arrived with the first group and entered the air lock. At intervals of a minute or two, the others arrived. When the entire party was clustered in the lock, the last tug holding to the hull in preparation for the return trip, Reynolds signaled that it was time to move out.

"Wait a minute," one of the men called. "We're not all here. Acton and Dodd went back to the tug to get suits."

"Then they'll have to stay there," Reynolds said. "The air is pure here—nobody needs a suit."

"But," said another man, pinching his nose. "This smell. It's awful."

Reynolds smiled. He had barely noticed the odor. Compared to the stench of the first few days, this was nothing today. "The aliens won't talk if you're wearing suits. They have a taboo against artificial communication. The smell gets better as you go farther inside. Until then, hold your nose, breathe through your mouth."

"It's making me almost sick," confided a man at Reynolds' elbow. "You're sure what you say is true, Doctor?"

"Cross my heart," Reynolds said. The two men who had left to fetch the suits returned. Reynolds wasted another minute lecturing them.

"Stop enjoying yourself so much," Kelly whispered when they were at last under way.

Before they reached the first of the tight passages where crawling was necessary, three men had dropped away, dashing back toward the tug. Working from a hasty map given him by the aliens, he was leading the party toward a section of the ship where he had never been before. The walk was less difficult than usual. In most places a man could walk comfortably and the ceilings were high enough to accommodate the aliens themselves. Reynolds ignored the occasional shouted exclamation from the men behind. He steered a silent course toward his destination.

The room, when they reached it, was huge, big as a basketball gymnasium, the ceiling lost in the deep shadows above. Turning, Reynolds counted the aliens present: fifteen . . . twenty . . . thirty . . . forty . . . forty-five . . . forty-six. That had to be about all. He wondered if this was the full crew.

Then he counted his own people: twenty-two. Better than he had expected—only six lost en route, victims of the smell.

He spoke directly to the alien who stood in front of the others. "Greetings," he said. The alien wasn't Vergnan, but it could have been Jonathon.

From behind, he heard, "They're just like giraffes."

"And they even seem intelligent," said another.

"Exceedingly so. Their eyes."

"And friendly too."

"Hello, Reynolds," the alien said. "Are these the ones?"

"Jonathon?" asked Reynolds.

"Yes."

"These are the ones."

"They are your leaders—they wish to question my people?"

"They do."

"May I serve as our spokesman in order to save time?"

"Of course," Reynolds said. He turned and faced his party, looking from face to face, hoping to spot a single glimmer of intelligence, no matter how minute. But he found nothing. "Gentlemen?" he said. "You heard?"

"His name is Jonathon?" said one.

"It is a convenient expression. Do you have a real question?"

"Yes," the man said. He continued speaking to Reynolds. "Where is your homeworld located?"

Jonathon ignored the man's rudeness and promptly named a star.

"Where is that?" the man asked, speaking directly to the alien now.

Reynolds told him it lay some thirty light-years from Earth. As a star, it was very much like the sun, though somewhat larger.

"Exactly how many miles in a light-year?" a man wanted to know.

Reynolds tried to explain. The man claimed he understood, though Reynolds remained skeptical.

It was time for another question.

"Why have you come to our world?"

"Our mission is purely one of exploration and discovery," Jonathon said.

"Have you discovered any other intelligent races besides our own?"

"Yes. Several."

This answer elicited a murmur of surprise from the men. Reynolds wondered who they were, how they had been chosen for this mission. Not what they were, but who. What made them tick. He knew what they were: politicians, NASA bureaucrats, a sprinkling of real scientists. But who?

"Are any of these people aggressive?" asked a man, almost certainly a politician. "Do they pose a threat to you—or—or to us?"

"No," Jonathon said. "None."

Reynolds was barely hearing the questions and answers now. His attention was focused upon Jonathon's eyes. He had stopped blinking now. The last two questions—the ones dealing with intelligent life forms—he had told the truth. Reynolds thought he was beginning to understand. He had underestimated these creatures. Plainly, they had encountered other races during their travels before coming to Earth. They were experienced. Jonathon was lying—yes—but unlike before, he was lying well, only when the truth would not suffice.

"How long do you intend to remain in orbit about our moon?"

"Until the moment you and your friends leave our craft. Then we shall depart."

This set up an immediate clamor among the men. Waving his arms furiously, Reynolds attempted to silence them. The man who had been unfamiliar with the term "light-year" shouted out an invitation for Jonathon to visit Earth.

This did what Reynolds himself could not do. The others fell silent in order to hear Jonathon's reply.

"It is impossible," Jonathon said. "Our established schedule requires us to depart immediately."

"Is it this man's fault?" demanded a voice. "He should have asked you himself long before now."

"No," Jonathon said. "I could not have come—or any of my people—because we were uncertain of your peaceful intentions. Not until we came to know Reynolds well did we fully comprehend the benevolence of your race." The alien blinked rapidly now.

He stopped during the technical questions. The politicians and bureaucrats stepped back to speak among themselves and the scientists came forward. Reynolds was amazed at the intelligence of their questions. To this extent at least, the expedition had not been wholly a farce.

Then the questions were over and all the men came forward to listen to Jonathon's last words.

"We will soon return to our homeworld and when we do we shall tell the leaders of our race of the greatness and glory of the human race. In passing here, we have come to know your star and through it you people who live beneath its soothing rays. I consider your visit here a personal honor to me as an individual. I am sure my brothers share my pride and only regret an inability to utter their gratitude."

Then Jonathon ceased blinking and looked hard at Reynolds. "Will you be going too?"

"No," Reynolds said. "I'd like to talk to you alone if I can."

"Certainly," Jonathon said.

Several of the men in the party protested to Kelly or O'Hara, but there was nothing they could do. One by one they left the chamber to wait in the corridor. Kelly was the last to leave. "Don't be a fool," she cautioned.

"I won't," he said.

When the men had gone, Jonathon took Reynolds away from the central room. It was only a brief walk to the old room where they had always met before. As if practicing a routine, Jonathon promptly marched to the farthest wall and stood there waiting. Reynolds smiled. "Thank you," he said.

"You are welcome."

"For lying to them. I was afraid they would offend you with their stupidity. I thought you would show your contempt by lying badly, offending them in return. I underestimated you. You handled them very well."

"But you have something you wish to ask of me?"

"Yes," Reynolds said. "I want you to take me away with you."

As always, Jonathon remained expressionless. Still, for a long time, it said nothing. Then, "Why do you wish this? We shall never return here."

"I don't care. I told you before: I am not typical of my race. I can never be happy here."

"But are you typical of my race? Would you not be unhappy with us?"

"I don't know. But I'd like to try."

"It is impossible," Jonathon said.

"But—but—why?"

"Because we have neither the time nor the abilities to care for you. Our mission is a most desperate one. Already, during our absence, our homeworld may have gone mad. We must hurry. Our time is growing brief. And you will not be of any help to us. I am sorry, but you know that is true."

"I can talk to the stars."

"No," Jonathon said. "You cannot."

"But I did."

"Vergnan did. Without him, you could not."

"Your answer is final? There's no one else I can ask? The captain?"

"I am the captain."

Reynolds nodded. He had carried his suitcases and crates all this way and now he would have to haul them home again. Home? No, not home. Only the moon. "Could you find out if they left a tug for me?" he asked.

"Yes. One moment."

Jonathon rippled lightly away, disappearing into the corridor. Reynolds turned and looked at the walls. Again, as he stared, the rainbow patterns appeared to shift and dance and swirl of their own volition. Watching this, he felt sad, but his sadness was not that of grief. It was the sadness of emptiness and aloneness. This emptiness had so long been a part of him that he sometimes forgot it was there. He knew it now. He knew, whether consciously aware of it or not, that he had spent the past ten years of his life searching vainly for a way of filling this void. Perhaps even more than that: perhaps his whole life had been nothing more than a search for that one moment of real completion. Only twice had he ever really come close. The first time had been on Mars. When he had lived and watched while the others had died. Then he had not been alone or empty. And the other time had been right here in this very room—with Vergnan. Only twice in his life had he been allowed to approach the edge of true meaning. Twice in fifty-eight long and endless years. Would it ever happen again? When? How?

Jonathon returned, pausing in the doorway. "A pilot is there," it said.

Reynolds went toward the door, ready to leave. "Are you still planning to visit our sun?" he asked.

"Oh, yes. We shall continue trying, searching. We know nothing else. You do not believe—even after what Vergnan showed you—do you, Reynolds?"

"No, I do not believe."

"I understand," Jonathon said. "And I sympathize. All of us—even I—sometimes we have doubts."

Reynolds continued forward into the corridor. Behind, he heard a heavy clipping noise and turned to see Jonathon coming after him. He waited for the alien to join him and then they walked together. In the narrow corridor, there was barely room for both.

Reynolds did not try to talk. As far as he could see, there was nothing left to be said that might possibly be said in so short a time as that which remained. Better to say nothing, he thought, than to say too little.

The air lock was open. Past it, Reynolds glimpsed the squat bulk of the shuttle tug clinging to the creased skin of the starship.

There was nothing left to say. Turning to Jonathon, he said, "Good-bye," and as he said it, for the first time he wondered about what he was going back to. More than likely, he would find himself a hero once again. A celebrity. But that was all right: fame was fleeting; it was bearable. Two hundred forty thousand miles was still a great distance. He would be all right.

As if reading his thoughts, Jonathon asked, "Will you be remaining here or will you return to your homeworld?"

The question surprised Reynolds; it was the first time the alien had ever evidenced a personal interest in him. "I'll stay here. I'm happier."

"And there will be a new director?"

"Yes. How did you know that? But I think I'm going to be famous again. I can get Kelly retained."

"You could have the job yourself," Jonathon said.

"But I don't want it. How do you know all this? About Kelly and so on?"

"I listen to the stars," Jonathon said in its high warbling voice.

"They are alive, aren't they?" Reynolds said suddenly.

"Of course. We are permitted to see them for what they are. You do not. But you are young."

"They are balls of ionized gas. Thermonuclear reactions."

The alien moved, shifting its neck as though a joint lay in the middle of it. Reynolds did not understand the gesture. Nor would he ever. Time had run out at last.

Jonathon said, "When they come to you, they assume a disguise you can see. That is how they spend their time in this universe. Think of them as doorways."

"Through which I cannot pass."

"Yes."

Reynolds smiled, nodded and passed into the lock. It contracted behind him, engulfing the image of his friend. A few moments of drifting silence, then the other end of the lock furled open.

The pilot was a stranger. Ignoring the man, Reynolds dressed, strapped himself down and thought about Jonathon. What was it that it had said? I listen to the stars. Yes, and the stars had told it that Kelly had been fired?

He did not like that part. But the part he liked even less was this: when it said it, Jonathon had not blinked.

(1) It had been telling the truth. (2) It could lie without flicking a lash. Choose one.

Reynolds did, and the tug fell toward the moon.

George Turner

George Turner (1916–   ) is the most influential Australian SF writer and critic. From the 1960s onward he was a leading contemporary Australian novelist who also wrote SF criticism. It wasn't until the mid-'70s that he turned to writing science fiction. His first SF novel, *Beloved Son* (1978), published when he was in his early sixties, was recognized as an important debut, and he has gone on to write a number of first-rate SF novels, including *The Sea and Summer* (1987, published as *Drowning Towers* in the U.S.), which won the Arthur C. Clarke Award. *Beloved Son* involves interstellar travel, a post-holocaust civilization in the 21st century, and genetic engineering—this last has remained one of the principal concerns of his fiction, in recent works such as *Brain Child* (1991), *The Destiny Makers* (1993), and *Genetic Soldier* (1994).

Turner's literary execution is contoured by deeply held moral convictions and his life as a contemporary novelist. "I prefer to maintain a low key in my own work," says Turner. "To this end I have concentrated on simple, staple SF ideas, mostly those which have become conventions in the genre, injected without background or discussion into stories on the understanding that readers know all they need to know about such things. My SF method remains the same as for my mainstream novels—set characters in motion in speculative situation and let them work out their destinies with a minimum of auctorial interference."

His future societies have a satisfying complexity, portraying class conflict and economic disparities in a gritty, realistic fashion absent from most American science fiction. While American science fiction generally sees space as simply the new frontier, Turner, the Australian, envisions it as an alien place with a strange and different culture, one with its own moral imperatives and structures—as he envisions the future on Earth as operating under other moral structures different from ours today.

He has written comparatively few short SF stories, less than a dozen to date. This one is about the conflict of values between cultures in the future, and has intriguing resonances with James Tiptree, Jr.'s "Beam Us Home."

I STILL CALL AUSTRALIA HOME

The past is another country; they do things differently there.
                                        —L. P. Hartley

1

The complement of *Starfarer* had no idea, when they started out, of how long they might be gone. They searched the sky, the three hundred of them, men and women, black and brown and white and yellow, and in thirty years landed on forty planets whose life-support parameters appeared—from distant observation—close to those of Earth.

Man, they discovered, might fit his own terrestrial niche perfectly, but those parameters for his existence were tight and inelastic. There were planets where they could have dwelt in sealed environments, venturing out only in special suits, even one planet where they could have existed comfortably through half its year but been burned and suffocated in the other half. They found not one where they could establish a colony of mankind.

In thirty years they achieved nothing but an expectable increase in their numbers and this was a factor in their decision to return home. The ship was becoming crowded and, in the way of crowded tenements, something of a slum.

So they headed for Earth; and, at the end of the thirty-first year, took up a precessing north-south orbit allowing them a leisurely overview, day by day, of the entire planet.

This was wise. They had spent thirty years in space, travelling between solar systems at relativistic speeds, and reckoned that about six hundred local years had passed since they set out. They did not know what manner of world they might find.

They found, with their instruments, that the greenhouse effect had subsided slowly during the centuries, aided by the first wisps of galactic cloud heralding the new ice age, but that the world was still warmer than the interregnal norm. The ozone layer seemed to have healed itself, but the desert areas were still formidably large although the spread of new pasture and forest was heartening.

What they did not see from orbit was the lights of cities by night and this did not greatly surprise them. The world they had left in a desperate search for new habitat had been an ant heap of ungovernable, unsupportable billions whose numbers were destined to shrink drastically if any were to survive at all. The absence of lights suggested that the population problem had solved itself in grim fashion.

They dropped the ship into a lower orbit just outside the atmosphere and brought in the spy cameras.

There were people down there, all kinds of people. The northern hemisphere was home to nomadic tribes, in numbers like migratory nations; the northern temperate zone had become a corn belt, heavily farmed and guarded by soldiers in dispersed forts, with a few towns and many villages; the equatorial jungles were, no doubt, home to hunter-gatherers but their traces were difficult to see; there were signs of urban communities, probably trading centres, around the seacoasts but no evidence of transport networks or lighting by night and no sounds of electronic transmission. Civilisation had regressed, not unexpectedly.

They chose to inspect Australia first because it was separated from the larger landmasses and because the cameras showed small farming communities and a few townlets. It was decided to send down a Contact Officer to inspect and report back.

The ship could not land. It had been built in space and could live only in space; planetary gravity would have warped its huge but light-bodied structure beyond repair. Exploratory smallcraft could have been despatched, but it was reasoned that a crew of obviously powerful supermen might create an untrusting reserve among the inhabitants, even an unhealthy regard for gods or demons from the sky. A single person, powerfully but unobtrusively armed, would a suitable ambassador.

They sent a woman, Nugan Johnson, not because she happened to be Australian but because she was a Contact Officer, and it was her rostered turn for duty.

They chose a point in the south of the continent because it was autumn in the hemisphere, and an average daily temperature of twenty-six C would be bearable, and dropped her by tractor beam on the edge of a banana grove owned by Mrs Flighty Jones, who screamed and fled.

2

Flighty, in the English of her day, meant something like *scatterbrained*. Her name was, in fact, Hallo-Mary (a rough—very rough—descendant of Ave Maria), but she was a creature of fits and starts, so much so that the men at the bottling shed made some fun of her before they were convinced that she had seen *something*, and called the Little Mother of the Bottles.

"There was I, counting banana bunches for squeeging into baby pap, when it goes hissss-bump behind me."

"What went hiss-bump?"

"It did."

"What was it?" Little Mother wondered if the question was unfair to Flighty wits.

"I don't know." Having no words, she took refuge in frustrated tears. She had inherited the orchard but not the self-control proper to a proprietary woman.

In front of the men! Little Mother sighed and tried again. "What did it look like? What shape?"

Flighty tried hard. "Like a bag. With legs. And a glass bowl on top. And it bounced. That's what made the bump. And it made a noise."

"What sort of noise?"

"Just a noise." She thought of something else. "You know the pictures on the library wall? In the holy stories part? The ones where the angels go up? Well, like the angels."

Little Mother knew that the pictures did not represent angels, whatever the congregation were told. Hiding trepidation, she sent the nearest man for Top Mother.

Top Mother came, and listened . . . and said, as though visitations were nothing out of the way, "We will examine the thing that hisses and bumps. The men may come with us in case their strength is needed." That provided at least a bodyguard.

The men were indeed a muscular lot, and also a superstitious lot, but they were expected to show courage when the women claimed protection. They picked up whatever knives and mashing clubs lay to hand and tried to look grim. Man-to-man was a bloodwarming event but man-to-whatisit had queasy overtones. They agreed with Little Mother's warning: "There could be danger."

"There might be greater danger later on if we do *not* investigate. Lead the way, Hallo-Mary." A Top Mother did not use nicknames.

Flighty was now thoroughly terrified and no longer sure that she had seen anything, but Top Mother took her arm and pushed her forward. Perhaps it had gone away; perhaps it had bounced up and up . . .

It had not gone anywhere. It had sat down and pushed back its glass bowl and revealed itself, by its cropped hair, as a man.

"A man," murmured Top Mother, who knew that matriarchy was a historical development and not an evolutionary given. She began to think like the politician which at heart she was. A *man* from—from *outside*—could be a social problem.

The men, who were brought up to revere women but often resented them—except during the free-fathering festivals—grinned and winked at each other and wondered what the old girl would do.

The old girl said, "Lukey! Walk up and observe him."

Lukey started off unwillingly, then noticed that three cows grazed unconcernedly not far from the man in a bag and took heart to cross the patch of pasture at the orchard's edge.

At a long arm's length he stood, leaned forward and sniffed. He was forest bred and able to sort out the man in a bag's scents from the norms about him and, being forest bred, his pheromone sense was better than rudimentary. He came so close that Nugan could have touched him and said, "Just another bloody woman!" The stranger should have been a man, a sex hero!

He called back to Top Mother, "It's only a woman with her hair cut short."

They all crowded forward across the pasture. Females were always peaceable—unless you really scratched their pride.

The hiss Flighty had heard had been the bootjets operating to break the force of a too-fast landing by an ineptly handled tractor beam; the bump had been the reality of a contact that wrenched an ankle. Even the bounce was almost real as she hopped for a moment on one leg. The noise was Nugan's voice through a speaker whose last user had left it tuned to baritone range, a hearty, "Shit! Goddam shit!" before she sat down and became aware of a dumpy figure vanishing among columns of what she remembered vaguely as banana palms. Not much of a start for good PR.

She thought first to strip the boot and bind her ankle, then that she should not be caught minus a boot if the runaway brought unfriendly reinforcements. She did not fear the village primitives; though she carried no identifiable weapons, the thick gloves could spit a variety of deaths through levelled fingers. However, she had never killed a civilised organism and had no wish to do so; her business was to prepare a welcome home.

The scents of the air were strange but pleasant, as the orbital analysis had affirmed; she folded the transparent *fishbowl* back into its neck slot. She became aware of animals nearby. Cows. She recognised them from pictures though she had been wholly city bred in an era of gigantic cities. They took no notice of her. Fascinated and unafraid, she absorbed a landscape of grass and tiny flowers in the grass, trees and shrubs and a few vaguely familiar crawling and hopping insects. The only strangeness was the spaciousness stretching infinitely on all sides, a thing that the lush Ecological Decks of *Starfarer* could not mimic, together with the sky like a distant ceiling with wisps of cloud. Might it rain on her? She scarcely remembered rain.

Time passed. It was swelteringly hot but not as hot as autumn in the greenhouse streets.

They came at last, led by a tall woman in a black dress—rather, a robe cut to enhance dignity though it was trimmed off at the knees. She wore a white headdress like something starched and folded in the way of the old nursing tradition and held together by a brooch. She was old, perhaps in her sixties, but she had presence and the dress suggested status.

She clutched another woman by the arm, urging her forward, and Nugan recognised the clothing, like grey denim jeans, that fled through the palms. Grey Denim Jeans pointed and planted herself firmly in a determined no-further pose. Madam In Black gestured to the escort and spoke a few words.

Nugan became aware of the men and made an appreciative sound unbecoming in a middle-aged matron past child-bearing years. These men wore only G-strings and they were *men*. Not big men but shapely, muscular and very male. *Or am I so accustomed to Starfarer crew that any change rings a festival bell? Nugan, behave!*

The man ordered forward came warily and stopped a safe arm's length from her, sniffing. Nugan examined him. *If I were, even looked, twenty years younger* . . . He spoke suddenly in a resentful, blaming tone. The words were strange (of course they must be) yet hauntingly familiar; she thought that part of the sentence was "dam-dam she!"

She kept quiet. Best to observe and wait. The whole party, led by Madam In Black, came across the pasture. They stopped in front of her, fanning out in silent inspection. The men smelled mildly of sweat, but that was almost a pleasure; after thirty years of propinquity, *Starfarer*'s living quarters stank of sweat.

Madam In Black said something in a voice of authority that seemed part of her. It sounded a little like "Oo're yah?"—interrogative with a clipped note to it; the old front-of-the-mouth Australian vowels had vanished in the gulf of years. It should mean, by association, *Who are you?* but in this age might be a generalised, *Where are you from?*, even, *What are you doing here?*

Nugan played the oldest game in language lesson, tapping her chest and saying, "Nugan. I—Nugan."

Madam In Black nodded and tapped her own breast. "Ay Tup-Ma."

"Tupma?"

"Dit—Tup-Ma, Yah Nuggorn?"

"Nugan."

The woman repeated, "Nugan," with a fair approximation of the old vowels and followed with, "Wurriya arta?"

Nugan made a guess at vowel drift and consonant elision and came up with, *Where are you out of?* meaning, Where do you come from?

They must know, she thought, that something new is in the sky. A ship a kilometre long has been circling for weeks with the sun glittering on it at dawn and twilight. They can't have lost all contact with the past; there must be stories of the bare bones of history . . .

She pointed upwards and said, "From the starship."

The woman nodded as if the statement made perfect sense and said, "Stair-boot."

Nugan found herself fighting sudden tears. *Home, home, HOME has not forgotten us.* Until this moment she had not known what Earth meant to her, swimming in the depths of her shipbound mind. "Yes, stairboot. We say starship."

The woman repeated, hesitantly, "Stairsheep?" She tried again, reaching for the accent, "Starship! I say it right?"

"Yes, you say it *properly.*"

The woman repeated, "Prupperly. Ta for that. It is old-speak. I read some of that but not speak—only small bit."

So not everything had been lost. There were those who had rescued and preserved the past. Nugan said, "You are quite good."

Tup-Ma blushed with obvious pleasure. "Now we go." She waved towards the banana grove.

"I can't." A demonstration was needed. Nugan struggled upright, put the injured foot to the ground and tried for a convincing limp. That proved easy; the pain made her gasp and she sat down hard.

"Ah! You bump!"

"Indeed I bump." She unshackled the right boot and broke the seals before fascinated eyes and withdrew a swelling foot.

"We carry."

We meant two husky males with wrists clasped under her, carrying her through the grove to a large wooden shed where more near-naked men worked at vats and tables. They sat on a table and brought cold water (*How do they cool it? Ice? Doubtful.*) and a thick yellow grease which quite miraculously eased the pain somewhat (*A native pharmacopoeia?*) and stout, unbleached bandages to swathe her foot tightly.

She saw that in other parts of the shed the banana flesh was being mashed into long wooden moulds. Then it was fed into glass cylinders whose ends were capped, again with glass, after a pinch of some noisome-looking fungus was added. (*Preservative? Bacteriophage? Why not?*) A preserving industry, featuring glass rather than metal; such details helped to place the culture.

Tup-Ma called, "Lukey!" and the man came forward to be given a long instruction in which the word *Stair-boot* figured often. He nodded and left the shed at a trot.

"Lukey go—goes—to tell Libary. We carry you there."

"Who is Libary?"

The woman thought and finally produced, "Skuller. Old word, I think."

"Scholar? Books? Learning?"

"Yes, yes, books. Scho-lar. Ta." Ta? Of course—thank you. Fancy the child's word persisting.

"You will eat, please?"

Nugan said quickly, "No, thank you. I have this." She dug out a concentrate pack and swallowed one tablet before the uncomprehending Tup-Ma. She dared not risk local food before setting up the test kit, enzymes and once-harmless proteins could change so much. They brought a litter padded like a mattress and laid her on it. Four pleasantly husky men carried it smoothly, waist-high, swinging gently along a broad path towards low hills, one of which was crowned by a surprisingly large building from which smoke plumes issued.

"Tup-Ma goodbyes you."

"Goodbye, Tup-Ma. And ta."

3

It was a stone building, even larger than it had seemed. But that was no real wonder; the medieval stone masons had built cathedrals far more ornate than this squared-off warehouse of a building. It was weathered dirty grey but was probably yellow sandstone, of which there had been quarries in Victoria. Sandstone is easily cut and shaped even with soft iron tools.

There were windows, but the glass seemed not to be of high quality, and a small doorway before which the bearers set down the litter. A thin man of indeterminate middle age stood there, brown eyes examining her from a dark, clean shaven face. He wore a loose shirt, wide-cut, ballooning shorts and sandals, and he smiled brilliantly at her. He was a full-blooded Aborigine.

He said, "Welcome to the Library, Starwoman," with unexceptionable pronunciation though the accent was of the present century.

She sat up. "The language still lives."

He shook his head. "It is a dead language but scholars speak it, as many of yours spoke Latin. Or did that predate your time? There are many uncertainties."

"Yes, Latin was dead. My name is Nugan."

"I am Libary."

"Libary?"

"If you would be pedantic, but the people call me Libary. It is both name and title. I preside." His choice of words, hovering between old-fashioned and donnish, made her feel like a child before a tutor, yet he seemed affable.

He gave an order in the modern idiom and the bearers carried her inside. She gathered an impression of stone walls a metre thick, pierced by sequent doors which formed a temperature lock. The moist heat outside was balanced by an equally hot but dry atmosphere inside. She made the connection at once, having a student's reverence for books. The smoke she had seen was given off by a low-temperature furnace stoked to keep the interior air dry and at a reasonably even temperature. This was more than a scholars' library; it was the past, preserved by those who knew its value.

She was carried past open doorways, catching glimpses of bound volumes behind glass, of a room full of hanging maps and once of a white man at a lectern, touching his book with gloved hands.

She was set down on a couch in a rather bare room furnished mainly by a desk of brilliantly polished wood which carried several jars of coloured inks, pens which she thought had split nibs and a pile of thick, greyish paper. (*Unbleached paper? Pollution free? A psychic prohibition from old time?*)

The light came through windows, but there were oil lamps available with shining parabolic reflectors. And smoke marks on the ceiling. Electricity slept still.

The carriers filed out. Libary sat himself behind the desk. "We have much to say to each other."

Nugan marvelled, "You speak so easily. Do you use the old English all the time?"

"There are several hundred scholars in Libary. Most speak the old tongue. We practise continually."

"In order to read the old books?"

"That, yes." He smiled in a fashion frankly conspirational. "Also it allows private discussion in the presence of the uninstructed."

Politics, no doubt—the eternal game that has never slept in all of history. "In front of Tup-Ma, perhaps?"

"A few technical expressions serve to thwart her understanding. But the Tup-Ma is no woman's fool."

"*The* Tup-Ma? I thought it was her name."

"Her title. Literally, Top Mother. As you would have expressed it, Mother Superior."

"A nun!"

Libary shrugged. "She has no cloister and the world is her convent. Call her priest rather than a nun."

"She has authority?"

"She has great authority." He looked suddenly quizzical. "She is very wise. She sent you to me before you should fall into error."

"Error? You mean, like sin?"

"That also, but I speak of social error. It would be easy. Yours was a day of free thinking and irresponsible doing in a world that could not learn discipline for living. This Australian world is a religious matriarchy. It is fragile when ideas can shatter and dangerous when the women make hard decisions."

It sounded like too many dangers to evaluate at once. Patriarchy and equality she could deal with—in theory—but matriarchy was an unknown quantity in history. He had given his warning and waited silently on her response.

She pretended judiciousness. "That is interesting." He waited, smiling faintly. She said, to gain time, "I would like to remove this travel suit. It is hot."

He nodded, stood, turned away.

"Oh, I'm fully dressed under it. You may watch."

He turned back to her and she pressed the release. The suit split at the seams and crumpled round her feet. She stepped out, removed the gloves with their concealed armament and revealed herself in close-cut shirt and trousers and soft slippers. The damaged ankle hurt less than she had feared.

Libary was impressed but not amazed. "One must expect ingenious invention." He felt the crumpled suit fabric. "Fragile."

She took a small knife from her breast pocket and slit the material, which closed up seamlessly behind the blade. Libary said, "Beyond our capability."

"We could demonstrate—"

"No doubt." His interruption was abrupt, uncivil. "There is little we need." He changed direction. "I think Nugan is of Koori derivation."

"Possibly from Noongoon or Nungar or some such. You might know better than I."

His dark face flashed a smile. "I don't soak up old tribal knowledge while the tribes themselves preserve it in their enclaves."

"Enclaves?"

"We value variety of culture." He hesitated, then added, "Under the matriarchal aegis which covers all."

"All the world."

"Most of it."

That raised questions. "You communicate with the whole world? From space we detected no radio, no electronic signals at all."

"Wires on poles and radiating towers, as in the books? Their time has not come yet."

A queer way of phrasing it. "But you hinted at global communication, even global culture."

"The means are simple. Long ago the world was drawn together by trading vessels; so it is today. Ours are very fast; we use catamaran designs of great efficiency, copied from your books. The past does not offer much but there are simple things we take—things we can make and handle by simple means." He indicated the suit. "A self-healing cloth would require art beyond our talent."

"We could show—" But could they? Quantum chemistry was involved and electro-molecular physics and power generation . . . Simple products were not at all simple.

Libary said, "We would not understand your showing. Among your millions of books, few are of use. Most are unintelligible because of the day of simple explanation was already past in your era. We strain to comprehend what you would find plain texts, and we fail. Chemistry, physics—those disciplines of complex numeration and incomprehensible signs and arbitrary terms—are beyond our understanding."

She began to realise that unintegrated piles of precious but mysterious books are not knowledge.

He said, suddenly harsh, "Understanding will come at its own assimilable pace. You can offer us nothing."

"Surely . . . "

"Nothing! You destroyed a world because you could not control your greed for a thing you called progress but which was no more than a snapping up of all that came to hand or to mind. You destroyed yourselves by inability to control your breeding. You did not ever cry *Hold!* for a decade or a century to unravel the noose of a self-strangling culture. You have nothing to teach. You knew little that mattered when sheer existence was at stake."

Nugan sat still, controlling anger. *You don't know how we fought to stem the tides of population and consumption and pollution; how each success brought with it a welter of unforeseen disasters; how impossible it was to coordinate a world riven by colour, nationality, political creed, religious belief and economic strata.*

Because she had been reared to consult intelligence rather than emotion, she stopped thought in mid-tirade. *Oh, you are right. These were the impossible troubles brought by greed and irresponsible use of a finite world. We begged our own downfall. Yet . . .*

"I think," she said, "you speak with the insolence of a lucky survival. You exist only because we did. Tell me how your virtue saved mankind."

Libary bowed his head slightly in apology. "I regret anger and implied contempt." His eyes met hers again. "But I will not pretend humility. We rebuilt the race. In which year did you leave Earth?"

"In twenty-one eighty-nine. Why?"

"In the last decades before the crumbling. How to express it succinctly? Your world was administered by power groups behind national boundaries, few ruling many, pretending to a mystery termed *democracy* but ruling by decree. Do I read the history rightly?"

"Yes." It was a hard admission. "Well, it was beginning to seem so. Oppression sprang from the need to ration food. We fed fifteen billion only by working land and sea until natural fertility cycles were exhausted, and that only at the cost of eliminating other forms of life. We were afraid when the insects began to disappear . . ."

"Rightly. Without insects, nothing flourishes."

"There was also the need to restrict birth, to deny birth to most of the world. When you take away the right to family from those who have nothing else and punish savagely contravention of the population laws . . . " She shrugged hopelessly.

"You remove the ties that bind, the sense of community, the need to consider any but the self. Only brute force remains."

"Yes."

"And fails as it has always failed."

"Yes. What happened after we left?"

Libary said slowly, "At first, riots. Populations rose against despots, or perhaps against those forced by circumstances into despotism. But ignorant masses cannot control a state; bureaucracies collapsed, supply fell into disarray and starvation set in. Pack leaders—not to be called soldiers—fought for arable territory. Then great fools unleashed biological weaponry—I think that meant toxins and bacteria and viruses, whatever such things may have been—and devastated nations with plague and pestilence. There was a time in the northern hemisphere called by a term I read only as Heart of Winter. Has that meaning for you?"

"A time of darkness and cold and starvation?"

"Yes."

"Nuclear winter. They must have stopped the bombing in the nick of time. It could only have been tried by a madman intent on ruling the ruins."

"We do not know his name—their names—even which country. Few records were kept after that time. No machines, perhaps, and no paper."

"And then?"

"Who knows? Cultural darkness covers two centuries. Then history begins again; knowledge is reborn. Some of your great cities saw the darkness falling and sealed their libraries and museums in hermetic vaults. This building houses the contents of the Central Libary of Melbourne; there are others in the world and many yet to be discovered. Knowledge awaits deciphering but there is no hurry. This is, by and large, a happy world."

Sophisticated knowledge was meaningless here. They could not, for instance, create electronic communication until they had a broad base of metallurgy, electrical theory and a suitable mathematics. Text books might as well have been written in cipher.

"And," Libary said, "there were the Ambulant Scholars. They set up farming communities for self support, even in the Dark Age, while they preserved the teachings and even some of the books of their ancestors. They visited each other and established networks around the world. When they set up schools, the new age began."

"Like monks of the earlier Dark Age, fifteen hundred years before."

"So? It has happened before?"

"At least once and with less reason. Tell me about the rise of women to power."

Libary chuckled. "Power? Call it that but it is mostly manipulation. The men don't mind being ruled; they get their own way in most things and women know how to bow with dignity when caught in political error. It is a system of giving and taking wherein women give the decisions and take the blame for their mistakes. The men give them children—under certain rules—and take responsibility for teaching them when maternal rearing is completed."

She made a stab in the dark. "Women established their position by taking control of the birth rate."

"Shrewdly thought, nearly right. They have a mumbo jumbo of herbs and religious observances and fertility periods but in fact it is all contraception, abortion and calculation. Some men believe, more are sceptical, but it results in attractive sexual rituals and occasional carnivals of lust, so nobody minds greatly." He added offhandedly, "Those who cannot restrain their physicality are killed by the women."

That will give Starfarer pause for thought.

"I think," said Libary, "that the idea was conceived by the Ambulant Scholars and preached in religious guise—always a proper approach to basically simple souls who need a creed to cling to. So, you see, the lesson of overpopulation has been learned and put to work."

"This applies across the planet?"

"Not yet, but it will. America is as yet an isolated continent. Our Ambulant Scholars wielded in the end a great deal of respected authority."

"And now call yourselves Librarians?"

His black face split with pleasure. "It is so good to speak with a quick mind."

"Yet a day will come when population will grow again beyond proper maintenance."

"We propose that it shall not. Your machines and factories will arrive in their own good time, but our present interest is in two subjects you never applied usefully to living: psychology and philosophy. Your thinking men and women studied profoundly and made their thoughts public, but who listened? There is a mountain of the works of those thinkers to be sifted and winnowed and applied. Psychology is knowledge of the turbulent self; philosophy is knowledge of the ideals of which that self is capable. Weave these together and there appears a garment of easy discipline wherein the self is fulfilled and the world becomes its temple, not just a heap of values for ravishing. We will solve the problem of population."

Nugan felt, with the uneasiness of someone less than well prepared, that they would. Their *progress* would lie in directions yet unthought of.

"Now," Libary said, "would you please tell me how you came to Earth without a transporting craft?"

"I was dropped by tractor beam."

"A—beam?" She had surprised him at last. "A ray of light that carries a burden?"

"Not light. Monopoles."

"What are those?"

"Do you have magnets? Imagine a magnet with only one end, so that the attraction goes on in a straight line. It is very powerful. Please don't ask how it works because I don't know. It is not in my field."

Libary said moodily, "I would not wish to know. Tell me, rather, what you want here."

Want? Warnings rang in Nugan's head but she could only plough ahead. "After six hundred years we have come home! And Earth is far more beautiful than we remember it to be."

His dark eyebrows rose. "Remember? Are you six hundred years old?"

Explanation would be impossible. She said, despairingly, "Time in heaven is slower than time on Earth. Our thirty years among the stars are six centuries of your time. Please don't ask for explanation. It is not magic; it is just so."

"Magic is unnecessary in a sufficiently wonderful universe. Do you tell me that you do not understand the working of your everyday tools?"

"I don't understand the hundredth part. Knowledge is divided among specialists; nobody knows all of even common things."

Libary considered in silence, then sighed lightly and said, "Leave that and return to the statement that you have come home. This is not your home."

"Not the home we left. It has changed."

"Your home has gone away. For ever."

The finality of his tone must have scattered her wits, she thought later; it roused all the homesickness she had held in check and she said quickly, too quickly, "We can rebuild it."

The black face became still, blank. She would have given years of life to recall the stupid words. He said at last, "After all I have told you of resistance to rapid change you propose to redesign our world!"

She denied without thinking, "No! You misunderstand me!" In her mind she pictured herself facing *Starfarer*'s officers, stumbling out an explanation, seeing disbelief that a trained Contact could be such a yammering fool.

"Do I? Can you mean that your people wish to live as members of our society, in conditions they will see as philosophically unrewarding and physically primitive?"

He knew she could not mean any such thing. She tried, rapidly, "A small piece of land, isolated, perhaps an island, a place where we could live on our own terms. Without contact. You would remain—unspoiled."

Insulting, condescending habit of speech, truthful in its meaning, revealing and irrevocable!

"You will live sequestered? Without travelling for curiosity's sake, without plundering resources for your machines, without prying into our world and arguing with it? In that case, why not stay between the stars?"

Only truth remained. "We left Earth to found new colonies. Old Earth seemed beyond rescue; only new Earths could perpetuate a suffocating race."

"So much we know. The books tell it."

Still she tried: "We found no new Earth. We searched light-years of sky for planets suitable for humans. We found the sky full of planets similar to Earth— but only similar. Man's range of habitable conditions is very narrow. We found planets a few degrees too hot for healthy existence or a few degrees too cool to support a terrestrial ecology, others too seismically young or too aridly old, too deficient in oxygen or too explosively rich in hydrogen, too low in carbon dioxide to support a viable plant life or unbearably foul with methane or lacking an ozone layer. Parent stars, even of G-type, flooded surfaces with overloads of ultraviolet radiation, even gamma radiation, or fluctuated in minute but lethal instabilities. We visited forty worlds in thirty years and found not one where we could live. Now you tell me we are not welcome in our own home!"

"I have told you it is not your home. You come to us out of violence and decay; you are conditioned against serenity. You would be only an eruptive force in a world seeking a middle way. You would debate our beliefs, corrupt our young men by offering toys they do not need, tempt the foolish to extend domination over space and time—and in a few years destroy what has taken six centuries to build."

Anger she could have borne but he was reasonable—as a stone wall is reasonable and unbreachable.

"Search!" he said. "Somewhere in such immensity must be what you seek. You were sent out with a mission to propagate mankind, but in thirty years you betray it."

She burst out, "Can't you understand that we *remember* Earth! After thirty years in a steel box we want to come home."

"I do understand. You accepted the steel box; now you refuse the commitment."

She pleaded, "Surely six hundred people are not too many to harbour? There must be small corners—"

He interrupted, "There are small corners innumerable but not for you. Six hundred, you say, but you forget the books with their descriptions of the starships. You forget that we know of the millions of ova carried in the boxes called cryogenic vaults, of how in a generation you would be an army surging out of its small corner to dominate the culture whose careful virtues mean nothing to you. Go back to your ship, Nugan. Tell your people that time has rolled over them, that their home has vanished."

She sat between desperation and fulmination while he summoned the bearers. Slowly she resumed the travel suit.

From the hilltop she saw a world unrolled around her, stirring memory and calling the heart. It should not be lost for a pedantic Aboriginal's obstinacy.

"I will talk with your women!"

"They may be less restrained than I, Nugan. The Tup-Ma's message said you were to be instructed and sent away. My duty is done."

She surrendered to viciousness. "We'll come in spite of you!"

"Then we will wipe you out as a leprous infection."

She laughed, pointed a gloved finger and a patch of ground glowed red, then white. "Wipe us out?"

He told her, "That will not fight the forces of nature we can unleash against you. Set your colony on a hill and we will surround it with bushfires, a weapon your armoury is not equipped to counter. Set it in a valley and we will show you how a flash flood can be created. Force us at your peril."

All her Contact training vanished in the need to assert. "You have not seen the last of us."

He said equably, "I fear that is true. I fear for you, Nugan, and all of yours."

She tongued the switch at mouth level and the helmet sprang up and over her head, its creases smoothing invisibly out. She had a moment's unease at the thought of the Report Committee on *Starfarer*, then she tongued the microphone switch. "Jack!"

"Here, love. So soon?"

"Yes, so damned soon!" She looked once at the steady figure of Libary, watching and impassive, then gave the standard call for return: "Lift me home, Jack."

Hurtling into the lonely sky, she realised what she had said and began silently to weep.

Alexander Kuprin

Translated by Leland Fetzer

Alexander Kuprin (1879–1938) is the first Russian writer to incorporate the influence of H. G. Wells, in this 1913 story, and to provide a model for later Russian writers such as Evgeny Zamiatin. Kuprin is also clearly influenced by other literature, including various stories of adventure and shipwreck. (Perhaps, also, Poe's *Narrative of Arthur Gordon Pym*.)

Zamiatin said in his enthusiastic essay on H. G. Wells in 1922, "Of course, science fiction could enter the field of fine literature only in the last decades, when truly fantastic potentialities unfolded before science and technology . . . true science fiction clothed in literary form will be found only at the end of the nineteenth century . . . The petrified life of the old, prerevolutionary Russia produced almost no examples of social fantasies or science fiction, as indeed it could not. Perhaps the only representatives of this genre in the recent history of our literature are Kuprin, with his 'The Liquid Sun,' and Bogdanov. . . ."

This is a story that could easily have appeared twenty-five or thirty years later in *Amazing Stories* as a genre story without causing a ripple—and been seen as innovative. It did not, however, appear in English translation until the early 1980s in an academic collection, so it has not been part of the main genre dialogue for decades. It is about the idea of radical transformation of human society through science and technology. Russian and American science fiction share a central fascination with this idea. In the rest of the world, this idea is generally treated ironically, with great suspicion, or as a recipe for disaster.

LIQUID SUNSHINE

I, Henry Dibble, turn to the truthful exposition of certain important and extraordinary events in my life with the greatest concern and absolutely understandable hesitation. Much of what I find essential to put to paper will, without doubt, arouse astonishment, doubt, and even disbelief in the future reader of my account. For this I have long been prepared, and I find such an attitude to my memoirs completely plausible and logical. I must myself admit that even to me those years spent in part in travel and in part on the six-thousand-foot summit of the volcano Cayambe in the South American Republic of Ecuador often seem not to have been actual events in my life, but only a strange and fantastic dream or the ravings of a transient cataclysmic madness.

But the absence of four fingers on my left hand, recurring headaches, and the eye ailment which goes by the common name of night blindness, these incontrovertible phenomena compel me to believe that I was in fact a witness to the most astonishing events in world history. And, finally, it is not madness, not a dream, not a delusion, that punctually three times a year from the firm E. Nideston and Son, 451 Regent Street, I receive 400 pounds sterling. This allowance was generously left to me by my teacher and patron, one of the greatest men in all of human history, who perished in the terrible wreck of the Mexican schooner *Gonzalez*.

I completed studies in the Mathematical Department with special studies in Physics and Chemistry at the Royal University in the year . . . That, too, is yet another persistent reminder of my adventures. In addition to the fact that a pulley or a chain took the fingers of my left hand at the time of the catastrophe, in addition to the damage to my optic nerves, etc., as I fell into the sea I received, not knowing when nor how, a sharp blow on the right upper quarter of my skull. That blow left hardly any external sign but it is strangely reflected in my mind, specifically in my powers of recall. I can remember well words, faces, localities, sounds, and the sequence of events, but I have forgotten forever all numbers and personal names, addresses, telephone numbers, and historical dates; the years, months, and days which marked my personal life have disappeared without a trace, scientific formulae, although I am able to deal with them without difficulty in logical fashion, have fled, and both the names of those I have known and know now have disappeared, and this circumstance is very painful to me. Unfortunately, I did not then maintain a diary, but two or three notebooks which have survived, and a few old letters aid me to a certain degree to orient myself.

Briefly, I completed my studies and received the title Master of Physics two, three, four, or perhaps even five years before the beginning of the twentieth century. Precisely at that time the husband of my elder sister, Maude, a farmer of Norfolk who periodically had loaned me material support and even more important moral support, took ill and died. He firmly believed that I would continue my scientific career at one of the English universities and that in time I would shine as a luminary to cast a ray of glory on his modest family. He was healthy, sanguine, strong as a bull, could drink, write a verse, and box—a lad in the spirit of good old merry England. He died as the result of a stroke one night after consuming one-fourth of a Berkshire mutton roast, which he seasoned with a strong sauce: a bottle of whiskey and two gallons of Scotch light beer.

His predictions and expectations were not fulfilled. I did not join the scientific ranks. Even more, I was not fortunate enough to find the position of a teacher or a tutor in a private or public school; rather, I fell into the vicious, implacable, furious, cold, wearisome world of failure. Oh! who, besides the rare spoiled darlings, has not known and felt on his shoulders this stupid, ridiculous, blind blow of fate? But it abused me for too lengthy a time.

Neither at factories nor at scientific agencies—nowhere could I find a place for myself. Usually I arrived too late: the position was already taken.

In many cases I became convinced that I had fallen into some dark and suspicious conspiracy. Even more often I was paid nothing for two or three months of labor and thrown onto the street like a kitten. One cannot say that I was excessively indecisive, shy, unenterprising, or, on the other hand, sensitive, vain or refractory. No, it was simply that the circumstances of life were against me.

But I was above all an Englishman and I held myself as a gentleman and a representative of the greatest nation in the world. The thought of suicide in this terrible period of my life never came to mind. I fought against the injustice of fate with cold, sober persistence and with the unshakable faith that never, never would an Englishman be a slave. And fate, finally, surrendered in the face of my Anglo-Saxon courage.

I lived then in the most squalid of all the squalid lanes in Bethel Green, in the God-forsaken East End, dwelling behind a chintz curtain in the home of a dock worker, a coal hauler. I paid him four shillings a month for the place, and in addition I helped his wife with the cooking, taught his three oldest children to read and write, and also scrubbed the kitchen and the backstairs. My hosts always cordially invited me to eat with them, but I had decided not to burden their beggar's budget. I dined, rather, in the dark basement and God knows how many cats', dogs', and horses' lives lay on my black conscience. But my landlord, Mr. John Johnson, requited my natural tact with attentiveness: when there was much work on the East End docks and not enough workmen and the wages reached extraordinary heights, he always managed to find a place for me to load heavy cargoes where with no difficulty I could earn eight or ten shillings in a day. It was unfortunate that this handsome, kind, and religious man became intoxicated every Sunday without fail and when he did so he displayed a great inclination toward fisticuffs.

In addition to my duties as cook and occasional work on the docks, I essayed numerous other ridiculous, onerous, and peculiar professions. I helped clip poodles and cut the tails from fox terriers, clerked in a sausage store when its owner was absent, catalogued old libraries, counted the earnings at horse races, at times gave lessons in mathematics, psychology, fencing, theology, and even dancing, copied off the most tedious reports and infantile stories, watched coach horses when the drivers were eating ham and drinking beer; once, in uniform, I spread rugs and raked the sand between acts in a circus, worked as a sandwich man, and even fought as boxer, a middleweight, translated from German to English and vice versa, composed tombstone inscriptions, and what else did I not do! To be candid, thanks to my inexhaustible energy and temperate habits I was never in particular need. I had a stomach like a camel, I weighed 150 pounds without my clothes, had good hands, slept well and was cheerful in temperament. I had so adjusted to poverty and to its unavoidable deprivations, that occasionally I could not only send a little money to my younger sister, Esther, who had been abandoned in Dublin with her two children by her Irish husband, and actor, a drunkard, a liar, a tramp, and a rake—but I also followed the sciences and public life closely, read newspapers and scholarly journals, bought used books, and belonged to rental libraries. I even managed to make two minor inventions: a very cheap device which would warn a railroad engineer in fog or snow of a closed switch ahead, and an unusual, long-lasting welding flame which burned hydrogen. I must say that I did not enjoy the income from these inventions—others did. But I remained true to science, like a knight to his lady, and I never abandoned the belief that the time would come when my beloved would summon me to her chamber with her bright smile.

That smile shone upon me in the most unexpected and commonplace fashion. One foggy autumn morning my landlord, the good Mr. Johnson, went to a neighboring shop for hot water and milk for his children. He returned with a radiant face, the odor of whiskey on his breath, and a newspaper in his hand. He gave me the newspaper, still damp and smelling of ink, and, pointing out an entry marked with a line from the edge of his dirty nail, exclaimed:

"Look, old man. As easy as I can tell anthracite from coke, I know that these lines are for you, lad."

I read, not without interest, the following announcement:

"The solicitors 'E. Nideston and Son,' 451 Regent Street, seek an individual for an equatorial voyage to a location where he must remain for not less than three years engaged in scientific pursuits. Conditions: age, 22 to 30 years, English citizenship, faultless health, discrete, sober and forbearing, must know one, or yet better, two other European languages (French and German), must be a bachelor, and so far as it is possible, free of family and other ties to his native land. Beginning salary: 400 pounds sterling per year. A university education is desirable, and in particular a gentleman knowing theoretical and applied chemistry and physics has an advantage in obtaining the position. Applicants are to call between nine and ten in the morning." I am able to quote this advertisement with such assurance since it is still preserved among my few papers, although I copied it off in haste and has been subject to the action of sea water.

"Nature has given you long legs, son, and good lungs," Johnson said, approvingly pounding my back. "Start up the engine and full steam ahead. No doubt there will be many more young gentlemen there of irreproachable health and honorable character than at Derby. Anne, make him a sandwich with meat and preserves. Perhaps he will have to wait his turn in line for five hours. Well, I wish you luck, my friend. Onward, brave England!"

I arrived barely in time at Regent Street. Silently I thanked nature for my good legs. As he opened the door the porter with indifferent familiarity said: "Your luck, mister. You got the last chance," and promptly fixed on the outside doors the fateful announcement: "The advertised opening is now closed to applicants."

In the darkened, cramped, and rather dirty reception room—such are almost all the reception rooms belonging to the magicians of the City who deal in millions—were about ten men who had come before me. They sat about the walls on dark, time-polished, soiled wooden benches, above which, at the height of a sitting man's head, the ancient wallpaper displayed a wide, dirty, band. Good God, what a pitiful collection of hungry, ragged men, driven by need, sick and broken, had gathered here, like a parade of monsters! Involuntarily my heart contracted with pity and wounded self-esteem. Sallow faces, averted, malicious, envious, suspicious glances from under lowered brows, trembling hands, tatters, the smell of poverty, cheap tobacco, and fumes of alcohol long since drunk. Some of these young gentlemen were not yet seventeen years of age while others were past fifty. One after another, like pale shades, they drifted into the office and returned from there looking like drowned men only lately removed from the water. I felt both sickened and ashamed to admit to myself that I was infinitely healthier and stronger than all of them taken together.

Finally my turn came. Someone invisible opened the door from the other side and shouted abruptly and disgustedly in an exasperated voice:

"Number eighteen, and Allah be praised, the last!"

I entered the office, nearly as neglected as the reception room, different only that it was papered in peeling checked paper; it had two side chairs, a couch, and two easy chairs on which sat two middle-aged gentlemen of apparently the same medium height, but the elder of the two, in a long coat was slim, swarthy, and seemingly stern, while the other, dressed in a new jacket with silken lapels, was fair, plump, blue-eyed and sat at his ease one leg placed upon the other.

I gave my name and bowed not deeply, but respectfully. Then, seeing that I was not to be offered a seat, I was at the point of taking a place on the couch.

"Wait," said the swarthy one, "First remove your coat and vest. There is a doctor here who will examine you."

I remembered the clause in the advertisement which referred to irreproachable health, and I silently removed my outer garments. The florid stout man lazily freed himself from his chair and placing his arms around me he pressed his ear to my chest.

"Well, at least we have one with clean linen," he said casually.

He listened to my lungs and heart, tapped my spine and chest with his fingers, sat me down and checked the reflexes of my knees, and finally said lazily:

"As fit as a fiddle. He hasn't eaten too well recently, however. But that is nothing and all that is required is two weeks of good food. To his good fortune, I find no traces of exhaustion from over-indulgences in athletics as is common among our young men. In a word, Mr. Nideston, I present you a gentleman, a fortunate, almost perfect example of the healthy Anglo-Saxon race. May I assume that I am no longer needed?"

"You are free, doctor," said the solicitor. "But can you, may I be assured, visit us tomorrow morning, if I require your professional advice?"

"Oh, Mr. Nideston, I am always at your service."

When we were alone, the solicitor sat opposite me and peered intently into my face. He had little sharp eyes the color of a coffee bean with quite yellow whites. Every now and then when he looked directly at you, it seemed as though diminutive sharp and bright needles issued from those tiny blue pupils.

"Let us talk," he said abruptly. "Your name, origins, and place of birth?"

I answered him in the same expressionless and laconic fashion.

"Education?"

"The Royal University."

"Subject of study?"

"Department of Mathematics, in particular, Physics."

"Foreign languages?"

"I know German comparatively well. I understand when French is not spoken too rapidly, I can put together a few score essential expressions, and I read it without difficulty."

"Relatives and their social position?"

"Is that of any importance to you, Mr. Nideston?"

"To me? Of supreme unimportance. But I act in the interests of a third party."

I described the situations of my two sisters. During my speech he attentively inspected his nails, and then threw two needles at me from his eyes, asking:

"Do you drink? And how much?"

"Sometimes at dinner I drink a half pint of beer."

"A bachelor?"

"Yes, sir."

"Do you have any intention of commiting that blunder? Of marrying?"

"Oh, no."

"Any present love affairs?"

"No, sir."

"How do you support yourself?"

I answered that question briefly and fairly, omitting, for the sake of brevity, five or six of my latest casual professions.

"So," he said, when I had finished, "do you need money?"

"No. My stomach is full and I am adequately clothed. I always find work. So far as it is possible I follow recent developments in science. I am convinced that sooner or later I will find my opportunity."

"Would you like money in advance? A loan?"

"No, that is not my practice. I don't take money from anyone . . . But we're not finished."

"Your principles are commendable. Perhaps we can come to an agreement. Give me your address and I will inform you, and probably very soon, of our decision. Good-bye."

"Excuse me, Mr. Nideston," I responded. "I have answered all your questions, even the most delicate, with complete candor. May I ask you one question?"

"Please."

"What is the purpose of the journey?"

"Oho! Are you concerned about that?"

"We may assume that I am."

"The purpose of the journey is purely scientific."

"That is not an adequate answer."

"Not adequate?" Mr. Nideston abruptly shouted at me, and his coffee eyes poured out sheaves of needles. "Not adequate? Do you have the insolence to assume that the firm of Nideston and Son now in existence for one hundred and fifty years and respected by all of England's commercial establishments would suggest anything dishonorable or which might compromise you? Or that we would undertake any enterprise without possessing reliable guarantees beforehand that it is unconditionally legal?"

"Oh, sir, I have no doubt of that," I responded in confusion.

"Very well, then," he interrupted me and immediately became tranquil, like a stormy sea spread with oil. "But you see, first of all I am bound by the proviso that you not be informed of any substantial details of the journey until you are aboard the steamship out of Southampton . . ."

"Bound where?" I asked suddenly.

"For the time being I cannot tell you. And secondly, the purpose of your journey (if indeed it comes to pass) is not completely clear even to me."

"Strange," said I.

"Passing strange," the solicitor willingly agreed. "But I may also inform you, if you so desire, that it will be fantastic, grandiose, unprecedented, splendid, and audacious to the point of madness!"

Now it was my turn to say "Hmmm," and this I did with a certain restraint.

"Wait," Mr. Nideston exclaimed with sudden fervor. "You are young. I am twenty-five or thirty years older than you. You are not at all astonished by many of the greatest accomplishments of the human mind, but if, when I was your age, someone had predicted that I would work in the evenings by the light of invisible electricity which flowed through wires or that I would converse with an acquaintance at a distance of eighty miles, that I would see moving, laughing human figures on a screen, that I would send telegraph messages without the benefit of wires, and so on, and so on, then I would have waged my honor, my freedom, my career against one pint of bad London beer that I was confronted with a madman."

"You mean the project involves some new invention or a great discovery?"

"If you wish, yes. But I ask you, do not view me with distrust or suspicion. What would you say, for example, if a great genius were to appeal to your young energy, strength, and knowledge, a genius who, we will assume, is engaged with a problem—to create a pleasing, nutritious, economical food out of the elements found in the air? If you were provided the opportunity to labor for the sake of the future organization and adornment of the earth? To dedicate your talents and spiritual energies to the happiness of future generations? What would you say? Here is an example at hand. Look out the window."

Involuntarily I arose under the spell of his compelling, swift gesture and looked through the clouded glass. There, over the streets, hung a black-rust-gray fog, like dirty cotton from heaven to earth. In it only dimly could be perceived the wavering glow from the street lights. It was eleven o'clock in the morning.

"Yes, yes, look," said Mr. Nideston. "Look carefully. Now assume that a gifted, disinterested man is summoning you to a great project to ameliorate and beautify the earth. He tells you that everything that is on the earth depends on the mind, will, and hands of man. He tells you that if God in his righteous anger has turned his face away from man, then man's measureless mind will come to his own aid. This man will tell you that fogs, disease, climatic extremes, winds, volcanic eruptions—they are all subject to the influence and control of the human will—and that finally the earth could become a paradise and its existence extended by several hundred thousand years. What would you say to that man?"

"But what if he who presents me with this radiant dream is wrong? What if I find myself a dumb plaything in the hands of a monomaniac? A capricious madman?"

Mr. Nideston rose, and, presenting me his hand as a sign of farewell, said firmly:

"No. Aboard the steamship in two or three months from now (if we can come to an agreement) I will inform you of the name of that scientist and the meaning of his great task, and you will remove your hat as a mark of your great reverence for the man and his ideas. But I, unfortunately, Mr. Dibble, am a layman. I am only a solicitor—the guardian and representative of others' interests."

After this interview I had almost no doubt that fate, finally, had grown tired of my fixed inspection of her unbending spine and had decided to show me her mysterious face. Therefore, that same evening with the help of my small savings I produced a banquet of extraordinary luxury, which consisted of a roast, a punch, plum pudding and hot chocolate which was enjoyed in addition to myself by the worthy couple, the elder Johnsons, and, I do not remember exactly—six or seven of the younger Johnsons. My left shoulder was quite blue and out of joint from the friendly pounding of my good landlord who sat next to me on my left.

And I was not wrong. The next evening I received a telegram: "Call at noon tomorrow. 451 Regent Street, Nideston."

I arrived punctually at the appointed time. He was not in his office, but a servant who had been forewarned led me to a small room in a restaurant located around the corner at a distance of two hundred paces. Mr. Nideston was there alone. At first he was not that ebullient, and perhaps even poetic, man who had spoken with me so fervently about the future happiness of mankind two days earlier. No, once more he was that dry and laconic solicitor who on the occasion of our first meeting that morning had so commandingly instructed me to remove my outer clothing and had questioned me like a police inspector.

"Good day. Sit down," he said indicating a chair. "It is my lunch hour, a time I have at my disposal. Although my firm is called 'Nideston and Son' I am in fact a bachelor and a lonely man. And so—would you care to dine? To drink?"

I thanked him and asked for tea and toast. Mr. Nideston ate at leisure, sipped an old port and from time to time transfixed me with the bright needles of his eyes. Finally, he wiped his lips, threw down his napkin, and asked:

"Then, you are agreed?"

"To buy a pig in a poke?" I asked in turn.

"No," he said loudly and angrily. "The previous conditions remain in force. Before your departure to the tropics you will receive as much information as I am empowered to give you. If this is not satisfactory, you may, on your part, refuse to sign the contract and I will pay you a recompense for the time which you have employed in fruitless conversations with me."

I observed him carefully. At that moment he was engaged in an effort to crack two nuts, the right hand enveloping the knuckles of the left. The sharp needles of his eyes were concealed behind the curtain of his brows. And suddenly, as though in a moment of illumination, I perceived all the soul of that man—the strange soul of a formalist and a gambler, the narrow specialist and an extraordinarily expansive temperament, the slave of his counting house traditions and at the same time a secret searcher for adventures, a pettifogger, ready for two pennies to put his opponent in prison for a long sentence, and at the same time an eccentric capable of sacrificing the wealth acquired in dozens of years of unbroken labor for the sake of the shadow of a beautiful idea. This thought passed through me like lightning. And Nideston, suddenly, as though we had been united by some invisible current, opened his eyes, with a great effort crushed the nuts into tiny fragments and smiled at me with an open, childlike, almost mischievous smile.

"When all is said and done, you are risking little, my dear Mr. Dibble. Before you leave for the tropics I will give you several commissions on the continent. These commissions will not require from you any particular scientific knowledge, but they will demand great mechanical accuracy, precision, and foresight. You will need no more than about two months, perhaps a week more or less than that. You are to accept in various European locations certain expensive and very fragile optical glasses as well as several extremely delicate and sensitive physical instruments. I entrust to your care, agility, and skills their packing, delivery to the railroad, and sea and rail transport. You must agree that it would mean nothing to a drunken sailor or porter to throw a crate into the hold and smash into fragments a doubly convex lens over which dozens of men have worked for dozens of years . . ."

"An observatory!" I thought joyfully. "Of course, it's an observatory! What happiness! At last I have my elusive fate by the forelock."

I could see that he had guessed my thoughts and his eyes became yet merrier.

"We will not discuss the remuneration for this, your first, task. We will come to agreement on details, of course, as I can see from your expression. But," and then he suddenly laughed heedlessly, like a child, "I want to turn your attention to a very curious fact. Look, through these fingers have passed ten or twenty thousand curious cases, some of them involving very large sums. Several times I have made a fool of myself, and that in spite of all our subtle casuistic precision and diligence. But, imagine that every time that I have rejected all the tricks of my craft and looked a man straight in the eye, as I am now looking at you, I have never gone wrong and never had cause for repentance. And so?"

His eyes were clear, firm, trusting and affectionate. At that second this little swarthy, wrinkled, yellow-faced man indeed took my heart into his hands and conquered it.

"Good," I said. "I believe you. From this time I am at your disposal."

"Oh, why so fast?" Mr. Nideston said genially. "You have plenty of time. We still have time to drink a bottle of claret together." He pulled the cord for the waiter. "But please put your personal affairs in order, and this evening at eight o'clock you will leave with the tide on board the steamship *The Lion and the Magdalene* to which I will in time deliver your itinerary, drafts on various banks, and money for your personal expenses. My dear young man, I drink to your health and your successes. If only," he suddenly exclaimed with unexpected enthusiasm, "if only you knew how I envy you, my dear Mr. Dibble!"

In order to flatter him and in quite an innocent manner, I responded almost sincerely:

"What's detaining you, my dear Mr. Nideston? I swear that in spirit you are as young as I."

The swarthy solicitor lowered his long delicately modeled nose into his claret cup, was silent for a moment and suddenly said with a sigh of feeling:

"Oh, my dear Mr. Dibble! My office, which has existed nearly from the time of the Plantagenets, the honor of my firm, my ancestors, thousands of ties connecting me with my clients, associates, friends, and enemies . . . I couldn't name it all . . . This means you have no doubts?"

"No."

"Well, let us drink a toast and sing 'Rule, Britannia'!"

And we drank a toast and sang—I almost a boy, yesterday a tramp, and that dry man of business, whose influence extended from the gloom of his dirty office to touch the fates of European powers and business magnates—we sang together in the most improbable and unsteady voices in all the world:

> *"Rule, Britannia!*
> *Britannia, rules the waves!*
> *Britons never, never, never will be slaves!"*

A servant entered, and turning politely to Mr. Nideston, he said:

"Excuse me, sir. I listened to your singing with genuine pleasure. I have heard nothing more pleasing even in the Royal Opera, but next to you in the adjoining room is a meeting of lovers of French medieval music. Perhaps I should not refer to them as gentlemen . . . but they all have very discriminating ears."

"You are no doubt correct," the solicitor answered gently. "And therefore I ask you to accept as a keepsake this round yellow object with the likeness of our good king."

Here is a brief list of the cities and the laboratories which I visited after I crossed the Channel. I copy them out in entirety from my notebook: The Pragemow concern in Paris; Repsold in Hamburg; Zeiss, Schott Brothers, and Schlattf in Jena; in Munich the Frauenhof concern and the Wittschneider Optical Institute and also the Mertz laboratory there; Schick in Berlin, and also Bennech and Basserman. And also, not distant in Potsdam, the superb branch of the Pragemow concern which operates in conjunction with the essential and enlightened support of Dr. E. Hartnack.

The itinerary composed by Mr. Nideston was extraordinarily precise and included train schedules and the addresses of inexpensive but comfortable English hotels. He had drawn it up in his own hand. And here, too, one was aware of his strange and unpredictable character. On the corner of one of the pages he had written in pencil in his angular, firm hand: "If Chance and Co. were real

Englishmen they would have not abandoned their concern and it would not be necessary for us to obtain lenses and instruments from the French and Germans with names like Schnurbartbindhalter."

I will admit, not in a spirit of boasting, that everywhere I bore myself with the requisite weight and dignity, because many times in critical moments in my ears I heard Mr. Nideston's terrible goat's voice singing, "Britons never, never, never will be slaves."

But, too, I must say that I cannot complain about any lack of attentiveness and courtesy on the part of the learned scientists and famous technicians whom I met. My letters of recommendation signed with large, black, completely illegible flourishes and reinforced below with Mr. Nideston's precise signature served as a magic wand in my hands which opened all doors and all hearts for me. With unremitting and deep-felt concern I watched the manufacture and polishing of convex and curving lenses and the production of the most delicate, complex and beautiful instruments which gleamed with brass and steel, shining with all their screws, tubing, and machined metal. When in one of the most famous workshops of the globe I was shown an almost complete fifty-inch mirror which had required at least two or three years of final polishing—my heart stood still and my breath caught, so overcome was I with delight and awe at the power of the human mind.

But I was also rendered very uneasy by the persistent curiosity of these serious, learned men who in turn attempted to ascertain the mysterious purpose of my patron whose name I did not know. Sometimes subtly and artfully, sometimes crudely and directly, they attempted to extract from me the details and goal of my journey, the addresses of the firms with which I had business, the type and function of our orders to other workshops, etc., etc. But, firstly, I remembered well Mr. Nideston's very serious warnings about indiscretions; secondly, what could I answer even if I wished to? I myself knew nothing and was feeling my way, as though at night in an unknown forest. I was accepting, after verifying drawings and calculations, some kind of strange optical glasses, metal tubing of various sizes, calculators, small-scale propellors, miniaturized cylinders, shutters, heavy glass retorts of a strange form, pressure gauges, hydraulic presses, a host of electrical devices which I had never seen before, several powerful microscopes, three chronometers and two underwater diving suits with helmets. One thing became obvious to me: the strange enterprise which I served had nothing to do with the construction of an observatory, and on the basis of the objects which I was accepting I found it absolutely impossible to guess the purpose which they were to serve. My only concern was to ensure that they were packed with great care and I constantly devised ingenious devices which protected them from vibrations, concussion, and deformation.

I freed myself from impertinent questions by suddenly falling silent, and not saying a word I would look with stony eyes directly at the face of my interrogator. But one time I was compeled to resort to very persuasive eloquence: a fat, insolent Prussian dared to offer me a bribe of two thousand Marks if I would reveal to him the secret of our enterprise. This happened in Berlin in my own room on the fourth floor of my hotel. I succinctly and sternly informed that stout insolent creature that he spoke with an English gentleman. He neighed like a Percheron, slapped me familiarly on the back and exclaimed:

"Oh, come now, my good man, let's forget these jokes. We both understand what they mean. Do you think that I have not offered you enough? But we, like intelligent men of the world, can come to an agreement, I am sure . . ."

His vulgar tone and crude gestures displeased me inordinately. I opened the great window of my room and pointing below at the pavement I said firmly:

"One word more, and you will not find it necessary to employ the elevator to leave this floor. One, two, three . . ."

Pale, cowed, and enraged, he cursed hoarsely in his harsh Berlin accent, and on his way out slammed the door so hard that the floor of my apartment trembled and objects leaped upon the table.

My last visit on the continent was to Amsterdam. There I was to transmit my letters of recommendation to the two owners of two world famous diamond cutting firms, Maas and Daniels, respectively. They were intelligent, polite, dignified, and sceptical Jews. When I visited them in turn, Daniels first of all said to me slyly: "Of course you have a commission also for Mr. Maas." And Maas, as soon as he read the letter addressed to him, said with a query in his voice, "You have no doubt spoken with Mr. Daniels?"

Both of them displayed the greatest reserve and suspicion in their relations with me; they consulted together, sent off simple and coded telegrams, put to me the most subtle and detailed questions about my personal life, and so on. They both visited me on the day of my departure. A kind of Biblical dignity could be perceived in their words and movements.

"Excuse us, young man, and do not consider it a sign of our distrust that we inform you," said the older and more imposing, Daniels, "that on the route Amsterdam–London all steamships are alive with international thieves of the highest skill. It is true that we hold in strictest confidence the execution of your worthy commission, but who can be assured that one or two of these enterprising, intelligent, at times almost brilliant international knights of commerce will not manage to discover our secret? Therefore, we have not considered it excessive to surround you with an invisible but faithful police guard. You, perhaps, will not even notice them. You know that caution is never unwanted. Will you not agree that we and your associates would be much relieved if that which you transport were under reliable, observant, and ceaseless observation during the entire voyage? This is not a matter of a leather cigarette case, but two objects which cost together approximately one million three hundred thousand francs and which are unique in all the world, and perhaps in all the universe."

I, in the most sincere and concerned tone, hastened to assure the worthy diamond cutter of my complete agreement with his wise and farsighted words. Apparently, my trust inclined him even more in my favor, and he asked in a low voice, in which I detected a quaver, an expression of awe:

"Would you like to see them?"

"If that is convenient, then please," I said, barely able to conceal my curiosity and perplexity.

Both the Jews almost simultaneously, with the expression of priests performing a holy ritual, took out of the side pockets of their long frock coats two small boxes—Daniels' was of oak while that of Maas was of red morocco; they carefully unfastened the gold clasps and lifted the lids. Both boxes were lined in white velvet and at first to me they appeared to be empty. It was only when I had bent close over them and looked closely that I saw two round, convex, totally colorless lenses of extraordinary purity and transparency, which would have been almost invisible except for their delicate, round, precise outlines.

"Astonishing workmanship!" I exclaimed, ecstatically. "Undoubtedly the polishing of glass in this manner must have required much expenditure of time."

"Young man!" said Daniels in a startled whisper. "They are not glass, they are two diamonds. The one from my shop weighs thirty and one-half carats and the diamond of Mr. Maas in all weighs seventy-four carats."

I was so stunned that I lost my usual composure.

"Diamonds? Diamonds cut into spheres? But that's a miracle such as I have never seen or heard. Man has never succeeded in producing anything like them!"

"I have already told you that these objects are unique in all the world," the jeweler reminded me solemnly, "but, excuse me, I am somewhat puzzled by your surprise. Did you not know about them? Had you in fact never heard of them?"

"Never in my life. You know that the enterprise which I serve is a closely guarded secret. Not only I, but also Mr. Nideston, are unacquainted with it in detail. I know only that I am collecting parts and equipment in various locations in Europe for some kind of an enormous project, whose purpose and plan I—a scientist by training—as yet understand nothing."

Daniels looked intently at me with his calm capable eyes, light brown in color, and his Biblical face darkened.

"Yes, that is so," he said slowly and thoughtfully after a brief pause. "Apparently you know nothing more than we, but do I perceive, when I look into your eyes, that even if you were informed of the nature of the enterprise, you would not share your information with us?"

"I have given my word, Mr. Daniels," I said as softly as possible.

"Yes, that is so, that is so. Do not think, young man, that you have come to our city of canals and diamonds completely unknown."

The Jew smiled a thin smile.

"We are even aware of the manner in which you suggested an aerial journey out of your window to a certain individual with commercial connections."

"How could anyone have known of that incident except the two of us involved?" I said, astonished. "Apparently, that German swine could not keep his mouth closed."

The Jew's face became enigmatic. He slowly and significantly passed his hand down his long beard.

"You should know that the German said nothing about his humiliation. But we knew about it the next day. We must! We whose guarded fire-proof vaults contain our own and others' valuables sometimes worth hundreds of millions of francs, must maintain our own intelligence. Yes. And three days later Mr. Nideston also knew of your deed."

"That's going too far!" I exclaimed in confusion.

"You have lost nothing, my young Englishman. Rather you have gained. Do you know how Mr. Nideston responded when he heard of the Berlin incident? He said: 'I knew that Mr. Dibble, an excellent young man, would have done nothing else.' For my part I would like to congratulate Mr. Nideston and his patron on the fact that their interests have fallen into such faithful hands. Although ... Although ... Although this disrupts certain of our schemes, our plans, and our hopes."

"Yes," confirmed the taciturn Mr. Maas.

"Yes," repeated quietly the Biblical Mr. Daniels, and once more a sad expression passed over his face. "We were given these diamonds in almost the same form in which you now see them, but their surfaces, as they had only recently been removed from the matrix, were crude and rough. We ground them as patiently and lovingly as though they were a commission from an emperor. To express it more accurately; it was impossible to improve on them. But I, an old man, a craftsman and one of the great gem experts of the world, have long been tortured by one cursed question: who could give such a shape to a diamond? Moreover, look at the diamond—here is a lens—not a crack, not a blemish, not a bubble. This prince of diamonds must have been subjected to the greatest heat and pressure. And I," and here Daniels sighed sadly, "and I must admit that I had counted much on your arrival and your candor."

"Forgive me, but I am in no position . . ."

"That's enough, I understand. But we wish you a pleasant journey."

My ship left Amsterdam that evening. The agents who accompanied me were so skilled at their work that I did not know who among the passengers was my guard. But toward midnight when I wished to sleep and retired to my room, to my surprise I found there a bearded, broad-shouldered stranger whom I had never seen on deck. He stretched out, not on the spare bunk, but on the floor near the door where he spread out a coat and an inflatable rubber pillow and covered himself with a robe. Not without repressed anger I informed him that the entire cabin to its full extent including its cubic content of air belonged to me. But he responded calmly and with a good English accent:

"Do not be disturbed, sir. It is my duty to spend this night near you in the position of a faithful watchdog. May I add that here is a letter and a package from Mr. Daniels."

The old Jew had written briefly and affectionately:

Do not deny me a small pleasure: take as a souvenir of our meeting this ring I offer you. It is of no great value, but it will serve as an amulet to guard you from danger at sea. The inscription on it is ancient, and may indeed be in the language of the now extinct Incas.

Daniels

In the packet was a ring with a small flat ruby on whose surface were engraved wondrous signs.

Then my "watchdog" locked the cabin, laid a revolver next to him on the floor and seemingly fell instantly asleep.

"Thank you, my dear Mr. Dibble," Mr. Nideston said to me the next day, shaking my hand firmly. "You have excellently fulfilled all your commissions, which were at times difficult enough, employed your time well, and in addition have borne yourself with dignity. Now you may rest for a week and divert yourself as you wish. Sunday morning we shall dine together and then leave for Southampton and on Monday morning you will be at sea aboard *The Southern Cross*, a splendid steamer. Do not forget, may I remind you, to visit my clerk to receive your two months' salary and expenses, and during the next two days I will examine and re-pack all of your baggage. It is dangerous to trust another's hands, and I doubt if there is anyone in London as skilled as I in the packing of delicate objects."

On Sunday I bade farewell to kind Mr. John Johnson and his numerous family, leaving them to the sound of their best wishes for a happy journey. And on Monday morning Mr. Nideston and I were seated in the luxurious stateroom of the huge liner *The Southern Cross* where we drank coffee in expectation of my departure. A fresh breeze blew over the sea and green waves with white caps dashed against the thick glass of the portholes.

"I must inform you, my dear sir, that you will not be traveling alone," said Mr. Nideston. "A certain Mr. de Mon de Rique will be sailing with you. He is an electrician and mechanic with several years of irreproachable experience behind him and I have only the most favorable reports concerning his abilities. I feel no special affection for the lad, but it may well be in this case the voice of my own erroneous and baseless antipathy—an old man's eccentricity. His father was a Frenchman who took English citizenship and his mother was Irish but he himself has the blood of a Gaelic fighting cock in his veins. He is a dandy, handsome in a common sort of way, much taken with himself and his own appearance, and is fond of women's skirts. It was not I who selected him. I acted only in accordance with the instructions issued to me by Lord Charlesbury, your future director and mentor. De Mon de Rique will arrive in twenty or twenty-five minutes with the morning train from Cardiff and we shall speak with him. At any rate I advise you to establish good relations with him. Whether you like it or not you must live three or four years at his side on God-knows-what desert at the equator on the summit of the extinct volcano Cayambe, where you, white men, will be only five or six, while all the others will be Negroes, Mestizos, Indians and others of their ilk. Are you perhaps frightened at such a prospect? Remember, the choice is yours to make. We could at any moment tear up the contract you signed and return together by the eleven o'clock train to London. And I may assure you that this would in no wise reduce the respect and affection I feel for you."

"No, my dear Mr. Nideston, I see myself already on Cayambe," I said with laughter. "I yearn for regular employment, particularly if it involves science, and when I think of it I lick my chops like a starveling in front of a White Chapel sausage shop. I hope that my work will be interesting enough that I will not become bored and involved in petty concerns and personal differences."

"Oh, my dear sir, you will have much beautiful and lofty labor before you complete your scheme. The time has come to be open with you and I will enlighten you on some matters of which I am informed. Lord Charlesbury has been laboring now nine years on a plan of unheard of dimensions. He has decided at any costs to accomplish the transformation of the sun's rays into a gas and what is more—to compress that gas to an extraordinary degree at terribly low temperatures under colossal pressures into liquid form. If God grants him the power of completing his plan, then his discovery will have enormous consequences . . ."

"Enormous!" I repeated softly, subdued and awed by Mr. Nideston's words.

"That is all I know," said the solicitor. "No, I also know from a personal letter from Lord Charlesbury that he is closer than ever to the successful completion of his work and less than ever has any doubts about the rapid solution of his problem. I must tell you, my dear friend, that Lord Charlesbury is one of the great men of science, one of few touched with genius. In addition, he is a genuine aristocrat both in birth and in spirit, an unselfish and self-denying friend of mankind, a patient and considerate teacher, a charming conversationalist and a faithful friend. He is, moreover, the possessor of such attractive spiritual beauty that all hearts are attracted to him . . . But here is your traveling companion coming up the gang plank now," Mr. Nideston said, breaking off his enthusiastic speech. "Take this envelope. You will find in it your steamship tickets, your exact itinerary and money. You will be at sea for sixteen or seventeen days. Tomorrow you will be overcome by depression. For such an occasion I have acquired and deposited in your cabin thirty or so books. And in addition, in your baggage you will find a suitcase with a supply of warm clothing and boots. You did not know that you will be required to live in a mountain region with eternal snows. I attempted to select clothing of your size, but I was so afraid of making an error, that I preferred the larger size to the smaller. Also you will find among your things a small box with seasickness remedies. I do not in fact believe in them, but at any rate . . . do you suffer from seasickness?"

"Yes, but not to a particularly painful degree. And anyway, I have a talisman against all dangers at sea."

I showed him the ruby, Daniels' gift. He examined it carefully, shook his head and said thoughtfully:

"Somewhere I have seen such a stone as that, and it seems with the same inscription. But now I see the Frenchman has noticed us and is coming our way. With all my heart, my dear Dibble, I wish you a happy voyage, good spirits and health . . . Greetings, Mr. de Mon de Rique. May I introduce you: Mr. Dibble, Mr. de Mon de Rique, future colleagues and collaborators."

I personally was not particularly impressed by the dandy. He was tall, slender, effete and sleek, with a kind of grace in his movements, an indolent and flexible strength, such as we see in the great cats. He reminded me first of all of a Levantine with his beautiful velvety dark eyes and small gleaming black mustache, which was carefully trimmed over his classic pink mouth. We exchanged a few insignificant and polite phrases. But at that moment a bell rang above us and a whistle sounded, shaking the deck with its full powerful voice—the ship's whistle.

"Well, now, good-bye, gentlemen," said Mr. Nideston. "With all my heart I hope you will become friends. My greetings to Lord Charlesbury. May you have good weather during your crossing. Until we meet again."

He walked briskly down the gang plank, entered a waiting cab, waved affectionately in our direction for the last time, and without looking back disappeared from our sight. I did not know why, but I felt a kind of sadness, as though when that man disappeared I had lost a true and faithful helper and a moral support.

I remember little that was remarkable in our journey. I will say only that those seventeen days seemed as long to me as 170 years, and they were so monotonous and dreary that now from a distance they seem to me to be one endlessly long day.

De Mon de Rique and I met several times a day at dinner in the salon. We had no other close meetings. He was cooly polite with me and I in turn re-paid him with restrained courtesy, but I constantly felt he was not interested in me personally nor indeed in anyone else in the world. But, on the other hand, when our conversation touched upon our special fields, I was overwhelmed by his knowledge, his audacity, and the originality of his hypotheses, and what was important, by his ability to express his ideas in precise and picturesque language.

I tried to read the books which Mr. Nideston had left for me. Most of them were narrowly scientific works which dealt with the theory of light and optic lenses, observations on high and low temperatures, and the description of experiments on the concentration and liquefaction of gases. There were also several books devoted to the description of remarkable expeditions and two or three books about the equatorial countries of South America. But it was difficult to read because a heavy wind blew constantly and the steamship oscillated in long sliding glides. All the passengers gave their due to seasickness except de Mon de Rique, who in spite of his great height and delicate build conducted himself as well as an old sailor.

Finally, we arrived at Colón in the northern part of the isthmus of Panama. When I disembarked my legs were leaden and would not obey my will. According to Mr. Nideston's instructions we were personally to oversee the trans-shipment of our baggage to the train station and its loading into baggage cars. The most delicate and sensitive instruments we took with ourselves into our compartment. The precious polished diamonds were, of course, in my possession, but—it is now painful to admit this—I not only did not even show them to my companion, I never said a word to him about them.

Our journey henceforth was fatiguing and consequently of little interest. We traveled by railroad from Colón to Panama, from Panama we had two days' journey on the ancient quivering steamship *Gonzalez* to the Bay of Guayaquil, then on horseback and rail to Quito. In Quito, in accordance with Mr. Nideston's instruction we sought out the Equator Hotel where we found a party of guides and packers who were expecting us. We spent the night in the hotel and early in the morning, refreshed, we set off for the mountains. What intelligent, good, charming creatures—the mules. With their bells tinkling steadily, shaking their heads decorated with rings and plumes, carefully stepping on the uneven country roads with their long tumbler-shaped hooves, they calmly proceeded along the rim of the abyss over such defiles that involuntarly you closed your eyes and held to the horn of the high saddle.

We reached the snow about five that evening. The road widened and became level. It was obvious that people of a high civilization had labored over it. The sharp turns were always paralleled with a low stone barrier.

At six o'clock when we had passed through a short tunnel, we suddenly saw residences before us: several low white buildings over which proudly rose a white tower which resembled a Byzantine church spire or an observatory. Still higher into the sky rose iron and brick chimneys. A quarter of an hour later we arrived at our destination.

Out of a door belonging to a house larger and more spacious than the rest emerged to meet us a tall thin old man with a long, irreproachably white beard. He said he was Lord Charlesbury and greeted us with unfeigned kindness. It was hard to know his age from his appearance: fifty or seventy-five. His large, slightly protuberant blue eyes, the eyes of a pure Englishman, were as clear as a lad's, shining and penetrating. The clasp of his hand was firm, warm, and open, and his high broad forehead was notable for its delicate and noble lines. And as I admired his slender beautiful face and responded to his handshake it clearly seemed to me that one time long ago I had seen his visage and many times I had heard his name.

"I am infinitely pleased at your arrival," said Lord Charlesbury, climbing up the stairs with us. "Was your journey a pleasant one? And how is the good Mr. Nideston? A remarkable man, is he not? But you can answer all my questions at dinner. Now go refresh yourselves and put yourselves in order. Here is our major-domo, the worthy Sambo," and he indicated a portly old Negro who met us in the foyer. "He will show you to your rooms. We dine punctually at seven, and Sambo will inform you of our remaining schedule."

The worthy Sambo very politely, but without a shadow of servile ingratiation, took us to a small house nearby. Each of us was given three rooms—simple, but at the same time somehow exceptionally comfortable, bright, and cheerful. Our quarters were separated from each other by a stone wall and each had a separate entrance. For some reason I was pleased by this arrangement.

With indescribable pleasure I sank into a huge marble bath (thanks to the rocking of the steamship I had been deprived of this satisfaction, and in the hotels at Colón, Panama and Quito the baths would not have aroused the trust even of my friend John Johnson). But when I luxuriated in the warm water, took a cold shower, shaved, and then dressed with the greatest care I was ridden by the question: why was Lord Charlesbury's face so familiar? And what was it, something almost fabulous, it seemed to me, that I had heard about him? At times in some corner of my consciousness I dimly felt that I could remember something, but then it would disappear, as a light breath disappears from a polished steel surface.

From the window of my study I could see all of this strange settlement with its five or six buildings, a stable, a greenhouse with low sooty equipment sheds, a mass of air hoses, with cars drawn over narrow rails by vigorous sleek mules, with high steam cranes which were smoothly carrying through the air steel containers to be filled with coal and oil shale out of a series of dumps. Here and there workers were active, the majority of them half-naked, although the thermometer attached to the outside of my window showed a temperature below freezing, and who were of all colors: white, yellow, bronze, coffee, and gleaming black.

I observed and thought how a flaming will and colossal wealth had been able to transform the barren summit of the extinct volcano into a veritable outpost of civilization with a manufactory, a workshop, and a laboratory, to transport stone, wood and iron to an altitude of eternal snows, to bring water, to construct buildings and machines, to set into motion precious physical instruments, among which the two lenses alone which I had brought cost 1,300,000 francs, to hire dozens of workers and summon highly paid assistants . . . Once more there arose clearly in my mind the figure of Lord Charlesbury and suddenly—but wait! enlightenment suddenly came to my memory. I recalled very precisely how fifteen years earlier when I was still a green student at my school all the newspapers for months trumpeted various rumors concerning the disappearance of Lord Charlesbury, the English peer, the only scion of an ancient family, a famous scientist and a millionaire. His photograph was printed everywhere as well as conjectures on the causes of this strange event. Some took it as murder; others asserted that he had fallen under the influence of some malevolent hypnotist who for his evil purposes had removed the nobleman from England, leaving no traces; a third opinion held that the nobleman was in the hands of criminals who were holding him in expectation of a great ransom; a fourth opinion, and the most prescient one, asserted that the scientist had secretly undertaken an expedition to the North Pole.

Shortly later it became known that before his disappearance Lord Charlesbury very advantageously had liquidated all his lands, forests, parks, farms, coal and clay pits, castles, pictures, and other collections for cash, guided by a very acute and farsighted financial sense. But no one knew what had happened to this immense sum of money. When he disappeared there also disappeared, no one knew where, the famous Charlesbury diamonds, which were rightly the pride of all of England. No police, no private investigators were able to illuminate this strange affair. Within two months the press and society had forgotten him, diverted by other earthshaking interests. Only the learned journals which had dedicated many pages to the memory of the lost nobleman long continued to recount in great detail and with respectful deference his major scientific accomplishments in the study of light and heat and in particular in the expansion and contraction of gases, thermostatics, thermometrics, and thermodynamics, light refraction, the theory of lenses, and phosphorescence.

Outside resounded the drawn-out doleful sound of a gong. And then almost immediately someone knocked on my door and then entered a little cheerful Negro lad, as active as a monkey, who, bowing to me with a friendly smile, reported:

"Mister, I have been appointed by Lord Charlesbury to be at your service. Would you, sir, please come to dinner?"

On the table in my sitting room was a small, delicate bouquet of flowers in a porcelain vase. I selected a gardenia and inserted it into the lapel of my dinner-jacket. But just at that moment Mr. de Mon de Rique emerged from his door wearing a modest daisy in the buttonhole of his frock coat. I felt a kind of uneasy displeasure sweep over me. And even at that distant time there must have been in me still much shallow juvenile peevishness, because I was very pleased to see that Lord Charlesbury who met us in the salon was not wearing a frock coat but a dinner-jacket as was I.

"Lady Charlesbury will be with us shortly," he said, looking at his watch. "I suggest, gentlemen, that you join me for dinner. During the dinner and afterwards there will be two or three hours of free time to converse about business or whatever. May I add that there is a library, skittles, a billiard room and a smoking room here at your disposal. I ask you to utilize them at your discretion as with everything I possess here. I leave you complete freedom as to breakfast and lunch. And this is true also of dinner. But I know how valuable and fruitful is women's company for young Englishmen and therefore . . ."—he rose and indicated the door through which at that moment entered a slender, young, golden-haired woman escorted by another individual of the female sex, spare and sallow dressed all in black. "And therefore, Lady Charlesbury, I have the honor and the pleasure of introducing to you my future colleagues and, I hope, my friends, Mr. Dibble and Mr. de Mon de Rique."

"Miss Sutton," he said, addressing his wife's faded companion (later I discovered she was a distant relative and companion of Lady Charlesbury), "this is Mr. Dibble and Mr. de Mon de Rique. Please share with them your kindness and attention."

At dinner, which was both simple and refined, Lord Charlesbury revealed himself as a cordial host and a superb conversationalist. He inquired animatedly of political affairs, the latest journalistic and scientific news and the health of one or another public figures. By the way, as strange as it may seem, he appeared to be better informed on these subjects than either of us. In addition, his wine cellar turned out to be above praise.

From time to time I secretly glanced at Lady Charlesbury. She took hardly any part in the conversation, only lifting her dark lashes occasionally in the direction of a speaker. She was much younger, even very much younger, than her husband. Her pale face, untouched by any equatorial tan and distinguished by an unhealthy kind of beauty, was framed by thick golden hair, and she had dark, deep, serious, almost melancholy eyes. And all of her appearance, her attractive, very slim figure in white gauze and delicate white hands with long narrow fingers, was reminiscent of some rare and beautiful, but also perhaps poisonous and exotic flower grown without light in a moist dark conservatory.

But I also noticed that de Mon de Rique, who sat opposite me during the meal, often turned an emotional and meaningful glance from his beautiful eyes on our hostess, a glance which persisted perhaps, a half a second longer than propriety permitted. I found myself disliking him more and more: his soft well-groomed face and hands, his languid sweet eyes, which seemed to conceal something, his confident posture, movements, and tone of voice. In my male opinion he seemed repugnant, but I did not doubt for a moment that he possessed all the marks and attributes of an authentic, life-long, cruel, and indifferent conquerer of women's hearts.

After dinner when everyone had left for the salon and Mr. de Mon de Rique had asked permission to retire to the smoking room, I gave the case with the diamonds to Lord Charlesbury, saying:

"These are from Maas and Daniels in Amsterdam."

"You carried them with you?"

"Yes, sir."

"And you did well. These two stones are more valuable to me than all my laboratory."

He went to his study and returned with an eight-power glass. For a long time he carefully examined the diamonds under an electric lamp, and finally, returning them to the case, he said in a satisfied voice, although not without agitation.

"The polishing is above reproach. They are ideally precise. This evening I will check their curved surfaces with instruments employed to measure lenses. Tomorrow morning, Mr. Dibble, we shall fix them into place. Until ten o'clock I shall be occupied with your comrade, Mr. de Mon de Rique, showing him his future laboratory but at ten I ask you to wait for me in your quarters. I shall come for you. Ah, my dear Mr. Dibble, I feel that together we shall advance our project, one of the greatest enterprises ever undertaken by that noble creature, *Homo sapiens.*"

When he said this his eyes burned with a blue light and his hands stroked the lid of the case. And his wife continued to watch him with her deep, dark, fathomless eyes.

The next morning promptly at ten o'clock my doorbell rang and the smartly dressed Negro boy, bowing deeply, admitted Lord Charlesbury.

"You are ready, I'm pleased to see," said my patron in greeting. "I examined the things you brought yesterday and they all seem to be in excellent order. I thank you for your concern and diligence."

"Three-quarters of that honor, if not more, is due to Mr. Nideston, sir."

"Yes, a fine human being and a true friend," the nobleman said with a gracious smile. "But, now, if there is nothing to hinder you, shall we go to the laboratory?"

The laboratory turned out to be a massive round white building, something like a tower, crowned with the dome which had been the first thing to strike my eye when we emerged from the tunnel.

Wearing our coats we passed through a small anteroom lighted by a single electric lamp and then found ourselves in total darkness. But Lord Charlesbury flipped a switch near me and bright light in a moment flooded a huge round room with a regular hemispherical ceiling some forty feet above the floor. In the midst of the room rose something like a small glass room, which resembled those medical isolation rooms which have lately appeared at university clinics in operating rooms which provide the exceptional cleanliness and disinfected air required during long and complicated operations. From that glass chamber which contained strange equipment such as I had never seen before rose three solid copper cylinders. At a height of about twelve feet both of the cylinders split into three pipes of yet larger diameter; those, in turn, were divided into three and the upper ends of these final massive copper pipes touched the concave surface of the dome. A multitude of pressure gauges and levers, curved and straight steel shafts, valves, wiring, and hydraulic presses completed this extraordinary and, for me, absolutely stunning laboratory. Steep circular staircases, iron columns and beams, narrow catwalks with slender hand rails which crossed high above me, hanging electric lamps, a host of thick pendant fiber hoses and long copper pipes—all of this was wound together, fatiguing the eye and giving the impression of a chaos.

Surmising my state of mind, Lord Charlesbury said calmly:

"When a person for the first time sees what is for him a strange mechanism, such as the workings of a watch or a sewing machine, he at first throws up his hands in despair at their complexity. When I, for the first time, saw the disassembled parts of a bicycle, it seemed to me that even the most ingenious mechanic in the world could not assemble them. But a week later I myself put them together and then disassembled them, astonished at the simplicity of its construction. Please, listen to my explanations patiently. If at first you do not understand, do not hesitate to ask me as many questions as you wish. This will give me only pleasure.

"Thus, there are twenty-seven closely placed openings in the roof. And in these openings are inserted cylinders which you see high above you which emerge into the open air through doubly-concave lenses of great power and exceptional clarity. Perhaps you now understand the scheme. We collect the sun's rays in foci and then, thanks to a whole series of mirrors and optic lenses made according to my plans and calculations, we conduct them, at times concentrating them and at other times dispersing them, through a whole system of pipes until the lowest pipes release concentrated sunlight here under the insulated cover into this very narrow and strong cylinder made of vanadium steel in which there is a whole system of pistons equipped with shutters, something like in a camera, which allow absolutely no light to enter when they are closed. Finally to the free end of this major cylinder with its internal closures I attach in a vacuum a vessel in the shape of a retort in the throat of which there are also several valves. When it is necessary I can open these closures and then insert a threaded stopper into the neck of the retort, unfasten the vessel from the end of the cylinder and then I have a superb means of storing compressed solar emanations."

"This means that Hook and Euler and Young . . . ?"

"Yes," Lord Charlesbury interrupted me. "They, and Fresnel, and Cauchy, and Malus, and Huygens and even the great Arago—they were all wrong when they perceived the phenomenon of light as one of the elements of the earth's atmosphere. I will prove this to you in ten minutes in the most striking fashion. Only the wise old Descartes and the genius of geniuses, the divine Newton, were right. The words of Biot and Brewster have only sustained and confirmed my experiments, but this was only much after I began them. Yes! Now it is clear to me and it will be shortly to you also that sunlight is a dense stream of very small resilient bodies, like tiny balls, which with terrible force and energy move through space, transfixing in their course the mass of the earth's atmosphere . . . But we will talk about theory later. Now, to be methodical, I will demonstrate the procedures which you must perform every day. Let us go outside."

We left the laboratory, climbed a circular staircase almost to the roof of the dome and found ourselves on a bright open gallery which circled the entire spherical roof in a spiral and a half.

"You need not struggle to open in turn all the covers which protect the delicate lenses from dust, snow, hail, and birds," said Lord Charlesbury. "All the more so that even a very strong man could not do that. Simply pull this lever toward yourself, and all twenty-seven shutters will turn their fiber rings in identical circular grooves in a counter-clockwise direction, as though they were all being unscrewed. Now the covers are free of pressure. You will now press that foot pedal. Watch!"

Click! And twenty-seven covers, metal surfaces resounding, instantly opened outward revealing glass sparkling in the sunlight.

"Every morning, Mr. Dibble," the scientist went on, "you are to uncover the lenses and carefully wipe them off with a clean chamois. Observe how this is done."

And he, like an experienced workman, rapidly, carefully, almost affectionately wiped all the glasses with a bit of chamois wrapped in cigarette paper which he brought out of his pocket.

"Now, let us go back down," he went on. "I will show you your other responsibilities."

Below in the laboratory he continued his explanations:

"Then you are 'to catch the sun.' To do this, every day at noon check these two chronometers against the sun. By the way, I checked them myself yesterday. The method is, of course, known to you. Note the time. Take the average time of the two chronometers: 10 hours, 31 minutes, 10 seconds. Here are three curving levers: the largest marks the hour, the middle one is for minutes, the smallest for seconds. Note: I turn the large circle until the hand of the indicator shows ten o'clock. Ready. I place the middle lever a little forward to 36 minutes. So. I move the little lever—that is my own favorite—forward to 50 seconds. Now place this plug in the socket. You can hear how the gears are whining and grinding below you. That is a clock device beginning to move which will rotate the entire laboratory and its dome, instruments, lenses and the two of us to follow the movement of the sun. Observe the chronometers and you will see that we are approaching 10:30. Five seconds more. Now. Can you hear how the clock mechanism has changed its sound? Those are the minute gears beginning to turn. A few seconds more . . . Watch! One minute more! Now there's a new sound, which neatly and precisely is marking off the seconds. That's all. The sun has now been captured. But it's not over yet. Because of its bulkiness and quite understandable crudity the clock mechanism cannot be especially accurate. Therefore as often as possible check this dial which indicates its movement. Here are the hours, minutes, and seconds; here is the regulator—forward, back. On the basis of the chronometers which are extraordinarily precise you will be able, as often as it is possible, to correct the revolution of the laboratory to a tenth of a second.

"Now we have caught the sun. But that is not all we must do. The light has to pass through a vacuum, otherwise it would become heated and melt all our equipment. And therefore when it is in our closed vessels from which all the air has been pumped the light is almost as cold as when it was passing through the endless regions of space outside the earth's atmosphere. When you look closely you can see a control button for an electromagnetic coil. In each of the cylinders is a stopper around which is a steel band circled by a wire. I press the control button and the current flows into the wire. All the bands are instantly affected and the stoppers leave their seats. Now I pull a bronze lever which starts a vacuum pump, one line of which is connected to each of the cylinders. The finest dust, microscopic flecks of matter, are removed with the air. Look at the gauge F on which is a red line indicating the pressure limit. Listen through an acoustic tube leading into the pump; the hissing has ceased. The gauge now crosses the red line. Disconnect the electricity by pressing the same control button a second time; the steel bands no longer are activated. The stoppers in response to the attraction of the vacuum close tightly in their conic seats. Now the light is passing through an almost absolute vacuum. But that is not adequate for the precision our work requires. We can transform all our laboratory into a giant vacuum chamber; in time we will be working in underwater diving equipment. Air will flow through the fiber pipes and the waste air systematically removed to the outside. In the meantime the air will be pulled out of the laboratory by powerful pumps. Do you understand? You will be in the position of a diver with the only difference being that you will have a container with compressed gas on your back: in case of an accident, the equipment's malfunction, a leak in the hoses, or anything else, open a small valve on your helmet and you will have enough air to breathe for a quarter of an hour. You must only keep your wits about you and you will leave the laboratory fresh and smiling, like a blooming rose.

"We still must check very carefully the installation of the piping. All of the pipes are firmly joined but at places some triple-unions allow an infinitesimal amount of play, two or three millimeters, and this might prove to be a problem. There are thirteen such points and you must check them about three times a day, working downward. Therefore, let us climb these stairs."

We mounted narrow staircases and unsteady platforms to the very top of the dome. The teacher went ahead with a youthful step while I followed, not without effort, because this was new to me. At the union of the first three pipes he showed me a small cover which he opened with one turn of the hand and lifted back so that it was held precisely vertical by springs. Its reverse side was a rigid, silver, finely polished mirror with various incisions and numbers on its edge. Three parallel gold bands, thin, like telescopic hairs, nearly touching each other, cut the smooth surface of the mirror.

"This is a small well through which we covertly follow the flow of the light. The three bands are reflections from three internal mirrors. Combine them into one. No, you do it yourself. Here you see three minute screws to adjust the positions of the lenses. Here is a very strong magnifying glass. Combine the three light bands into one but in such a manner that the total ray of light falls on zero. It is not difficult to do. You will shortly be able to carry it out in one minute."

In fact, the mechanism was very compliant and three minutes later, barely touching the sensitive screws I combined the light bands into one sharp line which was almost painful to look at, and then I introduced it into a narrow incision at zero. Then I closed the cover and screwed it down. I adjusted the remaining twelve control wells alone without Lord Charlesbury's help. Every time I performed this operation it went more smoothly. But by the time we reached the second level of the laboratory my eyes so ached from the bright light that involuntarily the tears streamed down my face.

"Put on goggles. Here they are," said my chief, handing me a case.

But I could not approach the final cylinder which we were to adjust in its location inside the isolation chamber. My eyes would not accept the glare.

"Take some darker glasses," said Lord Charlesbury. "I have them in ten shades. Today we will attach the lenses which you brought yesterday to the main cylinder and then direct observation will be three times as difficult. Good. That's right. Now I am activating an internal piston. I'm opening the valve of a hydraulic pump. I'm also opening a valve with liquid carbon dioxide. Now the temperature inside the cylinder has reached 150 degrees centigrade and the pressure is equal to 20 atmospheres; the latter is indicated by a gauge, the former by a Witkowski thermometer which I have improved. The following is now underway in the cylinder: light is passing through it in a dense vertical stream of blinding brightness approximately the diameter of a pencil. The valve actuated by an electric current is opening and closing its shutter in one one-thousandth of a second. The valve sends the light on through a small, highly convex lens. From there the stream of light emerges yet denser, narrower, and brighter. There are five such valves and lenses in each cylinder. Under the compression of the last, smallest and most powerful piston, a needle-thin stream of light flows into the vessel, passing through three valves in series.

"That is the basis of my liquid sunlight collector," my teacher said triumphantly. "Now, in order that there can be no doubts at all, we will conduct an experiment. Press control button A. You have just stopped the movement of the valve. Lift that bronze lever. Now you have closed the interior covers of the collecting glasses in the building's dome. Turn the red valve as far as it will go, and lower handle C. The pressure is now released and the supply of carbon dioxide cut off. Now you must close the vessel. This is done by ten turns of that small rounded lever. Everything is now complete, my friend. Notice how I disconnect the receiver vessel from the cylinder. See, I have it in my hands now; it weighs no more than twenty pounds. Its internal shutters are controlled by minute screws on the exterior of the cylinder. I am now opening wide the first and largest shutter. Then the intermediate one. The final shutter I will open only one-half a micron. But, first, go and turn off the electric lights."

I obeyed and the room filled with impenetrable darkness.

"Now watch!" I heard Lord Charlesbury's voice from the other end of the laboratory. "I'm opening it!"

An extraordinary golden light, delicate, radiant, transparent, suddenly flooded the room, softly but clearly outlining its walls, gleaming equipment, and the figure of my teacher himself. And, at the same moment, I felt on my face and hands something like a warm breath of air. This phenomenon lasted not more than a second or a second and a half. Then heavy darkness concealed everything from my eyes.

"Lights, please!" exclaimed Lord Charlesbury and once more I saw him emerging from the door of the glass chamber. His face was pale, but illuminated by joy and pride.

"Those were only the first steps, a schoolboy's trials, the first seeds," he said exultantly. "That was not sunlight condensed into a gas, but only a compressed weightless substance. For months I have compressed sunlight in my containers, but not one of them has become heavier by the weight of a human hair. You saw that marvelous, steady, caressing light. Now do you believe in my project?"

"Yes," I answered heatedly, with profound conviction. "I believe in it and I bow before an invention of great genius."

"But let's go on. Still further on! We will lower the temperature inside the cylinder to minus 275 degrees centigrade, to absolute zero. We will raise the hydraulic pressure to thousands, twenty, thirty thousand times the earth's atmosphere. We will replace our eight-inch light collectors with powerful fifty-inch models. We will melt pounds of diamonds by a technique I have developed and pour them into lenses to the specifications we require and place them in our instruments . . . ! Perhaps I will not live to see the time when men will compress the sun's rays into a liquid form, but I believe and I feel that I will compress them to the density of a gas. I only want to see the hand on an electric scale move even one millimeter to the left—and I will be boundlessly happy.

"But time is passing. Let us lunch and then before dinner we will concern ourselves with the installation of our new diamond lenses. Beginning tomorrow we will work together. For a week you will be with me as an ordinary worker, as a simple, obedient helper. A week from now we will exchange roles. The third week I will give you a helper, to whom in my presence you will teach all the procedures with the instruments. Then I will give you complete freedom. I trust you," he said briskly with a captivating, charming smile and reached out to shake my hand.

I remember very well that evening and dinner with Lord Charlesbury. Lady Charlesbury was in a red silk dress and her red mouth against her pale, slightly weary face glowed like a purple flower, like an incandescent ember. De Mon de Rique, whom I saw at dinner for the first time that day, was alert, handsome, and elegant, as I had never seen him either before or afterwards, while I felt enervated and overwhelmed by the flood of impressions I had received during the day. At first I thought that he had spent the day at his customary, simple labors, mostly observations. But it was not I, but Lady Charlesbury who first drew our attention to the fact that the electrician's left hand was bandaged to above the knuckles. De Mon de Rique modestly recounted how he had scraped his hand as he was climbing down a wall with an insufficiently tightened safety belt. That evening he dominated the conversation, but gently and with tact. He told about his journeys to Abyssinia where he prospected for gold in the mountain valleys on the verge of the Sahara, about lion hunting, the races at Epsom, fox hunting in the north of England, and about Oscar Wilde, then becoming fashionable and with whom he was personally acquainted. He had a surprising and probably too rare conversational trait, which, I will add, I have never noticed in anyone else. When he told a story he was extremely abstracted: he never spoke of himself nor in his own voice. But by some mysterious means his personality, remaining in the background, was illuminated, now in mild, now in heroic half-tones.

Now he was looking at Lady Charlesbury much less frequently than she at him. Only from time to time his caressing and languid eyes passed over her from under his long, lowered lashes. But she hardly took her grave and mysterious eyes away from him. Her gaze followed the movements of his hands and head, his mouth and eyes. Strange! That evening she reminded me of a child's toy: a tin fish or a duck with a bit of iron in its mouth which involuntarily, obediently follows after a magnetized stick which compels it from a distance. Frequently in alarm I observed the expression on my host's face. But he was serenely high-spirited and composed.

After dinner when de Mon de Rique asked permission to smoke, Lady Charlesbury herself offered to play billiards with him. They left while the host and I made our way into his study.

"How about a game of chess," he said. "Do you play?"

"Indifferently, but always with pleasure."

"And do you know what else has happened? Let us have a glass of some lively wine."

He pressed a button.

"What is the occasion?" I asked.

"You already have guessed. Because, it seems to me, I have found in you an assistant, and, if fate wills it, someone to carry on my work."

"Oh, sir!"

"One minute. What drink would you prefer?"

"I'm ashamed to admit that I'm no expert in such matters."

"Very well, in such a case I will name four drinks which I love, and a fifth which I detest. Bordeaux wines, port, Scotch ale, and water. But I cannot bear champagne. And, therefore, let us drink Chateau-la-Rose. My dear Sambo," he commanded the butler who stood near, waiting, "a bottle of Chateau-la-Rose."

Lord Charlesbury, to my surprise, played rather poorly. I quickly checkmated his king. After our first game we abandoned play and once more spoke of my morning's impressions.

"Listen, my dear Dibble," said Lord Charlesbury, laying his little, warm and energetic hand on my knuckles. "You have undoubtedly many times heard that one may obtain an authentic and accurate opinion of a man at first glance. I believe that to be a grave error. Many times I have seen men with the faces of convicts, cheats, or perjurors—and by the way, you will meet your assistant in a few days—and they turned out to be honest, faithful in friendship, and attentive, courteous gentlemen. On the other hand, very rarely, a generous, charming face, adorned with gray hair and the flush of age, and honorable speech conceals, as it becomes clear, such a villain that any London hooligan is by comparison an innocent lamb with a pink ribbon round his neck. Now may I ask you to help me to solve a problem? Mr. de Mon de Rique so far has not been involved in any way in the completion of my scientific work. On his mother's side he is distantly related to me. Mr. Nideston, who has known him from childhood, informed me that de Mon de Rique was in a very difficult position (only not in the material sense). I immediately offered him a position which he accepted with a joy that testified to his precarious situation. I have heard tales about him, but I give no credence to rumors and gossip. He made absolutely no impression upon me when first we met. Perhaps this was because I have never met a person such as he. But for some reason it also seems to me that I have met millions of such men. Today I carefully observed him at work. I believe him to be clever, knowing, ingenious and industrious. In addition, he is cultured and can conduct himself well in any society, as it seems to me, and moreover, he is energetic and intelligent. But in one respect I have my doubts. Tell me frankly, dear Mr. Dibble, your opinion of him."

This unexpected and tactless question agitated and distressed me; to tell the truth I did not expect it at all.

"But, sir, I have none. Indeed, I don't know him as well as you and Mr. Nideston. I saw him for the first time on board the steamship *Southern Cross*, and during our journey we met and talked very rarely. And I must tell you that I suffered from seasickness the entire journey. But from our few meetings and conversations I have obtained approximately the same impression as you, sir: knowing, ingenious, energetic, eloquent, well-read and . . . a peculiar and perhaps very rare mixture, very cold-hearted but with a fervent imagination."

"You are right, Mr. Dibble, right. Beautifully said. My dear Mr. Sambo, bring another bottle of wine and then you may go. Thank you. I hardly expected any other evaluation from you. But I will return to my difficulty: should I inform him or not of what you witnessed today? Just imagine that a year or two will pass, perhaps less, and our dandy, our Adonis, our admirer of women, will suddenly become bored with his life on this God-forsaken volcano. I think that in such a case he would not come to me for my blessing and approval. Simply one beautiful morning he will pack his things and leave. The fact that I would be left without an assistant and a very valuable assistant at that is of secondary importance, but I cannot assure you that after he has arrived in the Old World he will not turn out to be loose-tongued, perhaps very innocently."

"Are you really concerned about this, sir?"

"I tell you frankly—I fear it very much! I am afraid of the notoriety, the publicity, and the invasion of reporters. I am afraid that some influential but talentless scientific reviewer who will base his attitude on a rejection of all new ideas and audacious conjectures will interpret my scheme to the public as a meaningless fantasy, the ravings of a madman. Finally, I am afraid most of all that some hungry upstart, a greedy failure, a talentless ignoramus will misunderstand my idea, and state, as has happened a thousand times, that it is his, thereby belittling, abusing and sullying something I have brought into the world in anguish and joy. Do you understand me, Mr. Dibble?"

"Completely, sir."

"If this happens, then I and my idea will perish. But what does this little 'I' mean when compared to my idea? I am deeply convinced that on the evening when in one of the huge London halls I order the lights extinguished and blind a selected audience of ten thousand with a stream of sunshine which will make flowers open and cause the birds to sing—that evening I will receive a million pounds for my cause. But, a trifle, an accident, an insignificant mistake, as I said, could destroy in a fateful manner the most selfless and grandiose idea. Therefore, I ask your opinion, should I trust Mr. de Mon de Rique or leave him in false and evasive ignorance? This is a dilemma which I cannot avoid without help. On one hand the possibility of a worldwide scandal and failure, and on the other a sure road for arousing a feeling of anger and revenge in a man thanks to my lack of trust in him. And so, Mr. Dibble?"

I wanted to give him the direct answer: "Tomorrow send this Narcissus with all honors back into the world and you can rest in peace." Now I regret deeply that a foolish sense of delicacy prevented me from giving that advice. Instead of saying this, I took on an air of cool correctness and answered:

"I hope you will not be angry with me, sir, if I decline to pass judgment on such a difficult matter."

Lord Charlesbury looked directly at me, shook his head sadly and said with a mirthless smile:

"Let's finish our wine and visit the billiard room. I would like to smoke a cigar."

In the billiard room we saw the following picture. De Mon de Rique was bent over the billiard table telling some lively tale, while Lady Charlesbury, leaning against the mantelpiece, laughed loudly. This struck me more than if I had seen her weeping. Lord Charlesbury inquired into the cause of the merriment, and when de Mon de Rique repeated his story about a certain vain aristocrat who acquired a tame leopard in a desire to pass himself off as an original and then was compelled to sit three hours in his room with the animal because he was so afraid of it, my patron laughed loud and long, like a child . . .

Everything in the world is inter-related in the strangest manner.

That evening in some inscrutable fashion combined the beginnings, the engagement and the tragic denouement of our lives.

The first two days of my existence at Cayambe I remember very well, but as for the rest, the closer they come to the end, the hazier they become. And therefore, with more reason I turn for help to my notebook. The seawater erased the first and last pages and in part the intervening pages also. But some of it, with difficulty, I can restore. Thus:

December 11. Today I rode on muleback with Lord Charlesbury into Quito to obtain copper wire. It happened that the subject of the material support of our project arose (it was not merely the result of my idle curiosity). Lord Charlesbury, who, it seemed to me, had long given me his full confidence, suddenly turned quickly in his saddle to face me and asked unexpectedly:

"You know Mr. Nideston?"

"Certainly, sir."

"A fine man, is he not so?"

"An excellent man."

"And is it not true, in the world, dry and something of a formalist?"

"Yes, sir. But he is also capable of great enthusiasm and even of high emotion."

"You are observant, Mr. Dibble," my mentor answered. "You should know that for fifteen years he has believed in me and my idea as stubbornly as a Mohammedan believes in his Kaaba. You know he is a London solicitor. He not only does not take any pay for my commissions, but long ago he offered to place his own private fortune at my disposal if I so wished. I am deeply convinced that he is the only eccentric left in old England. Therefore let us be of good cheer."

December 12. Today Lord Charlesbury for the first time showed me the force which drives the timing mechanism which turns the laboratory with the sun. It is obvious, simple, and ingenious. Down the slope of the extinct volcano a dressed basalt block weighing thirty-five tons suspended by a steel cable almost as thick as a man's leg moves on almost vertical rails. This weight puts the mechanism into motion. It functions exactly for eight hours and early in the morning an old blind mule raises this counterweight with the help of another cable and a system of blocks without any great effort.

December 20. Today I sat with Lord Charlesbury after dinner in the hothouse sunk in the heady odor of narcissi, pomegranates and tuberoses. Recently my patron has been very withdrawn and his eyes seemingly have begun to lose their beautiful youthful brightness. I take this to be the result of fatigue because we are working very hard now. I am sure that he has guessed nothing about *it*. He suddenly changed the subject of the conversation, as is his wont:

"Our work is the most selfless and honorable on earth. To think about the happiness of one's children or grandchildren is both natural and egotistical. But you and I are thinking of the lives and happiness of humanity so far in the future that they will not know of us nor of our poets, kings, or conquerers, about our language and religion, about our national borders or even the names of our countries. 'Not for those who are near but those who come later!' Isn't that what our most popular philosopher has said? I am willing to give all my strength to this unselfish and pure service to the distant future."

January 3. I went to Quito today to accept a shipment from London. My relationship with Mr. de Mon de Rique has become cold, almost inimical.

February. Today we completed the work of connecting all our piping with the containers of chilling solutions. A combination of ice and salt gives minus 21 degrees centigrade, dry ice and ether—minus 80 degrees, hydrogen—minus 118 degrees, vaporized dry ice—minus 130 degrees, and it seems that we will be able to reduce the atmospheric pressure indefinitely.

April. My assistant continues to arouse my interest. He is some kind of a Slav. A Russian, or a Pole, and, so it seems, an anarchist. He is intelligent and speaks English well, but it seems he prefers not to speak any language at all, but to remain silent. Here is his appearance: he is tall, thin, slightly round-shouldered; his hair is straight and long and falls onto his face in such a manner that his forehead takes the shape of a trapezoid, the narrow end up; he has a tilted nose with great open hairy, but delicate nostrils. His eyes are clear, gray, and boundlessly impertinent. He hears and understands everything that we say about the happiness of future generations and often smiles with a benevolent but contemptuous smile, which reminds me of the expression on the face of a large old bulldog watching a pack of yelping toy terriers. But his attitude toward my mentor—and this I not only know, but feel to the marrow of my bones—is one of boundless adoration. My colleague's attitude, de Mon de Rique's attitude, is quite different. He often speaks to the teacher about the idea of liquid sunshine with such false enthusiasm that I blush for shame and I fear that the technician is mocking our patron. And he is not interested in him at all as a man, and in the most discourteous manner and in the presence of his wife disparages his position as husband and master of the house, although this is unwise and contrary to common sense, the result of his perverted temperament and, perhaps, out of jealousy.

May. Let us hail the names of three talented Poles—Wrublewski, Olszewski, and Witkowski—and the man who completed their work, Dewar. Today we transformed helium into a liquid, and instantly reducing the pressure, reached a temperature of minus 272 degrees centigrade in our major cylinder and the dial on the electric scales for the first time moved, not one, but *five whole millimeters.* Silently, in solitude, I bow before you, my dear preceptor and teacher.

June 26. Apparently de Mon de Rique has come to believe in liquid sunshine—and now without sickening coyness and forced delight. At least today at dinner he made a remarkable statement. He said that in his opinion liquid sunshine would have a brilliant future as an explosive substance in mines or projectiles.

I objected, it is true, rather violently, in German: "You sound like a Prussian lieutenant."

But Lord Charlesbury responded succinctly and in a conciliatory tone: "Our dreams are not of destruction, but of creation."

June 27. I am writing in great agitation, my hands trembling. I worked late this evening in the laboratory, until two o'clock. It was a matter of urgency to install a cooling unit. As I was returning to my quarters the moon shone brightly. I was wearing warm sealskin boots and my footsteps on the frozen path could not be heard. My route lay in shadow. Reaching my door I stopped when I heard voices.

"Come in, Mary dear, for God's sake, come in for only a minute. What are you always afraid of? And don't you always discover that there's no reason to be afraid?"

And then I saw them both in the bright light of the southern moon. He had his arm around her waist, and her head lay passively on his shoulder. Oh, how beautiful they were at that moment!

"But your friend . . ." Lady Charlesbury said timorously.

"What kind of a friend is he?" de Mon de Rique laughed heedlessly. "He's only a boring and sentimental drudge who goes to bed every night at ten o'clock in order to arise at six. Mary, please come in, I beg you."

And both of them, their arms around each other, went onto the porch illuminated by the blue light of the moon and disappeared in an open door.

June 28. Evening. This morning I went to see Mr. de Mon de Rique, refused his proffered hand, would not sit down on the chair he offered and said quietly:

"I must tell you what I think of you, sir. I believe that you, sir, in a situation where we should work together cheerfully and selflessly for the sake of humanity, are conducting yourself in a most unworthy and shameful manner. Last night at two o'clock I saw you when you entered your quarters."

"Were you spying, you scoundrel?" shouted de Mon de Rique, and his eyes gleamed with a violet light, like a cat at night.

"No, I found myself in an impossible situation. I did not speak out, not because I did not want to cause you pain, but because I did not want to harm another person. But this gives me more reason than ever to tell you to your face that you, sir, are a villain and a sneak."

"You will pay for that with your blood with a weapon in your hands," shouted de Mon de Rique, leaping to his feet.

"No," I answered firmly. "First of all, we have no reason to fight except that I called you a villain, but not in the presence of witnesses, and secondly, because I am engaged in a great work of world-wide importance and I do not want to abandon it thanks to your ridiculous bullet until it is completed. Thirdly, would it not be easiest of all for you to pack your bags, mount the first mule available, leave for Quito, and then by your previous route return to hospitable England? Or did you dishonor someone or steal money there, Mr. Scoundrel?"

He leaped to the table and seized a leather whip which lay there.

"I'll kill you like a dog!" he roared.

But I remembered my old boxing skills. Acting quickly, I feinted with my left hand, and then hit him with my right below his chin. He cried out, spun like a top, and blood rushed out of his nose.

I walked out.

June 29. "Why is it that I haven't seen Mr. de Mon de Rique today?" Lord Charlesbury asked unexpectedly.

"It seems he isn't well," I answered, avoiding his eyes.

We were sitting together on the northern slope of the volcano. It was nine in the evening and the moon had not yet risen. Near us stood two porters and my mysterious helper, Peter. Against the quiet dark blue of the sky the slender electric lines, which we had installed that day, could hardly be seen. And on a great heap of stones rested receiver no. 6, firmly braced by basalt boulders, ready any second to open its shutters.

"Prepare the fuse," ordered Lord Charlesbury. "Roll the spool down the hill, I'm too tired and excited; give me your hand, help me down. This is good. And there is no risk of being blinded. Think on it, my dear Dibble, think on it, my dear boy, now the two of us, in the name of glory and the happiness of future mankind, will light all the world with sunshine concentrated in gaseous form. Ready! Light the fuse."

The fiery snake of the lighted fuse ran up the hill and disappeared over the edge of the deep defile in which we sat. Listening carefully I could hear the instantaneous click of contacts closing and the penetrating roar of motors. According to our calculations gaseous sunshine should issue from the containers next to the explosion sites at a rate of approximately six thousand feet per second. At that moment above our heads there was a flash of blinding sunlight, at which the trees below rustled, clouds turned pink in the sky, distant roofs and the windows of houses in Quito gleamed brightly, and the cocks in the village nearby began crowing.

When the light faded as quickly as it had appeared, my teacher pressed the button on a stop watch, turned his flashlight on it, and said:

"It burned for one minute and eleven seconds. This is a genuine triumph, Mr. Dibble. I assure you that within a year we will be able to fill immense reservoirs with heavy liquid golden sunshine, like mercury, and compel it to provide light, heat and drive all our machinery."

When we returned home that night about midnight we discovered that in our absence Lady Charlesbury and Mr. de Mon de Rique in the daylight hours soon after our departure had seemingly gone for a walk but then on mules saddled beforehand had left for the city of Quito below.

Lord Charlesbury remained true to himself. He said without bitterness, but sadly and in pain:

"Why didn't they say anything to me, why this deceit? Didn't I see that they loved each other? I would not have hindered them."

At this point my notes end, and at that they were so damaged by water that I could restore them only with the greatest difficulty and I cannot guarantee their accuracy. Nor can I in the future guarantee the reliability of my memory. But this is always the case: the closer I draw to the final resolution the more confused my recollections become.

For about twenty-five days we worked steadily in the laboratory filling more and more containers with solar gas. During this period we invented ingenious valves for our solar containers. We equipped each of them with a clock mechanism with a simple face, as on an alarm clock. Adjusting the dials of three cylinders we could obtain light over any given period of time, and lengthen the period of its combustion and its intensity from a dim half-hour of glimmer to an instantaneous explosion—depending on the time set. We worked without inspiration, almost unwillingly, but I must admit that this was the most productive time of my stay on Cayambe. But it all ended abruptly, fantastically, and horribly.

Once, early in August, Lord Charlesbury, even more tired and aged than usual, came to visit me in the laboratory; he said to me calmly and with distaste:

"My dear friend, I feel that my death is not far away, and old convictions are making themselves heard. I want to die and be buried in England. I will leave you some money, these buildings, the equipment, the land and this laboratory. The money, on the basis of what I have spent, should be ample for two or three years. You are younger and more active than I and perhaps you will obtain some results for your labors. Our dear Mr. Nideston would give his support at any time. Please think on it."

This man had become dearer to me than my father, mother, brother, wife or sister. And therefore I answered with deep assurance:

"Dear sir, I would not leave you for one minute."

He embraced me and kissed me on my forehead.

The next day he summoned all the workers and paying them two years in advance said that his work on Cayambe had come to an end and that day they were to leave Cayambe for the valley below.

They left carefree and ungrateful, anticipating the sweet proximity of drunkenness and dissipation in the innumerable taverns which swarmed in the city of Quito. Only my assistant, the silent Slav—an Albanian or a Siberian—tarried near the master. "I will stay with you as long as you or I am alive," he said. But Lord Charlesbury looked at him firmly, almost sternly and said:

"I am leaving for Europe, Mr. Peter."

"Then I will go with you."

"But you know what awaits you there, Mr. Peter."

"I know. A rope. But nonetheless I will not abandon you. I have always laughed in my heart at your sentimental concerns for men in the millions of years to come, but when I came to know you better I also learned that the more insignificant is mankind the more precious is man, and therefore I have stayed with you, like an old, homeless, embittered, hungry, and mangy dog turns to the first hand that sincerely caresses it. And therefore I will stay with you. That is all."

With astonishment and deep feeling I turned my eyes to this man whom I had always thought to be incapable of elevated feelings. But my teacher said to him softly and with authority:

"No, you must leave. Right now. I value your friendship and your tireless labors. But I'm leaving for my native land to die and the possibility that you might suffer would only darken my departure from this world. Be a man, Peter. Take this money, embrace me in farewell, and let us part."

I saw how they embraced and how blunt Peter kissed the hand of Lord Charlesbury several times and then left us, not turning back, almost at a run and disappeared around a nearby building.

I looked at my teacher: covering his face with his hands he was weeping . . .

Three days later we left on the old *Gonzalez* from Guayaquil for Panama. The sea was rough, but we had a following wind and to help out the small engine the captain had sails spread. Lord Charlesbury and I never left our cabins. I was seriously concerned about his condition and there were even times when I feared he was losing his mind. I observed him with helpless pity. I was especially troubled by the manner in which he invariably referred after every two or three phrases to container no. 216 which we had left behind on Cayambe, and every time he referred to it, he would say through tight lips: "Did I forget, how could I forget?" but then his speech would become melancholy and abstracted.

"Do not think," he said, "that a petty personal tragedy forced me to abandon my work and the persistent searches and inspirations which I have patiently worked out during the course of my conscious life. But circumstances jarred my thoughts. Recently I have much altered my ideas and judgments, but only on a different plane than before. If only you knew how difficult it has been to alter my view of life at the age of sixty-five. I have come to believe, or, more correctly, to feel, that the future of mankind is not worth our concern or our selfless work. Mankind, growing more degenerate every day, is becoming flabbier, more decadent, and hard-hearted. Society is falling under the power of the cruelest despotism in the world—capital. Trusts, manipulating the supply of meat, kerosene, and sugar, are creating a generation of fabulous millionaires and next to them millions of hungry unemployed thieves and murderers. And so it will be forever. And my idea of prolonging the sun's life for the earth will become the property of a handful of villains who will control it or employ my liquid sunshine in shells or bombs of unheard of power . . . No, I do not want that . . . Ah, my God! that container! How could I forget! How could I!" and Lord Charlesbury clapped his hands to his head.

"What troubles you, my dear teacher?" I asked.

"You see, kind Henry, . . . I fear that I have made a small but fateful mistake . . ."

But I heard no more. Suddenly in the east flashed an enormous golden flame. In a moment the sky and the sea were all agleam. Then followed a deafening roar and a burning whirlwind threw me to the deck.

I lost consciousness and revived only when I heard my teacher's voice above me.

"What?" asked Lord Charlesbury. "Are you blind?"

"Yes, I can see nothing, except rainbow-colored circles before my eyes. Was it some kind of a catastrophe, Professor? Why did you do it or allow it to happen? Didn't you foresee it?"

But he softly laid his beautiful little white hand on my shoulder and said in a deep and gentle voice (and from that touch and his confident tone I immediately was calmed):

"Don't you believe me? Wait a moment, close your eyes tightly and cover them with the palm of your right hand, and hold it there until I stop talking or until you catch a glimpse of light; then, before you open your eyes, put on these glasses which I am placing in your left hand. They are very dark. Listen to me. It seems that you have come to know me better in a brief time than anyone else close to me. It was only for your sake, my dear friend, that I did not take on my conscience a cruel and pointless experiment which might have brought death to tens of thousands of people. But what difference would the existence of these dissolute blacks, drunken Indians, and degenerate Spaniards have made? If the Republic of Ecuador with its intrigues, mercenary attitudes and revolutions were instantly transformed into a great door to Hell there would be no loss to science, the arts, or history. I am only a little sorry for my intelligent, patient, and affectionate mules. I will tell you candidly that I would have not hesitated for a second to sacrifice you and millions of lives to the triumph of my idea, if only I were convinced of its significance, but as I said only three minutes ago I have become totally disillusioned about the future generations' ability to love, to be happy and to sacrifice themselves. Do you think I could take revenge on a tiny part of humanity for my great philosophical error? But there is one thing for which I cannot forgive myself: that was a purely technical mistake, a mistake which could have been made by any workman. I am like a craftsman who has worked for twenty years with a complicated machine, and on the next day falls into melancholy over his family affairs, forgets his work, ignores the rhythm of his machine so that a belt parts and kills several unthinking workmen. You see, I have been tormented by the idea that thanks to my forgetfulness for the first time in twenty years I neglected to shut down the controls on container no. 216 and left it set at full power. And that realization, like a nightmare, pursued me on board this ship. And I was right. The container exploded and as a result the other storage units also. Once more it was my mistake. Rather than storing such great amounts of liquid sunshine I should have conducted preliminary experiments, it is true at the risk of my life, on the explosive capabilities of compressed light. Now, look in this direction," and he gently but firmly turned my head toward the east. "Remove your hand and then slowly, slowly open your eyes."

At that moment with extraordinary clarity, the way, they say, that occurs in the seconds before death, I saw a smoking red glow to the east, now contracting, now expanding, the steamship's listing deck, waves lashing over the railings, an angry, bloody sea and dark purple clouds in the sky and a beautiful calm face with a gray, silken beard and eyes which shone like mournful stars. A stifling hot wind blew from the shore.

"A fire?" I asked, turning slowly, as though in a dream, to face the south. There, above Cayambe's summit, stood a thick smoky column of fire cut by rapid flashes of lightning.

"No, that is the eruption of our good old volcano. The exploding liquid sunshine has stirred it into life. You must agree that it has enormous power! And to think it was all in vain."

I understood nothing . . . My head was spinning. And then I heard a strange voice near me, both gentle like a mother's voice and commanding like that of a dictator.

"Sit on this bale and do everything faithfully as I tell you. Here is a life belt, put it on and fasten it securely under your arms, but do not restrict your breathing; here is a flask of brandy which you are to place in your left chest pocket along with three bars of chocolate, and here is a waterproof envelope with money and letters. In a moment the *Gonzalez* will be swamped by a terrible wave, such as has rarely been seen since the time of the flood. Lie down on the ship's starboard side. That is so. Place your legs and arms around this railing. Very good. Your head should be behind this steel plate, which will prevent you from becoming deaf from the shock. When you feel the wave hitting the deck, hold your breath for twenty seconds and then throw yourself free, and may God help you! This is all I can wish and advise you. And if you are condemned to die so early and so stupidly . . . I would like to hear you forgive me. I would not say that to any other man, but I know you are an Englishman and a gentleman."

His words, said so calmly and with such dignity, aroused my own sense of self-control. I found enough strength to press his hand and answer calmly:

"You can believe, my dear teacher, that no pleasures in life could replace those happy hours which I spent working with you. I only want to know why you are taking no precautions for yourself?"

I can see him now, holding to a compass box, as the wind blew his clothes and his gray beard, so terrible against the red background of the erupting volcano. That second I noticed with surprise that the unbearably hot shore wind had ceased, but on the contrary a cold, gusty gale blew from the west and our craft nearly lay on its side.

"Oh!" exclaimed Lord Charlesbury indifferently, and waved his arm "I have nothing to lose. I am alone in this world. I have only one tie, that is you, and you I have put into deadly peril from which you have only one chance in a million to escape. I have a fortune, but I do not know what to do with it," and here his voice expressed a melancholy and gentle irony, "except to disperse it to the poor of County Norfolk and thereby increase the number of parasites and supplicants. I have knowledge, but you can see that it too has failed. I have energy but I have no way to employ it now. Oh, no, I will not commit suicide; if I am not condemned to die this night, I will employ the rest of my life in some garden on a bit of land not far from London. But if death comes," he removed his hat and it was strange to see his blowing hair, tossing beard, and kind, melancholy eyes and to hear his voice resounding like an organ, "but if death comes I shall commit my body and my soul to God, may He forgive the errors of my weak human mind."

"Amen," I said.

He turned his back to the wind and lighted a cigar. His dark figure defined sharply against the purple sky was a fantastic, and magnificent, sight. I could smell the odor of his fine Havana cigar.

"Make ready. There is yet only a minute or two. Are you afraid?"

"No . . . But the crew and the other passengers! . . ."

"While you were unconscious I warned them. Now there is not a sober man nor a lifebelt on the ship. I have no fear for you, for you have the talisman on your finger. I had one, too, but I have lost it. Oh, hold on! Henry! . . ."

I turned to the east and froze in horror. Toward our eggshell craft from the east roared an enormous wave as high as the Eiffel tower, black, with a rosy-white, frothing crest. Something crashed, shook . . . and it was as though the whole world fell onto the deck.

I lost consciousness once more and revived only several hours later on a little boat belonging to a fisherman who had rescued me. My damaged left hand was tied in a crude bandage and my head wrapped in rags. A month later, having recovered from my wounds and emotional shock I was on my way back to England.

This history of my strange adventure is complete. I must only add that I live modestly in the quietest part of London, needing nothing, thanks to the generosity of the late Lord Charlesbury. I occupy myself with the sciences and tutoring. Every Sunday Mr. Nideston and I alternate as hosts for dinner. We are bound by close ties of friendship, and our first toast is always to the memory of the great Lord Charlesbury.

H. Dibble

P.S. All the personal names in my tale are not authentic but invented by me for my purposes.

John Crowley

John Crowley (1942–   ) is the author of the classic fantasy novel *Little, Big* (1981), a monument of the genre and his masterpiece to date, and several SF novels, including the highly regarded *Engine Summer* (1979). He is currently teaching at Yale University and in 1987 embarked on a multi-volume work of the fantastic which began with *Aegypt* and continued with *Love and Sleep* (1994). He is among the most complex and literate of writers to emerge from the contemporary genre. Based upon his recent works, one might usefully consider him a postmodern writer somewhat in the vein of Thomas Pynchon, who sometimes writes in genre. His writing adds substance to critic Brian McHale's contention that contemporary science fiction is the "paraliterary shadow" of postmodernism.

He has written only a dozen or so short stories in the fantastic mode, and of them only a few are genre science fiction. This long piece is his best SF story to date. It was first published in his original collection of four stories, *Novelty* (1989). It is another SF story about time, in the same tradition as Jeschke's "The King and the Dollmaker." The idea that reality is somehow malleable, that a different future, even a different present, might result from some perhaps quite minor change in the past, has become a staple of science fiction since the 1930s. Here it is richly explored.

GREAT WORK OF TIME

I: THE SINGLE EXCURSION OF CASPAR LAST

If what I am to set down is a chronicle, then it must differ from any other chronicle whatever, for it begins, not in one time or place, but everywhere at once—or perhaps *everywhen* is the better word. It might be begun at any point along the infinite, infinitely broken coastline of time.

It might even begin within the forest in the sea: huge trees like American redwoods, with their roots in the black benthos, and their leaves moving slowly in the blue currents overhead. There it might end as well.

It might begin in 1893—or in 1983. Yes: it might be as well to begin with Last, in an American sort of voice (for we are all Americans now, aren't we?). Yes, Last shall be first: pale, fattish Caspar Last, on excursion in the springtime of 1983 to a far, far part of the Empire.

The tropical heat clothed Caspar Last like a suit as he disembarked from the plane. It was nearly as claustrophobic as the hours he had spent in the middle seat of a three-across; economy-class pew between two other cut-rate, one-week-excursion, plane-fare-and-hotel-room holiday-makers in monstrous good spirits. Like them, Caspar had taken the excursion because it was the cheapest possible way to get to and from this equatorial backwater. Unlike them, he hadn't come to soak up sun and molasses-dark rum. He didn't intend to spend all his time at the beach, or even within the twentieth century.

It had come down, in the end, to a matter of money. Caspar Last had never had money, though he certainly hadn't lacked the means to make it; with any application he could have made good money as a consultant to any of a dozen research firms, but that would have required a certain subjection of his time and thought to others, and Caspar was incapable of that. It's often said that genius can live in happy disregard of material circumstances, dress in rags, not notice its nourishment, and serve only its own abstract imperatives. This was Caspar's case, except that he wasn't happy about it: he was bothered, bitter, and rageful at his poverty. Fame he cared nothing for, success was meaningless except when defined as the solution to abstract problems. A great fortune would have been burdensome and useless. All he wanted was a nice bit of change.

He had decided, therefore, to use his "time machine" once only, before it and the principles that animated it were destroyed, for good he hoped. (Caspar always thought of his "time machine" thus, with scare-quotes around it, since it was not really a machine, and Caspar did not believe in time.) He would use it, he decided, to make money. Somehow.

The one brief annihilation of "time" that Caspar intended to allow himself was in no sense a test run. He knew that his "machine" would function as predicted. If he hadn't needed the money, he wouldn't use it at all. As far as he was concerned, the principles once discovered, the task was completed; like a completed jigsaw puzzle, it had no further interest; there was really nothing to do with it except gloat over it briefly and then sweep all the pieces randomly back into the box.

It was a mark of Caspar's odd genius that figuring out a scheme with which to make money out of the past (which was the only "direction" his "machine" would take him) proved almost as hard, given the limitations of his process, as arriving at the process itself.

He had gone through all the standard wish fulfillments and rejected them. He couldn't, armed with today's race results, return to yesterday and hit the daily double. For one thing it would take a couple of thousand in betting money to make it worth it, and Caspar didn't have a couple of thousand. More importantly, Caspar had calculated the results of his present self appearing at any point within the compass of his own biological existence, and those results made him shudder.

Similar difficulties attended any scheme that involved using money to make money. If he returned to 1940 and bought, say, two hundred shares of IBM for next to nothing: in the first place there would be the difficulty of leaving those shares somehow in escrow for his unborn self; there would be the problem of the alteration this growing fortune would have on the linear life he had actually lived; and where was he to acquire the five hundred dollars or whatever was needed in the currency of 1940? The same problem obtained if he wanted to return to 1623 and pick up a First Folio of Shakespeare, or to 1460 and a Gutenberg Bible: the cost of the currency he would need rose in relation to the antiquity, thus the rarity and value, of the object to be bought with it. There was also the problem of walking into a bookseller's and plunking down a First Folio he had just happened to stumble on while cleaning out the attic. In any case, Caspar doubted that anything as large as a book could be successfully transported "through time." He'd be lucky if he could go and return in his clothes.

Outside the airport, Caspar boarded a bus with his fellow excursionists, already hard at work with their cameras and index fingers as they rode through a sweltering lowland out of which concrete-block light industry was struggling to be born. The hotel in the capital was, as he expected, shoddy-American and intermittently refrigerated. He ceased to notice it, forwent the complimentary rum concoction promised with his tour, and after asking that his case be put in the hotel safe—extra charge for that, he noted bitterly—he went immediately to the Hall of Records in the government complex. The collection of old survey maps of the city and environs were more extensive than he had hoped. He spent most of that day among them searching for a blank place on the 1856 map, a place as naked as possible of buildings, brush, water, and that remained thus through the years. He discovered one, visited it by unmuffled taxi, found it suitable. It would save him from the awful inconvenience of "arriving" in the "past" and finding himself inserted into some local's wattle-and-daub wall. Next morning, then, he would be "on his way." If he had believed in time, he would have said that the whole process would take less than a day's time.

Before settling on this present plan, Caspar had toyed with the idea of bringing back from the past something immaterial: some knowledge, some secret that would allow him to make himself rich in his own present. Ships have gone down with millions in bullion: he could learn exactly where. Captain Kidd's treasure. Inca gold. Archaeological rarities buried in China. Leaving aside the obvious physical difficulties of these schemes, he couldn't be sure that their location wouldn't shift in the centuries between his glimpse of them and his "real" life span; and even if he could be certain, no one else would have much reason to believe him, and he didn't have the wherewithal to raise expeditions himself. So all that was out.

He had a more general, theoretical problem to deal with. Of course the very presence of his eidolon in the past would alter, in however inconsequential a way, the succeeding history of the world. The comical paradoxes of shooting one's own grandfather and the like neither amused nor intrigued him, and the chance he took of altering the world he lived in out of all recognition was constantly present to him. Statistically, of course, the chance of this present plan of his altering anything significantly, except his own personal fortunes, was remote to a high power. But his scruples had caused him to reject anything such as, say, discovering the Koh-i-noor diamond before its historical discoverers. No: what he needed to abstract from the past was something immensely trivial, something common, something the past wouldn't miss but that the present held in the highest regard; something that would take the briefest possible time and the least irruption of himself into the past to acquire; something he could reasonably be believed to possess through simple historical chance; and something tiny enough to survive the cross-time "journey" on his person.

It had come to him quite suddenly—all his ideas did, as though handed to him—when he learned that his great-great-grandfather had been a commercial traveler in the tropics, and that in the attic of his mother's house (which Caspar had never had the wherewithal to move out of) some old journals and papers of his still moldered. They were, when he inspected them, completely without interest. But the dates were right.

Caspar had left a wake-up call at the desk for before dawn the next morning. There was some difficulty about getting his case out of the safe, and more difficulty about getting a substantial breakfast served at that hour (Caspar expected not to eat during his excursion), but he did arrive at his chosen site before the horrendous tropical dawn broke, and after paying the taxi, he had darkness enough left in which to make his preparations and change into his costume. The costume—a linen suit, a shirt, hat, boots—had cost him twenty dollars in rental from a theatrical costumer, and he could only hope it was accurate enough not to cause alarm in 1856. The last item he took from his case was the copper coin, which had cost him quite a bit, as he needed one unworn and of the proper date. He turned it in his fingers for a moment, thinking that if, unthinkably, his calculations were wrong and he didn't survive this journey, it would make an interesting obol for Charon.

Out of the unimaginable chaos of its interminable stochastic fiction, Time thrust only one unforeseen oddity on Caspar Last as he, or something like him, appeared beneath a plantain tree in 1856: he had grown a beard almost down to his waist. It was abominably hot.

The suburbs of the city had of course vanished. The road he stood by was a muddy track down which a cart was being driven by a tiny and close-faced Indian in calico. He followed the cart, and his costume boots were caked with mud when at last he came into the center of town, trying to appear nonchalant and to remember the layout of the city as he had studied it in the maps. He wanted to speak to no one if possible, and he did manage to find the post office without affecting, however minutely, the heterogeneous crowd of blacks, Indians, and Europeans in the filthy streets. Having absolutely no sense of humor and very little imagination other than the most rigidly abstract helped to keep him strictly about his business and not to faint, as another might have, with wonder and astonishment at his translation, the first, last, and only of its kind a man would ever make.

"I would like," he said to the mulatto inside the brass and mahogany cage, "an envelope, please."

"Of course, sir."

"How long will it take for a letter mailed now to arrive locally?"

"Within the city? It would arrive in the afternoon post."

"Very good."

Caspar went to a long, ink-stained table, and with one of the steel pens provided, he addressed the envelope to Georg von Humboldt Last, Esq., Grand Hotel, City, in the approximation of an antique round hand that he had been practicing for weeks. There was a moment's doubt as he tried to figure how to fold up and seal the cumbersome envelope, but he did it, and gave this empty missive to the incurious mulatto. He slipped his precious coin across the marble to him. For the only moment of his adventure, Caspar's heart beat fast as he watched the long, slow brown fingers affix a stamp, cancel and date it with a pen-stroke, and drop it into a brass slot like a hungry mouth behind him.

It only remained to check into the Grand Hotel, explain about his luggage's being on its way up from the port, and sit silent on the hotel terrace, growing faint with heat and hunger and expectation, until the afternoon post.

The one aspect of the process Caspar had never been able to decide about was whether his eidolon's residence in the fiction of the past would consume any "time" in the fiction of the present. It did. When, at evening, with the letter held tight in his hand and pressed to his bosom, Caspar reappeared beardless beneath the plantain tree in the traffic-tormented and smoky suburb, the gaseous red sun was squatting on the horizon in the west, just as it had been in the same place in 1856.

He would have his rum drink after all, he decided.

"Mother," he said, "do you think there might be anything valuable in those papers of your great-grandfather's?"

"What papers, dear? Oh—I remember. I couldn't say. I thought once of donating them to a historical society. How do you mean, valuable?"

"Well, old stamps, for one thing."

"You're free to look, Caspar dear."

Caspar was not surprised (though he supposed the rest of the world was soon to be) that he found, among the faded, water-spotted diaries and papers, an envelope that bore a faint brown address—it had aged nicely in the next-to-no-time it had traveled "forward" with Caspar—and that had in its upper right-hand corner a one-penny magenta stamp, quite undistinguished, issued for a brief time in 1856 by the Crown Colony of British Guiana.

The asking price of the sole known example of this stamp, a "unique," owned by a consortium of wealthy men who preferred to remain anonymous, was a million dollars. Caspar Last had not decided whether it would be more profitable for him to sell the stamp itself, or to approach the owners of the unique, who would certainly pay a large amount to have it destroyed, and thus preserve their unique's uniqueness. It did seem a shame that the only artifact man had ever succeeded in extracting from the nonexistent past should go into the fire, but Caspar didn't really care. His own bonfire—the notes and printouts, the conclusions about the nature and transversability of time and the orthogonal logic by which it was accomplished—would be only a little more painful.

The excursion was over; the only one that remained to him was the brief but, to him, all-important one of his own mortal span. He was looking forward to doing it first class.

II: AN APPOINTMENT IN KHARTOUM

It might be begun very differently, though; and it might now be begun again, in a different time and place, like one of those romances by Stevenson, where different stories only gradually reveal themselves to be parts of a whole . . .

The paradox is acute, so acute that the only possible stance for a chronicler is to ignore it altogether, and carry on. This, the Otherhood's central resignation, required a habit of mind so contrary to ordinary cause-and-effect thinking as to be, literally, unimaginable. It would only have been in the changeless precincts of the Club they had established beyond all frames of reference, when deep in leather armchairs or seated all together around the long table whereon their names were carved, that they dared reflect on it at all.

Take, for a single but not a random instance, the example of Denys Winterset, twenty-three years old, Winchester, Oriel College, younger son of a well-to-do doctor and in 1956 ending a first year as assistant district commissioner of police in Bechuanaland.

He hadn't done strikingly well in his post. Though on the surface he was exactly the sort of man who was chosen, or who chose himself, to serve the Empire in those years—a respectable second at Oxford, a cricketer more steady than showy, a reserved, sensible, presentable lad with sound principles and few beliefs—still there was an odd strain in him. Too imaginative, perhaps; given to fits of abstraction, even to what his commissioner called "tears, idle tears." Still, he was resourceful and hardworking; he hadn't disgraced himself, and he was now on his way north on the Cape-to-Cairo Railroad, to take a month's holiday in Cairo and England. His anticipation was marred somewhat by a sense that, after a year in the veldt, he would no longer fit into the comfortable old shoe of his childhood home; that he would feel as odd and exiled as he had in Africa. Home had become a dream, in Bechuanaland; if, at home, Bechuanaland became a dream, then he would have no place real at all to be at home in; he would be an exile for good.

The high veldt sped away as he was occupied with these thoughts, the rich farmlands of Southern Rhodesia. In the saloon car a young couple, very evidently on honeymoon, watched expectantly for the first glimpse of the eternal rainbow, visible miles off, that haloed Victoria Falls. Denys watched them and their excitement, feeling old and wise. Americans, doubtless: they had that shy, inoffensive air of all Americans abroad, that wondering quality as of children let out from a dark and oppressive school to play in the sun.

"There!" said the woman as the train took a bend. "Oh, look, how beautiful!"

Even over the train's sound they could hear the sound of the falls now, like distant cannon. The young man looked at his watch and smiled at Denys. "Right on time," he said, and Denys smiled too, amused to be complimented on his railroad's efficiency. The Bulawayo Bridge—longest and highest span on the Cape-to-Cairo line—leapt out over the gorge. "My God, that's something," the young man said. "Cecil Rhodes built this, right?"

"No," Denys said. "He thought of it, but never lived to see it. It would have been far easier to build it a few miles up, but Rhodes pictured the train being washed in the spray of the falls as it passed. And so it was built here."

The noise of the falls was immense now, and weirdly various, a medley of cracks, thumps, and explosions playing over the constant bass roar, which was not so much like a noise at all as it was like an eternal deep-drawn breath. And as the train chugged out across the span, aimed at Cairo thousands of miles away, passing here the place so hard-sought-for a hundred years ago— the place where the Nile had its origin—the spray *did* fall on the train just as Cecil Rhodes had imagined it, flung spindrift hissing on the locomotive, drops speckling the window they looked out of and rainbowing in the white air. The young Americans were still with wonder, and Denys, too, felt a lifting of his heart.

At Khartoum, Denys bid the honeymooners farewell: they were taking the Empire Airways flying boat from here to Gibraltar, and the Atlantic dirigible home. Denys, by now feeling quite proprietary about his Empire's transportation services, assured them that both flights would also certainly be right on time, and would be as comfortable as the sleepers they were leaving, would serve the same excellent meals with the same white napery embossed with the same royal insignia. Denys himself was driven to the Grand Hotel. His Sudan Railways sleeper to Cairo left the next morning.

After a bath in a tiled tub large enough almost to swim in, Denys changed into dinner clothes (which had been carefully laid out for him on the huge bed— for whom had these cavernous rooms been built, a race of Kitcheners?) He reserved a table for one in the grill room and went down to the bar. One thing he *must* do in London, he thought, shooting his cuffs, was to visit his tailor. Bechuanaland had sweated off his college baby fat, and the tropics seemed to have turned his satin lapels faintly green.

The bar was comfortably filled, before the dinner hour, with men of several sorts and a few women, and with the low various murmur of their talk. Some of the men wore *white* dinner jackets—businessmen and tourists, Denys supposed—and a few even wore shorts with black shoes and stockings, a style Denys found inherently funny, as though a tailor had made a frightful error and cut evening clothes to the pattern of bush clothes. He ordered a whiskey.

Rarely in African kraals or in his bungalow or his whitewashed office did Denys think about his Empire: or if he did, it was in some local, even irritated way, of Imperial trivialities or Imperial red tape, the rain-rusted engines and stacks of tropic-mildewed paperwork that, collectively, Denys and his young associates called the White Man's Burden. It seemed to require a certain remove from the immediacy of Empire before he could perceive it. Only here (beneath the fans' ticking, amid the voices naming places—Kandahar, Durban, Singapore, Penang) did the larger Empire that Denys had never seen but had lived in in thought and feeling since childhood open in his mind. How odd, how far more odd really than admirable or deplorable that the small place which was his childhood, circumscribed and cozy—gray Westminster, chilly Trafalgar Square of the black umbrellas, London of the coal-smoked wallpaper and endless chimney pots— should have opened itself out so ceaselessly and for so long into huge hot places, subcontinents where rain never fell or never stopped, lush with vegetable growth or burdened with seas of sand or stone. Send forth the best ye breed: or at least large numbers of those ye breed. If one thought how odd it was—and if one thought then of what should have been natural empires, enormous spreads of restless real property like America or Russia turning in on themselves, making themselves into what seemed (to Denys, who had never seen them) to be very small places: then it did seem to be Destiny of a kind. Not a Destiny to be proud of, particularly, nor ashamed of either, but one whose compelling inner logic could only be marveled at.

Quite suddenly, and with poignant vividness, Denys saw himself, or rather felt himself once more to be, before his nursery fire, looking into the small glow of it, with animal crackers and cocoa for tea, listening to Nana telling tales of her brother the sergeant, and the Afghan frontier, and the now-dead king he served—listening, and feeling the Empire ranged in widening circles around him: first Harley Street, outside the window, and then Buckingham Palace, where the king lived; and the country then into which the trains went, and then the cold sea, and the Possessions, and the Commonwealth, stretching ever farther outward, worldwide: but always with his small glowing fire and his comfort and wonder at the heart of it.

So, there he is: a young man with the self-possessed air of an older, in evening clothes aged prematurely in places where evening clothes had not been made to go; thinking, if it could be called thinking, of a nursery fire; and about to be spoken to by the man next down the bar. If his feelings could be summed up and spoken, they were that, however odd, there is nothing more real, more pinioned by acts great and small, more clinker-built of time and space and filled brimful of this and that, than is the real world in which his five senses and his memories had their being; and that this was deeply satisfying.

"I beg your pardon," said the man next down the bar.

"Good evening," Denys said.

"My name is Davenant," the man said. He held out a square, blunt-fingered hand, and Denys drew himself up and shook it. "You are, I believe, Denys Winterset?"

"I am," Denys said, searching the smiling face before him and wondering from where he was known to him. It was a big, square, high-fronted head, a little like Bernard Shaw's, with ice-blue eyes of that twinkle; it was crowned far back with a neat hank of white hair, and was crossed above the broad jaw with upright white mustaches.

"You don't mind the intrusion?" the man said. "I wonder if you know whether the grub here is as good as once it was. It's been some time since I last ate a meal in Khartoum."

"The last time I did so was a year ago this week," Denys said. "It was quite good."

"Excellent," said Davenant, looking at Denys as though something about the young man amused him. "In that case, if you have no other engagement, may I ask your company?"

"I have no other engagement," Denys said; in fact he had rather been looking forward to dining alone, but deference to his superiors (of whom this man Davenant was surely in some sense one) was strong in him. "Tell me, though, how you come to know my name."

"Oh, well, there it is," Davenant said. "One has dealings with the Colonial Office. One sees a face, a name is attached to it, one files it but doesn't forget—that sort of thing. Part of one's job."

A civil servant, an inspector of some kind. Denys felt the sinking one feels on running into one's tutor in a wine bar: the evening not well begun. "They may well be crowded for dinner," he said.

"I have reserved a quiet table," said the smiling man, lifting his glass to Denys.

The grub was, in fact, superior. Sir Geoffrey Davenant was an able teller of tales, and he had many to tell. He was, apparently, no such dull thing as an inspector for the Colonial Office, though just what office he did fill Denys couldn't determine. He seemed to have been "attached to" or "had dealings with" or "gone about for" half the establishments of the Empire. He embodied, it seemed to Denys, the entire strange adventure about which Denys had been thinking when Sir Geoffrey had first spoken to him.

"So," Sir Geoffrey said, filling their glasses from a bottle of South African claret—no harm in being patriotic, he'd said, for one bottle—"so, after some months of stumbling about Central Asia and making myself useful one way or another, I was to make my way back to Sadiya. I crossed the Tibetan frontier disguised as a monk—"

"A monk?"

"Yes. Having lost all my gear in Manchuria, I could do the poverty part quite well. I had a roll of rupees, the films, and a compass hidden inside my prayer wheel. Mine didn't whiz around then with the same sanctity as the other fellows', but no matter. After adventures too ordinary to describe—avalanches and so on—I managed to reach the monastery at Rangbok, on the old road up to Everest. Rather near collapse. I was recovering a bit and thinking how to proceed when there was a runner with a telegram. From my superior at Ch'eng-tu. WARN DAVENANT MASSACRE SADIYA, it said. The Old Man then was famously closemouthed. But this was particularly unhelpful, as it did not say who had massacred whom—or why." He lifted the silver cover of a dish, and found it empty.

"This must have been a good long time ago," Denys said.

"Oh, yes," Davenant said, raising his ice-blue eyes to Denys. "A good long time ago. That was an excellent curry. Nearly as good as at Veeraswamy's, in London—which is, strangely, the best in the world. Shall we have coffee?"

Over this, and brandy and cigars, Sir Geoffrey's stories modulated into reflections. Pleasant as his company was, Denys couldn't overcome a sensation that everything Sir Geoffrey said to him was rehearsed, laid on for his entertainment, or perhaps his enlightenment, and yet with no clue in it as to why he had thus been singled out.

"It amuses me," Sir Geoffrey said, "how constant it is in human nature to think that things might have gone on differently from the way they did. In a man's own life, first of all: how he might have taken this or that very different route, except for this or that accident, this or that slight push—if he'd only known then, and so on. And then in history as well, we ruminate endlessly, if, what if, if only . . . The world seems always somehow malleable to our minds, or to our imaginations anyway."

"Strange you should say so," Denys said. "I was thinking, just before you spoke to me, about how very solid the world seems to me, how very—real. And—if you don't mind my thrusting it into your thoughts—you never did tell me how it is you come to know my name; or why it is you thought good to invite me to that excellent dinner."

"My dear boy," Davenant said, holding up his cigar as though to defend his innocence.

"I can't think it was chance."

"My dear boy," Davenant said in a different tone, "if anything is, that was not. I will explain all. You were on that train of thought. If you will have patience while it trundles by."

Denys said nothing further. He sipped his coffee, feeling a dew of sweat on his forehead.

"History," said Sir Geoffrey. "Yes. Of course the possible worlds we make don't compare to the real one we inhabit—not nearly so well furnished, or tricked out with details. And yet still somehow better. More satisfying. Perhaps the novelist is only a special case of a universal desire to reshape, to 'take this sorry scheme of things entire,' smash it into bits, and 'remold it nearer to the heart's desire'—as old Khayyám says. The egoist is continually doing it with his own life. To dream of doing it with history is no more useful a game, I suppose, but as a game, it shows more sport. There are rules. You can be more objective, if that's an appropriate world." He seemed to grow pensive for a moment. He looked at the end of his cigar. It had gone out, but he didn't relight it.

"Take this Empire," he went on, drawing himself up somewhat to say it. "One doesn't want to be mawkish, but one has served it. Extended it a bit, made it more secure; done one's bit. You and I. Nothing more natural, then, if we have worked for its extension in the future, to imagine its extension in the past. We can put our finger on the occasional bungle, the missed chance, the wrong man in the wrong place, and so on, and we think: if I had only been there, seen to it that the news went through, got the guns there in time, forced the issue at a certain moment—well. But as long as one is dreaming, why stop? A favorite instance of mine is the American civil war. We came very close, you know, to entering that war on the Confederacy's side."

"Did we."

"I think we did. Suppose we had. Suppose we had at first dabbled—sent arms—ignored Northern protests—then got deeper in; suppose the North declared war on us. It seems to me a near certainty that if we had entered the war fully, the South would have won. And I think a British presence would have mitigated the slaughter. There was a point, you know, late in that war, when a new draft call in the North was met with terrible riots. In New York several Negroes were hanged, just to show how little their cause was felt."

Denys had partly lost the thread of this story, unable to imagine himself in it. He thought of the Americans he had met on the train. "Is that so," he said.

"Once having divided the States into two nations, and having helped the South to win, we would have been in place, you see. The fate of the West had not yet been decided. With the North much diminished in power—well, I imagine that by now we, the Empire, would have recouped much of what we lost in 1780."

Denys contemplated this. "Rather stirring," he said mildly. "Rather cold-blooded, too. Wouldn't it have meant condoning slavery? To say nothing of the lives lost. British, I mean."

"Condoning slavery—for a time. I've no doubt the South could have been bullied out of it. Without, perhaps, the awful results that accompanied the Northerners doing it. The eternal resentment. The backlash. The near genocide of the last hundred years. And, in my vision, there would have been a net savings in red men." He smiled. "Whatever might be said against it, the British Empire does not wipe out populations wholesale, as the Americans did in their West. I often wonder if that sin isn't what makes the Americans so gloomy now, so introverted."

Denys nodded. He believed implicitly that his Empire did not wipe out populations wholesale. "Of course," he said, "there's no telling what exactly would have been the result. If we'd interfered as you say."

"No," Sir Geoffrey said. "No doubt whatever result it *did* have would have to be reshaped as well. And the results of that reshaping reshaped, too, the whole thing subtly guided all along its way toward the result desired—after all, if we can imagine how we might want to alter the past we do inherit, so we can imagine that any past might well be liable to the same imagining; that stupidities, blunders, shortsightedness, would occur in any past we might initiate. Oh, yes, it would all have to be reshaped, with each reshaping. . . ."

"The possibilities are endless," Denys said, laughing. "I'm afraid the game's beyond me. I say let the North win—since in any case we can't do the smallest thing about it."

"No," Davenant said, grown sad again, or reflective; he seemed to feel what Denys said deeply. "No, we can't. It's just—just too long ago." With great gravity he relit his cigar. Denys, at the oddness of this response, seeing Sir Geoffrey's eyes veiled, thought: *Perhaps he's mad.* He said, joining the game, "Suppose, though. Suppose Cecil Rhodes hadn't died young, as he did. . . ."

Davenant's eyes caught cold fire again, and his cigar paused in midair. "Hm?" he said with interest.

"I only meant," Denys said, "that your remark about the British not wiping out peoples wholesale was perhaps not tested. If Rhodes had lived to build his empire—hadn't he already named it Rhodesia—I imagine he would have dealt fairly harshly with the natives."

"Very harshly," said Sir Geoffrey.

"Well," Denys said, "I suppose I mean that it's not always evil effects that we inherit from these past accidents."

"Not at all," said Sir Geoffrey. Denys looked away from his regard, which had grown, without losing a certain cool humor, intense. "Do you know, by the way, that remark of George Santayana—the American philosopher—about the British Empire, about young men like yourself? 'Never,' he said, 'never since the Athenians has the world been ruled by such sweet, just, boyish masters.' "

Denys, absurdly, felt himself flush with embarrassment.

"I don't ramble," Sir Geoffrey said. "My trains of thought carry odd goods, but all headed the same way. I want to tell you something, about that historical circumstance, the one you've touched on, whose effects we inherit. Evil or good I will leave you to decide.

"Cecil Rhodes died prematurely, as you say. But not before he had amassed a very great fortune, and laid firm claims to the ground where that fortune would grow far greater. And also not before he had made a will disposing of that fortune."

"I've heard stories," Denys said.

"The stories you have heard are true. Cecil Rhodes, at his death, left his entire fortune, and its increase, to found and continue a secret society which should, by whatever means possible, preserve and extend the British Empire. His entire fortune."

"I have never believed it," Denys said, momentarily feeling untethered, like a balloon: afloat.

"For good reason," Davenant said. "If such a society as I describe were brought into being, its very first task would be to disguise, cast doubt upon, and quite bury its origins. Don't you think that's so? In any case it's true what I say: the society was founded; is secret; continues to exist; is responsible, in some large degree at least, for the Empire we now know, in this year of grace 1956, IV Elizabeth II, the Empire on which the sun does not set."

The veranda where the two men sat was nearly deserted now; the night was loud with tropical noises that Denys had come to think of as silence, but the human noise of the town had nearly ceased.

"You can't know that," Denys said. "If you knew it, if you were privy to it, then you wouldn't say it. Not to me." He almost added: *Therefore you're not in possession of any secret, only a madman's certainty.*

"I *am* privy to it," Davenant said. "I am myself a member. The reason I reveal the secret to you—and you see, here we are, come to you and my odd knowledge of you, at last, as I promised—the reason I reveal it to you is because I wish to ask you to join it. To accept from me an offer of membership."

Denys said nothing. A dark waiter in white crept close, and was waved away by Sir Geoffrey.

"You are quite properly silent," Sir Geoffrey said. "Either I am mad, you think, in which case there is nothing to say; or what I am telling you is true, which likewise leaves you nothing to say. Quite proper. In your place I would be silent also. In your place I was. In any case I have no intention of pressing you for an answer now. I happen to know, by a roundabout sort of means that if I explained to you would certainly convince you I was mad, that you will seriously consider what I've said to you. Later. On your long ride to Cairo: there will be time to think. In London. I ask nothing from you now. Only . . ."

He reached into his waistcoat pocket. Denys watched, fascinated: would he draw out some sign of power, a royal charter, some awesome seal? No: it was a small metal plate, with a strip of brown ribbon affixed to it, like a bit of recording tape. He turned it in his hands thoughtfully. "The difficulty, you see, is that in order to alter history and bring it closer to the heart's desire, it would be necessary to stand outside it altogether. Like Archimedes, who said that if he had a lever long enough, and a place to stand, he could move the world."

He passed the metal plate to Denys, who took it reluctantly.

"A place to stand, you see," Sir Geoffrey said. "A place to stand. I would like you to keep that plate about you, and not misplace it. It's in the nature of a key, though it mayn't look it; and it will let you into a very good London club, though it mayn't look it either, where I would like you to call on me. If, even out of simple curiosity, you would like to hear more of us." He extinguished his cigar. "I am going to describe the rather complicated way in which that key is to be used—I really do apologize for the hugger-mugger, but you will come to understand—and then I am going to bid you good evening. Your train is an early one? I thought so. My own departs at midnight. I possess a veritable Bradshaw's of the world's railroads in this skull. Well. No more. I will just sign this— oh, don't thank me. Dear boy: don't thank me."

When he was gone, Denys sat a long time with his cold cigar in his hand and the night around him. The amounts of wine and brandy he had been given seemed to have evaporated from him into the humid air, leaving him feeling cool, clear, and unreal. When at last he rose to go, he inserted the flimsy plate into his waistcoat pocket; and before he went to bed, to lie a long time awake, he changed it to the waistcoat pocket of the pale suit he would wear next morning.

As Sir Geoffrey suggested he would, he thought on his ride north of all that he had been told, trying to reassemble it in some more reasonable, more everyday fashion: as all day long beside the train the sempiternal Nile—camels, nomads, women washing in the barge canals, the thin line of palms screening the white desert beyond—slipped past. At evening, when at length he lowered the shade of his compartment window on the poignant blue sky pierced with stars, he thought suddenly: But how could he have know he would find me there, at the bar of the Grand, on that night of this year, at that hour of the evening, just as though we had some long-standing agreement to meet there?

If anything is chance, Davenant had said, that was not.

At the airfield at Ismailia there was a surprise: his flight home on the R101, which his father had booked months ago as a special treat for Denys, was to be that grand old airship's last scheduled flight. The oldest airship in the British fleet, commissioned in the year Denys was born, was to be—mothballed? Drydocked? Deflated? Denys wondered just what one did with a decommissioned airship larger than Westminster Cathedral.

Before dawn it was drawn from its great hangar by a crowd of white-clothed fellahin pulling at its ropes—descendants, Denys thought, of those who had pulled ropes at the Pyramids three thousand years ago, employed now on an object almost as big but lighter than air. It isn't because it is so intensely romantic that great airships must always arrive or depart at dawn or at evening, but only that then the air is cool and most likely to be still: and yet intensely romantic it remains. Denys, standing at the broad, canted windows, watched the ground recede—magically, for there was no sound of engines, no jolt to indicate liftoff, only the waving, cheering fellahin growing smaller. The band on the tarmac played "Land of Hope and Glory." Almost invisible to watchers on the ground—because of its heat-reflective silver dome—the immense ovoid turned delicately in the wind as it arose.

"Well, it's the end of an era," a red-faced man in a checked suit said to Denys. "In ten years they'll all be gone, these big airships. The propeller chaps will have taken over; and the jet aeroplane, too, I shouldn't wonder."

"I should be sorry to see that," Denys said. "I've loved airships since I was a boy."

"Well, they're just that little bit slower," the red-faced man said sadly. "It's all hurry-up, nowadays. Faster, faster. And for what? I put it to you: for what?"

Now with further gentle pushes of its Rolls-Royce engines, the R101 altered its attitude again; passengers at the lounge windows pointed out the Suez Canal, and the ships passing; Lake Mareotis; Alexandria, like a mirage; British North Africa, as far to the left as one cared to point; and the white-fringed sea. Champagne was being called for, traditional despite the hour, and the red-faced man pressed a glass on Denys.

"The end of an era," he said again, raising his flute of champagne solemnly.

And then the cloudscape beyond the windows shifted, and all Africa had slipped into the south, or into the imaginary, for they had already begun to seem the same thing to Denys. He turned from the windows and decided—the effort to decide it seemed not so great here aloft, amid the potted palms and the wicker, with this pale champagne—that the conversation he had had down in the flat lands far away must have been imaginary as well.

III: THE TALE OF THE PRESIDENT *PRO TEM*

The universe proceeds out of what it has been and into what it will be, inexorably, unstoppably, at the rate of one second per second, one year per year, forever. At right angles to its forward progress lie the past and the future. The future, that is to say, does not lie "ahead" of the present in the stream of time, but at a right angle to it: the future of any present moment can be projected as far as you like outward from it, infinitely in fact, but when the universe has proceeded further, and a new present moment has succeeded this one, the future of this one retreats with it into the what-has-been, forever outdated. It is similar but more complicated with the past.

Now within the great process or procession that the universe makes, there can be no question of "movement," either "forward" or "back." The very idea is contradictory. Any conceivable movement is into the orthogonal futures and pasts that fluoresce from the universe as it is; and from those orthogonal futures and pasts into others, and others, and still others, never returning, always moving at right angles to the stream of time. To the traveler, therefore, who does not ever return from the futures or pasts into which he has gone, it must appear that the times he inhabits grow progressively more remote from the stream of time that generated them, the stream that has since moved on and left his futures behind. Indeed, the longer he remains in the future, the farther off the traveler gets from the moment in actuality whence he started, and the less like actuality the universe he stands in seems to him to be.

It was thoughts of this sort, only inchoate as yet and with the necessary conclusions not yet drawn, that occupied the mind of the President *pro tem* of the Otherhood as he walked the vast length of an iron and glass railway station in the capital city of an aged empire. He stopped to take a cigar case from within the black Norfolk overcoat he wore, and a cigar from the case; this he lit, and with its successive blue clouds hanging lightly about his hat and head, he walked on. There were hominids at work on the glossy engines of the empire's trains that came and went from this terminus; hominids pushing with their long strong arms the carts burdened with the goods and luggage that the trains were to carry; hominids of other sorts, gathered in groups or standing singly at the barricades, clutched their tickets, waiting to depart, some aided by or waited upon by other species—too few creatures, in all, to dispel the extraordinary impression of smoky empty hugeness that the cast-iron arches of the shed made.

The President *pro tem* was certain, or at any rate retained a distinct impression, that at his arrival some days before there were telephones available for citizens to use, in the streets, in public places such as this (he seemed to see an example in his mind, a wooden box whose bright veneer was loosening in the damp climate, a complex instrument within, of enameled steel and heavy celluloid); but if there ever had been, there were none now. Instead he went in at a door above which a yellow globe was alight, a winged foot etched upon it. He chose a telegraph form from a stack of them on a long scarred counter, and with the scratchy pen provided he dashed off a quick note to the Magus in whose apartments he had been staying, telling him that he had returned late from the country and would not be with him till evening.

This missive he handed in at the grille, paying what was asked in large coins; then he went out, up the brass-railed stairs, and into the afternoon, into the quiet and familiar city.

It was the familiarity that had been, from the beginning, the oddest thing. The President *pro tem* was a man who, in the long course of his work for the Otherhood, had become accustomed to stepping out of his London club into a world not quite the same as the world he had left to enter that club. He was used to finding himself in a London—or a Lahore or a Laos—stripped of well-known monuments, with public buildings and private ways unknown to him, and a newspaper (bought with an unfamiliar coin found in his pocket) full of names that should not have been there, or missing events that should have been. But here—where nothing, nothing at all, was as he had known it, no trace remaining of the history he had come from—here where no man should have been able to take steps, where even Caspar Last had thought it not possible to take steps—the President *pro tem* could not help but feel easy: had felt easy from the beginning. He walked up the cobbled streets, his furled umbrella over his shoulder, troubled by nothing but the weird grasp that this unknown dark city had on his heart.

The rain that had somewhat spoiled his day in the country had ceased but had left a pale, still mist over the city, a humid atmosphere that gave to views down avenues a stage-set quality, each receding rank of buildings fainter, more vaguely executed. Trees, too, huge and weeping, still and featureless as though painted on successive scrims. At the great gates, topped with garlanded urns, of a public park, the President *pro tem* looked in toward the piled and sounding waters of a fountain and the dim towers of poplar trees. And as he stood resting on his umbrella, lifting the last of the cigar to his lips, someone passed by him and entered the park.

For a moment the President *pro tem* stood unmoving, thinking what an attractive person (boy? girl?) that had been, and how the smile paid to him in passing seemed to indicate a knowledge of him, a knowledge that gave pleasure or at least amusement; then he dropped his cigar end and passed through the gates through which the figure had gone.

That had *not* been a hominid who had smiled at him. It was not a Magus and surely not one of the draconics either. Why he was sure he could not have said: for the same unsayable reason that he knew this city in this world, this park, these marble urns, these leaf-littered paths. He was sure that the person he had seen belonged to a different species from himself, and different also from the other species who lived in this world.

At the fountain where the paths crossed, he paused, looking this way and that, his heart beating hard and filled absurdly with a sense of loss. The child (had it been a child?) was gone, could not be seen that way, or that way—but then was there again suddenly, down at the end of a yew alley, loitering, not looking his way. Thinking at first to sneak up on her, or him, along the sheltering yews, the President *pro tem* took a sly step that way; then, ashamed, he thought better of it and set off down the path at an even pace, as one would approach a young horse or a tame deer. The one he walked toward took no notice of him, appeared lost in thought, eyes cast down.

Indescribably lovely, the President *pro tem* thought: and yet at the same time negligent and easeful and ordinary. Barefoot, or in light sandals of some kind, light pale clothing that seemed to be part of her, like a bird's dress—and a wristwatch, incongruous, yet not really incongruous at all: someone for whom incongruity was inconceivable. A reverence—almost a holy dread—came over the President *pro tem* as he came closer: as though he had stumbled into a sacred grove. Then the one he walked toward looked up at him, which caused the President *pro tem* to stop still as if a gun had casually been turned on him.

He was known, he understood, to this person. She, or he, stared unembarrassed at the President *pro tem*, with a gaze of the most intense and yet impersonal tenderness, of compassion and amusement and calm interest all mixed; and almost imperceptibly shook her head *no* and smiled again: and the President *pro tem* lowered his eyes, unable to meet that gaze. When he looked up again, the person was gone.

Hesitantly the President *pro tem* walked to the end of the avenue of yews and looked in all directions. No one. A kind of fear flew over him, felt in his breast like the beat of departing wings. He seemed to know, for the first time, what those encounters with gods had been like, when there had been gods; encounters he had puzzled out of the Greek in school.

Anyway he was alone now in the park: he was sure of that. At length he found his way out again into the twilight streets.

By evening he had crossed the city and was climbing the steps of a tall town house, searching in his pockets for the key given him. Beside the varnished door was a small plaque, which said that within were the offices of the Orient Aid Society; but this was not in fact the case. Inside was a tall foyer; a glass-paneled door let him into a hallway wainscoted in dark wood. A pile of gumboots and rubber overshoes in a corner, macs and umbrellas on an ebony tree. Smells of tea, done with, and dinner cooking: a stew, an apple tart, a roast fowl. The tulip-shaped gas lamps along the hall were lit.

He let himself into the library at the hall's end; velvet armchairs regarded the coal fire, and on a drum table a tray of tea things consorted with the books and the papers. The President *pro tem* went to the low shelves that ran beneath the windows and drew out one volume of an old encyclopedia, buckram-bound, with marbled fore-edges and illustrations in brownish photogravure.

The Races. For some reason the major headings and certain other words were in the orthography he knew, but not the closely printed text. His fingers ran down the columns, which were broken into numbered sections headed by the names of species and subspecies. *Hominidae*, with three subspecies. *Draconiidae*, with four: here were etchings of skulls. And lastly *Sylphidae*, with an uncertain number of subspecies. Sylphidae, the Sylphids. Fairies.

"Angels," said a voice behind him. The President *pro tem* turned to see the Magus whose guest he was, recently risen no doubt, in a voluminous dressing gown richly figured. His beard and hair were so long and fine they seemed to float on the currents of air in the room, like filaments of thistledown.

" 'Angels,' is that what you call them?"

"What they would have themselves called," said the Magus. "What name they call themselves, among themselves, no one knows but they."

"I think I met with one this evening."

"Yes."

There was no photogravure to accompany the subsection on Sylphidae in the encyclopedia. "I'm sure I met with one."

"They are gathering, then."

"Not . . . not because of me?"

"Because of you."

"How, though," said the President *pro tem*, feeling again within him the sense of loss, of beating wings departing, "how, how could they have known, how . . ."

The Magus turned away from him to the fire, to the armchairs and the drum table. The President *pro tem* saw that beside one chair a glass of whiskey had been placed, and an ashtray. "Come," said the Magus. "Sit. Continue your tale. It will perhaps become clear to you: perhaps not." He sat then himself, and without looking back at the President *pro tem* he said: "Shall we go on?"

The President *pro tem* knew it was idle to dispute with his host. He did stand unmoving for the space of several heartbeats. Then he took his chair, drew the cigar case from his pocket, and considered where he had left off his tale in the dark of the morning.

"Of course," he said then, "Last knew: he knew, without admitting it to himself, as a good orthogonist must never do, that the world he had returned to from his excursion was not the world he had left. The past he had passed through on his way back was not 'behind' his present at all, but at a right angle to it; the future of that past, which he had to traverse in order to get back again, was not the same road, and 'back' was not where he got. The frame house on Maple Street which, a little sunburned, he reentered on his return was twice removed in reality from the one he had left a week before; the mother he kissed likewise.

"He knew that, for it was predicated by orthogonal logic, and orthogonal logic was in fact what Last had discovered—the transversability of time was only an effect of that discovery. He knew it, and despite his glee over his triumph, he kept his eye open. Sooner or later he would come upon something, something that would betray the fact that this world was not his.

"He could not have guessed it would be me."

The Magus did not look at the President *pro tem* as he was told this story; his pale gray eyes instead wandered from object to object around the great dark library but seemed to see none of them; what, the President *pro tem* wondered, did they see? He had at first supposed the race of Magi to be blind, from this habitual appearance of theirs; he now knew quite well that they were not blind, not blind at all.

"Go on," the Magus said.

"So," said the President *pro tem*, "Last returns from his excursion. A week passes uneventfully. Then one morning he hears his mother call: he has a visitor. Last, pretending annoyance at this interruption of his work (actually he was calculating various forms of compound interest on a half million dollars), comes to the door. There on the step is a figure in tweeds and a bowler hat, leaning on a furled umbrella: me.

" 'Mr. Last,' I said. 'I think we have business.'

"You could see by his expression that he knew I should not have been there, should not have had business with him at all. He really ought to have refused to see me. A good deal of trouble might have been saved if he had. There was no way I could force him, after all. But he didn't refuse; after a goggle-eyed moment he brought me in, up a flight of stairs (Mama waiting anxiously at the bottom), and into his study.

"Geniuses are popularly supposed to live in an atmosphere of the greatest confusion and untidiness, but this wasn't true of Last. The study—it was his bedroom, too—was of a monkish neatness. There was no sign that he worked there, except for a computer terminal, and even it was hidden beneath a cozy that Mama had made for it and Caspar had not dared to spurn.

"He was trembling slightly, poor fellow, and had no idea of the social graces. He only turned to me—his eyeglasses were the kind that oddly diffract the eyes behind and make them unmeetable—and said, 'What do you want?' "

The President *pro tem* caressed the ashtray with the tip of his cigar. He had been offered no tea, and he felt the lack. "We engaged in some preliminary fencing," he continued. "I told him what I had come to acquire. He said he didn't know what I was talking about. I said I thought he did. He laughed and said there must be some mistake. I said, no mistake, Mr. Last. At length he grew silent, and I could see even behind those absurd goggles that he had begun to try to account for me.

"Thinking out the puzzles of orthogonal logic, you see, is not entirely unlike puzzling out moves in chess: theoretically chess can be played by patiently working out the likely consequences of each move, and the consequences of those consequences, and so on; but in fact it is not so played, certainly not by master players. Masters seem to have a more immediate apprehension of possibilities, an almost visceral understanding of the, however rigorously mathematical, logic of the board and pieces, an understanding that they can act on without being able necessarily to explain. Whatever sort of mendacious and feckless fool Caspar Last was in many ways, he was a genius in one or two, and orthogonal logic was one of them.

" 'From when,' he said, 'have you come?'

" 'From not far on,' I answered. He sat then, resigned, stuck in a sort of check impossible to think one's way out of, yet not mated. 'Then,' he said, 'go back the same way you came.'

" 'I cannot,' I said, 'until you explain to me how it is done.'

" 'You know how,' he said, 'if you can come here to ask me.'

" 'Not until you have explained it to me. Now or later.'

" 'I never will,' he said.

" 'You will,' I said. 'You will have done already, before I leave. Otherwise I would not be here now asking. Let us,' I said, and took a seat myself, 'let us assume these preliminaries have been gone through, for they have been of course, and move ahead to the bargaining. My firm are prepared to make you a quite generous offer.'

"That was what convinced him that he must, finally, give up to us the processes he had discovered, which he really had firmly intended to destroy forever: the fact that I had come there to ask for them. Which meant that he had already somehow, somewhen, already yielded them up to us."

The President *pro tem* paused again, and lifted his untouched whiskey. "It was the same argument," he said, "the same incontrovertible argument, that was used to convince me once, too, to do a dreadful thing."

He drank, thoughtfully, or at least (he supposed) appearing thoughtful; more and more often as he grew older it happened that in the midst of an anecdote, a relation, even one of supreme importance, he would begin to forget what it was he was telling; the terrifically improbable events would begin to seem not only improbable but fictitious, without insides, the incidents and characters as false as in any tawdry cinema story, even his own part in them unreal: as though they happened to someone made up—certainly not to him who told them. Often enough he forgot the plot.

"You see," he said, "Last exited from a universe in which travel 'through time' was, apparently, either not possible, or possible only under conditions that would allow such travel to go undetected. That was apparent from the fact that no one, so far as Last knew, up to the time of his own single excursion, had ever detected it going on. No one, from Last's own future that is, had ever come 'back' and disrupted his present, or the past of his present: never ever. Therefore, if his excursion could take place, and he could 'return,' he would have to return to a different universe: a universe where time travel *had* taken place, a universe in which once-upon-a-time a man from 1983 had managed to insert himself into a minor colony of the British Crown one hundred and twenty-seven years earlier. What he couldn't know in advance was whether the universe he 'returned' to was one where time travel was a commonplace, an everyday occurrence, something, anyway, that could deprive his excursion of the value it had; or whether it was one in which one excursion only had taken place, his own. My appearance before him convinced him that it was, or was about to become, common enough: common enough to disturb his own peace and quiet, and alter in unforeseeable ways his comfortable present.

"There was only one solution, or one dash at a solution anyway. I might, myself, be a singularity in Last's new present. It was therefore possible that if he could get rid of me, I would take his process 'away' with me into whatever future I had come out of to get it, and thereupon never be able to find my way again to his present and disturb it or him. Whatever worlds I altered, they would not be his, not his anyway who struck the bargain with me: if each of them also contained a Last, who would suffer or flourish in ways unimaginable to the Last to whom I spoke, then those eidolons would have to make terms for themselves, that's all. The quantum angle obtruded by my coming, and then the one obtruded by my returning, divorced all those Lasts from him for all eternity: that is why, though the angle itself is virtually infinitesimal, it has always to be treated as a right angle.

"Last showed me, on his computer, after our bargain was struck and he was turning over his data and plans to me. I told him I would not probably grasp the theoretical basis of the process, however well I had or would come to manage the practical paradoxes of it, but he liked to show me. He first summoned up x-y coordinates, quite ordinary, and began by showing me how some surprising results were obtained by plotting on such coordinates an imaginary number, specifically the square root of minus one. The only way to describe what happens, he said, is that the plotted figure, one unit high, one unit wide, generates a shadow square of the same measurements 'behind' itself, in space undefined by the coordinates. It was with such tricks that he had begun; the orthogons he obtained had first started him thinking about the generation of inhabitable—if also somehow imaginary—pasts.

"Then he showed me what became of the orthogons so constructed if the upright axis were set in motion. Suppose (he said) that this vertical coordinate were in fact revolving around the axle formed by the other, horizontal coordinate. If it were so revolving, like an aeroplane propeller, we could not apprehend it, edge on as it is to us, so to speak; but what would that motion do to the plots we were making? And of course it was quite simple, given the proper instructions to the computer, to find out. And his orthogons—always remaining at right angles to the original coordinates—began to turn in the prop wash of the whole system's progress at one second per second out of the what-was and into the what-has-never-yet-been; and to generate, when one had come to see them, the paradoxes of orthogonal logic: the cyclonic storm of logic in which all travelers in that medium always stand; the one in which Last and I, I bending over his shoulder hat in hand, he with fat white fingers on his keys and eyeglasses slipping down his nose, stood even as we spoke: a storm as unfeelable as Last's rotating axis was unseeable."

The President *pro tem* tossed his extinguished cigar into the fading fire and crossed his arms upon his breast, weary; weary of the tale.

"I don't yet understand," the other said. "If he had been so adamant, why would he give up his secrets to you?"

"Well," said the President *pro tem*, "there was, also, the matter of money. It came down to that, in the end. We were able to make him a very generous offer, as I said."

"But he didn't need money. He had this stamp."

"Yes. So he did. Yes. We were able to pick up the stamp, too, from him, as part of the bargain. I think we offered him a hundred pounds. Perhaps it was more."

"I thought it was invaluable."

"Well, so did he, of course. And yet he was not really as surprised as one might have expected him to be, when he discovered it was not; when it turned out that the stamp he had gone to such trouble to acquire was in fact rather a common one. I seemed to see it in his face, the expectation of what he was likely to find, as soon as I directed him to look it up in his Scott's, if he didn't believe me. And there it was in Scott's: the one-penny magenta 1856, a nice

enough stamp, a stamp many collectors covet, and many also have in their al-
bums. He had begun breathing stertorously, staring down at the page. I'm afraid
he was suffering, rather, and I didn't like to observe it.

" 'Come,' I said to him. 'You knew it was possible.' And he did, of course.
'Perhaps it was something you did,' I said. 'Perhaps you bought the last one of
a batch, and the postmaster subsequently reordered, a thing he had not before
intended to do. Perhaps . . .' But I could see him think it: there needed to be
no such explanation. He needed to have made no error, nor to have influenced
the moment's shape in any way by his presence. The very act of his coming and
going was sufficient source of unpredictable, stochastic change: this world was
not his, and minute changes from his were predicated. But *this* change, this of
all possible changes . . .

"His hand had begun to shake, holding the volume of Scott's. I really wanted
now to get through the business and be off, but it couldn't be hurried. I knew
that, for I'd done it all before. In the end we acquired the stamp. And then
destroyed it, of course."

The President *pro tem* remembered: a tiny, momentary fire.

"It's often been observed," he said, "that the cleverest scientists are often the
most easily taken in by charlatans. There is a famous instance, famous in some
worlds, of a scientist who was brought to believe firmly in ghosts and ectoplasm,
because the medium and her manifestations passed all the tests the scientist
could devise. The only thing he didn't think to test for was conscious fraud. I
suppose it's because the phenomena of nature, or the entities of mathematics,
however puzzling and elusive they may be, are not after all bent on fooling the
observer; and so a motive that would be evident to the dullest of policemen
does not occur to the genius."

"The stamp," said the Magus.

"The stamp, yes. I'm not exactly proud of this part of the story. We were
convinced, though, that two *very* small wrongs could go a long way toward
making a very great right. And Last, who understood me and the 'firm' I represented to be capable of handling—at least in a practical way—the awful paradoxes of orthogony, did not imagine us to be also skilled, if anything more
skilled, at such things as burglary, uttering, fraud, and force. Of such contradictions is Empire made. It was easy enough for us to replace, while Last was off
in the tropics, one volume of his Scott's stamp catalog with another printed by
ourselves, almost identical to his but containing one difference. It was harder
waiting to see, once he had looked up his stamp in our bogus volume, if he
would then search out some other source to confirm what he found there. He
did not."

The Magus rose slowly from his chair with the articulated dignity, the waste-
less lion's motion, of his kind. He tugged the bell pull. He picked up the poker
then, and stood with his hand upon the mantel, looking down into the ruby ash
of the dying fire. "I would he had," he said.

The dark double doors of the library opened, and the servant entered noise-
lessly.

"Refresh the gentleman's glass," the Magus said without turning from the fire,
"and draw the drapes."

The President *pro tem* thought that no matter how long he lived in this world
he would never grow accustomed to the presence of draconics. The servant's
dark hand lifted the decanter, poured an exact dram into the glass, and stoppered
the bottle again; then his yellow eyes, irises slit like a cat's or a snake's, rose from

that task toward the next, the drawing of the drapes. Unlike the eyes of the Magi, these draconic eyes seemed to see and weigh everything—though on a single scale, and from behind a veil of indifference.

Their kind, the President *pro tem* had learned, had been servants for uncounted ages, though the Magus his host had said that once they had been masters, and men and the other hominids their slaves. And they still had, the President *pro tem* observed, that studied reserve which upper servants had in the world from which the President *pro tem* had come, that reserve which says: Very well, I will do your bidding, better than you could do it for yourself; I will maintain the illusion of your superiority to me, as no other creature could.

With a taper he lit at the fire, he lit the lamps along the walls and masked them with glass globes. Then he drew the drapes.

"I'll ring for supper," the Magus said, and the servant stopped at the sound of his voice. "Have it sent in." The servant moved again, crossing the room on narrow naked feet. At the doorway he turned to them, but only to draw the double doors closed together as he left.

For a time the Magus stood regarding the doors the great lizard had closed. Then: "Outside the City," he said, "in the mountains, they have begun to combine. There are more stories every week. In the old forests whence they first emerged, they have begun to collect on appointed days, trying to remember—for they are not really as intelligent as they look—trying to remember what it is they have lost, and to think of gaining it again. In not too long a time we will begin to hear of massacres. Some remote place; a country house; a more than usually careless man; a deed of unfamiliar horridness. And a sign left, the first sign: a writing in blood, or something less obvious. And like a spot symptomatic of a fatal disease, it will begin to spread."

The President *pro tem* drank, then said softly: "We didn't know, you know. We didn't understand that this would be the result." The drawing of the drapes, the lighting of the lamps, had made the old library even more familiar to the President *pro tem*: the dark varnished wood, the old tobacco smoke, the hour between tea and dinner; the draught that whispered at the window's edge, the bitter smell of the coal on the grate; the comfort of this velvet armchair's napless arms, of this whiskey. The President *pro tem* sat grasped by all this, almost unable to think of anything else. "We couldn't know."

"Last knew," the Magus said. "All false, all imaginary, all generated by the wishes and fears of others: all that I am, my head, my heart, my house. Not the world's doing, or time's, but yours." The opacity of his eyes, turned on the President *pro tem*, was fearful. "You have made me; you must unmake me."

"I'll do what I can," the President *pro tem* said. "All that I can."

"For centuries we have studied," the Magus said. "We have spent lifetimes—lifetimes much longer than yours—searching for the flaw in this world, the flaw whose existence we suspected but could not prove. I say 'centuries,' but those centuries have been illusory, have they not? We came, finally, to guess at you, down the defiles of time, working your changes, which we can but suffer.

"We only guessed at you: no more than men or beasts can we Magi remember, once the universe has become different, that it was ever other than it is now. But I think the Sylphids can feel it change: can know when the changes are wrought. Imagine the pain for them."

That was a command: and indeed the President *pro tem* could imagine it, and did. He looked down into his glass.

"That is why they are gathering. They know already of your appearance; they have expected you. The request is theirs to make, not mine: that you put this world out like a light."

He stabbed with the poker at the settling fire, and the coals gave up blue flames for a moment. The mage's eyes caught the light, and then went out.

"I long to die," he said.

IV: CHRONICLES OF THE OTHERHOOD

Once past the door, or what might be considered the door, or what Sir Geoffrey Davenant had told him was a club, Denys Winterset was greeted by the Fellow in Economic History, a gentle, academic-looking man called Platt.

"Not many of the Fellows about, just now," he said. "Most of them fossicking about on one bit of business or another. I'm always here." He smiled, a vague, self-effacing smile. "Be no good out there. But they also serve, eh?"

"Will Sir Geoffrey Davenant be here?" Denys asked him. He followed Platt through what did seem to be a gentlemen's club of the best kind: dark-paneled, smelling richly of leather upholstery and tobacco.

"Davenant, oh, yes," said Platt. "Davenant will be here. All the executive committee will get here, if they can. The President—*pro tem.*" He turned back to look at Denys over his half-glasses. "All our presidents are *pro tem.*" He led on. "There'll be dinner in the executive committee's dining room. After dinner we'll talk. You'll likely have questions." At that Denys almost laughed. He felt made of questions, most of them unputtable in any verbal form.

Platt stopped in the middle of the library. A lone Fellow in a corner by a green-shaded lamp was hidden by the *Times* held up before him. There was a fire burning placidly in the oak-framed fireplace; above it, a large and smoke-dimmed painting: a portrait of a chubby, placid man in a hard collar, thinning blond hair, eyes somehow vacant. Platt, seeing Deny's look, said: "Cecil Rhodes."

Beneath the portrait, carved into the mantelpiece, were words; Denys took a step closer to read them:

> *To Ruin the Great Work of Time*
> *& Cast the Kingdoms old*
> *Into another mould.*

"Marvell," Platt said. "That poem about Cromwell. Don't know who chose it. It's right, though. I look at it often, working here. Now. It's down that corridor, if you want to wash your hands. Would you care for a drink? We have some time to kill. Ah, Davenant."

"Hullo, Denys," said Sir Geoffrey, who had lowered his *Times.* "I'm glad you've come."

"I think we all are," said Platt, taking Denys's elbow in a gentle, almost tender grasp. "Glad you've come."

He had almost not come. If it had been merely an address, a telephone number he'd been given, he might well not have; but the metal card with its brown strip was like a string tied round his finger, making it impossible to forget he had been invited. Don't lose it, Davenant had said. So it lay in his waistcoat pocket; he touched it whenever he reached for matches there; he tried shifting it to other pockets, but wherever it was on his person he felt it. In the end he decided to use it, as much to get rid of its importunity as for any other reason—so he told himself. On a wet afternoon he went to the place Davenant had told him of, the Orient Aid Society, and found it as described, a sooty French-Gothic building, one of those private houses turned to public use, with a discreet brass plaque by the door indicating that within some sort of business is done, one can't imagine what; and inside the double doors, in the vestibule, three telephone boxes, looking identical, the first of which had the nearly invisible slit by the door. His heart for some reason beat slow and hard as he inserted the card within this slot—it was immediately snatched away, like a ticket on the Underground—and entered the box and closed the door behind him.

Though nothing moved, he felt as though he had stepped onto a moving footpath, or onto one of those trick floors in a fun house that slide beneath one's feet. He was going somewhere. The sensation was awful. Beginning to panic, he tried to get out, not knowing whether that might be dangerous, but the door would not open, and its glass could not be seen out of either. It had been transparent from outside but was somehow opaque from within. He shook the door handle fiercely. At that moment the nonmobile motion reversed itself sickeningly, and the door opened. Denys stepped out, not into the vestibule of the Orient Aid Society, but into the foyer of a club. A dim, old-fashioned foyer, with faded Turkey carpet on the stairs, and an aged porter to greet him; a desk, behind which pigeonholes held members' mail; a stand of umbrellas. It was reassuring, almost absurdly so, the "then I woke up" of a silly ghost story. But Denys didn't feel reassured, or exactly awake either.

"Evening, sir."

"Good evening."

"Still raining, sir? Take your things?"

"Thank you."

A member was coming toward him down the long corridor: Platt.

"Sir?"

Denys turned back to the porter. "Your key, sir," the man said, and gave him back the metal plate with the strip of brown ribbon on it.

"Like a lift," Davenant told him as they sipped whiskey in the bar. "Alarming, somewhat, I admit; but imagine using a lift for the first time, not knowing what its function was. Closed inside a box; sensation of movement; the doors open, and you are somewhere else. Might seem odd. Well, this is the same. Only you're not somewhere else: not exactly."

"Hm," Denys said.

"Don't dismiss it, Sir Geoffrey," said Platt. "It *is* mighty odd." He said to Denys: "The paradox is acute: it is. Completely contrary to the usual cause-and-effect thinking we all do, can't stop doing really, no matter how hard we try to adopt other habits of mind. Strictly speaking it is unthinkable: unimaginable. And yet there it is."

"Yes," Davenant said. "To ignore, without ever forgetting, the heart of the matter: that's the trick. I've met monks, Japanese, Tibetan, who know the techniques. They can be learned."

"We speak of the larger paradox," Platt said to Denys. "The door you came in by being only a small instance. The great instance being, of course, the Otherhood's existence at all: we here now sitting and talking of it."

But Denys was not talking of it. He had nothing to say. To be told that in entering the telephone box in the Orient Aid Society he had effectively exited from time and entered a precinct outside it, revolving between the actual and the hypothetical, not quite existent despite the solidity of its parquet floor and the truthful bite of its whiskey; to be told that in these changeless and atemporal halls there gathered a society—"not quite a brotherhood," Davenant said; "that would be mawkish, and untrue of these chaps; we call it an Otherhood"—of men and women who by some means could insert themselves into the stream of the past, and with their foreknowledge alter it, and thus alter the future of that past, the future in which they themselves had their original being; that in effect the world Denys had come from, the world he knew, the year 1956, the whole course of things, the very cast and flavor of his memories, were dependent on the Fellows of this Society, and might change at any moment, though if they did he would know nothing of it; and that he was being asked to join them in their work—he heard the words, spoken to him with a frightening casualness; he felt his mind fill with the notions, though not able to do anything that might be called thinking about them; and he had nothing to say.

"You can see," Sir Geoffrey said, looking not at Denys but into his whiskey, "why I didn't explain all this to you in Khartoum. The words don't come easily. Here, in the Club, outside all frames of reference, it's possible to explain. To describe, anyway. I suppose if we hadn't a place like this, we should all go mad."

"I wonder," said Platt, "whether we haven't, despite it." He looked at no one. "Gone mad, I mean."

For a moment no one spoke further. The barman glanced at them, to see if their silence required anything of him. Then Platt spoke again. "Of course there are restrictions," he said. "The chap who discovered it was possible to change one's place in time, an American, thought he had proved that it was only possible to displace oneself into the past. In a sense, he was correct. . . ."

"In a sense," Sir Geoffrey said. "Not quite correct. The possibilities are larger than he supposed. Or rather will suppose, all this from your viewpoint is still to happen—which widens the possibilities right there, you see, one man's future being as it were another man's past. (You'll get used to it, dear boy, shall we have another of these?) The past, as it happens, is the only sphere of time we have any interest in; the only sphere in which we can do good. So you see there are natural limits: the time at which this process was made workable is the forward limit; and the rear limit we have made the time of the founding of the Otherhood itself. By Cecil Rhodes's will, in 1893."

"Be pointless, you see, for the Fellows to go back before the Society existed," said Platt. "You can see that."

"One further restriction," said Sir Geoffrey. "A house rule, so to speak. We forbid a man to return to a time he has already visited, at least in the same part of the world. There is the danger—a moment's thought will show you I'm right—of bumping into oneself on a previous, or successive, mission. Unnerving, let me tell you. Unnerving completely. The trick is hard enough to master as it is."

Denys found voice. "Why?" he said. "And why me?"

"Why," said Sir Geoffrey, "is spelled out in our founding charter: to preserve and extend the British Empire in all parts of the world, and to strengthen it against all dangers. Next, to keep peace in the world, insofar as this is compatible with the first; our experience has been that it usually is the same thing. And lastly to keep fellowship among ourselves, this also subject to the first, though any conflict is unimaginable, I should hope, bickering aside."

"The Society was founded to be secret," Platt said. "Rhodes liked that idea—a sort of Jesuits of the Empire. In fact there was no real need for secrecy, not until—well, not until the Society became the Otherhood. This jaunting about in other people's histories would not be understood. So secrecy *is* important. Good thing on the whole that Rhodes insisted on it. And for sure he wouldn't have been displeased at the Society's scope. He wanted the world for England. And more. 'The moon, too,' he used to say. 'I often think of the moon.' "

"Few know of us even now," Sir Geoffrey said. "The Foreign Office, sometimes. The PM. Depending on the nature of H.M. Government at any moment, we explain more, or less. Never the part about time. That is for us alone to know. Though some have guessed a little, over the years. It's not even so much that we wish to act in secret—that was just Rhodes's silly fantasy—but well, it's just damned difficult to explain, don't you see?"

"And the Queen knows of us," Platt said. "Of course."

"I flew back with her, from Africa, that day," Davenant said. "After her father had died. I happened to be among the party. I told her a little then. Didn't want to intrude on her grief, but—it seemed the moment. In the air, over Africa. I explained more later. Plucky girl," he added. "Plucky." He drew his watch out. "And as for the second part of your question—why you?—I shall ask you to reserve that one, for a moment. We'll dine upstairs . . . Good heavens, look at the time."

Platt swallowed his drink hastily. "I remember Lord Cromer's words to us when I was a schoolboy at Leys," he said. " 'Love your country,' he said, 'tell the truth, and don't dawdle.' "

"Words to live by," Sir Geoffrey said, examining the bar chit doubtfully and fumbling for a pen.

The drapes were drawn in the executive dining room; the members of the executive committee were just taking their seats around a long mahogany table, scarred around its edge with what seemed to be initials and dates. The members were of all ages; some sunburned, some pale, some in evening clothes of a cut unfamiliar to Denys; among them were two Indians and a Chinaman. When they were all seated, Denys beside Platt, there were several seats empty. A tall woman with severe gray hair but eyes somehow kind took the head of the table.

"The President *pro tem*," she said as she sat, "is not returned, apparently, from his mission. I'll preside, if there are no objections."

"Oh, balls," said a broad-faced man with the tan of a cinema actor. "Don't give yourself airs, Huntington. Will we really need any presiding?"

"Might be a swearing-in," Huntington said mildly, pressing the bell beside her and not glancing at Denys. "In any case, best to keep up the forms. First order of business—the soup."

It was a mulligatawny, saffrony and various; it was followed by a whiting, and that by a baron of claret-colored beef. Through the clashings of silverware and crystal Denys listened to the table's talk, little enough of which he could understand: only now and then he felt—as though he were coming horribly in two—the import of the Fellows' conversation: that history was malleable, time a fiction; that nothing was necessarily as he supposed it must be. How could they bear that knowledge? How could he?

"Mr. Deng Fa-shen, there," Platt said quietly to him, "is our physicist. Orthogonal physics—as opposed to orthogonal logic—is his invention. What makes this club possible. The mechanics of it. Don't ask me to explain."

Deng Fa-shen was a fine-boned, parchment-colored man with gentle fox's eyes. Denys looked from him to the two Indians in silk. Platt said, as though reading Denys's thought: "The most disagreeable thing about old Rhodes and the Empire of his day was its racialism, of course. Absolutely unworkable, too. Nothing more impossible to sustain than a world order based on some race's supposed inherent superiority." He smiled. "It isn't the only part of Rhodes's scheme that's proved unworkable."

The informal talk began to assemble itself, with small nudges from the woman at the head of the table (who did her presiding with no pomp and few words), around a single date: 1914. Denys knew something of this date, though several of the place names spoken of (the Somme, Jutland, Gallipoli—wherever that was) meant nothing to him. Somehow, in some possible universe, 1914 had changed everything; the Fellows seemed intent on changing 1914, drawing its teeth, teeth that Denys had not known it had—or might still have once had: he felt again the sensation of coming in two, and sipped wine.

"Jutland," a Fellow was saying. "All that's needed is a bit more knowledge, a bit more jump on events. Instead of a foolish stalemate, it could be a solid victory. Then, blockade; war over in six months . . ."

"Who's our man in the Admiralty now? Carteret, isn't it? Can he—"

"Carteret," said the bronze-faced man, "was killed the last time around at Jutland." There was a silence; some of the Fellows seemed to be aware of this, and some taken by surprise. "Shows the foolishness of that kind of thinking," the man said. "Things have simply gone too far by then. That's my opinion."

Other options were put forward. That moment in what the Fellows called the Original Situation was searched for into which a small intrusion might be made, like a surgical incision, the smallest possible intrusion that would have the proper effect; then the succeeding Situation was searched, and the Situation following that, the Fellows feeling with enormous patience and care into the workings of the past and its possibilities, like a blind man weaving. At length a decision seemed to be made, without fuss or a vote taken, about this place Gallipoli, and a Turkish soldier named Mustapha Kemal, who would be apprehended and sequestered in a quick action that took or would take place there; the sun-bronzed man would see, or had seen, to it; and the talk, after a reflective moment, turned again to anecdote and speculation.

Denys listened to the stories, of desert treks and dangerous negotiations, men going into the wilderness of a past catastrophe with a precious load of penicillin or of knowledge, to save one man's life or end another's; to intercept one trivial telegram, get one bit of news through, deflect one column of troops—removing one card from the ever-building possible future of some past moment and seeing the whole of it collapse silently, unknowably, even as another was building, just as fragile but happier: he looked into the faces of the Fellows, knowing that no ruthless stratagem was beyond them, and yet knowing also that they were men of honor, with a great world's peace and benefit in their trust, though the world couldn't know it; and he felt an odd but deep thrill of privilege to be here now, wherever that was—the same sense of privilege that, as a boy, he had expected to feel (and as a man had laughed at himself for expecting to feel) upon being admitted to the ranks of those who—selflessly, though not without reward—had been chosen or had chosen themselves to serve the Empire. "The difference you make makes all the difference," his headmasterish commissioner was fond of telling Denys and his fellows; and it was a joke among them that, in their form-filling, their execution of tedious and sometimes absurd directives, they were following in the footsteps of Gordon and Milner, Warren Hastings and Raffles of Singapore. And yet—Denys perceived it with a kind of inward stillness, as though his heart flowed instead of beating—a difference *could* be made. Had been made. Went on being made, in many times and places, without fuss, without glory, with rewards for others that those others could not recognize or even imagine. He crossed his knife and fork on his plate and sat back slowly.

"This 1914 business has its tricksome aspects," Platt said to him. "Speaking in large terms, not enough can really be done within our time frames. The Situation that issues in war was firmly established well before: in the founding of the German Empire under Prussian leadership. Bismarck. There's the man to get to, or to his financiers, most of whom were Jewish—little did they know, and all that. Even Sedan is too late, and not enough seems to be able to be made, or unmade, out of the Dreyfus affair, though that *does* fall within our provenance. No," he said. "It's all just too long ago. If only ... Well, no use speculating, is there? Make the best of it, and shorten the war; make it less catastrophic at any rate, a short, sharp shaking-out—above all, win it quickly. We must do the best we can."

He seemed unreconciled.

Denys said: "But I don't understand. I mean, of course I wouldn't expect to understand it as you do, but ... well, you *did* do all that. I mean we studied 1914 in school—the guns of August and all that, the 1915 peace, the Monaco Conference. What I mean is ..." He became conscious that the Fellows had turned their attention to him. No one else spoke. "What I mean to say is that I know you solved the problem, and how you solved it, in a general way; and I don't see why it remains to be solved. I don't see why you're worried." He laughed in embarrassment, looking around at the faces that looked at him.

"You're right," said Sir Geoffrey, "that you don't understand." He said it smiling, and the others were, if not smiling, patient and not censorious. "The logic of it is orthogonal. I can present you with an even more paradoxical instance. In fact I intend to present you with it; it's the reason you're here."

"The point to remember," the woman called Huntington said (as though to the whole table, but obviously for Denys's instruction), "is that here—in the Club—nothing has yet happened except the Original Situation. All is still to do: all that we have done, all still to do."

"Precisely," said Geoffrey. "All still to do." He took from his waistcoat pocket an eyeglass, polished it with his napkin, and inserted it between cheek and eyebrow. "You had a question, in the bar. You asked *why me*, meaning, I suppose, why is it you should be nominated to this Fellowship, why you and not another."

"Yes," said Denys. He wanted to go on, list what he knew of his inadequacies, but kept silent.

"Let me, before answering your question, ask you this," said Sir Geoffrey. "Supposing that you were chosen by good and sufficient standards—supposing that a list had been gone over carefully, and your name was weighed; supposing that a sort of competitive examination has been passed by you—would you then accept the nomination?"

"I—" said Denys. All eyes were on him, yet they were not somehow expectant; they awaited an answer they knew. Denys seemed to know it, too. He swallowed. "I hope I should," he said.

"Very well," Sir Geoffrey said softly. "Very well." He took a breath. "Then I shall tell you that you have in fact been chosen by good and sufficient standards. Chosen, moreover, for a specific mission, a mission of the greatest importance; a mission on which the very existence of the Otherhood depends. No need to feel flattered; I'm sure you're a brave lad, and all that, but the criteria were not entirely your sterling qualities, whatever they should later turn out to be.

"To explain what I mean, I must further acquaint you with what the oldest, or rather earliest, of the Fellows call the Original Situation.

"You recall our conversation in Khartoum. I told you no lie then; it is the case, in that very pleasant world we talked in, that good year 1956, fourth of a happy reign, on that wide veranda overlooking a world at peace—it is the case, I say, in that world and in most possible worlds like it, that Cecil Rhodes died young, and left the entire immense fortune he had won in the Scramble for the founding of a secret society, a society dedicated to the extension of that Empire which had his entire loyalty. The then Government's extreme confusion over this bequest, their eventual forming of a society—not without some embarrassment and doubt—a society from which this present Otherhood descends; still working toward the same ends, though the British Empire is not now what Rhodes thought it to be, nor the world either in which it has its hegemony— well, one of the Fellows is working up or will work up that story, insofar as it can be told, and it is, as I say, a true one.

"But there is a situation in which it is not true. In that situation which we call Original—the spine of time from which all other possibilities fluoresce— Cecil Rhodes, it appears, changed his mind."

Sir Geoffrey paused to light a cigar. The port was passed him. A cloud of smoke issued from his mouth. "Changed his mind, you see," he said, dispersing the smoke with a wave. "He did not die young, he lived on. His character mellowed, perhaps, as the years fell away; his fortune certainly diminished. It may be that Africa disappointed him, finally; his scheme to take over Tanganyika and join the Cape-to-Cairo with a single All-Red railroad line had ended in failure . . ."

Denys opened his mouth to speak; he had only a week before taken that line. He shut his mouth again.

"Whatever it was," Sir Geoffrey said, "he changed his mind. His last will left his fortune—what was left of it—to his old university, a scholarship fund to allow Americans and others of good character to study in England. No secret society. No Otherhood."

There was a deep silence at the table. No one had altered his casual position, yet there was a stillness of utter attention. Someone poured for Denys, and the liquid rattle of port into his glass was loud.

"Thus the paradox," Sir Geoffrey said. "For it is only the persuasions of the Otherhood that alter this Original Situation. The Otherhood must reach its fingers into the past, once we have learned how to do so; we must send our agents down along the defiles of time and intercept our own grandfather there, at the very moment when he is about to turn away from the work of generating us.

"And persuade him not to, you see; cause him—cause him not to turn away from that work of generation. Yes, cause him not to turn away. And thus ensure our own eventual existence."

Sir Geoffrey pushed back his chair and rose. He turned toward the sideboard, then back again to Denys. "Did I hear you say 'That's madness'?" he asked.

"No," Denys said.

"Oh," Sir Geoffrey said. "I thought you spoke. Or thought I remembered you speaking." He turned again to the sideboard, and returned again to the table with his cigar clenched in his teeth and a small box in his hands. He put this on the table. "You do follow me thus far," he said, his hands on the box and his eyes regarding Denys from under their curling brows.

"Follow you?"

"The man had to die," Sir Geoffrey said. He unlatched the box. "It was his moment. The moment you will find in any biography of him you pick up. Young, or anyway not old; at the height of his triumphs. It would have been downhill for him from there anyway."

"How," Denys asked, and something in his throat intruded on the question; it was a moment before he could complete it: "How did he die?"

"Oh, various ways," Sir Geoffrey said. "In the most useful version, he was shot to death by a young man he'd invited up to his house at Cape Town. Shot twice, in the heart, with a Webley .38-caliber revolver." He took from the box this weapon, and placed it with its handle toward Denys.

"That's madness," Denys said. His hands lay along the arms of his chair, drawing back from the gun. "You can't mean to say you went back and *shot* him, you . . ."

"Not we, dear boy," Sir Geoffrey said. "We, generally, yes; but specifically, not we. You."

"No."

"Oh, you won't be alone—not initially, at least. I can explain why it must be you and not another; I can expound the really quite dreadful paradox of it further, if you think it would help, though it seems to me best if, for now, you simply take our word for it."

Denys felt the corners of his mouth draw down, involuntarily, tightly; his lower lip wanted to tremble. It was a sign he remembered from early childhood: what had usually followed it was a fit of truculent weeping. That could not follow, here, now: and yet he dared not allow himself to speak, for fear he would be unable. For some time, then, no one spoke.

At the head of the table Huntington pushed her empty glass away.

"Mr. Winterset," she said gently. "I wonder if I might put in a word. Sit down, Davenant, will you, just for a moment, and stop looming over us. With your permission, Mr. Winterset—Denys—I should like to describe to you a little more broadly that condition of the world we call the Original Situation."

She regarded Denys with her sad eyes, then closed her fingers together before her. She began to speak, in a low voice which more than once Denys had to lean forward to catch. She told about Rhodes's last sad bad days; she told of Rhodes's chum, the despicable Dr. Jameson, and his infamous raid and the provocations that led to war with the Boers; of the shame of that war, the British defeats and the British atrocities, the brutal intransigence of both sides. She told how in those same years the European powers who confronted each other in Africa were also at work stockpiling arms and building mechanized armies of a size unheard of in the history of the world, to be finally let loose upon one another in August of 1914, unprepared for what was to become of them; armies officered by men who still lived in the previous century, but armed with weapons more dreadful than they could imagine. The machine gun: no one seemed to understand that the machine gun had changed war forever, and though the junior officers and Other Ranks soon learned it, the commanders never did. At the First Battle of the Somme wave after wave of British soldiers were sent against German machine guns, to be mown down like grain. There were a quarter of a million casualties in that battle. And yet the generals went on ordering massed attacks against machine guns for the four long years of the war.

"But they knew," Denys could not help saying. "They did know. Machine guns had been used against massed native armies for years, all over the Empire. In Afghanistan. In the Sudan. Africa. They knew."

"Yes," Huntington said. "They knew. And yet, in the Original Situation, they paid no attention. They went blindly on and made their dreadful mistakes. Why? How could they be so stupid, those generals and statesmen who in the world you knew behaved so wisely and so well? For one reason only: they lacked the help and knowledge of a group of men and women who had seen all those mistakes made, who could act in secret on what they knew, and who had the ear and the confidence of one of the governments—not the least stupid of them, either, mind you. And with all our help it was still a close-run thing."

"Damned close-run," Platt put in. "Still hangs in the balance, in fact."

"Let me go on," Huntington said.

She went on: long hands folded before her, eyes now cast down, she told how at the end a million men, a whole generation, lay dead on the European battle-field, among them men whom Denys might think the modern world could not have been made without. A grotesque tyranny calling itself Socialist had been imposed on a war-weakened Russian empire. Only the intervention of a fully mobilized United States had finally broken the awful deadlock—thereby altering the further history of the world unrecognizably. She told how the vindictive settlement inflicted on a ruined Germany (so unlike the wise dispositions of the Monaco Conference, which had simply reestablished the old pre-Bismarck patch-work of German states and princedoms) had rankled in the German spirit; how a madman had arisen and, almost unbelievably, had ridden a wave of resentment and anti-Jewish hysteria to dictatorship.

"Yes," Denys said. "*That* we didn't escape, did we? I remember that, or almost remember it; it was just before I can remember anything. Anti-Jewish riots all over Germany."

"Yes," said Huntington softly.

"Yes. Terrible. These nice funny Germans, all lederhosen and cuckoo clocks, and suddenly they show a terrible dark side. Thousands of Jews, some of them very highly placed, had to leave Germany. They lost everything. Synagogues attacked, professors fired. Even Einstein, I think, had to leave Germany for a time."

Huntington let him speak. When Denys fell silent, unable to remember more and feeling the eyes of the Fellows on him, Huntington began again. But the things she began to tell of now simply could not have happened, Denys thought; no, they were part of a monstrous, foul dream, atrocities on a scale only a psychopath could conceive, and only the total resources of a strong and perverted science achieve. When Einstein came again into the tale, and the world Huntington described drifted ignorantly and inexorably into an icy and permanent stalemate that could be broken only by the end of civilization, perhaps of life itself, Denys found a loathsome surfeit rising in his throat; he covered his face, he would hear no more.

"So you see," Huntington said, "why we think it possible that the life—nearly over, in any case—of one egotistical, racialist adventurer is worth the chance to alter that situation." She raised her eyes to Denys. "I don't say you need agree.

There *is* a sticky moral question, and I don't mean to brush it aside. I only say you see how we might think so."

Denys nodded slowly. He reached out and put his hand on the pistol that had been placed before him. He lifted his eyes and met those of Sir Geoffrey Davenant, which still smiled, though his mouth and his mustaches were grave.

What they were all telling him was that he could help create a better world than the original, which Huntington had described; but that was not how Denys perceived it. What Denys perceived was that reality—reality, the world he had come from, reality sun-shot and whole—was somehow under threat from a disgusting nightmare of death, ignorance, and torture, which could invade and replace it forever unless he acted. He did not think himself capable of interfering with the world to make it better; but to defend the world he knew, the world that with all its shortcomings was life and sustenance and sense and cleanly wakefulness—yes, that he could do. Would do, with all his strength.

Which is why, of course, it was he who had been chosen to do it. He saw that in Davenant's eyes.

And of course, if he refused, he could not then be brought here to be asked. If it was now possible for him to be asked to do this by the Otherhood, then he must have already consented, and done it. That, too, was in Davenant's silence. Denys looked down. His hand was on the Webley; and beside it, carved by a penknife into the surface of the table, almost obscured by later waxings, were the neat initials *D.W.*

"I always remember what Lord Milner said," Platt spoke into his ear. *"Everyone can help."*

V: THE TEARS OF THE PRESIDENT *PRO TEM*

"I remember," the President *pro tem* of the Otherhood said, "the light: a very clear, very pure, very cool light that seemed somehow potent but reserved, as though it could do terrible blinding things, and give an unbearable heat, if it chose—well, I'm not quite sure what I mean."

There was a midnight fug in the air of the library where the President *pro tem* retold his tale. The Magus to whom he told it did not look at him; his pale gray eyes moved from object to object around the room in the aimless idiot wandering that had at first caused the President *pro tem* to believe him blind.

"The mountain was called Table Mountain—a sort of high mesa. What a place that was then—I think the most beautiful in the Empire, and young then, but not raw; a peninsula simply made to put a city on, and a city being put there, beneath the mountain: and this piercing light.

"Our party put up at the Mount Nelson Hotel, perhaps a little grand for the travelers in electroplating equipment we were pretending to be, but the incognito wasn't really important, it was chiefly to explain the presence of the Last equipment among the luggage.

"A few days were spent in reconnaissance. But you see—this is continually the impossible thing to explain—in a sense those of the party who knew the outcome were only going through the motions of conferring, mapping their victim's movements, choosing a suitable moment and all that: for they knew the story; there was only one way for it to happen, if it was to happen at all. If it was *not* to happen, then no one could predict what was to happen instead; but so long as our party was there, and preparing it, it would evidently have to happen—or would have to have had to have happened."

The President *pro tem* suddenly missed his old friend Davenant, Davenant the witty and deep, who never bumbled over his tenses, never got himself stuck in a sentence such as that one; Davenant lost now with the others in the interstices of imaginary pasthood—or rather about to be lost, in the near future, if the President *pro tem* assented to what was asked of him. "It was rather jolly," he said, "like a game rather, striving to bring about a result that you were sure had already been brought about; an old ritual, if you like, to which not much importance needed to be attached, so long as it was all done correctly . . ."

"I think," said the Magus, "you need not explain these feelings that you then had."

"Sorry," said the President *pro tem*. "The house was called Groote Schuur—that was the old Dutch name, which he'd revived, for a big granary that had stood on the property; the English had called it the Grange. It was built on the lower slopes of Devil's Peak, with a view up to the mountains, and out to sea as well. He'd only recently seen the need for a house—all his life in Africa he'd more or less pigged it in rented rooms, or stayed in his club or a hotel or even a tent pitched outside town. For a long time he roomed with Dr. Jameson, sleeping on a little truckle bed hardly big enough for his body. But now that he'd become Prime Minister, he felt it was time for something more substantial.

"It seemed to me that it would have been easier to take him out in the bush—the *bundas*; as the Matabele say. Hire a party of natives—wait till all are asleep—ambush. He often went out into the wilds with almost no protection. There was no question of honor involved—I mean, the man had to die, one way or the other, and the more explainably or accidentally the better. But I was quite wrong—I was myself, still young—and had to be put right: the one time that way was tried, the assassination initiated a punitive war against the native populations that lasted for twenty years, which ended only with the virtual extermination of the Matabele and Mashona peoples. Dreadful.

"No, it had to be the house; moreover, it had to be within a very brief span of time—a time when we knew he was there, when we knew where his will was, and *which* will it was—he made eight or nine in his lifetime—and when we knew, also, what assets were in his hands. Business and ownership were fluid things in those days; his partners were quick and subtle men; his sudden death might lose us all that we were intending to acquire by it in the way of a campaign chest, so to speak.

"So it had to be the house, in this week of this year, on this night. In fact orthogonal logic dictated it. Davenant was quite calmly sure of that. After all, that was the night when it had happened: and for sure we ought not to miss it."

That was an attempt at the sort of remark Davenant might make, and the President *pro tem* smiled at the Magus, who remained unmoved. The President *pro tem* thought it impossible that beings as wise as he knew the one before him to be, no matter how grave, could altogether lack any sense of humor. For himself, he had often thought that if he did not find funny the iron laws of orthogony he would go mad; but his jokes apparently amused only himself.

"It was not a question of getting to his house, or into it; he practically kept open house the year round, and his grounds could be walked upon by anyone. The gatekeepers were only instructed to warn walkers about the animals they might come across—he had brought in dozens of species, and he allowed all but the genuinely dangerous to roam at will. Wildebeest. Zebras. Impala. And 'human beings,' as he always called them, roamed at will, too; there were always some about. At dinner he had visitors from all over Africa, and from England and Europe as well; his bedrooms were often full. I think he hated to be alone. All of which provided a fine setting, you see, for a sensational—and insoluble— murder mystery: if only the man could be got alone, and escape made good then through these crowds of hangers-on.

"Our plan depended on a known proclivity of his, or rather two proclivities. The first was a taste he had for the company of a certain sort of a young man. He liked having them around him and could become very attached to them. There was never a breath of scandal in this—well, there was talk, but only talk. His 'angels,' people called them: good-looking, resourceful if not particularly bright, good all-rounders with a rough sense of fun—practical jokes, horseplay— but completely devoted and ready for anything he might ask them to do. He had a fair crowd of these fellows up at Groote Schuur just then. Harry Curry, his private secretary. Johnny Grimmer, a trooper who was never afraid to give him orders—like a madman's keeper, some people said, scolding him and brushing dust from his shoulders; he never objected. Bob Coryndon, another trooper. They'd all just taken on a butler for themselves, a sergeant in the Inniskillings: good-looking chap, twenty-three years old. Oddly, they had all been just that age when he'd taken an interest in them: twenty-three. Whether that was chance or his conscious choice we didn't know.

"The other proclivity was his quickness in decision-making. And this often involved the young men. The first expedition into Matabeleland had been headed up by a chap he'd met at his club one morning at breakfast just as the column was preparing for departure. Took to the chap instantly: liked his looks, liked his address. Gave him the job on the spot.

"That had worked out very well, of course—his choices often did. The pioneer column had penetrated into the heart of the *bundas*, the flag was flying over a settlement they called Fort Salisbury, and the whole of Matabeleland was in the process of being added to the Empire. Up at Groote Schuur they were kicking around possible names for the new country: Rhodia, perhaps, or Rhodesland, even Cecilia. It was that night that they settled on Rhodesia."

The President *pro tem* felt a moment's shame. There had been, when it came down to it, no doubt in his mind that what they had done had been the right thing to do: and in any case it had all happened a long time ago, more than a century ago in fact. It was not what was done, or that it had been done, only the moment of its doing, that was hard to relate: it was the picture in his mind, of an old man (though he was only forty-eight, he looked far older) sitting in the lamplight reading *The Boy's Own Paper*, as absorbed and as innocent in his absorption as a boy himself; and the vulnerable shine on his balding crown; and the tender and indifferent night: it was all that which raised a lump in the throat of the President *pro tem* and caused him to pause, and roll the tip of his cigar in the ashtray, and clear his throat before continuing.

"And so," he said, "we baited our hook. Rhodes's British South Africa Company was expanding, in the wake of the Fort Salisbury success. He was on the lookout for young men of the right sort. We presented him with one: good-

looking lad, public school, cricketer; just twenty-three years old. He was the bait.
The mole. The Judas."

And the bait had been taken, of course. The arrangement's having been keyed
so nicely to the man's nature, a nature able to be studied from the vantage point
of several decades on, it could hardly have failed. That the trick seemed so
fragile, even foolish, something itself out of *The Boy's Own Paper* or a story by
Henley, only increased the likelihood of its striking just the right note here: the
colored fanatic, Rhodes leaving his hotel after luncheon to return to Parliament,
the thug stepping out of the black noon shadows with a knife just as Rhodes
mounts his carriage steps—then the young man, handily by with a stout walking
stick (a gift of his father upon his departure for Africa)—the knife deflected,
the would-be assassin slinking off, the great man's gratitude. You must have
some reward. Not a bit, sir, anyone would have done the same; just lucky I was
nearby. Come to dinner at any rate—my house on the hill—anyone can direct
you. Allow me to introduce myself; my name is . . .

No need, sir, everyone knows Cecil Rhodes.

And your name is . . .

The clean hand put frankly forward, the tanned, open, boyish face smiling.
My name is Denys Winterset.

"So then you see," the President *pro tem* said, "the road was open. The road
up to Groote Schuur. The road that branches, in effect, to lead here: to us here
now speaking of it."

"And how many times since then," the Magus said, "has the world branched?
How many times has it been bent double, and broken? A thousand times, ten
thousand? Each time growing smaller, having to be packed into lesser space,
curling into itself like a snail's shell; growing ever weaker as the changes multiply,
and more liable to failure of its fabric: how many times?"

The President *pro tem* answered nothing.

"You understand, then," the Magus said to him, "what you will be asked: to
find the crossroads that leads this way and to turn the world from it."

"Yes."

"And how will you reply?"

The President *pro tem* had no better answer for this question, and he gave
none. He had begun to feel at once heavy as lead and disembodied. He arose
from his armchair, with some effort, and crossed the worn Turkish carpet to the
tall window.

"You must leave my house now," the Magus said, rising from his chair. "There
is much for me to do this night, if this world is to pass out of existence."

"Where shall I go?"

"They will find you. I think in not too long a time." Without looking back
he left the room.

The President *pro tem* pushed aside the heavy drape the draconic had drawn.
Where shall I go? He looked out the window into the square outside, deserted
at this late and rainy hour. It was an irregular square, the intersection of three
streets, filled with rain-wet cobbles as though with shiny eggs. It was old; it had
been the view out these windows for two centuries at the least; there was nothing
about it to suggest that it had not been the intersection of three streets for a
good many more centuries than that.

And yet it had not been there at all only a few decades earlier, when the
President *pro tem* had last walked the city outside the Orient Aid Society. Then
the city had been London; it was no more. These three streets, these cobbles,

had not been there in 1983; nor in 1893 either. Yet there they were, somewhere early in the twenty-first century; there they had been, too, for time out of mind, familiar no doubt to any dweller in this part of town, familiar for that matter to the President *pro tem* who looked out at them. In each of two lamp-lit cafés on two corners of the square, a man in a soft cap held a glass and looked out into the night, unsurprised, at home.

Someone had broken the rules: there simply was no other explanation.

There had been, of course, no way for anyone, not Deng Fa-shen, not Davenant, not the President *pro tem* himself, to guess what the President *pro tem* might come upon on this, the first expedition the Otherhood was making into the future: not only did the future not exist (Deng Fa-shen was quite clear about that), but, as Davenant reminded him, the Otherhood itself, supposing the continued existence of the Otherhood, would no doubt go busily on changing things in the past far and near—shifting the ground therefore of the future the President *pro tem* was headed for. Deng Fa-shen was satisfied that that future, the ultimate future, sum of all intermediate revisions, was the only one that could be plumbed, if any could; and that was the only one the Otherhood would want to glimpse: to learn how they would do, or would come to have done; to find out, as George V whispered on his death-bed, "How is the Empire."

("Only that isn't what he said," Davenant was fond of telling. "That's what he was, understandably, reported to have said, and what the Queen and the nurses convinced themselves they heard. But he was a bit dazed there at the end, poor good old man. What he said was not 'How is the Empire,' but 'What's at the Empire,' a popular cinema. I happened," he always added gravely, "to have been with him.")

The first question had been how far "forward" the Otherhood should press; those members who thought the whole scheme insane, as Platt did, voted for next Wednesday, and bring back the Derby winners please. Deng Fa-shen was not certain the thrust could be entirely calculated: the imaginary futures of imaginary pasts were not, he thought, likely to be under the control of even the most penetrating orthogonal engineering. Sometime in the first decades of the next century was at length agreed upon, a time just beyond the voyager's own mortal span—for the house rule seemed, no one could say quite why, to apply in both directions—and for as brief a stay as was consistent with learning what was up.

The second question—who was to be the voyager—the President *pro tem* had answered by fiat, assuming an executive privilege he just at that moment claimed to exist, and cutting off further debate. (Why exactly did he insist? I'm not certain why, except that it was not out of a sense of adventure, or of fun or curiosity: whatever of those qualities he may once have had had been much worn away in his rise to the Presidency *pro tem* of the Otherhood. A sense of duty may have been part of it. It may have been to forestall the others, out of a funny sort of premonition. Duty, and premonition: of what, though? Of what?)

"It'll be quite different from any of our imaginings, you know," Davenant said, who for some reason had not vigorously contested the President's decision. "The future of all possible pasts. I envy you, I do. I should rather like to see it for myself."

Quite different from any of our imaginings: very well. The President *pro tem* had braced himself for strangeness. What he had not expected was familiarity. Familiarity—cozy as an old shoe—was certainly different from his imaginings.

And yet what was it he was familiar with? He had stepped out of his club in London and found himself to be, not in the empty corridors of the Orient Aid Society that he knew well, but in private quarters of some kind that he had never seen before. It reminded him, piercingly, of a place he did know, but what place he could not have said: some don's rich but musty rooms, some wealthy and learned bachelor's digs. How had it come to be?

And how had it come to be lit by gas?

One of the pleasant side effects (most of the members thought it pleasant) of the Otherhood's endless efforts in the world had been a general retardation in the rate of material progress: so much of that progress had been, on the one hand, the product of the disastrous wars that it was the Otherhood's chief study to prevent, and on the other hand, American. The British Empire moved more slowly, a great beast without predators, and naturally conservative; it clung to proven techniques and could impose them on the rest of the world by its weight. The telephone, the motor car, the flying boat, the wireless, all were slow to take root in the Empire that the Otherhood shaped. And yet surely, the President *pro tem* thought, electricity was in general use in London in 1893, before which date no member could alter the course of things. And gas lamps lit this place.

Pondering this, the President *pro tem* had entered the somber and apparently little-used dining room and seen the draconic standing in the little butler's pantry: silent as a statue (asleep, the President *pro tem* would later deduce, with lidless eyes only seeming to be open); a polishing-cloth in his claw, and the silver before him; his heavy jaws partly open, and his weight balanced on the thick stub of tail. He wore a baize apron and black sleeve garters to protect his clothes.

Quite different from our imaginings: and yet no conceivable amount of tinkering with the twentieth century, just beyond which the President *pro tem* theoretically stood, could have brought forth this butler, in wing collar and green apron, the soft gaslight ashine on his bald brown head.

So someone had broken the rules. Someone had dared to regress beyond 1893 and meddle in the farther past. That was not, in itself, impossible; Caspar Last had done it on his first and only excursion. It had only been thought impossible for the Otherhood to do it, because it would have taken them "back" before the Otherhood's putative existence, and therefore before the Otherhood could have wrested the techniques of such travel from Last's jealous grip, a power they acquired by already having it—that was what the President *pro tem* had firmly believed.

But it was not, apparently, so. Somewhen in that stretch of years that fell between his entrance into the telephone box of the Club and his exit from it into this familiar and impossible world, someone—many someones, or someone many times—had gone "back" far before Rhodes's death: had gone back far enough to initiate this house, this city, these races who were not men.

A million years? It couldn't have been less. It didn't seem possible it could be less.

And who, then? Deng Fa-shen, the delicate, brilliant Chinaman, who had thoughts and purposes he kept to himself; the only one of them who might have been able to overcome the theoretical limits? Or Platt, who was never satisfied with what was possible within what he called "the damned parameters"?

Or Davenant. Davenant, who was forever quoting Khayyám: *Ah, Love, couldst*

*thou and I with Him conspire To take this sorry scheme of things entire; Would
we not smash it into pieces, then Remold it nearer to the heart's desire . . .*

"There is," said the Magus behind him, "one other you have not thought of."

The President *pro tem* let fall the drape and turned from the window. The
Magus stood in the doorway, a great ledger in his arms. His eyes did not meet
the President *pro tem*'s, and yet seemed to regard him anyway, like the blind
eyes of a statue.

One other . . . Yes, the President *pro tem* saw, there *was* one other who might
have done this. One other, not so good at the work perhaps as others, as Davenant for example, but who nonetheless would have been, or would come to
have been, in a position to take such steps. The President *pro tem* would not
have credited himself with the skill, or the nerve, or the dreadnought power. But
how else to account for the familiarity, the bottomless *suitability* to him of this
world he had never before seen?

"Between the time of your people's decision to plumb our world," said the
Magus, "and the time of your standing here within it, you must yourself have
brought it into being. I see no likelier explanation."

The President *pro tem* stood still with wonder at the efforts he was apparently
to prove capable of making. A million years at least: a million years. How had
he known where to begin? Where had he found, would he find, the time?

"Shall I ring," the Magus said, "or will you let yourself out?"

Deng Fa-shen had always said it, and anyone who traveled in them knew it to
be so: the imaginary futures and imaginary pasts of orthogony are imaginary only
in the sense that imaginary numbers (which they very much resemble) are imaginary. To a man walking within one, it alone is real, no matter how strange; it
is all the others, standing at angles to it, which exist only in imagination. Night-
long the President *pro tem* walked the city, with a measured and unhurried step,
but with a constant tremor winding round his rib cage, waiting for what would
become of him, and observing the world he had made.

Of course it could not continue to exist. It should not ever have come into
existence in the first place; his own sin (if it had been his) had summoned it
out of nonbeing, and his repentance must expunge it. The Magus who had taken
his confession (which the President *pro tem* had been unable to withhold from
him) had drawn that conclusion: it must be put out, like a light. And yet how
deeply the President *pro tem* wanted it to last forever; how deeply he believed
it *ought* to last forever.

The numinous and inhuman angels, about whom nothing could be said, beings with no ascertainable business among the lesser races and yet beings without whom, the President *pro tem* was sure, this world could not go on
functioning. They lived (endless?) lives unimaginable to men, and perhaps to
Magi, too, who yet sought continually for knowledge of them: Magi, highest of
the hominids, gentle and wise yet inflexible of purpose, living in simplicity and
solitude (Were there females? Where? Doing what?) and yet from their shabby
studies influencing, perhaps directing, the lives of mere men. The men, such as
himself, clever and busy, with their inventions and their politics and their affairs. The lesser hominids, strong, sweet-natured, comic, like placid trolls. The
draconics.

It was not simply a world inhabited by intelligent races of different kinds: it
was a harder thing to grasp than that. The lives of the races constituted different

universes of meaning, different constructions of reality; it was as though four or five different novels, novels of different kinds by different and differently limited writers, were to become interpenetrated and conflated: inside a gigantic Russian thing a stark and violent *policier*, and inside that something Dickensian, full of plot, humors, and eccentricity. Such an interlacing of mutually exclusive universes might be comical, like a sketch in *Punch*; it might be tragic, too. And it might be neither: it might simply be what is, the given against which all airy imaginings must finally be measured: reality.

Near dawn the President *pro tem* stood leaning on a parapet of worked stone that overlooked a streetcar roundabout. A car had just ended its journey there, and the conductor and the motorman descended, squat hominids in great-coats and peaked caps. With their long strong arms they began to swing the car around for its return journey. The President *pro tem* gazed down at this commonplace sight; his nose seemed to know the smell of that car's interior, his bottom to know the feel of its polished seats. But he knew also that yesterday there had not been streetcars in this city. Today they had been here for decades.

No, it was no good, the President *pro tem* knew: the fabric of this world he had made—if it had been he—was fatally weakened with irreality. It was a botched job: as though he were that god of the Gnostics who made the material world, a minor god unversed in putting time together with space. He had not worked well. And how could he have supposed it would be otherwise? What had got into him, that he had dared?

"No," said the angel who stood beside him. "You should not think that it was you."

"If not me," said the President *pro tem*, "then who?"

"Come," said the angel. She (I shall say "she") slipped a small cool hand within his hand. "Let's go over the tracks, and into the trees beyond that gate."

A hard and painful stone had formed in the throat of the President *pro tem*. The angel beside him led him like a daughter, like the daughter of old blind Oedipus. Within the precincts of the park—which apparently had its entrance or its entrances where the angels needed them to be—he was led down an avenue of yew and dim towers of poplar toward the piled and sounding waters of a fountain. They sat together on the fountain's marble lip.

"The Magus told me," the President *pro tem* began, "that you can feel the alterations that we make, back then. Is that true?"

"It's like the snap of a whip infinitely long," the angel said. "The whole length of time snapped and laid out differently: not only the length of time backward to the time of the change, but the length of the future forward. We felt ourselves come into being, oldest of the Old Races (though the last your changes brought into existence); we saw in that moment the aeons of our past, and we guessed our future, too."

The President *pro tem* took out his pocket handkerchief and pressed it to his face. He must weep, yet no tears came.

"We love this world—this only world—just as you do," she said. "We love it, and we cannot bear to feel it sicken and fail. Better that it not have been than that it die."

"I shall do all I can," said the President *pro tem*. "I shall find who has done this—I suppose I know who it was, if it wasn't me—and dissuade him. Teach him, teach him what I've learned, make him see . . ."

"You don't yet understand," the angel said with careful kindness but at the same time glancing at her wristwatch. "There is no one to tell. There is no one who went beyond the rules."

"There must have been," said the President *pro tem*. "You, your time, it just isn't that far along from ours, from mine! To make this world, this city, these races . . ."

"Not far along in time," said the angel, "but many times removed. You know it to be so: whenever you, your Otherhood, set out across the timelines, your passage generated random variation in the worlds you arrived in. Perhaps you didn't understand how those variations accumulate, here at the sum end of your journeyings."

"But the changes were so minute!" said the President *pro tem*. "Deng Fa-shen explained it. A molecule here and there, no more; the position of a distant star; some trivial thing, the name of a flower or a village. Too few, too small even to notice."

"They increase exponentially with every alteration—and your Otherhood has been busy since you last presided over them. Through the days random changes accumulate, tiny errors silting up like the blown sand that fills the streets of a desert city, that buries it at last."

"But why these changes?" asked the President *pro tem* desperately. "It can't have been chance that a world like this was the sum of those histories, it can't be. A world like *this* . . . "

"Chance, perhaps. Or it may be that as time grows softer the world grows more malleable by wishes. There is no reason to believe this, yet that is what we believe. You—all of you—could not have known that you were bringing this world into being; and yet this is the world you wanted."

She reached out to let the tossed foam of the fountain fall into her hand. The President *pro tem* thought of the bridge over the Zambezi, far away; the tossed foam of the Falls. It was true: this is what they had striven for: a world of perfect hierarchies, of no change forever. God, how they must have longed for it! The loneliness of continual change—no outback, no *bundas* so lonely. He had heard how men can be unsettled for days, for weeks, who have lived through earthquakes and felt the earth to be uncertain: what of his Fellows, who had felt time and space picked apart, never to be rewoven that way again, and not once but a hundred times? What of himself?

"I shall tell you what I see at the end of all your wishings," said the angel softly. "At the far end of the last changed world, after there is nothing left that can change. There is then only a forest, growing in the sea. I say 'forest' and I say 'sea,' though whether they are of the kind I know, or some other sort of thing, I cannot say. The sea is still and the forest is thick; it grows upward from the black bottom, and its topmost branches reach into the sunlight, which penetrates a little into the warm upper waters. That's all. There is nothing else anywhere forever. Your wishes have come true: the Empire is quiet. There is not, nor will there be, change anymore; never will one thing be confused again with another; higher for lower, better for lesser, master for servant. Perpetual Peace."

The President *pro tem* was weeping now, painful sobs drawn up from an interior he had long kept shut and bolted. Tears ran down his cheeks, into the corners of his mouth, under his hard collar. He knew what he must do, but not how to do it.

"The Otherhood cannot be dissuaded from this," the angel said, putting a hand on the wrist of the President *pro tem.* "For all of it, including our sitting here now, all of it—and the forest in the sea—is implicit in the very creation of the Otherhood itself."

"But then . . ."

"Then the Otherhood must be uncreated."

"I can't do that."

"You must."

"No, no, I can't." He had withdrawn from her pellucid gaze, horrified. "I mean it isn't because . . . if it must be done, it must be. But not by me."

"Why?"

"It would be against the rules given me. I don't know what the result would be. I can't imagine. I don't *want* to imagine."

"Rules?"

"The Otherhood came into being," said the President *pro tem*, "when a British adventurer, Cecil Rhodes, was shot and killed by a young man called Denys Winterset."

"Then you must return and stop that killing."

"But you don't see!" said the President *pro tem* in great distress. "The rules given the Otherhood forbid a Fellow from returning to a time and place that he formerly altered by his presence . . ."

"And . . ."

"And I am myself that same Denys Winterset."

The angel regarded the President *pro tem*—the Honorable Denys Winterset, fourteenth President *pro tem* of the Otherhood—and her translucent face registered a sweet surprise, as though the learning of something she had not known gave her pleasure. She laughed, and her laughter was not different from the plashing of the fountain by which they sat. She laughed and laughed, as the old man in his black coat and hat sat silent beside her, bewildered and afraid.

VI: THE BOY DAVID OF HYDE PARK CORNER

There are days when I seem genuinely to remember, and days when I do not remember at all: days when I remember only that sometimes I remember. There are days on which I think I recognize another like myself: someone walking smartly along the Strand or Bond Street, holding the *Times* under one arm and walking a furled umbrella with the other—a sort of military bearing, mustaches white (older than when I seem to have known him, but then so am I, of course), and cheeks permanently tanned by some faraway sun. I do not catch his eye, nor he mine, though I am tempted to stop him, to ask him . . . Later on I wonder—if I can remember to wonder—whether he, too, is making a chronicle, in his evenings, writing up the story: a story that can be told in any direction, starting from anywhere, leading on to a forest in the sea.

I won't look any longer into this chronicle I've compiled. I shall only complete it.

My name is Denys Winterset. I was born in London in 1933; I was the only son of a Harley Street physician, and my earliest memory is of coming upon my father in tears in his surgery: he had just heard the news that the R101 dirigible had crashed on its maiden flight, killing all those aboard.

We lived then above my father's offices, in a little building whose nursery I remember distinctly, though I was taken to the country with the other children of London when I was only six, and that building was knocked down by a bomb in 1940. A falling wall killed my mother; my father was on ambulance duty in the East End and was spared.

He didn't know quite what to do with me, nor I with myself; I have been torn all my life between the drive to discover what others whom I love and admire expect of me, and my discovery that then I don't want to do it, really. After coming down from the University I decided, out of a certain perversity which my father could not sympathize with, to join the Colonial Service. He could not fathom why I would want to fasten myself to an enterprise that everyone save a few antediluvian colonels and letter writers to the *Times* could see was a dead animal. And I couldn't explain. Psychoanalysis later suggested that it was quite simply because no one wanted me to do it. The explanation has since come to seem insufficient to me.

That was a strange late blooming of Empire in the decade after the war, when the Colonial Office took on factitious new life, and thousands of us went out to the Colonies. The Service became larger than it had been in years, swollen with ex-officers too accustomed to military life to do anything else, and with the innocent and the confused, like myself. I ended up a junior member of a transition team in a Central African country I shall not name, helping see to it that as much was given to the new native government as they could be persuaded to accept, in the way of a parliament, a well-disciplined army, a foreign service, a judiciary.

It was not after all very much. Those institutions that the British are sure no civilized nation can do without were, in the minds of many Africans who spoke freely to me, very like those exquisite japanned toffee-boxes from Fortnum & Mason that you used often to come across in native kraals, because the chieftains and shamans loved them so, to keep their juju in. Almost as soon as I arrived, it became evident that the commander in chief of the armed forces was impatient with the pace of things, and felt the need of no special transition to African, i.e., his own, control of the state. The most our Commission were likely to accomplish was to get the British population out without a bloodbath.

Even that would not be easy. We—we young men—were saddled with the duty of explaining to aged planters that there was no one left to defend their estates against confiscation, and that under the new constitution they hadn't a leg to stand on, and that despite how dearly their overseers and house people loved them, they ought to begin seeing what they could pack into a few small trunks. On the other hand, we were to calm the fears of merchants and diamond factors, and tell them that if they all simply dashed for it, they could easily precipitate a closing of the frontiers, with incalculable results.

There came a night when, more than usually certain that not a single Brit under my care would leave the country alive, nor deserved to either, I stood at the bar of the Planters' (just renamed the Republic) Club, drinking gin and Italian (tonic hadn't been reordered in weeks) and listening to the clacking of the fans. A fellow I knew slightly as a regular here saluted me; I nodded and returned to my thoughts. A moment later I found him next to me.

"I wonder," he said, "if I might have your ear for a moment."

The expression, in his mouth, was richly comic, or perhaps it was my exhaustion. He waited for my laughter to subside before speaking. He was called

Rossie, and he'd spent a good many years in Africa, doing whatever came to hand. He was one of those Englishmen whom the sun turns not brown but only gray and greasy; his eyes were always watery, the cups of his lids red and painful to look at.

"I am," he said at last, "doing a favor for a chap who would like your help."

"I'll do what I can," I said.

"This is a chap," he said, "who has been too long in this country, and would like to leave it."

"There are many in his situation."

"Not quite."

"What is his name?" I said, taking out a memorandum book. "I'll pass it on to the Commission."

"Just the point," Rossie said. He drew closer to me. At the other end of the bar loud laughter arose from a group consisting of a newly commissioned field marshal—an immense, glossy, nearly blue-black man—and his two colonels, both British, both small and lean. They laughed when the field marshal laughed, though their laugh was not so loud, nor their teeth so large and white.

"He'll want to tell you his name himself," Rossie said. "I've only brought the message. He wants to see you, to talk to you. I said I'd tell you. That's all."

"To tell us . . ."

"Not you, all of you. *You:* you."

I drank. The warm, scented liquor was thick in my throat. "Me?"

"What he asked me to ask you," Rossie said, growing impatient, "was would you come out to his place, and see him. It isn't far. He wanted you, no one else. He said I was to insist. He said you were to come alone. He'll send a boy of his. He said tell no one."

There were many reasons why a man might want to do business with the Commission privately. I could think of none why it should be done with me alone. I agreed, with a shrug. Rossie seemed immediately to put the matter out of his mind, mopped his red face, and ordered drinks for both of us. By the time they were brought we were already discussing the Imperial groundnut scheme, which was to have kept this young republic self-sufficient, but which, it was now evident, would do no such thing.

I too put what had been asked of me out of my mind, with enough success that when on a windless and baking afternoon a native boy shook me awake from a nap, I could not imagine why.

"Who are you? What are you doing in my bungalow?"

He only stared down at me, as though it were he who could not think why I should be there before him. Questions in his own language got no response either. At length he backed out the door, clearly wanting me to follow; and so I did, with the dread one feels on remembering an unpleasant task one has contrived to neglect. I found him outside, standing beside my Land-Rover, ready to get aboard.

"All right," I said. "Very well." I got into the driver's seat. "Point the way."

It was a small spread of tobacco and a few dusty cattle an hour's drive from town, a low bungalow looking beaten in the ocher heat. He gave no greeting as I alighted from the Land-Rover but stood in the shadows of the porch unmoving: as though he had stood so a long time. He went back into the house as I approached, and when I went in, he was standing against the netting of the window, the light behind him. That seemed a conscious choice. He was smiling, I could tell: a strange and eager smile.

"I've waited a long time for you," he said. "I don't mind saying."

"I came as quickly as I could," I said.

"There was no way for me to know, you see," he said, "whether you'd come at all."

"Your boy was quite insistent," I said. "And Mr. Rossie—"

"I meant: to Africa." His voice was light, soft, and dry. "There being so much less reason for it, now. I've wondered often. In fact I don't think a day has passed this year when I haven't wondered." Keeping his back to the sunward windows, he moved to sit on the edge of a creaking wicker sofa. "You'll want a drink," he said.

"No." The place was filled with the detritus of an African bachelor farmer's digs: empty paraffin tins, bottles, tools, hanks of rope and motor parts. He put a hand behind him without looking and put it on the bottle he was no doubt accustomed to find there. "I tried to think reasonably about it," he said, pouring a drink. "As time went on, and things began to sour here, I came to be more and more certain that no lad with any pluck would throw himself away down here. And yet I couldn't know. Whether there might not be some impulse, I don't know, traveling to you from—elsewhere. . . . I even thought of writing to you. Though whether to convince you to come or to dissuade you I'd no idea."

I sat, too. A cool sweat had gathered on my neck and the backs of my hands.

"Then," he said, "when I heard you'd come—well, I was afraid, frankly. I didn't know what to think." He dusted a fly from the rim of his glass, which he had not tasted. "You see," he said, "this was against the rules given me. That I—that I and—that you and I should meet."

Perhaps he's mad, I thought, and even as I thought it I felt intensely the experience called *déjà vu*, an experience I have always hated, hated like the nightmare. I steeled myself to respond coolly and took out my memorandum book and pencil. "I'm afraid you've rather lost me," I said—briskly I hoped. "Perhaps we'd better start with your name."

"Oh," he said, smiling again his mirthless smile, "not the hardest question first, please."

Without having, so far as I knew, the slightest reason for it, I began to feel intensely sorry for this odd dried jerky of a man, whose eyes alone seemed quick and shy. "All right," I said, "nationality, then. You are a British subject."

"Well, yes."

"Proof?" He answered nothing. "Passport?" No. "Army card? Birth certificate? Papers of any kind?" No. "Any connections in Britain? Relatives? Someone who could vouch for you, take you in?"

"No," he said. "None who could. None but you. It will have to be you."

"Now hold hard," I said.

"I don't know why I must," he said, rising suddenly and turning away to the window. "But I must. I must go back. I imagine dying here, being buried here, and my whole soul retreats in horror. I must go back. Even though I fear that, too."

He turned from the window, and in the sharp side light of the late afternoon his face was clearly the face of someone I knew. "Tell me," he said. "Mother and father. Your mother and father. They're alive?"

"No," I said. "Both dead."

"Very well," he said, "very well"; but it did not seem to be very well with him. "I'll tell you my story, then."

"I think you'd best do that."

"It's a long one."

"No matter." I had begun to feel myself transported, like a Sinbad, into somewhere that it were best I listen, and keep my counsel: and yet the first words of this specter's tale made that impossible.

"My name," he said, "is Denys Winterset."

I have come to believe, having had many years in which to think about it, that it must be as he said, that an impulse from somewhere else (he meant: some previous present, some earlier version of these circumstances) must press upon such a life as mine. That I chose the Colonial Service, that I came to Africa—and not just to Africa, but to that country: well, *if anything is chance, that was not*—as I understand Sir Geoffrey Davenant to have once said.

In that long afternoon, there where I perhaps could not have helped arriving eventually, I sat and perspired, listening—though it was for a long time very nearly impossible to hear what was said to me: an appointment in Khartoum some months from now, and some decades past; a club, outside all frames of reference; the Last equipment. It was quite like listening to the unfollowable logic of a madman, as meaningless as the roar of the insects outside. I only began to hear when this aged man, older than my grandfather, told me of something that he—that I—that he and I—had once done in boyhood, something secret, trivial really and yet so shameful that even now I will not write it down; something that only Denys Winterset could know.

"There now," he said, eyes cast down. "There now, you must believe me. You *will* listen. The world has not been as you thought it to be, any more than it was as I thought it to be, when I was as you are now. I shall tell you why: and we will hope that mine is the last story that need be told."

And so it was that I heard how he had gone up the road to Groote Schuur, that evening in 1893 (a young man then of course, only twenty-three), with the Webley revolver in his breast pocket as heavy as his heart, nearly sick with wonder and apprehension. The tropical suit he had been made to wear was monstrously hot, complete with full waistcoat and hard collar; the topee they insisted he use was as weighty as a crown. As he came in sight of the house, he could hear the awesome cries from the lion house, where the cats were evidently being given their dinner.

The big house appeared raw and unfinished to him, the trees yet ungrown and the great masses of scentless flowers—hydrangea, bougainvillaea, canna— that had smothered the place when last he had seen it, some decades later, just beginning to spread.

"Rhodes himself met me at the door—actually he happened to be going out for his afternoon ride—and welcomed me," he said. "I think the most striking thing about Cecil Rhodes, and it hasn't been noticed much, was his utter lack of airs. He was the least self-conscious man I have ever known; he did many things for effect, but he was himself entirely single: as whole as an egg, as the old French used to say.

" 'The house is yours,' he said to me. 'Use it as you like. We don't dress for dinner, as a rule; too many of the guests would be taken short, you see. Now some of the fellows are playing croquet in the Great Hall. Pay them no mind.'

"I remember little of that evening. I wandered the house; the great skins of animals, the heavy beams of teak, the brass chandeliers. I looked into the library, full of the specially transcribed and bound classics that Rhodes had ordered by the yard from Hatchard's: all the authorities that Gibbon had consulted in writing the *Decline and Fall*. All of them: that had been Rhodes's order.

"Dinner was a long and casual affair, entirely male—Rhodes had not even any female servants in the house. There was much toasting and hilarity about the successful march into Matabeleland, and the foundation of a fort, which news had only come that week; but Rhodes seemed quiet at the table's head, even melancholy: many of his closest comrades were gone with the expeditionary column, and he seemed to miss them. I do remember that at one point the conversation turned to America. Rhodes contended—no one disputed him— that if we (he meant the Empire, of course) had not lost America, the peace of the world could have been secured forever. 'Forever,' he said. 'Perpetual Peace.' And his pale opaque eyes were moist.

"How I comported myself at table—how I joined the talk, how I kept up conversations on topics quite unfamiliar to me—none of that do I recall. It helped that I was supposed to have been only recently arrived in Africa: though one of Rhodes's band of merry men looked suspiciously at my sun-browned hands when I said so.

"As soon as I could after dinner, I escaped from the fearsome horseplay that began to develop among those left awake. I pleaded a touch of sun and was shown to my room. I took off the hateful collar and tie (not without difficulty) and lay on the bed otherwise fully clothed, alert and horribly alone. Perhaps you can imagine my thoughts."

"No," I said. "I don't think I can."

"No. Well. No matter. I must have slept at last; it seemed to be after midnight when I opened my eyes and saw Rhodes standing in the doorway, a candlestick in his hand.

" 'Asleep?' he asked softly.

" 'No,' I answered. 'Awake.'

" 'Can't sleep either,' he said. 'Never do, much.' He ventured another step into the room. 'You ought to come out, see the sky,' he said. 'Quite spectacular. As long as you're up.'

"I rose and followed him. He was without his coat and collar; I noticed he wore carpet slippers. One button of his wide braces was undone; I had the urge to button it for him. Pale starlight fell in blocks across the black and white tiles of the hall, and the huge heads of beasts were mobile in the candlelight as we passed. I murmured something about the grandness of his house.

" 'I told my architect,' Rhodes answered. 'I said I wanted the big and simple— the barbaric, if you like.' The candle flame danced before him. 'Simple. The truth is always simple.'

"The chessboard tiles of the hall continued out through the wide doors onto the veranda—the *stoep* as the old Dutch called it. At the frontier of the *stoep* great pillars divided the night into panels filled with clustered stars, thick and near as vine blossoms. From far off came a long cry as of pain: a lion, awake.

"Rhodes leaned on the parapet, looking into the mystery of the sloping lawns beyond the *stoep*. 'That's good news, about the chaps up in Matabeleland,' he said a little wistfully.

" 'Yes.'

" 'Pray God they'll all be safe.'

" 'Yes.'

" '*Zambesia*,' he said after a moment. "What d'you think of that?'

" 'I beg your pardon?'

" 'As a name. For this country we'll be building. *Beyond the Zambesi*, you see.'

" 'It's a fine name.'

"He fell silent a time. A pale, powdery light filled the sky: false dawn. 'They shall say, in London,' he said, ' "Rhodes has taken for the Empire a country larger than Europe, at not a sixpence of cost to us, and we shall have that, and Rhodes shall have six feet by four feet." '

"He said this without bitterness, and turned from the parapet to face me. The Webley was pointed toward him. I had rested my (trembling) right hand on my left forearm, held up before me.

" 'Why, what on earth,' he said.

" 'Look,' I said.

"Drawing his look slowly away from me, he turned again. Out in the lawn, seeming in that illusory light to be but a long leap away, a male lion stood unmoving.

" 'The pistol won't stop him,' I said, 'but it will deflect him. If you will go calmly through the door behind me, I'll follow.'

"Rhodes backed away from the rail, and without haste or panic turned and walked past me into the house. The lion, ochre in the blue night, regarded him with a lion's expression, at once aloof and concerned, and returned his look to me. I thought I smelled him. Then I saw movement in the young trees beyond. I thought for a moment that my lion must be an illusion, or a dream, for he took no notice of these sounds—the crush of a twig, a soft voice—but at length he did turn his eyes from me to them. I could see the dim figure of a gamekeeper in a wide-awake hat, carrying a rifle, and Negroes with nets and poles: they were closing in carefully on the escapee. I stood for a moment longer, still poised to shoot, and then beat my own retreat into the house.

"Lights were being lit down the halls, voices calling: a lion does not appear on the lawn every night. Rhodes stood looking, not out the window, but at me. With deep embarrassment I clumsily pocketed the Webley (*I* knew what it had been given to me for, after all, even if he did not), and only then did I meet Rhodes's eyes.

"I shall never forget their expression, those pale eyes: a kind of exalted wonder, almost a species of adoration.

" 'That's twice now in one day,' he said, 'that you have kept me from harm. You must have been sent, that's all. I really believe you have been sent.'

"I stood before him staring, with a horror dawning in my heart such as, God willing, I shall never feel again. I knew, you see, what it meant that I had let slip the moment: that now I could not go back the way I had come. The world had opened for an instant, and I and my companions had gone down through it to this time and place; and now it had closed over me again, a seamless whole. I had no one and nothing; no Last equipment awaited me at the Mount Nelson Hotel; the Otherhood could not rescue me, for I had canceled it. I was entirely alone.

"Rhodes, of course, knew nothing of this. He crossed the hall to where I stood, with slow steps, almost reverently. He embraced me, a sudden great bear hug. And do you know what he did then?"

"What did he do?"

"He took me by the shoulders and held me at arm's length, and he insisted that I stay there with him. In effect, he offered me a job. For life, if I wanted it."

"What did you do?"

"I took it." He had finished his drink, and poured more. "I took it. You see, I simply had no place else to go."

Afternoon was late in the bungalow where we sat together, day hurried away with this tale. "I think," I said, "I shall have that drink now, if it's no trouble."

He rose and found a glass; he wiped the husk of a bug from it and filled it from his bottle. "It has always astonished me," he said, "how the mind, you know, can construct with lightning speed a reasonable, if quite mistaken, story to account for an essentially unreasonable event: I have had more than one occasion to observe this process.

"I was sure, instantly sure, that a lion which had escaped from Rhodes's lion house had appeared on the lawn at Groote Schuur just at the moment when I tried, but could not bring myself, to murder Cecil Rhodes. I can still see that cat in the pale light of predawn. And yet I cannot know if that is what happened, or if it is only what my mind has substituted for what did happen, which cannot be thought about.

"I am satisfied in my own mind—having had a lifetime to ponder it—that it cannot be possible for one to meet oneself on a trip into the past or future: that is a lie, invented by the Otherhood to forestall its own extinction, which was, however, inevitable.

"But I dream, sometimes, that I am lying on the bed at Groote Schuur, and a man enters—it is not Rhodes, but a man in a black coat and a bowler hat, into whose face I look as into a rotted mirror, who tells me impossible things.

"And I know that in fact there was no lion house at Groote Schuur. Rhodes wanted one, and it was planned, but it was never built."

In the summer of that year Rhodes—alive, alive-oh—went on expedition up into Pondoland, seeking concessions from an intransigent chief named Sicgau. Denys Winterset—this one, telling me the tale—went with him.

"Rhodes took Sicgau out into a field of mealies where he had had us set up a Maxim gun. Rhodes and the chief stood in the sun for a moment, and then Rhodes gave a signal; we fired the Maxim for a few seconds and mowed down much of the field. The chief stood unmoving for a long moment after the silence returned. Rhodes said to him softly: 'You see, this is what will happen to you and all your warriors if you give us any further trouble.'

"As a stratagem, that seemed to me both sporting and thrifty. It worked, too. But we were later to use the Maxims against men and not mealies. Rhodes knew that the Matabele had finally to be suppressed, or the work of building a white state north of the Zambezi would be hopeless. A way was found to intervene in a quarrel the Matabele were having with the Mashona, and in not too long we were at war with the Matabele. They were terribly, terribly brave; they were, after all, the first eleven in those parts, and they believed with reason that no one could withstand their leaf-bladed spears. I remember how they would come against the Maxims, and be mown down like the mealies, and fall back, and muster for another attack. Your heart sank; you prayed they would go away, but they would not. They came on again, to be cut down again. These puzzled, bewildered faces: I cannot forget them.

"And Christ, such drivel was written in the papers then, about the heroic stand of a few beleaguered South African police against so many battle-crazed natives! The only one who saw the truth was the author of that silly poem—Belloc, was it? You know—'Whatever happens, we have got/The Maxim gun, and they have not.' It was as simple as that. The truth, Rhodes said, is always simple."

He took out a large pocket-handkerchief and mopped his face and his eyes; no doubt it was hot, but it seemed to me that he wept. Tears, idle tears.

"I met Dr. Jameson during the Matabele campaign," he continued. "Leander Starr Jameson. I think I have never met a man—and I have met many wicked and twisted ones—whom I have loathed so completely and so instantly. I had hardly heard of him, of course; he was already dead and unknown in this year as it had occurred in my former past, the only version of these events I knew. Jameson was a great lover of the Maxim; he took several along on the raid he made into the Transvaal in 1896, the raid that would eventually lead to war with the Boers, destroy Rhodes's credit, and begin the end of Empire: so I have come to see it. The fool.

"I took no part in that war, thank God. I went north to help put the railroad through: Cape-to-Cairo." He smiled, seemed almost about to laugh, but did not; only mopped his face again. It was as though I were interrogating him, and he were telling me all this under the threat of the rubber truncheon or the rack. I wanted him to stop, frankly; only I dared say nothing.

"I made up for a lack of engineering expertise by my very uncertain knowledge of where and how, one day, the road would run. The telegraph had already reached Uganda; next stop was Wadi Halfa. The rails would not go through so easily. I became a sort of scout, leading the advance parties, dealing with the chieftains. The Maxim went with me, of course. I learned the weapon well."

Here there came another silence, another inward struggle to continue. I was left to picture what he did not say: *That which I did I should not have done; that which I should have done I did not do.*

"Rhodes gave five thousand pounds to the Liberal party to persuade them not to abandon Egypt: for there his railroad must be hooked to the sea. But then of course came the end of the whole scheme in German Tanganyika: no Cape-to-Cairo road. Germany was growing great in the world; the Germans wanted to have an Empire of their own. It finished Rhodes.

"By that time I was a railroad expert. The nonexistent Uganda Railroad was happy to acquire my services: I had a reputation, among the blacks, you see . . . I think there was a death for every mile of that road as it went through the jungle to the coast: rinderpest, fever, Nanda raids. We would now and then hang a captured Nanda warrior from the telegraph poles, to discourage the others. By the time the rails reached Mombasa, I was an old man; and Cecil Rhodes was dead."

He died of his old heart condition, the condition that had brought him out to Africa in the first place. He couldn't breathe in the awful heat of that summer of 1902, the worst anyone could remember; he wandered from room to room at Groote Schuur, trying to catch his breath. He lay in the darkened drawing room and could not breathe. They took him down to his cottage by the sea, and put ice between the ceiling and the iron roof to cool it; all afternoon the punkahs spooned the air. Then, suddenly, he decided to go to England. April was there: April showers. A cold spring: it seemed that could heal him. So a cabin was fitted out for him aboard a P&O liner, with electric fans and refrigerating pipes and oxygen tanks.

He died on the day he was to sail. He was buried at that place on the Matopos, the place he had chosen himself; buried facing north.

"He wanted the heroes of the Matabele campaign to be buried there with him. I could be one, if I chose; only I think my name would not be found among the register of those who fought. I think my name does not appear at all in history: not in the books of the Uganda Railroad, not in the register of the Mount Nelson Hotel for 1893. I have never had the courage to look."

I could not understand this, though it sent a cold shudder between my shoulder blades. The Original Situation, he explained, could not be returned to; but it could be restored, as those events that the Otherhood brought about were one by one come upon in time, and then not brought about. And as the Original Situation was second by second restored, the whole of his adventure in the past was continually worn away into nonbeing, and a new future replaced his old past ahead of him.

"You must imagine how it has been for me," he said, his voice now a whisper from exertion and grief. "To everyone else it seemed only that time went on— history—the march of events. But to me it has been otherwise. It has been the reverse of the nightmare from which you wake in a sweat of relief to find that the awful disaster has not occurred, the fatal step was not taken: for I have seen the real world gradually replaced by this other, nightmare world, which everyone else assumes is real, until nothing in past or present is as I knew it to be; until I am like the servant in Job: *I only am escaped to tell thee.*"

March 8, 1983

I awoke again this morning from the dream of the forest in the sea: a dream without people or events in it, or anything whatever except the gigantic dendrites, vast masses of pale leaves, and the tideless waters, light and sunshot toward the surface, darkening to impenetrability down below. It seemed there were schools of fish, or flocks of birds, in the leaves, something that faintly disturbed them, now and then; otherwise, stillness.

No matter that orthogonal logic refutes it, I cannot help believing that my present succeeds in time the other presents and futures that have gone into making it. I believe that as I grow older I come to incorporate the experiences I have had as an older man in pasts (and futures) now obsolete: as though in absolute time I continually catch up with myself in the imaginary times that fluoresce from it, gathering dreamlike memories of the lives I have lived therein. Somewhere God (I have come to believe in God; there was simply no existing otherwise) is keeping these universes in a row, and sees to it that they happen in succession, the most recently generated one last—and so felt to be last, no matter where along it I stand.

I remember, being now well past the age that he was then, the Uganda Railroad, the Nanda arrows, all the death.

I remember the shabby library and the coal fire, the encyclopedia in another orthography; the servant at the double doors.

I think that in the end, should I live long enough, I shall remember nothing but the forest in the sea. That is the terminus: complete strangeness that is at the same time utterly changeless; what cannot be becoming all that has ever been.

I took him out myself, in the end, abandoning my commission to do so, for there was no way that he could have crossed the border by himself, without papers, a nonexistent man. And it was just at that moment, as we motored up through the Sudan past Wadi Halfa, that the Anglo-French expeditionary force took Port Said. The Suez incident, that last hopeless spasm of Empire, was taking its inevitable course. Inevitable: I have not used the word before.

When we reached the Canal, the Israelis had already occupied the east bank. The airport at Ismailia was a shambles, the greater part of the Egyptian Air

Force shot up, planes scattered in twisted attitudes like dead birds after a storm. We could find no plane to take us. *He* had gone desperately broody, wide-eyed and speechless, useless for anything. I felt as though in a dream where one is somehow saddled with an idiot brother one had not had before.

And yet it was only the confusion and mess that made my task possible at all, I suppose. There were so many semiofficial and unofficial British scurrying or loafing around Port Said when we entered the city that our passage was unremarked. We went through the smoke and dust of that famously squalid port like two ghosts—two ghosts progressing through a ghost city at the retreating edge of a ghost of empire. And the crunch of broken glass continually underfoot.

We went out on an old oiler attached to the retreating invasion fleet, which had been ordered home having accomplished nothing except, I suppose, the end of the British Empire in Africa. He stood on the oiler's boat deck and watched the city grow smaller and said nothing. But once he laughed, his dry, light laugh: it made me think of the noise that Homer says the dead make. I asked the reason.

"I was remembering the last time I went out of Africa," he said. "On a day much like this. Very much like this. This calm weather; this sea. Nothing else the same, though. Nothing else." He turned to me smiling, and toasted me with an imaginary glass. "The end of an era," he said.

March 10

My chronicle seems to be degenerating into a diary.

I note in the *Times* this morning the sale of the single known example of the 1856 magenta British Guiana, for a sum far smaller than was supposed to be its worth. Neither the names of the consortium that sold it nor the names of the buyers were made public. I see in my mind's eye a small, momentary fire.

I see now that there is no reason why this story should come last, no matter my feeling, no matter that in Africa he hoped it would. Indeed there is no reason why it should even fall last in this chronicling, nor why the world, the sad world in which it occurs, should be described as succeeding all others—it does not, any more than it precedes them. For the sake of a narrative only, perhaps; perhaps, like God, we cannot live without narrative.

I used to see him, infrequently, in the years after we both came back from Africa: he didn't die as quickly as we both supposed he would. He used to seek me out, in part to borrow a little money—he was living on the dole and on what he brought out of Africa, which was little enough. I stood him to tea now and then and listened to his stories. He'd appear at our appointed place in a napless British Warm, ill-fitting, as his eyeglasses and National Health false teeth were also. I imagine he was terribly lonely. I know he was.

I remember the last time we met, at a Lyons teashop near the Marble Arch. I'd left the Colonial Service, of course, under a cloud, and taken a position teaching at a crammer's in Holborn until something better came along (nothing ever did; I recently inherited the headmaster's chair at the same school; little has changed there over the decades but the general coloration of the students).

"This curious fancy haunts me," he said to me on that occasion. "I picture the Fellows, all seated around the great table in the executive committee's dining room; only it is rather like Miss Havisham's, you know, in Dickens: the roast beef has long since gone foul, and the silver tarnished, and the draperies rotten; and the Fellows dead in their chairs, or mad, dust on their evening clothes, the port dried up in their glasses. Huntington. Davenant. The President *pro tem*."

He stirred sugar in his tea (he liked it horribly sweet; so, of course, do I). "It's not true, you know, that the Club stood somehow at a nexus of possibilities, amid multiplying realities. If that were so, then what the Fellows did would be trivial or monstrous or both: generating endless new universes just to see if they could get one to their liking. No: it is we, out here, who live in but one of innumerable possible worlds. In there, they were like a man standing at the north pole, whose only view, wherever he looks, is south: they looked out upon a single encompassing reality, which it was their opportunity—no, their duty, as they saw it—to make as happy as possible, as free from the calamities they knew of as they could make it.

"Well, they were limited people, more limited than their means to work good or evil. That which they did they should not have done. And yet what they hoped for us was not despicable. The calamities they saw were real. Anyone who could would try to save us from them: as a mother would pull her child, her foolish child, from the fire. They ought to be forgiven; they ought."

I walked with him up toward Hyde Park Corner. He walked now with agonizing slowness, as I will, too, one day; it was a rainy autumn Sunday, and his pains were severe. At Hyde Park Corner he stopped entirely, and I thought perhaps he could go no farther: but then I saw that he was studying the monument that stands there. He went closer to it, to read what was written on it.

I have myself more than once stopped before this neglected monument. It is a statue of the boy David, a memorial to the Machine Gun Corps, and was put up after the First World War. Some little thought must have gone into deciding how to memorialize that arm which had changed war forever; it seemed to require a religious sentiment, a quote from the Bible, and one was found. Beneath the naked boy are written words from Kings:

> Saul has slain his thousands
> But David his tens of thousands.

He stood in the rain, in his vast coat, looking down at these words, as though reading them over and over; and the faint rain that clung to his cheeks mingled with his tears:

> Saul has slain his thousands
> But David his tens of thousands.

I never saw him again after that day, and I did not seek for him: I think it unlikely he could have been found.

AFTERWORD

Much of the impulse and many of the details of the preceding come from the second and third volumes of Jan Morris's enthralling chronicle of the rise and decline of the British Empire, *Pax Britannica* (1968) and *Farewell the Trumpets* (1978). I hope she will forgive the author the liberties he has taken, and accept his gratitude for the many hours she has allowed him to spend dawdling in a world more fantastical than any he could himself invent.

The story of Rhodes's death and many details of his character and conversation are taken from Sarah Gertrude Millin's elegant and neglected biography *Cecil Rhodes* (London, 1933).

The story of Rhodes in Pondoland, along with much else that was suggestive, comes from John Ellis's book *The Social History of the Machine Gun* (1975).

For an introduction to that book, for his convincing analysis of the possibilities and limits of what I have called orthogonal logic, and in general for his infectious enthusiasm for notions, the author's thanks to Bob Chasell (hi, Bob).

Robert Silverberg

Robert Silverberg (1935–   ) is the author of many SF novels and stories. He has published more than twenty collections of his short fiction. His most famous novels include *Dying Inside* (1972), one of the most impressive SF novels of character, and *Lord Valentine's Castle* (1980), the first of a series of popular fantasy works somewhat in the tradition of Jack Vance.

Silverberg is one of the leading conscious literary craftsmen of the genre in the last forty years. Of particular interest is his anthology *Robert Silverberg's Worlds of Wonder* (1987), which is perhaps the best single discussion, with examples, of the craft of SF writing. It includes an essay on this story that clearly lines out the conscious literary choices involved in the composition of "Sundance."

The range and breadth of Silverberg's vision, as well as his legendary facility, put him in the top rank of SF writers in the contemporary period. If there is a continuum from the pole of sentiment to the pole of artifice, Silverberg's work, when it errs, errs in the direction of artifice. In "Sundance," however, it seems to me Silverberg achieves a fine balance. It is a story of an American Indian in the future on another planet finding himself, and also a formal experiment in technique within genre boundaries.

SUNDANCE

Today you liquidated about 50,000 Eaters in Sector A, and now you are spending an uneasy night. You and Herndon flew east at dawn, with the green-gold sunrise at your backs, and sprayed the neural pellets over a thousand hectares along the Forked River. You flew on into the prairie beyond the river, where the Eaters have already been wiped out, and had lunch sprawled on that thick, soft carpet of grass where the first settlement is expected to rise. Herndon picked some juiceflowers, and you enjoyed half an hour of mild hallucinations. Then, as you headed toward the copter to begin an afternoon of further pellet spraying, he said suddenly, "Tom, how would you feel about this if it turned out that the Eaters weren't just animal pests? That they were *people*, say, with a language and rites and a history and all?"

You thought of how it had been for your own people.

"They aren't," you said.

"Suppose they were. Suppose the Eaters—"

"They aren't. Drop it."

Herndon has this streak of cruelty in him that leads him to ask such questions. He goes for the vulnerabilities; it amuses him. All night now his casual remark has echoed in your mind. Suppose the Eaters . . . supposed the Eaters . . . suppose . . . suppose . . .

You sleep for a while, and dream, and in your dreams you swim through rivers of blood.

Foolishness. A feverish fantasy. You know how important it is to exterminate the Eaters fast, before the settlers get here. They're just animals, and not even harmless animals at that; ecology-wreckers is what they are, devourers of oxygen-liberating plants, and they have to go. A few have been saved for zoological study. The rest must be destroyed. Ritual extirpation of undesirable beings, the old old story. But let's not complicate our job with moral qualms, you tell yourself. Let's not dream of rivers of blood.

The Eaters don't even *have* blood, none that could flow in rivers, anyway. What they have is, well, a kind of lymph that permeates every tissue and transmits nourishment along the interfaces. Waste products go out the same way, osmotically. In terms of process, it's structurally analogous to your own kind of circulatory system, except there's no network of blood vessels hooked to a master pump. The life-stuff just oozes through their bodies as though they were amoebas or sponges or some other low-phylum form. Yet they're definitely high-phylum in nervous system, digestive setup, limb-and-organ template, etc. Odd, you think. The thing about aliens is that they're alien, you tell yourself, not for the first time.

The beauty of their biology for you and your companions is that it lets you exterminate them so neatly.

You fly over the grazing grounds and drop the neural pellets. The Eaters find and ingest them. Within an hour the poison has reached all sectors of the body. Life ceases; a rapid breakdown of cellular matter follows, the Eater literally falling apart molecule by molecule the instant that nutrition is cut off; the lymph-like stuff works like acid; a universal lysis occurs; flesh and even the bones, which are cartilaginous, dissolve. In two hours, a puddle on the ground. In four, nothing at all left. Considering how many millions of Eaters you've scheduled for extermination here, it's sweet of the bodies to be self-disposing. Otherwise what a charnel house this world would become!

Suppose the Eaters . . .

Damn Herndon. You almost feel like getting a memory-editing in the morning. Scrape his stupid speculations out of your head. If you dared. If you dared.

In the morning he does not dare. Memory-editing frightens him; he will try to shake free of his newfound guilt without it. The Eaters, he explains to himself, are mindless herbivores, the unfortunate victims of human expansionism, but not really deserving of passionate defense. Their extermination is not tragic; it's just too bad. If Earthmen are to have this world, the Eaters must relinquish it. There's a difference, he tells himself, between the elimination of the Plains Indians from the American prairie in the nineteenth century and the destruction of the bison on that same prairie. One feels a little wistful about the slaughter of the thundering herds; one regrets the butchering of millions of the noble brown woolly beasts, yes. But one feels outrage, not mere wistful regret, at what was done to the Sioux. There's a difference. Reserve your passions for the proper cause.

He walks from his bubble at the edge of the camp toward the center of things. The flagstone path is moist and glistening. The morning fog has not yet lifted, and every tree is bowed, the long, notched leaves heavy with droplets of water. He pauses, crouching, to observe a spider-analog spinning its asymmetrical web. As he watches, a small amphibian, delicately shaded turquoise, glides as inconspicuously as possible over the mossy ground. Not inconspicuously enough; he gently lifts the little creature and puts it on the back of his hand. The gills flutter in anguish, and the amphibian's sides quiver. Slowly, cunningly, its color changes until it matches the coppery tone of the hand. The camouflage is excellent. He lowers his hand and the amphibian scurries into a puddle. He walks on.

He is forty years old, shorter than most of the other members of the expedition, with wide shoulders, a heavy chest, dark glossy hair, a blunt, spreading nose. He is a biologist. This is his third career, for he has failed as an anthropologist and as a developer of real estate. His name is Tom Two Ribbons. He has been married twice but has had no children. His great-grandfather died of alcoholism; his grandfather was addicted to hallucinogens; his father had compulsively visited cheap memory-editing parlors. Tom Two Ribbons is conscious that he is failing a family tradition, but he has not yet found his own mode of self-destruction.

In the main building he discovers Herndon, Julia, Ellen, Schwartz, Chang, Michaelson, and Nichols. They are eating breakfast; the others are already at work. Ellen rises and comes to him and kisses him. Her short soft yellow hair tickles his cheeks. "I love you," she whispers. She has spent the night in Michaelson's bubble. "I love you," he tells her, and draws a quick vertical line of affection between her small pale breasts. He winks at Michaelson, who nods, touches the tops of two fingers to his lips, and blows them a kiss. We are all good friends here, Tom Two Ribbons thinks.

"Who drops pellets today?" he asks.

"Mike and Chang," says Julia. "Sector C."

Schwartz says, "Eleven more days and we ought to have the whole peninsula clear. Then we can move inland."

"If our pellet supply holds up," Chang points out.

Herndon says, "Did you sleep well, Tom?"

"No," says Tom. He sits down and taps out his breakfast requisition. In the west, the fog is beginning to burn off the mountains. Something throbs in the back of his neck. He has been on this world nine weeks now, and in that time it has undergone its only change of season, shading from dry weather to foggy. The mists will remain for many months. Before the plains parch again, the Eaters will be gone and the settlers will begin to arrive. His food slides down the chute and he seizes it. Ellen sits beside him. She is a little more than half his age; this is her first voyage; she is their keeper of records, but she is also skilled at editing. "You look troubled," Ellen tells him. "Can I help you?"

"No. Thank you."

"I hate it when you get gloomy."

"It's a racial trait," says Tom Two Ribbons.

"I doubt that very much."

"The truth is that maybe my personality reconstruct is wearing thin. The trauma level was so close to the surface. I'm just a walking veneer, you know."

Ellen laughs prettily. She wears only a sprayon half-wrap. Her skin looks damp; she and Michaelson have had a swim at dawn. Tom Two Ribbons is thinking of asking her to marry him, when this job is over. He has not been married since the collapse of the real estate business. The therapist suggested divorce as part of the reconstruct. He sometimes wonders where Terry has gone and whom she lives with now. Ellen says, "You seem pretty stable to me, Tom."

"Thank you," he says. She is young. She does not know.

"If it's just a passing gloom I can edit it out in one quick snip."

"Thank you," he says. "No."

"I forgot. You don't like editing."

"My father—"

"Yes?"

"In fifty years he pared himself down to a thread," Tom Two Ribbons says. "He had his ancestors edited away, his whole heritage, his religion, his wife, his sons, finally his name. Then he sat and smiled all day. Thank you, no editing."

"Where are you working today?" Ellen asks.

"In the compound, running tests."

"Want company? I'm off all morning."

"Thank you, no," he says, too quickly. She looks hurt. He tries to remedy his unintended cruelty by touching her arm lightly and saying, "Maybe this afternoon, all right? I need to commune a while. Yes?"

"Yes," she says, and smiles, and shapes a kiss with her lips.

After breakfast he goes to the compound. It covers a thousand hectares east of the base; they have bordered it with neutral-field projectors at intervals of eighty meters, and this is a sufficient fence to keep the captive population of two hundred Eaters from straying. When all the others have been exterminated, this study group will remain. At the southwest corner of the compound stands a lab bubble from which the experiments are run: metabolic, psychological, physiological, ecological. A stream crosses the compound diagonally. There is a low ridge of grassy hills at its eastern edge. Five distinct corpses of tightly clustered knifeblade trees are separated by patches of dense savanna. Sheltered beneath the grass are the oxygen-plants, almost completely hidden except for the photosynthetic spikes that jut to heights of three or four meters at regular intervals, and for the lemon-colored respiratory bodies, chest high, that make the grassland sweet and dizzying with exhaled gases. Through the fields move the Eaters in a straggling herd, nibbling delicately at the respiratory bodies.

Tom Two Ribbons spies the herd beside the stream and goes toward it. He stumbles over an oxygen-plant hidden in the grass but deftly recovers his balance and, seizing the puckered orifice of the respiratory body, inhales deeply. His despair lifts. He approaches the Eaters. They are spherical, bulky, slow-moving creatures, covered by masses of coarse orange fur. Saucer-like eyes protrude above narrow rubbery lips. Their legs are thin and scaly, like a chicken's, and their arms are short and held close to their bodies. They regard him with bland lack of curiosity. "Good morning, brothers!" is the way he greets them this time, and he wonders why.

I noticed something strange today. Perhaps I simply sniffed too much oxygen in the fields; maybe I was succumbing to a suggestion Herndon planted; or possibly it's the family masochism cropping out. But while I was observing the Eaters in the compound, it seemed to me, for the first time, that they were behaving intelligently, that they were functioning in a ritualized way.

I followed them around for three hours. During that time they uncovered half a dozen outcroppings of oxygen-plants. In each case they went through a stylized pattern of action before starting to munch. They:

Formed a straggly circle around the plants.

Looked toward the sun.

Looked toward their neighbors on left and right around the circle.

Made fuzzy neighing sounds *only* after having done the foregoing.

Looked toward the sun again.

Moved in and ate.

If this wasn't a prayer of thanksgiving, a saying of grace, then what was it? And if they're advanced enough spiritually to say grace, are we not therefore committing genocide here? Do chimpanzees say grace? Christ, we wouldn't even wipe out chimps the way we're cleaning out the Eaters! Of course, chimps don't interfere with human crops, and some kind of coexistence would be possible, whereas Eaters and human agriculturalists simply can't function on the same planet. Nevertheless, there's a moral issue here. The liquidation effort is predicated on the assumption that the intelligence level of the Eaters is about on par with that of oysters, or, at best, sheep. Our consciences stay clear because our poison is quick and painless and because the Eaters thoughtfully dissolve upon dying, sparing us the mess of incinerating millions of corpses. But if they pray—

I won't say anything to the others just yet. I want more evidence—hard, objective. Films, tapes, record cubes. Then we'll see. What if I can show that we're exterminating intelligent beings? My family knows a little about genocide, after all, having been on the receiving end just a few centuries back. I doubt that I could halt what's going on here. But at the very least I could withdraw from the operation. Head back to Earth and stir up public outcries.

I hope I'm imagining this.

I'm not imagining a thing. They gather in circles; they look to the sun; they neigh and pray. They're only balls of jelly on chicken-legs, but they give thanks for their food. Those big round eyes now seem to stare accusingly at me. Our tame herd here knows what's going on: that we have descended from the stars to eradicate their kind, and that they alone will be spared. They have no way of fighting back or even of communicating their displeasure, but they *know*. And hate us. Jesus, we have killed two million of them since we got here, and in a metaphorical sense I'm stained with blood, and what will I do, what can I do?

I must move very carefully, or I'll end up drugged and edited.

I can't let myself seem like a crank, a quack, an agitator. I can't stand up and *denounce!* I have to find allies. Herndon, first. He surely is onto the truth; he's the one who nudged *me* to it, that day we dropped pellets. And I thought he was merely being vicious in his usual way!

I'll talk to him tonight.

He says, "I've been thinking about that suggestion you made. About the Eaters. Perhaps we haven't made sufficiently close psychological studies. I mean, if they really *are* intelligent—"

Herndon blinks. He is a tall man with glossy dark hair, a heavy beard, sharp cheekbones. "Who says they are, Tom?"

"You did. On the far side of the Forked River, you said—"

"It was just a speculative hypothesis. To make conversation."

"No, I think it was more than that. You really believed it."

Herndon looks troubled. "Tom, I don't know what you're trying to start, but don't start it. If I for a moment believed we were killing intelligent creatures, I'd run for an editor so fast I'd start an implosion wave."

"Why did you ask me that thing, then?" Tom Two Ribbons says.

"Idle chatter."

"Amusing yourself by kindling guilts in somebody else? You're a bastard, Herndon. I mean it."

"Well, look, Tom, if I had any idea that you'd get so worked up about a hypothetical suggestion—" Herndon shakes his head. "The Eaters aren't intelligent beings. Obviously. Otherwise we wouldn't be under orders to liquidate them."

"Obviously," says Tom Two Ribbons.

Ellen said, "No, I don't know what Tom's up to. But I'm pretty sure he needs a rest. It's only a year and a half since his personality reconstruct, and he had a pretty bad breakdown back then."

Michaelson consulted a chart. "He's refused three times in a row to make his pellet-dropping run. Claiming he can't take time away from his research. Hell, we can fill in for him, but it's the idea that he's ducking chores that bothers me."

"What kind of research is he doing?" Nichols wanted to know.

"Not biological," said Julia. "He's with the Eaters in the compound all the time, but I don't see him making any tests on them. He just watches them."

"And talks to them," Chang observed.

"And talks, yes," Julia said.

"About what?" Nichols asked.

"Who knows?"

Everyone looked at Ellen. "You're closest to him," Michaelson said. "Can't you bring him out of it?"

"I've got to know what he's in, first," Ellen said. "He isn't saying a thing."

You know that you must be very careful, for they outnumber you, and their concern for your welfare can be deadly. Already they realize you are disturbed, and Ellen has begun to probe for the source of the disturbance. Last night you lay in her arms and she questioned you, obliquely, skillfully, and you knew what she is trying to find out. When the moons appeared she suggested that you and she stroll in the compound, among the sleeping Eaters. You declined, but she sees that you have become involved with the creatures.

You have done probing of your own—subtly, you hope. And you are aware that you can do nothing to save the Eaters. An irrevocable commitment has been made. It is 1876 all over again; these are the bison, these are the Sioux, and they must be destroyed, for the railroad is on its way. If you speak out here, your friends will calm you and pacify you and edit you, for they do not see what you see. If you return to Earth to agitate, you will be mocked and recommended for another reconstruct. You can do nothing. You can do nothing.

You cannot save, but perhaps you can record.

Go out into the prairie. Live with the Eaters; make yourself their friend; learn their ways. Set it down, a full account of their culture, so that at least that much will not be lost. You know the techniques of field anthropology. As was done for your people in the old days, do now for the Eaters.

He finds Michaelson. "Can you spare me for a few weeks?" he asks.

"Spare you, Tom? What do you mean?"

"I've got some field studies to do. I'd like to leave the base and work with Eaters in the wild."

"What's wrong with the ones in the compound?"

"It's the last chance with wild ones, Mike. I've got to go."

"Alone, or with Ellen?"

"Alone."

Michaelson nods slowly. "All right, Tom. Whatever you want. Go. I won't hold you here."

I dance in the prairie under the green-gold sun. About me the Eaters gather. I am stripped; sweat makes my skin glisten; my heart pounds. I talk to them with my feet, and they understand.

They understand.

They have a language of soft sounds. They have a god. They know love and awe and rapture. They have rites. They have names. They have a history. Of all this I am convinced.

I dance on thick grass.

How can I reach them? With my feet, with my hands, with my grunts, with my sweat. They gather by the hundreds, by the thousands, and I dance. I must not stop. They cluster about me and make their sounds. I am a conduit for strange forces. My great-grandfather should see me now! Sitting on his porch in Wyoming, the firewater in his hand, his brain rotting—see me now, old one! See the dance of Tom Two Ribbons! I talk to these strange ones with my feet under a sun that is the wrong color. I dance. I dance.

"Listen to me," I say. "I am your friend, I alone, the only one you can trust. Trust me, talk to me, teach me. Let me preserve your ways, for soon the destruction will come."

I dance, and the sun climbs, and the Eaters murmur.

There is the chief. I dance toward him, back, toward, I bow, I point to the sun, I imagine the being that lives in that ball of flame, I imitate the sounds of these people, I kneel, I rise, I dance. Tom Two Ribbons dances for you.

I summon skills my ancestors forgot. I feel the power flowing in me. As they danced in the days of the bison, I dance now, beyond the Forked River.

I dance, and now the Eaters dance too. Slowly, uncertainly, they move toward me, they shift their weight, lift leg and leg, sway about. "Yes, like that!" I cry. "Dance!"

We dance together as the sun reaches noon height.

Now their eyes are no longer accusing. I see warmth and kinship. I am their brother, their redskinned tribesman, he who dances with them. No longer do they seem clumsy to me. There is a strange ponderous grace in their movements. They dance. They dance. They caper about me. Closer, closer, closer!

We move in holy frenzy.

They sing, now, a blurred hymn of joy. They throw forth their arms, unclench their little claws. In unison they shift weight, left foot forward, right, left, right. Dance, brothers, dance, dance, dance! They press against me. Their flesh quivers; their smell is a sweet one. They gently thrust me across the field, to a part of the meadow where the grass is deep and untrampled. Still dancing, we seek the oxygen-plants, and find clumps of them beneath the grass, and they make their prayer and seize them with their awkward arms, separating the respiratory bodies from the photosynthetic spikes. The plants, in anguish, release floods of oxygen. My mind reels. I laugh and sing. The Eaters are nibbling the lemon-colored perforated globes, nibbling the stalks as well. They thrust their plants at me. It is a religious ceremony, I see. Take from us, eat with us, join with us, this is the body, this is the blood, take, eat, join. I bend forward and put a lemon-colored globe to my lips. I do not bite; I nibble, as they do, my teeth slicing away the skin of the globe. Juice spurts into my mouth while oxygen drenches my nostrils. The Eaters sing hosannas. I should be in full paint for this, paint of my forefathers, feathers too, meeting their religion in the regalia of what should have been mine. Take, eat, join. The juice of the oxygen-plant flows in my veins. I embrace my brothers. I sing, and as my voice leaves my lips it becomes an arch that glistens like new steel, and I pitch my song lower, and the arch turns to tarnished silver. The Eaters crowd close. The scent of their bodies is fiery red to me. Their soft cries are puffs of steam. The sun is very warm; its rays are tiny jagged pings of puckered sound, close to the top of my range of hearing, plink! plink! plink! The thick grass hums to me, deep and rich, and the wind hurls points of flame along the prairie. I devour another oxygen-plant, and then a third. My brothers laugh and shout. They tell me of their gods, the god of warmth, the god of food, the god of pleasure, the god of death, the god of holiness, the god of wrongness, and the others. They recite for me the names of their kings, and I hear their voices as splashes of green mold on the clean sheet of the sky. They instruct me in their holy rites. I must remember this, I tell myself, for when it is gone it will never come again. I continue to dance. They continue to dance. The color of the hills becomes rough and coarse, like abrasive gas. Take, eat, join. Dance. They are so gentle!

I hear the drone of the copter, suddenly.

It hovers far overhead. I am unable to see who flies in it. "No!" I scream. "Not here! Not these people! Listen to me! This is Tom Two Ribbons! Can't you hear me? I'm doing a field study here! You have no right—!"

My voice makes spirals of blue moss edged with red sparks. They drift upward and are scattered by the breeze.

I yell, I shout, I bellow. I dance and shake my fists. From the wings of the copter the jointed arms of the pellet-distributors unfold. The gleaming spigots extend and whirl. The neural pellets rain down into the meadow, each tracing a blazing track that lingers in the sky. The sound of the copter becomes a furry carpet stretching to the horizon, and my shrill voice is lost in it.

The Eaters drift away from me, seeking the pellets, scratching at the roots of the grass to find them. Still dancing, I leap into their midst, striking the pellets from their hands, hurling them into the stream, crushing them to powder. The Eaters growl black needles at me. They turn away and search for more pellets. The copter turns and flies off, leaving a trail of dense oily sound. My brothers are gobbling the pellets eagerly.

There is no way to prevent it.

Joy consumes them and they topple and lie still. Occasionally a limb twitches; then even this stops. They begin to dissolve. Thousands of them melt on the prairie, sinking into shapelessness, losing spherical forms, flattening, ebbing into the ground. The bonds of the molecules will no longer hold. It is the twilight of protoplasm. They perish. They vanish. For hours I walk the prairie. Now I inhale oxygen; now I eat a lemon-colored globe. Sunset begins with the ringing of leaden chimes. Black clouds make brazen trumpet calls in the east and the deepening wind is a swirl of coaly bristles. Silence comes. Night falls. I dance. I am alone.

The copter comes again, and they find you, and you do not resist as they gather you in. You are beyond bitterness. Quietly you explain what you have done and what you have learned, and why it is wrong to exterminate these people. You describe the plant you have eaten and the way it affects your senses, and as you talk of the blessed synesthesia, the texture of the wind and the sound of the clouds and the timbre of the sunlight, they nod and smile and tell you not to worry, that everything will be all right soon, and they touch something cold to your forearm, so cold that it is a whir and a buzz and the deintoxicant sinks into your vein and soon the ecstasy drains away, leaving only the exhaustion and the grief.

He says, "We never learn a thing, do we? We export all our horrors to the stars. Wipe out the Armenians, wipe out the Jews, wipe out the Tasmanians, wipe out the Indians, wipe out everyone who's in the way, and then come here and do the same damned murderous thing. You weren't with me out there. You didn't dance with them. You didn't see what a rich, complex culture the Eaters have. Let me tell you about their tribal structure. It's dense: seven levels of matrimonial relationships, to begin with, and an exogamy factor that requires—"

Softly Ellen says, "Tom, darling, nobody's going to harm the Eaters."

"And the religion," he goes on. "Nine gods, each one an aspect of *the* god. Holiness and wrongness both worshiped. They have hymns, prayers, a theology. And we, the emissaries of the god of wrongness—"

"We're not exterminating them," Michaelson says. "Won't you understand that, Tom? This is all a fantasy of yours. You've been under the influence of drugs, but now we're clearing you out. You'll be clean in a little while. You'll have perspective again."

"A fantasy?" he says bitterly. "A drug dream? I stood out in the prairie and saw you drop pellets. And I watched them die and melt away. I didn't dream that."

"How can we convince you?" Chang asks earnestly. "What will make you believe? Shall we fly over the Eater country with you and show you how many millions there are?"

"But how many millions have been destroyed?" he demands.

They insist that he is wrong. Ellen tells him again that no one has ever desired to harm the Eaters. "This is a scientific expedition, Tom. We're here to *study* them. It's a violation of all we stand for to injure intelligent lifeforms."

"You admit that they're intelligent?"

"Of course. That's never been in doubt."

"Then why drop the pellets?" he asks. "Why slaughter them?"

"None of that has happened, Tom," Ellen says. She takes his hand between her cool palms. "Believe us. Believe us."

He says bitterly, "If you want me to believe you, why don't you do the job properly? Get out the editing machine and go to work on me. You can't simply *talk* me into rejecting the evidence of my own eyes."

"You were under drugs all the time," Michaelson says.

"I've never taken drugs! Except for what I ate in the meadow, when I danced—and that came after I had watched the massacre going on for weeks and weeks. Are you saying that it's a retroactive delusion?"

"No, Tom," Schwartz says. "You've had this delusion all along. It's part of your therapy, your reconstruct. You came here programmed with it."

"Impossible," he says.

Ellen kisses his fevered forehead. "It was done to reconcile you to mankind, you see. You had this terrible resentment of the displacement of your people in the nineteenth century. You were unable to forgive the industrial society for scattering the Sioux, and you were terribly full of hate. Your therapist thought that if you could be made to participate in an imaginary modern extermination, if you could come to see it as a necessary operation, you'd be purged of your resentment and able to take your place in society as—"

He thrusts her away. "Don't talk idiocy! If you knew the first thing about reconstruct therapy, you'd realize that no reputable therapist could be so shallow. There are no one-to-one correlations in reconstructs. No, don't touch me. Keep away. Keep away."

He will not let them persuade him that this is merely a drug-born dream. It is no fantasy, he tells himself, and it is no therapy. He rises. He goes out. They do not follow him. He takes a copter and seeks his brothers.

Again I dance. The sun is much hotter today. The Eaters are more numerous. Today I wear paint, today I wear feathers. My body shines with my sweat. They dance with me, and they have a frenzy in them that I have never seen before. We pound the trampled meadow with our feet. We clutch for the sun with our hands. We sing, we shout, we cry. We will dance until we fall.

This is no fantasy. These people are real, and they are intelligent, and they are doomed. This I know.

We dance. Despite the doom, we dance.

My great-grandfather comes and dances with us. He too is real. His nose is like a hawk's, not blunt like mine, and he wears the big headdress, and his muscles are like cords under his brown skin. He sings, he shouts, he cries.

Others of my family join us.

We eat the oxygen-plants together. We embrace the Eaters. We know, all of us, what it is to be hunted.

The clouds make music and the wind takes on texture and the sun's warmth has color.

We dance. We dance. Our limbs know no weariness.

The sun grows and fills the whole sky, and I see no Eater now, only my own people, my father's fathers across the centuries, thousands of gleaming skins, thousands of hawk's noses, and we eat the plants, and we find sharp sticks and thrust them into our flesh, and the sweet blood flows and dries in the blaze of the sun, and we dance, and we dance, and some of us fall from weariness, and we dance, and the prairie is a sea of bobbing headdresses, an ocean of feathers, and we dance, and my heart makes thunder, and my knees become water, and the sun's fire engulfs me, and I dance, and I fall, and I dance, and I fall, and I fall, and I fall.

Again they find you and bring you back. They give you the cool snout on your arm to take the oxygen-plant drug from your veins, and then they give you something else so you will rest. You rest and you are very calm. Ellen kisses you and you stroke her soft skin, and then the others come in and they talk to you, saying soothing things, but you do not listen, for you are searching for realities. It is not an easy search. It is like falling through many trapdoors, looking for the one room whose floor is not hinged. Everything that has happened on this planet is your therapy, you tell yourself, designed to reconcile an embittered aborigine to the white man's conquest; nothing is really being exterminated here. You reject that and fall through and realize that this must be the therapy of your friends; they carry the weight of accumulated centuries of guilts and have come here to shed that load, and you are here to ease them of their burden, to draw their sins into yourself and give them forgiveness. Again you fall through, and see that the Eaters are mere animals who threaten the ecology and must be removed; the culture you imagined for them is your hallucination, kindled out of old churnings. You try to withdraw your objections to this necessary extermination, but you fall through again and discover that there is no extermination except in your mind, which is troubled and disordered by your obsession with the crime against your ancestors, and you sit up, for you wish to apologize to these friends of yours, these innocent scientists whom you have called murderers. And you fall through.

Frank Herbert

Frank Herbert (1920–1986) is the author of *Dune* (1965), the single most popular SF novel of the century, according to some published polls of readers. In response to that popularity he wrote a number of sequels in the 1970s and 1980s. Herbert was a journalist (he was proud to show a picture of the Army–McCarthy hearings with himself in the front row) and an articulate public speaker. His first major impact came in the 1950s with his impressive novel *The Dragon in the Sea* (1956), which is an intense psychological examination of a small crew enclosed together in a submarine; it forecast an international oil crisis, and Cold War–style submarine oil theft.

Herbert's fiction is often intellectual and discursive, but he was also concerned with dramatic storytelling. He was particularly fascinated by technology and the idea of progress, yet his stories are always grounded in a political and social awareness that made him especially relevant and popular in the 1960s and '70s.

One of his major themes was the evolution of intelligence, artificial or organic. He was influential in the founding of the ecology movement, which he popularized through works such as *Dune,* this story, and *Hellstrom's Hive* (1973). He was the main speaker advertised at the first Earth Day celebration. "Greenslaves" was later expanded into the novel, *The Green Brain* (1966). As opposed to many stories of this type, it has only gained in pertinence since its original publication. It is a stunning ecological parable set in the rain forest of South America.

GREENSLAVES

He looked pretty much like the bastard offspring of a Guarani Indio and some backwoods farmer's daughter, some *sertanista* who had tried to forget her enslavement to the *encomendero* system by "eating the iron"—which is what they call lovemaking through the grill of a consel gate.

The type-look was almost perfect except when he forgot himself while passing through one of the deeper jungle glades.

His skin tended to shade down to green then, fading him into the background of leaves and vines, giving a strange disembodiment to the mud-gray shirt and ragged trousers, the inevitable frayed straw hat and rawhide sandals soled with pieces cut from worn tires.

Such lapses became less and less frequent the farther he got from the Parana headwaters, the *sertao* hinterland of Goyaz where men with his bang-cut black hair and glittering dark eyes were common.

By the time he reached *bandeirantes* country, he had achieved almost perfect control over the chameleon effect.

But now he was out of the jungle growth and into the brown dirt tracks that separated the parceled farms of the resettlement plan. In his own way, he knew he was approaching the *bandeirante* checkpoints, and with an almost human gesture, he fingered the *cedula de gracias al sacar*, the certificate of white blood, tucked safely beneath his shirt. Now and again, when humans were not near, he practiced speaking aloud the name that had been chosen for him—"Antonio Raposo Tavares."

The sound was a bit stridulate, harsh on the edges, but he knew it would pass. It already had. Goyaz Indios were notorious for the strange inflection of their speech. The farm folk who had given him a roof and fed him the previous night had said as much.

When their questions had become pressing, he had squatted on the doorstep and played his flute, the *qena* of the Andes Indian that he carried in a leather purse hung from his shoulder. He had kept the sound to a conventional non-dangerous pitch. The gesture of the flute was a symbol of the region. When a Guarani put flute to nose and began playing, that was a sign words were ended.

The farm folk had shrugged and retired.

Now, he could see red-brown rooftops ahead and the white crystal shimmering of a *bandeirante* tower with its aircars alighting and departing. The scene held an odd hive-look. He stopped, finding himself momentarily overcome by the touch of instincts that he knew he had to master or fail in the ordeal to come.

He united his mental identity then, thinking, *We are greenslaves subservient to the greater whole.* The thought lent him an air of servility that was like a shield against the stares of the humans trudging past all around him. His kind knew many mannerisms and had learned early that servility was a form of concealment.

Presently, he resumed his plodding course toward the town and the tower.

The dirt track gave way to a two-lane paved market road with its footpaths in the ditches on both sides. This, in turn, curved alongside a four-deck commercial transport highway where even the footpaths were paved. And now there were groundcars and aircars in greater number, and he noted that the flow of people on foot was increasing.

Thus far, he had attracted no dangerous attention. The occasional snickering side-glance from natives of the area could be safely ignored, he knew. Probing stares held peril, and he had detected none. The servility shielded him.

The sun was well along toward mid-morning and the day's heat was beginning to press down on the earth, raising a moist hothouse stink from the dirt beside the pathway, mingling the perspiration odors of humanity around him.

And they were around him now, close and pressing, moving slower and slower as they approached the checkpoint bottleneck. Presently, the forward motion stopped. Progress resolved itself into shuffle and stop, shuffle and stop.

This was the critical test now and there was no avoiding it. He waited with something like an Indian's stoic patience. His breathing had grown deeper to compensate for the heat, and he adjusted it to match that of the people around him, suffering the temperature rise for the sake of blending into his surroundings.

Andes Indians didn't breathe deeply here in the lowlands.

Shuffle and stop.

Shuffle and stop.

He could see the checkpoint now.

Fastidious *bandeirantes* in sealed white cloaks with plastic helmets, gloves, and boots stood in a double row within a shaded brick corridor leading into the town. He could see sunlight hot on the street beyond the corridor and people hurrying away there after passing the gantlet.

The sight of that free area beyond the corridor sent an ache of longing through all the parts of him. The suppression warning flashed out instantly on the heels of that instinctive reaching emotion.

No distraction could be permitted now; he was into the hands of the first *bandeirante*, a hulking blond fellow with pink skin and blue eyes.

"Step along now! Lively now!" the fellow said.

A gloved hand propelled him toward two *bandeirantes* standing on the right side of the line.

"Give this one an extra treatment," the blond giant called. "He's from the upcountry by the look of him."

The other two *bandeirantes* had him now, one jamming a breather mask over his face, the other fitting a plastic bag over him. A tube trailed from the bag out to machinery somewhere in the street beyond the corridor.

"Double shot!" one of the *bandeirantes* called.

Fuming blue gas puffed out the bag around him, and he took a sharp, gasping breath through the mask.

Agony!

The gas drove through every multiple linkage of his being with needles of pain.

We must not weaken, he thought.

But it was a deadly pain, killing. The linkages were beginning to weaken.

"Okay on this one," the bag handler called.

The mask was pulled away. The bag was slipped off. Hands propelled him down the corridor toward the sunlight.

"Lively now! Don't hold up the line."

The stink of the poison gas was all around him. It was a new one—a dissembler. They hadn't prepared him for this poison!

Now, he was into the sunlight and turning down a street lined with fruit stalls, merchants bartering with customers or standing fat and watchful behind their displays.

In his extremity, the fruit beckoned to him with the promise of life-saving sanctuary for a few parts of him, but the integrating totality fought off the lure. He shuffled as fast as he dared, dodging past the customers, through the knots of idlers.

"You like to buy some fresh oranges?"

An oily dark hand thrust two oranges toward his face.

"Fresh oranges from the green country. Never been a bug anywhere near these."

He avoided the hand, although the odor of the oranges came near overpowering him.

Now, he was clear of the stalls, around a corner down a narrow side street. Another corner and he saw far away to his left, the lure of greenery in open country, the free area beyond the town.

He turned toward the green, increasing his speed, measuring out the time still available to him. There was still a chance. Poison clung to his clothing, but fresh air was filtering through the fabric—and the thought of victory was like an antidote.

We can make it yet!

The green drew closer and closer—trees and ferns beside a river bank. He heard the running water. There was a bridge thronging with foot traffic from converging streets.

No help for it: he joined the throng, avoided contact as much as possible. The linkages of his legs and back were beginning to go, and he knew the wrong kind of blow could dislodge whole segments. He was over the bridge without disaster. A dirt track led off the path and down toward the river.

He turned toward it, stumbled against one of two men carrying a pig in a net slung between them. Part of the shell on his right upper leg gave way and he could feel it begin to slip down inside his pants.

The man he had hit took two backward steps, almost dropped the end of the burden.

"Careful!" the man shouted.

The man at the other end of the net said: "Damn drunks."

The pig set up a squirming, squealing distraction.

In this moment, he slipped past them onto the dirt track leading down toward the river. He could see the water down there now, boiling with aeration from the barrier filters.

Behind him, one of the pig carriers said: "I don't think he was drunk, Carlos. His skin felt dry and hot. Maybe he was sick."

The track turned around an embankment of raw dirt dark brown with dampness and dipped toward a tunnel through ferns and bushes. The men with the pig could no longer see him, he knew, and he grabbed at his pants where the part of his leg was slipping, scurried into the green tunnel.

Now, he caught sight of his first mutated bee. It was dead, having entered the barrier vibration area here without any protection against that deadliness. The bee was one of the butterfly type with iridescent yellow and orange wings. It lay in the cup of a green leaf at the center of a shaft of sunlight.

He shuffled past, having recorded the bee's shape and color. They had considered the bees as a possible answer, but there were serious drawbacks to this course. A bee could not reason with humans, that was the key fact. And humans had to listen to reason soon, else all life would end.

There came the sound of someone hurrying down the path behind him, heavy footsteps thudding on the earth.

Pursuit . . . ?

He was reduced to a slow shuffling now and soon it would be only crawling progress, he knew. Eyes searched the greenery around him for a place of concealment. A thin break in the fern wall on his left caught his attention. Tiny human footprints led into it—children. He forced his way through the ferns, found himself on a low narrow path along the embankment. Two toy aircars, red and blue, had been abandoned on the path. His staggering foot pressed them into the dirt.

The path led close to a wall of black dirt festooned with creepers, around a sharp turn and onto the lip of a shallow cave. More toys lay in the green gloom at the cave's mouth.

He knelt, crawled over the toys into the blessed dankness, lay there a moment, waiting.

The pounding footsteps hurried past a few feet below.

Voices reached up to him.

"He was headed toward the river. Think he was going to jump in?"

"Who knows? But I think me for sure he was sick."

"Here; down this way. Somebody's been down this way."

The voices grew indistinct, blended with the bubbling sound of the river.

The men were going on down the path. They had missed his hiding place. But why had they pursued him? He had not seriously injured the one by stumbling against him. Surely, they did not suspect.

Slowly, he steeled himself for what had to be done, brought his specialized parts into play and began burrowing into the earth at the end of the cave. Deeper and deeper he burrowed, thrusting the excess dirt behind and out to make it appear the cave had collapsed.

Ten meters in he went before stopping. His store of energy contained just enough reserve for the next stage. He turned on his back, scattering the dead parts of his legs and back, exposing the queen and her guard cluster to the dirt beneath his chitinous spine. Orifices opened at his thighs, exuded the cocoon foam, the soothing green cover that would harden into a protective shell.

This was victory; the essential parts had survived.

Time was the thing now—ten and one half days to gather new energy, go through the metamorphosis and disperse. Soon, there would be thousands of him—each with its carefully mimicked clothing and identification papers and appearance of humanity.

Identical—each of them.

There would be other checkpoints, but not as severe; other barriers, lesser ones.

This human copy had proved a good one. They had learned many things from study of their scattered captives and from the odd crew directed by the red-haired human female they'd trapped in the *sertao*. How strange she was: like a queen and not like a queen. It was so difficult to understand human creatures, even when you permitted them limited freedom . . . almost impossible to reason with them. Their slavery to the planet would have to be proved dramatically, perhaps.

The queen stirred near the cool dirt. They had learned new things this time about escaping notice. All of the subsequent colony clusters would share that knowledge. One of them—at least—would get through to the city by the Amazon "River Sea" where the death-for-all originated. One had to get through.

Senhor Gabriel Martinho, prefect of the Mato Grosso Barrier Compact, paced his study, muttering to himself as he passed the tall, narrow window that admitted the evening sunlight. Occasionally, he paused to glare down at his son, Joao, who sat on a tapir-leather sofa beneath one of the tall bookcases that lined the room.

The elder Martinho was a dark wisp of a man, limb thin, with gray hair and cavernous brown eyes above an eagle nose, slit mouth, and boot-toe chin. He wore old style black clothing as befitted his position, his linen white against the black, and with golden cuffstuds glittering as he waved his arms.

"I am an object of ridicule!" he snarled.

Joao, a younger copy of the father, his hair still black and wavy, absorbed the statement in silence. He wore a *bandeirante*'s white coverall suit sealed into plastic boots at the calf.

"An object of ridicule!" the elder Martinho repeated.

It began to grow dark in the room, the quick tropic darkness hurried by thunderheads piled along the horizon. The waning daylight carried a hazed blue cast. Heat lightning spattered the patch of sky visible through the tall window, sent dazzling electric radiance into the study. Drumming thunder followed. As though that were the signal, the house sensors turned on lights wherever there were humans. Yellow illumination filled the study.

The Prefect stopped in front of his son. "Why does my own son, a *bandeirante*, a jefe of the Irmandades, spout these Carsonite stupidities?"

Joao looked at the floor between his boots. He felt both resentment and shame. To disturb his father this way, that was a hurtful thing, with the elder Martinho's delicate heart. But the old man was so blind!

"Those rabble farmers laughed at me," the elder Martinho said. "I told them we'd increase the green area by ten thousand hectares this month, and they laughed. 'Your own son does not even believe this!' they said. And they told me some of the things you had been saying."

"I am sorry I have caused you distress, Father," Joao said. "The fact that I'm *a bandeirante . . .* " He shrugged. "How else could I have learned the truth about this extermination program?"

His father quivered.

"Joao! Do you sit there and tell me you took a false oath when you formed your Irmandades band?"

"That's not the way it was, Father."

Joao pulled a sprayman's emblem from his breast pocket, fingered it. "I believed it . . . then. We could shape mutated bees to fill every gap in the insect ecology. This I believed. Like the Chinese, I said: 'Only the useful shall live!' But that was several years ago, Father, and since then I have come to realize we don't have a complete understanding of what usefulness means."

"It was a mistake to have you educated in North America," his father said. "That's where you absorbed this Carsonite heresy. It's all well and good for *them* to refuse to join the rest of the world in the Ecological Realignment; they do not have as many million mouths to feed. But my own son!"

Joao spoke defensively: "Out in the red areas you see things, Father. These things are difficult to explain. Plants look healthier out there and the fruit is . . ."

"A purely temporary thing," his father said. "We will shape bees to meet whatever need we find. The destroyers take food from our mouths. It is very simple. They must die and be replaced by creatures which serve a function useful to mankind."

"The birds are dying, Father," Joao said.

"We are saving the birds! We have specimens of every kind in our sanctuaries. We will provide new foods for them to . . ."

"But what happens if our barriers are breached . . . before we can replace the population of natural predators? What happens then?"

The elder Martinho shook a thin finger under his son's nose. "This is nonsense! I will hear no more of it! Do you know what else those *mameluco* farmers said? They said they have seen *bandeirantes* reinfesting the green areas to prolong their jobs! That is what they said. This, too, is nonsense—but it is a natural consequence of defeatist talk just such as I have heard from you tonight. And every setback we suffer adds strength to such charges!"

"Setbacks, Father?"

"I have said it: setbacks!"

Senhor Prefect Martinho turned, paced to his desk and back. Again, he stopped in front of his son, placed hands on hips. "You refer to the Piratininga, of course?"

"You accuse me, Father?"

"Your Irmandades were on that line."

"Not so much as a flea got through us!"

"Yet, a week ago the Piratininga was green. Now, it is crawling. Crawling!"

"I cannot watch every *bandeirante* in the Mato Grosso," Joao protested. "If they . . ."

"The IEO gives us only six months to clean up," the elder Martinho said. He raised his hands, palms up; his face was flushed. "Six months! Then they throw an embargo around all Brazil—the way they have done with North America." He lowered his hands. "Can you imagine the pressures on me? Can you imagine the things I must listen to about the *bandeirantes* and especially about my own son?"

Joao scratched his chin with the sprayman's emblem. The reference to the International Ecological Organization made him think of Dr. Rhin Kelly, the IEO's lovely field director. His mind pictured her as he had last seen her in the A' Chigua nightclub at Bahia—red-haired, green-eyed . . . so lovely and strange. But she had been missing almost six weeks now—somewhere in the *sertao*—and there were those who said she must be dead.

Joao looked at his father. If only the old man weren't so excitable. "You excite yourself needlessly, Father," he said. "The Piratininga was not a full barrier, just a . . ."

"Excite myself!"

The Prefect's nostrils dilated; he bent toward his son. "Already we have gone past two deadlines. We gained an extension when I announced you and the *bandeirantes* of Diogo Alvarez had cleared the Piratininga. How do I explain now that it is reinfested, that we have the work to do over?"

Joao returned the sprayman's emblem to his pocket. It was obvious he'd not be able to reason with his father this night. Frustration sent a nerve quivering along Joao's jaw. The old man had to be told, though; someone had to tell him. And someone of his father's stature had to get back to the Bureau, shake them up there and make *them* listen.

The Prefect returned to his desk, sat down. He picked up an antique crucifix, one that the great Aleihadinho had carved in ivory. He lifted it, obviously seeking to restore his serenity, but his eyes went wide and glaring. Slowly, he returned the crucifix to its position on the desk, keeping his attention on it.

"Joao," he whispered.

It's his heart! Joao thought.

He leaped to his feet, rushed to his father's side. "Father! What is it?"

The elder Martinho pointed, hand trembling.

Through the spiked crown of thorns, across the agonized ivory face, over the straining muscles of the Christ figure crawled an insect. It was the color of the ivory, faintly reminiscent of a beetle in shape, but with a multi-clawed fringe along its wings and thorax, and with furry edging to its abnormally long antennae.

The elder Martinho reached for a roll of papers to smash the insect, but Joao put out a hand restraining him. "Wait. This is a new one. I've never seen anything like it. Give me a handlight. We must follow it, find where it nests."

Senhor Prefect Martinho muttered under his breath, withdrew a small Permalight from a drawer of the desk, handed the light to his son.

Joao peered at the insect, still not using the light. "How strange it is," he said. "See how it exactly matches the tone of the ivory."

The insect stopped, pointed its antennae toward the two men.

"Things have been seen," Joao said. "There are stories. Something like this was found near one of the barrier villages last month. It was inside the green area, on a path beside a river. Two farmers found it while searching for a sick man." Joao looked at his father. "They are very watchful of sickness in the newly green regions, you know. There have been epidemics . . . and that is another thing."

"There is no relationship," his father snapped. "Without insects to carry disease, we will have less illness."

"Perhaps," Joao said, and his tone said he did not believe it.

Joao returned his attention to the insect. "I do not think our ecologists know all they say they do. And I mistrust our Chinese advisors. They speak in such flowery terms of the benefits from eliminating useless insects, but they will not let us go into their green areas and inspect. Excuses. Always excuses. I think they are having troubles they do not wish us to know."

"That's foolishness," the elder Martinho growled, but his tone said this was not a position he cared to defend. "They are honorable men. Their way of life is closer to our socialism than it is to the decadent capitalism of North America. Your trouble is you see them too much through the eyes of those who educated you."

"I'll wager this insect is one of the spontaneous mutations," Joao said. "It is almost as though they appeared according to some plan. Find me something in which I may capture this creature and take it to the laboratory."

The elder Martinho remained standing by his chair. "Where will you say it was found?"

"Right here," Joao said.

"You will not hesitate to expose me to more ridicule?"

"But Father . . ."

"Can't you hear what they will say? In his own home this insect is found. It is a strange new kind. Perhaps he breeds them there to reinfest the green."

"Now *you* are talking nonsense, father. Mutations are common in a threatened species. And we cannot deny there is threat to insect species—the poisons, the barrier vibrations, the traps. Get me a container, Father. I cannot leave this creature, or I'd get a container myself."

"And you will tell where it was found?"

"I can do nothing else. We must cordon off this area, search it out. This could be . . . an accident . . ."

"Or a deliberate attempt to embarrass me."

Joao took his attention from the insect, studied his father. *That* was a possibility, of course. The Carsonites had friends in many places . . . and some were fanatics who would stoop to any scheme. Still . . .

Decision came to Joao. He returned his attention to the motionless insect. His father had to be told, had to be reasoned with at any cost. Someone whose voice carried authority had to get down to the Capitol and make them listen.

"Our earliest poisons killed off the weak and selected out those insects immune to this threat," Joao said. "Only the immune remained to breed. The poisons we use now . . . some of them do not leave such loopholes and the deadly vibrations at the barriers . . ." He shrugged. "This is a form of beetle, Father. I will show you a thing."

Joao drew a long, thin whistle of shiny metal from his pocket. "There was a time when this called countless beetles to their deaths. I had merely to tune it across their attraction spectrum." He put the whistle to his lips, blew while turning the end of it.

No sound audible to human ears came from the instrument, but the beetle's antennae writhed.

Joao removed the whistle from his mouth.

The antennae stopped writhing.

"It stayed put, you see," Joao said. "And there are indications of malignant intelligence among them. The insects are far from extinction, Father . . . and they are beginning to strike back."

"Malignant intelligence, pah!"

"You must believe me, Father," Joao said. "No one else will listen. They laugh and say we are too long in the jungle. And where is our evidence? And they say such stories could be expected from ignorant farmers but not from *bandeirantes*. You must listen, Father, and believe. It is why I was chosen to come here . . . because you are my father and you might listen to your own son."

"Believe what?" the elder Martinho demanded, and he was the Prefect now, standing erect, glaring coldly at his son.

"In the *sertao* of Goyaz last week," Joao said, "Antonil Lisboa's *bandeirante* lost three men who . . ."

"Accidents."

"They were killed with formic acid and oil of copahu."

"They were careless with their poisons. Men grow careless when they . . ."

"Father! The formic acid was a particularly strong type, but still recognizable as having been . . . or being of a type manufactured by insects. And the men were drenched with it. While the oil of copahu . . ."

"You imply that insects such as this . . ." The Prefect pointed to the motion-less creature on the crucifix. ". . . blind creatures such as this . . ."

"They're not blind, Father."

"I did not mean literally blind, but without intelligence," the elder Martinho said. "You cannot be seriously implying that these creatures attacked humans and killed them."

"We have yet to discover precisely how the men were slain," Joao said. "We have only their bodies and the physical evidence at the scene. But there have been other deaths, Father, and men missing and we grow more and more certain that . . ."

He broke off as the beetle crawled off the crucifix onto the desk. Immediately, it darkened to brown, blending with the wood surface.

"Please, Father. Get me a container."

"I will get you a container only if you promise to use discretion in your story of where this creature was found," the Prefect said.

"Father, I . . ."

The beetle leaped off the desk far out into the middle of the room, scuttled to the wall, up the wall, into a crack beside a window.

Joao pressed the switch of the handlight, directed its beam into the hole which had swallowed the strange beetle.

"How long has this hole been here, Father?"

"For years. It was a flaw in the masonry . . . an earthquake, I believe."

Joao turned, crossed to the door in three strides, went through an arched hallway, down a flight of stone steps, through another door and short hall, through a grillwork gate and into the exterior garden. He set the handlight to full intensity, washed its blue glare over the wall beneath the study window.

"Joao, what are you doing?"

"My job, Father," Joao said. He glanced back, saw that the elder Martinho had stopped just outside the gate.

Joao returned his attention to the exterior wall, washed the blue glare of light on the stones beneath the window. He crouched low, running the light along the ground, peering behind each clod, erasing all shadows.

His searching scrutiny passed over the raw earth, turned to the bushes, then the lawn.

Joao heard his father come up behind.

"Do you see it, son?"

"No, Father."

"You should have allowed me to crush it."

From the outer garden that bordered the road and the stone fence, there came a piercing stridulation. It hung on the air in almost tangible waves, making Joao think of the hunting cry of jungle predators. A shiver moved up his spine. He turned toward the driveway where he had parked his airtruck, sent the blue glare of light stabbing there.

He broke off, staring at the lawn. "What is that?"

The ground appeared to be in motion, reaching out toward them like the curling of a wave on a beach. Already, they were cut off from the house. The wave was still some ten paces away, but moving in rapidly.

Joao stood up, clutched his father's arm. He spoke quietly, hoping not to alarm the old man further. "We must get to my truck, Father. We must run across them."

"Them?"

"Those are like the insect we saw inside, father—millions of them. Perhaps they are not beetles, after all. Perhaps they are like army ants. We must make it to the truck. I have equipment and supplies there. We will be safe inside. It is a *bandeirante* truck, Father. You must run with me. I will help you."

They began to run, Joao holding his father's arm, pointing the way with the light.

Let his heart be strong enough, Joao prayed.

They were into the creeping waves of insects then, but the creatures leaped aside, opening a pathway which closed behind the running men.

The white form of the airtruck loomed out of the shadows at the far curve of the driveway about fifteen meters ahead.

"Joao . . . my heart," the elder Martinho gasped.

"You can make it," Joao panted. "Faster!" He almost lifted his father from the ground for the last few paces.

They were at the wide rear door into the truck's lab compartment now. Joao yanked open the door, slapped the light switch, reached for a spray hood and poison gun. He stopped, stared into the yellow-lighted compartment.

Two men sat there—*sertao* Indians by the look of them, with bright glaring eyes and bang-cut black hair beneath straw hats. They looked to be identical twins—even to the mud-gray clothing and sandals, the leather shoulder bags. The beetle-like insects crawled around them, up the walls, over the instruments and vials.

"What the devil?" Joao blurted.

One of the pair held a qena flute. He gestured with it, spoke in a rasping, oddly inflected voice: "Enter. You will not be harmed if you obey."

Joao felt his father sag, caught the old man in his arms. How light he felt! Joao stepped up into the truck, carrying his father. The elder Martinho breathed in short, painful gasps. His face was a pale blue and sweat stood out on his forehead.

"Joao," he whispered. "Pain . . . my chest."

"Medicine, Father," Joao said. "Where is your medicine?"

"House," the old man said.

"It appears to be dying," one of the Indians rasped.

Still holding his father in his arms, Joao, whirled toward the pair, blazed: "I don't know who you are or why you loosed those bugs here, but my father's dying and needs help. Get out of my way!"

"Obey or both die," said the Indian with the flute.

"He needs his medicine and a doctor," Joao pleaded. He didn't like the way the Indian pointed that flute. The motion suggested the instrument was actually a weapon.

"What part has failed?" asked the other Indian. He stared curiously at Joao's father. The old man's breathing had become shallow and rapid.

"It's his heart," Joao said. "I know you farmers don't think he's acted fast enough for . . ."

"Not farmers," said the one with the flute. "Heart?"

"Pump," said the other.

"Pump." The Indian with the flute stood up from the bench at the front of the lab, gestured down. "Put . . . Father here."

The other one got off the bench, stood aside.

In spite of fear for his father, Joao was caught by the strange look of this pair, the fine, scale-like lines in their skin, the glittering brilliance of their eyes.

"Put Father here," repeated the one with the flute, pointing at the bench. "Help can be . . ."

"Attained," said the other one.

"Attained," said the one with the flute.

Joao focused now on the masses of insects around the walls, the waiting quietude in their ranks. They *were* like the one in the study.

The old man's breathing was now very shallow, very rapid.

He's dying, Joao thought in desperation.

"Help can be attained," repeated the one with the flute. "If you obey, we will not harm."

The Indian lifted his flute, pointed it at Joao like a weapon. "Obey."

There was no mistaking the gesture.

Slowly, Joao advanced, deposited his father gently on the bench.

The other Indian bent over the elder Martinho's head, raised an eyelid. There was a professional directness about the gesture. The Indian pushed gently on the dying man's diaphragm, removed the Prefect's belt, loosened his collar. A stubby brown finger was placed against the artery in the old man's neck.

"Very weak," the Indian rasped.

Joao took another, closer look at this Indian, wondering at the sertao backwoodsman who behaved like a doctor.

"We've got to get him to a hospital," Joao said. "And his medicine in . . ."

"Hospital," the Indian agreed.

"Hospital?" asked the one with the flute.

A low, stridulate hissing came from the other Indian.

"Hospital," said the one with the flute.

That stridulate hissing! Joao stared at the Indian beside the Prefect. The sound had been reminiscent of the weird call that had echoed across the lawn.

The one with the flute poked him, said: "You will go into front and maneuver this . . ."

"Vehicle," said the one beside Joao's father.

"Vehicle," said the one with the flute.

"Hospital?" Joao pleaded.

"Hospital," agreed the one with the flute.

Joao looked once more to his father. The other Indian already was strapping the elder Martinho to the bench in preparation for movement. How competent the man appeared in spite of his backwoods look.

"Obey," said the one with the flute.

Joao opened the door into the front compartment, slipped through, feeling the other one follow. A few drops of rain spattered darkly against the curved windshield. Joao squeezed into the operator's seat, noted how the Indian crouched behind him, flute pointed and ready.

A *dart gun of some kind*, Joao guessed.

He punched the ignitor button on the dash, strapped himself in while waiting for the turbines to build up speed. The Indian still crouched behind him, vulnerable now if the airtruck were spun sharply. Joao flicked the communications switch on the lower left corner of the dash, looked into the tiny screen there giving him a view of the lab compartment. The rear doors were open. He closed them by hydraulic remote. His father was securely strapped to the bench now, Joao noted, but the other Indian was equally secured.

The turbines reached their whining peak. Joao switched on the lights, engaged the hydrostatic drive. The truck lifted six inches, angled upward as Joao increased pump displacement. He turned left onto the street, lifted another two meters to increase speed, headed toward the lights of a boulevard.

The Indian spoke beside his ear: "You will turn toward the mountain over there." A hand came forward, pointing to the right.

The Alejandro Clinic is there in the foothills, Joao thought.

He made the indicated turn down the cross street angling toward the boulevard.

Casually, he gave pump displacement another boost, lifted another meter and increased speed once more. In the same motion, he switched on the intercom to the rear compartment, tuned for the spare amplifier and pickup in the compartment beneath the bench where his father lay.

The pickup, capable of making a dropped pin sound like a cannon, gave forth only a distant hissing and rasping. Joao increased amplification. The instrument should have been transmitting the old man's heartbeats now, sending a noticeable drum-thump into the forward cabin.

There was nothing.

Tears blurred Joao's eyes, and he shook his head to clear them.

My father is dead, he thought. *Killed by these crazy backwoodsmen.*

He noted in the dashscreen that the Indian back there had a hand under the elder Martinho's back. The Indian appeared to be massaging the dead man's back, and a rhythmic rasping matched the motion.

Anger filled Joao. He felt like diving the airtruck into an abutment, dying himself to kill these crazy men.

They were approaching the outskirts of the city, and ring-girders circled off to the left giving access to the boulevard. This was an area of small gardens and cottages protected by over-fly canopies.

Joao lifted the airtruck above the canopies, headed toward the boulevard.

To the clinic, yes, he thought. *But it is too late.*

In that instant, he realized there were no heartbeats at all coming from that rear compartment—only that slow, rhythmic grating, a faint susurration and a cicada-like hum up and down scale.

"To the mountains, there," said the Indian behind him.

Again, the hand came forward to point off to the right.

Joao, with that hand close to his eyes and illuminated by the dash, saw the scale-like parts of a finger shift position slightly. In that shift, he recognized the scale-shapes by their claw fringes.

The beetles!

The finger was composed of linked beetles working in unison!

Joao turned, stared into the *Indian's* eyes, seeing now why they glistened so: they were composed of thousands of tiny facets.

"Hospital, there," the creature beside him said, pointing.

Joao turned back to the controls, fighting to keep from losing composure. They were not Indians . . . they weren't even human. They were insects—some kind of hive-cluster shaped and organized to mimic a man.

The implications of this discovery raced through his mind. How did they support their weight? How did they feed and breathe?

How did they speak?

Everything had to be subordinated to the urgency of getting this information and proof of it back to one of the big labs where the facts could be explored.

Even the death of his father could not be considered now. He had to capture one of these things, get out with it.

He reached overhead, flicked on the command transmitter, set its beacon for a homing call. *Let some of my Irmaos be awake and monitoring their sets,* he prayed.

"More to the right," said the creature behind him.

Again, Joao corrected course.

The moon was high overhead now, illuminating a line of *bandeirante* towers off to the left. The first barrier.

They would be out of the green area soon and into the gray—then, beyond that, another barrier and the great red that stretched out in reaching fingers through the Goyaz and the Mato Grosso. Joao could see scattered lights of Resettlement Plan farms ahead, and darkness beyond.

The airtruck was going faster than he wanted, but Joao dared not slow it. They might become suspicious.

"You must go higher," said the creature behind him.

Joao increased pump displacement, raised the nose. He leveled off at three hundred meters.

More *bandeirante* towers loomed ahead, spaced at closer intervals. Joao picked up the barrier signals on his meters, looked back at the *Indian*. The dissembler vibrations seemed not to affect the creature.

Joao looked out his side window and down. No one would challenge him, he knew. This was a *bandeirante* airtruck headed *into* the red zone . . . and with its transmitter sending out a homing call. The men down there would assume he was a bandleader headed out on a contract after a successful bid—and calling his men to him for the job ahead.

He could see the moon-silvered snake of the São Francisco winding off to his left, and the lesser waterways like threads raveled out of the foothills.

I must find the nest—where we're headed, Joao thought. He wondered if he dared turn on his receiver—but if his men started reporting in . . . No. That could make the creatures suspect; they might take violent counter-action.

My men will realize something is wrong when I don't answer, he thought. *They will follow.*

If any of them hear my call.

Hours droned past.

Nothing but moonlighted jungle sped beneath them now, and the moon was low on the horizon, near setting. This was the deep red region where broadcast poisons had been used at first with disastrous results. This was where the wild mutations had originated. It was here that Rhin Kelly had been reported missing.

This was the region being saved for the final assault, using a mobile barrier line when that line could be made short enough.

Joao armed the emergency charge that would separate the front and rear compartments of the truck when he fired it. The stub wings of the front compartment and its emergency rocket motors could get him back into *bandeirante* country.

With the *specimen* sitting behind him safely subdued, Joao hoped.

He looked up through the canopy, scanned the horizon as far as he could. Was that moonlight glistening on a truck far back to the right? He couldn't be sure.

"How much farther?" Joao asked.

"Ahead," the creature rasped.

Now that he was alert for it, Joao heard the modulated stridulation beneath that voice.

"But how long?" Joao asked. "My father . . ."

"Hospital for . . . the father . . . ahead," said the creature.

It would be dawn soon, Joao realized. He could see the first false line of light along the horizon behind. This night had passed so swiftly. Joao wondered if these creatures had injected some time-distorting drug into him without his knowing. He thought not. He was maintaining himself in the necessities of the moment. There was no time for fatigue or boredom when he had to record every landmark half-visible in the night, sense everything there was to sense about these creatures with him.

How did they coordinate all those separate parts?

Dawn came, revealing the plateau of the Mato Grosso. Joao looked out his windows. This region, he knew, stretched across five degrees of latitude and six degrees of longitude. Once, it had been a region of isolated *fazendas* farmed by independent blacks and by *sertanistos* chained to the *encomendero* plantation system. It was hardwood jungles with narrow rivers with banks overgrown by lush trees and ferns, savannahs, and tangled life.

Even in this age it remained primitive, a fact blamed largely on insects and disease. It was one of the last strongholds of *teeming* insect life, if the International Ecological Organization's reports could be believed.

Supplies for the *bandeirantes* making the assault on this insect stronghold would come by way of São Paulo, by air and by transport on the multi-decked highways, then on antique diesel trains to Itapira, on river runners to Bahus and by airtruck to Registo and Leopoldina on the Araguaya.

This area crawled with insects: wire worms in the roots of the savannahs, grubs digging in the moist black earth, hopping beetles, dart-like angita wasps, chalcis flies, chiggers, sphecidae, braconidae, fierce hornets, white termites, hemipteric crawlers, blood roaches, thrips, ants, lice, mosquitoes, mites, moths, exotic butterflies, mantidae—and countless unnatural mutations of them all.

This would be an expensive fight—unless it were stopped . . . because it already had been lost.

I mustn't think that way, Joao told himself. *Out of respect for my father.*

Maps of the IEO showed this region in varied intensities of red. Around the red ran a ring of gray with pink shading where one or two persistent forms of insect life resisted man's poisons, jelly flames, astringents, sonitoxics—the combination of flamant couroq and supersonics that drove insects from their hiding places into waiting death—and all the mechanical traps and lures in the *bandeirante* arsenal.

A grid map would be placed over this area and each thousand-acre square offered for bid to the independent bands to deinfest.

We bandeirantes *are a kind of ultimate predator,* Joao thought. *It's no wonder these creatures mimic us.*

But how good, really, was the mimicry? he asked himself. And how deadly to the predators?

"There," said the creature behind him, and the multipart hand came forward to point toward a black scarp visible ahead in the gray light of morning.

Joao's foot kicked a trigger on the floor releasing a great cloud of orange dye-fog beneath the truck to mark the ground and forest for a mile around under this spot. As he kicked the trigger, Joao began counting down the five-second delay to the firing of the separation charge.

It came in a roaring blast that Joao knew would smear the creature behind him against the rear bulkhead. He sent the stub wings out, fed power to the rocket motors and back hard around. He saw the detached rear compartment settling slowly earthward above the dye cloud, its fall cushioned as the pumps of the hydrostatic drive automatically compensated.

I will come back, Father, Joao thought. *You will be buried among family and friends.*

He locked the controls, twisted in the seat to see what had happened to his captive.

A gasp escaped Joao's lips.

The rear bulkhead crawled with insects clustered around something white and pulsing. The mud-gray shirt and trousers were torn, but insects already were repairing it, spinning out fibers that meshed and sealed on contact. There was a yellow-like extrusion near the pulsing white, and a dark brown skeleton with familiar articulation.

It looked like a human skeleton—but chitinous.

Before his eyes, the thing was reassembling itself, the long, furry antennae burrowing into the structure and interlocking.

The flute-weapon was not visible, and the thing's leather pouch had been thrown into the rear corner, but its eyes were in place in their brown sockets, staring at him. The mouth was re-forming.

The yellow sac contracted, and a voice issued from the half-formed mouth.

"You must listen," it rasped.

Joao gulped, whirled back to the controls, unlocked them and sent the cab into a wild, spinning turn.

A high-pitched rattling buzz sounded behind him. The noise seemed to pick up every bone in his body and shake it. Something crawled on his neck. He slapped at it, felt it squash.

All Joao could think of was escape. He stared frantically out at the earth beneath, seeing a blotch of white in a savannah off to his right and, in the same instant, recognizing another airtruck banking beside him, the insignia of his own Irmandades band bright on its side.

The white blotch in the savannah was resolving itself into a cluster of tents with an IEO orange and green banner flying beside them.

Joao dove for the tents, praying the other airtruck would follow.

Something stung his cheek. They were in his hair—biting, stinging. He stabbed the braking rockets, aimed for open ground about fifty meters from the tent. Insects were all over the inside of the glass now, blocking his vision. Joao said a silent prayer, hauled back on the control arm, felt the cab mush out, touch ground, skidding and slewing across the savannah. He kicked the canopy release before the cab stopped, broke the seal on his safety harness and launched himself up and out to land sprawling in grass.

He rolled through the grass, feeling the insect bites like fire over every exposed part of his body. Hands grabbed him and he felt a jelly hood splash across his face to protect it. A voice he recognized as Thome of his own band said: "This way, Johnny! Run!" They ran.

He heard a spraygun fire: "Whooosh!"

And again.

And again.

Arms lifted him and he felt a leap.

They landed in a heap and a voice said: "Mother of God! Would you look at that!"

Joao clawed the jelly hood from his face, sat up to stare across the savannah. The grass seethed and boiled with insects around the uptilted cab and the airtruck that had landed beside it.

Joao looked around him, counted seven of his Irmaos with Thome, his chief sprayman, in command.

Beyond them clustered five other people, a red-haired woman slightly in front, half turned to look at the savannah and at him. He recognized the woman immediately: Dr. Rhin Kelly of the IEO. When they had met in the A' Chigua nightclub in Bahia, she had seemed exotic and desirable to Joao. Now, she wore a field uniform instead of gown and jewels, and her eyes held no invitation at all.

"I see a certain poetic justice in this . . . traitors," she said.

Joao lifted himself to his feet, took a cloth proffered by one of his men, wiped off the last of the jelly. He felt hands brushing him, clearing dead insects off his coveralls. The pain of his skin was receding under the medicant jelly, and now he found himself dominated by puzzled questioning as he recognized the mood of the IEO personnel.

They were furious and it was directed at him . . . and at his fellow Irmandades.

Joao studied the woman, noting how her green eyes glared at him, the pink flush to her skin.

"Dr. Kelly?" Joao said.

"If it isn't Joao Martinho, jefe of the Irmandades," she said, "the traitor of the Piratininga."

"They are crazy, that is the only thing, I think," said Thome.

"Your pets turned on you, didn't they?" she demanded.

"And wasn't that inevitable?"

"Would you be so kind as to explain," Joao said.

"I don't need to explain," she said. "Let your friends out there explain." She pointed toward the rim of jungle beyond the savannah.

Joao looked where she pointed, saw a line of men in *bandeirante* white standing untouched amidst the leaping, boiling insects in the jungle shadow. He took a pair of binoculars from around the neck of one of his men, focused on the figures. Knowing what to look for made the identification easy.

"Tommy," Joao said.

His chief sprayman, Thome, bent close, rubbing at an insect sting on his swarthy cheek.

In a low voice, Joao explained what the figures at the jungle edge were.

"Aieeee," Thome said.

An Irmandade on Joao's left crossed himself.

"What was it we leaped across coming in here?" Joao asked.

"A ditch," Thome said. "It seems to be filled with couroq jelly . . . an insect barrier of some kind."

Joao nodded. He began to have unpleasant suspicions about their position here. He looked at Rhin Kelly. "Dr. Kelly, where are the rest of your people? Surely there are more than five in an IEO field crew."

Her lips compressed, but she remained silent.

"So?" Joao glanced around at the tents, seeing their weathered condition. "And where is your equipment, your trucks and lab huts and jitneys?"

"Funny thing you should ask," she said, but there was uncertainty atop the sneering quality of her voice. "About a kilometer into the trees over there . . ." She nodded to her left. ". . . is a wrecked jungle truck containing most of our . . . equipment, as you call it. The track spools of our truck were eaten away by acid."

"Acid?"

"It smelled like oxalic," said one of her companions, a blond Nordic with a scar beneath his right eye.

"Start from the beginning," Joao said.

"We were cut off here almost six weeks ago," said the blond man. "Something got our radio, our truck—they looked like giant chiggers and they can shoot an acid spray about fifteen meters."

"There's a glass case containing three dead specimens in my lab tent," said Dr. Kelly.

Joao pursued his lips, thinking. "So?"

"I heard part of what you were telling your men there," she said. "Do you expect us to believe that?"

"It is of no importance to me what you believe," Joao said. "How did you get here?"

"We fought our way in here from the truck using *caramuru* cold-fire spray," said the blond man. "We dragged along what supplies we could, dug a trench around our perimeter, poured in the couroq powder, added the jell compound and topped it off with our *copahu* oil . . . and here we sat."

"How many of you?" Joao asked.

"There were fourteen of us," said the man.

Joao rubbed the back of his neck where the insect stings were again beginning to burn. He glanced around at his men, assessing their condition and equipment, counted four spray rifles, saw the men carried spare charge cylinders on slings around their necks.

"The airtruck will take us," he said. "We had better get out of here."

Dr. Kelly looked out to the savannah, said: "I think it has been too late for that since a few seconds after you landed, *bandeirante*. I think in a day or so there'll be a few less traitors around. You're caught in your own trap."

Joao whirled to stare at the airtruck, barked: "Tommy! Vince! Get . . ." He broke off as the airtruck sagged to its left.

"It's only fair to warn you," said Dr. Kelly, "to stay away from the edge of the ditch unless you first spray the opposite side. They can shoot a stream of acid at least fifteen meters . . . and as you can see . . ." She nodded toward the airtruck. ". . . the acid eats metal."

"You're insane," Joao said. "Why didn't you warn us immediately?"

"Warn you?"

Her blond companion said: "Rhin, perhaps we . . ."

"Be quiet, Hogar," she said, and turned back to Joao. "We lost nine men to your playmates." She looked at the small band of Irmandades. "Our lives are little enough to pay now for the extinction of eight of you . . . traitors."

"You *are* insane," Joao said.

"Stop playing innocent, *bandeirante*," she said. "We have seen your companions out there. We have seen the new playmates you bred . . . and we understand that you were too greedy; now your game has gotten out of hand."

"You've not seen my Irmaos doing these things," Joao said. He looked at Thome. "Tommy, keep an eye on these insane ones." He lifted the spray rifle from one of his men, took the man's spare charges, indicated the other three armed men. "You—come with me."

"Johnny, what do you do?" Thome asked.

"Salvage the supplies from the truck," Joao said. He walked toward the ditch nearest the airtruck, laid down a hard mist of foamal beyond the ditch, beckoned the others to follow and leaped the ditch.

Little more than an hour later, with all of them acid-burned—two seriously— the Irmandades retreated back across the ditch. They had salvaged less than a fourth of the equipment in the truck, and this did not include a transmitter.

"It is evident the little devils went first for the communications equipment," Thome said. "How could they tell?"

Joao said: "I do not want to guess." He broke open a first aid box, began treating his men. One had a cheek and shoulder badly splashed with acid. Another was losing flesh off his back.

Dr. Kelly came up, helped him treat the men, but refused to speak, even to answering the simplest question.

Finally, Joao touched up a spot on his own arm, neutralizing the acid and covering the burn with flesh-tape. He gritted his teeth against the pain, stared at Rhin Kelly. "Where are these chigua you found?"

"Go find them yourself!" she snapped.

"You are a blind, unprincipled megalomaniac," Joao said, speaking in an even voice. "Do not push me too far."

Her face went pale and the green eyes blazed.

Joao grabbed her arm, hauled her roughly toward the tents. "Show me these chigua!"

She jerked free of him, threw back her red hair, stared at him defiantly. Joao faced her, looked her up and down with a calculating slowness.

"Go ahead, do violence to me," she said, "I'm sure I couldn't stop you."

"You act like a woman who wants . . . needs violence," Joao said. "Would you like me to turn you over to my men? They're a little tired of your raving."

Her face flamed. "You would not dare!"

"Don't be so melodramatic," he said, "I wouldn't give you the pleasure."

"You insolent . . . you . . ."

Joao showed her a wolfish grin, said: "Nothing you say will make me turn you over to my men!"

"Johnny."

It was Thome calling.

Joao turned, saw Thome talking to the Nordic IEO man who had volunteered information. What had she called him? Hogar.

Thome beckoned.

Joao crossed to the pair, bent close as Thome signaled secrecy.

"The gentleman here says the female doctor was bitten by an insect that got past their barrier's fumes."

"Two weeks ago," Hogar whispered.

"She has not been the same since," Thome said. "We humor her, jefe, no?"

Joao wet his lips with his tongue. He felt suddenly dizzy and too warm.

"The insect that bit her was similar to the ones that were on you," Hogar said, and his voice sounded apologetic.

They are making fun of me! Joao thought.

"I give the orders here!" he snapped.

"Yes, jefe," Thome said. "But you . . ."

"What difference does it make who gives the orders?"

It was Dr. Kelly close behind him.

Joao turned, glared at her. How hateful she looked . . . in spite of her beauty.

"What's the difference?" she demanded. "We'll all be dead in a few days anyway." She stared out across the savannah. "More of your friends have arrived."

Joao looked to the forest shadow, saw more human-like figures arriving. They appeared familiar and he wondered what it was—something at the edge of his mind, but his head hurt. Then he realized they looked like *sertao* Indians, like the pair who had lured him here. There were at least a hundred of them, apparently identical in every visible respect.

More were arriving by the second.

Each of them carried a qena flute.

There was something about the flutes that Joao felt he should remember.

Another figure came advancing through the *Indians*, a thin man in a black suit, his hair shiny silver in the sunlight.

"Father!" Joao gasped.

I'm sick, he thought. *I must be delirious.*

"That looks like the Prefect," Thome said. "Is it not so, Ramon?"

The Irmandade he addressed said: "If it is not the Prefect, it is his twin. Here, Johnny. Look with the glasses."

Joao took the glasses, focused on the figure advancing toward them through the grass. The glasses felt so heavy. They trembled in his hands and the figure coming toward them was blurred.

"I cannot see!" Joao muttered and he almost dropped the glasses.

A hand steadied him, and he realized he was reeling.

In an instant of clarity, he saw that the line of *Indians* had raised their flutes, pointing at the IEO camp. That buzzing-rasping that had shaken his bones in the airtruck cab filled the universe around him. He saw his companions begin to fall.

In the instant before his world went blank, Joao heard his father's voice calling strongly: "Joao! Do not resist! Put down your weapons!"

The trampled grassy earth of the campsite, Joao saw, was coming up to meet his face.

It cannot be my father, Joao thought. *My father is dead and they've copied him . . . mimicry, nothing more.*

Darkness.

There was a dream of being carried, a dream of tears and shouting, a dream of violent protests and defiance and rejection.

He awoke to yellow-orange light and the figure who could not be his father bending over him, thrusting a hand out, saying: "Then examine my hand if you don't believe!"

But Joao's attention was on the face behind his father. It was a giant face, baleful in the strange light, its eyes brilliant and glaring with pupils within pupils. The face turned, and Joao saw it was no more than two centimeters thick. Again, it turned, and the eyes focused on Joao's feet.

Joao forced himself to look down, began trembling violently as he saw he was half enveloped in a foaming green cocoon, that his skin shared some of the same tone.

"Examine my hand!" ordered the old-man figure beside him.

"He has been dreaming." It was a resonant voice that boomed all around him, seemingly coming from beneath the giant face. "He has been dreaming," the voice repeated. "He is not quite awake."

With an abrupt, violent motion, Joao reached out, clutched the proffered hand.

It felt warm . . . human.

For no reason he could explain, tears came to Joao's eyes.

"Am I dreaming?" he whispered. He shook his head to clear away the tears.

"Joao, my son," said his father's voice.

Joao looked up at the familiar face. It *was* his father and no mistake. "But . . . your heart," Joao said.

"My pump," the old man said. "Look." And he pulled his hand away, turned to display where the back of his black suit had been cut away, its edges held by some gummy substance, and a pulsing surface of oily yellow between those cut edges.

Joao saw the hair-fine scale lines, the multiple shapes, and he recoiled.

So it was a copy, another of their tricks.

The old man turned back to face him. "The old pump failed and they gave me a new one," he said. "It shares my blood and lives off me and it'll give me a few more years. What do you think our bright IEO specialists will say about the *usefulness* of that?"

"Is it really you?" Joao demanded.

"All except the pump," said the old man. "They had to give you and some of the others a whole new blood system because of all the corrosive poison that got into you."

Joao lifted his hands, stared at them.

"They know medical tricks we haven't even dreamed about," the old man said. "I haven't been this excited since I was a boy. I can hardly wait to get back and . . . Joao! What is it?"

Joao was thrusting himself up, glaring at the old man. "We're not human anymore if . . . We're not human!"

"Be still, son!" the old man ordered.

"If this is true," Joao protested, "they're in control." He nodded toward the giant face behind his father. "They'll *rule* us!"

He sank back, gasping. "We'll be their slaves."

"Foolishness," rumbled the drum voice.

Joao looked at the giant face, growing aware of the fluorescent insects above it, seeing that the insects clung to the ceiling of a cave, noting finally a patch of night sky and stars where the fluorescent insects ended.

"What is a slave?" rumbled the voice.

Joao looked beneath the face where the voice originated, saw a white mass about four meters across, a pulsing yellow sac protruding from it, insects crawling over it, into fissures along its surface, back to the ground beneath. The face appeared to be held up from that white mass by a dozen of round stalks, their scaled surfaces betraying their nature.

"Your attention is drawn to our way of answering your threat to us," rumbled the voice, and Joao saw that the sound issued from the pulsing yellow sac. "This is our brain. It is vulnerable, very vulnerable, weak, yet strong . . . just as your brain. Now, tell me what is a slave?"

Joao fought down a shiver of revulsion, said: "I'm a slave now; I'm in bondage to you."

"Not true," rumbled the voice. "A slave is one who must produce wealth for another, and there is only one true wealth in all the universe—living time. Are we slaves because we have given your father more time to live?"

Joao looked up to the giant, glittering eyes, thought he detected amusement there.

"The lives of all those with you have been spared or extended as well," drummed the voice. "That makes us your slaves, does it not?"

"What do you take in return?"

"Ah hah!" the voice fairly barked. "Quid pro quo! You are, indeed, our slaves as well. We are tied to each other by a bond of mutual slavery that cannot be broken—never could be."

"It is very simple once you understand it," Joao's father said.

"Understand what?"

"Some of our kind once lived in greenhouses and their cells remembered the experience," rumbled the voice. "You know about greenhouses, of course?" It turned to look out at the cave mouth where dawn was beginning to touch the world with gray. "That out there, that is a greenhouse, too." Again, it looked down at Joao, the giant eyes glaring. "To sustain life, a greenhouse must achieve a delicate balance—enough of this chemical, enough of that one, another substance available when needed. What is poison one day can be sweet food the next."

"What's all this to do with slavery?" Joao demanded.

"Life has developed over millions of years in this greenhouse we call Earth," the voice rumbled. "Sometimes it developed in the poison excrement of other life . . . and then that poison became necessary to it. Without a substance produced by the wire worm, that savannah grass out there would die . . . in time. Without substances produced by . . . insects, your kind of life would die. Sometimes, just a faint trace of the substance is needed, such as the special copper compound produced by the arachnids. Sometimes, the substance must subtly change each time before it can be used by a life-form at the end of the chain. The more different forms of life there are, the more life the greenhouse can support. This is the lesson of the greenhouse. The successful greenhouse must grow many times many forms of life. The more forms of life it has, the healthier it is."

"You're saying we have to stop killing insects," Joao said. "You're saying we have to let you take over."

"We say you must stop killing yourselves," rumbled the voice. "Already, the Chinese are . . . I believe you would call it: *reinfesting* their land. Perhaps they will be in time, perhaps not. Here, it is not too late. There . . . they were fast and thorough . . . and they may need help."

"You . . . give us no proof," Joao said.

"There will be time for proof, later," said the voice. "Now, join your woman friend outside; let the sun work on your skin and the chlorophyll in your blood, and when you come back, tell me if the sun is your slave."

Jack Vance

John Holbrook Vance (1916–   ) is one of the premier stylists of science fiction, popular world-wide and influential on other writers for six decades. His book *The Dying Earth* (1950), set in a fantastically distant future, is one of the classics of genre science fiction. It is also one of those genre-stretching works that blur the borders between science fiction and fantasy, in the manner of the *Weird Tales* writers of the 1920s and '30s. He has written award-winning mysteries under his full name, and as Ellery Queen (many of the later novels of Queen were written by SF writers such as Theodore Sturgeon, Avram Davidson, and Vance). He is a huge man, a lover of hot jazz and writing, but also a carpenter by trade who was still, in the 1980s, building and rebuilding his own house.

Vance found his writing voice early and hit his stride in the 1950s. Since then he has produced a continuing stream of exquisite work, much of it brilliant. Critics often praise his intricacies and ironies, his subtle wit, his settings and atmospherics. Yet his characters are usually motivated by common passions, no matter how nicely expressed, and his plots are clever. He is still writing distinctive novels of fantasy and SF and winning genre awards in the mid-'90s. He is most often at his best in the novel form, but this piece is one of his later novellas, pure Vance compressed and distilled.

RUMFUDDLE

I

From *Memoirs and Reflections*, by Alan Robertson:

Often I hear myself declared humanity's preeminent benefactor, though the jocular occasionally raise a claim in favor of the original serpent. After all circumspection I really cannot dispute the judgment. My place in history is secure; my name will persist as if it were printed indelibly across the sky. All of which I find absurd but understandable. For I have given wealth beyond calculation. I have expunged deprivation, famine, overpopulation, territorial constriction: All the first-order causes of contention have vanished. My gifts go freely and carry with them my personal joy, but as a reasonable man (and for lack of other restrictive agency), I feel that I cannot relinquish all control, for when has the human animal ever been celebrated for abnegation and self-discipline?

We now enter an era of plenty and a time of new concerns. The old evils are gone: we must resolutely prohibit a flamboyant and perhaps unnatural set of new vices.

The three girls gulped down breakfast, assembled their homework, and departed noisily for school.

Elizabeth poured coffee for herself and Gilbert. He thought she seemed pensive and moody. Presently she said, "It's so beautiful here. . . . We're very lucky, Gilbert."

"I never forget it."

Elizabeth sipped her coffee and mused a moment, following some vagrant train of thought. She said, "I never liked growing up. I always felt strange—different from the other girls. I really don't know why."

"It's no mystery. Everyone for a fact is different."

"Perhaps . . . But Uncle Peter and Aunt Emma always acted as if I were more different than usual. I remember a hundred little signals. And yet I was such an ordinary little girl . . . Do you remember when you were little?"

"Not very well." Gilbert Duray looked out the window he himself had glazed, across green slopes and down to the placid water his daughters had named the Silver River. The Sounding Sea was thirty miles south; behind the house stood the first trees of the Robber Woods.

Duray considered his past. "Bob owned a ranch in Arizona during the 1870s: one of his fads. The Apaches killed my father and mother. Bob took me to the ranch, and then when I was three he brought me to Alan's house in San Francisco, and that's where I was brought up."

Elizabeth sighed. "Alan must have been wonderful. Uncle Peter was so grim. Aunt Emma never told me anything. Literally, not anything! They never cared the slightest bit for me, one way or the other . . . I wonder why Bob brought the subject up—about the Indians and your mother and father being scalped and all . . . He's such a strange man."

"Was Bob here?"

"He looked in a few minutes yesterday to remind us of his Rumfuddle. I told him I didn't want to leave the girls. He said to bring them along."

"Hah!"

"I told him I didn't want to go to his damn Rumfuddle with or without the girls. In the first place, I don't want to see Uncle Peter, who's sure to be there . . ."

II

From *Memoirs and Reflections:*

I insisted then and I insist now that our dear old Mother Earth, so soiled and toil-worn, never be neglected. Since I pay the piper (in a manner of speaking), I call the tune, and to my secret amusement I am heeded most briskly the world around, in the manner of bellboys, jumping to the command of an irascible old gentleman who is known to be a good tipper. No one dares to defy me. My whims become actualities; my plans progress.

Paris, Vienna, San Francisco, St. Petersburg, Venice, London, Dublin, surely will persist, gradually to become idealized essences of their former selves, as wine in due course becomes the soul of the grape. What of the old vitality? The shouts and curses, the neighborhood quarrels, the raucous music, the vulgarity? Gone, all gone! (But easy of reference at any of the cognates.) Old Earth is to be a gentle, kindly world, rich in treasures and artifacts, a world of old places—old inns, old roads, old forests, old palaces—where folk come to wander and dream, to experience the best of the past without suffering the worst.

Material abundance can now be taken for granted: Our resources are infinite. Metal, timber, soil, rock, water, air: free for anyone's taking. A single commodity remains in finite supply: human toil.

Gilbert Duray, the informally adopted grandson of Alan Robertson, worked on the Urban Removal Program. Six hours a day, four days a week, he guided a trashing machine across deserted Cuperinto, destroying tract houses, service stations, and supermarkets. Knobs and toggles controlled a steel hammer at the end of a hundred-foot boom; with a twitch of the finger, Duray toppled powerpoles, exploded picture windows, smashed siding and stucco, exploded picture windows, smashed siding and stucco, pulverized concrete. A disposal rig crawled fifty feet behind. The detritus was clawed upon a conveyor belt, carried to a twenty-foot orifice, and dumped with a rush and a rumble into the Apathetic Ocean. Aluminum siding, asphalt shingles, corrugated fiber-glass, TV's and barbecues, Swedish Modern furniture, Book-of-the-Month selections, concrete patio-tiles, finally the sidewalk and street itself: all to the bottom of the Apathetic Ocean. Only the trees remained, a strange eclectic forest stretching as far as the eye could reach: liquidambar and Scotch pine; Chinese pistachio, Atlas cedar, and ginkgo; white birch and Norway maple.

At one o'clock Howard Wirtz emerged from the caboose, as they called the small locker room at the rear of the machine. Wirtz had homesteaded a Miocene world; Duray, with a wife and three children, had preferred the milder environment of a contemporary semicognate: the popular Type A world on which man had never evolved.

Duray gave Wirtz the work schedule. "More or less like yesterday—straight out Persimmon to Walden, then right a block and back."

Wirtz, a dour and laconic man, acknowledged the information with a jerk of the head. On his Miocene world he lived alone, in a houseboat on a mountain lake. He harvested wild rice, mushrooms, and berries; he shot geese, groundfowl, deer, young bison, and had once informed Duray that after his five-year work-time he might just retire to his lake and never appear on Earth again, except maybe to buy clothes and ammunition. "Nothing here I want, nothing at all."

Duray had given a derisive snort. "And what will you do with all your time?"

"Hunt, fish, eat, and sleep, maybe sit on the front deck."

"Nothing else?"

"I just might learn to fiddle. Nearest neighbor is fifteen million years away."

"You can't be too careful, I suppose."

Duray descended to the ground and looked over his day's work: a quarter-mile swath of desolation. Duray, who allowed his subconscious few extravagances, nevertheless felt a twinge for the old times, which, for all their disadvantages, at least had been lively. Voices, bicycle bells, the barking of dogs, the slamming of doors, still echoed along Persimmon Avenue. The former inhabitants presumably preferred their new homes. The self-sufficient had taken private worlds; the more gregarious lived in communities on worlds of every description: as early as the Carboniferous, as current as the Type A. A few had even returned to the now-uncrowded cities. An exciting era to live in: a time of flux. Duray, thirty-four years old, remembered no other way of life; the old existence, as exemplified by Persimmon Avenue, seemed antique, cramped, constricted.

He had a word with the operator of the trashing machine; returning to the caboose, Duray paused to look through the orifice across the Apathetic Ocean.

A squall hung black above the southern horizon, toward which a trail of broken lumber drifted, ultimately to wash up on some unknown pre-Cambrian shore. There never would be an inspector sailing forth to protest; the world knew no life other than mollusks and algae, and all the trash of Earth would never fill its submarine gorges. Duray tossed a rock through the gap and watched the alien water splash up and subside. Then he turned away and entered the caboose.

Along the back wall were four doors. The second from the left was marked "G. DURAY." He unlocked the door, pulled it open, and stopped short, staring in astonishment at the blank back wall. He lifted the transparent plastic flap that functioned as an air-seal and brought out the collapsed metal ring that had been the flange surrounding his passway. The inner surface was bare metal; looking through, he saw only the interior of the caboose.

A long minute passed. Duray stood staring at the useless ribbon as if hypnotized, trying to grasp the implications of the situation. To his knowledge no passway had ever failed, unless it had been purposefully closed. Who would play him such a spiteful trick? Certainly not Elizabeth. She detested practical jokes and if anything, like Duray himself, was perhaps a trifle too intense and literal-minded. He jumped down from the caboose and strode off across Cupertino Forest: a sturdy, heavy-shouldered man of about average stature. His features were rough and uncompromising; his brown hair was cut crisply short; his eyes glowed golden-brown and exerted an arresting force. Straight, heavy eyebrows crossed his long, thin nose like the bar of a T; his mouth, compressed against some strong inner urgency, formed a lower horizontal bar. All in all, not a man to be trifled with, or so it would seem.

He trudged through the haunted grove, preoccupied by the strange and inconvenient event that had befallen him. What had happened to the passway? Unless Elizabeth had invited friends out to Home, as they called their world, she was alone, with the three girls at school . . . Duray came out upon Stevens Creek Road. A farmer's pickup truck halted at his signal and took him into San Jose, now little more than a country town.

At the transit center he dropped a coin in the turnstile and entered the lobby. Four portals designated "LOCAL," "CALIFORNIA," "NORTH AMERICA," and "WORLD" opened in the walls, each portal leading to a hub on Utilis.*

Duray passed into the "California" hub, found the "Oakland" portal, returned to the Oakland Transit Center on Earth, passed back through the "Local" portal to the "Oakland" hub on Utilis, and returned to Earth through the "Montclair West" portal to a depot only a quarter mile from Thornhill School,† to which Duray walked.

---

*Utilis: a world cognate to Paleocene Earth, where, by Alan Robertson's decree, all the industries, institutions, warehouses, tanks, dumps, and commercial offices of old Earth were now located. The name Utilis, so it had been remarked, accurately captured the flavor of Alan Robertson's pedantic, quaint, and idealistic personality.

†Alan Robertson had proposed another specialized world, to be known as Tutelar, where the children of all the settled worlds should receive their education in a vast array of pedagogical facilities, To his hurt surprise, he encountered a storm of wrathful opposition from parents. His scheme was termed mechanistic, vast, dehumanizing, repulsive. What better world for schooling than old Earth itself? Here was the source of all tradition; let Earth become Tutelar! So insisted the parents, and Alan Robertson had no choice but to agree.

In the office Duray identified himself to the clerk and requested the presence of his daughter Dolly.

The clerk sent forth a messenger who, after an interval, returned alone. "Dolly Duray isn't at school."

Duray was surprised; Dolly had been in good health and had set off to school as usual. He said, "Either Joan or Ellen will do as well."

The messenger again went forth and again returned. "Neither one is in their classrooms, Mr. Duray. All three of your children are absent."

"I can't understand it," said Duray, now fretful. "All three set off to school this morning."

"Let me ask Miss Haig. I've just come on duty." The clerk spoke into a telephone, listened, then turned back to Duray. "The girls went home at ten o'clock. Mrs. Duray called for them and took them back through the passway."

"Did she give any reason whatever?"

"Miss Haig says no; Mrs. Duray just told her she needed the girls at home."

Duray stifled a sigh of baffled irritation. "Could you take me to their locker? I'll use their passway to get home."

"That's contrary to school regulations, Mr. Duray. You'll understand, I'm sure."

"I can identify myself quite definitely," said Duray. "Mr. Carr knows me well. As a matter of fact, my passway collapsed, and I came here to get home."

"Why don't you speak to Mr. Carr?"

"I'd like to do so."

Duray was conducted into the principal's office, where he explained his predicament. Mr. Carr expressed sympathy and made no difficulty about taking Duray to the children's passway.

They went to a hall at the back of the school and found the locker numbered 382. "Here we are," said Carr. "I'm afraid that you'll find it a tight fit." He unlocked the metal door with his master key and threw it open. Duray looked inside and saw only the black metal at the back of the locker. The passway, like his own, had been closed.

Duray drew back and for a moment could find no words.

Carr spoke in a voice of polite amazement. "How very perplexing! I don't believe I've ever seen anything like it before! Surely the girls wouldn't play such a silly prank!"

"They know better than to touch the passway," Duray said gruffly. "Are you sure that this is the right locker?"

Carr indicated the card on the outside of the locker, where three names had been typed: "DOROTHY DURAY, JOAN DURAY, ELLEN DURAY." "No mistake," said Carr, "and I'm afraid that I can't help you any further. Are you in common residency?"

"It's our private homestead."

Carr nodded with lips judiciously pursed, to suggest that insistence upon so much privacy seemed eccentric. He gave a deprecatory little chuckle. "I suppose if you isolate yourself to such an extent, you more or less must expect a series of emergencies."

"To the contrary," Duray said crisply. "Our life is uneventful, because there's no one to bother us. We love the wild animals, the quiet, the fresh air. We wouldn't have it any differently."

Carr smiled a dry smile. "Mr. Robertson has certainly altered the lives of us all. I understand that he is your grandfather?"

"I was raised in his household. I'm his nephew's foster son. The blood relationship isn't all that close."

III

From *Memoirs and Reflections:*

I early became interested in magnetic fluxes and their control. After taking my degree, I worked exclusively in this field, studying all varieties of magnetic envelopes and developing controls over their formation. For many years my horizons were thus limited, and I lived a placid existence.

Two contemporary developments forced me down from my "ivory castle." First: the fearful overcrowding of the planet and the prospect of worse to come. Cancer already was an affliction of the past; heart diseases were under control; I feared that in another ten years immortality might be a practical reality for many of us, with a consequent augmentation of population pressure.

Secondly, the theoretical work done upon "black holes" and "white holes" suggested that matter compacted in a "black hole" broke through a barrier to spew forth from a "white hole" in another universe. I calculated pressures and considered the self-focusing magnetic sheaths, cones, and whorls with which I was experimenting. Through their innate properties these entities constricted themselves to apexes of a cross section indistinguishable from a geometric point. What if two or more cones (I asked myself) could be arranged in contraposition to produce an equilibrium? In this condition charged particles must be accelerated to near light-speed and at the mutual focus constricted and impinged together. The pressures thus created, though of small scale, would be far in excess of those characteristic of the "black holes": to unknown effect.

I can now report that the mathematics of the multiple focus are a most improbable thicket, and the useful service I enforced upon what I must call a set of absurd contradictions is one of my secrets. I know that thousands of scientists, at home and abroad, are attempting to duplicate my work; they are welcome to the effort. None will succeed. Why do I speak so positively? This is my other secret.

Duray marched back to the Montclair West depot in a state of angry puzzlement. There were four passways to Home, of which two were closed. The third was located in his San Francisco locker: the "front door," so to speak. The last and the original orifice was cased, filed, and indexed in Alan Robertson's vault.

Duray tried to deal with the problem in rational terms. The girls would never tamper with the passways. As for Elizabeth, no more than the girls would she consider such an act. At least Duray could imagine no reason that would so urge or impel her. Elizabeth, like himself, a foster child, was a beautiful, passionate woman, tall, dark-haired, with lustrous dark eyes and a wide mouth that tended to curve in an endearingly crooked grin. She was also responsible, loyal, careful, industrious; she loved her family and Riverview Manor. The theory of erotic intrigue seemed to Duray as incredible as the fact of the closed passways. Though for a fact, Elizabeth was prone to wayward and incomprehensible moods. Suppose Elizabeth had received a visitor who for some sane or insane purpose had forced her to close the passway? . . . Duray shook his head in frustration, like a harassed bull. The matter no doubt had some simple cause. Or on the other hand, Duray reflected, the cause might be complex and intricate. The thought, by some obscure connection, brought before him the image of his nominal foster father, Alan Robertson's nephew, Bob Robertson. Duray gave his head a nod of gloomy asseveration, as if to confirm a fact he long ago should have suspected. He went to the phone booth and called Bob Robertson's apartment in San Francisco. The screen glowed white and an instant later displayed Bob Robertson's alert, clean, and handsome face. "Good afternoon, Gil. Glad you called; I've been anxious to get in touch with you."

Duray became warier than ever. "How so?"

"Nothing serious, or so I hope. I dropped by your locker to leave off some books that I promised Elizabeth, and I noticed through the glass that your passway is closed. Collapsed. Useless."

"Strange," said Duray. "Very strange indeed. I can't understand it. Can you?"

"No . . . not really."

Duray thought he detected a subtlety of intonation. His eyes narrowed in concentration. "The passway at my rig was closed. The passway at the girls' school was closed. Now you tell me that the downtown passway is closed."

Bob Robertson grinned. "That's a pretty broad hint, I would say. Did you and Elizabeth have a row?"

"No."

Bob Robertson rubbed his long aristocratic chin. "A mystery. There's probably some very ordinary explanation."

"Or some very extraordinary explanation."

"True. Nowadays a person can't rule out anything. By the way, tomorrow night is the Rumfuddle, and I expect both you and Elizabeth to be on hand."

"As I recall," said Duray, "I've already declined the invitation." The Rumfuddlers were a group of Bob's cronies. Duray suspected that their activities were not altogether wholesome. "Excuse me; I've got to find an open passway, or Elizabeth and the kids are marooned."

"Try Alan," said Bob. "He'll have the original in his vault."

Duray gave a curt nod. "I don't like to bother him, but that's my last hope."

"Let me know what happens," said Bob Robertson. "And if you're at loose ends, don't forget the Rumfuddle tomorrow night. I mentioned the matter to Elizabeth, and she said she'd be sure to attend."

"Indeed. And when did you consult Elizabeth?"

"A day or so ago. Don't look so damnably gothic, my boy."

"I'm wondering if there's a connection between your invitation and the closed passways. I happen to know that Elizabeth doesn't care for your parties."

Bob Robertson laughed with easy good grace. "Reflect a moment. Two events occur. I invite you and wife Elizabeth to the Rumfuddle. This is event one. Your passways close up, which is event two. By a feat of structured absurdity you equate the two and blame me. Now is that fair?"

"You call it 'structured absurdity,'" said Duray. "I call it instinct."

Bob Robertson laughed again. "You'll have to do better than that. Consult Alan, and if for some reason he can't help you, come to the Rumfuddle. We'll rack our brains and either solve your problem or come up with new and better ones." He gave a cheery nod, and before Duray could roar an angry expostulation, the screen faded.

Duray stood glowering at the screen, convinced that Bob Robertson knew much more about the closed passways than he admitted. Duray went to sit on a bench. . . . If Elizabeth had closed him away from Home, her reasons must

have been compelling indeed. But unless she intended to isolate herself permanently from Earth, she would leave at least one passway ajar, and this must
be the master orifice in Alan Robertson's vault.

Duray rose to his feet, somewhat heavily, and stood a moment, head bent and
shoulders hunched. He gave a surly grunt and returned to the phone booth,
where he called a number known to not more than a dozen persons.

The screen glowed white while the person at the other end of the line scrutinized his face. . . . The screen cleared, revealing a round pale face from which
pale blue eyes stared forth with a passionless intensity. "Hello, Ernest," said
Duray. "Is Alan busy at the moment?"

"I don't think he's doing anything particular—except resting."

Ernest gave the last two words a meaningful emphasis. "I've got some problems," said Duray. "What's the best way to get in touch with him?"

"You'd better come up here. The code is changed. It's MHF now."

"I'll be there in a few minutes."

Back in the "California" hub on Utilis, Duray went into a side chamber lined
with private lockers, numbered and variously marked with symbols, names, colored flags, or not marked at all. Duray went to Locker 122, and, ignoring the
keyhole, set the code lock to the letters MHF. The door opened; Duray stepped
into the locker and through the passway to the High Sierra headquarters of Alan
Robertson.

IV

From *Memoirs and Reflections:*

If one basic axiom controls the cosmos, it must be this:

*In a situation of infinity every possible condition occurs, not once, but an infinite number of
times.*

There is no mathematical nor logical limit to the number of dimensions. Our perceptions
assure us of three only, but many indications suggest otherwise: parapsychic occurrences of
a hundred varieties, the "white holes," the seemingly finite state of our own universe, which,
by corollary, asserts the existence of others.

Hence, when I stepped behind the lead slab and first touched the button, I felt confident of
success; failure would have surprised me!

But (and here lay my misgivings) what sort of success might I achieve?

Suppose I opened a hole into the interplanetary vacuum?

The chances of this were very good indeed; I surrounded the machine in a strong membrane
to prevent the air of Earth from rushing off into the void.

Suppose I discovered a condition totally beyond imagination?

My imagination yielded no safeguards.

I proceeded to press the button.

Duray stepped out into a grotto under damp granite walls. Sunlight poured into
the opening from a dark-blue sky. This was Alan Robertson's link to the outside
world; like many other persons, he disliked a passway opening directly into his
home. A path led fifty yards across bare granite mountainside to the lodge. To
the west spread a great vista of diminishing ridges, valleys, and hazy blue air; to

the east rose a pair of granite crags, with snow caught in the saddle between. Alan Robertson's lodge was built just below the timberline, beside a small lake fringed with tall dark firs. The lodge was built of rounded granite stones, with a wooden porch across the front; at each end rose a massive chimney.

Duray had visited the lodge on many occasions; as a boy he had scaled both of the crags behind the house, to look wonderingly off across the stillness, which on old Earth had a poignant breathing quality different from the uninhabited solitudes of worlds such as Home.

Ernest came to the door: a middle-aged man with an ingenuous face, small white hands, and soft, damp, mouse-colored hair. Ernest disliked the lodge, the wilderness, and solitude in general; he nevertheless would have suffered tortures before relinquishing his post as subaltern to Alan Robertson. Ernest and Duray were almost antipodal in outlook. Ernest thought Duray brusque, indelicate, a trifle coarse, and probably not disinclined to violence as an argumentative adjunct. Duray considered Ernest, when he thought of him at all, as the kind of man who takes two bites out of a cherry. Ernest had never married; he showed no interest in women, and Duray, as a boy, had often fretted at Ernest's overcautious restrictions.

In particular Ernest resented Duray's free and easy access to Alan Robertson. The power to restrict or admit those countless persons who demanded Alan Robertson's attention was Ernest's most cherished perquisite, and Duray denied him the use of it by simply ignoring Ernest and all his regulations. Ernest had never complained to Alan Robertson for fear of discovering that Duray's influence exceeded his own. A wary truce existed between the two, each conceding the other his privileges.

Ernest performed a polite greeting and admitted Duray into the lodge. Duray looked around the interior, which had not changed during his lifetime: varnished plank floors with red, black, and white Navaho rugs, massive pine furniture with leather cushions, a few shelves of books, a half-dozen pewter mugs on the mantle over the big fireplace—a room almost ostentatiously bare of souvenirs and mementos. Duray turned back to Ernest: "Whereabouts is Alan?"

"On his boat."

"With guests?"

"No," said Ernest, with a faint sniff of disapproval. "He's alone, quite alone."

"How long has he been gone?"

"He just went through an hour ago. I doubt if he's left the dock yet. What is your problem, if I may ask?"

"The passways to my world are closed. All three. There's only one left, in the vault."

Ernest arched his flexible eyebrows. "Who closed them?"

"I don't know. Elizabeth and the girls are alone, so far as I know."

"Extraordinary," said Ernest in a flat metallic voice. "Well, then, come along." He led the way down a hall to a back room. With his hand on the knob, Ernest paused and looked back over his shoulder. "Did you mention the matter to anyone? Robert, for instance?"

"Yes," said Duray curtly, "I did. Why do you ask?"

Ernest hesitated a fraction of a second. "No particular reason. Robert occasionally has a somewhat misplaced sense of humor, he and his Rumfuddlers." He spoke the word with a hiss of distaste.

Duray said nothing of his own suspicions. Ernest opened the door; they entered a large room illuminated by a skylight. The only furnishing was a rug on the varnished floor. Into each wall opened four doors. Ernest went to one of these doors, pulled it open, and made a resigned gesture. "You'll probably find Alan at the dock."

Duray looked into the interior of a rude hut with palm-frond walls, resting on a platform of poles. Through the doorway he saw a path leading under sunlit green foliage toward a strip of white beach. Surf sparkled below a layer of dark-blue ocean and a glimpse of the sky. Duray hesitated, rendered wary by the events of the morning. Anyone and everyone was suspect, even Ernest, who now gave a quiet sniff of contemptuous amusement. Through the foliage Duray glimpsed a spread of sail; he stepped through the passway.

V

From *Memoirs and Reflections*:

Man is a creature whose evolutionary environment has been the open air. His nerves, muscles, and senses have developed across three million years in intimate contiguity with natural earth, crude stone, live wood, wind, and rain. Now this creature is suddenly—on the geologic scale, instantaneously—shifted to an unnatural environment of metal and glass, plastic and plywood, to which his psychic substrata lack all compatibility. The wonder is not that we have so much mental instability but so little. Add to this the weird noises, electrical pleasures, bizarre colors, synthetic foods, abstract entertainments! We should congratulate ourselves on our durability.

I bring this matter up because, with my little device—so simple, so easy, so flexible—I have vastly augmenter the load upon our poor primeval brain, and for a fact many persons find the instant transition from one locale to another unsettling, and even actively unpleasant.

Duray stood on the porch of the cabin, under a vivid green canopy of sunlit foliage. The air was soft and warm and smelled of moist vegetation. He stood listening. The mutter of the surf came to his ears and from a far distance a single birdcall.

Duray stepped down to the ground and followed the path under tall palm trees to a riverbank. A few yards downstream, beside a rough pier of poles and planks, floated a white-and-blue ketch, sails hoisted and distended to a gentle breeze. On the deck stood Alan Robertson, on the point of casting off the mooring lines. Duray hailed him; Alan Robertson turned in surprise and vexation, which vanished when he recognized Duray. "Hello, Gil, glad you're here! For a moment I thought it might be someone to bother me. Jump aboard; you're just in time for a sail."

Duray somberly joined Alan Robertson on the boat. "I'm afraid I am here to bother you."

"Oh?" Alan Robertson raised his eyebrows in instant solicitude. He was a man of no great height, thin, nervously active. Wisps of rumpled white hair fell over his forehead; mild blue eyes inspected Duray with concern, all thoughts of sailing forgotten. "What in the world has happened?"

"I wish I knew. If it were something I could handle myself, I wouldn't bother you."

"Don't worry about me; there's all the time in the world for sailing. Now tell me what's happened."

"I can't get through to Home. All the passways are closed off. Why and how I have no idea. Elizabeth and the girls are out there alone; at least I think they're *out there*."

Alan Robertson rubbed his chin. "What an odd business! I can certainly understand your agitation. . . . You think Elizabeth closed the passways?"

"It's unreasonable—but there's no one else."

Alan Robertson turned Duray a shrewd, kindly glance. "No little family upsets? Nothing to cause her despair and anguish?"

"Absolutely nothing. I've tried to reason things out, but I draw a blank. I thought that maybe someone—a man had gone through to visit her and decided to take over, but if this were the case, why did she come to the school for the girls? That possibility is out. A secret love affair? Possible but so damn unlikely. Since she wants to keep me off the planet, her only motive could be to protect me or herself or the girls from danger of some sort. Again this means that another person is concerned in the matter. Who? How? Why? I spoke to Bob. He claims to know nothing about the situation, but he wants me to come to his damned Rumfuddle, and he hints very strongly that Elizabeth will be on hand. I can't prove a thing against Bob, but I suspect him. He's always had a taste for odd jokes."

Alan Robertson gave a lugubrious nod. "I won't deny that." He sat down in the cockpit and stared off across the water. "Bob has a complicated sense of humor, but he'd hardly close you away from your world. . . . I hardly think that your family is in actual danger, but of course we can't take chances. The possibility exists that Bob is not responsible, that something uglier is afoot." He jumped to his feet. "Our obvious first step is to use the master orifice in the vault." He looked a shade regretfully toward the ocean. "My little sail can wait. . . . A lovely world this: not fully cognate with Earth—a cousin, so to speak. The fauna and flora are roughly contemporary except for man. The hominids have never developed."

The two men returned up the path, Alan Robertson chatting lightheartedly: "Thousands and thousands of worlds I've visited, and looked into even more, but do you know I've never hit upon a good system of classification. There are exact cognates—of course we're never sure exactly *how* exact they are. These cases are relatively simple but then the problems begin . . . Bah! I don't think about such things anymore. I know that when I keep all the determinates at zero, the cognates appear. Overintellectualizing is the bane of this and every other era. Show me a man who deals only with abstraction, and I'll show you the dead futile end of evolution." Alan Robertson chuckled. "If I could control the machine tightly enough to produce real cognates, our troubles would be over . . . Much confusion, of course. I might step through into the cognate world immediately as a true cognate Alan Robertson steps through into our world, with net effect of zero. An amazing business, really; I never tire of it. . . ."

They returned to the transit room of the mountain lodge. Ernest appeared almost instantly. Duray suspected he had been watching through the passway.

Alan Robertson said briskly, "We'll be busy for an hour or two, Ernest. Gilbert is having difficulties, and we've got to set things straight."

Ernest nodded somewhat grudgingly, or so it seemed to Duray. "The progress report on the Ohio Plan has arrived. Nothing particularly urgent."

"Thank you, Ernest, I'll see to it later. Come along, Gilbert; let's get to the bottom of this affair." They went to door No. 1 and passed through to the Utilis hub. Alan Robertson led the way to a small green door with a three-dial coded lock, which he opened with a flourish. "Very well, in we go." He carefully locked the door behind them, and they walked the length of a short hall. "A shame that I must be so cautious," said Alan Robertson. "You'd be astonished at the outrageous requests otherwise sensible people make of me. I sometimes become exasperated . . . Well, it's understandable, I suppose."

At the end of the hall Alan Robertson worked the locking dials of a red door. "This way, Gilbert; you've been through before." They stepped through a passway into a hall that opened into a circular concrete chamber fifty feet in diameter, located, so Duray knew, deep under the Mad Dog Mountains of the Mojave Desert. Eight halls extended away into the rock; each hall communicated with twelve aisles. The center of the chamber was occupied by a circular desk twenty feet in diameter; here six clerks in white smocks worked at computers and collating machines. In accordance with their instructions they gave Alan Robertson neither recognition nor greeting.

Alan Robertson went up to the desk, at which signal the chief clerk, a solemn young man bald as an egg, came forward. "Good afternoon, sir."

"Good afternoon, Harry. Find me the index for 'Gilbert Duray,' on my personal list."

The clerk bowed smartly. He went to an instrument and ran his fingers over a bank of keys; the instrument ejected a card that Harry handed to Alan Robertson. "There you are, sir."

Alan Robertson showed the card to Duray, who saw the code: "4:8:10/6:13: 29."

"That's your world," said Alan Robertson. "We'll soon learn how the land lies. This way, to Radiant four." He led the way down the hall, turned into the aisle numbered "8," and proceeded to Stack 10. "Shelf six," said Alan Robertson. He checked the card. "Drawer thirteen . . . here we are." He drew forth the drawer and ran his fingers along the tabs. "Item twenty-nine. This should be Home." He brought forth a metal frame four inches square and held it up to his eyes. He frowned in disbelief. "We don't have anything here either." He turned to Duray a glance of dismay. "This is a serious situation!"

"It's no more than I expected," said Duray tonelessly.

"All this demands some careful thought." Alan Robertson clicked his tongue in vexation. "Tst, tst, tst." He examined the identification plaque at the top of the frame. "Four: eight: ten/six: thirteen: twenty-nine," he read. "There seems to be no question of error." He squinted carefully at the numbers, hesitated, then slowly replaced the frame. On second thought he took the frame forth once more. "Come along, Gilbert," said Alan Robertson. "We'll have a cup of coffee and think this matter out."

The two returned to the central chamber, where Alan Robertson gave the empty frame into the custody of Harry the clerk. "Check the records, if you please," said Alan Robertson. "I want to know how many passways were pinched off the master."

Harry manipulated the buttons of his computer. "Three only, Mr. Robertson."

"Three passways and the master—four in all?"

"That's right, sir."

"Thank you, Harry."

VI

From *Memoirs and Reflections:*

I recognized the possibility of many cruel abuses, but the good so outweighed the bad that I thrust aside all thought of secrecy and exclusivity. I consider myself not Alan Robertson but, like Prometheus, an archetype of Man, and my discovery must serve all men.

But caution, caution, caution!

I sorted out my ideas. I myself coveted the amplitude of a private, personal world; such a yearning was not ignoble, I decided. Why should not everyone have the same if he so desired, since the supply was limitless? Think of it! The wealth and beauty of an entire world: mountains and plains, forests and flowers, ocean cliffs and crashing seas, winds and clouds—all beyond value, yet worth no more than a few seconds of effort and a few watts of energy.

I became troubled by a new idea. Would everyone desert old Earth and leave it a vile junk-heap? I found the concepts intolerable. . . . I exchange access to a world for three to six years of remedial toil, depending upon occupancy.

A lounge overlooked the central chamber. Alan Robertson gestured Duray to a seat and drew two mugs of coffee from a dispenser. Settling in a chair, he turned his eyes up to the ceiling. "We must collect our thoughts. The circumstances are somewhat unusual; still, I have lived with unusual circumstances for almost fifty years.

"So then: the situation. We have verified that there are only four passways to Home. These four passways are closed, though we must accept Bob's word in regard to your downtown locker. If this is truly the case, if Elizabeth and the girls are still on Home, you will never see them again."

"Bob is mixed up in this business. I could swear to nothing, but—"

Alan Robertson held up his hand. "I will talk to Bob; this is the obvious first step." He rose to his feet and went to the telephone in the corner of the lounge. Duray joined him. Alan spoke into the screen. "Get me Robert Robertson's apartment in San Francisco."

The screen glowed white. Bob's voice came from the speaker. "Sorry, I'm not at home. I have gone out to my world Fancy, and I cannot be reached. Call back in a week, unless your business is urgent, in which case call back in a month."

"Mmph," said Alan Robertson, returning to his seat. "Bob is sometimes a trifle too flippant. A man with an under-extended intellect . . ." He drummed his fingers on the arm of his chair. "Tomorrow night is his party? What does he call it? A Rumfuddle?"

"Some such nonsense. Why does he want me? I'm a dead dog; I'd rather be home building a fence."

"Perhaps you had better plan to attend the party."

"That means, submit to his extortion."

"Do you want to see your wife and family again?"

"Naturally. But whatever he has in mind won't be for my benefit, or Elizabeth's."

"You're probably right there. I've heard one or two unsavory tales regarding the Rumfuddlers. . . . The fact remains that the passways are closed. All four of them."

Duray's voice became harsh. "Can't you open a new orifice for us?"

Alan Robertson gave his head a sad shake. "I can tune the machine very finely. I can code accurately for the 'Home' class of worlds and as closely as necessary approximate a particular world-state. But at each setting, no matter how fine the tuning, we encounter an infinite number of worlds. In practice, inaccuracies in the machine, backlash, the gross size of electrons, the very difference between one electron and another, make it difficult to tune with absolute precision. So even if we tuned exactly to the 'Home' class, the probability of opening into your particular Home is one of an infinite number: in short, negligible."

Duray stared off across the chamber. "Is it possible that space once entered might tend to open more easily a second time?"

Alan Robertson smiled. "As to that, I can't say. I suspect not, but I really know so little. I see no reason why it should be so."

"If we can open into a world precisely cognate, I can at least learn why the passways are closed."

Alan Robertson sat up in his chair. "Here is a valid point. Perhaps we can accomplish something in this regard." He glanced humorously sidewise at Duray. "On the other hand—consider this situation. We create access into a 'Home' almost exactly cognate to your own—so nearly identical that the difference is not readily apparent. You find there an Elizabeth, a Dolly, a Joan, and an Ellen indistinguishable from your own, and a Gilbert marooned on Earth. You might even convince yourself that this is your very own Home."

"I'd know the difference," said Duray shortly, but Alan Robertson seemed not to hear.

"Think of it! An infinite number of Homes isolated from Earth, an infinite number of Elizabeths, Dollys, Joans, and Ellens marooned, an infinite number of Gilbert Durays trying to regain access . . . The sum effect might be a wholesale reshuffling of families, with everyone more or less good-natured about the situation. I wonder if this could be Bob's idea of a joke to share with his Rumfuddlers."

Duray looked sharply at Alan Robertson, wondering whether the man was serious. "It doesn't sound funny and I wouldn't be very good-natured."

"Of course not," said Alan Robertson hastily. "An afterthought—in rather poor taste, I'm afraid."

"In any event, Bob hinted that Elizabeth would be at the damned Rumfuddle. If that's the case, she must have closed the passways from this side."

"A possibility," Alan Robertson conceded, "but unreasonable. Why should she seal you away from Home?"

"I don't know, but I'd like to find out."

Alan Robertson slapped his hands down upon his shanks and jumped to his feet, only to pause once more. "You're sure you want to look into these cognates? You might see things you wouldn't like."

"So long as I know the truth, I don't care whether I like it or not."

"So be it."

The machine occupied a room behind the balcony. Alan Robertson surveyed the device with pride and affection. "This is the fourth model, and probably optimum; at least I don't see any place for significant improvement. I use a hundred and sixty-seven rods converging upon the center of the reactor sphere. Each rod produces a quotum of energy and is susceptible to several types of adjustment to cope with the very large number of possible states. The number of particles to pack the universe full is on the order of ten raised to the power of sixty; the possible permutations these particles would number two raised to the power of ten raised to the power of sixty. The universe, of course, is built of many different particles, which makes the final number of possible, or let us say, thinkable states a number like two raised to the power of ten raised to the power of sixty, all times x, where x is the number of particles under consideration. A large, unmanageable number, which we need not consider, because the conditions we deal with—the possible variations of planet Earth—are far fewer."

"Still a very large number," said Duray.

"Indeed yes. But again the sheer unmanageable bulk is swept away by a self-normalizing property of the machine. In what I call floating neutral, the machine reaches the closest cognate—which is to say, that infinite class of perfect cognates. In practice, because of infinitesimal inaccuracies, 'floating neutral' reaches cognates more or less imperfect, perhaps by no more than the shape of a single grain of sand. Still, 'floating neutral' provides a natural base, and by adjusting the controls, we reach cycles at an ever greater departure from base. In practice I search out a good cycle and strike a large number of passways, as many as a hundred thousand. So now to our business." He went to a porthole at the side. "Your code number, what was it now?"

Duray brought forth the card and read the numbers: "Four: eight:ten/six:thirteen:twenty-nine."

"Very good. I give the code to the computer, which searches the files and automatically adjusts the machine. Now then, step over here; the process releases dangerous radiation."

The two stood behind lead slabs. Alan Robertson touched a button; watching through a periscope, Duray saw a spark of purple light and heard a small groaning, gasping sound seeming to come from the air itself.

Alan Robertson stepped forth and walked to the machine. In the delivery tray rested an extensible ring. He picked up the ring and looked through the hole. "This seems to be right." He handed the ring to Duray. "Do you see anything you recognize?"

Duray put the ring to his eye. "That's Home."

"Very good. Do you want me to come with you?"

Duray considered. "The time is now?"

"Yes. This is a time-neutral setting."

"I think I'll go alone."

Alan Robertson nodded. "Whatever you like. Return as soon as you can, so I'll know you're safe."

Duray frowned at him sidewise. "Why shouldn't I be safe? No one is there but my family."

"Not *your* family. The family of a cognate Gilbert Duray. The family may not be absolutely identical. The cognate Duray may not be identical. You can't be sure exactly what you will find—so be careful."

VII

From *Memoirs and Reflections:*

When I think of my machine and my little forays in and out of infinity, and idea keeps recurring to me which is so rather terrible that I close it out of my mind, and I will not even mention it here.

Duray stepped out upon the soil of Home and stood praising the familiar landscape. A vast meadow drenched in sunlight rolled down to wide Silver River. Above the opposite shore rose a line of low bluffs, with copses of trees in the hollows. To the left, the landscape seemed to extend indefinitely and at last become indistinct in the blue haze of distance. To the right, the Robber Woods ended a quarter mile from where Duray stood. On a flat beside the forest, on the bank of a small stream, stood a house of stone and timber: a sight that seemed to Duray the most beautiful one he had ever seen. Polished glass windows sparkled in the sunlight; banks of geraniums glowed green and red. From the chimney rose a wisp of smoke.

The air smelled cool and sweet but seemed—so Duray imagined—to carry a strange tang, different—so he imagined—from the meadow-scent of his own Home. Duray started forward, then halted. The world was his own, yet not his own. If he had been conscious of the fact, would he have recognized the strangeness? Nearby rose an outcrop of weathered gray field-rock: a rounded mossy pad on which he had sat only two days before, contemplating the building of a dock. He walked over and looked down at the stone. Here he had sat; here were the impressions of his heels in the soil; here was the pattern of moss from which he had absently scratched a fragment. Duray bent close. The moss was whole. The man who had sat here, the cognate Duray, had not scratched at the moss. So then: The world was perceptibly different from his own.

Duray was relieved and yet vaguely disturbed. If the world had been the exact simulacrum of his own, he might have been subjected to unmanageable emotions—which still might be the case. He walked toward the house, along the path that led down to the river. He stepped up to the porch. On a deck chair was a book: *Down There: A Study of Satanism,* by J. K. Huysmans. Elizabeth's tastes were eclectic. Duray had not previously seen the book; was it perhaps that Bob Robertson had put through the parcel delivery?

Duray went into the house. Elizabeth stood across the room. She had evidently watched him coming up the path. She said nothing; her face showed no expression.

Duray halted, somewhat at a loss as to how to address this familiar-strange woman. "Good afternoon," he said at last.

Elizabeth allowed a wisp of a smile to show. "Hello, Gilbert."

At least, thought Duray, on cognate worlds the same language was spoken. He studied Elizabeth. Lacking prior knowledge, would he have perceived her to be someone different from his own Elizabeth? Both were beautiful women: tall and slender, with curling black shoulder-length hair, worn without artifice. Their skin was pale, with a dusky undertone; their mouths were wide, passionate, stubborn. Duray knew his Elizabeth to be a woman of explicable moods, and this Elizabeth was doubtless no different—yet somehow a difference existed that Duray could not define, deriving perhaps from the strangeness of her atoms, the stuff of a different universe. He wondered if she sensed the same difference in him.

He asked, "Did you close off the passways?"

Elizabeth nodded, without change of expression.

"Why?"

"I thought it the best thing to do," said Elizabeth in a soft voice.

"That's no answer."

"I suppose not. How did you get here?"

"Alan made an opening."

Elizabeth raised her eyebrows. "I thought that was impossible."

"True. This is a different world to my own. Another Gilbert Duray built this house. I'm not your husband."

Elizabeth's mouth dropped in astonishment. She swayed back a step and put her hand up to her neck: a mannerism Duray could not recall in his own Elizabeth. The sense of strangeness came ever more strongly upon him. He felt an intruder. Elizabeth was watching him with a wide-eyed fascination. She said in a hurried mutter: "I wish you'd leave, go back to your own world; do!"

"If you've closed off all the passways, you'll be isolated," growled Duray. "Marooned, probably forever."

"Whatever I do," said Elizabeth, "it's not your affair."

"It is my affair, if only for the sake of the girls. I won't allow them to live and die alone out here."

"The girls aren't here," said Elizabeth in a flat voice. "They are where neither you nor any other Gilbert Duray will find them. So now go back to your own world, and leave me in whatever peace my soul allows me."

Duray stood glowering at the fiercely beautiful woman. He had never heard his own Elizabeth speak so wildly. He wondered if on his own world another Gilbert Duray similarly confronted his own Elizabeth, and as he analyzed his feelings toward this woman before him, he felt a throb of annoyance. A curious situation. He said in a quiet voice, "Very well. You and my own Elizabeth have decided to isolate yourselves. I can't imagine your reasons."

Elizabeth gave a wild laugh. "They're real enough."

"They may be real now, but ten years from now or forty years from now they may seem unreal. I can't give you access to your own Earth, but if you wish, you can use the—"

Elizabeth turned away and went to look out over the passway to the Earth from which I've just come, and you need never see me again."

Duray spoke to her back. "We've never had secrets between us, you and I— or I mean, Elizabeth and I. Why now? Are you in love with some other man?"

Elizabeth gave a snort of sardonic amusement. "Certainly not . . . I'm disgusted with the entire human race."

"Which presumably includes me."

"It does indeed, and myself as well."

"And you won't tell me why?"

Elizabeth, still looking out the window, wordlessly shook her head.

"Very well," said Duray in a cold voice. "Will you tell me where you've sent the girls? They're mine as much as yours, remember."

"These particular girls aren't yours at all."

"That may be, but the effect is the same."

Elizabeth said tonelessly: "If you want to find your own particular girls, you'd better find your own particular Elizabeth and ask her. I can only speak for myself. . . . To tell you the truth, I don't like being part of a composite person, and

I don't intend to act like one. I'm just me. You're you, a stranger, whom I've never seen before in my life. So I wish you'd leave."

Duray strode from the house, out into the sunlight. He looked once around the wide landscape, then gave his head a surely shake and marched off along the path.

VIII

From *Memoirs and Reflections*:

The past is exposed for our scrutiny; we can wander the epochs like lords through a garden, serene in our purview. We argue with the noble sages, refuting their laborious concepts, should we be so unkind. Remember (at least) two things. First: The more distant from now, the less precise our conjunctures, the less our ability to strike to any given instant. We can break in upon yesterday at a stipulated second; during the Eocene, plus or minus ten years is the limit of our accuracy; as for the Cretaceous or earlier, an impingement with three hundred years of a given date can be considered satisfactory. Secondly: The past we broach is never our own past but at best the past of a cognate world, so that any illumination cast upon historical problems is questionable and perhaps deceptive. We cannot plumb the future; the process involves a negative flow of energy, which is inherently impractical. An instrument constructed of antimatter has been jocularly recommended but would yield no benefit to us. The future, thankfully, remains forever shrouded.

"Aha, you're back!" exclaimed Alan Robertson. "What did you learn?"

Duray described the encounter with Elizabeth. "She makes no excuse for what she's done; she shows hostility, which doesn't seem real, especially since I can't imagine a reason for it."

Alan Robertson had no comment to make.

"The woman isn't my wife, but their motivations must be the same. I can't think of one sensible explanation for conduct so strange, let alone two."

"Elizabeth seemed normal this morning?" asked Alan Robertson.

"I noticed nothing unusual."

Alan Robertson went to the control panel of his machine. He looked over his shoulder at Duray. "What time do you leave for work?"

"About nine."

Alan Robertson set one dial and turned two others until a ball of green light balanced, wavering, precisely halfway along a glass tube. He signaled Duray behind the lead slab and touched the button. From the center of the machine came the impact of 167 colliding nodules of force and the groan of rending dimensional fabric.

Alan Robertson brought forth the new passway. "The time is morning. You'll have to decide for yourself how to handle the situation. You can try to watch without being seen; you can say that you have paperwork to catch up on, that Elizabeth should ignore you and go about her normal routine, while you unobtrusively see what happens."

Duray frowned. "Presumably for each of these worlds there is a Gilbert Duray who finds himself in my fix. Suppose each tries to slip inconspicuously into someone else's world to learn what is happening. Suppose each Elizabeth catches him in the act and furiously accuses the man she believes to be her husband of spying on her—this in itself might be the source of Elizabeth's anger."

"Well, be as discreet as you can. Presumably you'll be several hours, so I'll go back to the boat and putter about. Locker five in my private hub yonder; I'll leave the door open."

Once again Duray stood on the hillside above the river, with the rambling stone house built by still another Gilbert Duray two hundred yards along the slope. From the height of the sun, Duray judged local time to be about nine o'clock—somewhat earlier than necessary. From the chimney of the stone house rose a wisp of smoke; Elizabeth had built a fire in the kitchen fireplace. Duray stood reflecting. This morning in his own house Elizabeth had built no fire. She had been on the point of striking a match and then had decided that the morning was already warm. Duray waited ten minutes, to make sure that the local Gilbert Duray had departed, then set forth toward the house. He paused by the big flat stone to inspect the pattern of moss. The crevice seemed narrower than he remembered, and the moss was dry and discolored. Duray took a deep breath. The air, rich with the odor of grasses and herbs, again seemed to carry an odd, unfamiliar scent. Duray proceeded slowly to the house, uncertain whether, after all, he was engaged in a sensible course of action.

He approached the house. The front door was open. Elizabeth came to look out at him in surprise. "That was a quick day's work!"

Duray said lamely, "The rig is down for repairs. I thought I'd catch up on some paper work. You go ahead with whatever you were doing."

Elizabeth looked at him curiously. "I wasn't doing anything in particular."

He followed Elizabeth into the house. She wore soft black slacks and an old gray jacket; Duray tried to remember what his own Elizabeth had worn, but the garments had been so familiar that he could summon no recollection.

Elizabeth poured coffee into a pair of stoneware mugs, and Duray took a seat at the kitchen table, trying to decide how this Elizabeth differed from his own—if she did. This Elizabeth seemed more subdued and meditative; her mouth might have been a trifle softer. "Why are you looking at me so strangely?" she asked suddenly.

Duray laughed. "I was merely thinking what a beautiful girl you are."

Elizabeth came to sit in his lap and kissed him, and Duray's blood began to flow warm. He restrained himself; this was not his wife; he wanted no complications. And if he yielded to temptations of the moment, might not another Gilbert Duray visiting his own Elizabeth do the same . . . He scowled.

Elizabeth, finding no surge of ardor, went to sit in the chair opposite. For a moment she sipped her coffee in silence. Then she said, "Just as soon as you left, Bob called through."

"Oh?" Duray was at once attentive. "What did he want?"

"That foolish party of his—the Rubble-menders or some such thing. He wants us to come."

"I've already told him no three times."

"I told him no again. His parties are always so peculiar. He said he wanted us to come for a very special reason, but he wouldn't tell me the reason. I told him, 'Thank you but no.' "

Duray looked around the room. "Did he leave any books?"

"No. Why should he leave me books?"

"I wish I knew."

"Gilbert," said Elizabeth, "you're acting rather oddly."

"Yes, I suppose I am." For a fact Duray's mind was whirling. Suppose now he went to the school passway, brought the girls home from school, then closed off all the passways, so that once again he had an Elizabeth and three daughters, more or less his own; then the conditions he had encountered would be satisfied. And another Gilbert Duray, now happily destroying the tract houses of Cupertino, would find himself bereft. . . . Duray recalled the hostile conduct of the previous Elizabeth. The passways in that particular world had certainly not been closed off by an intruding Duray. . . . A startling possibility came to his mind. Suppose a Duray had come to the house and, succumbing to temptation, had closed off all passways except that one communicating with his own world; suppose then that Elizabeth, discovering the imposture, had killed him . . . The theory had a grim plausibility and totally extinguished whatever inclination Duray might have had for making the world his home.

Elizabeth said, "Gilbert, why are you looking at me with that strange expression?"

Duray managed a feeble grin. "I guess I'm just in a bad mood this morning. Don't mind me. I'll go make out my report." He went into the wide cool living room, at once familiar and strange, and brought out the work-records of the other Gilbert Duray. . . . He studied the handwriting: like his own, firm and decisive, but in some indefinable way different—perhaps a trifle more harsh and angular. The three Elizabeths were not identical, nor were the Gilbert Durays.

An hour passed. Elizabeth occupied herself in the kitchen; Duray pretended to write a report.

A bell sounded. "Somebody at the passway," said Elizabeth.

Duray said, "I'll take care of it."

He went to the passage room, stepped through the passway, looked through the peephole—into the large, bland sun-tanned face of Bob Robertson.

Duray opened the door. For a moment he and Bob Robertson confronted each other. Bob Robertson's eyes narrowed. "Why, hello, Gilbert. What are you doing home?"

Duray pointed to the parcel Bob Robertson carried. "What do you have there?"

"Oh, these?" Bob Robertson looked down at the parcel as if he had forgotten it. "Just some books for Elizabeth."

Duray found it hard to control his voice. "You're up to some mischief, you and your Rumfuddlers. Listen, Bob. Keep away from me and Elizabeth. Don't call here, and don't bring around any books. Is this definite enough?"

Bob raised his sun-bleached eyebrows. "Very definite, very explicit. But why the sudden rage? I'm just friendly old Uncle Bob."

"I don't care what you call yourself; stay away from us."

"Just as you like, of course. But do you mind explaining this sudden decree of banishment?"

"The reason is simple enough. We want to be left alone."

Bob made a gesture of mock despair. "All this over a simple invitation to a simple little party, which I'd really like you to come to."

"Don't expect us. We won't be there."

Bob's face suddenly went pink. "You're coming a very high horse over me, my lad, and it's a poor policy. You might just get hauled up with a jerk. Matters aren't all the way you think they are."

"I don't care a rap one way or another," said Duray. "Good-bye." He closed the locker door and backed through the passway. He returned into the living room.

Elizabeth called from the kitchen. "Who was it, dear?"

"Bob Robertson, with some books."

"Books? Why books?"

"I didn't trouble to find out. I told him to stay away. After this, if he's at the passway, don't open it."

Elizabeth looked at him intently. "Gil—you're so strange today! There's something about you that almost scares me."

"Your imagination is working too hard."

"Why should Bob trouble to bring me books? What sort of books? Did you see?"

"Demonology. Black magic. That sort of thing."

"Mmf. Interesting—but not all *that* interesting. . . . I wonder if a world like ours, where no one has ever lived, would have things like goblins and ghosts?"

"I suspect not," said Duray. He looked toward the door. There was nothing more to be accomplished here, and it was time to return to his own Earth. He wondered how to make a graceful departure. And what would occur when the Gilbert Duray now working his rig came home?

Duray said, "Elizabeth, sit down in this chair here."

Elizabeth slowly slid into the chair at the kitchen table and watched him with a puzzled gaze.

"This may come as a shock," he said. "I am Gilbert Duray, but not your personal Gilbert Duray. I'm his cognate."

Elizabeth's eyes widened to lustrous dark pools.

Duray said, "On my own world Bob Robertson caused me and my Elizabeth trouble. I came here to find out what he had done and why and to stop him from doing it again."

Elizabeth asked, "What has he done?"

"I still don't know. He probably won't bother you again. You can tell your personal Gilbert Duray whatever you think best, or even complain to Alan."

"I'm bewildered by all this!"

"No more so than I." He went to the door. "I've got to leave now. Good-bye."

Elizabeth jumped to her feet and came impulsively forward. "Don't say good-bye. It was such a lonesome sound, coming from you. . . . It's like my own Gilbert saying good-bye."

"There's nothing else to do. Certainly I can't follow my inclinations and move in with you. What good are two Gilberts? Who'd get to sit at the head of the table?"

"We could have a round table," said Elizabeth. "Room for six or seven. I like my Gilberts."

"Your Gilberts like their Elizabeths." Duray sighed and said, "I'd better go now."

Elizabeth held out her hand. "Good-bye, cognate Gilbert."

IX

From *Memoirs and Reflections*:

The Oriental world-view differs from our own—specifically my own—in many respects, and I was early confronted with a whole set of dilemmas. I reflected upon Asiatic apathy and its obverse, despotism; warlords and brain-laundries: indifference to disease, filth, and suffering; sacred apes and irresponsible fecundity.

I also took note of my resolve to use my machine in the service of all men.

In the end I decided to make the "mistake" of many before me; I proceeded to impose my own ethical point of view upon the Oriental lifestyle.

Since this was precisely what was expected of me, since I would have been regarded as a fool and a mooncalf had I done otherwise, since the rewards of cooperation far exceeded the gratifications of obduracy and scorn, my programs are a wonderful success, at least to the moment of writing.

Duray walked along the riverbank toward Alan Robertson's boat. A breeze sent twinkling cat's-paws across the water and bellied the sails that Alan Robertson had raised to air; the boat tugged at the mooring lines.

Alan Robertson, wearing white shorts and a white hat with a loose, flapping brim, looked up from the eye he had been splicing at the end of a halyard. "Aha, Gil! You're back. Come aboard and have a bottle of beer."

Duray seated himself in the shade of the sail and drank half the beer at a gulp. "I still don't know what's going on—except that one way or another Bob is responsible. He came while I was there. I told him to clear out. He didn't like it."

Alan Robertson heaved a melancholy sigh. "I realize that Bob has the capacity for mischief."

"I still can't understand how he persuaded Elizabeth to close the passways. He brought out some books, but what effect could they have?"

Alan Robertson was instantly interested. "What were the books?"

"Something about satanism, black magic; I couldn't tell you much else."

"Indeed, indeed!" muttered Alan Robertson. "Is Elizabeth interested in the subject?"

"I don't think so. She's afraid of such things."

"Rightly so. Well, well, that's disturbing." Alan Robertson cleared his throat and made a delicate gesture, as if beseeching Duray to geniality and tolerance. "Still, you mustn't be too irritated with Bob. He's prone to his little mischiefs, but—"

" 'Little mischiefs'!" roared Duray. "Like locking me out of my home and marooning my wife and children? That's going beyond mischief!"

Alan Robertson smiled. "Here, have another beer; cool off a bit. Let's reflect. First, the probabilities. I doubt if Bob has really marooned Elizabeth and the girls or caused Elizabeth to do so."

"Then why are all the passways broken?"

"That's susceptible to explanation. He has access to the vaults; he might have substituted a blank for your master orifice. There's one possibility, at least."

Duray could hardly speak for rage. At last he cried out: "He has no right to do this!"

"Quite right, in the largest sense. I suspect that he only wants to induce you to his Rumfuddle."

"And I don't want to go, expecially when he's trying to put pressure on me."

"You're a stubborn man, Gil. The easy way, of course, would be to relax and look in on the occasion. You might even enjoy yourself."

Duray glared at Alan Robertson. "Are you suggesting that I attend the affair?"

"Well—no. I merely proposed a possible course of action."

Duray drank more beer and glowered out across the river. Alan Robertson said, "In a day or so, when this business is clarified, I think that we—all of us— should go off on a lazy cruise, out there among the islands. Nothing to worry us, no bothers, no upsets. The girls would love such a cruise."

Duray grunted. "I'd like to see them again before I plan any cruises. What goes on at these Rumfuddler events?"

"I've never attended. The members laugh and joke and eat and drink and gossip about the worlds they've visited and show each other movies: that sort of thing. Why don't we look in on last year's party? I'd be interested myself."

Duray hesitated. "What do you have in mind?"

"We'll set the dials to a year-old cognate to Bob's world, Fancy, and see precisely what goes on. What do you say?"

"I suppose it can't do any harm," said Duray grudgingly.

Alan Robertson rose to his feet. "Help me get these sails in."

X

From *Memoirs and Reflections:*

The problems that long have harassed historians have now been resolved. Who were the Cro-Magnons; where did they evolve? Who were the Etruscans? Where were the legendary cities of the proto-Sumerians before they migrated to Mesopotamia? Why the identity between the ideographs of Easter Island and Mohenjo Daro? All these fascinating questions have now been settled and reveal to us the full scope of our early history. We have preserved the library at old Alexandria from the Mohammedans and the Inca codices from the Christians. The Guanches of the Canaries, the Ainu of Hokkaido, the Mandans of Missouri, the blond Kaffirs of Bhutan: All are now known to us. We can chart the development of every language syllable by syllable, from the earliest formulation to the present. We have identified the Hellenic heroes, and I myself have searched the haunted forests of the ancient North and, in their own stone keeps, met face to face those mighty men who generated the Norse myths.

Standing before his machine, Alan Robertson spoke in a voice of humorous self-deprecation. "I'm not as trusting and forthright as I would like to be; in fact I sometimes feel shame for my petty subterfuges, and now I speak in reference to Bob. We all have our small faults, and Bob certainly does not lack his share. His imagination is perhaps his greatest curse: He is easily bored and sometimes tends to overreach himself. So while I deny him nothing, I also make sure that I am in a position to counsel or even remonstrate, if need be. Whenever I open a passway to one of his formulae, I unobstrusively strike a duplicate which I keep in my private file. We will find no difficulty in visiting a cognate to Fancy."

Duray and Alan Robertson stood in the dusk, at the end of a pale white beach. Behind them rose a low basalt cliff. To their right, the ocean reflected the afterglow and a glitter from the waning moon; to the left, palms stood black against the sky. A hundred yards along the beach dozens of fairy lamps had been strung between the trees to illuminate a long table laden with fruit, confections, punch in crystal bowls. Around the table stood several dozen men and women in animated conversation; music and the sounds of gaiety came down the beach to Duray and Alan Robertson.

"We're in good time," said Alan Robertson. He reflected a moment. "No doubt we'd be quite welcome; still, it's probably best to remain inconspicuous. We'll just stroll unobtrusively down the beach, in the shadow of the trees. Be careful not to stumble or fall, and no matter what you see or hear, do nothing! Discretion is essential; we want no awkward confrontations."

Keeping to the shade of the foliage, the two approached the merry group. Fifty yards distant, Alan Robertson held up his hand to signal a halt. "This is as close as we need approach; most of the people you know, or more accurately, their cognates. For instance, there is Royal Hart, and there is James Parham and Elizabeth's aunt, Emma Bathurst, and her uncle Peter and Maude Granger and no end of other folk."

"They all seem very gay."

"Yes, this is an important occasion for them. You and I are surly outsiders who can't understand the fun."

"Is this all they do, eat and drink and talk?"

"I think not," said Alan Robertson. "Notice yonder. Bob seems to be preparing a projection screen. Too bad that we can't move just a bit closer." Alan Robertson peered through the shadows. "But we'd better take no chances; if we were discovered, everyone would be embarrassed."

They watched in silence. Presently Bob Robertson went to the projection equipment and touched a button. The screen became alive with vibrating rings of red and blue. Conversations halted; the group turned toward the screen. Bob Robertson spoke, but his words were inaudible to the two who watched from the darkness. Bob Robertson gestured to the screen, where now appeared the view of a small country town, as if seen from an airplane. Surrounding was flat farm country, a land of wide horizons; Duray assumed the location to be somewhere in the Middle West. The picture changed to show the local high school, with students sitting on the steps. The scene shifted to the football field, on the day of a game—a very important game, to judge from the conduct of the spectators. The local team was introduced; one by one the boys ran out on the field to stand blinking into the autumn sunlight; then they ran off to the pregame huddle.

The game began; Bob Robertson stood by the screen in the capacity of an expert commentator, pointing to one or another of the players, analyzing the play. The game proceeded, to the manifest pleasure of the Rumfuddlers. At half time the bands marched and countermarched, then play resumed. Duray became bored and made fretful comments to Alan Robertson, who only said: "Yes, yes; probably so" and "My word, the agility of that halfback!" and "Have you noticed the precision of the line-play? Very good indeed!" At last the final quarter ended; the victorious team stood under a sign reading:

THE SHOWALTER TORNADOES
CHAMPIONS OF TEXAS
1951

The players came forward to accept trophies; there was a last picture of the team as a whole, standing proud and victorious; then the screen burst out into a red and gold starburst and went blank. The Rumfuddlers rose to their feet and congratulated Bob Robertson, who laughed modestly and went to the table for a goblet of punch.

Duray said disgustedly, "Is this one of Bob's famous parties? Why does he make such a tremendous occasion of the affair? I expected some sort of debauch."

Alan Robertson said, "Yes, from our standpoint at least, the proceedings seem somewhat uninteresting. Well, if your curiosity is satisfied, shall we return?"

"Whenever you like."

Once again in the lounge under the Mad Dog Mountains, Alan Robertson said: "So now and at last we've seen one of Bob's famous Rumfuddles. Are you still determined not to attend the occasion of tomorrow night?"

Duray scowled. "If I have to go to reclaim my family. I'll do so. But I just might lose my temper before the evening is over."

"Bob has gone too far," Alan Robertson declared. "I agree with you there. As for what we saw tonight, I admit to a degree of puzzlement."

"Only a degree? Do you understand it at all?"

Alan Robertson shook his head with a somewhat cryptic smile. "Speculation is pointless. I suppose you'll spend the night with me at the lodge?"

"I might as well," grumbled Duray. "I don't have anywhere else to go."

Alan Robertson clapped him on the back. "Good lad. We'll put some steaks on the fire and turn our problems loose for the night."

XI

From *Memoirs and Reflections:*

When I first put the Mark I machine into operation, I suffered great fears. What did I know of the forces that I might release? . . . With all adjustments at dead neutral, I punched a passway into a cognate Earth. This was simple enough—in fact, almost anticlimactic . . . Little by little I learned to control my wonderful toy; our own world and all its past phases became familiar to me. What of other worlds? I am sure that in due course we will move instantaneously from world to world, from galaxy to galaxy, using a special space-traveling hub on Utilis. At the moment I am candidly afraid to punch through passways at blind random. What if I opened into the interior of a sun? Or into the center of a black hole? Or into an antimatter universe? I would certainly destroy myself and the machine and conceivably Earth itself.

Still, the potentialities are too entrancing to be ignored. With painstaking precautions and a dozen protective devices, I will attempt to find my way to new worlds, and for the first time interstellar travel will be a reality.

Alan Robertson and Duray sat in the bright morning sunlight beside the flinty-blue lake. They had brought their breakfast out to the table and now sat drinking coffee. Alan Robertson made cheerful conversation for the two of them. "These last few years have been easier on me; I've relegated a great deal of responsibility. Ernest and Henry know my policies as well as I do, if not better; and they're never frivolous or inconsistent." Alan Robertson chuckled. "I've worked two miracles: first, my machine, and second, keeping the business as simple as it is. I refuse to keep regular hours; I won't make appointments; I don't keep records;

I pay no taxes; I exert great political and social influence, but only informally; I simply refuse to be bothered with administrative detail, and consequently I find myself able to enjoy life."

"It's a wonder some religious fanatic hasn't assassinated you," said Duray sourly.

"No mystery there! I've given them all their private worlds, with my best regards, and they have no energy left for violence! And as you know, I walk with a very low silhouette. My friends hardly recognize me on the street." Alan Robertson waved his hand. "No doubt you're more concerned with your immediate quandary. Have you come to a decision regarding the Rumfuddle?"

"I don't have any choice," Duray muttered. "I'd prefer to wring Bob's neck. If I could account for Elizabeth's conduct, I'd feel more comfortable. She's not even remotely interested in black magic. Why did Bob bring her books on satanism?"

"Well—the subject is inherently fascinating," Alan Robertson suggested, without conviction. "The name Satan derives from the Hebrew word for 'adversary'; it never applied to a real individual. 'Zeus,' of course, was an Aryan chieftain of about 3500 B.C., while 'Woden' lived somewhat later. He was actually 'Othinn,' a shaman of enormous personal force who did things with his mind that I can't do with the machine. . . . But again I'm rambling."

Duray gave a silent shrug.

"Well, then, you'll be going to the Rumfuddle," said Alan Robertson, "by and large the best course, whatever the consequences."

"I believe that you know more than you're telling me."

Alan Robertson smiled and shook his head. "I've lived with too much uncertainty among my cognate and near-cognate worlds. Nothing is sure; surprises are everywhere. I think the best plan is to fulfill Bob's requirements. Then if Elizabeth is indeed on hand, you can discuss the event with her."

"What of you? Will you be coming?"

"I am of two minds. Would you prefer that I came?"

"Yes," said Duray. "You have more control over Bob than I do."

"Don't exaggerate my influence! He is a strong man, for all his idleness. Confidentially, I'm delighted that he occupies himself with games rather than . . ." Alan Robertson hesitated.

"Rather than what?"

"Than that his imagination should prompt him to less innocent games. Perhaps I have been overingenuous in this connection. We can only wait and see."

XII

From *Memoirs and Reflections:*

If the past is a house of many chambers, then the present is the most recent coat of paint.

At four o'clock Duray and Alan Robertson left the lodge and passed through Utilis to the San Francisco depot. Duray had changed into a somber dark suit; Alan Robertson wore a more informal costume: blue jacket and pale-gray trousers. They went to Bob Robertson's locker, to find a panel with the sign "NOT

HOME! FOR THE RUMFUDDLE GO TO ROGER WAILLE'S LOCKER, RC 3-96, AND PASS THROUGH TO EKSHAYAN!"

The two went on to Locker RC 3-96, where a sign read: "RUMFUDDLERS: PASS! ALL OTHERS: AWAY!"

Duray shrugged contemptuously, and parting the curtain, looked through the passway into a rustic lobby of natural wood, painted in black, red, yellow, blue, and white floral designs. An open door revealed an expanse of open land and water glistening in the afternoon sunlight. Duray and Alan Robertson passed through, crossed the foyer, and looked out upon a vast, slow river flowing from north to south. A rolling plain spread eastward away and over the horizon. The western bank of the river was indistinct in the afternoon glitter. A path led north to a tall house of eccentric architecture. A dozen domes and cupolas stood against the sky; gables and ridges created a hundred unexpected angles. The walls showed a fish-scale texture of hand-hewn shingles; spiral columns supported the second- and third-story entablatures, where wolves and bears, carved in vigorous curves and masses, snarled, fought, howled, and danced. On the side overlooking the river a pergola clothed with vines cast a dappled shade; here sat the Rumfuddlers.

Alan Robertson looked at the house, up and down the river, across the plain. "From the architecture, the vegetation, the height of the sun, the characteristic haze, I assume the river to be either the Don or the Volga, and yonder the steppes. From the absence of habitation, boats, and artifacts, I would guess the time to be early historic—perhaps 2,000 or 3,000 B.C., a colorful era. The inhabitants of the steppes are nomads; Scyths to the east, Celts to the west, and to the north the homeland of the Germanic and Scandinavian tribes; and yonder the mansion of Roger Waille, and very interesting, too, after the extravagant fashion of the Russian baroque. And, my word! I believe I see an ox on the spit! We may even enjoy our little visit!"

"You do as you like," muttered Duray. "I'd just as soon eat at home."

Alan Robertson pursed his lips. "I understand your point of view, of course, but perhaps we should relax a bit. The scene is majestic; the house is delightfully picturesque; the roast beef is undoubtedly delicious; perhaps we should meet the situation on its own terms."

Duray could find no adequate reply and kept his opinions to himself.

"Well, then," said Alan Robertson, "equability is the word. So now let's see what Bob and Roger have up their sleeves." He set off along the path to the house, with Duray sauntering morosely a step or two behind.

Under the pergola a man jumped to his feet and flourished his hand; Duray recognized the tall, spare form of Bob Robertson. "Just in time," Bob called jocosely. "Not to early, not too late. We're glad you could make it."

"Yes, we found we could accept your invitation after all," said Alan Robertson. "Let me see, do I know anyone here? Roger, hello! . . . And William . . . Ah! the lovely Dora Gorski! . . . Cypriano . . ." He looked around the circle of faces, waving to his acquaintances.

Bob clapped Duray on the shoulder. "Really pleased you could come! What'll you drink? The locals distill a liquor out of fermented mare's milk, but I don't recommend it."

"I'm not here to drink," said Duray. "Where's Elizabeth?"

The corners of Bob's wide mouth twitched. "Come now, old man; let's not be grim. This is the Rumfuddle! A time for joy and self-renewal! Go dance about a bit! Cavort! Pour a bottle of champagne over your head! Sport with the girls!"

Duray looked into the blue eyes for a long second. He strained to keep his voice even. "Where is Elizabeth?"

"Somewhere about the place. A charming girl, your Elizabeth! We're delighted to have you both!"

Duray swung away. He walked to the dark and handsome Roger Waille. "Would you be good enough to take me to my wife?"

Waille raised his eyebrows as if puzzled by Duray's tone of voice. "She is primping and gossiping. If necessary I suppose I could pull her away for a moment or two."

Duray began to feel ridiculous, as if he had been locked away from his world, subjected to harrassments and doubts, and made the butt of some obscure joke. "It's necessary," he said. "We're leaving."

"But you've just arrived!"

"I know."

Waille gave a shrug of amused perplexity and turned away toward the house. Duray followed. They went through a tall, narrow doorway into an entry-hall paneled with a beautiful brown-gold wood that Duray automatically identified as chestnut. Four high panes of tawny glass turned to the west filled the room with a smoky half-melancholy light. Oak settees, upholstered in leather, faced each other across a black, brown, and gray rug. Taborets stood at each side of the settees, and each supported an ornate golden candelabra in the form of conventionalized stag's heads. Waille indicated these last. "Striking, aren't they? The Scythians made them for me. I paid them in iron knives. They think I'm a great magician; and for a fact, I am." He reached into the air and plucked forth an orange, which he tossed upon a settee. "Here's Elizabeth now, and the other maenads as well."

Into the chamber came Elizabeth, with three other young women whom Duray vaguely recalled having met before. At the sight of Duray, Elizabeth stopped short. She essayed a smile and said in a light, strained voice, "Hello, Gil. You're here after all." She laughed nervously and, Duray felt, unnaturally. "Yes, of course you're here. I didn't think you'd come."

Duray glanced toward the other women, who stood with Waille, watching half expectantly. Duray said, "I'd like to speak to you alone."

"Excuse us," said Waille. "We'll go on outside."

They departed. Elizabeth looked longingly after them and fidgeted with the buttons of her jacket.

"Where are the children?" Duray demanded curtly.

"Upstairs, getting dressed." She looked down at her own costume, the festival raiment of a Transylvanian peasant girl: a green skirt embroidered with red and blue flowers, a white blouse, a black velvet vest, glossy black boots.

Duray felt his temper slipping; his voice was strained and fretful. "I don't understand anything of this. Why did you close the passways?"

Elizabeth attempted a flippant smile. "I was bored with routine."

"Oh? Why didn't you mention it to me yesterday morning? You didn't need to close the passways."

"Gilbert, please. Let's not discuss it."

Duray stood back, tongue-tied with astonishment. "Very well," he said at last. "We won't discuss it. You go up and get the girls. We're going home."

Elizabeth shook her head. In a neutral voice she said, "It's impossible. There's only one passway open. I don't have it."

"Who does? Bob?"

"I guess so; I'm not really sure."

"How did he get it? There were only four, and all four were closed."

"It's simple enough. He moved the downtown passway from our locker to another and left a blank in its place."

"And who closed off the other three?"

"I did."

"Why?"

"Because Bob told me to. I don't want to talk about it. I'm sick to death of the whole business." And she half whispered: "I don't know what I'm going to do with myself."

"I know what I'm going to do," said Duray. He turned toward the door.

Elizabeth held up her hands and clenched her fists against her breast. "Don't make trouble—please! He'll close our last passway!"

"Is that why you're afraid of him? If so—don't be. Alan wouldn't allow it."

Elizabeth's face began to crumple. She pushed past Duray and walked quickly out upon the terrace. Duray followed, baffled and furious. He looked back and forth across the terrace. Bob was not to be seen. Elizabeth had gone to Alan Robertson; she spoke in a hushed, urgent voice. Duray went to join them. Elizabeth became silent and turned away, avoiding Duray's gaze.

Alan Robertson spoke in a voice of easy geniality. "Isn't this a lovely spot? Look how the setting sun shines on the river!"

Roger Waille came by rolling a cart with ice, goblets, and a dozen bottles. He said: "Of all the places on all the Earths, this is my favorite. I call it Ekshayan, which is the Scythian name for this district."

A woman asked, "Isn't it cold and bleak in the winter?"

"Frightful!" said Waille. "The blizzards howl down from the north; then they stop, and the land is absolutely still. The days are short, and the sun comes up red as a poppy. The wolves slink out of the forests, and at dusk they circle the house. When a full moon shines, they howl like banshees, or maybe the banshees are howling! I sit beside the fireplace, entranced."

"It occurs to me," said Manfred Funk, "that each person, selecting a site for his home, reveals a great deal about himself. Even on old Earth, a man's home was ordinarily a symbolic simulacrum of the man himself; now, with every option available, a person's house is himself."

"This is very true," said Alan Robertson, "and certainly Roger need not fear that he has revealed any discreditable aspects of himself by showing us his rather grotesque home so the lonely steppes of prehistoric Russia."

Roger Waille laughed. "The grotesque house isn't me; I merely felt that it fitted its setting. . . . Here, Duray, you're not drinking. That's chilled vodka; you can mix it or drink it straight in the time-tested manner."

"Nothing for me, thanks."

"Just as you like. Excuse me; I'm wanted elsewhere." Waille moved away, rolling the cart. Elizabeth leaned as if she wanted to follow him, then remained beside Alan Robertson, looking thoughtfully over the river.

Duray spoke to Alan Robertson as if she were not there. "Elizabeth refuses to leave. Bob has hypnotized her."

"That's not true," said Elizabeth softly.

"Somehow, one way or another, he's forced her to stay. She won't tell me why."

"I want the passway back," said Elizabeth. But her voice was muffled and uncertain.

Alan Robertson cleared his throat. "I hardly know what to say. It's a very awkward situation. None of us wants to create a disturbance—"

"There you're wrong," said Duray.

Alan Robertson ignored the remark. "I'll have a word with Bob after the party. In the meantime I don't see why we shouldn't enjoy the company of our friends, and that wonderful roast ox! Who is that turning the spit? I know him from somewhere."

Duray could hardly speak for outrage. "After what he's done to us?"

"He's gone too far, much too far," Alan Robertson agreed. "Still, he's a flamboyant, feckless sort, and I doubt if he understands the full inconvenience he's caused you."

"He understands well enough. He just doesn't care."

"Perhaps so," said Alan Robertson sadly. "I had always hoped—but that's neither here nor there. I still feel that we should act with restraint. It's much easier not to do than to undo."

Elizabeth abruptly crossed the terrace and went to the front door of the tall house, where her three daughters had appeared—Dolly, twelve; Joan, ten; Ellen, eight—all wearing green, white, and black peasant frocks and glossy black boots. Duray thought they made a delightful picture. He followed Elizabeth across the terrace.

"It's Daddy," screamed Ellen, and threw herself in his arms. The other two, not to be outdone, did likewise.

"We thought you weren't coming to the party," cried Dolly. "I'm glad you did, though."

"So'm I."

"So'm I."

"I'm glad I came, too, if only to see you in these pretty costumes. Let's go see Grandpa Alan." He took them across the terrace, and after a moment's hesitation, Elizabeth followed. Duray became aware that everyone had stopped talking to look at him and his family, with, so it seemed, an extraordinary, even avid, curiosity, as if in expectation of some entertaining extravagance of conduct. Duray began to burn with emotion. Once, long ago, while crossing a street in downtown San Francisco, he had been struck by an automobile, suffering a broken leg and a fractured clavicle. Almost as soon as he had been knocked down, pedestrians came pushing to stare down at him, and Duray, looking up in pain and shock, had seen only the ring of white faces and intent eyes, greedy as flies around a puddle of blood. In hysterical fury he had staggered to his feet, striking out into every face within reaching distance, men and women alike. He hated them more than the man who had run him down: the ghouls who had come to enjoy his pain. Had he the miraculous power, he would have crushed them into a screaming bale of detestable flesh and hurled the bundle twenty miles out into the Pacific Ocean . . .

Some faint shadow of this emotion affected him now, but today he would provide them no unnatural pleasure. He turned a single glance of cool contempt around the group, then took his three eager-faced daughters to a bench at the back of the terrace. Elizabeth followed, moving like a mechanical object. She seated herself at the end of the bench and looked off across the river. Duray stared heavily back at the Rumfuddlers, compelling them to shift their gazes to where the ox roasted over a great bed of coals. A young man in a white jacket turned the spit; another basted the meat with a long-handled brush. A pair of Orientals carried out a carving table; another brought a carving set; a fourth wheeled out a cart laden with salads, round crusty loaves, trays of cheese and herrings. A fifth man, dressed as a Transylvanian gypsy, came from the house with a violin. He went to the corner of the terrace and began to play melancholy music of the steppes.

Bob Robertson and Roger Waille inspected the ox, a magnificent sight indeed. Duray attempted a stony detachment, but his nose was under no such strictures; the odor of the roast meat, garlic, and herbs tantalized him unmercifully. Bob Robertson returned to the terrace and held up his hands for attention; the fiddler put down his instrument. "Control your appetites; there'll still be a few minutes, during which we can discuss our next Rumfuddle. Our clever colleague Bernard Ulman recommends a hostelry in the Adirondacks: the Sapphire Lake Lodge. The hotel was built in 1902, to the highest standards of Edwardian comfort. The clientele is derived from the business community of New York. The cuisine is kosher; the management maintains an atmosphere of congenial gentility; the current date is 1930. Bernard has furnished photographs. Roger, if you please."

Waille drew back a curtain to reveal a screen. He manipulated the projection machine, and the hotel was displayed on the screen: a rambling, half-timbered structure overlooking several acres of park and a smooth lake.

"Thank you, Roger. I believe that we also have a photograph of the staff."

On the screen appeared a stiffly posed group of about thirty men and women, all smiling with various degrees of affability. The Rumfuddlers were amused; some among them tittered.

"Bernard gives a very favorable report as to the cuisine, the amenities, and the charm of the general area. Am I right, Bernard?"

"In every detail," declared Bernard Ulman. "The management is attentive and efficient; the clientele is well-established."

"Very good," said Bob Robertson. "Unless someone has a more entertaining idea, we will hold our next Rumfuddle at the Sapphire Lake Lodge. And now I believe that the roast beef should be ready—done to a turn, as the expression goes."

"Quite right," said Roger Waille. "Tom, as always, has done an excellent job at the spit."

The ox was lifted to the table. The carver set to work with a will. Duray went to speak to Alan Robertson, who blinked uneasily at his approach. Duray asked, "Do you understand the reason for these parties? Are you in on the joke?"

Alan Robertson spoke in a precise manner: "I certainly am not 'in on the joke,' as you put it." He hesitated, then said: "The Rumfuddlers will never again intrude upon your life or that of your family. I am sure of this. Bob became overexuberant; he exercised poor judgment, and I intend to have a quiet word with him. In fact, we have already exchanged certain opinions. At the moment your best interests will be served by detachment and unconcern."

Duray spoke with sinister politeness: "You feel, then, that I and my family should bear the brunt of Bob's jokes?"

"This is a harsh view of the situation, but my answer must be Yes."

"I'm not so sure. My relationship with Elizabeth is no longer the same. Bob has done this to me."

"To quote an old apothegm: 'Least said, soonest mended.' "

Duray changed the subject. "When Waille showed the photograph of the hotel staff, I thought some of the faces were familiar. Before I could be quite sure, the picture was gone."

Alan Robertson nodded unhappily. "Let's not develop the subject, Gilbert. Instead—"

"I'm into the situation too far," said Duray. "I want to know the truth."

"Very well, then," said Alan Robertson hollowly, "your instincts are accurate. The management of the Sapphire Lake Lodge, in cognate circumstances, has achieved an unsavory reputation. As you have guessed, they comprise the leadership of the National Socialist party during 1938 or thereabouts. The manager, of course, is Hitler, the desk clerk is Goebbels, the headwaiter is Göring, the bellboys are Himmler and Hess, and so on down the line. They are, of course, not aware of the activities of their cognates of other worlds. The hotel's clientele is for the most part Jewish, which brings a macabre humor to the situation."

"Undeniably," said Duray. "What of that Rumfuddlers party that we looked in on?"

"You refer to the high-school football team? The 1951 Texas champions, as I recall." Alan Robertson grinned. "And well they should be. Bob identified the players for me. Are you interested in the lineup?"

"Very much so."

Alan Robertson drew a sheet of paper from his pocket. "I believe—yes, this is it." He handed the sheet to Duray who saw a schematic lineup:

LE	LT	LG	C	RG	RT	RE
Achilles	Charle-magne	Hercules	Goliath	Samson	Richard the Lion-hearted	Billy the Kid

	Q	
	Machiavelli	
LHB		RHB
Sir Galahad		Geronimo
	FB	
	Cuchulain	

Duray returned the paper. "You approve of this?"

"I had best put it like this," said Alan Robertson, a trifle uneasily. "One day, chatting with Bob, I remarked that much travail could be spared the human race if the more notorious evildoers were early in their lives shifted to environments which afforded them constructive outlets for their energies. I speculated that having the competence to make such changes, it was perhaps our duty to do so. Bob became interested in the concept and formed his group, the Rumfuddlers, to serve the function I had suggested. In all candor I believe that Bob and his friends have been attracted more by the possibility of entertainment than by altruism, but the effect has been the same."

"The football players aren't evildoers," said Duray. "Sir Galahad, Charlemagne, Samson, Richard the Lion-hearted . . ."

"Exactly true," said Alan Robertson, "and I made this point to Bob. He asserted that all were brawlers and bullyboys, with the possible exception of Sir Galahad; that Charlemagne, for example, had conquered much territory to no particular achievement; that Achilles, a national hero to the Greeks, was a cruel enemy to the Trojans; and so forth. His justifications are somewhat specious perhaps . . . Still, these young men are better employed making touchdowns than breaking heads."

After a pause Duray asked: "How are these matters arranged?"

"I'm not entirely sure. I believe that by one means or another, the desired babies are exchanged with others of similar appearance. The child so obtained is reared in appropriate circumstances."

"The jokes seem elaborate and rather tedious."

"Precisely!" Alan Robertson declared. "Can you think of a better method to keep someone like Bob out of mischief?"

"Certainly," said Duray. "Fear of the consequences." He scowled across the terrace. Bob had stopped to speak to Elizabeth. She and the three girls rose to their feet.

Duray strode across the terrace. "What's going on?"

"Nothing of consequence," said Bob. "Elizabeth and the girls are going to help serve the guests." He glanced toward the serving table, then turned back to Duray. "Would you help with the carving?"

Duray's arm moved of its own volition. His fist caught Bob on the angle of the jaw and sent him reeling back into one of the white-coated Orientals, who carried a tray of food. The two fell into an untidy heap. The Rumfuddlers were shocked and amused and watched with attention.

Bob rose to his feet gracefully enough and gave a hand to the Oriental. Looking toward Duray, Bob shook his head ruefully. Meeting his glance, Duray noted a pale blue glint; then Bob once more became bland and debonair.

Elizabeth spoke in a low despairing voice: "Why couldn't you have done as he asked? It would have all been so simple."

"Elizabeth may well be right," said Alan Robertson.

"Why should she be right?" demanded Duray. "We are his victims! You've allowed him a taste of mischief, and now you can't control him!"

"Not true!" declared Alan Robertson. "I intend to impose rigorous curbs upon the Rumfuddlers, and I will be obeyed."

"The damage is done, so far as I am concerned," said Duray bitterly. "Come along, Elizabeth, we're going Home."

"We can't go Home. Bob has the passway."

Alan Robertson drew a deep sigh and came to a decision. He crossed to where Bob stood with a goblet of wine in one hand, massaging his jaw with the other. Alan Robertson spoke to Bob politely but with authority. Bob was slow in making a reply. Alan Robertson spoke again, sharply. Bob only shrugged. Alan Robertson waited a moment, then returned to Duray, Elizabeth, and the three children.

"The passway is at his San Francisco apartment," said Alan Robertson in a measured voice. "He will give it back to you after the party. He doesn't choose to go for it now."

Bob once more commanded the attention of the Rumfuddlers. "By popular request we replay the record of our last but one Rumfuddle, contrived by one of our most distinguished, diligent, and ingenious Rumfuddlers, Manfred Funk. The locale is the Red Barn, a roadhouse twelve miles west of Urbana, Illinois; the time is the late summer of 1926; the occasion is a Charleston dancing contest. The music is provided by the legendary Wolverines, and you will hear the fabulous cornet of Leon Bismarck Beiderbecke." Bob gave a wry smile, as if the music were not to his personal taste. "This was one of our most rewarding occasions, and here it is again."

The screen showed the interior of a dance-hall, crowded with excited young men and women. At the back of the stage sat the Wolverines, wearing tuxedos; to the front stood the contestants: eight dapper young men and eight pretty girls in short skirts. An announcer stepped forward and spoke to the crowd through a megaphone: "Contestants are numbered one through eight! Please, no encouragement from the audience. The prize is this magnificent trophy and fifty dollars cash; the presentation will be made by last year's winner, Boozy Horman. Remember, on the first number we eliminate four contestants, on the second number, two; and after the third number we select our winter. So then: Bix and the Wolverines and 'Sensation Rag'!"

From the band came music; from the contestants, agitated motion.

Duray asked, "Who are these people?"

Alan Robertson replied in an even voice: "The young men are locals and not important. But notice the girls: No doubt you find them attractive. You are not alone. They are Helen of Troy, Deirdre, Marie Antoinette, Cleopatra, Salome, Lady Godiva, Nefertiti, and Mata Hari."

Duray gave a dour grunt. The music halted; judging applause from the audience, the announcer eliminated Marie Antoinette, Cleopatra, Deirdre, Mata Hari, and their respective partners. The Wolverines played "Fidgety Feet"; the four remaining contestants danced with verve and dedication, but Helen and Nefertiti were eliminated. The Wolverines played "Tiger Rag." Salome and Lady Godiva and their young men performed with amazing zeal. After carefully appraising the volume of applause, the announcer gave his judgment to Lady Godiva and her partner. Large on the screen appeared a close-up view of the two happy faces; in an excess of triumphant joy they hugged and kissed each other. The screen went dim; after the vivacity of the Red Barn the terrace above the Don seemed drab and insipid.

The Rumfuddlers shifted in their seats. Some uttered exclamations to assert their gaiety; others stared out across the vast empty face of the river.

Duray glanced toward Elizabeth; she was gone. Now he saw her circulating among the guests with three other young women, pouring wine from Scythian decanters.

"It makes a pretty picture, does it not?" said a calm voice. Duray turned to find Bob standing behind him; his mouth twisted in an easy half-smile, but his eye glinted pale blue.

Duray turned away. Alan Robertson said, "This is not at all a pleasant situation, Bob, and in fact completely lacks charm."

"Perhaps at future Rumfuddles, when my face feels better, the charm will emerge. . . . Excuse me; I see that I must enliven the meeting." He stepped forward. "We have a final pastiche: oddments and improvisations, vignettes and glimpses, each in its own way entertaining and instructive. Roger, start the mechanism, if you please."

Roger Waille hesitated and glanced sidelong toward Alan Robertson.

"The item number is sixty-two, Roger," said Bob in a calm voice. Roger Waille delayed another instant, then shrugged and went to the projection machine.

"The material is new," said Bob, "hence I will supply a commentary. First we have an episode in the life of Richard Wagner, the dogmatic and occasionally irascible composer. This year is 1843; the place is Dresden. Wagner sets forth on a summer night to attend a new opera, *Der Sanger Krieg*, by an unknown composer. He alights from his carriage before the hall; he enters; he seats himself in his loge. Notice the dignity of his posture, the authority of his gestures! The music begins. Listen!" From the projector came the sound of music. "It is the overture," stated Bob. "But notice Wagner: Why is he stupefied? Why is he overcome with wonder? He listens to the music as if he has never heard it before. And in fact he hasn't; he has only just yesterday set down a few preliminary notes for this particular opus, which he planned to call *Tannhäuser*; today, magically, he hears it in its final form. Wagner will walk home slowly tonight, and perhaps in his abstraction he will kick the dog Schmutzi. . . . Now to a different scene: St. Petersburg in the year 1880 and the stables in back of the Winter Palace. The ivory and gilt carriage rolls forth to convey the czar and the czarina to a reception at the British Embassy. Notice the drivers: stern, well-groomed, intent at their business. Marx's beard is well-trimmed; Lenin's goatee is not so pronounced. A groom comes to watch the carriage roll away. He has a kindly twinkle in his eye, does Stalin." The screen went dim once more, then brightened to show a city street lined with automobile showrooms and used-car lots. "This is one of Shawn Henderson's projects. The four used-car lots are operated by men who in other circumstances were religious notables: prophets and so forth. That alert, keen-featured man in front of Quality Motors, for instance, is Mohammed. Shawn is conducting a careful survey, and at our next Rumfuddle he will report upon his dealings with these four famous figures."

Alan Robertson stepped forward, somewhat diffidently. He cleared his throat. "I don't like to play the part of spoilsport, but I'm afraid I have no choice. There will be no further Rumfuddles. Our original goals have been neglected, and I note far too many episodes of purposeless frivolity and even cruelty. You may wonder at what seems a sudden decision, but I have been considering the matter for several days. The Rumfuddles have taken a turn in an unwholesome direction and conceivably might become a grotesque new vice, which, of course, is far from our original ideal. I'm sure that every sensible person, after a few moments' reflection, will agree that now is the time to stop. Next week you may return to me all passways except those to worlds where you maintain residence."

The Rumfuddlers sat murmuring together. Some turned resentful glances toward Alan Robertson; others served themselves more bread and meat. Bob came over to join Alan and Duray. He spoke in an easy manner. "I must say that your admonitions arrive with all the delicacy of a lightning bolt. I can picture Jehovah smiting the fallen algels in a similar style."

Alan Robertson smiled. "Now, then, Bob, you're talking nonsense. The situations aren't at all similar. Jehovah struck out in fury; I impose my restriction in all goodwill in order that we can once again turn our energies to constructive ends."

Bob threw back his head and laughed. "But the Rumfuddlers have lost the habit of work. We only want to amuse ourselves, and after all, what is so noxious in our activities?"

"The trend is menacing, Bob." Alan Robertson's voice was reasonable. "Unpleasant elements are creeping into your fun, so stealthily that you yourself are unaware of them. For instance, why torment poor Wagner? Surely there was gratuitous cruelty, and only to provide you a few instants of amusement. And since the subject is in the air, I heartily deplore your treatment of Gilbert and Elizabeth. You have brought them both an extraordinary inconvenience, and in Elizabeth's case, actual suffering. Gilbert got something of his own back, and the balance is about even."

"Gilbert is far too impulsive," said Bob. "Self-willed and egocentric, as he always has been."

Alan held up his hand. "There is no need to go further into the subject, Bob. I suggest that you say no more."

"Just as you like, though the matter, considered as practical rehabilitation, isn't irrelevant. We can amply justify the work of the Rumfuddlers."

Duray asked quietly, "Just how do you mean, Bob?"

Alan Robertson made a peremptory sound, but Duray said, "Let him say what he likes and make an end to it. He plans to do so anyway."

There was a moment of silence. Bob looked across the terrace to where the three Orientals were transferring the remains of the beef to a service cart.

"Well?" Alan Robertson asked softly. "Have you made your choice?"

Bob held out his hands in ostensible bewilderment. "I don't understand you! I want only to vindicate myself and the Rumfuddlers. I think we have done splendidly. Today we have allowed Torquemada to roast a dead ox instead of a living heretic; Marquis de Sade has fulfilled his obscure urges by caressing seared flesh with a basting brush, and did you notice the zest with which Ivan the Terrible hacked up the carcass? Nero, who has real talent, played his violin. Attila, Genghis Khan, and Mao Tse-tung efficiently served the guests. Wine was poured by Messalina, Lucrezia Borgia, Delilah, and Gilbert's charming wife, Elizabeth. Only Gilbert failed to demonstrate his rehabilitation, but at least he provided us a touching and memorable picture: Gilles de Rais, Elizabeth Báthory, and their three virgin daughters. It was sufficient. In every case we have shown that rehabilitation is not an empty word."

"Not in every case," said Alan Robertson, "specifically that of your own."

Bob looked at him askance. "I don't follow you."

"No less than Gilbert are you ignorant of your background. I will now reveal the circumstances so that you may understand something of yourself and try to curb the tendencies which have made your cognate an exemplar of cruelty, stealth, and treachery."

Bob laughed: a brittle sound like cracking ice. "I admit to a horrified interest."

"I took you from a forest a thousand miles north of this very spot while I traced the phylogeny of the Norse gods. Your name was Loki. For reasons which are not now important I brought you back to San Francisco, and there you grew to maturity."

"So I am Loki."

"No. You are Bob Robertson, just as this is Gilbert Duray, and here is his wife, Elizabeth. Loki, Gilles de Rais, Elizabeth Báthory: These names applied to human material which has not functioned quite as well. Gilles de Rais, judging from all evidence, suffered from a brain tumor; he fell into his peculiar vices after a long and honorable career. The case of Princess Elizabeth Báthory is less clear, but one might suspect syphilis and consequent cerebral lesions."

"And what of poor Loki?" inquired Bob with exaggerated pathos.

"Loki seemed to suffer from nothing except a case of old-fashioned meanness."

Bob seemed concerned. "So that these qualities apply to me?"

"You are not necessarily identical to your cognate. Still, I advise you to take careful stock of yourself, and so far as I am concerned, you had best regard yourself as on probation."

"Just as you say." Bob looked over Alan Robertson's shoulder. "Excuse me; you've spoiled the party, and everybody is leaving. I want a word with Roger."

Duray moved to stand in his way, but Bob shouldered him aside and strode across the terrace, with Duray glowering at his back.

Elizabeth said in a mournful voice, "I hope we're at the end of all this."

Duray growled. "You should never have listened to him."

"I didn't listen; I read about it in one of Bob's books; I saw your picture; I couldn't—"

Alan Robertson intervened. "Don't harass poor Elizabeth; I consider her both sensible and brave; she did the best she could."

Bob returned. "Everything taken care of," he said cheerfully. "All except one or two details."

"The first of these is the return of the passway. Gilbert and Elizabeth—not to mention Dolly, Joan, and Ellen—are anxious to return to Home."

"They can stay here with you," said Bob. "That's probably the best solution."

"I don't plan to stay here," said Alan Robertson in mild wonder. "We are leaving at once."

"You must change your plans," said Bob. "I have finally become bored with your reproaches. Roger doesn't particularly care to leave his home, but he agrees that now is the time to make a final disposal of the matter."

Alan Robertson frowned in displeasure. "The joke is in very poor taste, Bob."

Roger Waille came from the house, his face somewhat glum. "They're all closed. Only the main gate is open."

Alan Robertson said to Gilbert: "I think that we will leave Bob and Roger to their Rumfuddle fantasies. When he returns to his senses, we'll get your passway. Come along, then, Elizabeth! Girls!"

"Alan," said Bob gently, "you're staying here. Forever. I'm taking over the machine."

Alan Robertson asked mildly: "How do you propose to restrain me? By force?"

"You can stay here alive or dead; take your choice."

"You have weapons, then?"

"I certainly do." Bob displayed a pistol. "There are also the servants. None have brain tumors or syphilis; they're all just plain bad."

Roger said in an awkward voice, "Let's go and get it over."

Alan Robertson's voice took on a harsh edge. "You seriously plan to maroon us here, without food?"

"Consider yourself marooned."

"I'm afraid that I must punish you, Bob, and Roger as well."

Bob laughed gaily. "You yourself are suffering from brain disease—megalomania. You haven't the power to punish anyone."

"I still control the machine, Bob."

"The machine isn't here. So now—"

Alan Robertson turned and looked around the landscape, with a frowning air of expectation. "Let me see. I'd probably come down from the main gate; Gilbert and a group from behind the house. Yes, here we are."

Down the path from the main portal, walking jauntily, came two Alan Robertsons with six men armed with rifles and gas grenades. Simultaneously from behind the house appeared two Gilbert Durays and six more men, similarly armed.

Bob stared in wonder. "Who are these people?"

"Cognates," said Alan, smiling. "I told you I controlled the machine, and so do all my cognates. As soon as Gilbert and I return to our Earth, we must similarly set forth and in our turn do our part on other worlds cognate to this . . . Roger, be good enough to summon your servants. We will take them back to Earth. You and Bob must remain here."

Waille gasped in distress. "Forever?"

"You deserve nothing better," said Alan Robertson. "Bob perhaps deserves worse." He turned to the cognate Alan Robertsons. "What of Gilbert's passway?"

Both replied, "It's in Bob's San Francisco apartment, in a box on the mantelpiece."

"Very good," said Alan Robertson. "We will now depart. Good-bye, Bob. Good-bye, Roger. I am sorry that our association ended on this rather unpleasant basis."

"Wait!" cried Roger. "Take me back with you!"

"Good-bye," said Alan Robertson. "Come along then, Elizabeth. Girls! Run on ahead!"

XIII

Elizabeth and the children had returned to Home; Alan Robertson and Duray sat in the lounge above the machine. "Our first step," said Alan Robertson, "is to dissolve our obligation. There are, of course, an infinite number of Rumfuddles at Ekshayans and an infinite number of Alans and Gilberts. If we visited a single Rumfuddle, we would, by the laws of probability, miss a certain number of the emergency situations. The total number of permutations, assuming that an infinite number of Alans and Gilberts makes a random choice among an infinite number of Ekshayans, is infinity raised to the infinite power. What percentage of this number yields blanks for any given Ekshayan, I haven't calculated. If we visited Ekshayans until we had by our own efforts rescued at least one Gilbert and Alan set, we might be forced to scour fifty or a hundred worlds or more. Or we might achieve our rescue on the first visit. The wisest course, I believe, is for you and I to visit, say, twenty Ekshayans. If each of the Alan and Gilbert sets does the same, then the chances for any particular Alan and Gilbert to be abandoned are one in twenty times nineteen times eighteen times seventeen, et cetera. Even then I think I will arrange that an operator check another five or ten thousand worlds to gather up that one lone chance . . ."

Philip Latham

Philip Latham is the pseudonym of Robert S. Richardson (1902–81), a distinguished astronomer who occasionally wrote articles under his own name, but published fiction between the 1940s and 1960s only under the Latham name. His stories characteristically feature astronomers, and until his later years always focused on science, especially theoretical physics embodied as fact.

From the flamboyant, apocalyptic astronomical fiction of Camille Flammarion in the late 19th century to the works of Fred Hoyle and Gregory Benford, working astronomers and astrophysicists have contributed stories of broad scope and cosmic speculation to the development of science fiction. The word "astronomical" is, after all, a synonym for very large in number or scale. Cosmology and astronomy are primary repositories of images for the SF genre, as was nature for the Romantic poets. And, of course, it is the astronomers who investigate the environments that are the literal settings of much science fiction. But it is also the teasing, ambiguous border between the physical and the metaphysical that astronomical science fiction often confronts, and that gives depth and emotional force to the cold and the distant. As in this story.

THE DIMPLE IN DRACO

There was never any doubt when quitting time came to the Institute for Cosmological Physics, Bill Backus reflected. Promptly at 4:53 P.M. the women all started heading for the powder room, whence shortly thereafter came the sound of water in turbulence. It was one of the zero points in this uneasy world.

For the third time he reached for the telephone and for the third time hesitated. It was 4:57 now. The girl at the switchboard always got sore if you kept her after five o'clock. Oh, well, the hell with her. He needed help. He seized the phone.

"Two-seven, please."

No answer . . . no answer . . . no . . .

"MacCready," came a noncommittal voice.

"Mac, this is Bill."

"Bill! It's so good to hear your voice!"

"Listen, Mac, I've got something down here in the measuring room I think will interest you."

"So's my wife. She's probably mixing it now."

"I'd like your opinion very much. Shouldn't take ten minutes."

One . . . two . . . three . . .

"All right. See you."

A few minutes later MacCready sauntered into the measuring room, hoisted one leg over a corner of the bench that ran along the wall, and applied a match to his pipe. When the tobacco was going to his satisfaction, he folded his arms and gazed expectantly at Bill.

"Here I am. Interest me."

Bill indicated the Toepfer measuring engine beside him.

"Plate's on there. Got it last week with the prime focus spectrograph. Six-hour exposure in the second order blue. I nearly froze. Coldest night in the memory of man—"

"You don't look so good," MacCready remarked.

"Maybe that's because I don't feel so good," Bill said. He rose and began pacing the floor. "Take a look at the plate, will you, and tell me what you think."

"But your feet seem better," MacCready added encouragingly.

"Yeah, they are better. Now will you look at the plate?"

MacCready laid aside his pipe and peered into the eyepiece.

"Nice spectrum," he said. "Real sharp lines."

"But *what* lines?" Bill cried. "I've been working on those lines for three days. Can't identify a single one." He ran his fingers through his black hair. "It's driving me crazy."

"Well, d'you have to get so dramatic about it?" MacCready asked. He gave the focusing screw a touch. "What is this famous object, anyhow?"

"Well, you see, that's what I don't know."

"*You don't know!*" MacCready stared at him. "Do you realize how much it cost the Institute to get this plate? Do you know that we have seventeen applications on file for time at this instrument? Applications from highly qualified individuals with no suspicion of insanity in their background. And then you take our giant eye, as the newspapers are pleased to call it, and bang away at any old—"

"Mac, shut up." Bill lit a cigarette. "I was after NGC 2146, that way-north nebula in Cepheus, I guess it is. This new night assistant was on that evening. Poor guy got all balled up. My fault as much as his. You wouldn't believe it possible, but he got set on the wrong side of the pole. Landed me over in Draco somewhere. I thought the setting looked kind of funny—"

"Couldn't you tell from your star field?"

"Well, I should, but the fields weren't so different. Anyhow—"

"—anyhow you goofed but you got *something*," MacCready finished for him. "By any chance would you have the vaguest notion what it is? Radio source? Interloper? QSG? Haro-Luyten object? Humason-Zwicky star? Have I left out anything?"

"All I know, it's got a spectrum nobody ever saw before."

"Then what are you griping about?" MacCready demanded. "That's *good*. Maybe this object's got the world's biggest red shift. You've probably dredged up some lines buried thousands of angstroms deep in the ultraviolet."

"Nope, won't suit, Mac. Remember the Houston meeting? It was agreed we're living in an exploding universe with a q-zero of 2.5. This thing's way off the beam—much too bright."

"You know what your problem is, Bill?" MacCready was suddenly serious. "You've always got to relate to somebody else. You're afraid to take your results just as they stand."

"But there must be an answer," Bill protested. "What else can it be?"

MacCready shrugged and fell to scrutinizing the plate again.

"Wouldn't surprise me if the answer's staring us right in the face," he said. "Only it's so simple we can't see it."

He moved the plate carriage a bit.

"Now you take these three big lines I see here . . . Why couldn't the one on my left be that HeII line at—what is it?—1640? And the one in the middle—"

"Oh, my gawd, don't you think I've been all through that search list?" Bill said wearily. "None of 'em's any good. I've tried a bunch of hundred-to-one shots. They're no good either. Nothing fits."

"Too bad." MacCready frowned slightly. "Strange . . . these lines are all in absorption, aren't they?"

"Here's my list of wavelengths," Bill said, handing him a sheet of paper. "They're the means of my measures on the machine and some runs with the electronic line-profile comparator. They ought to be pretty good."

"I'm sure they are," MacCready murmured. He shot a sudden glance at Bill. "You sure you set the grating in the right order spectrum?"

"Mac, I *couldn't* make a mistake like that."

"Congratulations."

There was a long silence broken only by an occasional motor starting up in the parking lot, and the steady rumble of traffic from the boulevard nearby. MacCready was the first to speak.

"After you got this plate, did you take another exposure on a familiar object, same spectrograph—same emulsion—same everything?"

"Yes."

"All right?"

"Yes."

"It was?"

"Yes!" Bill shouted. "In France it's *oui*. In Spanish it's *si*. In Russian it's *da*."

MacCready transferred his attention from the plate to Bill's list of wavelengths.

"You know, these three big lines remind me of something," he muttered. "But I'll confess I haven't the faintest notion what it is."

Bill looked completely deflated. He began pacing the room again, clasping and unclasping his hands behind him. MacCready seemed to have forgotten his existence.

Bill tossed away his cigarette.

"Well, thanks for coming down, Mac. I'd gotten to the end of my rope. Thought perhaps you could suggest something."

There was no response. Bill paced the floor for another five minutes.

"Well, I've got to go. We're having company tonight."

"Yeah, you run along," MacCready told him. "Leaving myself in a minute . . . just want to check one thing."

Bill was nearly out the door when MacCready called suddenly, "Bill."

"Yeah?"

"Call my wife, will you? Tell her I'll be a little late."

Bill had to wait forever before he got a break in the traffic at Los Robles. Why did he keep coming this way? he asked himself. There was no answer. You saw an opening—you took a deep breath—uttered a prayer—and if you were lucky you made it.

Turning north toward Hillhurst he saw that the signal at Cordova was going to be red, as usual. The signal was always red at Cordova. In the past five years he must have crossed Cordova going north at least two thousand times. There had been just three times by actual count when he had hit the green light. His confidence in the theory of probability had been badly shaken.

Through the tangle of varicolored lights, leering Santa Clauses, liquor advertisements, and five-pointed stars* of Bethlehem, Bill perceived a huge sign looming ahead, VILLAGE MARKET. *Click!* What was he supposed to do? What was he supposed to—Helen's grocery list, of course. Good old autohypnosis.

Within the Village Market the aisles were abustle with hausfrauen pushing metal carts, their vacant gaze reflecting the trancelike state induced by the sight of merchandise in profusion. Bill took a cart himself and went to work on Helen's grocery list, tracking down the various items by the awkward process of taking them in the order written. Occasionally when it seemed like a good idea he tossed in an extra item or two. How often he had come in for a fifty-nine-cent piece of cheese and departed laden down with a lot of junk he never originally had the slightest intention of buying. But who were we? Mere puppets moving at the bidding of the vast formless things that operate these huge pleasure domes of produce.

Helen wrote her shopping items in a code that might have baffled the best brains in Interpol. This time, however, it had been pretty clear sailing. He now had in the cart the "6 nce rd rpe toms" and the "2 pkes lmn jlo," and finally had reached the last item, "2 dz Ye Olde Eng Muffs." This sounded almost too easy. On any rational distribution system Olde English Muffins could hardly be anywhere else but in the bread section. He glanced at the Store Guide. Bread? . . . Bread? . . . Section 5. Where was he? Way over in 21 among Frozen Desserts and mouthwash. He deftly changed course and started bearing toward smaller numbers. 2 . . . 3 . . . 4 . . . 6 . . . 7. No 5! Must have missed it. Scan more carefully now . . . 2 . . . 3 . . . 4 . . . 6 . . . 7. Number 5 was absolutely and positively missing.

He looked around for a clerk, but there was none in sight. Neither was there any bread. He explored one aisle after another as fast as traffic permitted. There were shelves and bins loaded with pickles and olives, wieners and knockwurst, yoghurt and horseradish. But no Olde English Muffins. Well, he couldn't spend the evening pushing a metal cart around the Village Market. He picked up a box of Bixmix and headed for Checkers' Row.

The porch lights were already burning when he turned into the driveway. That was bad. It meant that even now company was ominously near. Closing the garage door, he noticed the stars of Auriga rising over the mountains to the north. How odd Capella looked, reddened almost to the color of Mars by the smoke and haze. Auriga had always been his favorite constellation. All the constellations had a background rich in mythological lore—except Auriga. Auriga was known as "the Charioteer." But where were his chariot and horse? Nobody knew. The stars of Auriga were meaningless.

"Well, where have *you* been?" Helen demanded, as he staggered into the kitchen with his load of groceries. She was a small woman whose early blond prettiness was beginning to show signs of wear under the ceaseless battering of suburbia: the Garden Club, the Art League, WAGS,† etc., etc.

"Where do you think?" Bill growled. "Picking up the stuff you forgot."

She started sorting over the groceries. "It shouldn't have taken—*Where's the muffins?*"

---

*Stars do not have points sticking out of them. Stars are spherical.
†Women Against Smog.

"Couldn't find 'em. Got Bixmix instead."

"Why couldn't you find them?"

"Hidden too well, I guess."

"Why, they're right by the bread."

"Couldn't find the bread either."

"Did you ask a clerk?"

"Didn't see any to ask."

"But there's always—"

"It's the truth!" he cried. "What do you want me to do? Lie to you?"

"Oh, do as you like. I don't care." With a resigned air she began putting away the various items. "Now hurry and change your clothes. They'll be here any minute."

He was scarcely halfway up the stairs when she came dashing after him. "Your feet! What's happened to your feet?"

"Don't know." He shrugged. "They just didn't hurt when I got up this morning."

"What did I tell you," Helen told him triumphantly. "You wouldn't go to see Dr. Levine. He's only the best orthopedic specialist in town but of course you know more than he does. If I hadn't made an appointment for you, you'd *never* have gone. Now admit it. Those arch supporters did help, didn't they?"

"If I'd worn those arch supporters one more day I wouldn't be ambulant now."

"But they must have done you *some* good." She regarded him with despair. "If it wasn't the arch supporters, what was it?"

Bill did not answer immediately. He leaned against the railing, gazing thoughtfully at some of Helen's abstract artwork on the opposite wall.

"Last night," he declared solemnly, "my feet were healed."

"Healed?"

He nodded. "What they called a miracle in the old days."

"So it was a miracle and not the arch supporters?"

"Why couldn't I be cured by a miracle?" he demanded angrily. "Other people are. People with their stomach and lungs eaten up by cancer. Suddenly they're all right. They rise from their bed and walk. They've got sworn medical testimony to prove it."

Helen hesitated uncertainly. "But you're not the miracle type."

"What's the matter with me?"

"I always supposed you had to be kind of on the saintly side."

He dismissed her objection with a wave of his hand.

"Merely a technicality." He closed his eyes for a few moments as if in meditation. "I hadn't intended to say anything about it, but for your information, I was healed by an angel who appeared in my room last night."

"So that was what I heard going on in there."

"She appeared over by the filing cabinet," Bill continued. "She was surrounded by a golden halo that illuminated the whole room. I thought I'd forgotten to turn the lights out at first." His voice dropped almost to a whisper. "She was no ordinary angel, either."

"It's so nice you got special attention."

"She had the most beautiful golden red hair." There was a faraway look in his eyes. "Her name was Edna."

"No last name?"

"Naturally I was somewhat startled at the sudden appearance of this apparition. 'What do you want?' I asked, in a voice that trembled.

" 'Have no fear, William,' she replied, approaching the bed. 'I have come to heal you. Not to harm you.'

" 'To heal me?' I whispered.

" 'Move over, William,' she said, 'so that I may touch you.'

"So I shoved over in the bed a little—"

His narrative was interrupted by the flash of headlights and the sound of a car pulling up in the driveway.

"There they are now!" Helen exclaimed. "And here I've been wasting my time talking to you about your feet and this redheaded angel."

Bill slowly mounted the stairs, his lips continuing to move inaudibly. In his room he stood for a while inspecting the place where he had recounted Edna's appearance. From the lower depths came the shriek of feminine voices raised in greeting interspersed with occasional masculine rumbles. Evidently the Nortons had picked up Bernice and Clem on the way over. Clem Tuttle was in advertising and Jim Norton was an agent for Inertia Acres, a real-estate project for the retired. Bernice Tuttle and Dottie Norton were among his favorite wives, but he found it hard to work up much enthusiasm for their husbands. It was while struggling into his shirt that it occurred to him that all the people they saw were friends of Helen's. Outside the office he had no friends.

Bill came downstairs, said hello all around, and made a quick exit to the kitchen to mix the cocktails. He put too much vodka into the martinis and had to drink a couple of glasses to provide more room for the vermouth. Back in the living room he had hoped to strike up a conversation with Bernice or Dottie, but the situation was hopeless. The girls were in ecstasy over Helen's Christmas tree, which was not a Christmas tree at all but a dead limb salvaged from the oak in the back yard. She had adorned its gnarled branches with blue and silver balls, with here and there an aerodynamically inadequate angel in flight. Since the girls were engaged, he was thrown upon the company of Jim and Clem, who were discussing the situation that had developed at Anoakia U., their old alma mater. It appeared that the quality of the faculty and student body had been steadily deteriorating since their departure in '41. Since Bill had never attended Anoakia U., and never had had much use for the place anyhow, he found the conversation less than fascinating. He sipped his cocktail, and moodily contemplated Bernice Tuttle's knees.

As if from a great distance he heard Helen calling him.

"Bill, telephone." He went into the hall, taking his glass with him. As he expected, it was Mac.

"Bill, what's your dispersion on that plate?"

"Hundred and ninety angstroms per millimeter."

"What kind of plate was it?"

"IIa-O, baked. Why?"

"Just checking, was all."

"Say, Mac, I explained to your wife it was my fault about getting home late."

"Well, as a matter of fact, I'm still at the office."

"Still at the office!" Bill went cold sober in an instant. "Mac, what do you know?"

"Nothing I want to talk about yet. But I think I'm gaining on it."

"Give me a ring—" But he had hung up.

Bill's mind was racing. Mac would never have called unless he was on to something big. A "critical" object that might settle the cosmological controversy once and for all. He gulped down the rest of his drink and casually strolled back to the living room. How petty they all were. Jim and Clem were thoroughly in agreement that autonomy was not for Anoakia U. The girls were deploring the Santa Claus situation that had developed at the various department stores around town. That Santa Claus at the Bon Marché, they must have got him from central casting! Did you get a whiff of his breath? And the way he talked to the children! Honestly, you'd have thought he was playing King Lear!

The soggy part of a Hillhurst evening came after dinner, when the guests were swollen with food, and the cocktails only a dull memory. There were two ways to endure the time till departure: (1) the men gathered at one end of the room and talked about their automobiles and their children, while the women went into a huddle at the other end and talked about their clothes and their children; or (2) somebody showed color slides of their trip to Hawaii last summer. One hostess had made a valiant attempt to break the pattern by handing out selected passages from Ovid and Chaucer to be read aloud, but some of the men had balked. But a few bold spirits still fought on. When her guests were comfortably relaxed over their coffee and liqueurs, Helen stepped to the center of the room and clapped her hands.

"Now I'm not going to let you sit around all evening," she informed them. "We're going to play a game called Three Answers. One person, called the Grand Inquisitor, asks the questions. The rest of us give the answers. We make up some sort of story and the Grand Inquisitor, by questioning us, tries to find the key to it."

This announcement was followed by a brief silence.

"Sounds like one of these fun things," Clem grunted, knocking the ashes from his cigar.

Jim raised his hand. "Mrs. Chairman, I would like to nominate my wife for Grand Inquisitor. She can beat any lie detector that was ever invented."

Dottie had a question. "How do we know what answers to give?"

"We answer as a group," Helen said. "The Grand Inquisitor can ask all the questions he likes. But we can only answer in three ways: yes, no, or maybe. I'll explain the details later. Now who'll be Grand Inquisitor?"

"I hereby nominate Bill Backus for G.I.," Clem said.

"Second the motion," Jim said promptly.

"Bill analyzes this deep space stuff all day," Clem said. "Ought to be easy for him.

"I'd *love* to be analyzed by Bill," Dottie cried.

"Well, darling, I guess you're Grand Inquisitor," Helen said. "Now go out in the kitchen and wait there till I call you."

Bill shuffled out to the kitchen, where he began picking at the remains of the turkey. From the front room came snatches of conversation and bursts of stifled laughter, but he was unable to distinguish any words. His mind kept going back to Mac at the office. It was nearly eleven. He had hoped to hear from him by this time if he knew anything exciting. Probably the whole thing had collapsed and Mac was home in bed. He had half a notion to give him a ring when he heard Helen calling him, "All right, you can come now."

Bill strode into the living room trying to assume the grim expression appropriate to a Grand Inquisitor. How to begin this crazy game? Try some questions of a general nature until he got a lead.

"Has Clem landed that brassiere account yet?"

"No," they responded in unison.

"Have Jim and Bernice run off together?"

"No."

"Was it some sort of crime?"

"Yes."

"Was the crime committed in this city?"

"Maybe."

"In this immediate area?"

"Yes."

"Was it a murder?"

"No."

"Something more ghastly?"

"Maybe."

This was tougher than he had anticipated. Why had Helen ever gotten him into this thing? How to proceed? They were gazing at him expectantly . . . gleefully . . .

"Was the person involved a man?"

"No."

"A woman?"

"No."

"An animal, then?"

"No."

No? What on earth . . . ? A suspicion began to dawn. Was it something on Earth?

"Was the victim a creature from outer space?"

"Yes!"

On the trail at last!

"Was it a creature from Mars?"

"No."

"Was it from Venus?"

"No."

"Mercury?"

"Maybe."

Not what he had expected, but keep on.

"Was it from Jupiter? Saturn? Uranus?"

"No! No! No!"

Well . . . there weren't many planets left. With elaborate casualness he inquired, "Did this creature, by any chance, come from Pluto?"

"Yes!" they shrieked.

At last!

"Is this Plutonian creature at present somewhere within the environs of this city?"

"Maybe."

"So you don't know?"

"Maybe."

Perhaps it would help if he knew more about the creature itself.

"Have you seen this creature?"

"Yes."

"Is it larger than man-size?"

"Yes."

"Is this creature affected adversely by the heat?"

"No."

A flash of inspiration.

"Is it in this house right now?"

"Maybe."

They were hedging now.

"Is it in the basement?"

"No."

"The attic?"

"No."

"The refrigerator?"

"No."

"Under the stairway?"

"Maybe."

Relentlessly he pursued the phantom creature over the house. But despite his best efforts it eluded him. He fancied he detected a hint of scorn . . . even contempt . . . in their eyes. Suddenly he recalled Mac's remark: *The answer may be staring us right in the face. Only it's so simple we can't see it.*

Go back . . . see if he had overlooked anything.

"You said this creature is also an inhabitant of Mercury?"

"Maybe."

"Then it *is* capable of withstanding a high temperature?"

"Yes."

He was groping for the next question when the telephone rang. *Mac!*

"Don't go. Be back in a minute."

It was Mac, all right.

"Well, Bill, I think I've got the answer." He sounded more relaxed. "But I'll be darned if I know what it means."

"Let me have it anyhow."

"Remember those three big lines I said reminded me of something? You naturally assumed they were ultraviolet lines Doppler-shifted into the visible. Only you couldn't identify 'em with anything in the UV. Neither could I. Wasted about two hours convincing myself of the fact."

He took about a three count.

"So, since I was all alone, I decided to play a crazy hunch. Bill, do you know what those lines are?"

"How the hell—"

"They're those three big ionized calcium lines in the infrared."

"*Infrared!*"

"This thing's got a velocity of about 0.6c."

"That wouldn't give so much of a redshift."

"Who said anything about a *red*shift? This is a *violet*shift. Bill, this thing is coming *our way.*"

"Get out!"

"Fact!"

"Mac, you can't screw up the whole universe that easy. Why, it contradicts everything we know. Besides, three lines aren't enough. You could force an agreement . . . a pretty good agreement."

"I'm sorry, Bill, but everything else fits, too. Your line at 3929 is 7699 of potassium . . . 4494 is 8806 of magnesium . . ."

"Mac, what does it *mean?*"

"From the geometry of the situation I would say it means there's a dimple in the expanding universe in the direction of Draco."

It was so long before he spoke again that Bill began to wonder if he'd hung up.

"I'm only giving you an answer, Bill. What it means is *your* problem."

Bill found his guests in various stages of relaxation when he returned to the living room. It was hard to get his mind on Hillhurst again.

"I'm afraid it's getting late," Bernice said. "Clem and I have to be up early tomorrow. We're driving to Carmel, you know."

"Oh, don't go," Helen protested.

"It's been such a lovely evening," Dottie told her. "But really—"

"Now wait a minute," Jim boomed, coming from the bathroom. "We've got to put the Grand Inquisitor straight first."

"Sure do," Clem chuckled. "Bill would toss all night."

Jim shook his head regretfully. "Bill, old boy, I'm afraid the game was rigged."

"Rigged?" He had only been half listening.

"You see," Jim went on, "if the last letter in the last word of a question was a vowel we all answered yes. If it was a consonant we answered no. And if it was a W or Y we answered maybe." He grinned. "Get it?"

It took a while.

"So I could have gone on asking questions forever," Bill said slowly. "And you could have gone on giving me answers forever. And I'd never have known any more than in the beginning."

"Afraid that's about the size of it," Jim said. He crunched out his cigar. "Well, Dottie, go get your costly mink . . ."

Bill accompanied his guests to the door, dutifully went through the ritual of parting, and waved as they went down the driveway.

Back in the living room Helen gazed listlessly at the remains of the hors d'oeuvres and the cigarette trays. "No use cleaning up tonight, I guess." She glanced at Bill standing by the north window. "What's the matter? Aren't you coming to bed?"

"I believe I'll stay down here for a while," he told her.

"I should think you'd be anxious to see your redheaded friend."

"Perhaps I am."

Helen paused at the stairs. "You didn't exactly sparkle tonight, did you?" she remarked. "What was the matter?"

"Tired, I guess."

"Who was it called?"

"MacCready."

"What did he want?"

"Oh . . . nothing."

"Nothing! When he calls after midnight!"

"It was about a dimple in Draco."

"A dimple—"

"Object's headed toward the Earth. Everything else is rushing away. Puts a dimple in the universe out in Draco."

"Headed toward the Earth! Very fast?"

Bill shrugged. "About six-tenths c—hundred thousand miles a second."

"You mean it's going to hit us?"

"Afraid not. You see, it's quite a ways off."

"How far?"

"Oh, hell, I don't know," he said impatiently. "A billion light-years maybe."

"Well, you don't need to be so disagreeable about it. I can ask, can't I?"

"It's like Job asking the Voice out of the Whirlwind how much torque He's got."

Helen stood without speaking for several moments, then turned and went slowly up the stairs. Bill waited until he heard her door close. Then he switched out the lights and drew the curtains away from the window.

Capella was far above the haze now, shining in the stars of Auriga with a golden reddish glow, as bright as the glow of Edna's hair. Suddenly Bill had the most intense sense of identity with Auriga. How lonely he must be up there among all those gods and monsters, the only one without a story. Did the old Charioteer ever ponder the meaning of his stars? If so, what were *his* answers? Or did he bother to ask questions anymore—when the answers had no meaning?

John Wyndham

John Wyndham is the pseudonym of John Beynon Harris (1903–69), an important British genre SF writer of the mid-century. His early career, during which he wrote under a variety of bylines, including John Beynon, John Beynon Harris, Wyndham Parkes, and others, overlapped that of Olaf Stapledon in the 1930s and early '40s; his later career, at which point he changed to the John Wyndham byline, overlapped the advent of Arthur C. Clarke in the late 1940s.

Wyndham and Clarke and Eric Frank Russell, all British SF authors, hit their stride as mature SF writers at about the same time and were major figures in '50s science fiction. "The new Wyndham," said Damon Knight in *In Search of Wonder* (1956), "has turned out to be something remarkably like H. G. Wells—not the wise-old-owl Wells, more interested in sermon than story, but the young Wells, with that astonishing, compelling gift of pure storytelling."

Wyndham is most famous for his disaster novels *The Day of the Triffids* (1951) and *The Midwich Cuckoos* (1957), both made into movies. His work ranged from pulp magazine adventure stories and serials in the 1930s to sophisticated and complex works such as this novella. His mature period began in 1950 and continued through 1961, after which he published little.

This story is arguably his best. It is a surprisingly advanced presentation of gender politics. It elicited enthusiastic comments at the time of its first publication in 1956 and shared a special Hugo Award (it was published with two other pieces, by William Golding and Mervyn Peake, in a book, *Sometime, Never,* that won a Hugo). Kingsley Amis, in a discussion of this story in *New Maps of Hell*, says, "The core of the story, occupying one third of its length, is a conversation . . . saying all that can be said for the notion that women would be better off without men and making what seem to me some fairly damaging criticisms of the contemporary female role."

CONSIDER HER WAYS

There was nothing but myself.

I hung in a timeless, spaceless, forceless void that was neither light, nor dark. I had entity, but no form; awareness, but no senses; mind, but no memory. I wondered, is this—this nothingness—my soul? And it seemed that I had wondered that always, and should go on wondering it for ever. . . .

But, somehow, timelessness ceased. I became aware that there was a force: that I was being moved, and that spacelessness had, therefore, ceased, too. There was nothing to show that I moved; I knew simply that I was being drawn. I felt happy because I knew there was something or someone to whom I wanted to be drawn. I had no other wish than to turn like a compass-needle and then fall through the void. . . .

But I was disappointed. No smooth, swift fall followed. Instead, other forces fastened on me. I was pulled this way, and then that. I did not know how I knew it; there was no outside reference, no fixed point, no direction even; yet I could feel that I was tugged hither and thither, as though against the resistance of some inner gyroscope. It was as if one force were in command of me for a time, only to weaken and lose me to a new force. Then I would seem to slide towards some unknown point, until I was arrested, and diverted upon another course. I wafted this way and that, with the sense of awareness continually growing firmer; and I wondered whether rival forces were fighting for me, good and evil, perhaps, or life and death. . . .

The sense of pulling back and forth became more definite until I was almost jerked from one course to another. Then, abruptly, the feeling of struggle finished. I had a sense of travelling faster and faster still, plunging like a wandering meteorite that had been trapped at last. . . .

"All right," said a voice. "Resuscitation was a little retarded, for some reason. Better make a note of that on her card. What's the number? Oh, only her fourth time. Yes, certainly make a note. It's all right. Here she comes!"

It was a woman's voice speaking, with a slightly unfamiliar accent. The surface I was lying on shook under me. I opened my eyes, saw the ceiling moving along above me, and let them close. Presently, another voice, again with an unfamiliar intonation, spoke to me:

"Drink this," she said.

A hand lifted my head, and a cup was pressed against my lips. After I had drunk the stuff I lay back with my eyes closed again. I dozed for a little while, and came out of it feeling stronger. For some minutes I lay looking up at the ceiling and wondering vaguely where I was. I could not recall any ceiling that was painted just this pinkish shade of cream. Then, suddenly, while I was still gazing up at the ceiling, I was shocked, just as if something had hit my mind a sharp blow. I was frighteningly aware that it was not just the pinkish ceiling that was *unfamiliar*—everything was unfamiliar. Where there should have been memories there was just a great gap. I had no idea who I was, or where I was; I could recall nothing of how or why I came to be here. . . . In a rush of panic I tried to sit up, but a hand pressed me back, and presently held the cup to my lips again.

"You're quite all right. Just relax," the same voice told me, reassuringly.

I wanted to ask questions, but somehow I felt immensely weary, and everything was too much trouble. The first rush of panic subsided, leaving me lethargic. I wondered what had happened to me—had I been in an accident, perhaps? Was this the kind of thing that happened when one was badly shocked? I did not know, and now for the moment I did not care: I was being looked after. I felt so drowsy that the questions could wait.

I suppose I dozed, and it may have been for a few minutes, or for an hour. I know only that when I opened my eyes again I felt calmer—more puzzled than alarmed—and I lay for a time without moving. I had recovered enough grasp now to console myself with the thought that if there had been an accident, at least there was no pain.

Presently I gained a little more energy, and, with it, curiosity to know where I was. I rolled my head on the pillow to see more of the surroundings.

A few feet away I saw a contrivance on wheels, something between a bed and a trolley. On it, asleep, with her mouth open, was the most enormous woman I had ever seen. I stared, wondering whether it was some kind of cage over her to take the weight of the covers that gave her the mountainous look, but the movement of her breathing soon showed me that it was not. Then I looked beyond her and saw two more trolleys, both supporting equally enormous women.

I studied the nearest one more closely, and discovered to my surprise that she was quite young—not more than twenty-two, or twenty-three, I guessed. Her face was a little plump, perhaps, but by no means over-fat; indeed, with her fresh, healthy young colouring and her short-cropped gold curls, she was quite pretty. I fell to wondering what curious disorder of the glands could cause such a degree of anomaly at her age.

Ten minutes or so passed, and there was a sound of brisk, business-like footsteps approaching. A voice inquired:

"How are you feeling now?"

I rolled my head to the other side, and found myself looking into a face almost level with my own. For a moment I thought its owner must be a child, then I saw that the features under the white cap were certainly not less than thirty years old. Without waiting for a reply she reached under the bed-clothes and took my pulse. Its rate appeared to satisfy her, for she nodded confidently.

"You'll be all right now, Mother," she told me.

I stared at her, blankly.

"The car's only just outside the door there. Do you think you can walk it?" she went on.

Bemusedly, I asked:

"What car?"

"Why, to take you home, of course," she said, with professional patience. "Come along now." And she pulled away the bedclothes.

I started to move, and looked down. What I saw there held me fixed. I lifted my arm. It was like nothing so much as a plump, white bolster with a ridiculous little hand attached at the end. I stared at it in horror. Then I heard a far-off scream as I fainted. . . .

When I opened my eyes again there was a woman—a normal-sized woman—in white overalls with a stethoscope round her neck, frowning at me in perplexity. The white-capped woman I had taken for a child stood beside her, reaching only a little above her elbow.

"—I don't know, Doctor," she was saying. "She just suddenly screamed and fainted."

"What is it? What's happened to me? I know I'm not like this—I'm not, I'm not," I said, and I could hear my own voice wailing the words.

The doctor went on looking puzzled.

"What does she mean?" she asked.

"I've no idea, Doctor," said the small one. "It was quite sudden, as if she'd had some kind of shock—but I don't know why."

"Well, she's been passed and signed-off, and, anyway, she can't stay here. We need the room," said the doctor. "I'd better give her a sedative."

"But what's happened? Who am I? There's something terribly wrong. I know I'm not like this. P-please t-tell me—" I implored her, and then somehow lost myself in a stammer and a muddle.

The doctor's manner became soothing. She laid a hand gently on my shoulder.

"That's all right, Mother. There's nothing to worry about. Just take things quietly. We'll soon have you back home."

Another white-capped assistant, no taller than the first, hurried up with a syringe, and handed it to the doctor.

"No!" I protested. "I want to know where I am. Who am I? Who are you? What's happened to me?" I tried to slap the syringe out of her hand, but both the small assistants flung themselves on my arm, and held on to it while she pressed in the needle.

It was a sedative, all right. It did not put me out, but it detached me. An odd feeling: I seemed to be floating a few feet outside myself and considering me with an unnatural calmness. I was able, or felt that I was able, to evaluate matters with intelligent clarity. Evidently I was suffering from amnesia. A shock of some kind had caused me to 'lose my memory,' as it is often put. Obviously it was only a very small part of my memory that had gone—just the personal part: who I was, what I was, where I lived—all the mechanism for day-to-day getting along seemed to be intact: I'd not forgotten how to talk, or how to think, and I seemed to have quite a well-stored mind to think with.

On the other hand there was a nagging conviction that everything about me was somehow *wrong*. I *knew*, somehow, that I'd never before seen the place I was in; I *knew*, too, that there was something queer about the presence of the two small nurses; above all, I *knew*, with absolute certainty, that this massive form lying here was not mine. I could not recall what face I ought to see in a mirror, not even whether it would be dark or fair, or old or young, but there was no shadow of doubt in my mind that, whatever it was like, it had never topped such a shape as I had now.

—And there were the other enormous young women, too. Obviously, it could not be a matter of glandular disorder in all of us, or there'd not be this talk of sending me 'home,' wherever that might be. . . .

I was still arguing the situation with myself in, thanks no doubt to the sedative, a most reasonable-seeming manner, though without making any progress at all, when the ceiling above my head began to move again, and I realized I was being wheeled along. Doors opened at the end of the room, and the trolley tilted a little beneath me as we went down a gentle ramp beyond.

At the foot of the ramp, an ambulance-like car, with pink coachwork polished until it gleamed, was waiting with the rear doors open. I observed interestedly that I was playing a part in a routine procedure. A team of eight diminutive attendants carried out the task of transferring me from the trolley to a sprung couch in the ambulance as if it were a kind of drill. Two of them lingered after the rest to tuck in my coverings and place another pillow behind my head. Then they got out, closing the doors behind them, and in a minute or two we started off.

It was at this point—and possibly the sedative helped in this, too—that I began to have an increasing sense of balance and a feeling that I was perceiving the situation. Probably there *had* been an accident, as I had suspected, but obviously my error, and the chief cause of my alarm, proceeded from my assumption that I was a stage further on than I actually was. I had assumed that after an interval I had recovered consciousness in these baffling circumstances, whereas the true state of affairs must clearly be that I had *not* recovered consciousness. I must be still in a suspended state, very likely with concussion, and this was a dream, or hallucination. Presently, I should wake up in conditions that would at least be sensible, if not necessarily familiar.

I wondered now that this consoling and stabilizing thought had not occurred to me before, and decided that it was the alarming sense of detailed reality that had thrown me into panic. It had been astonishingly stupid of me to be taken in to the extent of imagining that I really was a kind of Gulliver among rather over-size Lilliputians. It was quite characteristic of most dreams, too, that I should lack a clear knowledge of my identity, so we did not need to be surprised at that. The thing to do was to take an intelligent interest in all I observed: the whole thing must be chockful of symbolic content which it would be most interesting to work out later.

The discovery quite altered my attitude and I looked about me with a new attention. It struck me as odd right away that here was so much circumstantial detail, and all of it in focus—there was none of that sense of foreground in sharp relief against a muzzy, or even non-existent, background that one usually meets in a dream. Everything was presented with a most convincing, three-dimensional solidity. My own sensations, too, seemed perfectly valid. The injection, in particular, had been quite acutely authentic. The illusion of reality fascinated me into taking mental notes with some care.

The interior of the van, or ambulance, or whatever it was, was finished in the same shell-pink as the outside—except for the roof, which was powder-blue with a scatter of small silver stars. Against the front partition were mounted several cupboards, with plated handles. My couch, or stretcher, lay along the left side: on the other were two fixed seats, rather small, and upholstered in a semi-glazed material to match the colour of the rest. Two long windows on each side left little solid wall. Each of them was provided with curtains of a fine net, gathered back now in pink braid loops, and had a roller blind furled above it. Simply by turning my head on the pillow I was able to observe the passing scenery—though somewhat jerkily, for either the springing of the vehicle scarcely matched its appointments, or the road surface was bad: whichever the cause, I was glad my own couch was independently and quite comfortably sprung.

The external view did not offer a great deal of variety save in its hues. Our way was lined by buildings standing back behind some twenty yards of tidy lawn. Each block was three storeys high, about fifty yards long, and had a tiled roof of somewhat low pitch, suggesting a vaguely Italian influence. Structurally the blocks appeared identical, but each was differently coloured, with contrasting window-frames and doors, and carefully considered, uniform curtains. I could see no one behind the windows; indeed there appeared to be no one about at all except here and there a woman in overalls mowing a lawn, or tending one of the inset flowerbeds.

Further back from the road, perhaps two hundred yards away, stood larger, taller, more utilitarian-looking blocks, some of them with high, factory-type chimneys. I thought they might actually be factories of some kind, but at the distance, and because I had no more than fugitive views of them between the foreground blocks, I could not be sure.

The road itself seldom ran straight for more than a hundred yards at a stretch, and its windings made one wonder whether the buildings had not been more concerned to follow a contour line than a direction. There was little other traffic, and what there was consisted of lorries, large or small, mostly large. They were painted in one primary colour or another, with only a five-fold combination of letters and figures on their sides for further identification. In design they might have been any lorries anywhere.

We continued this uneventful progress at a modest pace for some twenty minutes, until we came to a stretch where the road was under repair. The car slowed, and the workers moved to one side, out of our way. As we crawled forward over the broken surface I was able to get a good look at them. They were all women or girls dressed in denim-like trousers, sleeveless singlets and working boots. All had their hair cut quite short, and a few wore hats. They were tall and broad-shouldered, bronzed and healthy-looking. The biceps of their arms were like a man's, and the hafts of their picks and shovels rested in the hard, strong hands of manual toilers.

They watched with concern as the car edged its way on to the rough patch, but when it drew level with them they transferred their attention, and jostled and craned to look inside at me.

They smiled widely, showing strong white teeth in their browned faces. All of them raised their right hands, making some sign to me, still smiling. Their good-will was so evident that I smiled back. They walked along, keeping pace with the crawling car, looking at me expectantly while their smiles faded into puz-zlement. They were saying something but I could not hear the words. Some of them insistently repeated the sign. Their disappointed look made it clear that I was expected to respond with more than a smile. The only way that occurred to me was to raise my own right hand in imitation of their gesture. It was at least a qualified success; their faces brightened though a rather puzzled look remained. Then the car lurched on to the made-up road again and their still somewhat troubled faces slid back as we speeded up to our former sedate pace. More dream symbols, of course—but certainly not one of the stock symbols from the book. What on earth, I wondered, could a party of friendly Amazons, equipped with navvying implements instead of bows, stand for in my subcon-scious? Something frustrated, I imagined. A suppressed desire to dominate? I did not seem to be getting much further along that line when we passed the last of the variegated but nevertheless monotonous blocks, and ran into open country.

The flower beds had shown me already that it was spring, and now I was able to look on healthy pastures, and neat arable fields already touched with green; there was a haze-like green smoke along the trim hedges, and some of the trees in the tidily placed spinneys were in young leaf. The sun was shining with a bright benignity upon the most precise countryside I had ever seen; only the cattle dotted about the fields introduced a slight disorder into the careful dis-positions. The farmhouses themselves were part of the pattern; hollow squares of neat buildings with an acre or so of vegetable garden on one side, an orchard on another, and a rickyard on a third. There was a suggestion of a doll's landscape about it—Grandma Moses, but tidied up and rationalized. I could see no ran-dom cottages, casually sited sheds, or unplanned outgrowths from the farm buildings. And what, I asked myself, should we conclude from this rather path-ological exhibition of tidiness? That I was a more uncertain person than I had supposed, one who was subconsciously yearning for simplicity and security? Well, well. . . .

An open lorry which must have been travelling ahead of us turned off down a lane bordered by beautifully laid hedges, towards one of the farms. There were half a dozen young women in it, holding implements of some kind; Amazons, again. One of them, looking back, drew the attention of the rest to us. They raised their hands in the same sign that the others had made, and then waved cheerfully. I waved back.

Rather bewildering, I thought: Amazons for domination and this landscape for passive security: the two did not seem to tie up very well.

We trundled on, at our unambitious pace of twenty miles an hour or so, for what I guessed to be three-quarters of an hour, with the prospect changing very little. The country undulated gently and appeared to continue like that to the foot of a line of low blue hills many miles away. The tidy farmhouses went by with almost the regularity of milestones, though with something like twice the frequency. Occasionally there were working-parties in the fields; more rarely, one saw individuals busy about the farms, and others hoeing with tractors, but they were all too far off for me to make out any details. Presently, however, came a change.

Off to the left of the road, stretching back at right angles to it for more than a mile, appeared a row of trees. At first I thought it just a wood, but then I noticed that the trunks were evenly spaced, and the trees themselves topped and pruned until they gave more the impression of a high fence.

The end of it came to within twenty feet of the road, where it turned, and we ran along beside it for almost half a mile until the car slowed, turned to the left, and stopped in front of a pair of tall gates. There were a couple of toots on the horn.

The gates were ornamental, and possibly of wrought iron under their pink paint. The archway that they barred was stucco-covered, and painted the same colour.

Why, I inquired of myself, this prevalence of pink, which I regard as a namby-pamby colour, anyway? Flesh-colour? Symbolic of an ardency for the flesh which I had insufficiently gratified? I scarcely thought so. Not pink. Surely a burning red. . . . I don't think I know anyone who can be really ardent in a pink way. . . .

While we waited, a feeling that there was something wrong with the gatehouse grew upon me. The structure was a single-storey building, standing against the left, inner side of the archway, and coloured to match it. The woodwork was pale blue, and there were white net curtains at the windows. The door opened, and a middle-aged woman in a white blouse-and-trouser suit came out. She was bare-headed, with a few grey locks in her short, dark hair. Seeing me, she raised her hand in the same sign the Amazons had used, though perfunctorily, and walked over to open the gates. It was only as she pushed them back to admit us that I suddenly saw how small she was—certainly not over four feet tall. And that explained what was wrong with the gatehouse: it was built entirely to her scale. . . .

I went on staring at her and her little house as we passed. Well, what about that? Mythology is rich in gnomes and 'little people', and they are fairly pervasive of dreams, too. Somebody, I was sure, must have decided that they are a standard symbol of something, but for the moment I could not recall what it was. Would it be repressed philo-progenitiveness, or was that too unsubtle? I stowed that away, too, for later contemplation and brought my attention back to the surroundings.

We were on our way, unhurriedly, along something more like a drive than a road, with surroundings that suggested a compromise between a public garden and a municipal housing estate. There were wide lawns of an unblemished velvet green, set here and there with flower beds, delicate groups of silver birch, and occasional larger, single trees. Among them stood pink, three-storey blocks, dotted about, seemingly to no particular plan.

A couple of the Amazon-types in singlets and trousers of a faded rust-red were engaged in planting-out a bed close beside the drive, and we had to pause while they dragged their handcart full of tulips onto the grass to let us pass. They gave me the usual salute and amiable grin as we went by.

A moment later I had a feeling that something had gone wrong with my sight, but as we passed one block we came in sight of another. It was white instead of pink, but otherwise exactly similar to the rest—except that it was scaled down by at least one-third. . . .

I blinked at it and stared hard, but it continued to seem just the same size.

A little further on, a grotesquely huge woman in pink draperies was walking slowly and heavily across a lawn. She was accompanied by three of the small, white-suited women looking, in contrast, like children, or very animated dolls: one was involuntarily reminded of tugs fussing round a liner.

I began to feel swamped: the proliferation and combination of symbols was getting well out of my class.

The car forked to the right, and presently we drew up before a flight of steps leading to one of the pink buildings—a normal-sized building, but still not free from oddity, for the steps were divided by a central balustrade; those to the left of it were normal, those to right, smaller and more numerous.

Three toots on the horn announced our arrival. In about ten seconds half a dozen small women appeared in the doorway and came running down the right-hand side of the steps. A door slammed as the driver got out and went to meet them. When she came into my range of view I saw that she was one of the little ones, too, but not in white as the rest were; she wore a shining pink suit like a livery that exactly matched the car.

They had a word together before they came round to open the door behind me, then a voice said brightly:

"Welcome, Mother Orchis. Welcome home."

The couch or stretcher slid back on runners, and between them they lowered it to the ground. One young woman whose blouse was badged with a pink St. Andrew's cross on the left breast leaned over me. She inquired considerately:

"Do you think you can walk, Mother?"

It did not seem the moment to inquire into the form of address. I was obviously the only possible target for the question.

"Walk?" I repeated. "Of course I can walk." And I sat up, with about eight hands assisting me.

'Of course' had been an overstatement. I realized that by the time I had been heaved to my feet. Even with all the help that was going on around me it was an exertion which brought on heavy breathing. I looked down at the monstrous form that billowed under my pink draperies, with a sick revulsion and a feeling that, whatever this particular mass of symbolism disguised, it was likely to prove a distasteful revelation later on. I tried a step. 'Walk' was scarcely the word for my progress. It felt like, and must have looked like, a slow series of forward surges. The women, at little more than my elbow height, fluttered about me like a flock of anxious hens. Once started, I was determined to go on, and I progressed with a kind of wave-motion, first across a few yards of gravel, and then, with ponderous deliberation, up the left-hand side of the steps.

There was a perceptible sense of relief and triumph all round as I reached the summit. We paused there a few moments for me to regain my breath, then we moved on into the building. A corridor led straight ahead, with three or four closed doors on each side; at the end it branched right and left. We took the left arm, and, at the end of it, I came face to face, for the first time since the hallucination had set in, with a mirror.

It took every volt of my resolution not to panic again at what I saw in it. The first few seconds of my stare were spent in fighting down a leaping hysteria.

In front of me stood an outrageous travesty, an elephantine female form, looking the more huge for its pink swathings. Mercifully, they covered everything but the head and hands, but these exposures were themselves another kind of shock, for the hands, though soft and dimpled and looking utterly out of proportion, were not uncomely, and the head and face were those of a girl.

She was pretty, too. She could not have been more than twenty-one, if that. Her curling fair hair was touched with auburn lights, and cut in a kind of bob. The complexion of her face was pink and cream, her mouth was gentle, and red without any artifice. She looked back at me, and at the little women anxiously clustering round me, from a pair of blue-green eyes beneath lightly arched brows. And this delicate face, this little Fragonard, was set upon that monstrous body: no less outrageously might a blossom of freesia sprout from a turnip.

When I moved my lips, hers moved; when I bent my arm, hers bent; and yet, once I got the better of that threatening panic, she ceased to be a reflection. She was nothing like me, so she must be a stranger whom I was observing, though in a most bewildering way. My panic and revulsion gave way to sadness, an aching pity for her. I could weep for the shame of it. I did. I watched the tears brim on her lower lids; mistily, I saw them overflow.

One of the little women beside me caught hold of my hand.

"Mother Orchis, dear, what's the matter?" she asked, full of concern.

I could not tell her: I had no clear idea myself. The image in the mirror shook her head, with tears running down her cheeks. Small hands patted me here and there; small, soothing voices encouraged me onward. The next door was opened for me and, amid concerned fussing, I was led into the room beyond.

We entered a place that struck me as a cross between a boudoir and a ward. The boudoir impression was sustained by a great deal of pink—in the carpet, coverlets, cushions, lampshades, and filmy window curtains; the ward motif, by an array of six divans, or couches, one of which was unoccupied.

It was a large enough room for six couches, separated by a chest, a chair and table for each, to be arranged on each side without an effect of crowding, and the open space in the middle was still big enough to contain several expansive easy chairs and a central table bearing an intricate flower-arrangement. A not displeasing scent faintly pervaded the place, and from somewhere came the subdued sound of a string quartette in a sentimental mood. Five of the bed-couches were already mountainously occupied. Two of my attendant party detached themselves and hurried ahead to turn back the pink satin cover on the sixth.

Faces from all the five other beds were turned towards me. Three of them smiling in welcome, the other two were less committal.

"Hallo, Orchis," one of them greeted me in a friendly tone. Then, with a touch of concern, she added: "What's the matter, dear? Did you have a bad time?"

I looked at her. She had a kindly, plumply pretty face, framed by light brown hair as she lay back against a cushion. The face looked about twenty-three or twenty-four years old. The rest of her was a huge mound of pink satin. I couldn't make any reply, but I did my best to return her smile as we passed.

Our convoy hove-to by the empty bed. After some preparation and positioning I was helped into it by all hands, and a cushion was arranged behind my head.

The exertion of my journey from the car had been considerable, and I was thankful to relax. While two of the little women pulled up the coverlet and arranged it over me, another produced a handkerchief and dabbed gently at my cheeks. She encouraged me:

"There you are, dear. Safely home again now. You'll be quite all right when you've rested a bit. Just try to sleep for a little."

"What's the matter with her?" inquired a forthright voice from one of the other beds. "Did she make a mess of it?"

The little woman with the handkerchief—she was the one who wore the St. Andrew's cross and appeared to be in charge of the operation—turned her head sharply.

"There's no need for that tone, Mother Hazel. Of course Mother Orchis had four beautiful babies—didn't you, dear?" she added to me. "She's just a bit tired after the journey, that's all."

"H'mph," said the girl addressed, in an unaccommodating tone, but she made no further comment.

A degree of fussing continued. Presently the small woman handed me a glass of something that looked like water, but had unsuspected strength. I spluttered a little at the first taste, but quickly felt the better for it. After a little more tidying and ordering, my retinue departed, leaving me propped against my cushion, with the eyes of the five other monstrous women dwelling upon me speculatively.

An awkward silence was broken by the girl who had greeted me as I came in.

"Where did they send you for your holiday, Orchis?"

"Holiday?" I asked blankly.

She and the rest stared at me in astonishment.

"I don't know what you're talking about," I told them.

They went on staring, stupidly, stolidly.

"It can't have been much of a holiday," observed one, obviously puzzled. "I'll not forget my last one. They sent me to the sea, and gave me a little car so that I could get about everywhere. Everybody was lovely to us, and there were only six Mothers there, including me. Did you go by the sea, or in the mountains?"

They were determined to be inquisitive, and one would have to make some answer sooner or later. I chose what seemed the simplest way out for the moment.

"I can't remember," I said. "I can't remember a thing. I seem to have lost my memory altogether."

That was not very sympathetically received, either.

"Oh," said the one who had been addressed as Hazel, with a degree of satisfaction. "I thought there was something. And I suppose you can't even remember for certain whether your babies were Grade One this time, Orchis?"

"Don't be stupid, Hazel," one of the others told her. "Of course they were Grade One. If they'd not been, Orchis wouldn't be back here now—she'd have been re-rated as a Class Two Mother, and sent to Whitewich." In a more kindly tone she asked me: "When did it happen, Orchis?"

"I—I don't know," I said. "I can't remember anything before this morning at the hospital. It's all gone entirely."

"Hospital!" repeated Hazel, scornfully.

"She must mean the Centre," said the other. "But do you mean to say you can't even remember *us*, Orchis?"

"No," I admitted, shaking my head. "I'm sorry, but everything before I came round in the Hosp—in the Centre—is all blank."

"That's queer," Hazel said, in an unsympathetic tone. "Do they know?"

One of the others took my part.

"Of course they're bound to know. I expect they don't think that remembering or not has anything to do with having Grade One babies. And why should it, anyway? But look, Orchis—"

"Why not let her rest for a bit," another cut in. "I don't suppose she's feeling too good after the Centre, and the journey, and getting in here. I never do myself. Don't take any notice of them, Orchis, dear. You just go to sleep for a bit. You'll probably find it's all quite all right when you wake up."

I accepted her suggestion gratefully. The whole thing was far too bewildering to cope with at the moment; moreover, I did feel exhausted. I thanked her for her advice, and lay back on my pillow. In so far as the closing of one's eyes can be made ostentatious, I made it so. What was more surprising was that, if one can be said to sleep within an hallucination or a dream, I slept. . . .

In the moment of waking, before opening my eyes, I had a flash of hope that I should find the illusion had spent itself. Unfortunately, it had not. A hand was shaking my shoulder gently, and the first thing that I saw was the face of the little women's leader, close to mine.

In the way of nurses she said:

"There, Mother Orchis, dear. You'll be feeling a lot better after that nice sleep, won't you?"

Beyond her, two more of the small women were carrying a long-legged bed-tray towards me. They set it down so that it bridged me and was convenient to reach. I stared at the load on it. It was, with no exception, the most enormous and nourishing meal I had ever seen put before one person. The first sight of it revolted me—but then I became aware of a schism within, for it did not revolt the physical form that I occupied: that, in fact, had a watering mouth, and was eager to begin. An inner part of me marvelled in a kind of semidetachment while the rest consumed two or three fish, a whole chicken, some slices of meat, a pile of vegetables, fruit hidden under mounds of stiff cream, and more than a quart of milk, without any sense of surfeit. Occasional glances showed me that the other 'Mothers' were dealing just as thoroughly with the contents of their similar trays.

I caught one or two curious looks from them, but they were too seriously occupied to take up their inquisition again at the moment. I wondered how to fend them off later, and it occurred to me that if only I had a book or a magazine I might be able to bury myself effectively, if not very politely, in it.

When the attendants returned, I asked the badged one if she could let me have something to read. The effect of such a simple request was astonishing: the two who were removing my tray all but dropped it. The one beside me gaped for an amazed moment before she collected her wits. She looked at me, first with suspicion and then with concern.

"Not feeling quite yourself yet, dear?" she suggested.

"But I am," I protested. "I'm quite all right now."

The look of concern persisted, however.

"If I were you I'd try to sleep again," she advised.

"But I don't want to. I'd just like to read quietly," I objected.

She patted my shoulder, a little uncertainly.

"I'm afraid you've had an exhausting time, Mother. Never mind, I'm sure it'll pass quite soon."

I felt impatient. "What's wrong with wanting to read?" I demanded.

She smiled a smug, professional-nurse smile.

"There, there, dear. Just you try to rest a little more. Why, bless me, what on earth would a Mother want with knowing how to read?"

With that she tidied my coverlet, and bustled away, leaving me to the wide-eyed stares of my five companions. Hazel gave a kind of contemptuous snigger; otherwise there was no audible comment for several minutes.

I had reached a stage where the persistence of the hallucination was beginning to wear away my detachment. I could feel that under a little more pressure I should be losing my confidence and starting to doubt its unreality. I did not at all care for its calm continuity: inconsequent exaggerations and jumps, foolish perspectives, indeed, any of the usual dream characteristics would have been reassuring; but, instead, it continued to present obvious nonsense, with an alarming air of conviction and consequence. Effects, for instance, were unmistakably following causes. I began to have an uncomfortable feeling that were one to dig deep enough one might begin to find logical causes for the absurdities, too. The integration was far too good for mental comfort—even the fact that I had enjoyed my meal as if I were fully awake, and was consciously feeling the better for it, encouraged the disturbing quality of reality.

"Read!" Hazel said suddenly, with a scornful laugh. "And write, too, I suppose?"

"Well, why not?" I retorted.

They all gazed at me more attentively than ever, and then exchanged meaningful glances among themselves. Two of them smiled at each other. I demanded irritably: "What on earth's wrong with that? Am I supposed not to be able to read or write, or something?"

One said kindly, soothingly:

"Orchis, dear. Don't you think it would be better if you were to ask to see the doctor? Just for a check-up?"

"No," I told her flatly. "There's nothing wrong with me. I'm just trying to understand. I simply ask for a book, and you all look at me as if I were mad. Why?"

After an awkward pause the same one said humouringly, and almost in the words of the little attendant:

"Orchis, dear, do try to pull yourself together. What sort of good would reading and writing be to a Mother? How could they help her to have better babies?"

"There are other things in life besides having babies," I said, shortly.

If they had been surprised before, they were thunderstruck now. Even Hazel seemed bereft of suitable comment. Their idiotic astonishment exasperated me and made me suddenly sick of the whole nonsensical business. Temporarily, I *did* forget to be the detached observer of a dream.

"Damn it," I broke out. "What is all this rubbish? Orchis! Mother Orchis!—for God's sake! Where am I? Is this some kind of lunatic asylum?"

I stared at them, angrily, loathing the sight of them, wondering if they were all in some spiteful complicity against me. Somehow I was quite convinced in my own mind that whoever, or whatever, I was, I was not a mother. I said so, forcibly, and then, to my annoyance, burst into tears.

For lack of anything else to use, I dabbed at my eyes with my sleeve. When I could see clearly again I found that four of them were looking at me with kindly concern. Hazel, however, was not.

"I said there was something queer about her," she told the others, triumphantly. "She's mad, that's what it is."

The one who had been most kindly disposed before, tried again:

"But, Orchis, *of course* you are a Mother. You're a Class One Mother—with three births registered. Twelve fine Grade One babies, dear. You *can't* have forgotten that!"

For some reason I wept again. I had a feeling that something was trying to break through the blankness in my mind; but I did not know what it was, only that it made me feel intensely miserable.

"Oh, this is cruel, cruel! Why can't I stop it? Why won't it go away and leave me?" I pleaded. "There's a horrible cruel mockery here—but I don't understand it. What's wrong with me? I'm not obsessional—I'm not—I—oh, can't somebody help me . . . ?"

I kept my eyes tight shut for a time, willing with all my mind that the whole hallucination should fade and disappear.

But it did not. When I looked again they were still there, their silly, pretty faces gaping stupidly at me across the revolting mounds of pink satin.

"I'm going to get out of this," I said.

It was a tremendous effort to raise myself to a sitting position. I was aware of the rest watching me, wide-eyed, while I made it. I struggled to get my feet round and over the side of the bed, but they were all tangled in the satin coverlet and I could not reach to free them. It was the true, desperate frustration of a dream. I heard my voice pleading: "Help me! Oh, Donald, darling, please help me. . . ."

And suddenly, as if the word "Donald" had released a spring, something seemed to click in my head. The shutter in my mind opened, not entirely, but enough to let me know who I was. I understood, suddenly, where the cruelty had lain.

I looked at the others again. They were still staring half-bewildered, half-alarmed. I gave up the attempt to move, and lay back on my pillows again.

"You can't fool me anymore," I told them. "I know who I am, now."

"But, Mother Orchis—" one began.

"Stop that," I snapped at her. I seemed to have swung suddenly out of self-pity into a kind of masochistic callousness. "I am *not* a mother," I said harshly. "I am just a woman who, for a short time, had a husband, and who hoped—but only hoped—that she would have babies by him."

A pause followed that; a rather odd pause, where there should have been at least a murmur. What I had said did not seem to have registered. The faces showed no understanding; they were as uncomprehending as dolls.

Presently, the most friendly one seemed to feel an obligation to break the silence. With a little vertical crease between her brows: "What," she inquired tentatively, "what is a husband?"

I looked hard from one face to another. There was no trace of guile in any of them; nothing but puzzled speculation such as one sometimes sees in a child's eyes. I felt close to hysteria for a moment; then I took a grip on myself. Very well, then, since the hallucination would not leave me alone, I would play it at its own game, and see what came of that. I began to explain with a kind of dead-pan, simple-word seriousness:

"A husband is a man whom a woman takes . . ."

Evidently, from their expressions I was not very enlightening. However, they let me go on for three or four sentences without interruption. Then, when I paused for breath, the kindly one chipped in with a point which she evidently felt needed clearing up:

"But what," she asked, in evident perplexity, "what is a man?"

A cool silence hung over the room after my exposition. I had an impression I had been sent to Coventry, or semi-Coventry, by them, but I did not bother to test it. I was too much occupied trying to force the door of my memory further open, and finding that beyond a certain point it would not budge.

I knew now that I was Jane. I had been Jane Summers, and had become Jane Waterleigh when I had married Donald.

I was—had been—twenty-four when we were married: just twenty-five when Donald was killed, six months later. And there it stopped. It seemed like yesterday, but I couldn't tell. . . .

Before that, everything was perfectly clear. My parents and friends, my home, my schools, my training, my job, as Dr. Summers, at the Wraychester Hospital. I could remember my first sight of Donald when they brought him in one evening with a broken leg—and all that followed. . . .

I could remember now the face that I ought to see in a looking-glass—and it was certainly nothing like that I had seen in the corridor outside—it should be more oval, with a complexion looking faintly sun-tanned; with a smaller, neater mouth; surrounded by chestnut hair that curled naturally; with brown eyes rather wide apart and perhaps a little grave as a rule.

I knew, too, how the rest of me should look—slender, long-legged, with small, firm breasts—a nice body but one that I had simply taken for granted until Donald gave me pride in it by loving it. . . .

I looked down at the repulsive mound of pink satin, and shuddered. A sense of outrage came welling up. I longed for Donald to comfort and pet me and love me and tell me it would be all right; that I wasn't as I was seeing myself at all, and that it *really* was a dream. At the same time I was stricken with horror at the thought that he should ever see me gross and obese like this. And then I remembered that Donald would never see me again at all—never anymore— and I was wretched and miserable, and the tears trickled down my cheeks again.

The five others just went on looking at me, wide-eyed and wondering. Half an hour passed, still in silence, then the door opened to admit a whole troop of the little women, all in white suits. I saw Hazel look at me, and then at the leader. She seemed about to speak, and then to change her mind. The little women split up, two to a couch. Standing one on each side, they stripped away the coverlet, rolled up their sleeves, and set to work at massage.

At first it was not unpleasant, and quite soothing. One lay back and relaxed. Presently, however, I liked it less: soon I found it offensive.

"Stop that!" I told the one on the right, sharply.

She paused, smiled at me amiably, though a trifle uncertainly, and then continued.

"I said stop it," I told her, pushing her away.

Her eyes met mine. They were troubled and hurt, although a professional smile still curved her mouth.

"I mean it," I added, curtly.

She continued to hesitate, and glanced across at her partner on the farther side of the bed.

"You, too," I told the other. "That'll do."

She did not even pause in her rhythm. The one on the right plucked a decision and returned. She restarted just what I had stopped. I reached out and pushed her, harder this time. There must have been a lot more muscle in that bolster of an arm than one would have supposed. The shove carried her half across the room, and she tripped and fell.

All movement in the room suddenly ceased. Everybody stared, first at her, and then at me. The pause was brief. They all set to work again. I pushed away the girl on the left, too, though more gently. The other one picked herself up. She was crying and she looked frightened, but she set her jaw doggedly and started to come back.

"You keep away from me, you little horrors," I told them threateningly.

That checked them. They stood off, and looked miserably at each other. The one with the badge of seniority fussed up.

"What's the trouble, Mother Orchis?" she inquired.

I told her. She looked puzzled.

"But that's quite right," she expostulated.

"Not for me. I don't like it, and I won't have it," I replied.

She stood awkwardly, at a loss.

Hazel's voice came from the other side of the room:

"Orchis is off her head. She's been telling us the most disgusting things. She's quite mad."

The little woman turned to regard her, and then looked inquiringly at one of the others. When the girl confirmed with a nod and an expression of distaste she turned back to me, giving me a searching inspection.

"You two go and report," she told my dicomfited masseuses.

They were both crying now, and they went wretchedly down the room together. The one in charge gave me another long, thoughtful look, and then followed them.

A few minutes later all the rest had packed up and gone. The six of us were alone again. It was Hazel who broke the ensuing silence.

"That was a bitchy piece of work. The poor little devils were only doing their job," she observed.

"If that's their job, I don't like it," I told her.

"So you just get them a beating, poor things. But I suppose that's the lost memory again. You wouldn't remember that a Servitor who upsets a Mother is beaten, would you?" she added sarcastically.

"Beaten?" I repeated, uneasily.

"Yes, beaten," she mimicked. "But you don't care what becomes of them, do you? I don't know what's happened to you while you were away, but whatever it was it seems to have produced a thoroughly nasty result. I never did care for you, Orchis, though the others thought I was wrong. Well, now we all know."

None of the rest offered any comment. The feeling that they shared her opinion was strong, but luckily I was spared confirmation by the opening of the door.

The senior attendant re-entered with half a dozen small myrmidons, but this time the group was dominated by a handsome woman of about thirty. Her appearance gave me immense relief. She was neither little, nor Amazonian, nor was she huge. Her present company made her look a little over-tall, perhaps, but I judged her at about five foot ten; a normal, pleasant-featured young woman with brown hair, cut somewhat short, and a pleated black skirt showing beneath white overalls. The senior attendant was almost trotting to keep up with her longer steps, and was saying something about delusions and 'only from the Centre today, Doctor.'

The woman stopped beside my couch while the smaller women huddled together, looking at me with some misgiving. She thrust a thermometer into my mouth and held my wrist. Satisfied on both these counts, she inquired:

"Headache? Any other aches or pains?"

"No," I told her.

She regarded me carefully. I looked back at her.

"What—?" she began.

"She's mad," Hazel put in from the other side of the room. "She says she's lost her memory and doesn't know us."

"She's been talking about horrid, disgusting things," added one of the others.

"She's got delusions. She thinks she can read and write," Hazel supplemented.

The doctor smiled at that.

"Do you?" she asked me.

"I don't see why not—but it should be easy enough to prove," I replied, brusquely.

She looked startled, a little taken aback, then she recovered her tolerant half-smile.

"All right," she said, humouring me.

She pulled a small notepad out of her pocket and offered it to me, with a pencil. The pencil felt a little odd in my hand; the fingers did not fall into place readily on it, nevertheless I wrote:

I'M ONLY TOO WELL AWARE THAT I HAVE DELUSIONS—AND
THAT YOU ARE PART OF THEM.

Hazel tittered as I handed the pad back.

The doctor's jaw did not actually drop, but her smile came right off. She looked at me very hard indeed. The rest of the room, seeing her expression, went quiet, as though I had performed some startling feat of magic. The doctor turned towards Hazel.

"What sort of things has she been telling you?" she inquired.

Hazel hesitated, then she blurted out:

"Horrible things. She's been talking about two human sexes—just as if we were like the animals. It was disgusting!"

The doctor considered a moment, then she told the senior attendant:

"Better get her along to the sick bay. I'll examine her there."

As she walked off there was a rush of little women to fetch a low trolley from the corner to the side of my couch. A dozen hands assisted me on to it, and then wheeled me briskly away.

"Now," said the doctor grimly, "let's get down to it. Who told you all this stuff about two human sexes? I want her name."

We were alone in a small room with a gold-dotted pink wallpaper. The attendants, after transferring me from the trolley to a couch again, had taken themselves off. The doctor was sitting with a pad on her knee and a pencil at the ready. Her manner was that of an unbluffable inquisitor.

I was not feeling tactful. I told her not to be a fool.

She looked staggered, flushed with anger for a moment, and then took a hold on herself. She went on:

"After you left the Clinic you had your holiday, of course. Now, where did they send you?"

"I don't know," I replied. "All I can tell you is what I told the others—that this hallucination, or delusion, or whatever it is, started in that hospital place you call the Centre."

With resolute patience she said:

"Look here, Orchis. You were perfectly normal when you left here six weeks ago. You went to the Clinic and had your babies in the ordinary way. *But* between then and now somebody has been filling your head with all this rubbish—and teaching you to read and write, as well. Now you are going to tell me who that somebody was. I warn you you won't get away with this loss of memory nonsense with me. If you are able to remember this nauseating stuff you told the others, then you're able to remember where you got it from."

"Oh, for heaven's sake, talk sense," I told her. She flushed again.

"I can find out from the Clinic where they sent you, and I can find out from the Rest Home who were your chief associates while you were there, but I don't want to waste time following up all your contacts, so I'm asking you to save trouble by telling me now. You might just as well. We don't want to have to make you talk," she concluded, ominously.

I shook my head.

"You're on the wrong track. As far as I am concerned this whole hallucination, including my connection with this Orchis, began somehow at the Centre—how it happened I can't tell you, and what happened to her before that just isn't there to be remembered."

She frowned, obviously disturbed.

"What hallucination?" she inquired, carefully.

"Why this fantastic set-up—and you, too." I waved my hand to include it all. "This revolting great body, all those little women, everything. Obviously it is all some projection of the subconscious—and the state of my subconscious is worrying me, for it's certainly no wish-fulfillment."

She went on staring at me, more worried now.

"Who on earth has been telling you about the subconscious and wish-fulfillments?" she asked uncertainly.

"I don't see why, even in an hallucination, I am expected to be an illiterate moron," I replied.

"But a Mother doesn't know anything about such things. She doesn't need to."

"Listen," I said. "I've told you, as I've told those poor grotesques in the other room, that I am not a Mother. What I am is just an unfortunate M.B. who is having some kind of nightmare."

"M.B.?" she inquired, vaguely.

"Bachelor of Medicine. I practise medicine," I told her.

She went on looking at me curiously. Her eyes wandered over my mountainous form, uncertainly.

"You are claiming to be a doctor?" she said, in an odd voice.

"Colloquially—yes," I agreed.

There was indignation mixed with bewilderment as she protested:

"But this is sheer nonsense! You were brought up and developed to be a Mother. You are a Mother. Just look at you!"

"Yes," I said, bitterly. "Just look at me!"

There was a pause.

"It seems to me," I suggested at last, "that, hallucination or not, we shan't get much further simply by going on accusing each other of talking nonsense. Suppose you explain to me what this place is, and who you think I am. It might jog my memory."

She countered that. "Suppose," she said, "that first you tell me what you can remember. It would give me more idea of what is puzzling you."

"Very well," I agreed, and launched upon a potted history of myself as far as I could recollect it—up to the time, that is to say, when Donald's aircraft crashed.

It was foolish of me to fall for that one. Of course, she had no intention of telling me anything. When she had listened to all I had to say, she went away, leaving me impotently furious.

I waited until the place quietened down. The music had been switched off. An attendant had looked in to inquire, with an air of polishing off the day's duties, whether there was anything I wanted, and presently there was nothing to be heard. I let a margin of half an hour elapse, and then struggled to get up—taking it by very easy stages this time. The greatest part of the effort was to get on to my feet from a sitting position, but I managed it at the cost of heavy breathing. Presently I crossed to the door, and found it unfastened. I held it a little open, listening. There was no sound of movement in the corridor, so I pulled it wide open, and set out to discover what I could about the place for myself. All the doors of the rooms were shut. Putting my ear close to them I could hear regular, heavy breathing behind some, but there were no other sounds in the stillness. I kept on, turning several corners, until I recognized the front door ahead of me. I tried the latch, and found that it was neither barred nor bolted. I paused again, listening for some moments, and then pulled it open and stepped outside.

The park-like garden stretched out before me, sharp-shadowed in the moonlight. Through the trees to the right was a glint of water, to the left was a house similar to the one behind me, with not a light showing in any of its windows.

I wondered what to do. Trapped in this huge carcase, all but helpless in it, there was very little I could do, but I decided to go on and at least find out what I could while I had the chance. I went forward to the edge of the steps that I had earlier climbed from the ambulance, and started down them cautiously, holding on to the balustrade.

"Mother," said a sharp, incisive voice behind me. "What are you doing?"

I turned and saw one of the little women, her white suit gleaming in the moonlight. She was alone. I made no reply, but took another step down. I could have wept at the outrage of the heavy, ungainly body, and the caution it imposed on me.

"Come back. Come back at once," she told me.

I took no notice. She came pattering down after me and laid hold of my draperies.

"Mother," she said again, "you must come back. You'll catch cold out here."

I started to take another step, and she pulled at the draperies to hold me back. I leant forward against the pull. There was a sharp tearing sound as the material gave. I swung round and lost my balance. The last thing I saw was the rest of the flight of steps coming up to meet me. . . .

As I opened my eyes a voice said:

"That's better, but it was very naughty of you, Mother Orchis, And lucky it wasn't a lot worse. Such a silly thing to do. I'm ashamed of you—really, I am."

My head was aching, and I was exasperated to find that the whole stupid business was still going on; altogether I was in no mood for reproachful drip. I told her to go to hell. Her small face goggled at me for a moment, and then became icily prim. She applied a piece of lint and plaster to the left side of my forehead, in silence, and then departed, stiffly.

Reluctantly, I had to admit to myself that she was perfectly right. What on earth had I been expecting to do—what on earth *could* I do, encumbered by this horrible mass of flesh? A great surge of loathing for it and a feeling of helpless frustration brought me to the verge of tears again. I longed for my own nice, slim body that pleased me and did what I asked of it. I remembered how Donald had once pointed to a young tree swaying in the wind, and introduced it to me as my twin sister. And only a day or two ago . . .

Then, suddenly, I made a discovery which brought me struggling to sit up. The blank part of my mind had filled up. I could remember everything. . . . The effort made my head throb, so I relaxed and lay back once more, recalling it all, right up to the point where the needle was withdrawn and someone swabbed my arm. . . .

But what had happened after that? Dreams and hallucinations I had expected . . . but not the sharp-focused, detailed sense of reality . . . not this state which was like a nightmare made solid. . . .

What, what in heaven's name, had they done to me . . . ?

I must have fallen asleep again soon, for when I opened my eyes again there was daylight outside, and a covey of little women had arrived to attend to my toilet.

They spread their sheets dexterously and rolled me this way and that with expert technique as they cleaned me up. I suffered their industry patiently, feeling the fresher for it, and glad to discover that the headache had all but gone.

When we were almost at the end of our ablutions there came a peremptory knock, and without invitation two figures, dressed in black uniforms with silver buttons, entered. They were the Amazon type, tall, broad, well set-up, and handsome. The little women dropped everything and fled with squeaks of dismay into the far corner of the room where they cowered in a huddle.

The two gave me the familiar salute. With an odd mixture of decision and deference one of them inquired:

"You are Orchis—Mother Orchis?"

"That's what they're calling me," I admitted.

The girl hesitated, then in a tone rather more pleading than ordering she said:

"I have orders for your arrest, Mother. You will please come with us."

An excited, incredulous twittering broke out among the little women in the corner. The uniformed girl quelled them with a look.

"Get the Mother dressed and make her ready," she commanded.

The little women came out of their corner hesitantly, directing nervous, propitiatory smiles towards the pair. The second one told them briskly, though not altogether unkindly:

"Come along now. Jump to it."

They jumped.

I was almost swathed in my pink draperies again when the doctor strode in. She frowned at the two in uniform.

"What's all this? What are you doing here?" she demanded.

The leader of the two explained.

"Arrest!" exclaimed the doctor. "Arrest a Mother! I never heard such nonsense. What's the charge?"

The uniformed girl said, a little sheepishly:

"She is accused of Reactionism."

The doctor simply stared at her.

"A Reactionist Mother! What'll you people think of next? Go on, get out, both of you."

The young woman protested:

"We have our orders, Doctor."

"Rubbish. There's no authority. Have you ever heard of a Mother being arrested?"

"No, Doctor."

"Well, you aren't going to make a precedent now. Go on."

The uniformed girl hesitated unhappily, then an idea occurred to her.

"If you would let me have a signed refusal to surrender the Mother . . . ?" she suggested helpfully.

When the two had departed, quite satisfied with their piece of paper, the doctor looked at the little women gloomily.

"You can't help tattling, you Servitors, can you? Anything you happen to hear goes through the lot of you like a fire in a cornfield, and makes trouble all round. Well, if I hear anymore of this I shall know where it comes from." She turned to me. "And you, Mother Orchis, will in future please restrict yourself to yes-and-no in the hearing of these nattering little pests. I'll see you again shortly. We want to ask you some questions," she added, as she went out, leaving a subdued, industrious silence behind her.

She returned just as the tray which had held my gargantuan breakfast was being removed, and not alone. The four women who accompanied her and looked as normal as herself were followed by a number of little women lugging in chairs which they arranged beside my couch. When they had departed, the five women, all in white overalls, sat down and regarded me as if I were an exhibit. One appeared to be much the same age as the first doctor, two nearer fifty, and one sixty, or more.

"Now, Mother Orchis," said the doctor, with an air of opening the proceedings, "it is quite clear that something highly unusual has taken place. Naturally we are interested to understand just what and, if possible, why. You don't need to worry about those police this morning—it was quite improper of them to come here at all. This is simply an inquiry—a scientific inquiry—to establish what has happened."

"You can't want to understand more than I do," I replied. I looked at them, at the room about me, and finally at my massive prone figure. "I am aware that all this must be an hallucination, but what is troubling me most is that I have always supposed that any hallucination must be deficient in at least one dimension—must lack reality to some of the senses. But this does not. I have all my senses, and can use them. Nothing is insubstantial: I am trapped in flesh that is, very palpably too, too solid. The only striking deficiency, so far as I can see, is reason—even symbolic reason."

The four other women stared at me in astonishment. The doctor gave them a sort of now-perhaps-you'll-believe-me glance, and then turned to me again.

"We'll start with a few questions," she said.

"Before you begin," I put in, "I have something to add to what I told you last night. It has come back to me."

"Perhaps the knock when you fell," she suggested, looking at my piece of plaster. "What were you trying to do?"

I ignored that. "I think I'd better tell you the missing part—it might help— a bit, anyway."

"Very well," she agreed. "You told me you were—er—married, and that your—er—husband was killed soon afterwards." She glanced at the others; their blankness of expression was somehow studious. "It was the part after that that was missing," she added.

"Yes," I said. "He was a test-pilot," I explained to them. "It happened six months after we were married—only one month before his contract was due to expire.

"After that, an aunt took me away for some weeks. I don't suppose I'll ever remember that part very well—I—I wasn't noticing anything very much. . . .

"But then I remember waking up one morning and suddenly seeing things differently, and telling myself that I couldn't go on like that. I knew I must have some work, something that would keep me busy.

"Dr. Hellyer, who is in charge of the Wraychester Hospital, where I was working before I married, told me he would be glad to have me with them again. I went back, and worked very hard, so that I did not have much time to think. That would be about eight months ago, now.

"Then one day Dr. Hellyer spoke about a drug that a friend of his had succeeded in synthesizing. I don't think he was really asking for volunteers, but I offered to try it out. From what he said it sounded as if the drug might have some quite important properties. It struck me as a chance to do something useful. Sooner or later, someone would try it, and as I didn't have any ties and didn't care very much what happened, anyway, I thought I might as well be the one to try it."

The spokeswoman doctor interrupted to ask:

"What was this drug?"

"It's called chuinjuatin," I told her. "Do you know it?"

She shook her head. One of the others put in:

"I've heard the name. What is it?"

"It's a narcotic," I told her. "The original form is in the leaves of a tree that grows chiefly in the South of Venezuela. The tribe of Indians who live there discovered it somehow, like others did quinine, and mescaline. And in much the same way they use it for orgies. Some of them sit and chew the leaves—they have to chew about six ounces of them—and gradually they go into a zombie-like, trance state. It lasts three or four days during which they are quite helpless and incapable of doing the simplest thing for themselves, so that other members of the tribe are appointed to look after them as if they were children, and to guard them.

"It's necessary to guard them because the Indian belief is that chuinjuatin liberates the spirit from the body, setting it free to wander anywhere in space and time, and the guardian's most important job is to see that no other wandering spirit shall slip into the body while the true owner is away. When the subjects recover they claim to have had wonderful mystical experiences. There seem to be no physical ill-effects, and no craving results from it. The mystical experiences, though, are said to be intense, and clearly remembered.

"Dr. Hellyer's friend had tested his synthesized chuinjuatin on a number of laboratory animals and worked out the dosage, and tolerances, and that kind of thing, but what he could not tell, of course, was what validity, if any, the reports of the mystical experiences had. Presumably they were the product of the drug's influence on the nervous system—but whether that effect produced a sensation of pleasure, ecstasy, awe, fear, horror, or any of a dozen more, it was impossible to tell without a human guinea-pig. So that was what I volunteered for."

I stopped. I looked at their serious, puzzled faces, at the billow of pink satin in front of me. . . .

"In fact," I added, "it appears to have produced a combination of the absurd, the incomprehensible, and the grotesque."

They were earnest women, these, not to be sidetracked. They were there to disprove an anomaly—if they could.

"I *see*," said the spokeswoman with an air of preserving reasonableness, rather than meaning anything. She glanced down at a paper on which she had made a note from time to time.

"Now, can you give us the time and date at which this experiment took place?"

I could, and did, and after that the questions went on and on and on. . . .

The least satisfactory part of it from my point of view was that even though my answers caused them to grow more uncertain of themselves as we went on, they did at least get them; whereas when I put a question it was usually evaded, or answered perfunctorily, as an unimportant digression.

They went on steadily, and only broke off when my next meal arrived. Then they went away, leaving me thankfully in peace—but little the wiser. I half-expected them to return, but when they did not I fell into a doze from which I was awakened by the incursion of a cluster of the little women once more. They brought a trolley with them, and in a short time were wheeling me out of the building on it—but not by the way I had arrived. This time we went down a ramp where another, or the same, pink ambulance waited at the bottom. When they had me safely loaded aboard three of them climbed in, too, to keep me company. They were chattering as they did so, and they kept it up inconsequentially, and almost incomprehensibly, for the whole hour and a half of the journey that ensued.

The countryside differed little from that I had already seen. Once we were outside the gates there were the same tidy fields and standardized farms. The occasional built-up areas were not extensive and consisted of the same types of blocks close by, and we ran on the same, not very good, road surfaces. There were groups of the Amazon types, and, more rarely, individuals, to be seen at work in the fields; the sparse traffic was lorries, large or small, and occasional buses, but with never a private car to be seen. My illusion, I reflected, was remarkably consistent in its details. Not a single group of Amazons, for instance, failed to raise its right hands in friendly, respectful greeting to the pink car.

Once, we crossed a cutting. Looking down from the bridge I thought at first that we were over the dried bed of a canal, but then I noticed a post leaning at a crazy angle among the grass and weeds: most of its attachments had fallen off, but there were enough left to identify it as a railway signal.

We passed through one concentration of identical blocks which was in size, though in no other way, quite a town, and then, two or three miles further on, ran through an ornamental gateway into a kind of park.

In one way it was not unlike the estate we had left, for everything was meticulously tended; the lawns like velvet, the flower beds vivid with spring blossoms, but it differed essentially in that the buildings were not blocks. They were houses, quite small for the most part, and varied in style, often no larger than roomy cottages. The place had a subduing effect on my small companions; for the first time they left off chattering, and gazed about them with obvious awe.

The driver stopped once to inquire the way of an overalled Amazon who was striding along with a hod on her shoulder. She directed us, and gave me a cheerful, respectful grin through the window, and presently we drew up again in front of a neat little two-storey Regency-style house.

This time there was no trolley. The little women, assisted by the driver, fussed over helping me out, and then half-supported me into the house, in a kind of buttressing formation.

Inside, I was manœuvred with some difficulty through a door on the left, and found myself in a beautiful room, elegantly decorated and furnished in the period-style of the house. A white-haired woman in a purple silk dress was sitting in a wing-chair beside a wood fire. Both her face and her hands told of considerable age, but she looked at me from keen, lively eyes.

"Welcome, my dear," she said, in a voice which had no trace of the quaver I half-expected.

Her glance went to a chair. Then she looked at me again, and thought better of it.

"I expect you'd be more comfortable on the couch," she suggested.

I regarded the couch—a genuine Georgian piece, I thought—doubtfully.

"Will it stand it?" I wondered.

"Oh, I think so," she said, but not too certainly.

The retinue deposited me there carefully, and stood by, with anxious expressions. When it was clear that, though it creaked, it was probably going to hold, the old lady shooed them away, and rang a little silver bell. A diminutive figure, a perfect parlourmaid three foot ten in height, entered.

"The brown sherry, please, Mildred," instructed the old lady. "You'll take sherry, my dear?" she added to me.

"Y-yes—yes, thank you," I said, faintly. After a pause I added: "You will excuse me, Mrs.—er—Miss—?"

"Oh, I should have introduced myself. My name is Laura—not Miss, or Mrs., just Laura. You, I know, are Orchis—Mother Orchis."

"So they tell me," I owned, distastefully.

We studied one another. For the first time since the hallucination had set in I saw sympathy, even pity, in someone else's eyes. I looked round the room again, noticing the perfection of details.

"This is—I'm not mad, am I?" I asked.

She shook her head slowly, but before she could reply the miniature parlourmaid returned, bearing a cut-glass decanter and glasses on a silver tray. As she poured out a glass for each of us I saw the old lady glance from her to me and back again, as though comparing us. There was a curious, uninterpretable expression on her face. I made an effort.

"Shouldn't it be madeira?" I suggested.

She looked surprised, and then smiled, and nodded appreciatively.

"I think you have accomplished the purpose of this visit in one sentence," she said.

The parlourmaid left, and we raised our glasses. The old lady sipped at hers and then placed it on an occasional table beside her.

"Nevertheless," she went on, "we had better go into it a little more. Did they tell you why they have sent you to me, my dear?"

"No." I shook my head.

"It is because I am a historian," she informed me. "Access to history is a privilege. It is not granted to many of us nowadays—and then somewhat reluctantly. Fortunately, a feeling that no branches of knowledge should be allowed to perish entirely still exists—though some of them are pursued at the cost of a certain political suspicion." She smiled deprecatingly, and then went on. "So when confirmation is required it is necessary to appeal to a specialist. Did they give you any report on their diagnosis?"

I shook my head again.

"I thought not. So like the profession, isn't it? Well, I'll tell you what they told me on the telephone from the Mother's Home, and we shall have a better idea of what we are about. I was informed that you have been interviewed by several doctors whom you have interested, puzzled—and, I suspect, distressed— very much, poor things. None of them has more than a minimum smattering of history, you see. Well, briefly, two of them are of the opinion that you are suffering from delusions of a schizophrenic nature: and three are inclined to think you are a genuine case of projected perception. It is an extremely rare condition. There are not more than three reliably documented cases, and one that is more debatable, they tell me; but of those confirmed two are associated with the drug chuinjuatin, and the third with a drug of very similar properties.

"Now, the majority of three found your answers coherent for the most part, and felt that they were authentically circumstantial. That is to say that nothing you told them conflicted directly with what they know, but, since they know so little outside their professional field, they found a great deal of the rest both hard to believe and impossible to check. Therefore, I, with my better means of checking, have been asked for my opinion."

She paused, and looked me over thoughtfully.

"I rather think," she added, "that this is going to be one of the most curiously interesting things that has happened to me in my quite long life—your glass is empty, my dear."

"Projected perception," I repeated wonderingly, as I held out my glass. "Now, if *that* were possible—"

"Oh, there's no doubt about the *possibility*. Those three cases I mentioned are fully authenticated."

"It might be that—almost," I admitted. "At least, in some ways it might be— but not in others. There *is* this nightmare quality. You seem perfectly normal to me, but look at me, myself—and at your little maid! There's certainly an element of delusion. I *seem* to be here, like this, and talking to you—but it can't really be so, so where am I?"

"I can understand, better than most, I think, how unreal this must seem to you. In fact, I have spent so much of my time in books that it sometimes seems unreal to me—as if I did not quite belong anywhere. Now, tell me, my dear, when were you born?"

I told her. She thought for a moment.

"H'm," she said. "George the Sixth—but you'd not remember the second big war?"

"No," I agreed.

"But you might remember the coronation of the next monarch? Whose was that?"

"Elizabeth—Elizabeth the Second. My mother took me to see the procession," I told her.

"Do you remember anything about it?"

"Not a lot really—except that it rained, nearly all day," I admitted.

We went on like that for a little while, then she smiled, reassuringly.

"Well, I don't think we need anymore to establish our point. I've heard about that coronation before—at secondhand. It must have been a wonderful scene in the Abbey." She mused a moment, and gave a little sigh. "You've been very patient with me, my dear. It is only fair that you should have your turn—but I'm afraid you must prepare yourself for some shocks."

"I think I must be inured after my last thirty-six hours—or what has appeared to be thirty-six hours," I told her.

"I doubt it," she said, looking at me seriously.

"Tell me," I asked her. "Please, explain it all—if you can."

"Your glass, my dear. Then I'll get the crux of it over." She poured for each of us, then she asked:

"What strikes you as the oddest feature of your experience, so far?"

I considered. "There's so much—"

"Might it not be that you have not seen a single man?" she suggested.

I thought back. I remembered the wondering tone of one of the Mothers asking: "What is a man?"

"That's certainly one of them," I agreed. "Where are they?"

She shook her head, watching me steadily.

"There aren't any, my dear. Not anymore. None at all."

I simply went on staring at her. Her expression was perfectly serious and sympathetic. There was no trace of guile there or deception while I struggled with the idea. At last I managed:

"But—but that's impossible! There must be some somewhere.... You couldn't—I mean, how—? I mean . . . ." My expostulation trailed off in confusion.

She shook her head.

"I know it must seem impossible to you, Jane—may I call you Jane? But it is so. I am an old woman now, nearly eighty, and in all my long life I have never seen a man—save in old pictures and photographs. Drink your sherry, my dear. It will do you good." She paused. "I'm afraid this upsets you."

I obeyed, too bewildered for further comment at the moment, protesting inwardly, yet not altogether disbelieving, for certainly I had not seen one man, nor sign of any. She went on quietly, giving me time to collect my wits:

"I can understand a little how you must feel. I haven't had to learn all my history entirely from books, you see. When I was a girl, sixteen or seventeen, I used to listen a lot to my grandmother. She was as old then as I am now, but her memory of her youth was still very good. I was able almost to see the places she talked about—but they were part of such a different world that it was difficult for me to understand how she felt. When she spoke about the young man she had been engaged to, tears would roll down her cheeks, even then—not just for him, of course, but for the whole world that she had known as a girl. I was sorry for her, although I could not really understand how she felt—How should I? But now that I am old, too, and have read so much, I am perhaps a little nearer to understanding her feelings, I think." She looked at me curiously. "And you, my dear. Perhaps you, too, were engaged to be married?"

"I was married—for a little time," I told her.

She contemplated that for some seconds, then:

"It must be a very strange experience to be owned," she remarked, reflectively.

"Owned?" I exclaimed, in astonishment.

"Ruled by a husband," she explained, sympathetically.

I stared at her.

"But it—it wasn't like that—it wasn't like that at all," I protested. "It was—" But there I broke off, with tears too close. To steer her away I asked:

"But what happened? What on earth happened to the men?"

"They all died," she told me. "They fell sick. Nobody could do anything for them, so they died. In little more than a year they were all gone—all but a very few."

"But surely—surely everything would collapse?"

"Oh, yes. Very largely it did. It was very bad. There was a dreadful lot of starvation. The industrial parts were the worst hit, of course. In the more backward countries and in rural areas women were able to turn to the land and till it to keep themselves and their children alive, but almost all the large organizations broke down entirely. Transport ceased very soon: petrol ran out, and no coal was being mined. It was quite a dreadful state of affairs because, although there were a great many women, and they had outnumbered the men, in fact, they had only really been important as consumers and spenders of money. So when the crisis came it turned out that scarcely any of them knew how to do any of the important things because they had nearly all been owned by men, and had to lead their lives as pets and parasites."

I started to protest, but her frail hand waved me aside.

"It wasn't their *fault*—not entirely," she explained. "They were caught up in a process, and everything conspired against their escape. It was a long process, going right back to the eleventh century, in Southern France. The Romantic conception started there as an elegant and amusing fashion for the leisured classes. Gradually, as time went on, it permeated through most levels of society, but it was not until the latter part of the nineteenth century that its commercial possibilities were intelligently perceived, and not until the twentieth that it was really exploited.

"At the beginning of the twentieth century women were starting to have their chance to lead useful, creative, interesting lives. But that did not suit commerce: it needed them much more as mass-consumers than as producers—except on the most routine levels. So Romance was adopted and developed as a weapon against their further progress and to promote consumption, and it was used intensively.

"Women must never for a moment be allowed to forget their sex, and compete as equals. Everything had to have a 'feminine angle' which must be different from the masculine angle, and be dinned in without ceasing. It would have been unpopular for manufacturers actually to issue an order 'back to the kitchen,' but there were other ways. A profession without a difference, called 'housewife,' could be invented. The kitchen could be glorified and made more expensive; it could be made to seem desirable, and it could be shown that the way to realize this heart's desire was through marriage. So the presses turned out, by the hundred thousand a week, journals which concentrated the attention of women ceaselessly and relentlessly upon selling themselves to some man in order that they might achieve some small, uneconomic unit of a home upon which money could be spent.

"Whole trades adopted the romantic approach and the glamour was spread thicker and thicker in the articles, the write-ups, and most of all in the advertisements. Romance found a place in everything that women might buy, from underclothes to motor-bicycles, from 'health' foods to kitchen stoves, from deodorants to foreign travel, until soon they were too bemused to be amused anymore.

"The air was filled with frustrated moanings. Women maundered in front of microphones yearning only to 'surrender,' and 'give themselves,' to adore and to be adored. The cinema most of all maintained the propaganda, persuading the main and important part of their audience, which was female, that nothing in life was worth achieving but dewy-eyed passivity in the strong arms of Romance. The pressure became such that the majority of young women spent all their leisure time dreaming of Romance, and the means of securing it. They were brought to a state of honestly believing that to be owned by some man and set down in a little brick box to buy all the things that the manufacturers wanted them to buy would be the highest form of bliss that life could offer."

"But—" I began to protest again. The old lady was now well launched, however, and swept on without a check.

"All this could not help distorting society, of course. The divorce-rate went up. Real life simply could not come near to providing the degree of romantic glamour which was being represented as every girl's proper inheritance. There was probably, in the aggregate, more disappointment, disillusion, and dissatisfaction among women than there had ever been before. Yet, with this ridiculous and ornamented ideal grained-in by unceasing propaganda, what could a conscientious idealist do but take steps to break up the short-weight marriage she had made, and seek elsewhere for the ideal which was hers, she understood, by right?

"It was a wretched state of affairs brought about by deliberately promoted dissatisfactions; a kind of rat-race with, somewhere safely out of reach, the glamourized romantic ideal always luring. Perhaps an exceptional few almost attained it, but, for all except those very few, it was a cruel, tantalizing sham on which they spent themselves, and of course their money, in vain."

This time I did get in my protest.

"But it wasn't like that. Some of what you say may be true—but that's all the superficial part. It didn't feel a bit like the way you put it. I was in it. I *know*."

She shook her head reprovingly.

"There is such a thing as being too close to make a proper evaluation. At a distance we are able to see more clearly. We can perceive it for what it was—a gross and heartless exploitation of the weaker-willed majority. Some women of education and resolution were able to withstand it, of course, but at a cost. There must always be a painful price for resisting majority pressure—even they could not always altogether escape the feeling that they might be wrong, and that the rat-racers were having the better time of it.

"You see, the great hopes for the emancipation of women with which the century had started had been outflanked. Purchasing-power had passed into the hands of the ill-educated and highly suggestible. The desire for Romance is essentially a selfish wish, and when it is encouraged to dominate every other it breaks down all corporate loyalties. The individual woman thus separated from, and yet at the same time thrust into competition with, all other women was almost defenceless; she became the prey of organized suggestion. When it was represented to her that the lack of certain goods or amenities would be fatal to Romance she became alarmed and, thus, eminently exploitable. She could only believe what she was told, and spent a great deal of time worrying about whether she was doing all the right things to encourage Romance. Thus, she became, in a new, a subtler way, more exploited, more dependent, and less creative than she had ever been before."

"Well," I said, "this is the most curiously unrecognizable account of my world that I have ever heard—it's like something copied, but with all the proportions wrong. And as for 'less creative'—well, perhaps families were smaller, but women still went on having babies. The population was still increasing."

The old lady's eyes dwelt on me a moment.

"You are undoubtedly a thought-child of your time, in some ways," she observed. "What makes you think there is anything creative about having babies? Would you call a plant-pot creative because seeds grow in it? It is a mechanical operation—and, like most mechanical operations, is most easily performed by the least intelligent. Now, bringing up a child, educating, helping her to become a person, that *is* creative. But unfortunately, in the time we are speaking of, women had, in the main, been successfully conditioned into bringing up their daughters to be unintelligent consumers, like themselves."

"But," I said helplessly, "I *know* the time. It's my time. This is all distorted."

"The perspective of history must be truer," she told me again, unimpressed, and went on: "But if what happened *had* to happen, then it chose a fortunate time to happen. A hundred years earlier, even fifty years earlier, it would very likely have meant extinction. Fifty years later might easily have been too late—it might have come upon a world in which all women were profitably restricted to domesticity and consumership. Luckily, however, in the middle of the century women were still entering the professions, and by far the greatest number of professional women was to be found in medicine—which is to say that they were only really numerous in, and skilled in, the very profession which immediately became of vital importance if we were to survive at all.

"I have no medical knowledge, so I cannot give you any details of the steps they took. All I can tell you is that there was intensive research on lines which will probably be more obvious to you than they are to me.

"A species, even our species, has great will to survive, and the doctors saw to it that the will had the means of expression. Through all the hunger, and the chaos, and the other privations, babies somehow continued to be born. That had to be. Reconstruction could wait: the priority was the new generation that would help in the reconstruction, and then inherit it. So babies were born: the girl babies lived, the boy babies died. That was distressing, and wasteful, too, and so, presently, only girl babies were born—again, the means by which that could be achieved will be easier for you to understand than for me.

"It is, they tell me, not nearly so remarkable as it would appear at first sight. The locust, it seems, will continue to produce female locusts without male, or any other kind of assistance; the aphis, too, is able to go on breeding alone and in seclusion, certainly for eight generations, perhaps more. So it would be a poor thing if we, with all our knowledge and powers of research to assist us, should find ourselves inferior to the locust and the aphis in this respect, would it not?"

She paused, looking at me somewhat quizzically for my response. Perhaps she expected amazed—or possibly shocked—disbelief. If so, I disappointed her: technical achievements have ceased to arouse simple wonder since atomic physics showed how barriers fall before the pressure of a good brainsteam. One can take it that most things are possible: whether they are desirable, or worth doing, is a different matter—and one that seemed to me particularly pertinent to her question. I asked her:

"And what is it that you have achieved?"

"Survival," she said, simply.

"Materially," I agreed. "I suppose you have. But when it has cost all the rest, when love, art, poetry, excitement, and physical joy have all been sacrificed to mere continued existence, what is left but a soulless waste? What reason is there any longer for survival?"

"As to the reason, I don't know—except that survival is a desire common to all species. I am quite sure that the reason for that desire was no clearer in the twentieth century than it is now. But, for the rest, why should you assume that they are gone. Did not Sappho write poetry? And your assumption that the possession of a soul depends upon a duality of sexes surprises me: it has so often been held that the two are in some sort of conflict, has it not?"

"As a historian who must have studied men, women, and motives you should have taken my meaning better," I told her.

She shook her head, with reproof. "You are so much the conditioned product of your age, my dear. They told you, on all levels, from the works of Freud to that of the most nugatory magazines for women, that it was sex, civilized into romantic love, that made the world go round—and you believed them. But the world continues to go round for others, too—for the insects, the fish, the birds, the animals—and how much do you suppose they know of romantic love, even in their brief mating-seasons? They hoodwinked you, my dear.

Between them they channelled your interests and ambitions along courses that were socially convenient, economically profitable, and almost harmless."

I shook my head.

"I just don't believe it. Oh, yes, you know something of my world—from the outside. But you don't understand it, or feel it."

"That's your conditioning, my dear," she told me, calmly.

Her repeated assumption irritated me. I asked:

"Suppose I were to believe what you say, what is it, then, that *does* make the world go round?"

"That's simple, my dear. It is the will to power. We have that as babies; we have it still in old age. It occurs in men and women alike. It is more fundamental, and more desirable, than sex; I tell you, you were misled—exploited, sublimated for economic convenience.

"After the disease had struck, women ceased, for the first time in history, to be an exploited class. Without male rulers to confuse and divert them they began to perceive that all true power resides in the female principle. The male had served only one brief useful purpose; for the rest of his life he was a painful and costly parasite.

"As they became aware of power, the doctors grasped it. In twenty years they were in full control. With them were the few women engineers, architects, lawyers, administrators, some teachers, and so on, but it was the doctors who held the keys of life and death. The future was in their hands and, as things began gradually to revive, they, together with the other professions, remained the dominant class and became known as the Doctorate. It assumed authority; it made the laws; it enforced them.

"There was opposition, of course. Neither the memory of the old days, nor the effect of twenty years of lawlessness, could be wiped out at once, but the doctors had the whip-hand—any woman who wanted a child had to come to them, and they saw to it that she was satisfactorily settled in a community. The roving gangs dwindled away, and gradually order was restored.

"Later on, they faced better organized opposition. There was a party which contended that the disease which had struck down the men had run its course, and the balance could, and should, be restored—they were known as Reactionists, and they became an embarrassment.

"Most of the Council of the Doctorate still had clear memories of a system which used every weakness of women, and had been no more than a more civilized culmination of their exploitation through the ages. They remembered how they themselves had only grudgingly been allowed to qualify for their careers. They were now in command: they felt no obligation to surrender their power and authority, and eventually, no doubt, their freedom to a creature whom they had proved to be biologically, and in all other ways, expendable. They refused unanimously to take a step that would lead to corporate suicide, and the Reactionists were proscribed as a subversive criminal organization.

"That, however, was just a palliative. It quickly became clear that they were attacking a symptom and neglecting the cause. The Council was driven to realize that it had an unbalanced society at its hands—a society that was capable of continuity, but was in structure, you might say, little more than the residue of a vanished form. It could not continue in that truncated shape and, as long as it tried to, disaffection would increase. Therefore, if power were to become stable, a new form suitable to the circumstances must be found.

"In deciding the shape it should take, the natural tendencies of the little-educated and uneducated woman were carefully considered—such qualities as her feeling for hierarchical principles and her disposition to respect artificial distinctions. You will no doubt recollect that in your own time any fool of a woman whose husband was ennobled or honoured at once acquired increased respect and envy from other women though she remained the same fool; and also, that any gathering or society of unoccupied women would soon become obsessionally enmeshed in the creation and preservation of social distinctions. Allied to this is the high value they usually place upon a feeling of security. Important, too, is the capacity for devoted self-sacrifice, and slavery to conscience within the canons of any local convention. We are naturally very biddable creatures. Most of us are happiest when we are being orthodox, however odd our customs may appear to an outsider; the difficulty in handling us lies chiefly in establishing the required standards of orthodoxy.

"Obviously, the broad outline of a system which was going to stand any chance of success would have to provide scope for these and other characteristic traits. It must be a scheme where the interplay of forces would preserve equilibrium and respect for authority. The details of such an organization, however, were less easy to determine.

"An extensive study of social forms and orders was undertaken, but for several years every plan put forward was rejected as in some way unsuitable. The architecture of that finally chosen was said, though I do not know with how much truth, to have been inspired by the Bible—a book at that time still unprohibited, and the source of much unrest. I am told that it ran something like: 'Go to the ant, thou sluggard; consider her ways.'

"The Council appears to have felt that this advice, suitably modified, could be expected to lead to a state of affairs which would provide most of the requisite characteristics.

"A four-class system was chosen as the basis, and strong differentiations were gradually introduced. These, now that they have become well established, greatly help to ensure stability: there is scope for ambition within one's class, but none for passing from one class to another. Thus, we have the Doctorate—the educated ruling-classes, fifty percent of whom are actually of the medical profession. The Mothers, whose title is self-explanatory. The Servitors, who are numerous and, for psychological reasons, small. The Workers, who are physically and muscularly strong, to do the heavier work. All the three lower classes respect the authority of the Doctorate. Both the employed classes revere the Mothers. The Servitors consider themselves more favoured in their tasks than the Workers; and the Workers tend to regard the puniness of the Servitors with a semi-affectionate contempt.

"So you see a balance has been struck, and though it works somewhat crudely as yet, no doubt it will improve. It seems likely, for instance, that it would be advantageous to introduce sub-divisions into the Servitor class before long, and the police are thought by some to be put at a disadvantage by having no more than a little education to distinguish them from the ordinary Worker . . ."

She went on explaining with increasing detail while the enormity of the whole process gradually grew upon me.

"Ants!" I broke in, suddenly. "The ant-nest! You've taken *that* for your model?"

She looked surprised, either at my tone, or the fact that what she was saying had taken so long to register.

"And why not?" she asked. "Surely it is one of the most enduring social patterns that nature has evolved—though of course some adaptation—"

"You're—are you telling me that only the Mothers have children?" I demanded.

"Oh, members of the Doctorate do, too, when they wish," she assured me.

"But—but."

"The Council decides the ratios," she went on to explain. "The doctors at the clinic examine the babies and allocate them suitably to the different classes. After that, of course, it is just a matter of seeing to their specialized feeding, glandular control, and proper training."

"But," I objected wildly, "what's it *for*? Where's the sense in it? What's the good of being alive, like that?"

"Well, what *is* the sense in being alive? You tell me," she suggested.

"But we're *meant* to love and be loved, to have babies we love by people we love."

"There's your conditioning again; glorifying and romanticizing primitive animalism. Surely you consider that we are superior to the animals?"

"Of course I do, but—"

"Love, you say, but what can you know of the love there can be between mother and daughter when there are no men to introduce jealousy? Do you know of any purer sentiment than the love of a girl for her little sisters?"

"But you don't understand," I protested again. "How should you understand a love that colours the whole world? How it centers in your heart and reaches out from there to pervade your whole being, how it can affect everything you are, everything you touch, everything you hear . . . It can hurt dreadfully, I know, oh, I know, but it can run like sunlight in your veins . . . It can make you a garden out of a slum; brocade out of rags; music out of speaking voice. It can show you a whole universe in someone else's eyes. Oh, you don't understand . . . you don't know . . . you can't. . . . Oh, Donald, darling, how can I show her what she's never even guessed at . . . ?"

There was an uncertain pause, but presently she said:

"Naturally, in your form of society it was necessary for you to be given such a conditioned reaction, but you can scarcely expect us to surrender our freedom, to connive at our own re-subjection by calling our oppressors into existence again."

"Oh, you *won't* understand. It was only the more stupid men and women who were continually at war with one another. Lots of us were complementary. We were pairs who formed units."

She smiled. "My dear, either you are surprisingly ill-informed on your own period, or else the stupidity you speak of was astonishingly dominant. Neither as myself, nor as a historian, can I consider that we should be justified in res-urrecting such a state of affairs. A primitive stage of our development has now given way to a civilized era. Woman, who is the vessel of life, had the misfortune to find man necessary for a time, but now she does so no longer. Are you sug-gesting that such a useless and dangerous encumbrance ought to be preserved, out of sheer sentimentality? I will admit that we have lost some minor conven-iences—you will have noticed, I expect, that we are less inventive mechanically, and tend to copy the patterns we have inherited; but that troubles us very little; our interests lie not in the inorganic, but in the organic and the sentient. Perhaps men could show us how to travel twice as fast, or how to fly to the moon, or how to kill more people more quickly; but it does not seem to us that such kinds of knowledge would be good payment for re-enslaving ourselves. No, our kind of world suits us better—all of us except a few Reactionists. You have seen our Servitors. They are a little timid in manner, perhaps, but are they oppressed, or sad? Don't they chatter among themselves as brightly and perkily as sparrows? And the Workers—those you called the Amazons—don't they look strong, healthy, and cheerful?"

"But you're robbing them all—robbing them of their birthright."

"You mustn't give me cant, my dear. Did not your social system conspire to rob a woman of her 'birthright' unless she married? You not only let her know it, but socially you rubbed it in: here, our Servitors and Workers do not know it, and they are not worried by a sense of inadequacy. Motherhood is the function of the Mothers, and understood as such."

I shook my head. "Nevertheless, they are being robbed.

A woman has a right to love—"

For once she was a little impatient as she cut me short.

"You keep repeating to me the propaganda of your age. The love you talk about, my dear, existed in your little sheltered part of the world by polite and profitable convention. You were scarcely ever allowed to see its other face, un-glamourized by Romance. You were never openly bought and sold, like livestock; you never had to sell yourself to the first comer in order to live; you did not happen to be one of the women who through the centuries screamed in agony and suffered and died under invaders in a sacked city—nor were you ever flung into a pit of fire to be saved from them; *you* were never compelled to suttee upon you dead husband's pyre; *you* did not have to spend your whole life imprisoned in a harem; *you* were never part of the cargo of a slave-ship; *you* never retained your own life only at the pleasure of your lord and master. . . .

"That is the other side—the age-long side. There is going to be no more of such things. They are finished at last. Dare you suggest that we should call them back, to suffer them all again?"

"But most of these things had already gone," I protested. "The world was getting better."

"Was it?" she said. "I wonder if the women of Berlin thought so when it fell? Was it, indeed?—or was it on the edge of a new barbarism?"

"But if you can only get rid of evil by throwing out the good, too, what is there left?"

"There is a great deal. Man was only a means to an end. We needed him in order to have babies. The rest of his vitality accounted for all the misery in the world. We are a great deal better off without him."

"So you really consider that you've improved on nature?"

"Tcha!" she said, impatient with my tone. "Civilization *is* improvement on nature. Would you want to live in a cave and have most of your babies die in infancy?"

"There are some things, some fundamental things—" I began, but she checked me, holding up her hand for silence.

Outside, the long shadows had crept across the lawns. In the evening quiet I could hear a choir of women's voices singing some little distance away. We listened for some minutes until the song was finished.

"Beautiful!" said the old lady. "Could angels themselves sing more sweetly? They sound happy enough, don't they? Our own lovely children—two of my granddaughters are there among them. They are happy, and they've reason to be happy: they're not growing up into a world where they must gamble on the goodwill of some man to keep them; they'll never need to be servile before a lord and master; they'll never stand in danger of rape and butchery, either. Listen to them!"

Another song had started and came lilting lightly to us out of the dusk.

"Why are you crying?" the old lady asked me as it ended.

"I know it's stupid—I don't really believe any of this is what it seems to be—so I suppose I'm crying for all you would have lost if it were true," I told her. "There should be lovers out there under the trees; they should be listening hand in hand to that song while they watch the moon rise. But there are no lovers now, there won't be any more. . . ." I looked back at her.

"Did you ever read the lines: 'Full many a flower is born to blush unseen, and waste its sweetness on the desert air'? Can't you feel the forlornness of this world you've made? Do you *really* not understand?" I asked.

"I know you've only seen a little of us, but do *you* not begin to understand what it can be like when women are no longer forced to fight one another for the favours of men?" she countered.

We talked on while the dusk gave way to darkness and the lights of other houses started to twinkle through the trees. Her reading had been wide. It had given her even an affection for some periods of the past, but her approval of her own era was unshaken. She felt no aridity in it. Always it was my 'conditioning' which prevented me from seeing that the golden age of woman had begun at last.

"You cling to too many myths," she told me. "You speak of a full life, and your instance is some unfortunate woman hugging her chains in a suburban villa. Full life, fiddlesticks! But it was convenient for the traders that she could be made to think so. A truly full life would be an exceedingly short one, in any form of society."

And so on. . . .

At length, the little parlourmaid reappeared to say that my attendants were ready to leave when it should be convenient. But there was one thing I very much wanted to know before I left. I put the question to the old lady.

"Please tell me. How did it—how could it—happen?"

"Simply by accident, my dear—though it was the kind of accident that was entirely the product of its time. A piece of research which showed unexpected, secondary results, that's all."

"But how?"

"Rather curiously—almost irrelevantly, you might say. Did you ever hear of a man called Perrigan?"

"Perrigan?" I repeated. "I don't think so; it's an uncommon name."

"It became very commonly known indeed," she assured me. "Doctor Perrigan was a biologist, and his concern was the extermination of rats—particularly the brown rat, which used to do a great deal of expensive damage.

"His approach to the problem was to find a disease which would attack them fatally. In order to produce it he took as his basis a virus infection often fatal to rabbits—or, rather, a group of virus infections that were highly selective, and also unstable since they were highly liable to mutation. Indeed, there was so much variation in the strains that when infection of rabbits in Australia was tried, it was only at the sixth attempt that it was successful; all the earlier strains died out as the rabbits developed immunity. It was tried in other places, too, though with indifferent success until a still more effective strain was started in France, and ran through the rabbit population of Europe.

"Well, taking some of these viruses as a basis, Perrigan induced new mutations by irradiation and other means, and succeeded in producing a variant that would attack rats. That was not enough, however, and he continued his work until he had a strain that had enough of its ancestral selectivity to attack only the brown rat, and with great virulence.

"In that way he settled the question of a long-standing pest, for there are no brown rats now. But something went amiss. It is still an open question whether the successful virus mutated again, or whether one of his earlier experimental viruses was accidentally liberated by escaped 'carrier' rats, but that's academic. The important thing is that somehow a strain capable of attacking human beings got loose, and that it was already widely disseminated before it was traced—also, that once it was free, it spread with devastating speed; too fast for any effective steps to be taken to check it.

"The majority of women were found to be immune; and of the ten percent or so whom it attacked over eight percent recovered. Among men, however, there was almost no immunity, and the few recoveries were only partial. A few men were preserved by the most elaborate precautions, but they could not be kept confined forever, and in the end the virus, which had a remarkable capacity for dormancy, got them, too."

Inevitably several questions of professional interest occurred to me, but for an answer she shook her head.

"I'm afraid I can't help you there. Possibly the medical people will be willing to explain," she said, but her expression was doubtful.

I maneuvered myself into a sitting position on the side of the couch.

"I see," I said. "Just an accident—yes, I suppose one could scarcely think of it happening any other way."

"Unless," she remarked, "unless one were to look upon it as divine intervention."

"Isn't that a little impious?"

"I was thinking of the Death of the Firstborn," she said, reflectively.

There did not seem to be an immediate answer to that. Instead, I asked:

"Can you honestly tell me that you never have the feeling that you are living in a dreary kind of nightmare?"

"Never," she said. "There was a nightmare—but it's over now. Listen!"

The voices of the choir, reinforced now by an orchestra, reached us distantly out of the darkened garden. No, they were not dreary: they even sounded almost exultant—but then, poor things, how were they to understand . . . ?

My attendants arrived and helped me to my feet. I thanked the old lady for her patience with me and her kindness. But she shook her head.

"My dear, it is I who am indebted to you. In a short time I have learnt more about the conditioning of women in a mixed society than all my books have been able to show me in the rest of my long life. I hope, my dear, that the doctors will find some way of enabling you to forget it and live happily here with us."

At the door I paused and turned, still helpfully shored up by my attendants.

"Laura," I said, using her name for the first time, "so many of your arguments are right—yet, over all, you're, oh, so *wrong*. Did you never read of lovers? Did you never, as a girl, sigh for a Romeo who would say: 'It is the east, and Laura is the sun!'?"

"I think not. Though I have read the play. A pretty, idealized tale—I wonder how much heartbreak it has given to how many would-be Juliets? But I would set a question against yours, my dear Jane. Did you ever see Goya's cycle of pictures called 'The Horrors of War'?"

The pink car did not return me to the 'Home'. Our destination turned out to be a more austere and hospital-like building where I was fussed into bed in a room alone. In the morning, after my massive breakfast, three new doctors visited me. Their manner was more social than professional, and we chatted amiably for half an hour. They had evidently been fully informed on my conversation with the old lady, and they were not averse to answering my questions. Indeed, they found some amusement in many of them, though I found none, for there was nothing consolingly vague in what they told me—it all sounded too disturbingly practicable, once the technique had been worked out. At the end of that time, however, their mood changed. One of them, with an air of getting down to business, said:

"You will understand that you present us with a problem. Your fellow Mothers, of course, are scarcely susceptible to Reactionist disaffection— though you have in quite a short time managed to disgust and bewilder them considerably—but on others less stable your influence might be more serious. It is not just a matter of what you may say; your difference from the rest is implicit in your whole attitude. You cannot help that, and, frankly, we do not see how you, as a woman of education, could possibly adapt yourself to the placid, unthinking acceptance that is expected of a Mother. You would quickly

feel frustrated beyond endurance. Furthermore, it is clear that the conditioning you have had under your system prevents you from feeling any goodwill
towards ours."

I took that straight; simply as a judgment without bias. Moreover, I could not
dispute it. The prospect of spending the rest of my life in pink, scented, soft-
musicked illiteracy, interrupted, one gathered, only by the production of quad-
ruplet daughters at regular intervals, would certainly have me violently unhinged
in a very short time.

"And so—what?" I asked. "Can you reduce this great carcass to normal shape
and size?"

She shook her head. "I imagine not—though I don't know that it has ever
been attempted. But even if it were possible, you would be just as much of a
misfit in the Doctorate—and far more of a liability as a Reactionist influence."

I could understand that, too.

"What, then?" I inquired.

She hesitated, then she said gently:

"The only practicable proposal we can make is that you should agree to a
hypnotic treatment which will remove your memory."

As the meaning of that came home to me I had to fight off a rush of panic.
After all, I told myself, they were being reasonable with me. I must do my best
to respond sensibly. Nevertheless, some minutes must have passed before I answered, unsteadily.

"You are asking me to commit suicide. My mind is my memories: they are
me. If I lose them I shall die, just as surely as if you were to kill my—this body."

They did not dispute that. How could they?

There is just one thing that makes my life worth living—knowing that you
loved me, my sweet, sweet Donald. It is only in my memory that you live now.
If you ever leave there you will die again—and forever.

"No!" I told them. "No! No!"

At intervals during the day small Servitors staggered in under the weight of my
meals. In between their visits I had only my thoughts to occupy me, and they
were not good company.

"Frankly," one of the doctors had put it to me, not unsympathetically, "we
can see no alternative. For years after it happened the annual figures of mental breakdowns were our greatest worry. Even though the women then could
keep themselves fully occupied with the tremendous amount of work that had
to be done, so many of them could not adjust. And we can't even offer you
work."

I knew that it was a fair warning she was giving me—and I knew that, unless
the hallucination which seemed to grow more real all the time could soon be
induced to dissolve, I was trapped.

During the long day and the following night I tried my hardest to get back
to the objectivity I had managed earlier, but I failed. The whole dialectic was
too strong for me now; my senses too consciously aware of my surroundings; the
air of consequence and coherence too convincingly persistent. . . .

When they had let me have twenty-four hours to think it over, the same trio
visited me again.

"I think," I told them, "that I understand better now. What you are offering
me is painless oblivion, in place of a breakdown followed by oblivion—and you
see no other choice."

"We don't," admitted the spokeswoman, and the other two nodded. "But, of course, for the hypnosis we shall need your co-operation."

"I realize that," I told her, "and I also see now that in the circumstances it would be obstinately futile to withhold it. So I—I—yes, I'm willing to give it—but on one condition."

They looked at me questioningly.

"It is this," I explained, "that you will try one other course first. I want you to give me an injection of chuinjuatin. I want it in precisely the same strength as I had it before—I can tell you the dose.

"You see, whether this is an intense hallucination, or whether it is some kind of projection which makes it seem very similar, it must have something to do with that drug. I'm sure it must—nothing remotely like this has ever happened to me before. So, I thought that if I could repeat the condition—or, would you say, believe myself to be repeating the condition?—there may be just a chance . . . I don't know. It may be simply silly . . . but even if nothing comes of it, it can't make things worse in any way now, can it? So, if you will let me try it . . . ?"

The three of them considered for some moments.

"I can see no reason why not . . ." said one.

The spokeswoman nodded.

"I shouldn't think there'll be any difficulty with authorization in the circumstances," she agreed. "If you want to try, well, it's fair to let you, but—I'd not count on it too much. . . ."

In the afternoon half a dozen small servitors arrived, bustling around, making me and the room ready, with anxious industry. Presently there came one more, scarcely tall enough to see over the trolley of bottles, trays, and phials which she pushed to my bedside.

The three doctors entered together. One of the little Servitors began rolling up my sleeve. The doctor who had done most of the talking looked at me, kindly, but seriously.

"This is a sheer gamble, you know that?" she said.

"I know. But it's my only chance. I'm willing to take it."

She nodded, picked up the syringe, and charged it while the little servitor swabbed my monstrous arm. She approached the bedside, and hesitated.

"Go on," I told her. "What is there for me here, anyway?"

She nodded, and pressed in the needle. . . .

Now, I have written the foregoing for a purpose. I shall deposit it with my bank, where it will remain unread unless it should be needed.

I have spoken of it to no one. The report on the effect of chuinjuatin—the one that I made to Dr. Hellyer where I described my sensation as simply one of floating in space—was false. The foregoing was my true experience.

I concealed it because after I came around, when I found that I was back in my own body in my normal world, the experience haunted me as vividly as if it had been actuality. The details were too sharp, too vivid, for me to get them out of my mind. It overhung me all the time, like a threat. It would not leave me alone. . . .

I did not dare to tell Dr. Hellyer how it worried me—he would have put me under treatment. If my other friends did not take it seriously enough to recommend treatment, too, then they would have laughed over it, and amused themselves at my expense interpreting the symbolism. So I kept it to myself.

As I went over parts of it again and again in detail, I grew angry with myself for not asking the old lady for more facts, things like dates, and details that could be verified. If, for instance, the thing should, by her account, have started two or three years ago, then the whole sense of threat would fall to pieces: it would all be discredited. But it had not occurred to me to ask that crucial question. . . . And then, as I went on thinking about it, I remembered that there was one, just one, piece of information that I could check, and I made inquiries. I wish now that I had not, but I felt forced to. . . .

So I have discovered that:

There *is* a Dr. Perrigan, he *is* a biologist, he does work with rabbits and rats. . . .

He is quite well known in his field. He has published papers on pest-control in a number of journals. It is no secret that he is evolving new strains of myxomatosis to attack rats; indeed, he has already developed a group of them and calls them mucosimorbus, though he has not yet succeeded in making them either stable or selective enough for general use. . . .

But I had never heard of this man or his work until his name was mentioned by the old lady in my 'hallucination.' . . .

I have given a great deal of thought to this whole matter. What sort of experience is it that I have recorded above? If it should be a kind of pre-vision of an inevitable, predestined future, then nothing anyone could do would change it. But this does not seem to me to make sense: it is what has happened, and is happening now, that determines the future. Therefore, there must be a great number of *possible* futures, each a possible consequence of what is being done now. It seems to me that under chuinjuatin I saw *one* of those futures. . . .

It was, I think, a warning of what *may* happen—unless it is prevented. . . .

The whole idea is so repulsive and misconceived, it amounts to such a monstrous aberration of the normal course, that failure to heed the warning would be neglect of duty to one's kind.

I shall, therefore, on my own responsibility and without taking any other person into my confidence, do my best to ensure that such a state as I have described *cannot* come about.

Should it happen that any other person is unjustly accused of doing, or of assisting me to do, what I intend to do, this document must stand in his defence. That is why I have written it.

It is my own unaided decision that Dr. Perrigan must not be permitted to continue his work.

(Signed) JANE WATERLEIGH.

The solicitor stared at the signature for some moments; then he nodded.

"And so," he said, "she then took her car and drove over to Perrigan's—with this tragic result.

"From the little I do know of her, I'd say that she probably did her best to persuade him to give up his work—though she can scarcely have expected any success with that. It is difficult to imagine a man who would be willing to give up the work of years on account of what must sound to him like a sort of gypsy's warning. So, clearly, she went prepared to fall back on direct action, if necessary. It looks as if the police are quite right when they suppose her to have shot him deliberately; but not so right when they suppose that she burnt the place down to hide evidence of the crime. The statement makes it pretty obvious that her main intention in doing that was to wipe out Perrigan's work."

He shook his head. "Poor girl! There's a clear conviction of duty in her last page or two: the sort of simplified clarity that drives martyrs on, regardless of consequences. She has never denied that she did it. What she wouldn't tell the police is *why* she did it."

He paused again, before he added: "Anyway, thank goodness for this document. It ought at least to save her life. I should be very surprised indeed if a plea of insanity could fail, backed up by this." He tapped the pile of manuscript with his finger. "It's a lucky thing she put off her intention of taking it to her bank."

Dr. Hellyer's face was lined and worried.

"I blame myself most bitterly for the whole thing," he said. "I never ought to have let her try the damned drug in the first place, but I thought she was over the shock of her husband's death. She was trying to keep her time fully occupied, and she was anxious to volunteer. You've met her enough to know how purposeful she can be. She saw it as a chance to contribute something to medical knowledge—which it was, of course. But I ought to have been more careful, and I ought to have seen afterwards that there was something wrong. The real responsibility for this thing runs right back to me."

"H'm," said the solicitor. "Putting that forward as a main line of defence isn't going to do you a lot of good professionally, you know, Hellyer."

"Possibly not. I can look after that when we come to it. The point is that I hold a responsibility for her as a member of my staff, if for no other reason. It can't be denied that, if I had refused her offer to take part in the experiment, this would not have happened. Therefore it seems to me that we ought to be able to argue a state of temporary insanity; that the balance of her mind was disturbed by the effects of the drug which I administered. And if we can get that as a verdict it will result in detention at a mental hospital for observation and treatment—perhaps quite a short spell of treatment."

"I can't say. We can certainly put it up to counsel and see what he thinks of it."

"It's valid, too," Hellyer persisted. "People like Jane don't do murder if they are in their right minds, not unless they're really in a corner, then they do it more cleverly. Certainly they don't murder perfect strangers. Clearly, the drug caused an hallucination sufficiently vivid to confuse her to a point where she was unable to make a proper distinction between the actual and the hypothetical. She got into a state where she believed the mirage was real, and acted accordingly."

"Yes. Yes, I suppose one might put it that way," agreed the solicitor. He looked down again at the pile of paper before him. "The whole account is, of course, unreasonable," he said, "and yet it is pervaded throughout with such an air of reasonableness. I wonder . . ." He paused pensively, and went on: "This expendability of the male, Hellyer. She doesn't seem to find it so much incredible, as undesirable. That seems odd in itself to a layman who takes the natural order for granted, but would you, as a medical scientist, say it was—well, not impossible, in theory?"

Dr. Hellyer frowned.

"That's very much the kind of question one wants more notice of. It would be very rash to proclaim it *impossible*. Considering it purely as an abstract problem, I can see two or three lines of approach. . . . Of course, if an utterly improbable situation were to arise calling for intensive research—research, that is, on the sort of scale they tackled the atom—well, who can tell . . . ?" He shrugged.

The solicitor nodded again.

"That's just what I was getting at," he observed. "Basically it is only just such a little way off the beam; quite near enough to possibility to be faintly disturbing. Mind you, as far as the defense is concerned, her air of thorough conviction, taken in conjunction with the near-plausibility of the thing, will probably help. But as far as I am concerned it is just that nearness that is enough to make me a trifle uneasy."

The doctor looked at him rather sharply.

"Oh, come! Really now! A hard-boiled solicitor, too! Don't tell me you're going in for fantasy-building. Anyway, if you are, you'll have to conjure up another one. If Jane, poor girl, has settled one thing, it is that there's no future in this particular fantasy. Perrigan's finished with, and all his work's gone up in smoke."

"H'm," said the solicitor again. "All the same, it would be more satisfactory if we knew of some way other than this"—he tapped the pile of papers—"some other way in which she is likely to have acquired a knowledge of Perrigan and his work. There is, as far as one knows, *no* other way in which he can have come into her orbit at all—unless, perhaps, she takes an interest in veterinary subjects?"

"She doesn't. I'm sure of that," Hellyer told him, shaking his head.

"Well, that, then, remains one slightly disturbing aspect. And there is another. You'll think it foolish of me, I'm sure—and no doubt time will prove you right to do so—but I have to admit I'd be feeling easier in my mind if Jane had been just a bit more thorough in her inquiries before she went into action."

"Meaning—?" asked Dr. Hellyer, looking puzzled.

"Only that she does not seem to have found out that there is a son. But there is, you see. He appears to have taken quite a close interest in his father's work, and is determined that it shan't be wasted. In fact he has already announced that he will do his best to carry it on with the very few specimens that were saved from the fire. . . .

"Laudably filial, no doubt. All the same it does disturb me a little to find that he, also, happens to be D.Sc., a biochemist; and that, very naturally, his name, too, is Perrigan. . . ."

Eddy C. Bertin

Eddy C. Bertin (1944–   ) lives in Flanders and is a leading Belgian SF and horror writer. He has published over 500 stories, over fifty in English, some Lovecraftian horror, some science fiction. He started writing at age thirteen, in Dutch, and published twenty-five books for adults between 1970 and 1986 in the Netherlands; he then switched to writing for children and young adults, and has published sixteen more books since 1986. He has in the past published poetry, translations, and 140 issues of his own *SF Guide* over eighteen years. He has written an SF future history trilogy that has not been published in English.

Most European countries have at least a few long-time science fiction writers, who have been producing fiction for decades. They are not always highly regarded internationally, but they have kept the international SF movement alive for its own sake for decades, in spite of the waves of literary fashion. Often they travel to meet other SF people at their own expense in other countries, and publish small press magazines to keep their own culture informed. Bertin is a distinguished representative of these men from the 1960s and the present. This story is a small jewel of a mood piece.

SOMETHING ENDING

You don't exist," was the first thing the ugly little fat man said to me as I entered the pub. He was seated on a barstool which was much too tall for someone his size, and his short stubby legs in their wrinkled trousers dangled freely without even touching the floor. He could hardly be called an attractive specimen of homo sapiens. His face looked like a sponge, with flabby cheeks and slobbering thin lips. His deep-sunken eyes were blurred by the amount of strong drinks he had had, and in these he showed an amazing appetite for variations, as indicated by the outstanding series of different empty glasses in front of him, and which he refused to let be taken away. The barman was eyeing him with open hostility and annoyance.

He looked me over once more, nodded, satisfied at his own reflection in the mirror, and repeated with more intonation: "No, you really don't exist." Satisfied with the approval of his mirror-image, he ordered another drink. There was no other place vacant, so I took the stool beside him, and since he made no gesture of buying me a drink, I ordered my own.

"You seem very certain of that," I said. Not that I cared very much what any fat drunk muttered to me, but I hate just sitting and drinking. I had been obliged to spent the evening in town, with no friends I cared to see, and no movie worth going to, either. In fact I had been preparing myself for a quiet evening at home with a good novel or maybe a rock-show on the tube, and a couple of good

Napoleon brandies, when Vodier had called me on the phone, asking if I were at home that evening. This had immediately resulted in my stating that I had to rush off to an urgent press-conference in a couple of minutes, and wouldn't be home till the next day. Vodier was a nice chap, but he had the irritating habit of hanging around till the early hours of the next morning, and his conversational habits were limited to one single subject: himself. Since I knew Vodier was liable to drive over anyway, just in the vague hope that my conference had been cancelled at the last instant, there was only one thing to do: get out as fast as possible. Which I had done.

Maybe this weirdo would bring some amusement in an otherwise dreary evening, and since there seemed to be no free female companionship available in this pub, I might as well make the best of it. Ghent is a nice city to live in, but it hasn't much to offer as nightlife, compared to Brussels or Antwerp, and I didn't feel like driving another couple of miles to find another more interesting café.

The stranger shook his head pityingly, murmuring: "Poor, poor chap, so utterly convinced that he really exists, that he has real life, and what is he in fact? Phut. Nothing. Zero. A hole. A vacuum."

"Can't say I ever thought about myself that way," I said grinning. "Maybe my reasoning is a bit confused, but I feel my hands here, flesh and bone, and here a head on top of my body. *Cogito ergo sum*, I think therefore I am. More, I FEEL that I am. Seems quite logical to me."

"Bloody nonsense," he said angrily. "You only BELIEVE that you exist; there's quite a difference between believing and being. You have no real proof of your existence. You're just a dummy; you may as well believe me. Knowing the truth about oneself always makes one happier, or so I've been told."

I laughed. The funny chap had his voice remarkably under control, but he clearly was completely stoned. You don't meet them often that way and still able to talk.

"All right, I don't exist," I grinned. "So what next? What makes you so goddamn sure anyway? If I don't exist, then why are you speaking to me?"

He looked me over with what surely must be the special look he reserved for people asking insane questions. "I am speaking to you because I want to," he said. "Because nothing exists except me and what I want. You are here because of me, you exist because I want you to exist here and now. I would have thought that was very simple to see, don't you? Oh, go to hell! One can't talk with someone of your kind. You understand nothing, accept nothing, bah."

He rose and dropped himself from his high seat of judgment. He threw some money at the barman and walked away, without saying as much as good night.

I concentrated on my drink and had two more, still thinking with amusement of the words of the funny madman. Then I drove home, got out and walked straight in the arms of a grinning Vodier, who had brought a crate of beer with him and kept me up till four o'clock in the morning.

The second time I ran into the funny-talking fat stranger was at quite a different place, at a charity ball of all things. It was one of those dry and hot evenings, which reassures you in advance that it will be raining like hell before the evening is done. The heat was unbearable in the dancing hall, and the fridge of the bar had chosen that exact evening to break down, so they had no ice cubes for the warm drinks. I decided to get a breath of fresh air on the terrace. And just guess who was standing there, his small hands on his back, staring up at the night stars? Yes, you got it right the first time. Mister You-don't-exist himself.

He looked over his shoulder as he heard my footsteps approaching and smiled amicably. He seemed sober this time.

"Hello, Mister Dummy," he said as a manner of greeting. "Made your mind up yet about whether or not you exist?"

"One day or other you're gonna get punched in the mouth if you speak to anyone like that," I said. For a moment I considered whether I should turn around and just walk away. After all he was no more than a bizarre but harmless weirdo. Still something about the fat little man intrigued me, and I decided to stay around for a couple of minutes. But he had already turned away from me and contemplated the night sky. He spoke again, this time more to himself, as if it were totally unimportant whether I listened or not.

"Nice shining stars up there," he said. "Specially the great sparkling one over there. You know, if I could stand up high enough and stretch my arms, I could just pick them right out of the sky. That specific star as well as all the other fake ones. It might convince you that I'm not crazy. And maybe then I would find out what's on the other side of that sky."

I shrugged. "Then why don't you just do that?"

He grinned. "It doesn't work," he said. "I tried it a couple of times, but they're faster than me. As soon as I stand on my toes, they just raise the sky a bit higher, out of my reach."

"So?" I asked. "First I don't exist. Now the sky is a curtain where you can pick the fake stars from. You do hold some pretty cranky ideas."

"Cranky?" He seemed shocked. "Wasn't it Shakespeare who said that the world's a stage? Or was that someone else? Not that it matters that much who said it, he or she surely had some idea about the truth of existence. But why am I bothering with you? One can't talk sense into an empty head. You're nothing, go away, shoo!"

"So, I am nothing. Well, just feel this hand. Feel the flesh, the muscles, the bones. That seems real enough to me. And you do hear me, don't you? So I can speak, too."

He smiled, all sympathy. "You got me all wrong, Mister. I am not talking about your material body. Of course that exists, just as this terrace and these stars exist for the time being. A window dummy exists, which doesn't means that he IS. The ego, the mind, the 'I' which you call 'me,' that doesn't exist. The material body you have, the streets over there, they are for real, too, but only temporary. They're make-believes, stage settings, just as the whole neighborhood. As soon as I'll be gone, they and you will stop existing. It's all here, because I am here. There must be air for me to breathe, there must be a terrace since I can't be standing here floating in empty air, and since I feel like talking to someone, you are here. If I decided to go to China now, this Europe would cease to exist the moment I left it. It would no longer be needed, since I would have left it."

This was just too much, and my laughing exploded in his face. It wasn't very polite, I admit, and it even might have been dangerous. You never know with a crazy; he didn't look aggressive, but you never know. But then, I was bigger than he, and I was certain that I could handle him if he tried to attack me. But he didn't.

"That's a good one," I said after I had stopped laughing. "Well, let me tell you that I know very well what I've been doing those last weeks, and I don't recall you being with me then or being in the neighborhood where I was."

"Artificial memories," he shrugged. "They're very good at them. They just put them inside your head so that you would be able to play your part as true-to-life as possible."

"They did, huh? And the rest of the world, all those other countries? I suppose they don't exist now since you aren't there?"

"Quite right," he said as if stating an indisputable fact. "They're just illusions, make-believes created to convince me that the world does exist. Tell me, were you ever really there? In China or Australia, in India or in Hungary?"

"Well no," I said. "I haven't been there. I wouldn't know why I should go there. But there are photographs, films, libraries . . ."

"Nonsense, it's all fake. You know only that small part of the world or even of this country in which you are, here and now. All the rest you know only by hearsay. I tell you, there is no world, no other countries, not even a real sky. It's just a stage curtain. Humanity, as such, is a dream. The only reality is my own being, and the stage they erect wherever I go. And of course all the dummies like yourself who only come into existence whenever I am near. People like you, and taxi drivers, and barkeepers, and cops, and traveling salesmen and house-wives . . . people . . ."

I gasped at him. He couldn't mean that, could he? If he did . . . well, I had met quite some weirdos in my life, but this one was really too much. He was ready for the men in the white suits to come and drag him away.

"The truth hurts, doesn't it?" he asked innocently. "But don't worry about it, Mister. After a while, you'll get used to being a third-rate character in the play I'm performing."

With these words, he turned and disappeared into the crowd inside.

During the following months, somehow or other, my thoughts often returned to the crazy little fellow. Strange how some crazies manage to sound too utterly convincing and logical, even while they're talking absolute nonsense. Like when he spoke of those other faraway countries which only existed on films and pho-tographs or just because others tell us they do exist. But, then, in the little man's mind, all those others were no more than animated showroom dummies them-selves, so it hardly mattered. Must be quite a frightening stage in his own mind, I thought, a world-wide theater in which performs one fat little ugly performer.

History tends to repeat itself, as they say, and so does this story, because when I met the stranger the third time, he was stone-drunk again. It was in another bar this time, one which had chairs small enough for him to sit on with his feet on the ground, which was as well, since I doubt if he would have managed his balance otherwise. I sat down in front of him, his eyes seemed more hidden below the ridges of fat than before, and he had to look three times before recognizing me.

"Oh, yes, it's you again," he said. "My own Mister Nothing. They must think quite a lot of your character for giving you three stage acts. Have a drink with me, since you're here anyway."

He seemed preoccupied and moody. We had a drink and then another one, but he didn't brighten. He did talk, however.

"I'm scared," he said in an appropriate stage whisper. "You see, I've started doubting my own existence. Suppose, just suppose that I, too, don't really exist?

What if I am no more than one of the dummies, a walking-talking-singing-drinking doll with a set of false memories? What sense would the world have then if it wasn't made for me? What if it is made and kept in existence for someone else? I couldn't bear that thought. If I was sure, I would have to hunt and kill that man or woman. But who knows? Maybe I would then cease to exist completely, as well as the rest of the world."

"That would be some problem indeed," I agreed.

"And it's not that fantastic at all," he continued. "I know, I have always known that I exist. But how can I prove it to myself? There is only one way to go about it: catch them! CATCH THEM AT IT! But how? I've tried everything possible so far. I went somewhere and suddenly changed direction. I bought a ticket to Africa and to London. But they're so fast, by the time the plane got there, they had built Africa and peopled it, complete with animals and tourists, just like in the traveler's catalogues. And when I got to London, they had already gotten it ready, except for part of the Tower, but they had their explanation ready: the Tower was being repaired just then. Everything turns out to be exactly as in the movies and pictures. They're good all right! It's almost as if they know in advance what I intend to do, or else they're just too damned fast and good at stage-building. They're smart, and they know I'm trying to catch them."

"THEY," I said. "You're always rambling about THEM. Who or what are THEY?"

"Isn't that clear yet? The builders, the owners of the stage, of course. They who hide themselves behind the sky-curtain, they who have built this world-theater and put me here in their play. You see, I think this is something like those intelligence tests they're always supposed to be doing with rats and mice and guinea pigs. They put them in a maze, and the food is at the other end of the maze. The guinea pig has to find its way through the corridors of the maze or it'll starve to death. Since the guinea pig has no gun to burn itself a straight way through the maze, it has to search, but at regular intervals they change the corridors of the maze, so the guinea pig has to adapt all the time in order to get to the food and survive. See, that's what I think I am. A rat in a maze, and they control the corridors. But I am more than a rat, I know they're THERE, and I intend to find out about them. I'm gonna burn myself through that maze in a straight line!"

"But why . . . would THEY go to all that trouble?"

"I don't know, but I have several ideas," he whispered. "Maybe all of this is just THAT: an experiment with a lower animal. A kind of reaction test. Maybe they just want to know how I'll work it all out, how fast I react to stimulations. And maybe . . . they're afraid of me. It isn't that silly, there must be a very logical reason for my being that all-important to them, to go to all that work and trouble. Maybe this is some kind of prison they've put me in, and they've taken some memories out of my mind, so I can't remember who I am or why I'm here. Maybe it's some kind of mental symbiosis: maybe they only exist because I exist, and MY being is their only reason for being. Maybe I'm a psychotic god, a lonely god, who has built a neurotic wall around himself and is now trying to get sane again. Maybe I even created THEM myself, so they could put me in their own play! As a snake eating its own tail. Maybe I am the one and only center of the universe, and therefore they—as my creations—are afraid of me."

He took a sip of his drink, and wiped his mouth with his sleeve. The drink was getting to him, his speech was becoming less clear every minute.

"But it'll be over soon now," he whispered. "I'm not that stupid, you see. I said I would burn my way through at them in a straight line, and that's what I'm gonna do. I've found the way to get them, the bastards!"

He ordered new drinks and bent lower so that I had trouble understanding his words. "I'm going to them damn stars," he whispered. "Sounds like nut talk, doesn't it? I don't look like a scientist or a spaceman, but I'm going anyway. Right through those fake stars, and then let them try to make a universe for me. I've been thinking about it for some time. I can't make a spaceship, but if I'm that important, then there must be other ways for me to get out of their maze. I've built a ship. Well, no, not exactly what you could call a spaceship. It's no more than just a hollow sphere with a chair in it. I can seal it airtight from the inside, and I'm taking oxygen tanks, food and drink. Probably I won't even need any of that, if the powers I've tapped inside my mind work out as I intend them to. Because I'm going to do it with my mind and nothing else."

He patted his head, grinning. "Yeah, ol' man, inside my head, there it is. Inside my brain, all the power I need to get at them. I've been reading up on such things as telekinesis, the transportation of matter by mental powers. Enough to lift the sphere and myself up to that damn sky, and burn through it. If there is only one really existing mind, which is mine, then that mind must possess those powers. I'm getting out of here tonight. You're the only one who knows now, and you're just another dummy, after all. Now once I'm through their sky-curtain let them try to keep up the illusion. Let them try to create real space, real stars, out there!"

"It's crazy." I said. "You need a real spaceship for that, engines, computers, technicians. It's an absurd idea!"

"Course it is," he agreed. "That's why it's genius. They'll never think of it before I get there and see for myself! You don't think I'm doing this without some preparations, do you? I've been testing my mental powers for weeks now, lifting tables, opening doors without touching them. Then other things, more heavy. Then giving them speed, always more speed! Oh, yes, I'm certain it'll work as I planned it. I just . . . FEEL it. I set my starting date for next month, so of course I'll be taking off tonight! I'll catch them all right when they're totally unprepared for me. But I thought I'd have a couple of drinks first, to test my courage. It may turn out to be a long trip if they try to create the universe when I'm coming, and I'm pretty sure they'll try. Even if I manage to drive my speed up towards the speed of light, it's still more than five light-years to the closest star, Alpha Centauri. But I may encounter them sooner than that."

When I left him, he was still drinking and muttering to himself how he'd finally get them, the bastards.

About eleven o'clock, I saw his sphere rising from the center of the city where I knew he lived. It was just a small, dark ball, which rose hesitatingly above the buildings, but then suddenly picked up speed, floating faster and faster towards the skies. It looked like a toy balloon, getting smaller and smaller, but it moved in one straight line up. He was going to burn his way through all right, just as he had said he would. He had left earlier than he had said, but I had expected that, too.

I waited till he had left the atmosphere, calculating the orbit he would follow to get away from earth and then the trajectory he would be following in the years to come, beyond the outer planets and into the void beyond, towards Alpha Centauri. I had already set the apparatus, and the projections of the outer planets and the stars would pass off satisfactorily on his eyes. There would be no errors. I still had time enough to catch up with him before he reached his destination. After all, I would have to be on the meeting committee.

"Boy, do your best," I thought. "You've wasted thirty-seven years down here: you should already be in the second-stage for a long time. Why doesn't your mind work faster, better?"

It wasn't my fault, nor my symbiont-wife's; our genes matched perfectly. Our getting a retarded child was just one of those things, it happens sometimes.

But now he HAD to succeed. He had left the nursery now, and was speeding towards the kindergarten. By then he would have figured it all out, he would have to! If he didn't he would be considered a total failure. I would be allowed no more children, and he . . . he would be erased from existence. The committee didn't lose its time with the unfit for the universe. They will be waiting for him, when he gets there, at Alpha Centauri, and I will be among them, unable to help him. He'll have to make it on his own, my son. And, though retarded, he hasn't been doing too badly after all. It was fortunate that they had at least let me work on the nursery years.

He has made a few errors and misjudgments, of course. What infant doesn't? He had drawn the wrong conclusion also when he had said that the world doesn't exist. When I do something, I do it well. There IS a real world. Now I'm beginning to tear it down.

Roger Zelazny

Roger Zelazny (1937–95) was among the leading SF writers to emerge in the 1960s. His body of work in that decade was enormously influential, particularly his twelve novellas, of which this is one. With the way paved by the impact of his early stories, his first novel, *This Immortal* (1966) shared the Hugo Award with Frank Herbert's *Dune*. Zelazny became one of the most popular and respected writers of that decade, with five more novels and a collection of novellas by 1970.

At the beginning of the 1970s he launched what was to become his most popular series of books with *Nine Princes in Amber* (1970). With the enormous popularity and financial success of the Amber books, Zelazny lost interest in experimentation with the novel form and limited his most intense aesthetic efforts to occasional short stories and novellas for most of the following twenty-five years. Novels such as *Doorways in the Sand* (1976), *Eye of Cat* (1982), and *A Night in the Lonesome October* (1993) stand out as exceptions. This novella, one of the works upon which his initial fame rests, is a powerful fusion of technology, psychology, and myths of godlike power.

HE WHO SHAPES

I

Lovely as it was, with the blood and all, Render could sense that it was about to end.

Therefore, each microsecond would be better off as a minute, he decided— and perhaps the temperature should be increased . . . Somewhere, just at the periphery of everything, the darkness halted its constriction.

Something, like a crescendo of subliminal thunders, was arrested at one raging note. That note was a distillate of shame and pain and fear.

The Forum was stifling.

Caesar cowered outside the frantic circle. His forearm covered his eyes but it could not stop the seeing, not this time.

The senators had no faces and their garments were spattered with blood. All their voices were like the cries of birds. With an inhuman frenzy they plunged their daggers into the fallen figure.

All, that is, but Render.

The pool of blood in which he stood continued to widen. His arm seemed to be rising and falling with a mechanical regularity and his throat might have been shaping birdcries, but he was simultaneously apart from and a part of the scene.

For he was Render, the Shaper.

Crouched, anguished and envious, Caesar wailed his protests.

"You have slain him! You have murdered Marcus Antonius—a blameless, useless fellow!"

Render turned to him and the dagger in his hand was quite enormous and quite gory.

"Aye," said he.

The blade moved from side to side. Caesar, fascinated by the sharpened steel, swayed to the same rhythm.

"Why?" he cried. "Why?"

"Because," answered Render, "he was a far nobler Roman than yourself."

"You lie! It is not so!"

Render shrugged and returned to the stabbing.

"It is not true!" screamed Caesar. "Not true!"

Render turned to him again and waved the dagger. Puppetlike, Caesar mimicked the pendulum of the blade.

"Not true?" smiled Render. "And who are you to question an assassination such as this? You are no one! You detract from the dignity of this occasion! Begone!"

Jerkily, the pink-faced man rose to his feet, his hair half-wispy, half-wetplastered, a disarray of cotton. He turned, moved away; and as he walked, he looked back over his shoulder.

He had moved far from the circle of assassins, but the scene did not diminish in size. It retained an electric clarity. It made him feel even further removed, ever more alone and apart.

Render rounded a previously unnoticed corner and stood before him, a blind beggar.

Caesar grasped the front of his garment.

"Have you an ill omen for me this day?"

"Beware!" jeered Render.

"Yes! Yes!" cried Caesar. " 'Beware!' That is good! Beware what?"

"The ides—"

"Yes? The ides—?"

"—of Octember."

He released the garment.

"What is that you say? What is October?"

"A month."

"You lie! There is no month of Octember!"

"And that is the date noble Caesar need fear—the non-existent time, the never-to-be-calendared occasion."

Render vanished around another sudden corner.

"Wait! Come back!"

Render laughed, and the Forum laughed with him. The birdcries became a chorus of inhuman jeers.

"You mock me!" wept Caesar.

The Forum was an oven, and the perspiration formed like a glassy mask over Caesar's narrow forehead, sharp nose and chinless jaw.

"I want to be assassinated too!" he sobbed. "It isn't fair!"

And Render tore the Forum and the senators and the grinning corpse of Antony to pieces and stuffed them into a black sack—with the unseen movement of a single finger—and last of all went Caesar.

•   •   •

Charles Render sat before the ninety white buttons and the two red ones, not really looking at any of them. His right arm moved, in its soundless sling, across the lap-level surface of the console—pushing some of the buttons, skipping over others, moving on, retracing its path to press the next in the order of the Recall Series.

Sensations throttled, emotions reduced to nothing, Representative Erikson knew the oblivion of the womb.

There was a soft click.

Render's hand had glided to the end of the bottom row of buttons. An act of conscious intent—will, if you like—was required to push the red button.

Render freed his arm and lifted off his crown of Medusa-hair leads and microminiature circuitry. He slid from behind his desk-couch and raised the hood. He walked to the window and transpared it, fingering forth a cigarette.

One minute in the ro-womb, he decided. *No more. This is a crucial one . . . Hope it doesn't snow till later—those clouds look mean. . . .*

It was smooth yellow trellises and high towers, glassy and gray, all smouldering into evening under a shale-colored sky; the city was squared volcanic islands, glowing in the end-of-day light, rumbling deep down under the earth; it was fat, incessant rivers of traffic, rushing.

Render turned away from the window and approached the great egg that lay beside his desk, smooth and glittering. It threw back a reflection that smashed all aquilinity from his nose, turned his eyes to gray saucers, transformed his hair into a light-streaked skyline; his reddish necktie became the wide tongue of a ghoul.

He smiled, reached across the desk. He pressed the second red button.

With a sigh, the egg lost its dazzling opacity and a horizontal crack appeared about its middle. Through the now-transparent shell, Render could see Erikson grimacing, squeezing his eyes tight, fighting against a return to consciousness and the thing it would contain. The upper half of the egg rose vertical to the base, exposing him knobby and pink on half-shell. When his eyes opened he did not look at Render. He rose to his feet and began dressing. Render used this time to check the ro-womb.

He leaned back across his desk and pressed the buttons: temperature control, full range, *check*; exotic sounds—he raised the earphone—*check*, on bells, on buzzes, on violin notes and whistles, on squeals and moans, on traffic noises and the sound of surf; *check*, on the feedback circuit—holding the patient's own voice, trapped earlier in analysis; *check*, on the sound blanket, the moisture spray, the odor banks; *check*, on the couch agitator and the colored lights, the taste stimulants . . .

Render closed the egg and shut off its power. He pushed the unit into the closet, palmed shut the door. The tapes had registered a valid sequence.

"Sit down," he directed Erikson.

The man did so, fidgeting with his collar.

"You have full recall," said Render, "so there is no need for me to summarize what occurred. Nothing can be hidden from me. I was there."

Erikson nodded.

"The significance of the episode should be apparent to you."

Erikson nodded again, finally finding his voice. "But was it valid?" he asked. "I mean, you constructed the dream and you controlled it, all the way. I didn't really *dream* it—in the way I would normally dream. Your ability to make things happen stacks the deck for whatever you're going to say—doesn't it?"

Render shook his head slowly, flicked an ash into the southern hemisphere of his globe-made-ashtray, and met Erikson's eyes.

"It is true that I supplied the format and modified the forms. You, however, filled them with an emotional significance, promoted them to the status of symbols corresponding to your problem. If the dream was not a valid analogue it would not have provoked the reactions it did. It would have been devoid of the anxiety-patterns which were registered on the tapes.

"You have been in analysis for many months now," he continued, "and everything I have learned thus far serves to convince me that your fears of assassination are without any basis in fact."

Erikson glared.

"Then why the hell do I have them?"

"Because," said Render, "you would like very much to be the subject of an assassination."

Erikson smiled then, his composure beginning to return.

"I assure you, doctor, I have never contemplated suicide, nor have I any desire to stop living."

He produced a cigar and applied a flame to it. His hand shook.

"When you came to me this summer," said Render, "you stated that you were in fear of an attempt on your life. You were quite vague as to why anyone should want to kill you—"

"My position! You can't be a Representative as long as I have and make no enemies!"

"Yet," replied Render, "it appears that you have managed it. When you permitted me to discuss this with your detectives I was informed that they could unearth nothing to indicate that your fears might have any real foundation. Nothing."

"They haven't looked far enough—or in the right places. They'll turn up something."

"I'm afraid not."

"Why?"

"Because, I repeat, your feelings are without any objective basis.—Be honest with me. Have you any information whatsoever indicating that someone hates you enough to want to kill you?"

"I receive many threatening letters . . ."

"As do all Representatives—and all of those directed to you during the past year have been investigated and found to be the work of cranks. Can you offer me *one* piece of evidence to substantiate your claims?"

Erikson studied the tip of his cigar.

"I came to you on the advice of a colleague," he said, "came to you to have you poke around inside my mind to find me something of that sort, to give my detectives something to work with.—Someone I've injured severely perhaps—or some damaging piece of legislation I've dealt with. . . ."

"—And I found nothing," said Render, "nothing, that is, but the cause of your discontent. Now, of course, you are afraid to hear it, and you are attempting to divert me from explaining my diagnosis—"

"I am not!"

"Then listen. You can comment afterward if you want, but you've poked and dawdled around here for months, unwilling to accept what I presented to you in a dozen different forms. Now I am going to tell you outright what it is, and you can do what you want about it."

"Fine."

"First," he said, "you would like very much to have an enemy or enemies—"

"Ridiculous!"

"—Because it is the only alternative to having friends—"

"I have lots of friends!"

"—Because nobody wants to be completely ignored, to be an object for whom no one has really strong feelings. Hatred and love are the ultimate forms of human regard. Lacking one, and unable to achieve it, you sought the other. You wanted it so badly that you succeeded in convincing yourself it existed. But there is always a psychic pricetag on these things. Answering a genuine emotional need with a body of desire-surrogates does not produce real satisfaction, but anxiety, discomfort—because in these matters the psyche should be an open system. You did not seek outside yourself for human regard. You were closed off. You created that which you needed from the stuff of your own being. You are a man very much in need of strong relationships with other people."

"Manure!"

"Take it or leave it," said Render. "I suggest you take it."

"I've been paying you half a year to help find out who wants to kill me. Now you sit there and tell me I made the whole thing up to satisfy a desire to have someone hate me."

"Hate you, or love you. That's right."

"It's absurd! I meet so many people that I carry a pocket recorder and a lapel-camera, just so I can recall them all. . . ."

"Meeting quantities of people is hardly what I was speaking of.—Tell me, *did* that dream sequence have a strong meaning for you?"

Erikson was silent for several tickings of the huge wall-clock.

"Yes," he finally conceded, "it did. But your interpretation of the matter is still absurd. Granting though, just for the sake of argument, that what you say is correct—what would I do to get out of this bind?"

Render leaned back in his chair.

"Rechannel the energies that went into producing the thing. Meet some people as yourself, Joe Erikson, rather than Representative Erikson. Take up something you can do with other people—something non-political, and perhaps somewhat competitive—and make some real friends or enemies, preferably the former. I've encouraged you to do this all along."

"Then tell me something else."

"Gladly."

"Assuming you *are* right, why is it that I am neither liked nor hated, and never have been? I have a responsible position in the Legislature. I meet people all the time. Why am I so neutral a—thing?"

Highly familiar now with Erikson's career, Render had to push aside his true thoughts on the matter, as they were of no operational value. He wanted to cite him Dante's observations concerning the trimmers—those souls who, denied heaven for their lack of virtue, were also denied entrance to hell for a lack of significant vices—in short, the ones who trimmed their sails to move them with every wind of the times, who lacked direction, who were not really concerned toward which ports they were pushed. Such was Erikson's long and colorless career of migrant loyalties, of political reversals.

Render said:

"More and more people find themselves in such circumstances these days. It is due largely to the increasing complexity of society and the depersonalization of the individual into a sociometric unit. Even the act of cathecting toward other persons has grown more forced as a result. There are so many of us these days."

Erikson nodded, and Render smiled inwardly.

Sometimes the gruff line, and then the lecture . . .

"I've got the feeling you could be right," said Erikson. "Sometimes I *do* feel like what you just described—a unit, something depersonalized. . . ."

Render glanced at the clock.

"What you choose to do about it from here is, of course, your own decision to make. I think you'd be wasting your time to remain in analysis any longer. We are now both aware of the cause of your complaint. I can't take you by the hand and show you how to lead your life. I can indicate, I can commiserate—but no more deep probing. Make an appointment as soon as you feel a need to discuss your activities and relate them to my diagnosis."

"I will," nodded Erikson, "and—damn that dream! It got to me. You can make them seem as vivid as waking life—more vivid. . . . It may be a long while before I can forget it."

"I hope so."

"Okay, doctor." He rose to his feet, extended a hand. "I'll probably be back in a couple weeks. I'll give this socializing a fair try." He grinned at the word he normally frowned upon. "In fact, I'll start now. May I buy you a drink around the corner, downstairs?"

Render met the moist palm which seemed as weary of the performance as a lead actor in too successful a play. He felt almost sorry as he said, "Thank you, but I have an engagement."

Render helped him on with his coat then, handed him his hat and saw him to the door.

"Well, good night."

"Good night."

As the door closed soundlessly behind him, Render recrossed the dark Astrakhan to his mahogany fortress and flipped his cigarette into the southern hemisphere of a globe ashtray. He leaned back in his chair, hands behind his head, eyes closed.

"Of course it was more real than life," he informed no one in particular, "I shaped it."

Smiling, he reviewed the dream sequence step by step, wishing some of his former instructors could have witnessed it. It had been well-constructed and powerfully executed, as well as being precisely appropriate for the case at hand. But then, he was Render, the Shaper—one of the two hundred or so special analysts whose own psychic makeup permitted them to enter into neurotic patterns without carrying away more than an esthetic gratification from the mimesis of aberrance—a Sane Hatter.

Render stirred his recollections. He had been analyzed himself, analyzed and passed upon as a granite-willed, ultra-stable outsider—tough enough to weather the basilisk gaze of a fixation, walk unscathed amidst the chimarae of perversions, force dark Mother Medusa to close her eyes before the caduceus of his art. His own analysis had not been difficult. Nine years before (it seemed much longer) he had suffered a willing injection of novocain into the most painful area of his spirit. It was after the auto wreck, after the death of Ruth, and of Miranda, their daughter, that he had begun to feel detached. Perhaps he did not want to recover certain empathies; perhaps his own world was now based upon a certain rigidity of feeling. If this was true, he was wise enough in the ways of the mind to realize it, and perhaps he had decided that such a world had its own compensations.

His son Peter was now ten years old. He was attending a school of quality, and he penned his father a letter every week. The letters were becoming progressively literate, showing signs of a precociousness of which Render could not but approve. He would take the boy with him to Europe in the summer.

As for Jill—Jill DeVille (what a luscious, ridiculous name!—he loved her for it)—she was growing if anything, more interesting to him. (He wondered if this was an indication of early middle age.) He was vastly taken by her unmusical nasal voice, her sudden interest in architecture, her concern with the unremovable mole on the right side of her otherwise well-designed nose. He should really call her immediately and go in search of a new restaurant. For some reason though, he did not feel like it.

It had been several weeks since he had visited his club, The Partridge and Scalpel, and he felt a strong desire to eat from an oaken table, alone, in the split-level dining room with the three fireplaces, beneath the artificial torches and the boars' heads like gin ads. So he pushed his perforated membership card into the phone-slot on his desk and there were two buzzes behind the voice-screen.

"Hello, Partridge and Scalpel," said the voice. "May I help you?"

"Charles Render," he said. "I'd like a table in about half an hour."

"How many will there be?"

"Just me."

"Very good, sir. Half an hour, then.—That's 'Render'?—R-e-n-d-er-?"

"Right."

"Thank you."

He broke the connection and rose from his desk. Outside, the day had vanished.

The monoliths and the towers gave forth their own light now. A soft snow, like sugar, was sifting down through the shadows and transforming itself into beads on the windowpane.

Render shrugged into his overcoat, turned off the lights, locked the inner office. There was a note on Mrs. Hedges' blotter.

Miss DeVille called, it said.

He crumpled the note and tossed it into the waste-chute. He would call her tomorrow and say he had been working until late on his lecture.

He switched off the final light, clapped his hat onto his head and passed through the outer door, locking it as he went. The drop took him to the sub-subcellar where his auto was parked.

It was chilly in the sub-sub, and his footsteps seemed loud on the concrete as he passed among the parked vehicles. Beneath the glare of the naked lights, his S-7 Spinner was a sleek gray cocoon from which it seemed turbulent wings might at any moment emerge. The double row of antennae which fanned forward from the slope of its hood added to this feeling. Render thumbed open the door.

He touched the ignition and there was the sound of a lone bee awakening in a great hive. The door swung soundlessly shut as he raised the steering wheel and locked it into place. He spun up the spiral ramp and came to a rolling stop before the big overhead.

As the door rattled upward he lighted his destination screen and turned the knob that shifted the broadcast map.—Left to right, top to bottom, section by section he shifted it, until he located the portion of Carnegie Avenue he desired. He punched out its coordinates and lowered the wheel. The car switched over to monitor and moved out onto the highway marginal. Render lit a cigarette.

Pushing his seat back into the centerspace, he left all the windows transparent. It was pleasant to half-recline and watch the oncoming cars drift past him like swarms of fireflies. He pushed his hat back on his head and stared upward.

He could remember a time when he had loved snow, when it had reminded him of novels by Thomas Mann and music by Scandinavian composers. In his mind now, though, there was another element from which it could never be wholly dissociated. He could visualize so clearly the eddies of milk-white coldness that swirled about his old manual-steer auto, flowing into its fire-charred interior to rewhiten that which had been blackened; so clearly—as though he had walked toward it across a chalky lakebottom—it, the sunken wreck, and he, the diver—unable to open his mouth to speak, for fear of drowning; and he knew, whenever he looked upon falling snow, that somewhere skulls were whitening. But nine years had washed away much of the pain, and he also knew that the night was lovely.

He was sped along the wide, wide roads, shot across high bridges, their surfaces slick and gleaming beneath his lights, was woven through frantic cloverleafs and plunged into a tunnel whose dimly glowing walls blurred by him like a mirage. Finally, he switched the windows to opaque and closed his eyes.

He could not remember whether he had dozed for a moment or not, which meant he probably had. He felt the car slowing, and he moved the seat forward and turned on the windows again. Almost simultaneously, the cut-off buzzer sounded. He raised the steering wheel and pulled into the parking dome, stepped out onto the ramp and left the car to the parking unit, receiving his ticket from that box-headed robot which took its solemn revenge on mankind by sticking forth a cardboard tongue at everyone it served.

As always, the noises were as subdued as the lighting. The place seemed to absorb sound and convert it into warmth, to lull the tongue with aromas strong enough to be tasted, to hypnotize the ear with the vivid crackle of the triple hearths. Render was pleased to see that his favorite table, in the corner off the right of the smaller fireplace, had been held for him. He knew the menu from memory, but he studied it with zeal as he sipped a Manhattan and worked up an order to match his appetite. Shaping sessions always left him ravenously hungry.

"Doctor Render . . . ?"

"Yes?" He looked up.

"Doctor Shallot would like to speak with you," said the waiter.

"I don't know anyone named Shallot," he said. "Are you sure he doesn't want Bender? He's a surgeon from Metro who sometimes eats here. . . ."

The waiter shook his head.

"No, sir—'Render'. See here?" He extended a three-by-five card on which Render's full name was typed in capital letters. "Doctor Shallot has dined here nearly every night for the past two weeks," he explained, "and on each occasion has asked to be notified if you came in."

"Hm?" mused Render. "That's odd. Why didn't he just call me at my office?"

The waiter smiled and made a vague gesture.

"Well, tell him to come on over," he said, gulping his Manhattan, "and bring me another of these."

"Unfortunately, Doctor Shallot is blind," explained the waiter. "It would be easier if you—"

"All right, sure." Render stood up, relinquishing his favorite table with a strong premonition that he would not be returning to it that evening.

"Lead on."

They threaded their way among the diners, heading up to the next level. A familiar face said "hello" from a table set back against the wall, and Render nodded a greeting to a former seminar pupil whose name was Jurgens or Jirkans or something like that.

He moved on, into the smaller dining room wherein only two tables were occupied. No, three. There was one set in the corner at the far end of the darkened bar, partly masked by an ancient suit of armor. The waiter was heading him in that direction.

They stopped before the table and Render stared down into the darkened glasses that had tilted upward as they approached. Doctor Shallot was a woman, somewhere in the vicinity of her early thirties. Her low bronze bangs did not fully conceal the spot of silver which she wore on her forehead like a caste-mark. Render inhaled, and her head jerked slightly as the tip of his cigarette flared. She appeared to be staring straight up into his eyes. It was an uncomfortable feeling, even knowing that all she could distinguish of him was that which her minute photoelectric cell transmitted to her visual cortex over the hair-fine wire implants attached to that oscillator convertor: in short, the glow of his cigarette.

"Doctor Shallot, this is Doctor Render," the waiter was saying.

"Good evening," said Render.

"Good evening," she said. "My name is Eileen and I've wanted very badly to meet you." He thought he detected a slight quaver in her voice. "Will you join me for dinner?"

"My pleasure," he acknowledged, and the waiter drew out the chair.

Render sat down, noting that the woman across from him already had a drink. He reminded the waiter of his second Manhattan.

"Have you ordered yet?" he inquired.

"No."

". . . And two menus—" he started to say, then bit his tongue.

"Only one," she smiled.

"Make it none," he amended, and recited the menu.

They ordered. Then:

"Do you always do that?"

"What?"

"Carry menus in your head."

"Only a few," he said, "for awkward occasions. What was it you wanted to see—talk to me about?"

"You're a neuroparticipant therapist," she stated, "a Shaper."

"And you are—?"

"—a resident in psychiatry at State Psych. I have a year remaining."

"You knew Sam Riscomb then."

"Yes, he helped me get my appointment. He was my adviser."

"He was a very good friend of mine. We studied together at Menninger."
She nodded.

"I'd often heard him speak of you—that's one of the reasons I wanted to meet you. He's responsible for encouraging me to go ahead with my plans, despite my handicap."

Render stared at her. She was wearing a dark green dress which appeared to be made of velvet. About three inches to the left of the bodice was a pin which might have been gold. It displayed a red stone which the outline of a goblet was cast. Or was it really two profiles that were outlined, staring through the stone at one another? It seemed vaguely familiar to him, but he could not place it at the moment. It glittered expensively in the dim light.

Render accepted his drink from the waiter.

"I want to become a neuroparticipant therapist," she told him.

And if she had possessed vision Render would have thought she was staring at him, hoping for some response in his expression. He could not quite calculate what she wanted him to say.

"I commend your choice," he said, "and I respect your ambition." He tried to put his smile into his voice. "It is not an easy thing, of course, not all of the requirements being academic ones."

"I know," she said. "But then, I have been blind since birth and it was not an easy thing to come this far."

"Since birth?" he repeated. "I thought you might have lost your sight recently. You did your undergrad work then, and went on through med school without eyes . . . That's—rather impressive."

"Thank you," she said, "but it isn't. Not really. I heard about the first neuroparticipants—Bartclmetz and the rest—when I was a child, and I decided then that I wanted to be one. My life ever since has been governed by that desire."

"What did you do in the labs?" he inquired. "—Not being able to see a specimen, look through a microscope . . . ? Or all that reading?"

"I hired people to read my assignments to me. I taped everything. The school understood that I wanted to go into psychiatry and they permitted a special arrangement for labs. I've been guided through the dissection of cadavers by lab assistants, and I've had everything described to me. I can tell things by touch . . . and I have a memory like yours with the menu," she smiled. " 'The quality of psychoparticipation phenomena can only be gauged by the therapist himself, at that moment outside of time and space as we normally know it, when he stands in the midst of a world erected from the stuff of another man's dreams, recognizes there the non-Euclidian architecture of aberrance, and then takes his patient by the hand and tours the landscape . . . If he can lead him back to the common earth, then his judgments were sound, his actions valid.' "

"From *Why No Psychometrics in This Place*," reflected Render.

"—by Charles Render, M.D."

"Our dinner is already moving in this direction," he noted, picking up his drink as the speed-cooked meal was pushed toward them in the kitchen-buoy.

"That's one of the reasons I wanted to meet you," she continued, raising her glass as the dishes rattled before her. "I want you to help me become a Shaper."

Her shaded eyes, as vacant as a statue's, sought him again.

"Yours is a completely unique situation," he commented. "There has never been a congenitally blind neuroparticipant—for obvious reasons. I'd have to consider all the aspects of the situation before I could advise you. Let's eat now, though. I'm starved."

"All right. But my blindness does not mean that I have never seen."

He did not ask her what she meant by that, because prime ribs were standing in front of him now and there was a bottle of Chambertin at his elbow. He did pause long enough to notice though, as she raised her left hand from beneath the table, that she wore no rings.

"I wonder if it's still snowing," he commented as they drank their coffee. "It was coming down pretty hard when I pulled into the dome."

"I hope so," she said, "even though it diffuses the light and I can't 'see' anything at all through it. I like to feel it falling about me and blowing against my face."

"How do you get about?"

"My dog, Sigmund—I gave him the night off," she smiled, "—he can guide me anywhere. He's a mutie Shepherd."

"Oh?" Render grew curious. "Can he talk much?"

She nodded.

"That operation wasn't as successful on him as on some of them, though. He has a vocabulary of about four hundred words, but I think it causes him pain to speak. He's quite intelligent. You'll have to meet him sometime."

Render began speculating immediately. He had spoken with such animals at recent medical conferences, and had been startled by their combination of reasoning ability and their devotion to their handlers. Much chromosome tinkering, followed by delicate embryo-surgery, was required to give a dog a brain capacity greater than a chimpanzee's. Several followup operations were necessary to produce vocal abilities. Most such experiments ended in failure, and the dozen or so puppies a year on which they succeeded were valued in the neighborhood of a hundred thousand dollars each. He realized then, as he lit a cigarette and held the light for a moment, that the stone in Miss Shallot's medallion was a genuine ruby. He began to suspect that her admission to a medical school might, in addition to her academic record, have been based upon a sizeable endowment to the college of her choice. Perhaps he was being unfair though, he chided himself.

"Yes," he said, "we might do a paper on canine neuroses. Does he ever refer to his father as 'that son of a female Shepherd'?"

"He never met his father," she said, quite soberly. "He was raised apart from other dogs. His attitude could hardly be typical. I don't think you'll ever learn the functional psychology of the dog from a mutie."

"I imagine you're right," he dismissed it. "More coffee?"

"No, thanks."

Deciding it was time to continue the discussion, he said, "So you want to be a Shaper. . . ."

"Yes."

"I hate to be the one to destroy anybody's high ambitions," he told her. "Like poison, I hate it. Unless they have no foundation at all in reality. Then I can be ruthless. So—honestly, frankly, and in all sincerity, I do not see how it could ever be managed. Perhaps you're a fine psychiatrist—but in my opinion, it is a physical and mental impossibility for you ever to become a neuroparticipant. As for my reasons—"

"Wait," she said. "Not here, please. Humor me. I'm tired of this stuffy place— take me somewhere else to talk. I think I might be able to convince you there *is* a way."

"Why not?" he shrugged. "I have plenty of time. Sure—you call it. Where?"

"Blindspin?"

He suppressed an unwilling chuckle at the expression, but she laughed aloud.

"Fine," he said, "but I'm still thirsty."

A bottle of champagne was tallied and he signed the check despite her protests. It arrived in a colorful "Drink While You Drive" basket, and they stood then, and she was tall, but he was taller.

Blindspin.

A single name of a multitude of practices centered about the auto-driven auto. Flashing across the country in the sure hands of an invisible chauffeur, windows all opaque, night dark, sky high, tires assailing the road below like four phantom buzzsaws—and starting from scratch and ending in the same place, and never knowing where you are going or where you have been—it is possible, for a moment, to kindle some feeling of individuality in the coldest brainpan, to produce a momentary awareness of self by virtue of an apartness from all but a sense of motion. This is because movement through darkness is the ultimate abstraction of life itself—at least that's what one of the Vital Comedians said, and everybody in the place laughed.

Actually, now, the phenomenon known as blindspin first became prevalent (as might be suspected) among certain younger members of the community, when monitored highways deprived them of the means to exercise their automobiles in some of the more individualistic ways which had come to be frowned upon by the National Traffic Control Authority. Something had to be done.

It was.

The first, disastrous reaction involved the simple engineering feat of disconnecting the broadcast control unit after one had entered onto a monitored highway. This resulted in the car's vanishing from the ken of the monitor and passing back into the control of its occupants. Jealous as a deity, a monitor will not tolerate that which denies its programmed omniscience: it will thunder and lightning in the Highway Control Station nearest the point of last contact, sending winged seraphs in search of that which has slipped from sight.

Often, however, this was too late in happening, for the roads are many and well-paved. Escape from detection was, at first, relatively easy to achieve.

Other vehicles, though, necessarily behave as if a rebel has no actual existence. Its presence cannot be allowed for.

Boxed-in on a heavily traveled section of roadway, the offender is subject to immediate annihilation in the event of any overall speedup or shift in traffic pattern which involves movement through his theoretically vacant position. This, in the early days of monitor-controls, caused a rapid series of collisions. Monitoring devices later became far more sophisticated, and mechanized cutoffs reduced the collision incidence subsequent to such an action. The quality of the pulpefactions and contusions which did occur, however, remained unaltered.

The next reaction was based on a thing which had been overlooked because it was obvious. The monitors took people where they wanted to go only because people told them they wanted to go there. A person pressing a random series of coordinates, without reference to any map, would either be left with a stalled automobile and a "RECHECK YOUR COORDINATES" light, or would suddenly be whisked away in any direction. The latter possesses a certain romantic appeal in that it offers speed, unexpected sights, and free hands. Also, it is perfectly legal; and it is possible to navigate all over two continents in this manner, if one is possessed of sufficient wherewithal and gluteal stamina.

As is the case in all such matters, the practice diffused upwards through the age brackets. School teachers who only drove on Sundays fell into disrepute as selling points for used autos. Such is the way a world ends, said the entertainer.

End or no, the car designed to move on monitored highways is a mobile efficiency unit, complete with latrine, cupboard, refrigerator compartment and gaming table. It also sleeps two with ease and four with some crowding. On occasion, three can be a real crowd.

Render drove out of the dome and into the marginal aisle. He halted the car.

"Want to jab some coordinates?" he asked.

"You do it. My fingers know too many."

Render punched random buttons. The Spinner moved onto the highway. Render asked speed of the vehicle then, and it moved into the high-acceleration lane.

The Spinner's lights burnt holes in the darkness. The city backed away fast; it was a smouldering bonfire on both sides of the road, stirred by sudden gusts of wind, hidden by white swirlings, obscured by the steady fall of gray ash. Render knew his speed was only about sixty percent of what it would have been on a clear, dry night.

He did not blank the windows, but leaned back and stared out through them. Eileen "looked" ahead into what light there was. Neither of them said anything for ten or fifteen minutes.

The city shrank to sub-city as they sped on. After a time, short sections of open road began to appear.

"Tell me what it looks like outside," she said.

"Why didn't you ask me to describe your dinner, or the suit of armor beside our table?"

"Because I tasted one and felt the other. This is different."

"There is snow falling outside. Take it away and what you have left is black."

"What else?"

"There is slush on the road. When it starts to freeze, traffic will drop to a crawl unless we outrun this storm. The slush looks like an old, dark syrup, just starting to get sugary on top."

"Anything else?"

"That's it, lady."

"Is it snowing harder or less hard than when we left the club?"

"Harder, I should say."

"Would you pour me a drink?" she asked him.

"Certainly."

They turned their seats inward and Render raised the table. He fetched two glasses from the cupboard.

"Your health," said Render, after he had poured.

"Here's looking at you."

Render downed his drink. She sipped hers. He waited for her next comment.

He knew that two cannot play at the Socratic game, and he expected more questions before she said what she wanted to say.

She said: "What is the most beautiful thing you have ever seen?"

Yes, he decided, he had guessed correctly.

He replied without hesitation: "The sinking of Atlantis."

"I was serious."

"So was I."

"Would you care to elaborate?"

"I sank Atlantis," he said, "personally.

"It was about three years ago. And God! it was lovely! It was all ivory towers and golden minarets and silver balconies. There were bridges of opal, and crimson pendants, and a milk-white river flowing between lemon-colored banks. There were jade steeples, and trees as old as the world tickling the bellies of clouds, and ships in the great sea-harbor of Xanadu, as delicately constructed as musical instruments, all swaying with the tides. The twelve princes of the realm held court in the dozen-pillared Colliseum of the Zodiac, to listen to a Greek tenor saxophonist play at sunset.

"The Greek, of course, was a patient of mine—paranoiac. The etiology of the thing is rather complicated, but that's what I wandered into inside his mind. I gave him free rein for a while, and in the end I had to split Atlantis in half and sink it full fathom five. He's playing again and you've doubtless heard his sounds, if you like such sounds at all. He's good. I still see him periodically, but he is no longer the last descendent of the greatest minstrel of Atlantis. He's just a fine, late twentieth-century saxman.

"Sometimes though, as I look back on the apocalypse I worked within his vision of grandeur, I experience a fleeting sense of lost beauty—because, for a single moment, his abnormally intense feelings were my feelings, and he felt that his dream was the most beautiful thing in the world."

He refilled their glasses.

"That wasn't exactly what I meant," she said.

"I know."

"I meant something real."

"It was more real than real, I assure you."

"I don't doubt it, but . . ."

"—But I destroyed the foundation you were laying for your argument. Okay, I apologize. I'll hand it back to you. Here's something that could be real:

"We are moving along the edge of a great bowl of sand," he said. "Into it, the snow is gently drifting. In the spring the snow will melt, the waters will run down into the earth, or be evaporated away by the heat of the sun. Then only the sand will remain. Nothing grows in the sand, except for an occasional cactus. Nothing lives here but snakes, a few birds, insects, burrowing things, and a wandering coyote or two. In the afternoon these things will look for shade. Any place where there's an old fence post or a rock or a skull or a cactus to block out the sun, there you will witness life cowering before the elements. But the colors are beyond belief, and the elements are more lovely, almost, than the things they destroy."

"There is no such place near here," she said.

"If I say it, then there is. Isn't there? I've seen it."

"Yes . . . you're right."

"And it doesn't matter if it's a painting by a woman named O'Keefe, or something right outside our window, does it? If I've seen it?"

"I acknowledge the truth of the diagnosis," she said. "Do you want to speak it for me?"

"No, go ahead."

He refilled the small glasses once more.

"The damage is in my eyes," she told him, "not my brain."

He lit her cigarette.

"I can see with other eyes if I can enter other brains."

He lit his own cigarette.

"Neuroparticipation is based upon the fact that two nervous systems can share the same impulses, the same fantasies. . . ."

"*Controlled* fantasies."

"I could perform therapy and at the same time experience genuine visual impressions."

"No," said Render.

"You don't know what it's like to be cut off from a whole area of stimuli! To know that a Mongoloid idiot can experience something you can never know— and that he cannot appreciate it because, like you, he was condemned before birth in a court of biological happenstance, in a place where there is no justice— only fortuity, pure and simple."

"The universe did not invent justice. Man did. Unfortunately, man must reside in the universe."

"I'm not asking the universe to help me—I'm asking you."

"I'm sorry," said Render.

"Why won't you help me?"

"At this moment you are demonstrating my main reason."

"Which is . . . ?"

"Emotion. This thing means far too much to you. When the therapist is in-phase with a patient he is narcoelectrically removed from most of his own bodily sensations. This is necessary—because his mind must be completely absorbed by the task at hand. It is also necessary that his emotions undergo a similar suspension. This, of course, is impossible in the one sense that a person always emotes to some degree. But the therapist's emotions are sublimated into a generalized feeling of exhilaration—or, as in my own case, into an artistic reverie. With you, however, the 'seeing' would be too much. You would be in constant danger of losing control of the dream."

"I disagree with you."

"Of course you do. But the fact remains that you would be dealing, and dealing constantly, with the abnormal. The power of a neurosis is unimaginable to ninety-nine point et cetera percent of the population, because we can never adequately judge the intensity of our own—let alone those of others, when we only see them from the outside. That is why no neuroparticipant will ever undertake to treat a full-blown psychotic. The few pioneers in that area are all themselves in therapy today. It would be like diving into a maelstrom. If the therapist loses the upper hand in an intense session, he becomes the Shaped rather than the Shaper. The synapses respond like a fission reaction when nervous impulses are artificially augmented. The transference effect is almost instantaneous.

"I did an awful lot of skiing five years ago. This is because I was a claustrophobe. I had to run and it took me six months to beat the thing—all because of one tiny lapse that occurred in a measureless fraction of an instant. I had to refer the patient to another therapist. And this was only a minor repercussion.—

If you were to go gaga over the scenery, girl, you could wind up in a rest home for life."

She finished her drink and Render refilled the glass. The night raced by. They had left the city far behind them, and the road was open and clear. The darkness eased more and more of itself between the falling flakes. The Spinner picked up speed.

"All right," she admitted, "maybe you're right. Still, though, I think you can help me."

"How?" he asked.

"Accustom me to seeing, so that the images will lose their novelty, the emotions wear off. Accept me as a patient and rid me of my sight-anxiety. Then what you have said so far will cease to apply. I will be able to undertake the training then, and give my full attention to therapy. I'll be able to sublimate the sight-pleasure into something else."

Render wondered.

Perhaps it could be done. It would be a difficult undertaking, though.

It might also make therapeutic history.

No one was really qualified to try it, because no one had ever tried it before.

But Eileen Shallot was a rarity—no, a unique item—for it was likely she was the only person in the world who combined the necessary technical background with the unique problem.

He drained his glass, refilled it, refilled hers.

He was still considering the problem as the "RECOORDINATE" light came on and the car pulled into a cutoff and stood there. He switched off the buzzer and sat there for a long while, thinking.

It was not often that other persons heard him acknowledge his feelings regarding his skill. His colleagues considered him modest. Offhand, though, it might be noted that he was aware that the day a better neuroparticipant began practicing would be the day that a troubled homo sapien was to be treated by something but immeasurably less than angels.

Two drinks remained. Then he tossed the emptied bottle into the backbin.

"You know something?" he finally said.

"What?"

"It might be worth a try."

He swiveled about then and leaned forward to recoordinate, but she was there first. As he pressed the buttons and the S-7 swung around, she kissed him. Below her dark glasses her cheeks were moist.

II

The suicide bothered him more than it should have, and Mrs. Lambert had called the day before to cancel her appointment. So Render decided to spend the morning being pensive. Accordingly, he entered the office wearing a cigar and a frown.

"Did you see . . . ?" asked Mrs. Hedges.

"Yes." He pitched his coat onto the table that stood in the far corner of the room. He crossed to the window, stared down. "Yes," he repeated, "I was driving by with my windows clear. They were still cleaning up when I passed."

"Did you know him?"

"I don't even know the name yet. How could I?"

"Priss Tully just called me—she's a receptionist for that engineering outfit up on the eighty-sixth. She says it was James Irizarry, and ad designer who had offices down the hall from them—That's a long way to fall. He must have been unconscious when he hit, huh? He bounced off the building. If you open the window and lean out you can see—off to the left there—where . . ."

"Never mind, Bennie. —Your friend have any idea why he did it?"

"Not really. His secretary came running up the hall, screaming. Seems she went in his office to see him about some drawings, just as he was getting up over the sill. There was a note on his board. 'I've had everything I wanted,' it said. 'Why wait around?' Sort of funny, huh? I don't mean *funny*. . . ."

"Yeah. —Know anything about his personal affairs?"

"Married. Coupla kids. Good professional rep. Lots of business. Sober as anybody. —He could afford an office in this building."

"Good Lord!" Render turned. "Have you got a case file there or something?"

"You know," she shrugged her thick shoulders, "I've got friends all over this hive. We always talk when things go slow. Prissy's my sister-in-law, anyhow—"

"You mean that if I dived through this window right now, my current biography would make the rounds in the next five minutes?"

"Probably," she twisted her bright lips into a smile, "give or take a couple. But don't do it today, huh? —You know, it would be kind of anticlimactic, and it wouldn't get the same coverage as a solus.

"Anyhow," she continued, "you're a mind-mixer. You wouldn't do it."

"You're betting against statistics," he observed. "The medical profession, along with attorneys, manages about three times as many as most other work areas."

"Hey!" She looked worried. "Go 'way from my window!"

"I'd have to go to work for Dr. Hanson then," she added, "and he's a slob."

He moved to her desk.

"I never know when to take you seriously," she decided.

"I appreciate your concern," he nodded, "indeed I do. As a matter of fact, I have never been statistic-prone—I should have repercussed out of the neuropy game four years ago."

"You'd be a headline, though," she mused. "All those reporters asking me about you . . . Hey, why do they do it, huh?"

"Who?"

"Anybody."

"How should I know, Bennie? I'm only a humble psyche-stirrer. If I could pinpoint a general underlying cause—and then maybe figure a way to anticipate the thing—why, it might even be better than my jumping, for newscopy. But I can't do it, because there is no single, simple reason—I don't think."

"Oh."

"About thirty-five years ago it was the ninth leading cause of death in the United States. Now it's number six for North and South America. I think it's seventh in Europe."

"And nobody will ever really know why Irizarry jumped?"

Render swung a chair backward and seated himself. He knocked an ash into her petite and gleaming tray. She emptied it into the waste-chute, hastily, and coughed a significant cough.

"Oh, one can always speculate," he said, "and one in my profession will. The first thing to consider would be the personality traits which might predispose a man to periods of depression. People who keep their emotions under rigid control, people who are conscientious and rather compulsively concerned with small matters . . ." He knocked another fleck of ash into her tray and watched as she reached out to dump it, then quickly drew her hand back again. He grinned an evil grin. "In short," he finished, "some of the characteristics of people in professions which require individual, rather than group performance—medicine, law, the arts."

She regarded him speculatively.

"Don't worry though," he chuckled, "I'm pleased as hell with life."

"You're kind of down in the mouth this morning."

"Pete called me. He broke his ankle yesterday in gym class. They ought to supervise those things more closely. I'm thinking of changing his school."

"Again?"

"Maybe. I'll see. The headmaster is going to call me this afternoon. I don't like to keep shuffling him, but I do want him to finish school in one piece."

"A kid can't grow up without an accident or two. It's—statistics."

"Statistics aren't the same thing as destiny, Bennie. Everybody makes his own."

"Statistics or destiny?"

"Both, I guess."

"I think that if something's going to happen, it's going to happen."

"I don't. I happen to think that the human will, backed by a sane mind can exercise some measure of control over events. If I didn't think so, I wouldn't be in the racket I'm in."

"The world's a machine—you know—cause, effect. Statistics do imply the prob—"

"The human mind is not a machine, and I do not know cause and effect. Nobody does."

"You have a degree in chemistry, as I recall. You're a scientist, Doc."

"So I'm a Trotskyite deviationist," he smiled, stretching, "and you were once a ballet teacher." He got to his feet and picked up his coat.

"By the way, Miss DeVille called, left a message. She said: 'How about St. Moritz?' "

"Too ritzy," he decided aloud. "It's going to be Davos."

Because the suicide bothered him more than it should have, Render closed the door to his office and turned off the windows and turned on the phonograph. He put on the desk light only.

How has the quality of human life been changed, he wrote, *since the beginnings of the industrial revolution?*

He picked up the paper and reread the sentence. It was the topic he had been asked to discuss that coming Saturday. As was typical in such cases he did not know what to say because he had too much to say, and only an hour to say it in.

He got up and began to pace the office, now filled with Beethoven's Eighth Symphony.

"The power to hurt," he said, snapping on a lapel microphone and activating his recorder, "has evolved in a direct relationship to technological advancement." His imaginary audience grew quiet. He smiled. "Man's potential for working simple mayhem has been multiplied by mass-production; his capacity for injuring the psyche through personal contacts has expanded in an exact ratio to improved communication facilities. But these are all matters of common knowledge, and are not the things I wish to consider tonight. Rather, I should like to discuss what I choose to call autopsychomimesis—the self-generated anxiety complexes which on first scrutiny appear quite similar to classic patterns, but which actually represent radical dispersions of psychic energy. They are peculiar to our times. . . ."

He paused to dispose of his cigar and formulate his next words.

"Autopsychomimesis," he thought aloud, "a self-perpetuated imitation complex—almost an attention-getting affair. —A jazzman, for example, who acted hopped-up half the time, even though he had never used an addictive narcotic and only dimly remembered anyone who had—because all the stimulants and tranquilizers of today are quite benign. Like Quixote, he aspired after a legend when his music alone should have been sufficient outlet for his tensions.

"Or my Korean War Orphan, alive today by virtue of the Red Cross and UNICEF and foster parents whom he never met. He wanted a family so badly that he made one up. And what then? —He hated his imaginary father and he loved his imaginary mother quite dearly—for he was a highly intelligent boy, and he too longed after the half-true complexes of tradition. Why?

"Today, everyone is sophisticated enough to understand the time-honored patterns of psychic disturbance. Today, many of the reasons for those disturbances have been removed—not as radically as my now-adult war orphan's, but with as remarkable an effect. We are living in a neurotic past. —Again, why? Because our present times are geared to physical health, security, and well-being. We have abolished hunger, though the backwoods orphan would still rather receive a package of food concentrates from a human being who cares for him than to obtain a warm meal from an automat unit in the middle of the jungle.

"Physical welfare is now every man's right in excess. The reaction to this has occurred in the area of mental health. Thanks to technology, the reasons for many of the old social problems have passed, and along with them went many of the reasons for psychic distress. But between the black of yesterday and the white of tomorrow is the great gray of today, filled with nostalgia and fear of the future, which cannot be expressed on a purely material plane, is now being represented by a willful seeking after historical anxiety-modes. . . ."

The phone-box buzzed briefly. Render did not hear it over the Eighth.

"We are afraid of what we do not know," he continued, "and tomorrow is a very great unknown. My own specialized area of psychiatry did not even exist thirty years ago. Science is capable of advancing itself so rapidly now that there is a genuine public uneasiness—I might even say 'distress'—as to the logical outcome: the total mechanization of everything in the world. . . ."

He passed near the desk as the phone buzzed again. He switched off his microphone and softened the Eighth.

"Hello?"

"Saint Moritz," she said.

"Davos," he replied firmly.

"Charlie, you are most exasperating!"

"Jill, dear—so are you."

"Shall we discuss it tonight?"

"There is nothing to discuss!"

"You'll pick me up at five, though?"

He hesitated, then:

"Yes, at five. How come the screen is blank?"

"I've had my hair fixed. I'm going to surprise you again."

He suppressed an idiot chuckle, said, "Pleasantly, I hope. Okay, see you then," waited for her "good-bye," and broke the connection.

He transpared the windows, turned off the light on his desk, and looked outside.

Gray again overhead, and many slow flakes of snow—wandering, not being blown about much—moving downward and then losing themselves in the tumult. . . .

He also saw, when he opened the window and leaned out, the place off to the left where Irizarry had left his next-to-last mark on the world.

He closed the window and listened to the rest of the symphony. It had been a week since he had gone blindspinning with Eileen. Her appointment was for one o'clock.

He remembered her fingertips brushing over his face, like leaves, or the bodies of insects, learning his appearance in the ancient manner of the blind. The memory was not altogether pleasant. He wondered why.

Far below, a patch of hosed pavement was blank once again; under a thin, fresh shroud of white, it was slippery as glass. A building custodian hurried outside and spread salt on it, before someone slipped and hurt themself.

Sigmund was the myth of Fenris come alive. After Render had instructed Mrs. Hedges, "Show them in," the door had begun to open, was suddenly pushed wider, and a pair of smoky yellow eyes stared in at him. The eyes were set in a strangely misshapen dog-skull.

Sigmund's was not a low canine brow, slanting up slightly from the muzzle; it was a high, shaggy cranium making the eyes appear even more deep-set than they actually were. Render shivered slightly at the size and aspect of that head. The muties he had seen had all been puppies. Sigmund was full-grown, and his gray-black fur had a tendency to bristle, which made him appear somewhat larger than a normal specimen of the breed.

He stared in at Render in a very un-doglike way and made a growling noise which sounded too much like, "Hello, doctor," to have been an accident.

Render nodded and stood.

"Hello, Sigmund," he said. "Come in."

The dog turned his head, sniffing the air of the room—as though deciding whether or not to trust his ward within its confines. Then he returned his stare to Render, dipped his head in an affirmative, and shouldered the door open. Perhaps the entire encounter had taken only one disconcerting second.

Eileen followed him, holding lightly to the double-leashed harness. The dog padded soundlessly across the thick rug—head low, as though he were stalking something. His eyes never left Render's.

"So this is Sigmund . . . ? How are you, Eileen?"

"Fine. —Yes, he wanted very badly to come along, and *I* wanted you to meet him."

Render led her to a chair and seated her. She unsnapped the double guide from the dog's harness and placed it on the floor. Sigmund sat down beside it and continued to stare at Render.

"How is everything at State Psych?"

"Same as always.—May I bum a cigarette, Doctor? I forgot mine."

He placed it between her fingers, furnished a light. She was wearing a dark blue suit and her glasses were flame blue. The silver spot on her forehead reflected the glow of his lighter; she continued to stare at that point in space after he had withdrawn his hand. Her shoulder-length hair appeared a trifle lighter than it had seemed on the night they met; today it was like a fresh-minted copper coin.

Render seated himself on the corner of his desk, drawing up his world-ashtray with his toe.

"You told me before that being blind did not mean that you had never seen. I didn't ask you to explain it then. But I'd like to ask you now."

"I had a neuroparticipation session with Dr. Riscomb," she told him, "before he had his accident. He wanted to accommodate my mind to visual impressions. Unfortunately, there was never a second session."

"I see. What did you do in that session?"

She crossed her ankles and Render noted they were well-turned.

"Colors, mostly. The experience was quite overwhelming."

"How well do you remember them? How long ago was it?"

"About six months ago—and I shall never forget them. I have even dreamed in color patterns since then."

"How often?"

"Several times a week."

"What sort of associations do they carry?"

"Nothing special. They just come into my mind along with other stimuli now—in a pretty haphazard way."

"How?"

"Well, for instance, when you ask me a question it's a sort of yellowish-orangish pattern that I 'see.' Your greeting was a kind of silvery thing. Now that you're just sitting there listening to me, saying nothing, I associate you with a deep, almost violet, blue."

Sigmund shifted his gaze to the desk and stared at the side panel.

Can he hear the recorder spinning inside? wondered Render. *And if he can, can he guess what it is and what it's doing?*

If so, the dog would doubtless tell Eileen—not that she was unaware of what was now an accepted practice—and she might not like being reminded that he considered her case as therapy, rather than a mere mechanical adaptation process. If he thought it would do any good (he smiled inwardly at the notion), he would talk to the dog in private about it.

Inwardly, he shrugged.

"I'll construct a rather elementary fantasy world then," he said finally, "and introduce you to some basic forms today."

She smiled; and Render looked down at the myth who crouched by her side, its tongue a piece of beefsteak hanging over a picket fence.

Is he smiling too?

"Thank you," she said.

Sigmund wagged his tail.

"Well then," Render disposed of his cigarette near Madagascar, "I'll fetch out the 'egg' now and test it. In the meantime," he pressed an unobtrusive button, "perhaps some music would prove relaxing."

She started to reply, but a Wagnerian overture snuffed out the words. Render jammed the button again, and there was a moment of silence during which he said, "Heh heh. Thought Respighi was next."

It took two more pushes for him to locate some Roman pines.

"You could have left him on," she observed. "I'm quite fond of Wagner."

"No thanks," he said, opening the closet, "I'd keep stepping in all those piles of leitmotifs."

The great egg drifted out into the office, soundless as a cloud. Render heard a soft growl behind as he drew it toward the desk. He turned quickly.

Like the shadow of a bird, Sigmund had gotten to his feet, crossed the room, and was already circling the machine and sniffing at it—tail taut, ears flat, teeth bared.

"Easy, Sig," said Render. "It's an Omnichannel Neural T & R Unit. It won't bite or anything like that. It's just a machine, like a car, or a teevee, or a dishwasher. That's what we're going to use today to show Eileen what some things look like."

"Don't like it," rumbled the dog.

"Why?"

Sigmund had no reply, so he stalked back to Eileen and laid his head in her lap.

"Don't like it," he repeated, looking up at her.

"Why?"

"No words," he decided. "We go home now?"

"No," she answered him. "You're going to curl up in the corner and take a nap, and I'm going to curl up in that machine and do the same thing—sort of."

"No good," he said, tail drooping.

"Go on now," she pushed him, "lie down and behave yourself."

He acquiesced, but he whined when Render blanked the windows and touched the button which transformed his desk into the operator's seat.

He whined once more—when the egg, connected now to an outlet, broke in the middle and the top slid back and up, revealing the interior.

Render seated himself. His chair became a contour couch and moved in halfway beneath the console. He sat upright and it moved back again, becoming a chair. He touched a part of the desk and half the ceiling disengaged itself, reshaped itself, and lowered to hover overhead like a huge bell. He stood and moved around to the side of the ro-womb. Respighi spoke of pines and such, and Render disengaged an earphone from beneath the egg and leaned back across his desk. Blocking one ear with his shoulder and pressing the microphone to the other, he played upon the buttons with his free hand. Leagues of surf drowned the tone poem; miles of traffic overrode it; a great clanging bell sent fracture lines running through it; and the feedback said: ". . . Now that you are just sitting there listening to me, saying nothing, I associate you with a deep, almost violet, blue. . . ."

He switched to the face mask and monitored, *one*—cinnamon, *two*—leaf mold, *three*—deep reptilian musk . . . and down through thirst, and the tastes of honey and vinegar and salt, and back on up through lilacs and wet concrete, a before-the-storm whiff of ozone, and all the basic olfactory and gustatory cues for morning, afternoon, and evening in the town.

The couch floated normally in its pool of mercury, magnetically stabilized by the walls of the egg. He set the tapes.

The ro-womb was in perfect condition.

"Okay," said Render, turning, "everything checks."

She was just placing her glasses atop her folded garments. She had undressed while Render was testing the machine. He was perturbed by her narrow waist, her large, dark-pointed breasts, her long legs. She was too well-formed for a woman her height, he decided.

He realized though, as he stared at her, that his main annoyance was, of course, the fact that she was his patient.

"Ready here," she said, and he moved to her side.

He took her elbow and guided her to the machine. Her fingers explored its interior. As he helped her enter the unit, he saw that her eyes were a vivid seagreen. Of this, too, he disapproved.

"Comfortable?"

"Yes."

"Okay then, we're set. I'm going to close it now. Sweet dreams."

The upper shell dropped slowly. Closed, it grew opaque, then dazzling. Render was staring down at his own distorted reflection.

He moved back in the direction of his desk.

Sigmund was on his feet, blocking the way.

Render reached down to pat his head, but the dog jerked it aside.

"Take me, with," he growled.

"I'm afraid that can't be done, old fellow," said Render. "Besides, we're not really going anywhere. We'll just be dozing, right here, in this room."

The dog did not seem mollified.

"Why?"

Render sighed. An argument with a dog was about the most ludicrous thing he could imagine when sober.

"Sig," he said, "I'm trying to help her learn what things look like. You doubt-less do a fine job guiding her around in this world which she cannot see—but she needs to know what it looks like now, and I'm going to show her."

"Then she, will not, need me."

"Of course she will." Render almost laughed. The pathetic thing was here bound so closely to the absurd thing that he could not help it. "I can't restore her sight," he explained. "I'm just going to transfer her some sight-abstractions—sort of lend her my eyes for a short time. Savvy?"

"No," said the dog. "Take mine."

Render turned off the music.

The whole mutie-master relationship might be worth six volumes, he decided, *in German.*

He pointed to the far corner.

"Lie down, over there, like Eileen told you. This isn't going to take long, and when it's all over you're going to leave the same way you came—you leading. Okay?"

Sigmund did not answer, but he turned and moved off to the corner, tail drooping again.

Render seated himself and lowered the hood, the operator's modified version of the ro-womb. He was alone before the ninety white buttons and the two red ones. The world ended in the blackness beyond the console. He loosened his necktie and unbuttoned his collar.

He removed the helmet from its receptacle and checked its leads. Donning it then, he swung the half-mask up over his lower face and dropped the darksheet down to meet with it. He rested his right arm in the sling, and with a single tapping gesture, he eliminated his patient's consciousness.

A Shaper does not press white buttons consciously. He wills conditions. Then deeply implanted muscular reflexes exert an almost imperceptible pressure against the sensitive arm-sling, which glides into the proper position and encourages an extended finger to move forward. A button is pressed. The sling moves on.

Render felt a tingling at the base of his skull; he smelled fresh-cut grass.

Suddenly he was moving up the great gray alley between the worlds.

After what seemed a long time, Render felt that he was footed on a strange Earth. He could see nothing; it was only a sense of presence that informed him he had arrived. It was the darkest of all the dark nights he had ever known.

He willed that the darkness disperse. Nothing happened.

A part of his mind came awake again, a part he had not realized was sleeping; he recalled whose world he had entered.

He listened for her presence. He heard fear and anticipation.

He willed color. First, red . . .

He felt a correspondence. Then there was an echo.

Everything became red; he inhabited the center of an infinite ruby.

Orange. Yellow. . . .

He was caught in a piece of amber.

Green now, and he added the exhalations of a sultry sea. Blue, and the coolness of evening.

He stretched his mind then, producing all the colors at once. They came in great swirling plumes.

Then he tore them apart and forced a form upon them.

An incandescent rainbow arced across the black sky.

He fought for browns and grays below him. Self-luminescent, they appeared—in shimmering, shifting patches.

Somewhere, a sense of awe. There was no trace of hysteria though, so he continued with the Shaping.

He managed a horizon, and the blackness drained away beyond it. The sky grew faintly blue, and he ventured a herd of dark clouds. There was resistance to his efforts at creating distance and depth, so he reinforced the tableau with a very faint sound of surf. A transference from an auditory concept of distance came slowly then, as he pushed the clouds about. Quickly, he threw up a high forest to offset a rising wave of acrophobia.

The panic vanished.

Render focused his attention on tall trees—oaks and pines, poplars and sycamores. He hurled them about like spears, in ragged arrays of greens and browns and yellows, unrolled a thick mat of morning-moist grass, dropped a series of gray boulders and greenish logs at irregular intervals, and tangled and twined the branches overhead, casting a uniform shade throughout the glen.

The effect was staggering. It seemed as if the entire world was shaken with a sob, then silent.

Through the stillness he felt her presence. He had decided it would be best to lay the groundwork quickly, to set up a tangible headquarters, to prepare a field for operations. He could backtrack later, he could repair and amend the results of the trauma in the sessions yet to come; but this much, at least, was necessary for a beginning.

With a start, he realized that the silence was not a withdrawal. Eileen had made herself immanent in the trees and the grass, the stones and the bushes; she was personalizing their forms, relating them to tactile sensations, sounds, temperatures, aromas.

With a soft breeze, he stirred the branches of the trees. Just beyond the bounds of seeing he worked out the splashing sounds of a brook.

There was a feeling of joy. He shared it.

She was bearing it extremely well, so he decided to extend the scope of the exercise. He let his mind wander among the trees, experiencing a momentary doubling of vision, during which time he saw an enormous hand riding in an aluminum carriage toward a circle of white.

He was beside the brook now and he was seeking her, carefully.

He drifted with the water. He had not yet taken on a form. The splashes became a gurgling as he pushed the brook through shallow places and over rocks. At his insistence, the waters became more articulate.

"Where are you?" asked the brook.

Here! Here!

Here!

. . . and here! replied the trees, the bushes, the stones, the grass.

"Choose one," said the brook, as it widened, rounded a mass of rock, then bent its way down a slope, heading toward a blue pool.

I cannot, was the answer from the wind.

"You must." The brook widened and poured into the pool, swirled about the surface, then stilled itself and reflected branches and dark clouds. "Now!"

Very well, echoed the wood, *in a moment.*

The mist rose above the lake and drifted to the bank of the pool.

"Now," tinkled the mist.

Here, then . . .

She had chosen a small willow. It swayed in the wind; it trailed its branches in the water.

"Eileen Shallot," he said, "regard the lake."

The breezes shifted; the willow bent.

It was not difficult for him to recall her face, her body. The tree spun as though rootless. Eileen stood in the midst of a quiet explosion of leaves; she stared, frightened, into the deep blue mirror of Render's mind, the lake.

She covered her face with her hands, but it could not stop the seeing.

"Behold yourself," said Render.

She lowered her hands and peered downward. Then she turned in every direction, slowly; she studied herself. Finally:

"I feel I am quite lovely," she said. "Do I feel so because you want me to, or is it true?"

She looked all about as she spoke, seeking the Shaper.

"It is true," said Render, from everywhere.

"Thank you."

There was a swirl of white and she was wearing a belted garment of damask. The light in the distance brightened almost imperceptibly. A faint touch of pink began at the base of the lowest cloudbank.

"What is happening there?" she asked, facing that direction.

"I am going to show you a sunrise," said Render, "and I shall probably botch it a bit—but then, it's my first professional sunrise under these circumstances."

"Where are *you*?" she asked.

"Everywhere," he replied.

"Please take on a form so that I can see you."

"All right."

"Your natural form."

He willed that he be beside her on the bank, and he was.

Startled by a metallic flash, he looked downward. The world receded for an instant, then grew stable once again. He laughed, and the laugh froze as he thought of something.

He was wearing the suit of armor which had stood beside their table in the Partridge and Scalpel on the night they met.

She reached out and touched it.

"The suit of armor by our table," she acknowledged, running her fingertips over the plates and the junctures. "I associated it with you that night."

". . . And you stuffed me into it just now," he commented. "You're a strong-willed woman."

The armor vanished and he was wearing his gray-brown suit and looseknit bloodclot necktie and a professional expression.

"Behold the real me," he smiled faintly. "Now, to the sunset. I'm going to use all the colors. Watch!"

They seated themselves on the green park bench which had appeared behind them, and Render pointed in the direction he had decided upon as east.

Slowly, the sun worked through its morning attitudes. For the first time in this particular world it shone down like a god, and reflected off the lake, and broke the clouds, and set the landscape to smouldering beneath the mist that arose from the moist wood.

Watching, watching intently, staring directly into the ascending bonfire, Eileen did not move for a long while, nor speak. Render could sense her fascination.

She was staring at the source of all light; it reflected back from the gleaming coin on her brow, like a single drop of blood.

Render said, "That is the sun, and those are clouds," and he clapped his hands and the clouds covered the sun and there was a soft rumble overhead, "and that is thunder," he finished.

The rain fell then, shattering the lake and tickling their faces, making sharp striking sounds on the leaves, then soft tapping sounds, dripping down from the branches overhead, soaking their garments and plastering their hair, running down their necks and falling into their eyes, turning patches of brown earth to mud.

A splash of lightning covered the sky, and a second later there was another peal of thunder.

". . . And this is a summer storm," he lectured. "You see how the rain affects the foliage and ourselves. What you just saw in the sky before the thunderclap was lightning."

". . . Too much," she said. "Let up on it for a moment, please."

The rain stopped instantly and the sun broke through the clouds.

"I have the damndest desire for a cigarette," she said, "but I left mine in another world."

As she said it one appeared, already lighted, between her fingers.

"It's going to taste rather flat," said Render strangely. He watched her for a moment, then:

"I didn't give you that cigarette," he noted. "You picked it from my mind."

The smoke laddered and spiraled upward, was swept away.

". . . Which means that, for the second time today, I have underestimated the pull of that vacuum in your mind—in the place where sight ought to be. You are assimilating these new impressions very rapidly. You're even going to the extent of groping after new ones. Be careful. Try to contain that impulse."

"It's like a hunger," she said.

"Perhaps we had best conclude this session now."

Their clothing was dry again. A bird began to sing.

"No, wait! Please! I'll be careful. I want to see more things."

"There is always the next visit," said Render. "But I suppose we can manage one more. Is there something you want very badly to see?"

"Yes. Winter. Snow."

"Okay," smiled the Shaper, "then wrap yourself in that fur-piece. . . ."

The afternoon slipped by rapidly after the departure of his patient. Render was in a good mood. He felt emptied and filled again. He had come through the first trial without suffering any repercussions. He decided that he was going to succeed. His satisfaction was greater than his fear. It was with a sense of exhilaration that he returned to working on his speech.

". . . And what is the power to hurt?" he inquired of the microphone.

"We live by pleasure and we live by pain," he answered himself. "Either can frustrate and either can encourage. But while pleasure and pain are rooted in biology, they are conditioned by society: thus are values to be derived. Because of the enormous masses of humanity, hectically changing positions in space every day throughout the cities of the world, there has come into necessary being a series of totally inhuman controls upon these movements. Every day they nibble their way into new areas—driving our cars, flying our planes, interviewing us, diagnosing our diseases—and I cannot even venture a moral judgment upon these intrusions. They have become necessary. Ultimately, they may prove salutary.

"The point I wish to make, however, is that we are often unaware of our own values. We cannot honestly tell what a thing means to us until it is removed from our life-situation. If an object of value ceases to exist, then the psychic energies which were bound up in it are released. We seek after new objects of value in which to invest this—mana, if you like, or libido, if you don't. And no one thing which has vanished during the past three or four or five decades was, in itself, massively significant; and no new thing which came into being during that time is massively malicious toward the people it has replaced or the people it in some manner controls. A society, though, is made up of many things, and when these things are changed too rapidly the results are unpredictable. An intense study of mental illness is often quite revealing as to the nature of the stresses in the society where the illness was made. If anxiety-patterns fall into special groups and classes, then something of the discontent of society can be learned from them. Karl Jung pointed out that when consciousness is repeatedly frustrated in a quest for values, it will turn its search to the unconscious; failing there, it will proceed to quarry its way into the hypothetical collective unconscious. He noted, in the postwar analyses of ex-Nazis, that the longer they searched for something to erect from the ruins of their lives—having lived through a period of classical iconoclasm, and then seen their new ideals topple as well—the longer they searched, the further back they seemed to reach into the collective unconscious of their people. Their dreams themselves came to take on patterns out of the Teutonic mythos.

"This, in a much less dramatic sense, is happening today. There are historical periods when the group tendency for the mind to turn in upon itself, to turn back, is greater than at other times. We are living in such a period of Quixotism, in the original sense of the term. This is because the power to hurt, in our time, is the power to ignore, to baffle—and it is no longer the exclusive property of human beings—"

A buzz interrupted him then. He switched off the recorder, touched the phone-box.

"Charles Render speaking," he told it.

"This is Paul Charter," lisped the box. "I am headmaster at Dilling."

"Yes?"

The picture cleared. Render saw a man whose eyes were set close together beneath a high forehead. The forehead was heavily creased; the mouth twitched as it spoke.

"Well, I want to apologize again for what happened. It was a faulty piece of equipment that caused—"

"Can't you afford proper facilities? Your fees are high enough."

"It was a *new* piece of equipment. It was a factory defect—"

"Wasn't there anybody in charge of the class?"

"Yes, but—"

"Why didn't he inspect the equipment? Why wasn't he on hand to prevent the fall?"

"He *was* on hand, but it happened too fast for him to do anything. As for inspecting the equipment for factory defects, that isn't his job. Look, I'm very sorry. I'm quite fond of your boy. I can assure you nothing like this will ever happen again."

"You're right, there. But that's because I'm picking him up tomorrow morning and enrolling him in a school that exercises proper safety precautions."

Render ended the conversation with a flick of his finger. After several minutes had passed he stood and crossed the room to his small wall safe, which was partly masked, though not concealed, by a shelf of books. It took only a moment for him to open it and withdraw a jewel box containing a cheap necklace and a framed photograph of a man resembling himself, though somewhat younger, and a woman whose upswept hair was dark and whose chin was small, and two youngsters between them—the girl holding the baby in her arms and forcing her bright bored smile on ahead. Render always stared for only a few seconds on such occasions, fondling the necklace, and then he shut the box and locked it away again for many months.

Whump! Whump! went the bass. *Tchg-tchg-tchga-tchg*, the gourds.

The gelatins splayed reds, greens, blues, and godawful yellows about the amazing metal dancers.

HUMAN? asked the marquee.

ROBOTS? (immediately below).

COME SEE FOR YOURSELF! (across the bottom, cryptically).

So they did.

Render and Jill were sitting at a microscopic table, thankfully set back against a wall, beneath charcoal caricatures of personalities largely unknown (there being so many personalities among the subcultures of a city of fourteen million people). Nose crinkled with pleasure, Jill stared at the present focal point of this particular subculture, occasionally raising her shoulders to ear level to add emphasis to a silent laugh or a small squeal, because the performers were just *too* human—the way the ebon robot ran his fingers along the silver robot's forearm as they parted and passed. . . .

Render alternated his attention between Jill and the dancers and a wicked-looking decoction that resembled nothing so much as a small bucket of whiskey sours strewn with seaweed (through which the Kraken might at any moment arise to drag some hapless ship down to its doom).

"Charlie, I think they're really people!"

Render disentangled his gaze from her hair and bouncing earrings.

He studied the dancers down on the floor, somewhat below the table area, surrounded by music.

There *could* be humans within those metal shells. If so, their dance was a thing of extreme skill. Though the manufacture of sufficiently light alloys was no problem, it would be some trick for a dancer to cavort so freely—and for so long a period of time, and with such effortless-seeming ease—within a head-to-toe suit of armor, without so much as a grate or a click or a clank.

Soundless . . .

They glided like two gulls; the larger, the color of polished anthracite, and the other, like a moonbeam falling through a window upon a silk-wrapped manikin.

Even when they touched there was no sound—or if there was, it was wholly masked by the rhythms of the band.

Whump-whump! Tchga-tchg!

Render took another drink.

Slowly, it turned into an apache-dance. Render checked his watch. Too long for normal entertainers, he decided. They must be robots. As he looked up again the black robot hurled the silver robot perhaps ten feet and turned his back on her.

There was no sound of striking metal.

Wonder what a setup like that costs? he mused.

"Charlie! There was no sound! How do they do that?"

"I've no idea," said Render.

The gelatins were yellow again, then red, then blue, then green.

"You'd think it would damage their mechanisms, wouldn't you?"

The white robot crawled back and the other swiveled his wrist around and around, a lighted cigarette between the fingers. There was laughter as he pressed it mechanically to his lipless faceless face. The silver robot confronted him. He turned away again, dropped the cigarette, ground it out slowly, soundlessly, then suddenly turned back to his partner. Would he throw her again? No . . .

Slowly then, like the great-legged birds of the East, they recommenced their movement, slowly, and with many turnings away.

Something deep within Render was amused, but he was too far gone to ask it what was funny. So he went looking for the Kraken in the bottom of the glass instead.

Jill was clutching his biceps then, drawing his attention back to the floor.

As the spotlight tortured the spectrum, the black robot raised the silver one high above his head, slowly, slowly, and then commenced spinning with her in that position—arms outstretched, back arched, legs scissored—very slowly, at first. Then faster.

Suddenly they were whirling with an unbelievable speed, and the gelatins rotated faster and faster.

Render shook his head to clear it.

They were moving so rapidly that they *had* to fall—human or robot. But they didn't. They were a mandala. They were a gray form uniformity. Render looked down.

Then slowing, and slower, slower. Stopped.

The music stopped.

Blackness followed. Applause filled it.

When the lights came on again the two robots were standing statue-like, facing the audience. Very, very slowly, they bowed.

The applause increased.

Then they turned and were gone.

The music came on and the light was clear again. A babble of voices arose. Render slew the Kraken.

"What d'you think of that?" she asked him.

Render made his face serious and said: "Am I a man dreaming I am a robot, or a robot dreaming I am a man?" He grinned, then added: "I don't know."

She punched his shoulder gaily at that and he observed that she was drunk.

"I am not," she protested. "Not much, anyhow. Not as much as you."

"Still, I think you ought to see a doctor about it. Like me. Like now. Let's get out of here and go for a drive."

"Not yet, Charlie. I want to see them once more, huh? Please?"

"If I have another drink I won't be able to see that far."

"Then order a cup of coffee."

"Yaagh!"

"Then order a beer."

"I'll suffer without."

There were people on the dance floor now, but Render's feet felt like lead. He lit a cigarette.

"So you had a dog talk to you today?"

"Yes. Something very disconcerting about that. . . ."

"Was she pretty?"

"It was a boy dog. And boy, was he ugly!"

"Silly. I mean his mistress."

"You know I never discuss cases, Jill."

"You told me about her being blind and about the dog. All I want to know is if she's pretty."

"Well . . . Yes and no." He bumped her under the table and gestured vaguely. "Well, you know . . ."

"Same thing all the way around," she told the waiter who had appeared suddenly out of an adjacent pool of darkness, nodded, and vanished as abruptly.

"There go my good intentions," sighed Render. "See how you like being examined by a drunken sot, that's all I can say."

"You'll sober up fast, you always do. Hippocratics and all that."

He sniffed, glanced at his watch.

"I have to be in Connecticut tomorrow. Pulling Pete out of that damned school. . . ."

She sighed, already tired of the subject.

"I think you worry too much about him. Any kid can bust an ankle. It's part of growing up. I broke my wrist when I was seven. It was an accident. It's not the school's fault, those things sometimes happen."

"Like hell," said Render, accepting his dark drink from the dark tray the dark man carried. "If they can't do a good job, I'll find someone who can."

She shrugged.

"You're the boss. All I know is what I read in the papers.

"—And you're still set on Davos, even though you know you meet a better class of people at Saint Moritz?" she added.

"We're going there to ski, remember? I like the runs better at Davos."

"I can't score any tonight, can I?"

He squeezed her hand.

"You always score with me, honey."

And they drank their drinks and smoked their cigarettes and held their hands until the people left the dance floor and filed back to their microscopic tables, and the gelatins spun round and round, tinting clouds of smoke from hell to sunrise and back again, and the bass went *whump!*

Tchga-tchga!

"Oh, Charlie! Here they come again!"

The sky was clear as crystal. The roads were clean. The snow had stopped.

Jill's breathing was the breathing of a sleeper. The S-7 raced across the bridges of the city. If Render sat very still he could convince himself that only his body was drunk; but whenever he moved his head the universe began to dance about him. As it did so, he imagined himself within a dream, and Shaper of it all.

For one instant this was true. He turned the big clock in the sky backward, smiling as he dozed. Another instant and he was awake again, and unsmiling.

The universe had taken revenge for his presumption. For one reknown moment with the helplessness which he had loved beyond helping, it had charged him the price of the lake-bottom vision once again; and as he had moved once more toward the wreck at the bottom of the world—like a swimmer, as unable to speak—he heard, from somewhere high over the Earth, and filtered down to him through the waters above the Earth, the howl of the Fenris Wolf as it prepared to devour the moon; and as this occurred, he knew that the sound was as like to the trump of a judgment as the lady by his side was unlike the moon. Every bit. In all ways. And he was afraid.

III

". . . The plain, the direct, and the blunt. This is Winchester Cathedral," said the guidebook. "With its floor-to-ceiling shafts, like so many huge tree trunks, it achieves a ruthless control over its spaces: the ceilings are flat; each bay, separated by those shafts, is itself a thing of certainty and stability. It seems, indeed, to reflect something of the spirit of William the Conqueror. Its disdain of mere elaboration and its passionate dedication to the love of another world would make it seem, too, an appropriate setting for some tale out of Mallory. . . ."

"Observe the scalloped capitals," said the guide. "In their primitive fluting they anticipated what was later to become a common motif. . . ."

"Faugh!" said Render—softly though, because he was in a group inside a church.

"Shh!" said Jill (Fotlock—that was her real last name) DeVille.

But Render was impressed as well as distressed.

Hating Jill's hobby, though, had become so much of a reflex with him that he would sooner have taken his rest seated beneath an oriental device which dripped water onto his head than to admit he occasionally enjoyed walking through the arcades and the galleries, the passages and the tunnels, and getting all out of breath climbing up the high twisty stairways of towers.

So he ran his eyes over everything, burned everything down by shutting them, then built the place up again out of the still smouldering ashes of memory, all so that at a later date he would be able to repeat the performance, offering the vision to his one patient who could see only in this manner. This building he disliked less than most. Yes, he would take it back to her.

The camera in his mind photographing the surroundings, Render walked with the others, overcoat over his arm, his fingers anxious to reach after a cigarette. He kept busy ignoring his guide, realizing this to be the nadir of all forms of human protest. As he walked through Winchester he thought of his last two sessions with Eileen Shallot. He recalled his almost unwilling Adam-attitude as he had named all the animals passing before them, led of course by the *one* she had wanted to see, colored fearsome by his own unease. He had felt pleasantly bucolic after boning up on an old Botany text and then proceeding to Shape and name the flowers of the fields.

So far they had stayed out of the cities, far away from the machines. Her emotions were still too powerful at the sight of the simple, carefully introduced objects to risk plunging her into so complicated and chaotic a wilderness yet; he would build her city slowly.

Something passed rapidly, high above the cathedral, uttering a sonic boom. Render took Jill's hand in his for a moment and smiled as she looked up at him. Knowing she verged upon beauty, Jill normally took great pains to achieve it. But today her hair was simply drawn back and knotted behind her head, and her lips and her eyes were pale; and her exposed ears were tiny and white and somewhat pointed.

"Observe the scalloped capitals," he whispered. "In their primitive fluting they anticipated what was later to become a common motif."

"Faugh!" said she.

"Shh!" said a sunburned little woman nearby, whose face seemed to crack and fall back together again as she pursed and unpursed her lips.

Later as they strolled back toward their hotel, Render said, "Okay on Winchester?"

"Okay on Winchester."

"Happy?"

"Happy."

"Good, then we can leave this afternoon."

"All right."

"For Switzerland. . . ."

She stopped and toyed with a button on his coat.

"Couldn't we just spend a day or two looking at some old chateaux first? After all, they're just across the channel, and you could be sampling all the local wines while I looked . . ."

"Okay," he said.

She looked up—a trifle surprised.

"What? No argument?" she smiled. "Where is your fighting spirit?—to let me push you around like this?"

She took his arm then and they walked on as he said, "Yesterday, while we were galloping about in the innards of that old castle, I heard a weak moan, and then a voice cried out, 'For the love of God, Montresor!' I think it was my fighting spirit, because I'm certain it was my voice. I've given up *der Geist der stets verneint. Pax vobiscum!* Let us be gone to France. *Alors!*"

"Dear Rendy, it'll only be another day or two. . . ."

"Amen," he said, "though my skis that were waxed are already waning."

So they did that, and on the morn of the third day, when she spoke to him of castles in Spain, he reflected aloud that while psychologists drink and only grow angry, psychiatrists have been known to drink, grow angry, and break things. Construing this as a veiled threat aimed at the Wedgewoods she had collected, she acquiesced to his desire to go skiing.

Free! Render almost screamed it.

His heart was pounding inside his head. He leaned hard. He cut to the left. The wind strapped at his face; a shower of ice crystals, like bullets of emery, fled by him, scraped against his cheek.

He was moving. Aye—the world had ended as Weissflujoch, and Dorftali led down and away from this portal.

His feet were two gleaming rivers which raced across the stark, curving plains; they could not be frozen in their course. Downward. He flowed. Away from all the rooms of the world. Away from the stifling lack of intensity, from the day's hundred spoon-fed welfares, from the killing pace of the forced amusements that hacked at the Hydra, leisure; away.

And as he fled down the run he felt a strong desire to look back over his shoulder, as though to see whether the world he had left behind and above had set one fearsome embodiment of itself, like a shadow, to trail along after him, hunt him down and drag him back to a warm and well-lit coffin in the sky, there to be laid to rest with a spike of aluminum driven through his will and a garland of alternating currents smothering his spirit.

"I hate you," he breathed between clenched teeth, and the wind carried the words back; and he laughed then, for he always analyzed his emotions, as a matter of reflex; and he added, "Exit Orestes, mad, pursued by the Furies. . . ."

After a time the slope leveled out and he reached the bottom of the run and had to stop.

He smoked one cigarette then and rode back up to the top so that he could come down it again for nontherapeutic reasons.

That night he sat before a fire in the big lodge, feeling its warmth soaking into his tired muscles. Jill massaged his shoulders as he played Rorschach with the flames, and he came upon a blazing goblet which was snatched away from him in the same instant by the sound of his name being spoken somewhere across the Hall of the Nine Hearths.

"Charles Render!" said the voice (only it sounded more like "Sharlz Runder"), and his head instantly jerked in that direction, but his eyes danced with too many afterimages for him to isolate the source of the calling.

"Maurice?" he queried after a moment. "Bartelmetz?"

"Aye," came the reply, and then Render saw the familiar grizzled visage, set neckless and balding above the red and blue shag sweater that was stretched mercilessly about the wine-keg rotundity of the man who now picked his way in their direction, deftly avoiding the strewn crutches and the stacked skis and the people who, like Jill and Render, disdained sitting in chairs.

Render stood, stretching, and shook hands as he came upon them.

"You've put on more weight," Render observed. "That's unhealthy."

"Nonsense, it's all muscle. How have you been, and what are you up to these days?" He looked down at Jill and she smiled back at him.

"This is Miss DeVille," said Render.

"Jill," she acknowledged.

He bowed slightly, finally releasing Render's aching hand.

". . . And this is Professor Maurice Bartelmetz of Vienna," finished Render, "a benighted disciple of all forms of dialectical pessimism, and a very distinguished pioneer in neuroparticipation—although you'd never guess it to look at him. I had the good fortune to be his pupil for over a year."

Bartelmetz nodded and agreed with him, taking in the Schnapsflasche Render brought forth from a small plastic bag, and accepting the collapsible cup which he filled to the brim.

"Ah, you are a good doctor still," he sighed. "You have diagnosed the case in an instant and you make the proper prescription. Nozdrovia!"

"Seven years in a gulp," Render acknowledged, refilling their glasses.

"Then we shall make time more malleable by sipping it."

They seated themselves on the floor, and the fire roared up through the great brick chimney as the logs burned themselves back to branches, to twigs, to thin sticks, ring by yearly ring.

Render replenished the fire.

"I read your last book," said Bartelmetz finally, casually, "about four years ago."

Render reckoned that to be correct.

"Are you doing any research work these days?"

Render poked lazily at the fire.

"Yes," he answered, "sort of."

He glanced at Jill, who was dozing with her cheek against the arm of the huge leather chair that held his emergency bag, the planes of her face all crimson and flickering shadow.

"I've hit upon a rather unusual subject and started with a piece of jobbery I eventually intend to write about."

"Unusual? In what way?"

"Blind from birth, for one thing."

"You're using the ONT&R?"

"Yes. She's going to be a Shaper."

"Verfluchter!—Are you aware of the possible repercussions?"

"Of course."

"You've heard of unlucky Pierre?"

"No."

"Good, then it was successfully hushed. Pierre was a philosophy student at the University of Paris, and was doing a dissertation on the evolution of consciousness. This past summer he decided it would be necessary for him to explore the mind of an ape, for purposes of comparing a moins-nausee mind with his own, I suppose. At any rate, he obtained illegal access to an ONT&R and to the mind of our hairy cousin. It was never ascertained how far along he got in exposing the animal to the stimulibank, but it is to be assumed that such items as would not be immediately trans-subjective between man and ape—traffic sounds and so weiter—were what frightened the creature. Pierre is still residing in a padded cell, and all his responses are those of a frightened ape.

"So, while he did not complete his own dissertation," he finished, "he may provide significant material for someone else's."

Render shook his head.

"Quite a story," he said softly, "but I have nothing that dramatic to contend with. I've found an exceedingly stable individual—a psychiatrist, in fact—one who's already spent time in ordinary analysis. She wants to go into neuroparticipation—but the fear of a sight-trauma was what was keeping her out. I've been gradually exposing her to a full range of visual phenomena. When I've finished she should be completely accommodated to sight, so that she can give her full attention to therapy and not be blinded by vision, so to speak. We've already had four sessions."

"And?"

". . . And it's working fine."

"You are certain about it?"

"Yes, as certain as anyone can be in these matters."

"Mm-hm," said Bartelmetz. "Tell me, do you find her excessively strong-willed? By that I mean, say, perhaps an obsessive-compulsive pattern concerning anything to which she's been introduced so far?"

"No."

"Has she ever succeeded in taking over control of the fantasy?"

"No!"

"You lie," he said simply.

Render found a cigarette. After lighting it, he smiled.

"Old father, old artificer," he conceded, "age has not withered your perceptiveness. I may trick me, but never you.—Yes, as a matter of fact, she *is* very difficult to keep under control. She is not satisfied just to see. She wants to Shape things for herself already. It's quite understandable—both to her and to me—but conscious apprehension and emotional acceptance never do seem to get together on things. She has become dominant on several occasions, but I've succeeded in resuming control almost immediately. After all, I *am* master of the bank."

"Hm," mused Bartelmetz. "Are you familiar with a Buddhist text—*Shankara's Catechism?*"

"I'm afraid not."

"Then I lecture you on it now. It posits—obviously not for therapeutic purposes—a true ego and a false ego. The true ego is that part of man which is immortal and shall proceed on to nirvana: the soul, if you like. Very good. Well, the false ego, on the other hand, is the normal mind, bound round with the illusions—the consciousness of you and me and everyone we have ever known professionally. Good?—Good. Now, the stuff this false ego is made up of they call skandhas. These include the feelings, the perceptions, the aptitudes, consciousness itself, and even the physical form. Very unscientific. Yes. Now they are not the same thing as neuroses, or one of Mr. Ibsen's life-lies, or an hallucination—no, even though they are all wrong, being parts of a false thing to begin with. Each of the five skandhas is a part of the eccentricity that we call identity—then on top come the neuroses and all the other messes which follow after and keep us in business. Okay?—Okay. I give you this lecture because I need a dramatic term for what I will say, because I wish to say something dramatic. View the skandhas as lying at the bottom of the pond; the neuroses, they are ripples on the top of the water; the 'true ego,' if there is one, is buried deep beneath the sand at the bottom. So. The ripples fill up the-the—*zwischenwelt*—between the object and the subject. The skandhas are a part of the subject, basic, unique, the stuff of his being.—So far, you are with me?"

"With many reservations."

"Good. Now I have defined my term somewhat, I will use it. You are fooling around with skandhas, not simple neuroses. You are attempting to adjust this woman's overall conception of herself and of the world. You are using the ONT&R to do it. It is the same thing as fooling with a psychotic or an ape. All may seem to go well, but—at any moment, it is possible you may do something, show her some sight, or some way of seeing which will break in upon her selfhood, break a skandha—and pouf!—it will be like breaking through the bottom of the pond. A whirlpool will result, pulling you—where? I do not want you for a patient, young man, young artificer, so I counsel you not to proceed with this experiment. The ONT&R should not be used in such a manner."

Render flipped his cigarette into the fire and counted on his fingers:

"One," he said, "you are making a mystical mountain out of a pebble. All I am doing is adjusting her consciousness to accept an additional area of perception. Much of it is simple transference work from the other senses—Two, her emotions were quite intense initially because it *did* involve a trauma—but we've passed that stage already. Now it is only a novelty to her. Soon it will be a commonplace—Three, Eileen is a psychiatrist herself; she is educated in these matters and deeply aware of the delicate nature of what we are doing— Four, her sense of identity and her desires, or her skandhas, or whatever you want to call them, are as firm as the Rock of Gibraltar. Do you realize the intense application required for a blind person to obtain the education she has obtained? It took a will of ten-point steel and the emotional control of an ascetic as well—"

"—And if something that strong should break, in a timeless moment of anxiety," smiled Bartelmetz sadly, "may the shades of Sigmund Freud and Karl Jung walk by your side in the valley of darkness.

"—And five," he added suddenly, staring into Render's eyes. "Five," he ticked it off on one finger. "Is she pretty?"

Render looked back into the fire.

"Very clever," sighed Bartelmetz. "I cannot tell whether you are blushing or not, with the rosy glow of the flames upon your face. I fear that you are, though, which would mean that you are aware that you yourself could be the source of the inciting stimulus. I shall burn a candle tonight before a portrait of Adler and pray that he give you the strength to compete successfully in your duel with your patient."

Render looked at Jill, who was still sleeping. He reached out and brushed a lock of her hair back into place.

"Still," said Bartelmetz, "if you do proceed and all goes well, I shall look forward with great interest to the reading of your work. Did I ever tell you that I have treated several Buddhists and never found a 'true ego'?"

Both men laughed.

Like me but not like me, that one on a leash, smelling of fear, small, gray, and unseeing. *Rrowl* and he'll choke on his collar. His head is empty as the oven till. She pushes the button and it makes dinner. Make talk and they never understand, but they are like me. One day I will kill one—why . . . ? Turn here.

"Three steps. Up. Glass doors. Handle to right."

Why? Ahead, drop-shaft. Gardens under, down. Smells nice, there. Grass, wet dirt, trees, and clean air. I see. Birds are recorded though. I see all. I.

"Dropshaft. Four steps."

Down Yes. Want to make loud noises in throat, feel silly. Clean, smooth, many of trees. God . . . She likes sitting on bench chewing leaves smelling smooth air. Can't see them like me. Maybe now, some . . . ? No.

Can't Bad Sigmund me on grass, trees, here. Must hold it. Pity. Best place . . .

"Watch for steps."

Ahead. To right, to left, to right, to left, trees and grass now. Sigmund sees. Walking . . . Doctor with machine gives her his eyes. *Rrowl* and he will not choke. No fearsmell.

Dig deep hole in ground, bury eyes. God is blind. Sigmund to see. Her eyes now filled, and he is afraid of teeth. Will make her to see and take her high up in the sky to see, away. Leave me here, leave Sigmund with none to see, alone. I will dig a deep hole in the ground . . .

It was after ten in the morning when Jill awoke. She did not have to turn her head to know that Render was already gone. He never slept late. She rubbed her eyes, stretched, turned onto her side and raised herself on her elbow. She squinted at the clock on the bedside table, simultaneously reaching for a cigarette and her lighter.

As she inhaled, she realized there was no ashtray. Doubtless Render had moved it to the dresser because he did not approve of smoking in bed. With a sigh that ended in a snort she slid out of the bed and drew on her wrap before the ash grew too long.

She hated getting up, but once she did she would permit the day to begin and continue on without lapse through its orderly progression of events.

"Damn him," she smiled. She had wanted her breakfast in bed, but it was too late now.

Between thoughts as to what she would wear, she observed an alien pair of skis standing in the corner. A sheet of paper was impaled on one. She approached it.

"Join me?" asked the scrawl.

She shook her head in an emphatic negative and felt somewhat sad. She had been on skis twice in her life and she was afraid of them. She felt that she should really try again, after his being a reasonably good sport about the chateaux, but she could not even bear the memory of the unseemly downward rushing—which, on two occasions, had promptly deposited her in a snowbank— without wincing and feeling once again the vertigo that had seized her during the attempts.

So she showered and dressed and went downstairs for breakfast.

All nine fires were already roaring as she passed the big hall and looked inside. Some red-faced skiers were holding their hands up before the blaze of the central hearth. It was not crowded though. The racks held only a few pairs of dripping boots, bright caps hung on pegs, moist skis stood upright in their place beside the door. A few people were seated in the chairs set further back toward the center of the hall, reading papers, smoking, or talking quietly. She saw no one she knew, so she moved on toward the dining room.

As she passed the registration desk the old man who worked there called out her name. She approached him and smiled.

"Letter," he explained, turning to a rack. "Here it is," he announced, handing it to her. "Looks important."

It had been forwarded three times, she noted. It was a bulky brown envelope, and the return address was that of her attorney.

"Thank you."

She moved off to a seat beside the big window that looked out upon a snow garden, a skating rink, and a distant winding trail dotted with figures carrying skis over their shoulders. She squinted against the brightness as she tore open the envelope.

Yes, it was final. Her attorney's note was accompanied by a copy of the divorce decree. She had only recently decided to end her legal relationship to Mr. Fotlock, whose name she had stopped using five years earlier, when they had separated. Now that she had the thing, she wasn't sure exactly what she was going to do with it. It would be a hell of a surprise for dear Rendy, though, she decided. She would have to find a reasonably innocent way of getting the information to him. She withdrew her compact and practiced a "Well?" expression. Well, there would be time for that later, she mused. Not too much later, though. . . . Her thirtieth birthday, like a huge black cloud, filled an April but four months distant. Well . . . She touched her quizzical lips with color, dusted more powder over her mole, and locked the expression within her compact for future use.

In the dining room she saw Doctor Bartelmetz, seated before an enormous mound of scrambled eggs, great chains of dark sausages, several heaps of yellow toast, and a half-emptied flask of orange juice. A pot of coffee steamed on the warmer at his elbow. He leaned slightly forward as he ate, wielding his fork like a windmill blade.

"Good morning," she said.

He looked up.

"Miss DeVille—Jill . . . Good morning." He nodded at the chair across from him. "Join me, please."

She did so, and when the waiter approached she nodded and said, "I'll have the same thing, only about ninety percent less."

She turned back to Bartelmetz.

"Have you seen Charles today?"

"Alas, I have not," he gestured, open-handed, "and I wanted to continue our discussion while his mind was still in the early stages of wakefulness and somewhat malleable. Unfortunately," he took a sip of coffee, "he who sleeps well enters the day somewhere in the middle of its second act."

"Myself, I usually come in around intermission and ask someone for a synopsis," she explained. "So why not continue the discussion with me?—I'm always malleable, and my skandhas are in good shape."

Their eyes met, and he took a bite of toast.

"Aye," he said, at length, "I had guessed as much. Well—good. What do you know of Render's work?"

She adjusted herself in the chair.

"Mm. He being a special specialist in a highly specialized area, I find it difficult to appreciate the few things he does say about it. I'd like to be able to look inside other people's minds sometimes—to see what they're thinking about *me*, of course—but I don't think I could stand staying there very long. Especially," she gave a mock-shudder, "the mind of somebody with—problems. I'm afraid I'd be too sympathetic or too frightened or something. Then, according to what I've read—pow!—like sympathetic magic, it would be my problem.

"Charles never has problems though," she continued, "at least, none that he speaks to me about. Lately I've been wondering, though. That blind girl and her talking dog seem to be too much with him."

"Talking dog?"

"Yes, her seeing-eye dog is one of those surgical mutants."

"How interesting. . . . Have you ever met her?"

"Never."

"So," he mused.

"Sometimes a therapist encounters a patient whose problems are so akin to his own that the sessions become extremely mordant," he noted. "It has always been the case with me when I treat a fellow-psychiatrist. Perhaps Charles sees in this situation a parallel to something which has been troubling him personally. I did not administer his personal analysis. I do not know all the ways of his mind, even though he was a pupil of mine for a long while. He was always self-contained, somewhat reticent; he could be quite authoritative on occasion, however.—What are some of the other things which occupy his attention these days?"

"His son Peter is a constant concern. He's changed the boy's school five times in five years."

Her breakfast arrived. She adjusted her napkin and drew her chair closer to the table.

"And he has been reading case histories of suicides recently, and talking about them, and talking about them, and talking about them."

"To what end?"

She shrugged and began eating.

"He never mentioned why," she said, looking up again. "Maybe he's writing something. . . ."

Bartelmetz finished his eggs and poured more coffee.

"Are you afraid of this patient of his?" he inquired.

"No . . . Yes," she responded, "I am."

"Why?"

"I am afraid of sympathetic magic," she said, flushing slightly.

"Many things could fall under that heading."

"Many indeed," she acknowledged. And, after a moment, "We are united in our concern for his welfare and in agreement as to what represents the threat. So, may I ask a favor?"

"You may."

"Talk to him again," she said. "Persuade him to drop the case."

He folded his napkin.

"I intend to do that after dinner," he stated, "because I believe in the ritualistic value of rescue-motions. They shall be made."

Dear Father-image,

Yes, the school is fine, my ankle is getting that way, and my classmates are a congenial lot. No, I am not short on cash, undernourished, or having difficulty fitting into the new curriculum. Okay?

The building I will not describe, as you have already seen the macabre thing. The grounds I cannot describe, as they are currently residing beneath cold white sheets. Brr! I trust yourself to be enjoying the arts wint'rish. I do not share your enthusiasm for summer's opposite, except within picture frames or as an emblem on ice-cream bars.

The ankle inhibits my mobility and my roommate has gone home for the week-end—both of which are really blessings (saith Pangloss), for I now have the opportunity to catch up on some reading. I will do so forthwith.
Prodigally,
Peter

Render reached down to pat the huge head. It accepted the gesture stoically, then turned its gaze up to the Austrian whom Render had asked for a light, as if to say, "Must I endure this indignity?" The man laughed at the expression, snapping shut the engraved lighter on which Render noted the middle initial to be a small 'v.'

"Thank you," he said, and to the dog: "What is your name?"

"Bismark," it growled.

Render smiled.

"You remind me of another of your kind," he told the dog. "One Sigmund, by name, a companion and guide to a blind friend of mine, in America."

"My Bismark is a hunter," said the young man. "There is no quarry that can outthink him, neither the deer nor the big cats."

The dog's ears pricked forward and he stared up at Render with proud, blazing eyes.

"We have hunted in Africa and the northern and southwestern parts of America. Central America, too. He never loses the trail. He never gives up. He is a beautiful brute, and his teeth could have been made in Solingen."

"You are indeed fortunate to have such a hunting companion."

"I hunt," growled the dog. "I follow . . . Sometimes, I have, the kill . . ."

"You would not know of the one called Sigmund then, or the woman he guides—Miss Eileen Shallot?" asked Render.

The man shook his head.

"No, Bismark came to me from Massachusetts, but I was never to the Center personally. I am not acquainted with other mutie handlers."

"I see. Well, thank you for the light. Good afternoon."

"Good afternoon . . ."

"Good, after, noon . . ."

Render strolled on up the narrow street, hands in his pockets. He had excused himself and not said where he was going. This was because he had had no destination in mind. Bartelmetz' second essay at counseling had almost led him to say things he would later regret. It was easier to take a walk than to continue the conversation.

On a sudden impulse he entered a small shop and bought a cuckoo clock which had caught his eye. He felt certain that Bartelmetz would accept the gift in the proper spirit. He smiled and walked on. *And what was that letter to Jill which the desk clerk had made a special trip to their table to deliver at dinnertime?* he wondered. It had been forwarded three times, and its return address was that of a law firm. Jill had not even opened it, but had smiled, overtipped the old man, and tucked it into her purse. He would have to hint subtly as to its contents. His curiosity so aroused, she would be sure to tell him out of pity.

The icy pillars of the sky suddenly seemed to sway before him as a cold wind leaped down out of the north. Render hunched his shoulders and drew his head further below his collar. Clutching the cuckoo clock, he hurried back up the street.

·   ·   ·

That night the serpent which holds its tail in its mouth belched, the Fenris Wolf made a pass at the moon, the little clock said "cuckoo" and tomorrow came on like Manolete's last bull, shaking the gate of horn with the bellowed promise to tread a river of lions to sand.

Render promised himself he would lay off the gooey fondue.

Later, much later, when they skipped through the skies in a kite-shaped cruiser, Render looked down upon the darkened Earth dreaming its cities full of stars, looked up at the sky where they were all reflected, looked about him at the tape-screens watching all the people who blinked into them, and at the coffee, tea, and mixed drink dispensers who sent their fluids forth to explore the insides of the people they required to push their buttons, then looked across at Jill, whom the old buildings had compelled to walk among their walls—because he knew she felt he should be looking at her then—felt his seat's demand that he convert it into a couch, did so, and slept.

IV

Her office was full of flowers, and she liked exotic perfumes. Sometimes she burned incense.

She liked soaking in overheated pools, walking through falling snow, listening to too much music, played perhaps too loudly, drinking five or six varieties of liqueurs (usually reeking of anise, sometimes touched with wormwood) every evening. Her hands were soft and lightly freckled. Her fingers were long and tapered. She wore no rings.

Her fingers traced and retraced the floral swellings on the side of her chair as she spoke into the recording unit.

"... Patient's chief complaints on admission were nervousness, insomnia, stomach pains, and a period of depression. Patient has had a record of previous admissions for short periods of time. He had been in this hospital in 1995 for a manic depressive psychosis, depressed type, and he returned here again, 2-3-96. He was in another hospital, 9-20-97. Physical examination revealed a BP of 170/100. He was normally developed and well-nourished on the date of examination, 12-11-98. On this date patient complained of chronic backache, and there was noted some moderate symptoms of alcohol withdrawal. Physical examination further revealed no pathology except that the patient's tendon reflexes were exaggerated but equal. These symptoms were the result of alcohol withdrawal. Upon admission he was shown to be not psychotic, neither delusional nor hallucinated. He was well-oriented as to place, time, and person. His psychological condition was evaluated and he was found to be somewhat grandiose and expansive and more than a little hostile. He was considered a potential troublemaker. Because of his experience as a cook, he was assigned to work in the kitchen. His general condition then showed definite improvement. He is less tense and is cooperative. Diagnosis: Manic depressive reaction (external precipitating stress unknown). The degree of psychiatric impairment is mild. He is considered competent. To be continued on therapy and hospitalization."

She turned off the recorder then and laughed. The sound frightened her. Laughter is a social phenomenon and she was alone. She played back the recording then, chewing on the corner of her handkerchief while the soft, clipped words were returned to her. She ceased to hear them after the first dozen or so.

When the recorder stopped talking she turned it off. She was alone. She was very alone. She was so damned alone that the little pool of brightness which occurred when she stroked her forehead and faced the window—that little pool of brightness suddenly became the most important thing in the world. She wanted it to be immense. She wanted it to be an ocean of light. Or else she wanted to grow so small herself that the effect would be the same: she wanted to drown in it.

It had been three weeks, yesterday . . .

Too long, she decided, *I should have waited. No! Impossible! But what if he goes as Riscomb went? No! He won't. He would not. Nothing can hurt him. Never. He is all strength and armor. But—but we should have waited till next month to start. Three weeks . . . Sight withdrawal—that's what it is. Are the memories fading? Are they weaker? (What does a tree look like? Or a cloud—I can't remember! What is red? What is green? God! It's hysterical! I'm watching and I can't stop it!—Take a pill! A pill!*

Her shoulders began to shake. She did not take a pill though, but bit down harder on the handkerchief until her sharp teeth tore through its fabric.

"Beware," she recited a personal beatitude, "those who hunger and thirst after justice, for we *will* be satisfied.

"And beware the meek," she continued, "for we shall attempt to inherit the Earth.

"And beware . . ."

There was a brief buzz from the phone-box. She put away her handkerchief, composed her face, turned the unit on.

"Hello . . . ?"

"Eileen, I'm back. How've you been?"

"Good, quite well in fact. How was your vacation?"

"Oh, I can't complain. I had it coming for a long time. I guess I deserve it. Listen, I brought some things back to show you—like Winchester Cathedral. You want to come in this week? I can make it any evening."

Tonight. No. I want it too badly. It will set me back if he sees . . .

"How about tomorrow night?" she asked. "Or the one after?"

"Tomorrow will be fine," he said. "Meet you at the P & S, around seven?"

"Yes, that would be pleasant. Same table?"

"Why not?—I'll reserve it."

"All right. I'll see you then."

"Good-bye."

The connection was broken.

Suddenly, then, at that moment, colors swirled again through her head; and she saw trees—oaks and pines, poplars and sycamores—great, and green and brown, and iron-colored; and she saw wads of fleecy clouds, dipped in paintpots, swabbing a pastel sky; and a burning sun, and a small willow tree, and a lake of a deep, almost violet, blue. She folded her torn handkerchief and put it away.

She pushed a button beside her desk and music filled the office: Scriabin. Then she pushed another button and replayed the tape she had dictated, half-listening to each.

Pierre sniffed suspiciously at the food. The attendant moved away from the tray and stepped out into the hall, locking the door behind him. The enormous salad waited on the floor. Pierre approached cautiously, snatched a handful of lettuce, gulped it.

He was afraid.

If only the steel would stop crashing and crashing against steel, somewhere in that dark night . . . If only . . .

Sigmund rose to his feet, yawned, stretched. His hind legs trailed out behind him for a moment, then he snapped to attention and shook himself. She would be coming home soon. Wagging his tail slowly, he glanced up at the human-level clock with the raised numerals, verified his feelings, then crossed the apartment to the teevee. He rose onto his hind legs, rested one paw against the table and used the other to turn on the set.

It was nearly time for the weather report and the roads would be icy.

"I have driven through countrywide graveyards," wrote Render, "vast forests of stone that spread further every day.

"Why does man so zealously guard his dead? Is it because this is the monumentally democratic way of immortalization, the ultimate affirmation of the power to hurt—that is to say, life—and the desire that it continue on forever? Unamuno has suggested that this is the case. If it is, then a greater percentage of the population actively sought immortality last year than ever before in history. . . ."

Tch-tchg, tchga-tchg!

"Do you think they're really people?"

"Naw, they're too good."

The evening was starglint and soda over ice. Render wound the S-7 into the cold sub-subcellar, found his parking place, nosed into it.

There was a damp chill that emerged from the concrete to gnaw like rats' teeth at their flesh. Render guided her toward the lift, their breath preceding them in dissolving clouds.

"A bit of a chill in the air," he noted.

She nodded, biting her lip.

Inside the lift, he sighed, unwound his scarf, lit a cigarette.

"Give me one, please," she requested, smelling the tobacco.

He did.

They rose slowly, and Render leaned against the wall, puffing a mixture of smoke and crystallized moisture.

"I met another mutie shep," he recalled, "in Switzerland. Big as Sigmund. A hunter though, and as Prussian as they come," he grinned.

"Sigmund likes to hunt, too," she observed. "Twice every year we go up to the North Woods and I turn him loose. He's gone for days at a time, and he's always quite happy when he returns. Never says what he's done, but he's never hungry. Back when I got him I guessed that he would need vacations from humanity to stay stable. I think I was right."

The lift stopped, the door opened and they walked out into the hall, Render guiding her again.

Inside his office, he poked at the thermostat and warm air sighed through the room. He hung their coats in the inner office and brought the great egg out from its nest behind the wall. He connected it to an outlet and moved to convert his desk into a control panel.

"How long do you think it will take?" she asked, running her fingertips over the smooth, cold curves of the egg. "The whole thing, I mean. The entire adaptation to seeing."

He wondered.

"I have no idea," he said, "no idea whatsoever, yet. We got off to a good start, but there's still a lot of work to be done. I think I'll be able to make a good guess in another three months."

She nodded wistfully, moved to his desk, explored the controls with finger strokes like ten feathers.

"Careful you don't push any of those."

"I won't. How long do you think it will take me to learn to operate one?"

"Three months to learn it. Six, to actually become proficient enough to use it on anyone, and an additional six under close supervision before you can be trusted on your own.—About a year altogether."

"Uh-huh." She chose a chair.

Render touched the seasons to life, and the phases of day and night, the breath of the country, the city, the elements that raced naked through the skies, and all the dozens of dancing cues he used to build worlds. He smashed the clock of time and tasted the seven or so ages of man.

"Okay," he turned, "everything is ready."

It came quickly, and with a minimum of suggestion on Render's part. One moment there was grayness. Then a dead-white fog. Then it broke itself apart, as though a quick wind had risen, although he neither heard nor felt a wind.

He stood beside the willow tree beside the lake, and she stood half-hidden among the branches and the lattices of shadow. The sun was slanting its way into evening.

"We have come back," she said, stepping out, leaves in her hair. "For a time I was afraid it had never happened, but I see it all again, and I remember now."

"Good," he said. "Behold yourself." And she looked into the lake.

"I have not changed," she said. "I haven't changed. . . ."

"No."

"But you have," she continued, looking up at him. "You are taller, and there is something different. . . ."

"No," he answered.

"I am mistaken," she said quickly. "I don't understand everything I see yet.

"I will, though."

"Of course."

"What are we going to do?"

"Watch," he instructed her.

Along a flat, no-colored river of road she just then noticed beyond the trees came the car. It came from the farthest quarter of the sky, skipping over the mountains, buzzing down the hills, circling through the glades, and splashing them with the colors of its voice—the gray and the silver of synchronized potency—and the lake shivered from its sounds, and the car stopped a hundred feet away, masked by the shrubberies; and it waited. It was the S-7.

"Come with me," he said, taking her hand. "We're going for a ride."

They walked among the trees and rounded the final cluster of bushes. She touched the sleek cocoon, its antennae, its tires, its windows—and the windows transpared as she did so. She stared through them at the inside of the car, and she nodded.

"It is your Spinner."

"Yes." He held the door for her. "Get in. We'll return to the club. The time is now. The memories are fresh, and they should be reasonably pleasant, or neutral."

"Pleasant," she said, getting in.

He closed the door, then circled the car and entered. She watched as he punched imaginary coordinates. The car leaped ahead and he kept a steady stream of trees flowing by them. He could feel the rising tension, so he did not vary the scenery. She swiveled her seat and studied the interior of the car.

"Yes," she finally said, "I can perceive what everything is."

She stared out the window again. She looked at the rushing trees. Render stared out and looked upon rushing anxiety patterns. He opaqued the windows.

"Good," she said, "thank you. Suddenly it was too much to see—all of it, moving past like a . . ."

"Of course," said Render, maintaining the sensations of forward motion. "I'd anticipated that. You're getting tougher, though."

After a moment, "Relax," he said, "relax now," and somewhere a button was pushed, and she relaxed, and they drove on, and on and on, and finally the car began to slow, and Render said, "Just for one nice, slow glimpse now, look out your window."

She did.

He drew upon every stimulus in the bank which could promote sensations of pleasure and relaxation, and he dropped the city around the car, and the windows became transparent, and she looked out upon the profiles of towers and a block of monolithic apartments, and then she saw three rapid cafeterias, an entertainment palace, a drugstore, a medical center of yellow brick with an aluminum Caduceus set above its archway, and a glassed-in high school, now emptied of its pupils, a fifty-pump gas station, another drugstore, and many more cars, parked or roaring by them, and people, people moving in and out of the doorways and walking before the buildings and getting into the cars and getting out of the cars; and it was summer, and the light of late afternoon filtered down upon the colors of the city and the colors of the garments the people wore as they moved along the boulevard, as they loafed upon the terraces, as they crossed the balconies, leaned on balustrades and windowsills, emerged from a corner kiosk, entered one, stood talking to one another; a woman walking a poodle rounded a corner; rockets went to and fro in the high sky.

The world fell apart then and Render caught the pieces.

He maintained an absolute blackness, blanketing every sensation but that of their movement forward.

After a time a dim light occurred, and they were still seated in the Spinner, windows blanked again, and the air as they breathed it became a soothing unguent.

"Lord," she said, "the world is so filled. Did I really see all of that?"

"I wasn't going to do that tonight, but you wanted me to. You seemed ready."

"Yes," she said, and the windows became transparent again. She turned away quickly.

"It's gone," he said. "I only wanted to give you a glimpse."

She looked, and it was dark outside now, and they were crossing over a high bridge. They were moving slowly. There was no other traffic. Below them were the Flats, where an occasional smelter flared like a tiny, drowsing volcano, spitting showers of orange sparks skyward; and there were many stars: they glistened on the breathing water that went beneath the bridge; they silhouetted by pinprick the skyline that hovered dimly below its surface. The slanting struts of the bridge marched steadily by.

"You have done it," she said, "and I thank you." Then: "Who are you, really?" (He must have wanted her to ask that.)

"I am Render," he laughed. And they wound their way through a dark, now-vacant city, coming at last to their club and entering the great parking dome.

Inside, he scrutinized all her feelings, ready to banish the world at a moment's notice. He did not feel he would have to, though.

They left the car, moved ahead. They passed into the club, which he had decided would not be crowded tonight. They were shown to their table at the foot of the bar in the small room with the suit of armor, and they sat down and ordered the same meal over again.

"No," he said, looking down, "it belongs over there."

The suit of armor appeared once again beside the table, and he was once again inside his gray suit and black tie and silver tie clasp shaped like a tree limb.

They laughed.

"I'm just not the type to wear a tin suit, so I wish you'd stop seeing me that way."

"I'm sorry," she smiled. "I don't know how I did that, or why."

"I do, and I decline the nomination. Also, I caution you once again. You are conscious of the fact that this is all an illusion. I had to do it that way for you to get the full benefit of the thing. For most of my patients though, it is the real item while they are experiencing it. It makes a counter-trauma or a symbolic sequence even more powerful. You are aware of the parameters of the game, however, and whether you want it or not this gives you a different sort of control over it than I normally have to deal with. Please be careful."

"I'm sorry. I didn't mean to."

"I know. Here comes the meal we just had."

"Ugh! It looks dreadful! Did we eat all that stuff?"

"Yes," he chuckled. "That's a knife, that's a fork, that's a spoon. That's roast beef, and those are mashed potatoes, those are peas, that's butter . . ."

"Goodness! I don't feel so well."

". . . And those are the salads, and those are the salad dressings. This is a brook trout—mm! These are French fried potatoes. This is a bottle of wine. Hmm—let's see—Romanee-Conti, since I'm not paying for it—and a bottle of Yquem for the trou—Hey!"

The room was wavering.

He bared the table, he banished the restaurant. They were back in the glade. Through the transparent fabric of the world he watched a hand moving along a panel. Buttons were being pushed. The world grew substantial again. Their emptied table was set beside the lake now, and it was still nighttime and summer, and the tablecloth was very white under the glow of the giant moon that hung overhead.

"That was stupid of me," he said. "Awfully stupid. I should have introduced them one at a time. The actual sight of basic, oral stimuli can be very distressing to a person seeing them for the first time. I got so wrapped up in the Shaping that I forgot the patient, which is just dandy! I apologize."

"I'm okay now. Really I am."

He summoned a cool breeze from the lake.

". . . And that is the moon," he added lamely.

She nodded, and she was wearing a tiny moon in the center of her forehead; it glowed like the one above them, and her hair and dress were all of silver.

The bottle of Romanée-Conti stood on the table, and two glasses.

"Where did that come from?"

She shrugged. He poured out a glassful.

"It may taste kind of flat," he said.

"It doesn't. Here—" She passed it to him.

As he sipped it he realized it had a taste—a *fruite* such as might be quashed from the grapes grown in the Isles of the Blest, a smooth, muscular *charnu*, and a *capiteux* centrifuged from the fumes of a field of burning poppies. With a start, he knew that his hand must be traversing the route of the perceptions, symphonizing the sensual cues of a transference and a counter-transference which had come upon him all unaware, there beside the lake.

"So it does," he noted, "and now it is time we returned."

"So soon? I haven't seen the cathedral yet. . . ."

"So soon."

He willed the world to end, and it did.

"It is cold out there," she said as she dressed, "and dark."

"I know. I'll mix us something to drink while I clear the unit."

"Fine."

He glanced at the tapes and shook his head. He crossed to his bar cabinet.

"It's not exactly Romanée-Conti," he observed, reaching for a bottle.

"So what? I don't mind."

Neither did he, at that moment. So he cleared the unit, they drank their drinks, he helped her into her coat and they left.

As they rode the lift down to the sub-sub he willed the world to end again, but it didn't.

Dad,

I hobbled from school to taxi and taxi to spaceport, for the local Air Force Exhibit—Outward, it was called. (Okay; I exaggerated the hobble. It got me extra attention though.) The whole bit was aimed at seducing young manhood into a five-year hitch, as I saw it. But it worked. I wanna join up. I wanna go Out There. Think they'll take me when I'm old enuf? I mean take me Out—not some crummy desk job. Think so?

I do.

There was this damn lite colonel ('scuse the French) who saw this kid lurching around and pressing his nose 'gainst the big windowpanes, and he decided to give him the subliminal sell. Great! He pushed me through the gallery and showed me all the pitchers of AF triumphs, from Moonbase to Marsport. He lectured me on the Great Traditions of the Service, and marched me into a flic room where the Corps had good clean fun on tape, wrestling one another in null-G "where it's all skill and no brawn," and making tinted water sculpture-work way in the middle of the air and doing dismounted drill on the skin of a cruiser. Oh joy!

Seriously though, I'd like to be there when they hit the Outer Five—and On Out. Not because of the bogus balonus in the throwaways, and suchlike crud, but because I think someone of sensibility should be along to chronicle the thing in the proper way. You know, raw frontier observer. Francis Parkman. Mary Austin, like that. So I decided I'm going.

The AF boy with the chicken stuff on his shoulders wasn't in the least way patronizing, gods be praised. We stood on the balcony and watched ships lift off and he told me to go forth and study real hard and I might be riding them someday. I did not bother to tell him that I'm hardly intellectually deficient and that I'll have my B.A. before I'm old enough to do anything with it, even join his Corps. I just watched the ships lift off and said, "Ten years from now I'll be looking down, not up." Then he told me how hard his own training had been, so I did not ask howcum he got stuck with a lousy dirt-side assignment like this one. Glad I didn't, now I think on it. He looked more like one of their ads than one of their real people. Hope I never look like an ad.

Thank you for the monies and the warm sox and Mozart's String Quintets, which I'm hearing right now. I wanna put in my bid for Luna instead of Europe next summer. Maybe . . . ? Possibly . . . ? Contingently . . . ? Huh?—If I can smash that new test you're designing for me . . . ? Anyhow, please think about it.

Your son,
Pete

"Hello. State Psychiatric Institute."

"I'd like to make an appointment for an examination."

"Just a moment. I'll connect you with the Appointment Desk."

"Hello. Appointment Desk."

"I'd like to make an appointment for an examination."

"Just a moment . . . What sort of examination."

"I want to see Doctor Shallot, Eileen Shallot. As soon as possible."

"Just a moment. I'll have to check her schedule . . . Could you make it at two o'clock next Tuesday?"

"That would be just fine."

"What is the name, please?"

"DeVille. Jill DeVille."

"All right, Miss DeVille. That's two o'clock, Tuesday."

"Thank you."

The man walked beside the highway. Cars passed along the highway. The cars in the high-acceleration lane blurred by.

Traffic was light.

It was 10:30 in the morning, and cold.

The man's fur-lined collar was turned up, his hands were in his pockets, and he leaned into the wind. Beyond the fence, the road was clean and dry.

The morning sun was buried in clouds. In the dirty light, the man could see the tree a quarter mile ahead.

His pace did not change. His eyes did not leave the tree. The small stones clicked and crunched beneath his shoes.

When he reached the tree he took off his jacket and folded it neatly.

He placed it upon the ground and climbed the tree.

As he moved out onto the limb which extended over the fence, he looked to see that no traffic was approaching. Then he seized the branch with both hands, lowered himself, hung a moment, and dropped onto the highway.

It was a hundred yards wide, the eastbound half of the highway.

He glanced west, saw there was still no traffic coming his way, then began to walk toward the center island. He knew he would never reach it. At this time of day the cars were moving at approximately one hundred sixty miles an hour in the high-acceleration lane. He walked on.

A car passed behind him. He did not look back. If the windows were opaqued, as was usually the case, then the occupants were unaware he had crossed their path. They would hear of it later and examine the front end of their vehicle for possible sign of such an encounter.

A car passed in front of him. Its windows were clear. A glimpse of two faces, their mouths made into O's, was presented to him, then torn from his sight. His own face remained without expression. His pace did not change. Two more cars rushed by, windows darkened. He had crossed perhaps twenty yards of highway.

Twenty-five . . .

Something in the wind, or beneath his feet, told him it was coming. He did not look.

Something in the corner of his eye assured him it was coming. His gait did not alter.

Cecil Green had the windows transpared because he liked it that way. His left hand was inside her blouse and her skirt was piled up on her lap, and his right hand was resting on the lever which would lower the seats. Then she pulled away, making a noise down inside her throat.

His head snapped to the left.

He saw the walking man

He saw the profile which never turned to face him fully. He saw that the man's gait did not alter.

Then he did not see the man.

There was a slight jar, and the windshield began cleaning itself. Cecil Green raced on.

He opaqued the windows.

"How . . . ?" he asked after she was in his arms again, and sobbing.

"The monitor didn't pick him up. . . ."

"He must not have touched the fence. . . ."

"He must have been out of his mind!"

"Still, he could have picked an easier way."

It could have been any face. . . . Mine?

Frightened, Cecil lowered the seats.

Charles Render was writing the "Necropolis" chapter for *The Missing Link Is Man*, which was to be his first book in over four years. Since his return he had set aside every Tuesday and Thursday afternoon to work on it, isolating himself in his office, filling pages with a chaotic longhand.

"There are many varieties of death, as opposed to dying . . ." he was writing, just as the intercom buzzed briefly, then long, then briefly again.

"Yes?" he asked it, pushing down on the switch.

"You have a visitor," and there was a short intake of breath between "a" and "visitor."

He slipped a small aerosol into his side pocket, then rose and crossed the office.

He opened the door and looked out.

"Doctor . . . Help . . ."

Render took three steps, then dropped to one knee.

"What's the matter?"

"Come—she is . . . sick," he growled.

"Sick? How? What's wrong?"

"Don't know. You come."

Render stared into the unhuman eyes.

"What kind of sick?" he insisted.

"Don't know," repeated the dog. "Won't talk. Sits. I . . . feel, she is sick."

"How did you get here?"

"Drove. Know the co, or, din, ates. . . . Left car, outside."

"I'll call her right now." Render turned.

"No good. Won't answer."

He was right.

Render returned to his inner office for his coat and medkit. He glanced out the window and saw where her car was parked, far below, just inside the entrance to the marginal, where the monitor had released it into manual control. If no one assumed that control a car was automatically parked in neutral. The other vehicles were passed around it.

So simple even a dog can drive one, he reflected. *Better get downstairs before a cruiser comes along. It's probably reported itself stopped there already. Maybe not, though. Might still have a few minutes grace.*

He glanced at the huge clock.

"Okay, Sig," he called out. "Let's go."

They took the lift to the ground floor, left by way of the front entrance and hurried to the car.

Its engine was still idling.

Render opened the passengerside door and Sigmund leaped in. He squeezed by him into the driver's seat then, but the dog was already pushing the primary coordinates and the address tabs with his paw.

Looks like I'm in the wrong seat.

He lit a cigarette as the car swept ahead into a U-underpass. It emerged on the opposite marginal, sat poised a moment, then joined the traffic flow. The dog directed the car into the high-acceleration lane.

"Oh," said the dog, "oh."

Render felt like patting his head at that moment, but he looked at him, saw that his teeth were bared, and decided against it.

"When did she start acting peculiar?" he asked.

"Came home from work. Did not eat. Would not answer me when I talked. Just sits."

"Has she ever been like this before?"

"No."

What could have precipitated it?—But maybe she just had a bad day. After all, he's only a dog—sort of.—No. He'd know. But what, then?

"How was she yesterday—and when she left home this morning?"

"Like always."

Render tried calling her again. There was still no answer.

"You did, it," said the dog.

"What do you mean?"

"Eyes. Seeing. You. Machine. Bad."

"No," said Render, and his hand rested on the unit of stun-spray in his pocket.

"Yes," said the dog, turning to him again. "You will, make her well . . . ?"

"Of course," said Render.

Sigmund stared ahead again.

Render felt physically exhilarated and mentally sluggish. He sought the con-fusion factor. He had had these feelings about the case since that first session. There was something very unsettling about Eileen Shallot; a combination of high intelligence and helplessness, of determination and vulnerability, of sensitivity and bitterness.

Do I find that especially attractive?—No. It's just the counter-transference, damn it!

"You smell afraid," said the dog.

"Then color me afraid," said Render, "and turn the page."

They slowed for a series of turns, picked up speed again, slowed again, picked up speed again. Finally, they were traveling along a narrow section of roadway through a semi-residential area of town. The car turned up a side street, pro-ceeded about half a mile further, clicked softly beneath its dashboard, and turned into the parking lot behind a high brick apartment building. The click must have been a special servomech which took over from the point where the monitor released it, because the car crawled across the lot, headed into its transparent parking stall, then stopped. Render turned off the ignition.

Sigmund had already opened the door on his side. Render followed him into the building, and they rode the elevator to the fiftieth floor. The dog dashed on ahead up the hallway, pressed his nose against a plate set low in a doorframe and waited. After a moment, the door swung several inches inward. He pushed it open with his shoulder and entered. Render followed, closing the door behind him.

The apartment was large, its walls pretty much unadorned, its color combi-nations unnerving. A great library of tapes filled one corner: a monstrous combination-broadcaster stood beside it. There was a wide bowlegged table set in front of the window, and a low couch along the right-hand wall; there was a closed door beside the couch; an archway to the left apparently led to other rooms. Eileen sat in an overstuffed chair in the far corner by the window. Sig-mund stood beside the chair.

Render crossed the room and extracted a cigarette from his case. Snapping open his lighter, he held the flame until her head turned in that direction.

"Cigarette?" he asked.

"Charles?"

"Right."

"Yes, thank you. I will."

She held out her hand, accepted the cigarette, put it to her lips.

"Thanks—What are you doing here?"

"Social call. I happened to be in the neighborhood."

"I didn't hear a buzz or a knock."

"You must have been dozing. Sig let me in."

"Yes, I must have." She stretched. "What time is it?"

"It's close to four-thirty."

"I've been home over two hours then. . . . Must have been very tired. . . ."

"How do you feel now?"

"Fine," she declared. "Care for a cup of coffee?"

"Don't mind if I do."

"A steak to go with it?"

"No, thanks."

"Barcardi in the coffee?"

"Sounds good."

"Excuse me, then. It'll only take a moment."

She went through the door beside the sofa and Render caught a glimpse of a large, shiny, automatic kitchen.

"Well?" he whispered to the dog.

Sigmund shook his head.

"Not same."

Render shook his head.

He deposited his coat on the sofa, folding it carefully about the medkit. He sat beside it and thought.

Did I throw too big a chunk of seeing at once? Is she suffering from depressive side-effects—say, memory repressions, nervous fatigue? Did I upset her sensory-adaptation syndrome somehow? Why have I been proceeding so rapidly anyway? There's no real hurry. Am I so damned eager to write the thing up?—Or am I doing it because she wants me to? Could she be that strong, consciously or unconsciously? Or am I that vulnerable—somehow?

She called him to the kitchen to carry out the tray. He set it on the table and seated himself across from her.

"Good coffee," he said, burning his lips on the cup.

"Smart machine," she stated, facing his voice.

Sigmund stretched out on the carpet next to the table, lowered his head between his forepaws, sighed and closed his eyes.

"I've been wondering," said Render, "whether or not there were any after effects to that last session—like increased synesthesiac experiences, or dreams involving forms, or hallucinations or . . ."

"Yes," she said flatly, "dreams."

"What kind?"

"That last session. I've dreamed it over, and over."

"Beginning to end?"

"No, there's no special order to the events. We're riding through the city, or over the bridge, or sitting at the table, or walking toward the car—just flashes, like that. Vivid ones."

"What sort of feelings accompany these—flashes?"

"I don't know, they're all mixed up."

"What are your feelings now, as you recall them?"

"The same, all mixed up."

"Are you afraid?"

"N-no. I don't think so."

"Do you want to take a vacation from the thing? Do you feel we've been proceeding too rapidly?"

"No. That's not it at all. It's—well, it's like learning to swim. When you finally learn how, why then you swim and you swim and you swim until you're all exhausted. Then you just lie there gasping in air and remembering what it was like, while your friends all hover and chew you out for overexerting yourself— and it's a good feeling, even though you do take a chill and there are pins and needles inside all your muscles. At least, that's the way I do things. I felt that way after the first session and after this last one. First Times are always very special times. . . . The pins and the needles are gone, though, and I've caught my breath again. Lord, I don't want to stop now! I feel fine."

"Do you usually take a nap in the afternoon?"

The ten red nails of her fingers moved across the tabletop as she stretched.

". . . Tired," she smiled, swallowing a yawn. "Half the staff's on vacation or sick leave and I've been beating my brains out all week. I was about ready to fall on my face when I left work. I feel all right now that I've rested, though."

She picked up her coffee cup with both hands, took a large swallow.

"Uh-huh," he said. "Good. I was a bit worried about you. I'm glad to see there was no reason."

She laughed.

"Worried? You've read Dr. Riscomb's notes on my analysis—and on the ONT&R trial—and you think I'm the sort to worry about? Ha! I have an operationally beneficent neurosis concerning my adequacy as a human being. It focuses my energies, coordinates my efforts toward achievement. It enhances my sense of identity. . . ."

"You do have on hell of a memory," he noted "That's almost verbatim."

"Of course."

"You had Sigmund worried today, too."

"Sig? How?"

The dog stirred uneasily, opened one eye.

"Yes," he growled, glaring up at Render. "He needs, a ride, home."

"Have you been driving the car again?"

"Yes."

"After I told you not to?"

"Yes."

"Why?"

"I was a, fraid. You would, not, answer me, when I talked."

"I was *very* tired—and if you ever take the car again, I'm going to have the door fixed so you can't come and go as you please."

"Sorry."

"There's nothing wrong with me."

"I, see."

"You are *never* to do it again."

"Sorry." His eye never left Render; it was like a burning lens.

Render looked away.

"Don't be too hard on the poor fellow," he said. "After all, he thought you were ill and he went for the doctor. Suppose he'd been right? You'd owe him thanks, not a scolding."

Unmollified, Sigmund glared a moment longer and closed his eye.

"He has to be told when he does wrong," she finished.

"I suppose," he said, drinking his coffee. "No harm done, anyhow. Since I'm here, let's talk shop. I'm writing something and I'd like an opinion."

"Great. Give me a footnote?"

"Two or three.—In your opinion, do the general underlying motivations that lead to suicide differ in different periods of history or in different cultures?"

"My well-considered opinion is no, they don't," she said. "Frustrations can lead to depressions or frenzies; and if these are severe enough, they can lead to self-destruction. You ask me about motivations and I think they stay pretty much the same. I feel this is a cross-cultural, cross-temporal aspect of the human condition. I don't think it could be changed without changing the basic nature of man."

"Okay. Check. Now, what of the inciting element?" he asked. "Let man be a constant, his environment is still a variable. If he is placed in an overprotective life-situation, do you feel it would take more or less to depress him—or stimulate him to frenzy—than it would take in a not so protective environment?"

"Hm. Being case-oriented, I'd say it would depend on the man. But I see what you're driving at: a mass predisposition to jump out windows at the drop of a hat—the window even opening itself for you, because you asked it to—the revolt of the bored masses. I don't like the notion. I hope it's wrong."

"So do I, but I was thinking of symbolic suicides too—functional disorders that occur for pretty flimsy reasons."

"Aha! Your lecture last month: autopsychomimesis. I have the tape. Well-told, but I can't agree."

"Neither can I, now. I'm rewriting that whole section—'Thanatos in Cloud-cuckooland,' I'm calling it. It's really the death-instinct moved nearer the surface."

"If I get you a scalpel and a cadaver, will you cut out the death-instinct and let me touch it?"

"Couldn't," he put the grin into his voice, "it would be all used up in a cadaver. Find me a volunteer though, and he'll prove my case by volunteering."

"Your logic is unassailable," she smiled. "Get us some more coffee, okay?"

Render went to the kitchen, spiked and filled the cups, drank a glass of water and returned to the living room. Eileen had not moved; neither had Sigmund.

"What do you do when you're not busy being a Shaper?" she asked him.

"The same things most people do—eat, drink, sleep, talk, visit friends and not-friends, visit places, read . . ."

"Are you a forgiving man?"

"Sometimes. Why?"

"Then forgive me. I argued with a woman today, a woman named De Ville."

"What about?"

"You—and she accused me of such things it were better my mother had not born me. Are you going to marry her?"

"No, marriage is like alchemy. It served an important purpose once, but I hardly feel it's here to stay."

"Good."

"What did you say to her?"

"I gave her a clinic referral card that said, 'Diagnosis:
Bitch. Prescription: Drug therapy and a tight gag.' "

"Oh," said Render, showing interest.

"She tore it up and threw it in my face."

"I wonder why?"

She shrugged, smiled, made a gridwork on the tablecloth.

" 'Fathers and elders, I ponder,' " sighed Render, " 'what is hell?' "

" 'I maintain it is the suffering of being unable to love,' " she finished. "Was Dostoevsky right?"

"I doubt it. I'd put him into group therapy myself. That'd be *real* hell for him—with all those people acting like his characters and enjoying it so."

Render put down his cup and pushed his chair away from the table.

"I suppose you must be going now?"

"I really should," said Render.

"And I can't interest you in food?"

"No."

She stood.

"Okay, I'll get my coat."

"I could drive back myself and just set the car to return."

"No! I'm frightened by the notion of empty cars driving around the city. I'd feel the thing was haunted for the next two and a half weeks.

"Besides," she said, passing through the archway, "you promised me Winchester Cathedral."

"You want to do it today?"

"If you can be persuaded."

As Render stood deciding, Sigmund rose to his feet. He stood directly before him and stared upward into his eyes. He opened his mouth and closed it, several times, but no sounds emerged. Then he turned away and left the room.

"No," Eileen's voice came back, "you will stay here until I return."

Render picked up his coat and put it on, stuffing the medkit into the far pocket.

As they walked up the hall toward the elevator Render thought he heard a very faint and very distant howling sound.

In this place, of all places, Render knew he was the master of all things.

He was at home on those alien worlds, without time, those worlds where flowers copulate and the stars do battle in the heavens, falling at last to the ground, bleeding, like so many split and shattered chalices, and the seas part to reveal stairways leading down, and arms emerge from caverns, waving torches that flame like liquid faces—a midwinter night's nightmare, summer go a-begging, Render knew—for he had visited those worlds on a professional basis for the better part of a decade. With the crooking of a finger he could isolate the sorcerers, bring them to trial for treason against the realm—aye, and he could execute them, could appoint their successors.

Fortunately, this trip was only a courtesy call. . . .

He moved forward through the glade, seeking her.

He could feel her awakening presence all about him.

He pushed through the branches, stood beside the lake. It was cold, blue, and bottomless, the lake, reflecting that slender willow which had become the station of her arrival.

"Eileen!"

The willow swayed toward him, swayed away.

"Eileen! Come forth!"

Leaves fell, floated upon the lake, disturbed its mirror-like placidity, distorted the reflections.

"Eileen?"

All the leaves yellowed at once then, dropped down into the water. The tree ceased its swaying. There was a strange sound in the darkening sky, like the humming of high wires on a cold day.

Suddenly there was a double file of moons passing through the heavens.

Render selected one, reached up and pressed it. The others vanished as he did so, and the world brightened; the humming went out of the air.

He circled the lake to gain a subjective respite from the rejection-action and his counter to it. He moved up along an aisle of pines toward the place where he wanted the cathedral to occur. Birds sang now in the trees. The wind came softly by him. He felt her presence quite strongly.

"Here, Eileen. Here."

She walked beside him then, green silk, hair of bronze, eyes of molten emerald;

she wore an emerald in her forehead. She walked in green slippers over the pine
needles, saying: "What happened?"

"You were afraid."

"Why?"

"Perhaps you fear the cathedral. Are you a witch?" he smiled.

"Yes, but it's my day off."

He laughed, and he took her arm, and they rounded an island of foliage, and
there was the cathedral reconstructed on a grassy rise, pushing its way above
them and above the trees, climbing into the middle air, breathing out organ
notes, reflecting a stray ray of sunlight from a plane of glass.

"Hold tight to the world," he said. "Here comes the guided tour."

They moved forward and entered.

" ' . . . With its floor-to-ceiling shafts, like so many huge tree trunks, it
achieves a ruthless control over its spaces,' " he said. "—Got that from the
guidebook. This is the north transept. . . ."

" 'Greensleeves.' " she said, "the organ is playing 'Greensleeves.' "

"So it is. You can't blame me for that though.—Observe the scalloped capitals—"

"I want to go nearer to the music."

"Very well. This way then."

Render felt that something was wrong. He could not put his finger on it.
Everything retained its solidity. . . .

Something passed rapidly then, high above the cathedral, uttering a sonic
boom. Render smiled at that, remembering now; it was like a slip of the tongue:
for a moment he had confused Eileen with Jill—yes, that was what had happened.

Why, then . . .

A burst of white was the altar. He had never seen it before, anywhere. All the
walls were dark and cold about them. Candles flickered in corners and high
niches. The organ chorded thunder under invisible hands.

Render knew that something was wrong.

He turned to Eileen Shallot, whose hat was a green cone towering up into the
darkness, trailing wisps of green veiling. Her throat was in shadow, but . . .

"That necklace—Where?"

"I don't know," she smiled.

The goblet she held radiated a rosy light. It was reflected from her emerald.
It washed him like a draft of cool air.

"Drink?" she asked.

"Stand still," he ordered.

He willed the walls to fall down. They swam in shadow.

"Stand still!" he repeated urgently. "Don't do anything. Try not even to think."

"—Fall down!" he cried. And the walls were blasted in all directions and the
roof was flung over the top of the world, and they stood amid ruins lighted by
a single taper. The night was black as pitch.

"Why did you do that?" she asked, still holding the goblet out toward him.

"Don't think. Don't think anything," he said. "Relax. You are very tired. As
that candle flickers and wanes so does your consciousness. You can barely keep
awake. You can hardly stay on your feet. Your eyes are closing. There is nothing
to see here anyway."

He willed the candle to go out. It continued to burn.

"I'm not tired. Please have a drink."

He heard organ music through the night. A different tune, one he did not recognize at first.

"I need your cooperation."

"All right. Anything."

"Look! The moon!" he pointed

She looked upward and the moon appeared from behind an inky cloud.

". . . And another, and another."

Moons, like strung pearls, proceeded across the blackness.

"The last one will be red," he stated.

It was.

He reached out then with his right index finger, slid his arm sideways along his field of vision, then tried to touch the red moon.

His arm ached, it burned. He could not move it.

"Wake up!" he screamed.

The red moon vanished, and the white ones.

"Please take a drink."

He dashed the goblet from her hand and turned away. When he turned back she was still holding it before him.

"A drink?"

He turned and fled into the night.

It was like running through a waist-high snowdrift. It was wrong. He was compounding the error by running—he was minimizing his strength, maximizing hers. It was sapping his energies, draining him.

He stood still in the midst of the blackness.

"The world around me moves," he said. "I am its center."

"Please have a drink." she said, and he was standing in the glade beside their table set beside the lake. The lake was black and the moon was silver, and high, and out of his reach. A single candle flickered on the table, making her hair as silver as her dress. She wore the moon on her brow. A bottle of Romanée-Conti stood on the white cloth beside a wide-brimmed wine glass. It was filled to overflowing, that glass, and rosy beads clung to its lip. He was very thirsty, and she was lovelier than anyone he had ever seen before, and her necklace sparkled, and the breeze came cool off the lake, and there was something—something he should remember. . . .

He took a step toward her and his armor clinked lightly as he moved. He reached toward the glass and his right arm stiffened with pain and fell back to his side.

"You are wounded!"

Slowly, he turned his head. The blood flowed from the open wound in his biceps and ran down his arm and dripped from his fingertips. His armor had been breached. He forced himself to look away.

"Drink this, love. It will heal you."

She stood.

Bruce Sterling

Bruce Sterling (1954–   ) is a journalist and SF writer who was the chief polemicist behind the launch of "cyberpunk" science fiction in the 1980s. Sterling's pseudonymous presentation (as Vincent Omniveritas) of the Movement, in his small press fanzine, *Cheap Truth,* and elsewhere, particularly in *Mirrorshades: the Cyberpunk Anthology,* invigorated science fiction in the 1980s. Sterling, William Gibson, Lewis Shiner, and John Shirley, the four central figures of the Movement, positioned themselves as radical reformers of hard science fiction, and attracted many followers and imitators. Sterling and Gibson, at least, became public figures far outside science fiction.

Now Sterling is a major voice of his generation, a successful revolutionary. His picture has been on the cover of *Wired.* His stories, from pure fantasy to hard science fiction, are collected in *Crystal Express* (1989) and *Globalhead: Stories* (1994). He has also published a novel in collaboration with William Gibson, *The Difference Engine* (1990).

Sterling, whose career in SF began in the mid-70s, began the major phase of his writing with his stories of the Shaper/Mech series in the early 1980s. Sterling's first novel, *Involution Ocean* (1977), was billed as "A Harlan Ellison Discovery," and is a work heavily influenced by the 1960s New Wave writers, particularly J. G. Ballard. His second novel, *The Artificial Kid* (1980), first showed serious interest in technological speculation. It escaped general notice in the early 1980s that Sterling had begun a series of stories rich in scientific speculation and technological detail set in a future solar system swarming with humanity and aliens. The first of these is "Swarm."

Then came *Schismatrix* (1985), the culmination of his "swarm" stories of the early 80s, one of the best SF novels of the decade. *Schismatrix* is in the tradition of van Vogtian SF adventure, artfully written to a literary standard far above the general run of hard science fiction, but definitely genre science fiction. The stories and the novel have recently been republished together as *Schismatrix Plus* (1996).

"Swarm" is thematically in the man versus machine tradition of SF stories of biological versus technological progress, one of the great intellectual and social conflicts of our century.

SWARM

I will miss your conversation during the rest of the voyage," the alien said. Captain-Doctor Simon Afriel folded his jeweled hands over his gold-embroidered waistcoat. "I regret it also, ensign," he said in the alien's own hissing language. "Our talks together have been very useful to me. I would have paid to learn so much, but you gave it freely."

"But that was only information," the alien said. He shrouded his bead-bright eyes behind thick nictitating membranes. "We Investors deal in energy, and precious metals. To prize and pursue mere knowledge is an immature racial trait." The alien lifted the long ribbed frill behind his pinhole-sized ears.

"No doubt you are right," Afriel said, despising him. "We humans are as children to other races, however; so a certain immaturity seems natural to us." Afriel pulled off his sunglasses to rub the bridge of his nose. The starship cabin was drenched in searing blue light, heavily ultraviolet. It was the light the Investors preferred, and they were not about to change it for one human passenger.

"You have not done badly," the alien said magnanimously. "You are the kind of race we like to do business with: young, eager, plastic, ready for a wide variety of goods and experiences. We would have contacted you much earlier, but your technology was still too feeble to afford us a profit."

"Things are different now," Afriel said. "We'll make you rich."

"Indeed," the Investor said. The frill behind his scaly head flickered rapidly, a sign of amusement. "Within two hundred years you will be wealthy enough to buy from us the secret of our starflight. Or perhaps your Mechanist faction will discover the secret through research."

Afriel was annoyed. As a member of Reshaped faction, he did not appreciate the reference to the rival Mechanists. "Don't put too much stock in mere technical expertise," he said. "Consider the aptitude for languages we Shapers have. It makes our faction a much better trading partner. To a Mechanist, all Investors look alike."

The alien hesitated. Afriel smiled. He had appealed to the alien's personal ambition with his last statement, and the hint had been taken. That was where the Mechanists always erred. They tried to treat all Investors consistently, using the same programmed routines each time. They lacked imagination.

Something would have to be done about the Mechanists, Afriel thought. Something more permanent than the small but deadly confrontations between isolated ships in the Asteroid Belt and the ice-rich Rings of Saturn. Both factions maneuvered constantly, looking for a decisive stroke, bribing away each other's best talent, practicing ambush, assassination, and industrial espionage.

Captain-Doctor Simon Afriel was a past master of these pursuits. That was why the Reshaped faction had paid the millions of kilowatts necessary to buy his passage. Afriel held doctorates in biochemistry and alien linguistics, and a master's degree in magnetic weapons engineering. He was thirty-eight years old and had been Reshaped according to the state of the art at the time of his conception. His hormonal balance had been altered slightly to compensate for long periods spent in free-fall. He had no appendix. The structure of his heart had been redesigned for greater efficiency, and his large intestine had been altered to produce the vitamins normally made by intestinal bacteria. Genetic engineering and rigorous training in childhood had given him an intelligence quotient of one hundred and eighty. He was not the brightest of the agents of the Ring Council, but he was one of the most mentally stable and the best trusted.

"It seems a shame," the alien said, "that a human of your accomplishments should have to rot for two years in this miserable, profitless outpost."

"The years won't be wasted," Afriel said.

"But why have you chosen to study the Swarm? They can teach you nothing, since they cannot speak. They have no wish to trade, having no tools or technology. They are the only spacefaring race that is essentially without intelligence."

"That alone should make them worthy of study."

"Do you seek to imitate them, then? You would make monsters of yourselves." Again the ensign hesitated. "Perhaps you could do it. It would be bad for business, however."

There came a fluting burst of alien music over the ship's speakers, then a screeching fragment of Investor language. Most of it was too high-pitched for Afriel's ears to follow.

The alien stood, his jeweled skirt brushing the tips of his clawed birdlike feet. "The Swarm's symbiote has arrived," he said.

"Thank you," Afriel said. When the ensign opened the cabin door, Afriel could smell the Swarm's representative; the creature's warm yeasty scent had spread rapidly through the starship's recycled air.

Afriel quickly checked his appearance in a pocket mirror. He touched powder to his face and straightened the round velvet hat on his shoulder-length reddish-blond hair. His earlobes glittered with red impact-rubies, thick as his thumbs' ends, mined from the Asteroid Belt. His knee-length coat and waistcoat were of gold brocade; the shirt beneath was of dazzling fineness, woven with red-gold thread. He had dressed to impress the Investors, who expected and appreciated a prosperous look from their customers. How could he impress this new alien? Smell, perhaps. He freshened his perfume.

Beside the starship's secondary airlock, the Swarm's symbiote was chittering rapidly at the ship's commander. The commander was an old and sleepy Investor, twice the size of most of her crewmen. Her massive head was encrusted in a jeweled helmet. From within the helmet her clouded eyes glittered like cameras.

The symbiote lifted on its six posterior legs and gestured feebly with its four clawed forelimbs. The ship's artificial gravity, a third again as strong as Earth's, seemed to bother it. Its rudimentary eyes, dangling on stalks, were shut tight against the glare. It must be used to darkness, Afriel thought.

The commander answered the creature in its own language. Afriel grimaced, for he had hoped that the creature spoke Investor. Now he would have to learn another language, a language designed for a being without a tongue.

After another brief interchange the commander turned to Afriel. "The symbiote is not pleased with your arrival," she told Afriel in the Investor language. "There has apparently been some disturbance here involving humans, in the recent past. However, I have prevailed upon it to admit you to the Nest. The episode has been recorded. Payment for my diplomatic services will be arranged with your faction when I return to your native star system."

"I thank Your Authority," Afriel said. "Please convey to the symbiote my best personal wishes, and the harmlessness and humility of my intentions—" He broke off short as the symbiote lunged toward him, biting him savagely in the calf of his left leg. Afriel jerked free and leaped backward in the heavy artificial gravity, going into a defensive position. The symbiote had ripped away a long shred of his pants leg; it now crouched quietly, eating it.

"It will convey your scent and composition to its nestmates," said the commander. "This is necessary. Otherwise you would be classed as an invader, and the Swarm's warrior caste would kill you at once."

Afriel relaxed quickly and pressed his hand against the puncture wound to stop the bleeding. He hoped that none of the Investors had noticed his reflexive action. It would not mesh well with his story of being a harmless researcher.

"We will reopen the airlock soon," the commander said phlegmatically, leaning back on her thick reptilian tail. The symbiote continued to munch the shred of cloth. Afriel studied the creature's neckless segmented head. It had a mouth and nostrils; it had bulbous atrophied eyes on stalks; there were hinged slats that might be radio receivers, and two parallel ridges of clumped wriggling antennae, sprouting among three chitinous plates. Their function was unknown to him.

The airlock door opened. A rush of dense, smoky aroma entered the departure cabin. It seemed to bother the half-dozen Investors, who left rapidly. "We will return in six hundred and twelve of your days, as by our agreement," the commander said.

"I thank Your Authority," Afriel said.

"Good luck," the commander said in English. Afriel smiled.

The symbiote, with a sinuous wriggle of its segmented body, crept into the airlock. Afriel followed it. The airlock door shut behind them. The creature said nothing to him but continued munching loudly. The second door opened, and the symbiote sprang through it, into a wide, round stone tunnel. It disappeared at once into the gloom.

Afriel put his sunglasses into a pocket of his jacket and pulled out a pair of infrared goggles. He strapped them to his head and stepped out of the airlock. The artificial gravity vanished, replaced by the almost imperceptible gravity of the Swarm's asteroid nest. Afriel smiled, comfortable for the first time in weeks. Most of his adult life had been spent in free-fall, in the Shapers' colonies in the Rings of Saturn.

Squatting in a dark cavity in the side of the tunnel was a disk-headed furred animal the size of an elephant. It was clearly visible in the infrared of its own body heat. Afriel could hear it breathing. It waited patiently until Afriel had launched himself past it, deeper into the tunnel. Then it took its place in the end of the tunnel, puffing itself up with air until its swollen head securely plugged the exit into space. Its multiple legs sank firmly into sockets in the walls.

The Investors' ship had left. Afriel remained here, inside one of the millions of planetoids that circled the giant star Betelgeuse in a girdling ring with almost five times the mass of Jupiter. As a source of potential wealth it dwarfed the entire solar system, and it belonged, more or less, to the Swarm. At least, no other race had challenged them for it within the memory of the Investors.

Afriel peered up the corridor. It seemed deserted, and without other bodies to cast infrared heat, he could not see very far. Kicking against the wall, he floated hesitantly down the corridor.

He heard a human voice. "Dr. Afriel!"

"Dr. Mirny!" he called out. "This way!"

He first saw a pair of young symbiotes scuttling toward him, the tips of their clawed feet barely touching the walls. Behind them came a woman wearing goggles like his own. She was young, and attractive in the trim, anonymous way of the genetically reshaped.

She screeched something at the symbiotes in their own language, and they halted, waiting. She coasted forward, and Afriel caught her arm, expertly stopping their momentum.

"You didn't bring any luggage?" she said anxiously.

He shook his head. "We got your warning before I was sent out. I have only the clothes I'm wearing and a few items in my pockets."

She looked at him critically. "Is that what people are wearing in the Rings these days? Things have changed more than I thought."

Afriel glanced at his brocaded coat and laughed. "It's a matter of policy. The Investors are always readier to talk to a human who looks ready to do business on a large scale. All the Shapers' representatives dress like this these days. We've stolen a jump on the Mechanists; they still dress in those coveralls."

He hesitated, not wanting to offend her. Galina Mirny's intelligence was rated at almost two hundred. Men and women that bright were sometimes flighty and unstable, likely to retreat into private fantasy worlds or become enmeshed in strange and impenetrable webs of plotting and rationalization. High intelligence was the strategy the Shapers had chosen in the struggle for cultural dominance, and they were obliged to stick to it, despite its occasional disadvantages. They had tried breeding the Superbright—those with quotients over two hundred—but so many had defected from the Shapers' colonies that the faction had stopped producing them.

"You wonder about my own clothing," Mirny said.

"It certainly has the appeal of novelty," Afriel said with a smile.

"It was woven from the fibers of a pupa's cocoon," she said. "My original wardrobe was eaten by a scavenger symbiote during the troubles last year. I usually go nude, but I didn't want to offend you by too great a show of intimacy."

Afriel shrugged. "I often go nude myself, I never had much use for clothes except for pockets. I have a few tools on my person, but most are of little importance. We're Shapers, our tools are here." He tapped his head. "If you can show me a safe place to put my clothes . . ."

She shook her head. It was impossible to see her eyes for the goggles, which made her expression hard to read. "You've made your first mistake, Doctor. There are no places of our own here. It was the same mistake the Mechanist agents made, the same one that almost killed me as well. There is no concept of privacy or property here. This is the Nest. If you seize any part of it for yourself—to store equipment, to sleep in, whatever—then you become an intruder, an enemy. The two Mechanists—a man and a woman—tried to secure an empty chamber for their computer lab. Warriors broke down their door and devoured them. Scavengers ate their equipment, glass, metal, and all."

Afriel smiled coldly. "It must have cost them a fortune to ship all that material here."

Mirny shrugged. "They're wealthier than we are. Their machines, their mining. They meant to kill me, I think. Surreptitiously, so the warriors wouldn't be upset by a show of violence. They had a computer that was learning the language of the springtails faster than I could."

"But you survived," Afriel pointed out. "And your tapes and reports—especially the early ones, when you still had most of your equipment—were of tremendous interest. The Council is behind you all the way. You've become quite a celebrity in the Rings, during your absence."

"Yes, I expected as much," she said.

Afriel was nonplused. "If I found any deficiency in them," he said carefully, "it was in my own field, alien linguistics." He waved vaguely at the two symbiotes who accompanied her. "I assume you've made great progress in communicating with the symbiotes, since they seem to do all the talking for the Nest."

She looked at him with an unreadable expression and shrugged. "There are at least fifteen different kinds of symbiotes here. Those that accompany me are called the springtails, and they speak only for themselves. They are savages, Doctor, who received attention from the Investors only because they can still talk. They were a spacefaring race once, but they've forgotten it. They discovered the Nest and they were absorbed, they became parasites." She tapped one of them on the head. "I tamed these two because I learned to steal and beg food better than they can. They stay with me now and protect me from the larger ones. They are jealous, you know. They have only been with the Nest for perhaps ten thousand years and are still uncertain of their position. They still think, and wonder sometimes. After ten thousand years there is still a little of that left to them."

"Savages," Afriel said. "I can well believe that. One of them bit me while I was still aboard the starship. He left a lot to be desired as an ambassador."

"Yes, I warned him you were coming," said Mirny. "He didn't much like the idea, but I was able to bribe him with food. . . . I hope he didn't hurt you badly."

"A scratch," Afriel said. "I assume there's no chance of infection."

"I doubt it very much. Unless you brought your own bacteria with you."

"Hardly likely," Afriel said, offended. "I have no bacteria. And I wouldn't have brought microorganisms to an alien culture anyway."

Mirny looked away. "I thought you might have some of the special genetically altered ones. . . . I think we can go now. The springtail will have spread your scent by mouth-touching in the subsidiary chamber, ahead of us. It will be spread throughout the Nest in a few hours. Once it reaches the Queen, it will spread very quickly."

She jammed her feet against the hard shell of one of the young springtails and launched herself down the hall. Afriel followed her. The air was warm and he was beginning to sweat under his elaborate clothing, but his antiseptic sweat was odorless.

They exited into a vast chamber dug from the living rock. It was arched and oblong, eighty meters long and about twenty in diameter. It swarmed with members of the Nest.

There were hundreds of them. Most of them were workers, eight-legged and furred, the size of Great Danes. Here and there were members of the warrior caste, horse-sized furry monsters with heavy fanged heads the size and shape of overstuffed chairs.

A few meters away, two workers were carrying a member of the sensor caste, a being whose immense flattened head was attached to an atrophied body that was mostly lungs. The sensor had great platelike eyes, and its furred chitin sprouted long coiled antennae that twitched feebly as the workers bore it along. The workers clung to the hollowed rock of the chamber walls with hooked and suckered feet.

A paddle-limbed monster with a hairless, faceless head came sculling past them, through the warm reeking air. The front of its head was a nightmare of sharp grinding jaws and blunt armored acid spouts. "A tunneler," Mirny said. "It can take us deeper into the Nest—come with me." She launched herself toward it and took a handhold on its furry, segmented back. Afriel followed her, joined by the two immature springtails, who clung to the thing's hide with their forelimbs. Afriel shuddered at the warm, greasy feel of its rank, damp fur. It continued to scull through the air, its eight fringed paddle feet catching the air like wings.

"There must be thousands of them," Afriel said.

"I said a hundred thousand in my last report, but that was before I had fully explored the Nest. Even now there are long stretches I haven't seen. They must number close to a quarter of a million. This asteroid is about the size of the Mechanists' biggest base—Ceres. It still has rich veins of carbonaceous material. It's far from mined out."

Afriel closed his eyes. If he was to lose his goggles, he would have to feel his way, blind, through these teeming, twitching, wriggling thousands. "The population's still expanding, then?"

"Definitely," she said. "In fact, the colony will launch a mating swarm soon. There are three dozen male and female alates in the chambers near the Queen. Once they're launched, they'll mate and start new Nests. I'll take you to see them presently." She hesitated. "We're entering one of the fungal gardens now."

One of the young springtails quietly shifted position. Grabbing the tunneler's fur with its forelimbs, it began to gnaw on the cuff of Afriel's pants. Afriel kicked it soundly, and it jerked back, retracting its eyestalks.

When he looked up again, he saw that had entered a second chamber, much larger than the first. The walls around, overhead, and below were buried under an explosive profusion of fungus. The most common types were swollen barrel-like domes, multibranched massed thickets, and spaghetti-like tangled extrusions that moved very slightly in the faint and odorous breeze. Some of the barrels were surrounded by dim mists of exhaled spores.

"You see those caked-up piles beneath the fungus, its growth medium?" Mirny said.

"Yes."

"I'm not sure whether it is a plant form or just some kind of complex biochemical sludge," she said. "The point is that it grows in sunlight, on the outside of the asteroid. A food source that grows in naked space! Imagine what that would be worth, back in the Rings."

"There aren't words for its value," Afriel said.

"It's inedible by itself," she said. "I tried to eat a very small piece of it once. It was like trying to eat plastic."

"Have you eaten well, generally speaking?"

"Yes. Our biochemistry is quite similar to the Swarm's. The fungus itself is perfectly edible. The regurgitate is more nourishing, though. Internal fermentation in the worker hindgut adds to its nutritional value."

Afriel stared. "You grow used to it," Mirny said. "Later I'll teach you how to solicit food from the workers. It's a simple matter of reflex tapping—it's not controlled by pheromones, like most of their behavior." She brushed a long lock of clumped and dirty hair from the side of her face. "I hope the pheromonal samples I sent back were worth the cost of transportation."

"Oh, yes," said Afriel. "The chemistry of them was fascinating. We managed to synthesize most of the compounds. I was part of the research team myself." He hesitated. How far did he dare trust her? She had not been told about the experiment he and his superiors had planned. As far as Mirny knew, he was a simple, peaceful researcher, like herself. The Shapers' scientific community was suspicious of the minority involved in military work and espionage.

As an investment in the future, the Shapers had sent researchers of each of the nineteen alien races described to them by the Investors. This had cost the Shaper economy many gigawatts of precious energy and tons of rare metals and isotopes. In most cases, only two or three researchers could be sent; in seven cases, only one. For the Swarm, Galina Mirny had been chosen. She had gone peacefully, trusting in her intelligence and her good intentions to keep her alive and sane. Those who had sent her had not known whether her findings would be of any use or importance. They had only known that it was imperative that she be sent, even alone, even ill-equipped, before some other faction sent their own people and possibly discovered some technique or fact of overwhelming importance. And Dr. Mirny had indeed discovered such a situation. It had made her mission into a matter of Ring security. That was why Afriel had come.

"You synthesized the compounds?" she said. "Why?"

Afriel smiled disarmingly. "Just to prove to ourselves that we could do it, perhaps."

She shook her head. "No mind-games, Dr. Afriel, please. I came this far partly to escape from such things. Tell me the truth."

Afriel stared at her, regretting that the goggles meant he could not meet her eyes. "Very well," he said. "You should know, then, that I have been ordered by the Ring Council to carry out an experiment that may endanger both our lives."

Mirny was silent for a moment. "You're from Security, then?"

"My rank is captain."

"I knew it. . . . I knew it when those two Mechanists arrived. They were so polite, and so suspicious—I think they would have killed me at once if they hadn't hoped to bribe or torture some secret out of me. They scared the life out of me, Captain Afriel. . . . You scare me, too."

"We live in a frightening world, Doctor. It's a matter of faction security."

"Everything's a matter of faction security with your lot," she said. "I shouldn't take you any farther, or show you anything more. This Nest, these creatures—they're not *intelligent*, Captain. They can't think, they can't learn. They're innocent, primordially innocent. They have no knowledge of good and evil. They have no knowledge of *anything*. The last thing they need is to become pawns in a power struggle within some other race, light-years away."

The tunneler had turned into an exit from the fungal chambers and was paddling slowly along in the warm darkness. A group of creatures like gray, flattened basketballs floated by from the opposite direction. One of them settled on Afriel's sleeve, clinging with frail whiplike tentacles. Afriel brushed it gently away, and it broke loose, emitting a stream of foul reddish droplets.

"Naturally I agree with you in principle, Doctor," Afriel said smoothly. "But consider these Mechanists. Some of their extreme factions are already more than half machine. Do you expect humanitarian motives from them? They're cold, Doctor—cold and soulless creatures who can cut a living man or woman to bits and never feel their pain. Most of the other factions hate us. They call us racist supermen. Would you rather that one of these cults do what we must do, and use the results against us?"

"This is double-talk." She looked away. All around them workers laden down with fungus, their jaws full and guts stuffed with it, were spreading out into the Nest, scuttling alongside them or disappearing into branch tunnels departing in every direction, including straight up and straight down. Afriel saw a creature much like a worker, but with only six legs, scuttle past in the opposite direction, overhead. It was a parasite mimic. How long, he wondered, did it take a creature to evolve to look like that?

"It's no wonder that we've had so many defectors, back in the Rings," she said sadly. "If humanity is so stupid as to work itself into a corner like you describe, then it's better to have nothing to do with them. Better to live alone. Better not to help the madness spread."

"That kind of talk will only get us killed," Afriel said. "We owe an allegiance to the faction that produced us."

"Tell me truly, Captain," she said. "Haven't you ever felt the urge to leave everything—everyone—all your duties and constraints, and just go somewhere to think it all out? Your whole world, and your part in it? We're trained so hard, from childhood, and so much is demanded from us. Don't you think it's made us lose sight of our goals, somehow?"

"We live in space," Afriel said flatly. "Space is an unnatural environment, and it takes an unnatural effort from unnatural people to prosper there. Our minds are our tools, and philosophy has to come second. Naturally I've felt those urges you mention. They're just another threat to guard against. I believe in an ordered society. Technology has unleashed tremendous forces that are ripping society apart. Some one faction must arise from the struggle and integrate things. We Shapers have the wisdom and restraint to do it humanely. That's why I do the work I do." He hesitated. "I don't expect to see our day of triumph. I expect to die in some brush-fire conflict, or through assassination. It's enough that I can foresee that day."

"But the arrogance of it, Captain!" she said suddenly. "The arrogance of your little life and its little sacrifice! Consider the Swarm, if you really want your humane and perfect order. Here it is! Where it's always warm and dark, and it smells good, and food is easy to get, and everything is endlessly and perfectly recycled. The only resources that are ever lost are the bodies of the mating swarms, and a little air. A Nest like this one could last unchanged for hundreds of thousands of years. Hundreds . . . of thousands . . . of years. Who, or what, will remember us and our stupid faction in even a thousand years?"

Afriel shook his head. "That's not a valid comparison. There is no such long view for us. In another thousand years we'll be machines, or gods." He felt the top of his head; his velvet cap was gone. No doubt something was eating it by now.

The tunneler took them deeper into the asteroid's honeycombed free-fall maze. They saw the pupal chambers, where pallid larvae twitched in swaddled silk; the main fungal gardens; the graveyard pits, where winged workers beat ceaselessly at the soupy air, feverishly hot from the heat of decomposition. Corrosive black fungus ate the bodies of the dead into coarse black powder, carried off by blackened workers themselves three-quarters dead.

Later they left the tunneler and floated on by themselves. The woman moved with the ease of long habit; Afriel followed her, colliding bruisingly with squeaking workers. There were thousands of them, clinging to ceiling, walls, and floor, clustering and scurrying at every conceivable angle.

Later still they visited the chamber of the winged princes and princesses, an echoing round vault where creatures forty meters long hung crooked-legged in midair. Their bodies were segmented and metallic, with organic rocket nozzles on their thoraxes, where wings might have been. Folded along their sleek backs were radar antennae on long sweeping booms. They looked more like interplanetary probes under construction than anything biological. Workers fed them ceaselessly. Their bulging spiracled abdomens were full of compressed oxygen.

Mirny begged a large chunk of fungus from a passing worker, deftly tapping its antennae and provoking a reflex action. She handed most of the fungus to the two springtails, who devoured it greedily and looked expectantly for more.

Afriel tucked his legs into a free-fall lotus position and began chewing with determination on the leathery fungus. It was tough, but tasted good, like smoked meat—a delicacy he had tasted only once. The smell of smoke meant disaster in a Shaper's colony.

Mirny maintained a stony silence. "Food's no problem," Afriel said. "Where do we sleep?"

She shrugged. "Anywhere . . . there are unused niches and tunnels here and there. I suppose you'll want to see the Queen's chamber next."

"By all means."

"I'll have to get more fungus. The warriors are on guard there and have to be bribed with food."

She gathered an armful of fungus from another worker in the endless stream, and they moved on. Afriel, already totally lost, was further confused in the maze of chambers and tunnels. At last they exited into an immense lightless cavern, bright with infrared heat from the Queen's monstrous body. It was the colony's central factory. The fact that it was made of warm and pulpy flesh did not conceal its essentially industrial nature. Tons of predigested fungal pap went into the slick blind jaws at one end. The rounded billows of soft flesh digested and processed it, squirming, sucking, and undulating, with loud machine-like churnings and gurglings. Out of the other end came an endless conveyor-like blobbed stream of eggs, each one packed in a thick hormonal paste of lubrication. The workers avidly licked the eggs clean and bore them off to nurseries. Each egg was the size of a man's torso.

The process went on and on. There was no day or night here in the lightless center of the asteroid. There was no remnant of a diurnal rhythm in the genes of these creatures. The flow of production was as constant and even as the working of an automated mine.

"This is why I'm here," Afriel murmured in awe. "Just look at this, Doctor. The Mechanists have cybernetic mining machinery that is generations ahead of ours. But here—in the bowels of this nameless little world—is a genetic technology that feeds itself, maintains itself, runs itself, efficiently, endlessly, mindlessly. It's the perfect organic tool. The faction that could use these tireless workers could make itself an industrial titan. And our knowledge of biochemistry is unsurpassed. We Shapers are just the ones to do it."

"How do you propose to do that?" Mirny asked with open skepticism. "You would have to ship a fertilized queen all the way to the solar system. We could scarcely afford that, even if the Investors would let us, which they wouldn't."

"I don't need an entire Nest," Afriel said patiently. "I only need the genetic information from one egg. Our laboratories back in the Rings could clone endless numbers of workers."

"But the workers are useless without the Nest's pheromones. They need chemical cues to trigger their behavior modes."

"Exactly," Afriel said. "As it so happens, I possess those pheromones, synthesized and concentrated. What I must do now is test them. I must prove that I can use them to make the workers do what I choose. Once I've proven it's possible, I'm authorized to smuggle the genetic information necessary back to the Rings. The Investors won't approve. There are, of course, moral questions involved, and the Investors are not genetically advanced. But we can win their approval back with the profits we make. Best of all, we can beat the Mechanists at their own game."

"You've carried the pheromones here?" Mirny said. "Didn't the Investors suspect something when they found them?"

"Now it's you who has made an error," Afriel said calmly. "You assume that the Investors are infallible. You are wrong. A race without curiosity will never explore every possibility, the way we Shapers did." Afriel pulled up his pants cuff and extended his right leg. "Consider this varicose vein along my shin. Circulatory problems of this sort are common among those who spend a lot of time in free-fall. This vein, however, has been blocked artificially and treated to reduce osmosis. Within the vein are ten separate colonies of genetically altered bacteria, each one specially bred to produce a different Swarm pheromone."

He smiled. "The Investors searched me very thoroughly, including X-rays. But the vein appears normal to X-rays, and the bacteria are trapped within compartments in the vein. They are indetectable. I have a small medical kit on my person. It includes a syringe. We can use it to extract the pheromones and test them. When the tests are finished—and I feel sure they will be successful, in fact I've staked my career on it—we can empty the vein and all its compartments. The bacteria will die on contact with air. We can refill the vein with the yolk from a developing embryo. The cells may survive during the trip back, but even if they die, they can't rot inside my body. They'll never come in contact with any agent of decay. Back in the Rings, we can learn to activate and suppress different genes to produce the different castes, just as is done in nature. We'll have millions of workers, armies of warriors if need be, perhaps even organic rocketships, grown from altered alates. If this works, who do you think will remember me then, eh? Me and my arrogant little life and little sacrifice?"

She stared at him; even the bulky goggles could not hide her new respect and even fear. "You really mean to do it, then."

"I made the sacrifice of my time and energy. I expect results, Doctor."

"But it's kidnapping. You're talking about breeding a slave race."

Afriel shrugged, with contempt. "You're juggling words, Doctor. I'll cause this colony no harm. I may steal some of its workers' labor while they obey my own chemical orders, but that tiny theft won't be missed. I admit to the murder of one egg, but that is no more a crime than a human abortion. Can the theft of one strand of genetic material be called 'kidnapping'? I think not. As for the scandalous idea of a slave race—I reject it out of hand. These creatures are genetic robots. They will no more be slaves than are laser drills or cargo tankers. At the very worst, they will be our domestic animals."

Mirny considered the issue. It did not take her long. "It's true. It's not as if a common worker will be staring at the stars, pining for its freedom. They're just brainless neuters."

"Exactly, Doctor."

"They simply work. Whether they work for us or the Swarm makes no difference to them."

"I see that you've seized on the beauty of the idea."

"And if it worked," Mirny said, "if it worked, our faction would profit astronomically."

Afriel smiled genuinely, unaware of the chilling sarcasm of his expression. "And the personal profit, Doctor . . . the valuable expertise of the first to exploit the technique." He spoke gently, quietly. "Ever see a nitrogen snowfall on Titan? I think a habitat of one's own there—larger, much larger than anything possible before. . . . A genuine city, Galina, a place where a man can scrap the rules and discipline that madden him. . . ."

"Now it's you who are talking defection, Captain-Doctor."

Afriel was silent for a moment, then smiled with an effort. "Now you've ruined my perfect reverie," he said. "Besides, what I was describing was the well-earned retirement of a wealthy man, not some self-indulgent hermitage. . . . There's a clear difference." He hesitated. "In any case, may I conclude that you're with me in this project?"

She laughed and touched his arm. There was something uncanny about the small sound of her laugh, drowned by a great organic rumble from the Queen's monstrous intestines. . . . "Do you expect me to resist your arguments for two long years? Better that I give in now and save us friction."

"Yes."

"After all, you won't do any harm to the Nest. They'll never know anything has happened. And if their genetic line is successfully reproduced back home, there'll never be any reason for humanity to bother them again."

"True enough," said Afriel, though in the back of his mind he instantly thought of the fabulous wealth of Betelgeuse's asteroid system. A day would come, inevitably, when humanity would move to the stars en masse, in earnest. It would be well to know the ins and outs of every race that might become a rival.

"I'll help you as best I can," she said. There was a moment's silence. "Have you seen enough of this area?"

"Yes." They left the Queen's chamber.

"I didn't think I'd like you at first," she said candidly. "I think I like you better now. You seem to have a sense of humor that most Security people lack."

"It's not a sense of humor," Afriel said sadly. "It's a sense of irony disguised as one."

There were no days in the unending stream of hours that followed. There were only ragged periods of sleep, apart at first, later together, as they held each other in free-fall. The sexual feel of skin and body became an anchor to their common humanity, a divided, frayed humanity so many light-years away that the concept no longer had any meaning. Life in the warm and swarming tunnels was the here and now; the two of them were like germs in a bloodstream, moving ceaselessly with the pulsing ebb and flow. Hours stretched into months, and time itself grew meaningless.

The pheromonal tests were complex, but not impossibly difficult. The first of the ten pheromones was a simple grouping stimulus, causing large numbers of workers to gather as the chemical was spread from palp to palp. The workers then waited for further instructions; if none were forthcoming, they dispersed. To work effectively, the pheromones had to be given in a mix, or series, like computer commands; number one, grouping, for instance, together with the third pheromone, a transferral order, which caused the workers to empty any given chamber and move its effects to another. The ninth pheromone had the best industrial possibilities; it was a building order, causing the workers to gather tunnelers and dredgers and set them to work. Others were annoying; the tenth pheromone provoked grooming behavior, and the workers' furry palps stripped off the remaining rags of Afriel's clothing. The eighth pheromone sent the workers off to harvest material on the asteroid's surface, and in their eagerness to observe its effects the two explorers were almost trapped and swept off into space.

The two of them no longer feared the warrior caste. They knew that a dose of the sixth pheromone would send them scurrying off to defend the eggs, just as it sent the workers to tend them. Mirny and Afriel took advantage of this and secured their own chambers, dug by chemically hijacked workers and defended by a hijacked airlock guardian. They had their own fungal gardens to refresh the air, stocked with the fungus they liked best, and digested by a worker they kept drugged for their own food use. From constant stuffing and lack of exercise the worker had swollen up into its replete form and hung from one wall like a monstrous grape.

Afriel was tired. He had been without sleep recently for a long time; how long, he didn't know. His body rhythms had not adjusted as well as Mirny's, and he was prone to fits of depression and irritability that he had to repress with an effort. "The Investors will be back sometime," he said. "Sometime soon."

Mirny was indifferent. "The Investors," she said, and followed the remark with something in the language of the springtails, which he didn't catch. Despite his linguistic training, Afriel had never caught up with her in her use of the spring-tails' grating jargon. His training was almost a liability; the springtail language had decayed so much that it was a pidgin tongue, without rules or regularity. He knew enough to give them simple orders, and with his partial control of the warriors he had the power to back it up. The springtails were afraid of him, and the two juveniles that Mirny had tamed had developed into fat, overgrown ty-rants that freely terrorized their elders. Afriel had been too busy to seriously study the springtails or the other symbiotes. There were too many practical matters at hand.

"If they come too soon, I won't be able to finish my latest study," she said in English.

Afriel pulled off his infrared goggles and knotted them tightly around his neck. "There's a limit, Galina," he said, yawning. "You can only memorize so much data without equipment. We'll just have to wait quietly until we can get back. I hope the Investors aren't shocked when they see me. I lost a fortune with those clothes."

"It's been so dull since the mating swarm was launched. If it weren't for the new growth in the alates' chamber, I'd be bored to death." She pushed greasy hair from her face with both hands. "Are you going to sleep?"

"Yes, if I can."

"You won't come with me? I keep telling you that this new growth is impor-tant. I think it's a new caste. It's definitely not an alate. It has eyes like an alate, but it's clinging to the wall."

"It's probably not a Swarm member at all, then," he said tiredly, humoring her. "It's probably a parasite, an alate mimic. Go on and see it, if you want to. I'll be here waiting for you."

He heard her leave. Without his infrareds on, the darkness was still not quite total; there was a very faint luminosity from the steaming, growing fungus in the chamber beyond. The stuffed worker replete moved slightly on the wall, rustling and gurgling. He fell asleep.

When he awoke, Mirny had not yet returned. He was not alarmed. First, he visited the original airlock tunnel, where the Investors had first left him. It was irrational—the Investors always fulfilled their contracts—but he feared that they would arrive someday, become impatient, and leave without him. The Investors would have to wait, of course. Mirny could keep them occupied in the short time it would take him to hurry to the nursery and rob a developing egg of its living cells. It was best that the egg be as fresh as possible.

Later he ate. He was munching fungus in one of the anterior chambers when Mirny's two tamed springtails found him. "What do you want?" he asked in their language.

"Food-giver no good," the larger one screeched, waving its forelegs in brainless agitation. "Not work, not sleep."

"Not move," the second one said. It added hopefully, "Eat it now?"

Afriel gave them some of his food. They ate it, seemingly more out of habit than real appetite, which alarmed him. "Take me to her," he told them.

The two springtails scurried off; he followed them easily, adroitly dodging and weaving through the crowds of workers. They led him several miles through the network, to the alates' chamber. There they stopped, confused. "Gone," the large one said.

The chamber was empty. Afriel had never seen it empty before, and it was very unusual for the Swarm to waste so much space. He felt dread. "Follow the food-giver," he said. "Follow the smell."

The springtails snuffled without much enthusiasm along one wall; they knew he had no food and were reluctant to do anything without an immediate reward. At last one of them picked up the scent, or pretended to, and followed it up across the ceiling and into the mouth of a tunnel.

It was hard for Afriel to see much in the abandoned chamber; there was not enough infrared heat. He leaped upward after the springtail.

He heard the roar of a warrior and the springtail's choked-off screech. It came flying from the tunnel's mouth, a spray of clotted fluid bursting from its ruptured head. It tumbled end over end until it hit the far wall with a flaccid crunch. It was already dead.

The second springtail fled at once, screeching with grief and terror. Afriel landed on the lip of the tunnel, sinking into a crouch as his legs soaked up momentum. He could smell the acrid stench of the warrior's anger, a pheromone so thick that even a human could scent it. Dozens of other warriors would group here within minutes, or seconds. Behind the enraged warrior he could hear workers and tunnelers shifting and cementing rock.

He might be able to control one enraged warrior, but never two, or twenty. He launched himself from the chamber wall and out an exit.

He searched for the other springtail—he felt sure he could recognize it, since it was so much bigger than the others—but he could not find it. With its keen sense of smell, it could easily avoid him if it wanted to.

Mirny did not return. Uncountable hours passed. He slept again. He returned to the alates' chamber; there were warriors on guard there, warriors that were not interested in food and brandished their immense serrated fangs when he approached. They looked ready to rip him apart; the faint reek of aggressive pheromones hung about the place like a fog. He did not see any symbiotes of any kind on the warriors' bodies. There was one species, a thing like a huge tick, that clung only to warriors, but even the ticks were gone.

He returned to his chambers to wait and think. Mirny's body was not in the garbage pits. Of course, it was possible that something else might have eaten her. Should he extract the remaining pheromone from the spaces in his vein and try to break into the alates' chamber? He suspected that Mirny, or whatever was left of her, was somewhere in the tunnel where the springtail had been killed. He had never explored that tunnel himself. There were thousands of tunnels he had never explored.

He felt paralyzed by indecision and fear. If he was quiet, if he did nothing, the Investors might arrive at any moment. He could tell the Ring Council anything he wanted about Mirny's death; if he had the genetics with him, no one would quibble. He did not love her; he respected her, but not enough to give up his life, or his faction's investment. He had not thought of the Ring Council in a long time, and the thought sobered him. He would have to explain his decision. . . .

He was still in a brown study when he heard a whoosh of air as his living airlock deflated itself. Three warriors had come for him. There was no reek of anger about them. They moved slowly and carefully. He knew better than to try to resist. One of them seized him gently in its massive jaws and carried him off.

It took him to the alates' chamber and into the guarded tunnel. A new, large chamber had been excavated at the end of the tunnel. It was filled almost to bursting by a black-splattered white mass of flesh. In the center of the soft speckled mass were a mouth and two damp, shining eyes, on stalks. Long tendrils like conduits dangled, writhing, from a clumped ridge above the eyes. The tendrils ended in pink, fleshy pluglike clumps.

One of the tendrils had been thrust through Mirny's skull. Her body hung in midair, limp as wax. Her eyes were open, but blind.

Another tendril was plugged into the braincase of a mutated worker. The worker still had the pallid tinge of a larva; it was shrunken and deformed, and its mouth had the wrinkled look of a human mouth. There was a blob like a tongue in the mouth, and white ridges like human teeth. It had no eyes.

It spoke with Mirny's voice. "Captain-Doctor Afriel . . ."

"Galina . . ."

"I have no such name. You may address me as Swarm."

Afriel vomited. The central mass was an immense head. Its brain almost filled the room.

It waited politely until Afriel had finished.

"I find myself awakened again," Swarm said dreamily. "I am pleased to see that there is no major emergency to concern me. Instead it is a threat that has become almost routine." It hesitated delicately. Mirny's body moved slightly in midair; her breathing was inhumanly regular. The eyes opened and closed. "Another young race."

"What are you?"

"I am the Swarm. That is, I am one of its castes. I am a tool, an adaptation; my specialty is intelligence. I am not often needed. It is good to be needed again."

"Have you been here all along? Why didn't you greet us? We'd have dealt with you. We meant no harm."

The wet mouth on the end of the plug made laughing sounds. "Like yourself, I enjoy irony," it said. "It is a pretty trap you have found yourself in, Captain-Doctor. You meant to make the Swarm work for you and your race. You meant to breed us and study us and use us. It is an excellent plan, but one we hit upon long before your race evolved."

Stung by panic, Afriel's mind raced frantically. "You're an intelligent being," he said. "There's no reason to do us any harm. Let us talk together. We can help you."

"Yes," Swarm agreed. "You will be helpful. Your companion's memories tell me that this is one of those uncomfortable periods when galactic intelligence is rife. Intelligence is a great bother. It makes all kinds of trouble for us."

"What do you mean?"

"You are a young race and lay great stock by your own cleverness," Swarm said. "As usual, you fail to see that intelligence is not a survival trait."

Afriel wiped sweat from his face. "We've done well," he said. "We came to you, and peacefully. You didn't come to us."

"I refer to exactly that," Swarm said urbanely. "This urge to expand, to explore, to develop, is just what will make you extinct. You naively suppose that you can continue to feed your curiosity indefinitely. It is an old story, pursued by countless races before you. Within a thousand years—perhaps a little longer—your species will vanish."

"You intend to destroy us, then? I warn you it will not be an easy task—"

"Again you miss the point. Knowledge is power! Do you suppose that fragile little form of yours—your primitive legs, your ludicrous arms and hands, your tiny, scarcely wrinkled brain—can *contain* all that power? Certainly not! Already your race is flying to pieces under the impact of your own expertise. The original human form is becoming obsolete. Your own genes have been altered, and you, Captain-Doctor, are a crude experiment. In a hundred years you will be a relic. In a thousand years you will not even be a memory. Your race will go the same way as a thousand others."

"And what way is that?"

"I do not know." The thing on the end of the Swarm's arm made a chuckling sound. "They have passed beyond my ken. They have all discovered something, learned something, that has caused them to transcend my understanding. It may be that they even transcend *being*. At any rate, I cannot sense their presence anywhere. They seem to do nothing, they seem to interfere in nothing; for all intents and purposes, they seem to be dead. Vanished. They may have become gods, or ghosts. In either case, I have no wish to join them."

"So then—so then you have—"

"Intelligence is very much a two-edged sword, Captain-Doctor. It is useful only up to a point. It interferes with the business of living. Life, and intelligence, do not mix very well. They are not at all closely related, as you childishly assume."

"But you, then—you are a rational being—"

"I am a tool, as I said." The mutated device on the end of its arm made a sighing noise. "When you began your pheromonal experiments, the chemical imbalance became apparent to the Queen. It triggered certain genetic patterns within her body, and I was reborn. Chemical sabotage is a problem that can best be dealt with by intelligence. I am a brain replete, you see, specially designed to be far more intelligent than any young race. Within three days I was fully self-conscious. Within five days I had deciphered these markings on my body. They are the genetically encoded history of my race . . . within five days and two hours I recognized the problem at hand and knew what to do. I am now doing it. I am six days old."

"What is it you intend to do?"

"Your race is a very vigorous one. I expect it to be here, competing with us, within five hundred years. Perhaps much sooner. It will be necessary to make a thorough study of such a rival. I invite you to join our community on a permanent basis."

"What do you mean?"

"I invite you to become a symbiote. I have here a male and a female, whose genes are altered and therefore without defects. You make a perfect breeding pair. It will save me a great deal of trouble with cloning."

"You think I'll betray my race and deliver a slave species into your hands?"

"Your choice is simple, Captain-Doctor. Remain an intelligent, living being, or become a mindless puppet, like your partner. I have taken over all the functions of her nervous system; I can do the same to you."

"I can kill myself."

"That might be troublesome, because it would make me resort to developing a cloning technology. Technology, though I am capable of it, is painful to me. I am a genetic artifact; there are fail-safes within me that prevent me from taking over the Nest for my own uses. That would mean falling into the same trap of progress as other intelligent races. For similar reasons, my life span is limited. I will live for only a thousand years, until your race's brief flurry of energy is over and peace resumes once more."

"Only a thousand years?" Afriel laughed bitterly. "What then? You kill off my descendants, I assume, having no further use for them."

"No. We have not killed any of the fifteen other races we have taken for defensive study. It has not been necessary. Consider that small scavenger floating by your head, Captain-Doctor, that is feeding on your vomit. Five hundred million years ago its ancestors made the galaxy tremble. When they attacked us, we unleashed their own kind upon them. Of course, we altered our side, so that they were smarter, tougher, and, naturally, totally loyal to us. Our Nests were the only world they knew, and they fought with a valor and inventiveness we never could have matched. . . . Should your race arrive to exploit us, we will naturally do the same."

"We humans are different."

"Of course."

"A thousand years here won't change us. You will die and our descendants will take over this Nest. We'll be running things, despite you, in a few generations. The darkness won't make any difference."

"Certainly not. You don't need eyes here. You don't need anything."

"You'll allow me to stay alive? To teach them anything I want?"

"Certainly, Captain-Doctor. We are doing you a favor, in all truth. In a thousand years your descendants here will be the only remnants of the human race. We are generous with our immortality; we will take it upon ourselves to preserve you."

"You're wrong, Swarm. You're wrong about intelligence, and you're wrong about everything else. Maybe other races would crumble into parasitism, but we humans are different."

"Certainly. You'll do it, then?"

"Yes. I accept your challenge. And I will defeat you."

"Splendid. When the Investors return here, the springtails will say that they have killed you, and will tell them to never return. They will not return. The humans should be the next to arrive."

"If I don't defeat you, they will."

"Perhaps." Again it sighed. "I'm glad I don't have to absorb you. I would have missed your conversation."

Nancy Kress

Nancy Kress (1948–) entered science fiction in the early 1980s but flowered by the early 90s. Kress's early novels were genre fantasy, but her short fiction, which gained her initial recognition, was SF, collected in *Trinity and Other Stories* (1985). Her most ambitious work, in which it became clear that she was determined to develop both character and science in her fiction, began with the novel *An Alien Light* (1988), and then *Brain Rose* (1990). Meanwhile, she continued to write an impressive body of short fiction, much of it collected in *The Aliens of Earth* (1993). With the publication of her Beggars novels (*Beggars in Spain* [1993], *Beggars and Choosers* [1994], and *Beggars Ride* [1996]), and in the technothriller *Oaths and Miracles* (1996), she showed the full strength of her powers.

Kress, as much as any SF writer today, is an heir to the tradition of H. G. Wells. Nowhere in her work is this more evident than in "Beggars in Spain" and the novels that have grown out of it. With this story, she began her magnum opus. In this story she deals with human and social evolution, with class and economic issues, and with ordinary characters, as Wells did in "A Story of the Days to Come."

BEGGARS IN SPAIN

With energy and sleepless vigilance go forward and give us victories.
—Abraham Lincoln, to Maj. Gen. Joseph Hooker, 1863

I

They sat stiffly on his antique Eames chairs, two people who didn't want to be here, or one person who didn't want to and one who resented the other's reluctance. Dr. Ong had seen this before. Within two minutes he was sure: the woman was the silently furious resister. She would lose. The man would pay for it later, in little ways, for a long time.

"I presume you've performed the necessary credit checks already," Roger Camden said pleasantly. "So let's get right on to details, shall we, Doctor?"

"Certainly," Ong said. "Why don't we start by your telling me all the genetic modifications you're interested in for the baby."

The woman shifted suddenly on her chair. She was in her late twenties—clearly a second wife—but already had a faded look, as if keeping up with Roger Camden was wearing her out. Ong could easily believe that. Mrs. Camden's hair was brown, her eyes were brown, her skin had a brown tinge that might have been pretty if her cheeks had had any color. She wore a brown coat, neither fashionable nor cheap, and shoes that looked vaguely orthopedic. Ong glanced at his records for her name: Elizabeth. He would bet people forgot it often.

Next to her, Roger Camden radiated nervous vitality, a man in late middle-age whose bullet-shaped head did not match his careful haircut and Italian-silk business suit. Ong did not need to consult his file to recall anything about Camden. A caricature of the bullet-shaped head had been the leading graphic of yesterday's on-line edition of the *Wall Street Journal*: Camden had led a major coup in cross-border data-atoll investment. Ong was not sure what cross-border data-atoll investment was.

"A girl," Elizabeth Camden said. Ong hadn't expected her to speak first. Her voice was another surprise: upper-class British. "Blond. Green eyes. Tall. Slender."

Ong smiled. "Appearance factors are the easiest to achieve, as I'm sure you already know. But all we can do about 'slenderness' is give her a genetic disposition in that direction. How you feed the child will naturally—"

"Yes, yes," Roger Camden said, "that's obvious. Now: intelligence. *High* intelligence. And a sense of daring."

"I'm sorry, Mr. Camden—personality factors are not yet understood well enough to allow genet—"

"Just testing," Camden said, with a smile that Ong thought was probably supposed to be lighthearted.

Elizabeth Camden said, "Musical ability."

"Again, Mrs. Camden, a disposition to be musical is all we can guarantee."

"Good enough," Camden said. "The full array of corrections for any potential gene-linked health problem, of course."

"Of course," Dr. Ong said. Neither client spoke. So far theirs was a fairly modest list, given Camden's money; most clients had to be argued out of contradictory genetic tendencies, alteration overload, or unrealistic expectations. Ong waited. Tension prickled in the room like heat.

"And," Camden said, "no need to sleep."

Elizabeth Camden jerked her head sideways to look out the window.

Ong picked a paper magnet off his desk. He made his voice pleasant. "May I ask how you learned whether that genetic-modification program exists?"

Camden grinned. "You're not denying it exists. I give you full credit for that, Doctor."

Ong held onto his temper. "May I ask how you learned whether the program exists?"

Camden reached into an inner pocket of his suit. The silk crinkled and pulled; body and suit came from different social classes. Camden was, Ong remembered, a Yagaiist, a personal friend of Kenzo Yagai himself. Camden handed Ong hard copy: program specifications.

"Don't bother hunting down the security leak in your data banks, Doctor—you won't find it. But if it's any consolation, neither will anybody else. Now." He leaned suddenly forward. His tone changed. "I know that you've created twenty children so far who don't need to sleep at all. That so far nineteen are healthy, intelligent, and psychologically normal. In fact, better than normal—they're all unusually precocious. The oldest is already four years old and can read in two languages. I know you're thinking of offering this genetic modification on the open market in a few years. All I want is a chance to buy it for my daughter *now*. At whatever price you name."

Ong stood. "I can't possibly discuss this with you unilaterally, Mr. Camden. Neither the theft of our data—"

"Which wasn't a theft—your system developed a spontaneous bubble regurgitation into a public gate, have a hell of a time proving otherwise—"

"—*nor* the offer to purchase this particular genetic modification lies in my sole area of authority. Both have to be discussed with the Institute's board of directors."

"By all means, by all means. When can I talk to them, too?"

"You?"

Camden, still seated, looked at him. It occurred to Ong that there were few men who could look so confident eighteen inches below eye level. "Certainly. I'd like the chance to present my offer to whoever has the actual authority to accept it. That's only good business."

"This isn't solely a business transaction, Mr. Camden."

"It isn't solely pure scientific research, either," Camden retorted. "You're a for-profit corporation here. *With* certain tax breaks available only to firms meeting certain fair-practice laws."

For a minute Ong couldn't think what Camden meant. "Fair-practice laws . . ."

". . . are designed to protect minorities who are suppliers. I know, it hasn't ever been tested in the case of customers, except for redlining in Y-energy installations. But it could be tested, Dr. Ong. Minorities are entitled to the same product offerings as nonminorities. I know the Institute would not welcome a court case, Doctor. None of your twenty genetic beta-test families is either black or Jewish."

"A court . . . but you're not black *or* Jewish!"

"I'm a different minority. Polish-American. The name was Kaminisky." Camden finally stood. And smiled warmly. "Look, it is preposterous. You know that, and I know that, and we both know what a grand time journalists would have with it anyway. And you know that I don't want to sue you with a preposterous case, just to use the threat of premature and adverse publicity to get what I want. I don't want to make threats at all, believe me I don't. I just want this marvelous advancement you've come up with for my daughter." His face changed, to an expression Ong wouldn't have believed possible on those particular features: wistfulness. "Doctor—do you know how much more I could have accomplished if I hadn't had to *sleep* all my life?"

Elizabeth Camden said harshly, "You hardly sleep now."

Camden looked down at her as if he had forgotten she was there. "Well, no, my dear, not now. But when I was young . . . college, I might have been able to finish college and still support . . . well. None of that matters now. What matters, Doctor, is that you and I and your board come to an agreement."

"Mr. Camden, please leave my office now."

"You mean before you lose your temper at my presumptuousness? You wouldn't be the first. I'll expect to have a meeting set up by the end of next week, whenever and wherever you say, of course. Just let my personal secretary, Diane Clavers, know the details. Anytime that's best for you."

Ong did not accompany them to the door. Pressure throbbed behind his temples. In the doorway Elizabeth Camden turned. "What happened to the twentieth one?"

"What?"

"The twentieth baby. My husband said nineteen of them are healthy and normal. What happened to the twentieth?"

The pressure grew stronger, hotter. Ong knew that he should not answer; that Camden probably already knew the answer even if his wife didn't; that he, Ong, was going to answer anyway; that he would regret the lack of self-control, bitterly, later.

"The twentieth baby is dead. His parents turned out to be unstable. They separated during the pregnancy, and his mother could not bear the twenty-four-hour crying of a baby who never sleeps."

Elizabeth Camden's eyes widened. "She killed it?"

"By mistake," Camden said shortly. "Shook the little thing too hard." He frowned at Ong. "Nurses, doctor. In shifts. You should have picked only parents wealthy enough to afford nurses in shifts."

"That's horrible!" Mrs. Camden burst out, and Ong could not tell if she meant the child's death, the lack of nurses, or the Institute's carelessness. Ong closed his eyes.

When they had gone, he took ten milligrams of cyclobenzaprine-III. For his back—it was solely for his back. The old injury hurting again. Afterward he stood for a long time at the window, still holding the paper magnet, feeling the pressure recede from his temples, feeling himself calm down. Below him Lake Michigan lapped peacefully at the shore; the police had driven away the homeless in another raid just last night, and they hadn't yet had time to return. Only their debris remained, thrown into the bushes of the lakeshore park: tattered blankets, newspapers, plastic bags like pathetic trampled standards. It was illegal to sleep in the park, illegal to enter it without a resident's permit, illegal to be homeless and without a residence. As Ong watched, uniformed park attendants began methodically spearing newspapers and shoving them into clean self-propelled receptacles.

Ong picked up the phone to call the president of Biotech Institute's board of directors.

Four men and three women sat around the polished mahogany table of the conference room. *Doctor, lawyer, Indian chief,* thought Susan Melling, looking from Ong to Sullivan to Camden. She smiled. Ong caught the smile and looked frosty. Pompous ass. Judy Sullivan, the Institute lawyer, turned to speak in a low voice to Camden's lawyer, a thin, nervous man with the look of being owned. The owner, Roger Camden, the Indian chief himself, was the happiest-looking person in the room. The lethal little man—what did it take to become that rich, starting from nothing? She, Susan, would certainly never know—radiated excitement. He beamed, he glowed, so unlike the usual parents-to-be that Susan was intrigued. Usually the prospective daddies and mommies—especially the daddies—sat there looking as if they were at a corporate merger. Camden looked as if he were at a birthday party.

Which, of course, he was. Susan grinned at him and was pleased when he grinned back. Wolfish, but with a sort of delight that could only be called innocent—what would he be like in bed? Ong frowned majestically and rose to speak.

"Ladies and gentlemen, I think we're ready to start. Perhaps introductions are in order. Mr. Roger Camden, Mrs. Camden are, of course, our clients. Mr. John Jaworski, Mr. Camden's lawyer. Mr. Camden, this is Judith Sullivan, the Institute's head of legal; Samuel Krenshaw, representing Institute director Dr. Brad Marsteiner, who unfortunately couldn't be here today; and Dr. Susan Melling, who developed the genetic modification affecting sleep. A few legal points of interest to both parties—"

"Forget the contracts for a minute," Camden interrupted. "Let's talk about the sleep thing. I'd like to ask a few questions."

Susan said, "What would you like to know?" Camden's eyes were very blue in his blunt-featured face; he wasn't what she had expected. Mrs. Camden, who apparently lacked both a first name and a lawyer, since Jaworski had been introduced as her husband's but not hers, looked either sullen or scared; it was difficult to tell which.

Ong said sourly, "Then perhaps we should start with a short presentation by Dr. Melling."

Susan would have preferred a Q&A, to see what Camden would ask. But she had annoyed Ong enough for one session. Obediently she rose.

"Let me start with a brief description of sleep. Researchers have known for a long time that there are actually three kinds of sleep. One is 'slow-wave sleep,' characterized on an EEG by delta waves. One is 'rapid-eye-movement sleep' or REM sleep, which is much lighter sleep and contains most dreaming. Together, these two make up 'core sleep.' The third type of sleep is 'optional sleep,' so-called because people seem to get along without it with no ill effects, and some short sleepers don't do it at all, sleeping naturally only three or four hours a night."

"That's me," Camden said. "I trained myself into it. Couldn't everybody do that?"

Apparently they were going to have a Q&A after all. "No. The actual sleep mechanism has some flexibility, but not the same amount for every person. The raphe nuclei on the brain stem—"

Ong said, "I don't think we need that level of detail, Susan. Let's stick to basics."

Camden said, "The raphe nuclei regulate the balance among neurotransmitters and peptides that lead to a pressure to sleep, don't they?"

Susan couldn't help it; she grinned. Camden, the laser-sharp ruthless financier, sat trying to look solemn, a third-grader waiting to have his homework praised. Ong looked sour. Mrs. Camden looked away, out the window.

"Yes, that's correct, Mr. Camden. You've done your research."

Camden said, "This is my *daughter*," and Susan caught her breath. When was the last time she had heard that note of reverence in anyone's voice? But no one in the room seemed to notice.

"Well, then," Susan said, "you already know that the reason people sleep is because a pressure to sleep builds up in the brain. Over the last twenty years, research has determined that's the *only* reason. Neither slow-wave sleep nor REM sleep serves functions that can't be carried on while the body and brain are awake. A lot goes on during sleep, but it can go awake just as well, if other hormonal adjustments are made.

"Sleep once served an important evolutionary function. Once Clem Premammal was done filling his stomach and squirting his sperm around, sleep kept him immobile and away from predators. Sleep was an aid to survival. But now it's a leftover mechanism, like the appendix. It switches on every night, but the need is gone. So we turn off the switch at its source, in the genes."

Ong winced. He hated it when she oversimplified like that. Or maybe it was the lightheartedness he hated. If Marsteiner were making this presentation, there'd be no Clem Pre-mammal.

Camden said, "What about the need to dream?"

"Not necessary. A leftover bombardment of the cortex to keep it on semialert in case a predator attacked during sleep. Wakefulness does that better."

"Why not have wakefulness instead, then? From the start of the evolution?"

He was testing her. Susan gave him a full, lavish smile, enjoying his brass. "I told you. Safety from predators. But when a modern predator attacks—say, a cross-border data-atoll investor—it's safer to be awake."

Camden shot at her, "What about the high percentage of REM sleep in fetuses and babies?"

"Still an evolutionary hangover. Cerebrum develops perfectly well without it."

"What about neural repair during slow-wave sleep?"

"That does go on. But it can go on during wakefulness, if the DNA is programmed to do so. No loss of neural efficiency, as far as we know."

"What about the release of human growth enzyme in such large concentrations during slow-wave sleep?"

Susan looked at him admiringly. "Goes on without the sleep. Genetic adjustments tie it to other changes in the pineal gland."

"What about the—"

"The *side effects?*" Mrs. Camden said. Her mouth turned down. "What about the bloody side effects?"

Susan turned to Elizabeth Camden. She had forgotten she was there. The younger woman stared at Susan, mouth still turned down at the corners.

"I'm glad you asked that, Mrs. Camden. Because there *are* side effects." Susan paused; she was enjoying herself. "Compared to their age mates, the nonsleep children—who have *not* had IQ genetic manipulation—are more intelligent, better at problem-solving, and more joyous."

Camden took out a cigarette. The archaic, filthy habit surprised Susan. Then she saw that it was deliberate: Roger Camden drawing attention to an ostentatious display to draw attention away from what he was feeling. His cigarette lighter was gold, monogrammed, innocently gaudy.

"Let me explain," Susan said. "REM sleep bombards the cerebral cortex with random neural firings from the brainstem; dreaming occurs because the poor besieged cortex tries so hard to make sense of the activated images and memories. It spends a lot of energy doing that. Without that energy expenditure, nonsleep cerebrums save the wear and tear and do better at coordinating real-life input. Thus—greater intelligence and problem-solving.

"Also, doctors have known for sixty years that antidepressants, which lift the mood of depressed patients, also suppress REM sleep entirely. What they have proved in the last ten years is that the reverse is equally true: suppress REM sleep and people don't *get* depressed. The nonsleep kids are cheerful, outgoing . . . *joyous*. There's no other word for it."

"At what cost?" Mrs. Camden said. She held her neck rigid, but the corners of her jaw worked.

"No cost. No negative side effects at all."

"So far," Mrs. Camden shot back.

Susan shrugged. "So far."

"They're only four years old! At the most!"

Ong and Krenshaw were studying her closely. Susan saw the moment the Camden woman realized it; she sank back into her chair, drawing her fur coat around her, her face blank.

Camden did not look at his wife. He blew a cloud of cigarette smoke. "Everything has costs, Dr. Melling."

She liked the way he said her name. "Ordinarily, yes. Especially in genetic modification. But we honestly have not been able to find any here, despite looking." She smiled directly into Camden's eyes. "Is it too much to believe that just once the universe has given us something wholly good, wholly a step forward, wholly beneficial? Without hidden penalties?"

"Not the universe. The intelligence of people like you," Camden said, surprising Susan more than anything that had gone before. His eyes held hers. She felt her chest tighten.

"I think," Dr. Ong said dryly, "that the philosophy of the universe may be beyond our concerns here. Mr. Camden, if you have no further medical questions, perhaps we can return to the legal points Ms. Sullivan and Mr. Jaworski have raised. Thank you, Dr. Melling."

Susan nodded. She didn't look again at Camden. But she knew what he said, how he looked, that he was there.

The house was about what she had expected, a huge mock Tudor on Lake Michigan north of Chicago. The land heavily wooded between the gate and the house, open between the house and the surging water. Patches of snow dotted the dormant grass. Biotech had been working with the Camdens for four months, but this was the first time Susan had driven to their home.

As she walked toward the house, another car drove up behind her. No, a truck, continuing around the curved driveway to a service entry at the side of the house. One man rang the service bell; a second began to unload a plastic-wrapped playpen from the back of the truck. White, with pink and yellow bunnies. Susan briefly closed her eyes.

Camden opened the door himself. She could see the effort not to look worried. "You didn't have to drive out, Susan—I'd have come into the city."

"No, I didn't want you to do that, Roger. Mrs. Camden is here?"

"In the living room." Camden led her into a large room with a stone fireplace. English country-house furniture; prints of dogs or boats, all hung eighteen inches too high: Elizabeth Camden must have done the decorating. She did not rise from her wing chair as Susan entered.

"Let me be concise and fast," Susan said. "I don't want to make this any more drawn out for you than I have to. We have all the amniocentesis, ultrasound, and Langston test results. The fetus is fine, developing normally for two weeks, no problems with the implant on the uterus wall. But a complication has developed."

"What?" Camden said. He took out a cigarette, looked at his wife, put it back unlit.

Susan said quietly, "Mrs. Camden, by sheer chance both your ovaries released eggs last month. We removed one for the gene surgery. By more sheer chance the second fertilized and implanted. You're carrying two fetuses."

Elizabeth Camden grew still. "Twins?"

"No," Susan said. Then she realized what she had said. "I mean, yes. They're twins, but nonidentical. Only one has been genetically altered. The other will be no more similar to her than any two siblings. It's a so-called 'normal' baby. And I know you didn't want a so-called normal baby."

Camden said, "No. I didn't."

Elizabeth Camden said, "I did."

Camden shot her a fierce look that Susan couldn't read. He took out the cigarette again, lit it. His face was in profile to Susan, thinking intently; she doubted he knew the cigarette was there or that he was lighting it. "Is the baby being affected by the other one's being there?"

"No," Susan said. "No, of course not. They're just . . . coexisting."

"Can you abort it?"

"Not without risk of aborting both of them. Removing the unaltered fetus might cause changes in the uterus lining that could lead to a spontaneous miscarriage of the other." She drew a deep breath. "There's that option, of course. We can start the whole process over again. But, as I told you at the time, you were very lucky to have the in vitro fertilization take on only the second try. Some couples take eight or ten tries. If we started all over, the process could be a lengthy one."

Camden said, "Is the presence of this second fetus harming my daughter? Taking away nutrients or anything? Or will it change anything for her later on in the pregnancy?"

"No. Except that there is a chance of premature birth. Two fetuses take up a lot more room in the womb, and if it gets too crowded birth can be premature. But the—"

"How premature? Enough to threaten survival?"

"Most probably not."

Camden went on smoking. A man appeared at the door. "Sir, London calling. James Kendall for Mr. Yagai."

"I'll take it." Camden rose. Susan watched him study his wife's face. When he spoke, it was to her. "All right, Elizabeth. All right." He left the room.

For a long moment the two women sat in silence. Susan was aware of disappointment; this was not the Camden she had expected to see. She became aware of Elizabeth Camden watching her with amusement.

"Oh, yes, Doctor. He's like that."

Susan said nothing.

"Completely overbearing. But not this time." She laughed softly, with excitement. "Two. Do you . . . do you know what sex the other one is?"

"Both fetuses are female."

"I wanted a girl, you know. And now I'll have one."

"Then you'll go ahead with the pregnancy."

"Oh, yes. Thank you for coming, Doctor."

She was dismissed. No one saw her out. But as she was getting into her car, Camden rushed out of the house, coatless. "Susan! I wanted to thank you. For coming all the way out here to tell us yourself."

"You already thanked me."

"Yes. Well. You're sure the second fetus is no threat to my daughter?"

Susan said deliberately, "Nor is the genetically altered fetus a threat to the naturally conceived one."

He smiled. His voice was low and wistful. "And you think that should matter to me just as much. But it doesn't. And why should I fake what I feel? Especially to you?"

Susan opened her car door. She wasn't ready for this, or she had changed her mind, or something. But then Camden leaned over to close the door, and his manner held no trace of flirtatiousness, no smarmy ingratiation. "I better order a second playpen."

"Yes."

"And a second car seat."

"Yes."

"But not a second night-shift nurse."

"That's up to you."

"And you." Abruptly he leaned over and kissed her, a kiss so polite and re-spectful that Susan was shocked. Neither lust nor conquest would have shocked her; this did. Camden didn't give her a chance to react; he closed the car door and turned back toward the house. Susan drove toward the gate, her hands shaky on the wheel until amusement replaced shock: it *had* been a deliberately distant, respectful kiss, an engineered enigma. And nothing else could have guaranteed so well that there would have to be another.

She wondered what the Camdens would name their daughters.

Dr. Ong strode the hospital corridor, which had been dimmed to half-light. From the nurse's station in Maternity a nurse stepped forward as if to stop him—it was the middle of the night, long past visiting hours—got a good look at his face, and faded back into her station. Around a corner was the viewing glass to the nursery. To Ong's annoyance, Susan Melling stood pressed against the glass. To his further annoyance, she was crying.

Ong realized that he had never liked the woman. Maybe not any women. Even those with superior minds could not seem to refrain from being made damn fools by their emotions.

"Look," Susan said, laughing a little, swiping at her face. "Doctor—*look*."

Behind the glass Roger Camden, gowned and masked, was holding up a baby in a white undershirt and pink blanket. Camden's blue eyes—theatrically blue; a man really should not have such garish eyes—glowed. The baby had a head covered with blond fuzz, wide eyes, pink skin. Camden's eyes above the mask said that no other child had ever had these attributes.

Ong said, "An uncomplicated birth?"

"Yes," Susan Melling sobbed. "Perfectly straightforward. Elizabeth is fine. She's asleep. Isn't she beautiful? He has the most adventurous spirit I've ever known." She wiped her nose on her sleeve; Ong realized that she was drunk. "Did I ever tell you that I was engaged once? Fifteen years ago, in med school? I broke it off because he grew to seem so ordinary, so boring. Oh, God, I shouldn't be telling you all this I'm sorry I'm sorry."

Ong moved away from her. Behind the glass Roger Camden laid the baby in a small wheeled crib. The nameplate said BABY GIRL CAMDEN #1. 5.9 POUNDS. A night nurse watched indulgently.

Ong did not wait to see Camden emerge from the nursery or to hear Susan Melling say to him whatever she was going to say. Ong went to have the OB paged. Melling's report was not, under the circumstances, to be trusted. A per-fect, unprecedented chance to record every detail of gene alteration with a nonaltered control, and Melling was more interested in her own sloppy emo-tions. Ong would obviously have to do the report himself, after talking to the OB. He was hungry for every detail. And not just about the pink-cheeked baby in Camden's arms. He wanted to know everything about the birth of the child in the other glass-sided crib: BABY GIRL CAMDEN #2 5.1 POUNDS. The dark-haired baby with the mottled red features, lying scrunched down in her pink blanket, asleep.

II

Leisha's earliest memory was of flowing lines that were not there. She knew they were not there because when she reached out her fist to touch them, her fist was empty. Later she realized that the flowing lines were light: sunshine slanting in bars between curtains in her room, between the wooden blinds in the dining room, between the crisscross lattices in the conservatory. The day she realized the golden flow was light she laughed out loud with the sheer joy of discovery, and Daddy turned from putting flowers in pots and smiled at her.

The whole house was full of light. Light bounded off the lake, streamed across the high white ceilings, puddled on the shining wooden floors. She and Alice moved continually through light, and sometimes Leisha would stop and tip back her head and let it flow over her face. She could feel it, like water.

The best light, of course, was in the conservatory. That's where Daddy liked to be when he was home from making money. Daddy potted plants and watered trees, humming, and Leisha and Alice ran between the wooden tables of flowers with their wonderful earthy smells, running from the dark side of the conservatory where the big purple flowers grew to the sunshine side with sprays of yellow flowers, running back and forth, in and out of the light. "Growth," Daddy said to her. "Flowers all fulfilling their promise. Alice, be careful! You almost knocked over that orchid." Alice, obedient, would stop running for a while. Daddy never told Leisha to stop running.

After a while the light would go away. Alice and Leisha would have their baths, and then Alice would get quiet, or cranky. She wouldn't play nice with Leisha, even when Leisha let her choose the game or even have all the best dolls. Then Nanny would take Alice to "bed," and Leisha would talk with Daddy some more until Daddy said he had to work in his study with the papers that made money. Leisha always felt a moment of regret that he had to go do that, but the moment never lasted very long, because Mamselle would arrive and start Leisha's lessons, which she liked. Learning things was so interesting! She could already sing twenty songs and write all the letters in the alphabet and count to fifty. And by the time lessons were done, the light had come back, and it was time for breakfast.

Breakfast was the only time Leisha didn't like. Daddy had gone to the office, and Leisha and Alice had breakfast with Mommy in the big dining room. Mommy sat in a red robe, which Leisha liked, and she didn't smell funny or talk funny the way she would later in the day, but, still, breakfast wasn't fun. Mommy always started with the Question.

"Alice, sweetheart, how did you sleep?"

"Fine, Mommy."

"Did you have any nice dreams?"

For a long time Alice said no. Then one day she said, "I dreamed about a horse. I was riding him." Mommy clapped her hands and kissed Alice and gave her an extra sticky bun. After that Alice always had a dream to tell Mommy.

Once Leisha said, "I had a dream, too. I dreamed light was coming in the window and it wrapped all around me like a blanket and then it kissed me on my eyes."

Mommy put down her coffee cup so hard that coffee sloshed out of it. "Don't lie to me, Leisha. You did not have a dream."

"Yes, I did," Leisha said.

"Only children who sleep can have dreams. Don't lie to me. You did not have a dream."

"Yes, I did! I did!" Leisha shouted. She could see it, almost: the light streaming in the window and wrapping around her like a golden blanket.

"I will not tolerate a child who is a liar. Do you hear me, Leisha—I won't tolerate it!"

"You're a liar!" Leisha shouted, knowing the words weren't true, hating herself because they weren't true but hating Mommy more, and that was wrong, too, and there sat Alice stiff and frozen with her eyes wide. Alice was scared and it was Leisha's fault.

Mommy called sharply, "Nanny! Nanny! Take Leisha to her room at once. She can't sit with civilized people if she can't refrain from telling lies."

Leisha started to cry. Nanny carried her out of the room. Leisha hadn't even had her breakfast. But she didn't care about that; all she could see while she cried was Alice's eyes, scared like that, reflecting broken bits of light.

But Leisha didn't cry long. Nanny read her a story and then played Data Jump with her, and then Alice came up and Nanny drove them both into Chicago to the zoo, where there were wonderful animals to see, animals Leisha could not have dreamed—nor Alice *either*. And by the time they came back Mommy had gone to her room, and Leisha knew that she would stay there with the glasses of funny-smelling stuff the rest of the day, and Leisha would not have to see her.

But that night she went to her mother's room.

"I have to go to the bathroom," she told Mamselle. Mamselle said, "Do you need any help?" maybe because Alice still needed help in the bathroom. But Leisha didn't, and she thanked Mamselle. Then she sat on the toilet for a minute even though nothing came, so that what she had told Mamselle wouldn't be a lie.

Leisha tiptoed down the hall. She went first into Alice's room. A little light in a wall socket burned near the "crib." There was no crib in Leisha's room. Leisha looked at her sister through the bars. Alice lay on her side with her eyes closed. The lids of the eyes fluttered quickly, like curtains blowing in the wind. Alice's chin and neck looked loose.

Leisha closed the door very carefully and went to her parents' room.

They didn't "sleep" in a crib but in a huge enormous "bed," with enough room between them for more people. Mommy's eyelids weren't fluttering; she lay on her back making a hrrr-hrrr sound through her nose. The funny smell was strong on her. Leisha backed away and tiptoed over to Daddy. He looked like Alice, except that his neck and chin looked even looser, folds of skin collapsed like the tent that had fallen down in the backyard. It scared Leisha to see him like that. Then Daddy's eyes flew open so suddenly that Leisha screamed.

Daddy rolled out of bed and picked her up, looking quickly at Mommy. But she didn't move. Daddy was wearing only his underpants. He carried Leisha out into the hall, where Mamselle came rushing up saying, "Oh, sir. I'm sorry, she just said she was going to the bathroom—"

"It's all right," Daddy said. "I'll take her with me."

"No!" Leisha screamed, because Daddy was only in his underpants and his neck had looked all funny and the room smelled bad because of Mommy. But Daddy carried her into the conservatory, set her down on a bench, wrapped himself in a piece of green plastic that was supposed to cover up plants, and sat down next to her.

"Now, what happened, Leisha? What were you doing?"

Leisha didn't answer.

"You were looking at people sleeping, weren't you?" Daddy said, and because his voice was softer Leisha mumbled, "Yes." She immediately felt better; it felt good not to lie.

"You were looking at people sleeping because you don't sleep and you were curious, weren't you? Like Curious George in your book?"

"Yes," Leisha said. "I thought you said you made money in your study all night!"

Daddy smiled. "Not all night. Some of it. But then I sleep, although not very much." He took Leisha on his lap. "I don't need much sleep, so I get a lot more done at night than most people. Different people need different amounts of sleep. And a few, a very few, are like you. You don't need any."

"Why not?"

"Because you're special. Better than other people. Before you were born, I had some doctors help make you that way."

"Why?"

"So you could do anything you want to and make manifest your own individuality."

Leisha twisted in his arms to stare at him; the words meant nothing. Daddy reached over and touched a single flower growing on a tall potted tree. The flower had thick white petals like the cream he put in coffee, and the center was a light pink.

"See, Leisha—this tree made this flower. Because it *can*. Only this tree can make this kind of wonderful flower. That plant hanging up there can't, and those can't either. Only this tree. Therefore the most important thing in the world for this tree to do is grow this flower. The flower is the tree's individuality—that means just *it*, and nothing else—made manifest. Nothing else matters."

"I don't understand, Daddy."

"You will. Someday."

"But I want to understand *now*," Leisha said, and Daddy laughed with pure delight and hugged her. The hug felt good, but Leisha still wanted to understand.

"When you make money, is that your indiv . . . that thing?"

."Yes," Daddy said happily.

"Then nobody else can make money? Like only that tree can make that flower?"

"Nobody else can make it just the ways I do."

"What do you do with the money?"

"I buy things for you. This house, your dresses, Mamselle to teach you, the car to ride in."

"What does the tree do with the flower?"

"Glories in it," Daddy said, which made no sense. "Excellence is what counts, Leisha. Excellence supported by individual effort. And that's *all* that counts."

"I'm cold, Daddy."

"Then I better bring you back to Mamselle."

Leisha didn't move. She touched the flower with one finger. "I want to sleep, Daddy."

"No, you don't, sweetheart. Sleep is just lost time, wasted life. It's a little death."

"Alice sleeps."

"Alice isn't like you."

"Alice isn't special?"

"No. You are."

"Why didn't you make Alice special, too?"

"Alice made herself. I didn't have a chance to make her special."

The whole thing was too hard. Leisha stopped stroking the flower and slipped off Daddy's lap. He smiled at her. "My little questioner. When you grow up, you'll find your own excellence, and it will be a new order, a specialness the world hasn't ever seen before. You might even be like Kenzo Yagai. He made the Yagai generator that powers the world."

"Daddy, you look funny wrapped in the flower plastic." Leisha laughed. Daddy did, too. But then she said, "When I grow up, I'll make my specialness find a way to make Alice special, too," and Daddy stopped laughing.

He took her back to Mamselle, who taught her to write her name, which was so exciting she forgot about the puzzling talk with Daddy. There were six letters, all different, and together they were *her name*. Leisha wrote it over and over, laughing, and Mamselle laughed, too. But later, in the morning, Leisha thought again about the talk with Daddy. She thought of it often, turning the unfamiliar words over in and over in her mind like small hard stones, but the part she thought about most wasn't a word. It was the frown on Daddy's face when she told him she would use her specialness to make Alice special, too.

Every week Dr. Melling came to see Leisha and Alice, sometimes alone, sometimes with other people. Leisha and Alice both liked Dr. Melling, who laughed a lot and whose eyes were bright and warm. Often Daddy was there, too. Dr. Melling played games with them, first with Alice and Leisha separately and then together. She took their pictures and weighed them. She made them lie down on a table and stuck little metal things to their temples, which sounded scary but wasn't because there were so many machines to watch, all making interesting noises, while you were lying there. Dr. Melling was as good at answering questions as Daddy. Once Leisha said, "Is Dr. Melling a special person? Like Kenzo Yagai?" And Daddy laughed and glanced at Dr. Melling and said, "Oh, yes, indeed."

When Leisha was five, she and Alice started school. Daddy's driver took them every day into Chicago. They were in different rooms, which disappointed Leisha. The kids in Leisha's room were all older. But from the first day she adored school, with its fascinating science equipment and electronic drawers full of math puzzlers and other children to find countries on the map with. In half a year she had been moved to yet a different room, where the kids were still older, but they were nonetheless nice to her. Leisha started to learn Japanese. She loved drawing the beautiful characters on thick white paper. "The Sauley School was a good choice," Daddy said.

But Alice didn't like the Sauley School. She wanted to go to school on the same yellow bus as cook's daughter. She cried and threw her paints on the floor at the Sauley School. Then Mommy came out of her room—Leisha hadn't seen her for a few weeks, although she knew Alice had—and threw some candlesticks from the mantelpiece on the floor. The candlesticks, which were china, broke. Leisha ran to pick up the pieces while Mommy and Daddy screamed at each other in the hall by the big staircase.

"She's my daughter, too. And I say she can go!"

"You don't have the right to say anything about it! A weepy drunk, the most rotten role model possible for both of them . . . and I thought I was getting a fine English aristocrat."

"You got what you paid for. Nothing! Not that you ever needed anything from me or anybody else."

"Stop it!" Leisha cried. "Stop it!" and there was silence in the hall. Leisha cut her fingers on the china; blood streamed onto the rug. Daddy rushed in and picked her up. "Stop it," Leisha sobbed, and didn't understand when Daddy said quietly, "*You* stop it, Leisha. Nothing *they* do should touch you at all. You have to be at least that strong."

Leisha buried her head in Daddy's shoulder. Alice transferred to Carl Sandburg Elementary School, riding there on the yellow school bus with cook's daughter.

A few weeks later Daddy told them that Mommy was going away for a few weeks to a hospital, to stop drinking so much. When Mommy came out, he said, she was going to live somewhere else for a while. She and Daddy were not happy. Leisha and Alice would stay with Daddy, and they would visit Mommy sometimes. He told them this very carefully, finding the right words for truth. Truth was very important, Leisha already knew. Truth was being true to your self, your specialness. Your individuality. An individual respected facts, and so always told the truth.

Mommy, Daddy did not say but Leisha knew, did not respect facts.

"I don't want Mommy to go away," Alice said. She started to cry. Leisha thought Daddy would pick Alice up, but he didn't. He just stood there looking at them both.

Leisha put her arms around Alice. "It's all right, Alice. It's all right! We'll make it all right! I'll play with you all the time we're not in school so you don't miss Mommy."

Alice clung to Leisha. Leisha turned her head so she didn't have to see Daddy's face.

III

Kenzo Yagai was coming to the United States to lecture. The title of his talk, which he would give in New York, Los Angeles, Chicago, and Washington, with a repeat in Washington as a special address to Congress, was "The Further Political Implications of Inexpensive Power." Leisha Camden, eleven years old, was going to have a private introduction after the Chicago talk, arranged by her father.

She had studied the theory of cold fusion at school, and her Global Studies teacher had traced the changes in the world resulting from Yagai's patented, low-cost applications of what had, until him, been unworkable theory. The rising prosperity of the Third World, the last death throes of the old communist systems, the decline of the oil states, the renewed economic power of the United States. Her study group had written a news script, filmed with the school's professional-quality equipment, about how a 1985 American family lived with expensive energy costs and a belief in tax-supported help, while a 2019 family lived with cheap energy and a belief in the contract as the basis of civilization. Parts of her own research puzzled Leisha.

"Japan thinks Kenzo Yagai was a traitor to his own country," she said to Daddy at supper.

"No," Camden said. "*Some* Japanese think that. Watch out for generalizations, Leisha. Yagai patented and marketed Y-energy first in the United States because here there were at least the dying embers of individual enterprise. Because of his invention, our entire country has slowly swung back toward an individual meritocracy, and Japan has slowly been forced to follow."

"Your father held that belief all along," Susan said. "Eat your peas, Leisha." Leisha ate her peas. Susan and Daddy had only been married less than a year; it still felt a little strange to have her there. But nice. Daddy said Susan was a valuable addition to their household: intelligent, motivated, and cheerful. Like Leisha herself.

"Remember, Leisha," Camden said. "A man's worth to society and to himself doesn't rest on what he thinks other people should do or be or feel, but on himself. On what he can actually do, and do well. People trade what they do well, and everyone benefits. The basic tool of civilization is the contract. Contracts are voluntary and mutually beneficial. As opposed to coercion, which is wrong."

"The strong have no right to take anything from the weak by force," Susan said. "Alice, eat your peas, too, honey."

"Nor the weak to take anything by force from the strong," Camden said. "That's the basis of what you'll hear Kenzo Yagai discuss tonight, Leisha."

Alice said, "I don't like peas."

Camden said, "Your body does. They're good for you."

Alice smiled. Leisha felt her heart lift; Alice didn't smile much at dinner anymore. "My body doesn't have a contract with the peas."

Camden said, a little impatiently, "Yes, it does. Your body benefits from them. Now eat."

Alice's smile vanished. Leisha looked down at her plate. Suddenly she saw a way out. "No, Daddy, look—Alice's body benefits, but the peas don't. It's not a mutually beneficial consideration—so there's no contract. Alice is right!"

Camden let out a shout of laughter. To Susan he said, "Eleven years old . . . *eleven*." Even Alice smiled, and Leisha waved her spoon triumphantly, light glinting off the bowl and dancing silver on the opposite wall.

But, even so, Alice did not want to go hear Kenzo Yagai. She was going to sleep over at her friend Julie's house; they were going to curl their hair together. More surprisingly, Susan wasn't coming, either. She and Daddy looked at each other a little funny at the front door, Leisha thought, but Leisha was too excited to think about this. She was going to hear *Kenzo Yagai*.

Yagai was a small man, dark and slim. Leisha liked his accent. She liked, too, something about him that took her awhile to name. "Daddy," she whispered in the half-darkness of the auditorium, "he's a joyful man."

Daddy hugged her in the darkness.

Yagai spoke about spirituality and economics. "A man's spirituality—which is only his dignity as a man—rests on his own efforts. Dignity and worth are not automatically conferred by aristocratic birth—we have only to look at history to see that. Dignity and worth are not automatically conferred by inherited wealth—a great heir may be a thief, a wastrel, cruel, an exploiter, a person who leaves the world much poorer than he found it. Nor are dignity and worth automatically conferred by existence itself—a mass murderer exists, but is of negative worth to his society and possess no dignity in his lust to kill.

"No, the only dignity, the only spirituality, rests on what a man can achieve with his own efforts. To rob a man of the chance to achieve, and to trade what he achieves with others, is to rob him of his spiritual dignity as a man. This is why communism has failed in our time. *All* coercion—all force to take from a man his own efforts to achieve—causes spiritual damage and weakens a society. Conscription, theft, fraud, violence, welfare, lack of legislative representation—*all* rob a man of his chance to choose, to achieve on his own, to trade the results of his achievement with others. Coercion is a cheat. It produces nothing new. Only freedom—the freedom to achieve, the freedom to trade freely the results of achievement—creates the environment proper to the dignity and spirituality of man."

Leisha applauded so hard her hands hurt. Going backstage with Daddy, she thought she could hardly breathe. Kenzo Yagai!

But backstage was more crowded than she had expected. There were cameras everywhere. Daddy said, "Mr. Yagai, may I present my daughter Leisha," and the cameras moved in close and fast—on *her*. A Japanese man whispered something in Kenzo Yagai's ear, and he looked more closely at Leisha. "Ah, yes."

"Look over here, Leisha," someone called, and she did. A robot camera zoomed so close to her face that Leisha stepped back, startled. Daddy spoke very sharply to someone, then to someone else. The cameras didn't move. A woman suddenly knelt in front of Leisha and thrust a microphone at her. "What does it feel like to never sleep, Leisha?"

"What?"

Someone laughed. The laugh was not kind. "Breeding geniuses . . ."

Leisha felt a hand on her shoulder. Kenzo Yagai gripped her very firmly, pulled her away from the cameras. Immediately, as if by magic, a line of Japanese men formed behind Yagai, parting only to let Daddy through. Behind the line, the three of them moved into a dressing room, and Kenzo Yagai shut the door.

"You must not let them bother you, Leisha," he said in his wonderful accent. "Not ever. There is an old Oriental proverb: 'The dogs bark, but the caravan moves on.' You must never let your individual caravan be slowed by the barking of rude or envious dogs."

"I won't," Leisha breathed, not sure yet what the words really meant, knowing there was time later to sort them out, to talk about them with Daddy. For now she was dazzled by Kenzo Yagai, the actual man himself, who was changing the world without force, without guns, with trading his special individual efforts. "We study your philosophy at my school, Mr. Yagai."

Kenzo Yagai looked at Daddy. Daddy said, "A private school. But Leisha's sister also studies it, although cursorily, in the public system. Slowly, Kenzo, but it comes. It comes." Leisha noticed that he did not say why Alice was not here tonight with them.

Back home, Leisha sat in her room for hours, thinking over everything that had happened. When Alice came home from Julie's the next morning, Leisha rushed toward her. But Alice seemed angry about something.

"Alice—what is it?"

"Don't you think I have enough to put up with at school already?" Alice shouted. "Everybody knows, but at least when you stayed quiet it didn't matter too much. They'd stopped teasing me. Why did you have to do it?"

"Do what?" Leisha said, bewildered.

Alice threw something at her: a hard-copy morning paper, on newsprint flimsier than the Camden system used. The paper dropped open at Leisha's feet. She stared at her own picture, three columns wide, with Kenzo Yagai. The headline said, YAGAI AND THE FUTURE: ROOM FOR THE REST OF US? Y-ENERGY INVENTOR CONFERS WITH "SLEEP-FREE" DAUGHTER OF MEGA-FINANCIER ROGER CAMDEN.

Alice kicked the paper. "It was on TV last night, too—on TV. I work hard not to look stuck-up or creepy, and you go and do this! Now Julie probably won't even invite me to her slumber party next week." She rushed up the broad curving stairs toward her room.

Leisha looked down at the paper. She heard Kenzo Yagai's voice in her head: "The dogs bark, but the caravan moves on." She looked at the empty stairs. Aloud she said, "Alice—your hair looks really pretty curled like that."

IV

"I want to meet the rest of them," Leisha said. "Why have you kept them from me this long?"

"I haven't kept them from you at all," Camden said. "Not offering is not the same as denial. Why shouldn't you be the one to do the asking? You're the one who now wants it."

Leisha looked at him. She was fifteen, in her last year at the Sauley School. "Why didn't you offer?"

"Why should I?"

"I don't know," Leisha said. "But you gave me everything else."

"Including the freedom to ask for what you want."

Leisha looked for the contradiction and found it. "Most things that you provided for my education I didn't ask for, because I didn't know enough to ask and you, as the adult, did. But you've never offered the opportunity for me to meet any of the other sleepless mutants—"

"Don't use that word," Camden said sharply.

"—so either you must think it was not essential to my education or else you had another motive for not wanting me to meet them."

"Wrong," Camden said. "There's a third possibility. That I think meeting them is essential to your education, that I do not want you to, but this issue provided a chance to further the education of your self-initiative by waiting for you to ask."

"All right," Leisha said, a little defiantly; there seemed to be a lot of defiance between them lately, for no good reason. She squared her shoulders. Her new breasts thrust forward. "I'm asking. How many of the Sleepless are there, who are they, and where are they?"

Camden said, "If you're using that term—'the Sleepless'—you've already done some reading on your own. So you probably know that there are 1,082 of you so far in the United States, a few more in foreign countries, most of them in major metropolitan areas. Seventy-nine are in Chicago, most of them still small children. Only nineteen anywhere are older than you."

Leisha didn't deny reading any of this. Camden leaned forward in his study chair to peer at her. Leisha wondered if he needed glasses. His hair was completely gray now, sparse and stiff, like lonely broomstraws. The *Wall Street Journal* listed him among the hundred richest men in America; *Women's Wear Daily* pointed out that he was the only billionaire in the country who did not move in the society of international parties, charity balls, and personal jets. Camden's jet ferried him to business meetings around the world, to the chairmanship of the Yagai Economics Institute, and to very little else. Over the years he had grown richer, more reclusive, and more cerebral. Leisha felt a rush of her old affection.

She threw herself sideways into a leather chair, her long slim legs dangling over the arm. Absently she scratched a mosquito bite on her thigh. "Well, then, I'd like to meet Richard Keller." He lived in Chicago and was the beta-test Sleepless closest to her own age. He was seventeen.

"Why ask me? Why not just go?"

Leisha thought there was a note of impatience in his voice. He liked her to explore things first, then report on them to him later. Both parts were important.

Leisha laughed. "You know what, Daddy? You're predictable."

Camden laughed, too. In the middle of the laugh Susan came in.

"He certainly is not. Roger, what about that meeting in Buenos Aires Thursday? Is it on or off?" When he didn't answer, her voice grew shriller. "Roger? I'm talking to you!"

Leisha averted her eyes. Two years ago Susan had finally left genetic research to run Camden's house and schedule; before that she had tried hard to do both. Since she had left Biotech, it seemed to Leisha, Susan had changed. Her voice was tighter. She was more insistent that cook and the gardener follow her directions exactly, without deviation. Her blond braids had become stiff sculptured waves of platinum.

"It's on," Roger said.

"Well, thanks for at least answering. Am I going?"

"If you like."

"I like."

Susan left the room. Leisha rose and stretched. Her long legs rose on tiptoe. It felt good to reach, to stretch, to feel sunlight from the wide windows wash over her face. She smiled at her father and found him watching her with an unexpected expression.

"Leisha—"

"What?"

"See Keller. But be careful."

"Of what?"

But Camden wouldn't answer.

The voice on the phone had been noncommittal. "Leisha Camden? Yes, I know who you are. Three o'clock on Thursday?" The house was modest, a thirty-year-old Colonial on a quiet suburban street where small children on bicycles could be watched from the front window. Few roofs had more than one Y-energy cell. The trees, huge old sugar maples, were beautiful.

"Come in," Richard Keller said.

He was no taller than she, stocky, with a bad case of acne. Probably no genetic alterations except sleep, Leisha guessed. He had thick dark hair, a low forehead, and bushy black brows. Before he closed the door Leisha saw him stare at her car and driver, parked in the driveway next to a rusty ten-speed bike.

"I can't drive yet," she said. "I'm still fifteen."

"It's easy to learn," Keller said. "So, you want to tell me why you're here?"

Leisha liked his directness. "To meet some other Sleepless."

"You mean you never have? Not any of us?"

"You mean the rest of you know each other?" She hadn't expected that.

"Come to my room, Leisha."

She followed him to the back of the house. No one else seemed to be home. His room was large and airy, filled with computers and filing cabinets. A rowing machine sat in one corner. It looked like a shabbier version of the room of any bright classmate at the Sauley School, except there was more space without a bed. She walked over to the computer screen.

"Hey—you working on Boesc equations?"

"On an application of them."

"To what?"

"Fish migration patterns."

Leisha smiled. "Yeah—that would work. I never thought of that."

Keller seemed not to know what to do with her smile. He looked at the wall, then at her chin. "You interested in Gaea patterns? In the environment?"

"Well, no," Leisha confessed. "Not particularly. I'm going to study politics at Harvard. Prelaw. But of course we had Gaea patterns at school."

Keller's gaze finally came unstuck from her face. He ran a hand through his dark hair. "Sit down, if you want."

Leisha sat, looking appreciatively at the wall posters, shifting green on blue, like ocean currents. "I like those. Did you program them yourself?"

"You're not at all what I pictured," Keller said.

"How did you picture me?"

He didn't hesitate. "Stuck-up. Superior. Shallow, despite your IQ."

She was more hurt than she had expected to be.

Keller blurted, "You're the only one of the Sleepless who's really rich. But you already know that."

"No, I don't. I've never checked."

He took the chair beside her, stretching his stocky legs straight in front of him, in a slouch that had nothing to do with relaxation. "It makes sense, really. Rich people don't have their children genetically modified to be superior—they think any offspring of theirs is already superior. By their values. And poor people can't afford it. We Sleepless are upper-middle class, no more. Children of professors, scientists, people who value brains and time."

"My father values brains and time," Leisha said. "He's the biggest supporter of Kenzo Yagai."

"Oh, Leisha, do you think I don't already know that? Are you flashing me or what?"

Leisha said with great deliberateness, "I'm *talking* to you." But the next minute she could feel the hurt break through on her face.

"I'm sorry," Keller muttered. He shot off his chair and paced to the computer, back. "I *am* sorry. But I don't . . . I don't understand what you're doing here."

"I'm lonely," Leisha said, astonished at herself. She looked up at him. "It's true. I'm lonely. I am. I have friends and Daddy and Alice—but no one really knows, really understands—what? I don't know what I'm saying."

Keller smiled. The smile changed his whole face, opened up its dark planes to the light. "I do. Oh, do I. What do you do when they say, 'I had such a dream last night!'?"

"Yes!" Leisha said. "But that's even really minor—it's when I say, 'I'll look that up for you tonight,' and they get that funny look on their face that means 'She'll do it while I'm asleep.' "

"But that's even really minor," Keller said. "It's when you're playing basketball in the gym after supper and then you go to the diner for food and then you say, 'Let's have a walk by the lake,' and they say, 'I'm really tired. I'm going home to bed now.' "

"But that's really minor," Leisha said, jumping up. "It's when you really are absorbed by the movie and then you get the point and it's so goddamn beautiful you leap up and say, 'Yes! Yes!' and Susan says, 'Leisha, really—you'd think nobody but you ever enjoyed anything before.' "

"Who's Susan?" Keller said.

The mood was broken. But not really; Leisha could say "my stepmother" without much discomfort over what Susan had promised to be and what she had become. Keller stood inches from her, smiling that joyous smile, understanding, and suddenly relief washed over Leisha so strong that she walked straight into him and put her arms around his neck, tightening them only when she felt his startled jerk. She started to sob—she, Leisha, who never cried.

"Hey," Richard said. "Hey."

"Brilliant," Leisha said, laughing. "Brilliant remark."

She could feel his embarrassed smile. "Wanta see my fish migration curves instead?"

"No," Leisha sobbed, and he went on holding her, patting her back awkwardly, telling her without words that she was home.

Camden waited up for her, although it was past midnight. He had been smoking heavily. Through the blue air he said quietly,

"Did you have a good time, Leisha?"

"Yes."

"I'm glad," he said, and put out his last cigarette and climbed the stairs—slowly, stiffly; he was nearly seventy now—to bed.

They went everywhere together for nearly a year: swimming, dancing, to the museums, the theater, the library. Richard introduced her to the others, a group of twelve kids between fourteen and nineteen, all of them intelligent and eager. All Sleepless.

Leisha learned.

Tony's parents, like her own, had divorced. But Tony, fourteen, lived with his mother, who had not particularly wanted a Sleepless child, while his father, who had, acquired a red hovercar and a young girlfriend who designed ergonomic chairs in Paris. Tony was not allowed to tell anyone—relatives, schoolmates—that he was Sleepless. "They'll think you're a freak," his mother said, eyes averted from her·son's face. The one time Tony disobeyed her and told a friend that he never slept, his mother beat him. Then she moved the family to a new neighborhood. He was nine years old.

Jeanine, almost as long-legged and slim as Leisha, was training for the Olympics in ice skating. She practiced twelve hours a day, hours no Sleeper still in high school could ever have. So far the newspapers had not picked up the story. Jeanine was afraid that if they did they would somehow not let her compete.

Jack, like Leisha, would start college in September. Unlike Leisha, he had already started his career. The practice of law had to wait for law school; the practice of investment required only money. Jack didn't have much, but his precise financial analyses parlayed $600 saved from summer jobs to $3,000 through stock-market investing, then to $10,000, and then he had enough to qualify for information-fund speculation. Jack was fifteen, not old enough to make legal investments; the transactions were all in the name of Kevin Baker, the oldest of the Sleepless, who lived in Austin. Jack told Leisha, "When I hit eighty-four percent profit over two consecutive quarters, the data analysts logged onto me. They were just sniffing. Well, that's their job, even when the overall amounts are actually small. It's the patterns they care about. If they take the trouble to cross-reference data banks and come up with the fact that Kevin is a Sleepless, will they try to stop us from investing somehow?"

"That's paranoid," Leisha said.

"No, it's not," Jeanine said. "Leisha, you don't *know*."

"You mean because I've been protected by my father's money and caring," Leisha said. No one grimaced; all of them confronted ideas openly, without shadowy allusions. Without dreams.

"Yes," Jeanine said. "Your father sounds terrific. And he raised you to think that achievement should not be fettered—Jesus Christ, he's a Yagaiist. Well, good. We're glad for you." She said it without sarcasm. Leisha nodded. "But the world isn't always like that. They hate us."

"That's too strong," Carol said. "Not hate."

"Well, maybe," Jeanine said. "But they're different from us. We're better, and they naturally resent that."

"I don't see what's natural about it," Tony said. "Why shouldn't it be just as natural to admire what's better? We do. Does any one of us resent Kenzo Yagai for his genius? Or Nelson Wade, the physicist? Or Catherine Raduski?"

"We don't resent them because we *are* better," Richard said. "Q.E.D."

"What we should do is have our own society," Tony said. "Why should we allow their regulations to restrict our natural, honest achievements? Why should Jeanine be barred from skating against them and Jack from investing on their same terms just because we're Sleepless? Some of them are brighter than others of them. Some have greater persistence. Well, we have greater concentration, more biochemical stability, and more time. All men are not created equal."

"Be fair, Tony—no one has been barred from anything yet," Jeanine said.

"But we will be."

"*Wait.*" Leisha said. She was deeply troubled by the conversation. "I mean, yes, in many ways we're better. But you quoted out of context, Tony. The Declaration of Independence doesn't say all men are created equal in ability. It's talking about rights and power—it means that all are created equal *under the law.* We have no more right to a separate society or to being free of society's restrictions than anyone else does. There's no other way to freely trade one's efforts, unless the same contractual rules apply to all."

"Spoken like a true Yagaiist," Richard said, squeezing her hand.

"That's enough intellectual discussion for me," Carol said, laughing. "We've been at this for hours. We're at the beach, for Chrissake. Who wants to swim with me?"

"I do," Jeanine said. "Come on, Jack."

All of them rose, brushing sand off their suits, discarding sunglasses. Richard pulled Leisha to her feet. But just before they ran into the water, Tony put his skinny hand on her arm. "One more question, Leisha. Just to think about. If we achieve better than most other people, and we trade with the Sleepers when it's mutually beneficial, making no distinction there between the strong and the weak—what obligation do we have to those so weak they don't have anything to trade with us? We're already going to give more than we get—do we have to do it when we get nothing at all? Do we have to take care of their deformed and handicapped and sick and lazy and shiftless with the products of our work?"

"Do the Sleepers have to?" Leisha countered.

"Kenzo Yagai would say no. He's a Sleeper."

"He would say they would receive the benefits of contractual trade even if they aren't direct parties to the contract. The whole world is better fed and healthier because of Y-energy."

"Come on," Jeanine yelled. "Leisha, they're dunking me. Jack, you stop that. Leisha, help me!"

Leisha laughed. Just before she grabbed for Jeanine, she caught the look on Richard's face, on Tony's: Richard frankly lustful, Tony angry. At her. But why? What had she done, except argue in favor of dignity and trade?

Then Jack threw water on her, and Carol pushed Jack into the warm spray, and Richard was there with his arms around her, laughing.

When she got the water out of her eyes, Tony was gone.

Midnight. "Okay," Carol said. "Who's first?"

The six teenagers in the bramble clearing looked at each other. A Y-lamp, kept on low for atmosphere, cast weird shadows across their faces and over their bare legs. Around the clearing Roger Camden's trees stood thick and dark, a wall between them and the closest of the estate's outbuildings. It was very hot. August air hung heavy, sullen. They had voted against bringing an air-conditioned Y-field because this was a return to the primitive, the dangerous; let it be primitive.

Six pairs of eyes stared at the glass in Carol's hand.

"Come *on*," she said. "Who wants to drink up?" Her voice was jaunty, theatrically hard. "It was difficult enough to get this."

"How *did* you get it?" said Richard, the group member—except for Tony—with the least influential family contacts, the least money. "In a drinkable form like that?"

"My cousin Brian is a pharmaceutical supplier to the Biotech Institute. He's curious." Nods around the circle; except for Leisha, they were Sleepless precisely because they had relatives somehow connected to Biotech. And everyone was curious. The glass held interleukin-1, an immune-system booster, one of many substances that as a side effect induced the brain to swift and deep sleep.

Leisha stared at the glass. A warm feeling crept through her lower belly, not unlike the feeling when she and Richard made love.

Tony said, "Give it to me!"

Carol did. "Remember—you only need a little sip."

Tony raised the glass to his mouth, stopped, looked at them over the rim with his fierce eyes. He drank.

Carol took back the glass. They all watched Tony. Within a minute he lay on the rough ground; within two, his eyes closed in sleep.

It wasn't like seeing parents sleep, siblings, friends. It was Tony. They looked away, didn't meet each other's eyes. Leisha felt the warmth between her legs tug and tingle, faintly obscene.

When it was her turn, she drank slowly, then passed the glass to Jeanine. Her head turned heavy, as if it were being stuffed with damp rags. The trees at the edge of the clearing blurred. The portable lamp blurred, too—it wasn't bright and clean anymore but squishy, blobby; if she touched it, it would smear. Then darkness swooped over her brain, taking it away: *taking away her mind.* "Daddy!" She tried to call, to clutch for him, but then the darkness obliterated her.

Afterward they all had headaches. Dragging themselves back through the woods in the thin morning light was torture, compounded by an odd shame. They didn't touch each other. Leisha walked as far away from Richard as she could. It was a whole day before the throbbing left the base of her skull or the nausea her stomach.

There had not even been any dreams.

"I want you to come with me tonight," Leisha said, for the tenth or twelfth time. "We both leave for college in just two days; this is the last chance. I really want you to meet Richard."

Alice lay on her stomach across her bed. Her hair, brown and lusterless, fell around her face. She wore an expensive yellow jump suit, silk by Ann Patterson, which rucked up in wrinkles around her knees.

"Why? What do you care if I meet Richard or not?"

"Because you're my sister," Leisha said. She knew better than to say "my twin." Nothing got Alice angry faster.

"I don't want to." The next moment Alice's face changed. "Oh, I'm sorry, Leisha—I didn't mean to sound so snotty. But . . . but I don't want to."

"It won't be all of them. Just Richard. And just for an hour or so. Then you can come back here and pack for Northwestern."

"I'm not going to Northwestern."

Leisha stared at her.

Alice said, "I'm pregnant."

Leisha sat on the bed. Alice rolled onto her back, brushed the hair out of her eyes, and laughed. Leisha's ears closed against the sound. "Look at you," Alice said. "You'd think it was *you* who was pregnant. But you never would be, would you, Leisha? Not until it was the proper time. Not you."

"How?" Leisha said. "We both had our caps put in . . ."

"I had the cap removed," Alice said.

"You wanted to get pregnant?"

"Damn flash I did. And there's not a thing Daddy can do about it. Except, of course, cut off all credit completely, but I don't think he'll do that, do you?" She laughed again. "Even to me?"

"But, Alice . . . why? Not just to anger Daddy."

"No," Alice said. "Although you would think of that, wouldn't you? Because I want something to love. Something of my *own*. Something that has nothing to do with this house."

Leisha thought of her and Alice running through the conservatory, years ago, her and Alice darting in and out of the sunlight. "It hasn't been so bad growing up in this house."

"Leisha, you're stupid. I don't know how anyone so smart can be so stupid. Get out of my room! Get out!"

"But, Alice . . . *a baby* . . ."

"Get out!" Alice shrieked. "Go to Harvard. Go be successful. Just get out!"

Leisha jerked off the bed. "Gladly! You're irrational, Alice. You don't think ahead; you don't plan a *baby* . . ." But she could never sustain anger. It dribbled away, leaving her mind empty. She looked at Alice, who suddenly put out her arms. Leisha went into them.

"You're the baby," Alice said wonderingly. "You *are*. You're so . . . I don't know what. You're a baby."

Leisha said nothing. Alice's arms felt warm, felt whole, felt like two children running in and out of sunlight. "I'll help you, Alice. If Daddy won't."

Alice abruptly pushed her away. "I don't need your help."

Alice stood. Leisha rubbed her empty arms, fingertips scraping across opposite elbows. Alice kicked the empty, open truck in which she was supposed to pack for Northwestern and then abruptly smiled, a smile that made Leisha look away. She braced herself for more abuse. But what Alice said, very softly, was, "Have a good time at Harvard."

V

She loved it.

From the first sight of Massachusetts Hall, older than the United States by a half century, Leisha felt something that had been missing in Chicago: Age. Roots. Tradition. She touched the bricks of Widener Library, the glass cases in the Peabody Museum, as if they were the grail. She had never been particularly sensitive to myth or drama; the anguish of Juliet seemed to her artificial, that of Willy Loman merely wasteful. Only King Arthur, struggling to create a better social order, had interested her. But now, walking under the huge autumn trees, she suddenly caught a glimpse of a force that could span generations, fortunes left to endow learning and achievement the benefactors would never see, individual effort spanning and shaping centuries to come. She stopped and looked at the sky through the leaves, at the buildings solid with purpose. At such moments she thought of Camden, bending the will of an entire genetic-research institute to create her in the image he wanted.

Within a month she had forgotten all such mega-musings.

The workload was incredible, even for her. The Sauley School had encouraged individual exploration at her own pace; Harvard knew what it wanted from her, at its pace. In the last twenty years, under the academic leadership of a man who in his youth had watched Japanese economic domination with dismay, Harvard had become the controversial leader of a return to hard-edged learning of facts, theories, applications, problem solving, intellectual efficiency. The school accepted one out of every two hundred applications from around the world. The daughter of England's prime minister had flunked out her first year and been sent home.

Leisha had a single room in a new dormitory, the dorm because she had spent so many years isolated in Chicago and was hungry for people, the single so she would not disturb anyone else when she worked all night. Her second day, a boy from down the hall sauntered in and perched on the edge of her desk.

"So you're Leisha Camden."

"Yes."

"Sixteen years old."

"Almost seventeen."

"Going to outperform us all, I understand, without even trying."

Leisha's smile faded. The boy stared at her from under lowered downy brows. He was smiling, his eyes sharp. From Richard and Tony and the others, Leisha had learned to recognize the anger that presented itself as contempt.

"Yes," Leisha said coolly. "I am."

"Are you sure? With your pretty little-girl hair and your mutant little-girl brain?"

"Oh, leave her alone, Hannaway," said another voice. A tall blond boy, so thin his ribs looked like ripples in brown sand, stood in jeans and bare feet, drying his wet hair. "Don't you ever get tired of walking around being an asshole?"

"Do you?" Hannaway said. He heaved himself off the desk and started toward the door. The blond moved out of his way. Leisha moved into it.

"The reason I'm going to do better than you," she said evenly, "is because I have certain advantages you don't. Including sleeplessness. And then after I 'outperform' you I'll be glad to help you study for your tests so that you can pass, too."

The blond, drying his ears, laughed. But Hannaway stood still, and into his eyes came an expression that made Leisha back away. He pushed past her and stormed out.

"Nice going, Camden," the blond said. "He deserved that."

"But I meant it," Leisha said. "I will help him study."

The blond lowered his towel and stared. "You did, didn't you? You meant it."

"Yes! Why does everybody keep questioning that?"

"Well," the boy said, "*I* don't. You can help me if I get into trouble." Suddenly he smiled. "But I won't."

"Why not?"

"Because I'm just as good at anything as you are, Leisha Camden."

She studied him. "You're not one of us. Not Sleepless."

"Don't have to be. I know what I can do. Do, be, create, trade."

She said, delighted, "You're a Yagaiist!"

"Of course." He held out his hand. "Stewart Sutter. How about a fishburger in the Yard?"

"Great," Leisha said. They walked out together, talking excitedly.

When people stared at her she tried not to notice. She was here. At Harvard. With space ahead of her, time to learn, and with people like Stewart Sutter who accepted and challenged her.

All the hours he was awake.

She became totally absorbed in her classwork. Roger Camden drove up once, walking the campus with her, listening, smiling. He was more at home than Leisha would have expected: he knew Stewart Sutter's father, Kate Addams's grandfather. They talked about Harvard, business, Harvard, the Yagai Economics Institute, Harvard. "How's Alice?" Leisha asked once, but Camden said that he didn't know; she had moved out and did not want to see him. He made her an allowance through his attorney. While he said this, his face remained serene.

Leisha went to the Homecoming Ball with Stewart, who was also majoring in prelaw but was two years ahead of Leisha. She took a weekend trip to Paris with Kate Addams and two other girlfriends, taking the Concorde III. She had a fight with Stewart over whether the metaphor of superconductivity could apply to Yagaiism, a stupid fight they both knew was stupid but had anyway, and afterward they became lovers. After the fumbling sexual explorations with Richard, Stewart was deft, experienced, smiling faintly as he taught her how to have an orgasm both by herself and with him. Leisha was dazzled.

"It's so *joyful*," she said, and Stewart looked at her with a tenderness she knew was part disturbance but didn't know why.

At midsemester she had the highest grades in the freshman class. She got every answer right on every single question on her midterms. She and Stewart went out for a beer to celebrate, and when they came back Leisha's room had been destroyed. The computer was smashed, the data banks wiped, hard copies and books smoldering in a metal wastebasket. Her clothes were ripped to pieces, her desk and bureau hacked apart. The only thing untouched, pristine, was the bed.

Stewart said, "There's no way this could have been done in silence. Everyone on the floor—hell, on the floor *below*—had to know. Someone will talk to the police." No one did. Leisha sat on the edge of the bed, dazed, and looked at the remnants of her homecoming gown. The next day Dave Hannaway gave her a long, wide smile.

Camden flew east again, taut with rage. He rented her an apartment in Cambridge with E-lock security and a bodyguard named Toshio. After he left Leisha fired the bodyguard but kept the apartment. It gave her and Stewart more privacy, which they used to endlessly discuss the situation. It was Leisha who argued that it was an aberration, an immaturity.

"There have always been haters, Stewart. Hate Jews, hate blacks, hate immigrants, hate Yagaiists who have more initiative and dignity than you do. I'm just the latest object of hatred. It's not new, it's not remarkable. It doesn't mean any basic kind of schism between the Sleepless and Sleepers."

Stewart sat up in bed and reached for the sandwiches on the night stand. "Doesn't it? Leisha, you're a different kind of person entirely. More evolutionarily fit, not only to survive but to prevail. Those other 'objects of hatred' you cite except Yagaiists—they were all powerless in their societies. They occupied *inferior* positions. You, on the other hand—all three Sleepless in Harvard Law are on the *Law Review*. All of them. Kevin Baker, your oldest, has already founded a successful bio-interface software firm and is making money, a lot of it. Every Sleepless is making superb grades, none have psychological problems, all are healthy—and most of you aren't even adults yet. How much hatred do you think you're going to encounter once you hit the big-stakes world of finance and business and scarce endowed chairs and national politics?"

"Give me a sandwich," Leisha said. "Here's my evidence you're wrong: you yourself. Kenzo Yagai. Kate Addams. Professor Lane. My father. Every Sleeper who inhabits the world of fair trade, mutually beneficial contracts. And that's most of you, or at least most of you who are worth considering. You believe that competition among the most capable leads to the most beneficial trades for everyone, strong and weak. Sleepless are making real and concrete contributions to society, in a lot of fields. That has to outweigh the discomfort we cause. We're *valuable* to you. You know that."

Stewart brushed crumbs off the sheets. "Yes. I do. Yagaiists do."

"Yagaiists run the business and financial and academic worlds. Or they will. In a meritocracy, they *should*. You underestimate the majority of people, Stew. Ethics aren't confined to the ones out front."

"I hope you're right," Stewart said. "Because, you know, I'm in love with you." Leisha put down her sandwich.

"Joy," Stewart mumbled into her breasts. "You are joy."

When Leisha went home for Thanksgiving, she told Richard about Stewart. He listened tight-lipped.

"A Sleeper."

"A *person*," Leisha said. "A good, intelligent, achieving person."

"Do you know what your good intelligent achieving Sleepers have done, Leisha? Jeanine has been barred from Olympic skating. 'Genetic alteration, analogous to steroid abuse to create an unsportsmanlike advantage.' Chris Devereaux's left Stanford. They trashed his laboratory, destroyed two years' work in memory-formation proteins. Kevin Baker's software company is fighting a nasty advertising campaign, all underground, of course, about kids using software designed by 'nonhuman minds.' Corruption, mental slavery, satanic influences: the whole bag of witch-hunt tricks. Wake up, Leisha!"

They both heard his words. Moments dragged by. Richard stood like a boxer, forward on the balls of his feet, teeth clenched. Finally he said, very quietly, "Do you love him?"

"Yes," Leisha said. "I'm sorry."

"Your choice," Richard said coldly. "What do you do while he's asleep? Watch?"

"You make it sound like a perversion!"

Richard said nothing. Leisha drew a deep breath. She spoke rapidly but calmly, a controlled rush: "While Stewart is asleep I work. The same as you do. Richard—don't do this. I didn't mean to hurt you. And I don't want to lose the group. I believe the Sleepers are the same species as we are—are you going to punish me for that? Are you going to *add* to the hatred? Are you going to tell me that I can't belong to a wider world that includes all honest, worthwhile people whether they sleep or not? Are you going to tell me that the most important division is by genetics and not by economic spirituality? Are you going to force me into an artificial choice, 'us' or 'them'?"

Richard picked up a bracelet. Leisha recognized it: she had given it to him in the summer. His voice was quiet. "No. It's not a choice." He played with the gold links a minute, then looked up at her. "Not yet."

By spring break, Camden walked more slowly. He took medicine for his blood pressure, his heart. He and Susan, he told Leisha, were getting a divorce. "She changed, Leisha, after I married her. You saw that. She was independent and productive and happy, and then after a few years she stopped all that and became a shrew. A whining shrew." He shook his head in genuine bewilderment. "You saw the change."

Leisha had. A memory came to her: Susan leading her and Alice in "games" that were actually controlled cerebral-performance tests. Susan's braids dancing around her sparkling eyes. Alice had loved Susan, then, as much as Leisha had.

"Dad, I want Alice's address."

"I told you up at Harvard, I don't have it," Camden said. He shifted in his chair, the impatient gesture of a body that never expected to wear out. In January

Kenzo Yagai had died of pancreatic cancer; Camden had taken the news hard. "I make her allowance through an attorney. By her choice."

"Then I want the address of the attorney."

The attorney, however, refused to tell Leisha where Alice was. "She doesn't want to be found, Ms. Camden. She wanted a complete break."

"Not from me," Leisha said.

"Yes," the attorney said, and something flickered behind his eyes, something she had last seen in Dave Hannaway's face.

She flew to Austin before returning to Boston, making her a day late for classes. Kevin Baker saw her instantly, canceling a meeting with IBM. She told him what she needed, and he set his best datanet people on it, without telling them why. Within two hours she had Alice's address from the attorney's electronic files. It was the first time, she realized, that she had ever turned to one of the Sleepless for help, and it had been given instantly. Without trade.

Alice was in Pennsylvania. The next weekend Leisha rented a hovercar and driver—she had learned to drive, but only groundcars as yet—and went to High Ridge, in the Appalachian Mountains.

It was an isolated hamlet, twenty-five miles from the nearest hospital. Alice lived with a man named Ed, a silent carpenter twenty years older than she, in a cabin in the woods. The cabin had water and electricity but no news net. In the early spring light the earth was raw and bare, slashed with icy gullies. Alice and Ed apparently worked at nothing. Alice was eight months pregnant.

"I didn't want you here," she said to Leisha. "So why are you?"

"Because you're my sister."

"God, look at you. Is that what they're wearing at Harvard? Boots like that? When did you become fashionable, Leisha? You were always too busy being intellectual to care."

"What's this all about, Alice? Why here? What are you doing?"

"Living," Alice said. "Away from dear Daddy, away from Chicago, away from drunken broken Susan—did you know she drinks? Just like Mom. He does that to people. But not to me. I got out. I wonder if you ever will."

"Got out? To *this*?"

"I'm happy," Alice said angrily. "Isn't that what it's supposed to be about? Isn't that the aim of your great Kenzo Yagai—happiness through individual effort?"

Leisha thought of saying that Alice was making no efforts that she could see. She didn't say it. A chicken ran through the yard of the cabin. Behind, the Appalachian Mountains rose in layers of blue haze. Leisha thought what this place must have been like in winter: cut off from the world where people strived toward goals, learned, changed.

"I'm glad you're happy, Alice."

"Are you?"

"Yes."

"Then I'm glad, too," Alice said, almost defiantly. The next moment she abruptly hugged Leisha, fiercely, the huge hard mound of her belly crushed between them. Alice's hair smelled sweet, like fresh grass in sunlight.

"I'll come see you again, Alice."

"Don't," Alice said.

VI

SLEEPLESS MUTIE BEGS FOR REVERSAL OF GENE TAMPERING, screamed the headline in the Food Mart. "PLEASE LET ME SLEEP LIKE REAL PEOPLE!" CHILD PLEADS.

Leisha typed in her credit number and pressed the news kiosk for a printout, although ordinarily she ignored the electronic tabloids. The headline went on circling the kiosk. A Food Mart employee stopped stacking boxes on shelves and watched her. Bruce, Leisha's bodyguard, watched the employee.

She was twenty-two, in her final year at Harvard Law, editor of the *Law Review*, ranked first in her class. The next three were Jonathan Cocchiara, Len Carter, and Martha Wentz. All Sleepless.

In her apartment she skimmed the printout. Then she accessed the Groupnet run from Austin. The files had more news stories about the child, with comments from other Sleepless, but before she could call them up Kevin Baker came online himself, on voice.

"Leisha. I'm glad you called. I was going to call you."

"What's the situation with this Stella Bevington, Kev? Has anybody checked it out?"

"Randy Davies. He's from Chicago, but I don't think you've met him; he's still in high school. He's in Park Ridge; Stella's in Skokie. Her parents wouldn't talk to him—were pretty abusive, in fact—but he got to see Stella face-to-face anyway. It doesn't look like an abuse case, just the usual stupidity: parents wanted a genius child, scrimped and saved, and now they can't handle that she *is* one. They scream at her to sleep, get emotionally abusive when she contradicts them, but so far no violence."

"Is the emotional abuse actionable?"

"I don't think we want to move on it yet. Two of us will keep in close touch with Stella—she does have a modem, and she hasn't told her parents about the net—and Randy will drive out weekly."

Leisha bit her lip. "A tabloid shitpiece said she's seven years old."

"Yes."

"Maybe she shouldn't be left there. I'm an Illinois resident, I can file an abuse grievance from here if Candy's got too much in her briefcase. . . ." *Seven years old.*

"No. Let it sit awhile. Stella will probably be all right. You know that."

She did. Nearly all of the Sleepless stayed "all right," no matter how much opposition came from the stupid segment of society. And it was only the stupid segment, Leisha argued—a small if vocal minority. Most people could, and would, adjust to the growing presence of the Sleepless, when it became clear that that presence included not only growing power but growing benefits to the country as a whole.

Kevin Baker, now twenty-six, had made a fortune in microchips so revolutionary that artificial intelligence, once a debated dream, was yearly closer to reality. Carolyn Rizzolo had won the Pulitzer Prize in drama for her play *Morning Light*. She was twenty-four. Jeremy Robinson had done significant work in superconductivity applications while still a graduate student at Stanford. William Thaine, *Law Review* editor when Leisha first came to Harvard, was now in private practice. He had never lost a case. He was twenty-six, and the cases were becoming important. His clients valued his ability more than his age.

But not everyone reacted that way.

Kevin Baker and Richard Keller had started the datanet that bound the Sleepless into a tight group, constantly aware of each other's personal fights. Leisha Camden financed the legal battles, the educational costs of Sleepless whose parents were unable to meet them, the support of children in emotionally bad situations. Rhonda Lavelier got herself licensed as a foster mother in California, and whenever possible the Group maneuvered to have small Sleepless who were removed from their homes assigned to Rhonda. The Group now had three ABA lawyers; within the next year they would gain four more, licensed to practice in five different states.

The one time they had not been able to remove an abused Sleepless child legally, they kidnapped him.

Timmy DeMarzo, four years old. Leisha had been opposed to the action. She had argued the case morally and pragmatically—to her they were the same thing—thus: if they believed in their society, in its fundamental laws and in their ability to belong to it as free-trading productive individuals, they must remain bound by the society's contractual laws. The Sleepless were, for the most part, Yagaiists. They should already know this. And if the FBI caught them, the courts and press would crucify them.

They were not caught.

Timmy DeMarzo—not even old enough to call for help on the datanet; they had learned of the situation through the automatic police-record scan Kevin maintained through his company—was stolen from his own backyard in Wichita. He had lived the last year in an isolated trailer in North Dakota; no place was too isolated for a modem. He was cared for by a legally irreproachable foster mother who had lived there all her life. The foster mother was second cousin to a Sleepless, a broad cheerful woman with a much better brain than her appearance indicated. She was a Yagaiist. No record of the child's existence appeared in any data bank: not the IRS's, not any school's, not even the local grocery store's computerized checkout slips. Food specifically for the child was shipped in monthly on a truck owned by a Sleepless in State College, Pennsylvania. Ten of the Group knew about the kidnapping, out of the total 3,428 born in the United States. Of that total, 2,691 were part of the Group via the net. Another 701 were as yet too young to use a modem. Only 36 Sleepless, for whatever reason, were not part of the Group.

The kidnapping had been arranged by Tony Indivino.

"It's Tony I wanted to talk to you about," Kevin said to Leisha. "He's started again. This time he means it. He's buying land."

She folded the tabloid very small and laid it carefully on the table. "Where?"

"Allegheny Mountains. In southern New York State. A lot of land. He's putting in the roads now. In the spring, the first buildings."

"Jennifer Sharifi still financing it?" She was the American-born daughter of an Arab prince who had wanted a Sleepless child. The prince was dead, and Jennifer, dark-eyed and multilingual, was richer than Leisha would one day be.

"Yes. He's starting to get a following, Leisha."

"I know."

"Call him."

"I will. Keep me informed about Stella."

She worked until midnight at the *Law Review*, then until four A.M. preparing her classes. From four to five she handled legal matters for the Group. At five A.M. she called Tony, still in Chicago. He had finished high school, done one semester at Northwestern, and at Christmas vacation he had finally exploded at his mother for forcing him to live as a Sleeper. The explosion, it seemed to Leisha, had never ended.

"Tony? Leisha."

"The answer is yes, yes, no, and go to hell."

Leisha gritted her teeth. "Fine. Now tell me the questions."

"Are you really serious about the Sleepless withdrawing into their own self-sufficient society? Is Jennifer Sharifi willing to finance a project the size of building a small city? Don't you think that's a cheat of all that can be accomplished by patient integration of the Group into the mainstream? And what about the contradictions of living in an armed restricted city and still trading with the Outside?"

"I would never tell *you* to go to hell."

"Hooray for you," Tony said. After a moment he added, "I'm sorry. That sounds like one of *them*."

"It's wrong for us, Tony."

"Thanks for not saying I couldn't pull it off."

She wondered if he could. "We're not a separate species, Tony."

"Tell that to the Sleepers."

"You exaggerate. There are haters out there, there are *always* haters, but to give up . . ."

"We're not giving up. Whatever we create can be freely traded: software, hardware, novels, information, theories, legal counsel. We can travel in and out. But we'll have a safe place to return *to*. Without the leeches who think we owe them blood because we're better than they are."

"It isn't a matter of owing."

"Really?" Tony said. "Let's have this out, Leisha. All the way. You're a Yagaiist—what do you believe in?"

"Tony . . ."

"*Do it*," Tony said, and in his voice she heard the fourteen-year-old Richard had introduced her to. Simultaneously, she saw her father's face: not as he was now, since the bypass, but as he had been when she was a little girl, holding her on his lap to explain that she was special.

"I believe in voluntary trade that is mutually beneficial. That spiritual dignity comes from supporting one's life through one's own efforts, and trading the results of those efforts in mutual cooperation throughout the society. That the symbol of this is the contract. And that we need each other for the fullest, most beneficial trade."

"Fine," Tony bit off. "Now what about the beggars in Spain?"

"The what?"

"You walk down a street in a poor country like Spain and you see a beggar. Do you give him a dollar?"

"Probably."

"Why? He's trading nothing with you. He has nothing to trade."

"I know. Out of kindness. Compassion."

"You see six beggars. Do you give them all a dollar?"

"Probably," Leisha said.

"You would. You see a hundred beggars and you haven't got Leisha Camden's money—do you give them each a dollar?"

"No."

"Why not?"

Leisha reached for patience. Few people could make her want to cut off a comm link; Tony was one of them. "Too draining on my own resources. My life has first claim on the resources I earn."

"All right. Now consider this. At Biotech Institute—where you and I began, dear pseudo sister—Dr. Melling has just yesterday—"

"Who?"

"Dr. Susan Melling. Oh, God, I completely forgot—she used to be married to your father!"

"I lost track of her," Leisha said. "I didn't realize she'd gone back to research. Alice once said . . . never mind. What's going on at Biotech?"

"Two crucial items, just released. Carla Dutcher has had first-month fetal genetic analysis. Sleeplessness is a dominant gene. The next generation of the Group won't sleep, either."

"We all knew that," Leisha said. Carla Dutcher was the world's first pregnant Sleepless. Her husband was a Sleeper. "The whole world expected that."

"But the press will have a windfall with it anyway. Just watch. 'Muties Breed!' 'New Race Set to Dominate Next Generation of Children!' "

Leisha didn't deny it. "And the second item?"

"It's sad, Leisha. We've just had our first death."

Her stomach tightened. "Who?"

"Bernie Kuhn. Seattle." She didn't know him. "A car accident. It looks pretty straightforward—he lost control on a steep curve when his brakes failed. He had only been driving a few months. He was seventeen. But the significance here is that his parents have donated his brain and body to Biotech, in conjunction with the pathology department at the Chicago Medical School. They're going to take him apart to get the first good look at what prolonged sleeplessness does to the body and brain."

"They should," Leisha said. "That poor kid. But what are you so afraid they'll find?"

"I don't know. I'm not a doctor. But whatever it is, if the haters can use it against us, they will."

"You're paranoid, Tony."

"Impossible. The Sleepless have personalities calmer and more reality-oriented than the norm. Don't you read the literature?"

"Tony—"

"What if you walk down that street in Spain and a hundred beggars each want a dollar and you say no and they have nothing to trade you, but they're so rotten with anger about what you have that they knock you down and grab it and then beat you out of sheer envy and despair?"

Leisha didn't answer.

"Are you going to say that's not a human scenario, Leisha? That it never happens?"

"It happens," Leisha said evenly. "But not all that often."

"Bullshit. Read more history. Read more *newspapers*. But the point is: what do you owe the beggars then? What does a good Yagaiist who believes in mutually beneficial contracts do with people who have nothing to trade and can only take?"

"You're not—"

"*What*, Leisha? In the most objective terms you can manage, what do we owe the grasping and nonproductive needy?"

"What I said originally. Kindness. Compassion."

"Even if they don't trade it back? Why?"

"Because . . ." She stopped.

"Why? Why do law-abiding and productive human beings owe anything to those who neither produce very much nor abide by laws? What philosophical or economic or spiritual justification is there for owing them anything? Be as honest as I know you are."

Leisha put her head between her knees. The question gaped beneath her, but she didn't try to evade it. "I don't know. I just know we do."

"Why?"

She didn't answer. After a moment Tony did. The intellectual challenge was gone from his voice. He said, almost tenderly, "Come down in the spring and see the site for Sanctuary. The buildings will be going up then."

"No," Leisha said.

"I'd like you to."

"No. Armed retreat is not the way."

Tony said, "The beggars are getting nastier, Leisha. As the Sleepless grow richer. And I don't mean in money."

"Tony—" she said, and stopped. She couldn't think what to say.

"Don't walk too many streets armed with just the memory of Kenzo Yagai."

In March, a bitterly cold March of winds whipping down the Charles River, Richard Keller came to Cambridge. Leisha had not seen him for four years. He didn't send her word on the Groupnet that he was coming. She hurried up the walk to her townhouse, muffled to the eyes in a red wool scarf against the snowy cold, and he stood there blocking the doorway. Behind Leisha, her bodyguard tensed.

"Richard! Bruce, it's all right; this is an old friend."

"Hello, Leisha."

He was heavier, sturdier looking, with a breadth of shoulder she didn't recognize. But the face was Richard's, older but unchanged: dark low brows, unruly dark hair. He had grown a beard.

"You look beautiful," he said.

She handed him a cup of coffee. "Are you here on business?" From the Groupnet she knew that he had finished his master's and had done outstanding work in marine biology in the Caribbean but had left that a year ago and disappeared from the net.

"No. Pleasure." He smiled suddenly, the old smile that opened up his dark face. "I almost forgot about that for a long time. Contentment, yes, we're all good at the contentment that comes from sustained work, but pleasure? Whim? Caprice? When was the last time you did something silly, Leisha?"

She smiled. "I ate cotton candy in the shower."

"Really? Why?"

"To see if it would dissolve in gooey pink patterns."

"Did it?"

"Yes. Lovely ones."

"And that was your last silly thing? When was it?"

"Last summer," Leisha said, and laughed.

"Well, mine is sooner than that. It's now. I'm in Boston for no other reason than the spontaneous pleasure of seeing you."

Leisha stopped laughing. "That's an intense tone for a spontaneous pleasure, Richard."

"Yup," he said, intensely. She laughed again. He didn't.

"I've been in India, Leisha. And China and Africa. Thinking, mostly. Watching. First I traveled like a Sleeper, attracting no attention. Then I set out to meet the Sleepless in India and China. There are a few, you know, whose parents were willing to come here for the operation. They pretty much are accepted and left alone. I tried to figure out why desperately poor countries—by our standards, anyway; over there Y-energy is mostly available only in big cities—don't have any trouble accepting the superiority of Sleepless, whereas Americans, with more prosperity than any time in history, build in resentment more and more."

Leisha said, "Did you figure it out?"

"No. But I figured out something else, watching all those communes and villages and kampongs. We are too individualistic."

Disappointment swept Leisha. She saw her father's face: *Excellence is what counts, Leisha. Excellence supported by individual effort. . . .* She reached for Richard's cup. "More coffee?"

He caught her wrist and looked up into her face. "Don't misunderstand me, Leisha. I'm not talking about work. We are too much individuals in the rest of our lives. Too emotionally rational. Too much alone. Isolation kills more than the free flow of ideas. It kills joy."

He didn't let go of her wrist. She looked down into his eyes, into depths she hadn't seen before: it was the feeling of looking into a mine shaft, both giddy and frightening, knowing that at the bottom might be gold or darkness. Or both.

Richard said softly, "Stewart?"

"Over long ago. An undergraduate thing." Her voice didn't sound like her own.

"Kevin?"

"No, never—we're just friends."

"I wasn't sure. Anyone?"

"No."

He let go of her wrist. Leisha peered at him timidly. He suddenly laughed. "Joy, Leisha." An echo sounded in her mind, but she couldn't place it and then it was gone and she laughed, too, a laugh airy and frothy as pink cotton candy in summer.

"Come home, Leisha. He's had another heart attack."

Susan Melling's voice on the phone was tired. Leisha said, "How bad?"

"The doctors aren't sure. Or say they're not sure. He wants to see you. Can you leave your studies?"

It was May, the last push toward her finals. The *Law Review* proofs were behind schedule. Richard had started a new business, marine consulting to Boston fishermen plagued with sudden inexplicable shifts in ocean currents, and was working twenty hours a day. "I'll come," Leisha said.

Chicago was colder than Boston. The trees were half budded. On Lake Michigan, filling the huge east windows of her father's house, whitecaps tossed up cold spray. Leisha saw that Susan was living in the house: her brushes on Camden's dresser, her journals on the credenza in the foyer.

"Leisha," Camden said. He looked old. Gray skin, sunken cheeks, the fretful and bewildered look of men who accepted potency like air, indivisible from their lives. In the corner of the room, on a small eighteenth-century slipper chair, sat a short, stocky woman with brown braids.

"*Alice.*"

"Hello, Leisha."

"*Alice.* I've looked for you. . . ." The wrong thing to say. Leisha had looked but not very hard, deterred by the knowledge that Alice had not wanted to be found. "How are you?"

"I'm fine," Alice said. She seemed remote, gentle, unlike the angry Alice of six years ago in the raw Pennsylvania hills. Camden moved painfully on the bed. He looked at Leisha with eyes that, she saw, were undimmed in their blue brightness.

"I asked Alice to come. And Susan. Susan came a while ago. I'm dying, Leisha."

No one contradicted him. Leisha, knowing his respect for facts, remained silent. Love hurt her chest.

"John Jaworski has my will. None of you can break it. But I wanted to tell you myself what's in it. The last few years I've been selling, liquidating. Most of my holdings are accessible now. I've left a tenth to Alice, a tenth to Susan, a tenth to Elizabeth, and the rest to you, Leisha, because you're the only one with the individual ability to use the money to its full potential for achievement."

Leisha looked wildly at Alice, who gazed back with her strange remote calm. "Elizabeth? My . . . mother? Is alive?"

"Yes," Camden said.

"You told me she was dead! Years and years ago."

"Yes. I thought it was better for you that way. She didn't like what you were, was jealous of what you could become. And she had nothing to give you. She would only have caused you emotional harm."

Beggars in Spain . . .

"That was wrong, Dad. You were *wrong*. She's my *mother . . .*" She couldn't finish the sentence.

Camden didn't flinch. "I don't think I was. But you're an adult now. You can see her if you wish."

He went on looking at her from his bright, sunken eyes, while around Leisha the air heaved and snapped. Her father had lied to her. Susan watched her closely, a small smile on her lips. Was she glad to see Camden fall in his daughter's estimation? Had she all along been that jealous of their relationship, of Leisha . . .

She was thinking like Tony.

The thought steadied her a little. But she went on staring at Camden, who went on staring implacably back, unbudged, a man positive even on his deathbed that he was right.

Alice's hand was on her elbow, Alice's voice so soft that no one but Leisha could hear. "He's done now, Leisha. And after a while you'll be all right."

Alice had left her son in California with her husband of two years, Beck Watrous, a building contractor she had met while waitressing in a resort on the Artificial Islands. Beck had adopted Jordan, Alice's son.

"Before Beck there was a real bad time," Alice said in her remote voice. "You know, when I was carrying Jordan I actually used to dream that he would be Sleepless? Like you. Every night I'd dream that, and every morning I'd wake up and have morning sickness with a baby that was only going to be a stupid nothing like me. I stayed with Ed—in Pennsylvania, remember? You came to see me there once—for two more years. When he beat me, I was glad. I wished Daddy could see. At least Ed was touching me."

Leisha made a sound in her throat.

"I finally left because I was afraid for Jordan. I went to California, did nothing but eat for a year. I got up to a hundred and ninety pounds." Alice was, Leisha estimated, five-foot-four. "Then I came home to see Mother."

"You didn't tell me," Leisha said. "You knew she was alive and you didn't tell me."

"She's in a drying-out tank half the time," Alice said, with brutal simplicity. "She wouldn't see you if you wanted to. But she saw me, and she fell slobbering all over me as her 'real' daughter, and she threw up on my dress. And I backed away from her and looked at the dress and knew it *should* be thrown up on, it was so ugly. Deliberately ugly. She started screaming how Dad had ruined her life, ruined mine, all for *you*. And do you know what I did?"

"What?" Leisha said. Her voice was shaky.

"I flew home, burned all my clothes, got a job, started college, lost fifty pounds, and put Jordan in play therapy."

The sisters sat silent. Beyond the window the lake was dark, unlit by moon or stars. It was Leisha who suddenly shook, and Alice who patted her shoulder.

"Tell me . . ." Leisha couldn't think what she wanted to be told, except that she wanted to hear Alice's voice in the gloom, Alice's voice as it was now, gentle and remote, without damage anymore from the damaging fact of Leisha's existence. Her very existence as damage. ". . . tell me about Jordan. He's five now? What's he like?"

Alice turned her head to look levelly into Leisha's eyes. "He's a happy, ordinary little boy. Completely ordinary."

Camden died a week later. After the funeral, Leisha tried to see her mother at the Brookfield Drug and Alcohol Abuse Center. Elizabeth Camden, she was told, saw no one except her only child, Alice Camden Watrous.

Susan Melling, dressed in black, drove Leisha to the airport. Susan talked deftly, determinedly, about Leisha's studies, about Harvard, about the *Review*. Leisha answered in monosyllables, but Susan persisted, asking questions, quietly insisting on answers: When would Leisha take her bar exams? Where was she interviewing for jobs? Gradually Leisha began to lose the numbness she had felt since her father's casket was lowered into the ground. She realized that Susan's persistent questioning was a kindness.

"He sacrificed a lot of people," Leisha said suddenly.

"Not me," Susan said. She pulled the car into the airport parking lot. "Only for a while there, when I gave up my work to do his. Roger didn't respect sacrifice much."

"Was he wrong?" Leisha said. The question came out with a kind of desperation she hadn't intended.

Susan smiled sadly. "No. He wasn't wrong. I should never have left my research. It took me a long time to come back to myself after that."

He does that to people, Leisha heard inside her head. Susan? Or Alice? She couldn't, for once, remember clearly. She saw her father in the old conservatory, potting and repotting the dramatic exotic flowers he had loved.

She was tired. It was muscle fatigue from stress, she knew; twenty minutes of rest would restore her. Her eyes burned from unaccustomed tears. She leaned her head back against the car seat and closed them.

Susan pulled the car into the airport parking lot and turned off the ignition. "There's something I want to tell you, Leisha."

Leisha opened her eyes. "About the will?"

Susan smiled tightly. "No. You really don't have any problems with how he divided the estate, do you? It seems to you reasonable. But that's not it. The research team from Biotech and Chicago Medical has finished its analysis of Bernie Kuhn's brain."

Leisha turned to face Susan. She was startled by the complexity of Susan's expression. Determination, and satisfaction, and anger, and something else Leisha could not name.

Susan said, "We're going to publish next week, in the *New England Journal of Medicine*. Security has been unbelievably restricted—no leaks to the popular press. But I want to tell you now, myself, what we found. So you'll be prepared."

"Go on," Leisha said. Her chest felt tight.

"Do you remember when you and the other Sleepless kids took interleukin-1 to see what sleep was like? When you were sixteen?"

"How did you know about that?"

"You kids were watched a lot more closely than you think. Remember the headache you got?"

"Yes." She and Richard and Tony and Carol and Jeanine . . . after her rejection by the Olympic Committee, Jeanine had never skated again. She was a kindergarten teacher in Butte, Montana.

"Interleukin-1 is what I want to talk about. At least, partly. It's one of a whole group of substances that boost the immune system. They stimulate the production of antibodies, the activity of white blood cells, and a host of other immunoenhancements. Normal people have surges of IL-1 released during the slow-wave phases of sleep. That means that they—we—are getting boosts to the immune system during sleep. One of the questions we researchers asked ourselves twenty-eight years ago was: will Sleepless kids who don't get those surges of IL-1 get sick more often?"

"I've never been sick," Leisha said.

"Yes, you have. Chicken pox and three minor colds by the end of your fourth year," Susan said precisely. "But in general you were all a very healthy lot. So we researchers were left with the alternative theory of sleep-driven immunoenhancement: that the burst of immune activity existed as a counterpart to a greater vulnerability of the body in sleep to disease, probably in some way connected to the fluctuations in body temperature during REM sleep. In other words, sleep *caused* the immune vulnerability that endogenous pyrogens like IL-1 counteract. Sleep was the problem; immune-system enhancements were the solution. Without sleep, there would be no problem. Are you following this?"

"Yes."

"Of course you are. Stupid question." Susan brushed her hair off her face. It was going gray at the temples. There was a tiny brown age spot beneath her right ear.

"Over the years we collected thousands—maybe hundreds of thousands—of Single Photon Emission Tomography scans of you and the other kids' brains, plus endless EEGs, samples of cerebrospinal fluid, and all the rest of it. But we couldn't really see inside your brains, really know what's going on in there. Until Bernie Kuhn hit that embankment."

"Susan," Leisha said, "give it to me straight. Without more buildup."

"You're not going to age."

"What?"

"Oh, cosmetically, yes. Gray hair, wrinkles, sags. But the absence of sleep peptides and all the rest of it affects the immune and tissue-restoration systems in ways we don't understand. Bernie Kuhn had a perfect liver. Perfect lungs, perfect heart, perfect lymph nodes, perfect pancreas, perfect medulla oblongata. Not just healthy or young—*perfect.* There's a tissue-regeneration enhancement that clearly derives from the operation of the immune system but is radically different from anything we ever suspected. Organs show no wear and tear—not even the minimal amount expected in a seventeen-year-old. They just repair themselves, perfectly, on and on . . . and on."

"For how long?" Leisha whispered.

"Who the hell knows? Bernie Kuhn was young—maybe there's some compensatory mechanism that cuts in at some point and you'll all just collapse, like an entire fucking gallery of Dorian Grays. But I don't think so. Neither do I think it can go on forever; no tissue regeneration can do that. But a long, long time."

Leisha stared at the blurred reflections in the car windshield. She saw her father's face against the blue satin of his casket, banked with white roses. His heart, unregenerated, had given out.

Susan said, "The future is all speculative at this point. We know that the peptide structures that build up the pressure to sleep in normal people resemble the components of bacterial cell walls. Maybe there's a connection between sleep and pathogen receptivity. We don't know. But ignorance never stopped the tabloids. I wanted to prepare you because you're going to get called supermen, *Homo perfectus,* who all knows what. Immortal."

The two women sat in silence. Finally Leisha said, "I'm going to tell the others. On our datanet. Don't worry about the security. Kevin Baker designed Groupnet; nobody knows anything we don't want them to."

"You're that well organized already?"

"Yes."

Susan's mouth worked. She looked away from Leisha. "We better go in. You'll miss your flight."

"Susan . . ."

"What?"

"Thank you."

"You're welcome," Susan said, and in her voice Leisha heard the thing she had seen before in Susan's expression and not been able to name: it was longing.

Tissue regeneration. A long, long time, sang the blood in Leisha's ears on the flight to Boston. *Tissue regeneration.* And, eventually: *immortal.* No, not that, she told herself severely. Not that. The blood didn't listen.

"You sure smile a lot," said the man next to her in first class, a business traveler who had not recognized Leisha. "You coming from a big party in Chicago?"

"No. From a funeral."

The man looked shocked, then disgusted. Leisha looked out the window at the ground far below. Rivers like microcircuits, fields like neat index cards. And on the horizon fluffy white clouds like masses of exotic flowers, blooms in a conservatory filled with light.

The letter was no thicker than any hard-copy mail, but hard-copy mail addressed by hand to either of them was so rare that Richard was nervous. "It might be explosive." Leisha looked at the letter on their hall credenza. MS. LIESHA CAMDEN. Block letters, misspelled.

"It looks like a child's writing," she said.

Richard stood with head lowered, legs braced apart. But his expression was only weary. "Perhaps deliberately like a child's. You'd be more open to a child's writing, they might have figured."

" 'They'? Richard, are we getting that paranoid?"

He didn't flinch from the question. "Yes. For the time being."

A week earlier the *New England Journal of Medicine* had published Susan's careful, sober article. An hour later the broadcast and datanet news had exploded in speculation, drama, outrage, and fear. Leisha and Richard, along with all the Sleepless on the Groupnet, had tracked and charted each of four components, looking for a dominant reaction: speculation ("The Sleepless may live for centuries, and this might lead to the following events . . ."); drama ("If a Sleepless marries only Sleepers, he may have lifetime enough for a dozen brides—and several dozen children, a bewildering blended family . . ."); outrage ("Tampering with the law of nature has only brought among us unnatural so-called people who will live with the unfair advantage of time: time to accumulate more kin, more power, more property than the rest of us could ever know . . ."); and fear ("How soon before the Superrace takes over?").

"They're all fear, of one kind or another," Carolyn Rizzolo finally said, and the Groupnet stopped their differentiated tracking.

Leisha was taking the final exams of her last year of law school. Each day comments followed her to the campus, along the corridors, and in the classroom; each day she forgot them in the grueling exam sessions, all students reduced to the same status of petitioner to the great university. Afterward, temporarily drained, she walked silently back home to Richard and the Groupnet, aware of the looks of people on the street, aware of her bodyguard, Bruce, striding between her and them.

"It will calm down," Leisha said. Richard didn't answer.

The town of Salt Springs, Texas, passed a local ordinance that no Sleepless could obtain a liquor license, on the grounds that civil rights statutes were built on the "all men were created equal" clause of the Declaration of Independence and Sleepless clearly were not covered. There were no Sleepless within a hundred miles of Salt Springs, and no one had applied for a new liquor license there for the past ten years, but the story was picked up by United Press and by Datanet News, and within twenty-four hours heated editorials appeared, on both sides of the issue, across the nation.

More local ordinances appeared. In Pollux, Pennsylvania, the Sleepless could be denied apartment rental on the grounds that their prolonged wakefulness would increase both wear and tear on the landlord's property and utility bills. In Cranston Estates, California, Sleepless were barred from operating twenty-four-hour businesses: "unfair competition." Iroquois County, New York, barred them from serving on county juries, arguing that a jury containing Sleepless, with their skewed idea of time, did not constitute "a jury of one's peers."

"All those statutes will be thrown out in superior courts," Leisha said. "But, God, the waste of money and docket time to do it!" A part of her mind noticed that her tone as she said this was Roger Camden's.

The state of Georgia, in which some sex acts between consenting adults were still a crime, made sex between a Sleepless and a Sleeper a third-degree felony, classing it with bestiality.

Kevin Baker had designed software that scanned the newsnets at high speed, flagged all stories involving discrimination or attacks on Sleepless, and categorized them by type. The files were available on Groupnet. Leisha read through them, then called Kevin. "Can't you create a parallel program to flag defenses of us? We're getting a skewed picture."

"You're right," Kevin said, a little startled. "I didn't think of it."

"Think of it," Leisha said, grimly. Richard, watching her, said nothing.

She was most upset by the stories about Sleepless children. Shunned at school, verbal abuse by siblings, attacks by neighborhood bullies, confused resentment from parents who had wanted an exceptional child but had not bargained on one who might live centuries. The school board of Cold River, Iowa, voted to bar Sleepless children from conventional classrooms because their rapid learning "created feelings of inadequacy in others, interfering with their education." The board made funds available for Sleepless to have tutors at home. There were no volunteers among the teaching staff. Leisha started spending as much time on Groupnet with the kids, talking to them all night long, as she did studying for her bar exams, scheduled for July.

Stella Bevington stopped using her modem.

Kevin's second program catalogued editorials urging fairness toward Sleepless. The school board of Denver set aside funds for a program in which gifted children, including the Sleepless, could use their talents and build teamwork through tutoring even younger children. Rive Beau, Louisiana, elected Sleepless Danielle du Cherney to the city council, although Danielle was twenty-two and technically too young to qualify. The prestigious medical research firm of Halley-Hall gave much publicity to their hiring of Christopher Amren, a Sleepless with a Ph.D. in cellular physics.

Dora Clarq, a Sleepless in Dallas, opened a letter addressed to her, and a plastic explosive blew off her arm.

Leisha and Richard stared at the envelope on the hall credenza. The paper was thick, cream-colored, but not expensive: the kind of paper made of bulky newsprint dyed the shade of vellum. There was no return address. Richard called Liz Bishop, a Sleepless who was majoring in criminal justice in Michigan. He had never spoken with her before—neither had Leisha—but she came on Groupnet immediately and told them how to open it, or she could fly up and do it if they preferred. Richard and Leisha followed her directions for remote detonation in the basement of the townhouse. Nothing blew up. When the letter was open, they took it out and read it:

Dear Ms. Camden,

You been pretty good to me and I'm sorry to do this but I quit. They are making it pretty hot for me at the union not officially but you know how it is. If I was you I wouldn't go to the union for another bodyguard I'd try to find one privately. But be careful. Again I'm sorry but I have to live too.
Bruce

"I don't know whether to laugh or cry," Leisha said. "The two of us getting all this equipment, spending hours on this set-up so an explosive won't detonate . . ."

"It's not as if I at least had a whole lot else to do," Richard said. Since the wave of anti-Sleepless sentiment, all but two of his marine-consultant clients, vulnerable to the marketplace and thus to public opinion, had canceled their accounts.

Groupnet, still up on Leisha's terminal, shrilled in emergency override. Leisha got there first. It was Tony.

"Leisha. I'll need your legal help, if you'll give it. They're trying to fight me on Sanctuary. Please fly down here."

Sanctuary was raw brown gashes in the late-spring earth. It was situated in the Allegheny Mountains of southern New York State, old hills rounded by age and covered with pine and hickory. A superb road led from the closest town, Belmont, to Sanctuary. Low, maintenance-free buildings, whose design was plain but graceful, stood in various stages of completion. Jennifer Sharifi, looking strained, met Leisha and Richard. "Tony wants to talk to you, but first he asked me to show you both around."

"What's wrong?" Leisha asked quietly. She had never met Jennifer before, but no Sleepless looked like that—pinched, spent, *weary*—unless the stress level was enormous.

Jennifer didn't try to evade the question. "Later. First look at Sanctuary. Tony respects your opinion enormously, Leisha; he wants you to see everything."

The dormitories each held fifty, with communal rooms for cooking, dining, relaxing, and bathing, and a warren of separate offices and studios and labs for work. "We're calling them 'dorms' anyway, despite the etymology," Jennifer said, trying to smile. Leisha glanced at Richard. The smile was a failure.

She was impressed, despite herself, with the completeness of Tony's plans for lives that would be both communal and intensely private. There was a gym, a small hospital—"By the end of next year, we'll have eighteen AMA-certified doctors, you know, and four are thinking of coming here"—a day-care facility, a school, an intensive-crop farm. "Most of our food will come in from the outside, of course. So will most people's jobs, although they'll do as much of them as possible from here, over datanets. We're not cutting ourselves off from the world—only creating a safe place from which to trade with it." Leisha didn't answer.

Apart from the power facilities, self-supported Y-energy, she was most impressed with the human planning. Tony had Sleepless interested from virtually every field they would need both to care for themselves and to deal with the outside world. "Lawyers and accountants come first," Jennifer said. "That's our first line of defense in safeguarding ourselves. Tony recognizes that most modern battles for power are fought in the courtroom and boardroom."

But not all. Last, Jennifer showed them the plans for physical defense. She explained them with a mixture of defiance and pride: every effort had been made to stop attackers without hurting them. Electronic surveillance completely circled the 150 square miles Jennifer had purchased—some *counties* were smaller than that, Leisha thought, dazed. When breached, a force field a half-mile within the E-gate activated, delivering electric shocks to anyone on foot—"But only on the *outside* of the field. We don't want any of our kids hurt." Unmanned penetration by vehicles or robots was identified by a system that located all moving metal above a certain mass within Sanctuary. Any moving metal that did not carry a special signaling device designed by Donna Pospula, a Sleepless who had patented important electronic components, was suspect.

"Of course, we're not set up for an air attack or an outright army assault," Jennifer said. "But we don't expect that. Only the haters in self-motivated hate." Her voice sagged.

Leisha touched the hard copy of the security plans with one finger. They troubled her. "If we can't integrate ourselves into the world . . . free trade should imply free movement."

"Yeah. Well," Jennifer said, such an uncharacteristic Sleepless remark—both cynical and inarticulate—that Leisha looked up. "I have something to tell you, Leisha."

"What?"

"Tony isn't here."

"Where is he?"

"In Allegheny County Jail. It's true we're having zoning battles about Sanctuary—zoning! In this isolated spot. But this is something else, something that just happened this morning. Tony's been arrested for the kidnapping of Timmy DeMarzo."

The room wavered. "FBI?"

"Yes."

"How . . . how did they find out?"

"Some agent eventually cracked the case. They didn't tell us how. Tony needs a lawyer, Leisha. Dana Monteiro has already agreed, but Tony wants you."

"Jennifer—I don't even take the bar exams until July."

"He says he'll wait. Dana will act as his lawyer in the meantime. Will you pass the bar?"

"Of course. But I already have a job lined up with Morehouse, Kennedy & Anderson in New York—" She stopped. Richard was looking at her hard, Jennifer gazing down at the floor. Leisha said quietly, "What will he plead?"

"Guilty," Jennifer said. "With—what is it called legally?—extenuating circumstances."

Leisha nodded. She had been afraid Tony would want to plead not guilty: more lies, subterfuge, ugly politics. Her mind ran swiftly over extenuating circumstances, precedents, tests to precedents. . . . They could use *Clements v. Voy* . . .

"Dana is at the jail now," Jennifer said. "Will you drive in with me?"

"Yes."

In Belmont, the county seat, they were not allowed to see Tony. Dana Monteiro, as his attorney, could go in and out freely. Leisha, not officially an attorney at all, could go nowhere. This was told them by a man in the D.A.'s office whose face stayed immobile while he spoke to them and who spat on the ground behind their shoes when they turned to leave, even though this left him with a smear of spittle on his courthouse floor.

Richard and Leisha drove their rental car to the airport for the flight back to Boston. On the way Richard told Leisha he was leaving her. He was moving to Sanctuary, now, even before it was functional, to help with the planning and building.

She stayed most of the time in her townhouse, studying ferociously for the bar exams or checking on the Sleepless children through Groupnet. She had not hired another bodyguard to replace Bruce, which made her reluctant to go outside very much; the reluctance in turn made her angry with herself. Once or twice a day she scanned Kevin's electronic news clippings.

There were signs of hope. The *New York Times* ran an editorial, widely reprinted on the electronic news services:

PROSPERITY AND HATRED: A LOGIC CURVE WE'D RATHER NOT SEE

The United States has never been a country that much values calm, logic, rationality. We have, as a people, tended to label these things "cold." We have, as a people, tended to admire feeling and action: we exalt in our stories and our memorials; not the creation of the Constitution but its defense at Iwo Jima; not the intellectual achievements of a Stephen Hawking but the heroic passion of a Charles Lindbergh; not the inventors of the monorails and computers that unite us but the composers of the angry songs of rebellion that divide us.

A peculiar aspect of this phenomenon is that it grows stronger in times of prosperity. The better off our citizenry, the greater their contempt for the calm reasoning that got them there, and the more passionate their indulgence in emotion. Consider, in the last century, the gaudy excesses of the Roaring Twenties and the antiestablishment contempt of the sixties. Consider, in our own century, the unprecedented prosperity brought about by Y-energy—and then consider that Kenzo Yagai, except to his followers, was seen as a greedy and bloodless logician, while our national adulation goes to neonihilist writer Stephen Castelli, to "feelie" actress Brenda Foss, and to daredevil gravity-well diver Jim Morse Luter.

But most of all, as you ponder this phenomenon in your Y-energy houses, consider the current outpouring of irrational feeling directed at the "Sleepless" since the publication of the joint findings of the Biotech Institute and the Chicago Medical School concerning Sleepless tissue regeneration.

Most of the Sleepless are intelligent. Most of them are calm, if you define that much-maligned word to mean directing one's energies into solving problems rather than to emoting about them. (Even Pulitzer Prize winner Carolyn Rizzolo gave us a stunning play of ideas, not of passions run amok.) All of them show a natural bent toward achievement, a bent given a decided boost by the one-third more time in their days to achieve in. Their achievements lie, for the most part, in logical fields rather than emotional ones: Computers. Law. Finance. Physics. Medical research. They are rational, orderly, calm, intelligent, cheerful, young, and possibly very long-lived.

And, in our United States of unprecedented prosperity, increasingly hated.

Does the hatred that we have seen flower so fully over the last few months really grow, as many claim, from the "unfair advantage" the Sleepless have over the rest of us in securing jobs, promotions, money, success? Is it really envy over the Sleepless' good fortune? Or does it come from something more pernicious, rooted in our tradition of shoot-from-the-hip American action: hatred of the logical, the calm, the considered? Hatred in fact of the superior mind?

If so, perhaps we should think deeply about the founders of this country: Jefferson, Washington, Paine, Adams—inhabitants of the Age of Reason, all. These men created our orderly and balanced system of laws precisely to protect the property and achievements created by the individual efforts of balanced and rational minds. The Sleepless may be our severest internal test yet of our own sober belief in law and order. No, the Sleepless were not "created equal," but our attitudes toward them should be examined with a care equal to our soberest jurisprudence. We may not like what we learn about our own motives, but our credibility as a people may depend on the rationality and intelligence of the examination.

Both have been in short supply in the public reaction to last month's research findings.

Law is not theater. Before we write laws reflecting gaudy and dramatic feelings, we must be very sure we understand the difference.

Leisha hugged herself, gazing in delight at the screen, smiling. She called the *New York Times*: who had written the editorial? The receptionist, cordial when she answered the phone, grew brusque. The *Times* was not releasing that information, "prior to internal investigation."

It could not dampen her mood. She whirled around the apartment, after days of sitting at her desk or screen. Delight demanded physical action. She washed dishes, picked up books. There were gaps in the furniture patterns where Richard had taken pieces that belonged to him; a little quieter now, she moved the furniture to close the gaps.

Susan Melling called to tell her about the *Times* editorial; they talked warmly for a few minutes. When Susan hung up, the phone rang again.

"Leisha? Your voice still sounds the same. This is Stewart Sutter."

"Stewart." She had not seen him for years. Their romance had lasted two years and then dissolved, not from any painful issue so much as from the press of both their studies. Standing by the comm terminal, hearing his voice, Leisha suddenly felt again his hands on her breasts in the cramped dormitory bed: all those years before she had found a good use for a bed. The phantom hands became Richard's hands, and a sudden pain pierced her.

"Listen," Stewart said. "I'm calling because there's some information I think you should know. You take your bar exams next week, right? And then you have a tentative job with Morehouse, Kennedy & Anderson."

"How do you know all that, Stewart?"

"Men's-room gossip. Well, not as bad as that. But the New York legal community—that part of it, anyway—is smaller than you think. And you're a pretty visible figure."

"Yes," Leisha said neutrally.

"Nobody has the slightest doubt you'll be called to the bar. But there is some doubt about the job with Morehouse, Kennedy. You've got two senior partners, Alan Morehouse and Seth Brown, who have changed their minds since this . . . flap. 'Adverse publicity for the firm,' 'turning law into a circus,' blah blah blah. You know the drill. But you've also got two powerful champions, Ann Carlyle and Michael Kennedy, the old man himself. He's quite a mind. Anyway, I wanted you to know all this so you can recognize exactly what the situation is and know whom to count on in the in-fighting."

"Thank you," Leisha said. "Stew . . . why do you care if I get it or not? Why should it matter to you?"

There was a silence on the other end of the phone. Then Stewart said, very low, "We're not all noodleheads out here, Leisha. Justice does still matter to some of us. So does achievement."

Light rose in her, a bubble of buoyant light.

Stewart said, "You have a lot of support here for that stupid zoning fight over Sanctuary, too. You might not realize that, but you do. What the parks commission crowd is trying to pull is . . . but they're just being used as fronts. You know that. Anyway, when it gets as far as the courts, you'll have all the help you need."

"Sanctuary isn't my doing. At all."

"No? Well, I meant the plural you."

"Thank you. I mean that. How are you doing?"

"Fine. I'm a daddy now."

"Really! Boy or girl?"

"Girl. A beautiful little bitch, drives me crazy. I'd like you to meet my wife sometime, Leisha."

"I'd like that," Leisha said.

She spent the rest of the night studying for her bar exams. The bubble stayed with her. She recognized exactly what it was: joy.

It was going to be all right. The contract, unwritten, between her and her society—Kenzo Yagai's society, Roger Camden's society—would hold. With dissent and strife and, yes, some hatred: she suddenly thought of Tony's beggars in Spain, furious at the strong because they themselves were not. Yes. But it would hold.

She believed that.

She did.

VII

Leisha took her bar exams in July. They did not seem hard to her. Afterward three classmates, two men and a woman, made a fakely casual point of talking to Leisha until she had climbed safely into a taxi whose driver obviously did not recognize her, or stop signs. The three were all Sleepers. A pair of undergraduates, clean-shaven blond men with the long faces and pointless arrogance of rich stupidity, eyed Leisha and sneered. Leisha's female classmate sneered back.

Leisha had a flight to Chicago the next morning. Alice was going to join her there. They had to clean out the big house on the lake, dispose of Roger's personal property, put the house on the market. Leisha had had no time to do it earlier.

She remembered her father in the conservatory, wearing an ancient flat-topped hat he had picked up somewhere, potting orchids and jasmine and passion flowers.

When the doorbell rang she was startled: she almost never had visitors. Eagerly, she turned on the outside camera—maybe it was Jonathan or Martha, back in Boston to surprise her, to celebrate—why hadn't she thought before about some sort of celebration?

Richard stood gazing up at the camera. He had been crying.

She tore open the door. Richard made no move to come in. Leisha saw that what the camera had registered as grief was actually something else: tears of rage.

"Tony's dead."

Leisha put out her hand, blindly. Richard did not take it.

"They killed him in prison. Not the authorities—the other prisoners. In the recreation yard. Murderers, rapists, looters, scum of the earth—and they thought they had the right to kill *him* because he was different."

Now Richard did grab her arm, so hard that something, some bone, shifted beneath the flesh and pressed on a nerve. "Not just different—*better*. Because he was better, because we all are, we goddamn just don't stand up and shout it out of some misplaced feeling for *their* feelings . . . God!"

Leisha pulled her arm free and rubbed it, numb, staring at Richard's contorted face.

"They beat him to death with a lead pipe. No one even knows how they got a lead pipe. They beat him on the back of the head and they rolled him over and—"

"Don't!" Leisha said. It came out a whimper.

Richard looked at her. Despite his shouting, his violent grip on her arm, Leisha had the confused impression that this was the first time he had actually seen her. She went on rubbing her arm, staring at him in terror.

He said quietly, "I've come to take you to Sanctuary, Leisha. Dan Walcott and Vernon Bulriss are in the car outside. The three of us will carry you out, if necessary. But you're coming. You see that, don't you? You're not safe here, with your high profile and your spectacular looks—you're a natural target if anyone is. Do we have to force you? Or do you finally see for yourself that we have no choice—the bastards have left us no choice—except Sanctuary?"

Leisha closed her eyes. Tony, at fourteen, at the beach. Tony, his eyes ferocious and alight, the first to reach out his hand for the glass of Interleukin-1. Beggars in Spain.

"I'll come."

She had never known such anger. It scared her, coming in bouts throughout the long night, receding but always returning again. Richard held her in his arms, sitting with their backs against the wall of her library, and his holding made no difference at all. In the living room Dan and Vernon talked in low voices.

Sometimes the anger erupted in shouting, and Leisha heard herself and thought, *I don't know you.* Sometimes it became crying, sometimes talking about Tony, about all of them. Not the shouting nor the crying nor the talking, eased her at all.

Planning did, a little. In a cold dry voice she didn't recognize, Leisha told Richard about the trip to close the house in Chicago. She had to go; Alice was already there. If Richard and Dan and Vernon put Leisha on the plane, and Alice met her at the other end with union bodyguards, she should be safe enough. Then she would change her return ticket from Boston to Belmont and drive with Richard to Sanctuary.

"People are already arriving," Richard said. "Jennifer Sharifi is organizing it, greasing the Sleeper suppliers with so much money they can't resist. What about this townhouse here, Leisha? Your furniture and terminal and clothes?"

Leisha looked around her familiar office. Law books lined the walls, red and green and brown, although most of the same information was on-line. A coffee cup rested on a printout on the desk. Beside it was the receipt she had requested from the taxi driver this afternoon, a giddy souvenir of the day she had passed her bar exams; she had thought of having it framed. Above the desk was a holographic portrait of Kenzo Yagai.

"Let it rot," Leisha said.

Richard's arm tightened around her.

"I've never seen you like this," Alice said, subdued. "It's more than just clearing out the house, isn't it?"

"Let's get on with it," Leisha said. She yanked a suit from her father's closet. "Do you want any of this stuff for your husband?"

"It wouldn't fit."

"The hats?"

"No," Alice said. "Leisha—what is it?"

"Let's just *do* it!" She yanked all the clothes from Camden's closet, piled them on the floor, scrawled FOR VOLUNTEER AGENCY on a piece of paper, and dropped it on top of the pile. Silently, Alice started adding clothes from the dresser, which already bore a taped paper scrawled ESTATE AUCTION.

The curtains were already down throughout the house; Alice had done that yesterday. She had also rolled up the rugs. Sunset glared redly on the bare wooden floors.

"What about your old room?" Leisha said. "What do you want there?"

"I've already tagged it," Alice said. "A mover will come Thursday."

"Fine. What else?"

"The conservatory. Sanderson has been watering everything, but he didn't really know what needed how much, so some of the plants are—"

"Fire Sanderson," Leisha said curtly. "The exotics can die. Or have them sent to a hospital, if you'd rather. Just watch out for the ones that are poisonous. Come on, let's do the library."

Alice sat slowly on a rolled-up rug in the middle of Camden's bedroom. She had cut her hair; Leisha thought it looked ugly, jagged brown spikes around her broad face. She had also gained more weight. She was starting to look like their mother.

Alice said, "Do you remember the night I told you I was pregnant? Just before you left for Harvard?"

"Let's do the library."

"Do you?" Alice said. "For God's sake, can't you just once listen to someone else, Leisha? Do you have to be so much like Daddy every single minute?"

"I'm not like Daddy!"

"The hell you're not. You're exactly what he made you. But that's not the point. Do you remember that night?"

Leisha walked over the rug and out the door. Alice simply sat. After a minute Leisha walked back in. "I remember."

"You were near tears," Alice said implacably. Her voice was quiet. "I don't even remember exactly why. Maybe because I wasn't going to college after all. But I put my arms around you, and for the first time in years—years, Leisha—I felt you really were my sister. Despite all of it—the roaming the halls all night and the show-off arguments with Daddy and the special school and the artificially long legs and golden hair—all that crap. You seemed to need me to hold you. You seemed to need me. You seemed to *need*."

"What are you saying?" Leisha demanded. "That you can only be close to someone if they're in trouble and need you? That you can only be a sister if I was in some kind of pain, open sores running? Is that the bond between you Sleepers? 'Protect me while I'm unconscious, I'm just as crippled as you are'?"

"No," Alice said. "I'm saying that *you* could be a sister only if you were in some kind of pain."

Leisha stared at her. "You're stupid, Alice."

Alice said calmly, "I know that. Compared to you, I am. I know that."

Leisha jerked her head angrily. She felt ashamed of what she had just said, and yet it was true, and they both knew it was true, and anger still lay in her like a dark void, formless and hot. It was the formless part that was the worst. Without shape, there could be no action; without action, the anger went on burning her, choking her.

Alice said, "When I was twelve, Susan gave me a dress for our birthday. You were away somewhere, on one of those overnight field trips your fancy progressive school did all the time. The dress was silk, pale blue, with antique lace—very beautiful. I was thrilled, not only because it was beautiful but because Susan had gotten it for me and gotten software for you. The dress was mine. Was, I thought, *me*." In the gathering gloom Leisha could barely make out her broad, plain features. "The first time I wore it a boy said, 'Stole your sister's dress, Alice? Snitched it while she was *sleeping?*' Then he laughed like crazy, the way they always did.

"I threw the dress away. I didn't even explain to Susan, although I think she would have understood. Whatever was yours was yours, and whatever wasn't yours was yours, too. That's the way Daddy set it up. The way he hard-wired it into our genes."

"You, too?" Leisha said. "You're no different from the other envious beggars?"

Alice stood up from the rug. She did it slowly, leisurely, brushing dust off the back of her wrinkled skirt, smoothing the print fabric. Then she walked over and hit Leisha in the mouth.

"Now do you see me as real?" Alice asked quietly.

Leisha put her hand to her mouth. She felt blood. The phone rang, Camden's unlisted personal line. Alice walked over, picked it up, listened, and held it calmly out to Leisha. "It's for you."

Numb, Leisha took it.

"Leisha? This is Kevin. Listen; something's happened. Stella Bevington called me, on the phone, not Groupnet; I think her parents took away her modem. I picked up the phone and she screamed, 'This is Stella! They're hitting me, he's drunk—' and then the line went dead. Randy's gone to Sanctuary—hell, they've *all* gone. You're closest to her; she's still in Skokie. You better get there fast. Have you got bodyguards you trust?"

"Yes," Leisha said, although she hadn't. The anger—finally—took form. "I can handle it."

"I don't know how you'll get her out of there," Kevin said. "They'll recognize you, they know she called somebody, they might even have knocked her out . . ."

"I'll handle it," Leisha said.

"Handle what?" Alice said.

Leisha faced her. Even though she knew she shouldn't, she said, "What your people do. To one of ours. A seven-year-old kid who's getting beaten up by her parents because she's Sleepless—because she's *better* than you are—" She ran down the stairs and out to the rental car she had driven from the airport.

Alice ran right down with her. "Not your car, Leisha. They can trace a rental car just like that. My car."

Leisha screamed. "If you think you're—"

Alice yanked open the door of her battered Toyota, a model so old the Y-energy cones weren't even concealed but hung like drooping jowls on either side. She shoved Leisha into the passenger seat, slammed the door, and rammed herself behind the wheel. Her hands were steady. "Where?"

Blackness swooped over Leisha. She put her head down, as far between her knees as the cramped Toyota would allow. Two—no, three—days since she had eaten. Since the night before the bar exams. The faintness receded, swept over her again as soon as she raised her head.

She told Alice the address in Skokie.

"Stay way in the back," Alice said. "And there's a scarf in the glove compartment—put it on. Low, to hide as much of your face as possible."

Alice had stopped the car along Highway 42. Leisha said. "This isn't—"

"It's a union quick-guard place. We have to look like we have some protection, Leisha. We don't need to tell him anything. I'll hurry."

She was out in three minutes with a huge man in a cheap dark suit. He squeezed into the front seat beside Alice and said nothing at all. Alice did not introduce him.

The house was small, a little shabby, with lights on downstairs, none upstairs. The first stars shone in the north, away from Chicago. Alice said to the guard, "Get out of the car and stand here by the car door—no, more in the light— and don't do anything unless I'm attacked in some way." The man nodded. Alice started up the walk. Leisha scrambled out of the backseat and caught her sister two-thirds of the way to the plastic front door.

"Alice, what the hell are you doing? *I* have to—"

"Keep your voice down," Alice said, glancing at the guard. "Leisha, *think*. You'll be recognized. Here, near Chicago, with a Sleepless daughter—these people have looked at your picture in magazines for years. They've watched long-range holovids of you. They know you. They know you're going to be a lawyer. Me they've never seen. I'm nobody."

"Alice—"

"For Chrissake, get back in the car!" Alice hissed, and pounded on the front door.

Leisha drew off the walk, into the shadow of a willow tree. A man opened the door. His face was completely blank.

Alice said, "Child Protection Agency. We got a call from a little girl, this number. Let me in."

"There's no little girl here."

"This is an emergency, priority one," Alice said. "Child Protection Act 186. Let me in!"

The man, still blank-faced, glanced at the huge figure by the car. "You got a search warrant?"

"I don't need one in a priority-one child emergency. If you don't let me in, you're going to have legal snarls like you never bargained for."

Leisha clamped her lips together. No one would believe that; it was legal gobbledygook. . . . Her lip throbbed where Alice had hit her.

The man stood aside to let Alice enter.

The guard started forward. Leisha hesitated, then let him. He entered with Alice.

Leisha waited, alone, in the dark.

In three minutes they were out, the guard carrying a child. Alice's broad face gleamed pale in the porch light. Leisha sprang forward, opened the car door, and helped the guard ease the child inside. The guard was frowning, a slow puzzled frown shot with wariness.

Alice said, "Here. This is an extra hundred dollars. To get back to the city by yourself."

"Hey . . ." the guard said, but he took the money. He stood looking after them as Alice pulled away.

"He'll go straight to the police," Leisha said despairingly. "He has to, or risk his union membership."

"I know," Alice said. "But by that time we'll be out of the car."

"Where?"

"At the hospital," Alice said.

"Alice, we can't—" Leisha didn't finish. She turned to the backseat. "Stella? Are you conscious?"

"Yes," said the small voice.

Leisha groped until her fingers found the rear-seat illuminator. Stella lay stretched out on the backseat, her face distorted with pain. She cradled her left arm in her right. A single bruise colored her face, above the left eye.

"You're Leisha Camden," the child said, and started to cry.

"Her arm's broken," Alice said.

"Honey, can you . . ." Leisha's throat felt thick; she had trouble getting the words out ". . . can you hold on till we get you to a doctor?"

"Yes," Stella said. "Just don't take me back there!"

"We won't," Leisha said. "Ever." She glanced at Alice and saw Tony's face.

Alice said, "There's a community hospital about ten miles south of here."

"How do you know that?"

"I was there once. Drug overdose," Alice said briefly. She drove hunched over the wheel, with the face of someone thinking furiously. Leisha thought, too, trying to see a way around the legal charge of kidnapping. They probably couldn't say the child came willingly: Stella would undoubtedly cooperate, but at her age and in her condition she was probably *non sui juris*, her word would have no legal weight. . . .

"Alice, we can't even get her into the hospital without insurance information. Verifiable on-line."

"Listen," Alice said, not to Leisha but over her shoulder, toward the backseat. "Here's what we're going to do, Stella. I'm going to tell them you're my daughter and you fell off a big rock you were climbing while we stopped for a snack at a roadside picnic area. We're driving from California to Philadelphia to see your grandmother. Your name is Jordan Watrous and you're five years old. Got that, honey?"

"I'm seven," Stella said. "Almost eight."

"You're a very large five. Your birthday is March twenty-third. Can you do this, Stella?"

"Yes," the little girl said. Her voice was stronger.

Leisha stared at Alice. "Can *you* do this?"

"Of course I can," Alice said. "I'm Roger Camden's daughter."

Alice half carried, half supported Stella into the emergency room of the small community hospital. Leisha watched from the car: the short stocky woman, the child's thin body with the twisted arm. Then she drove Alice's car to the farthest corner of the parking lot, under the dubious cover of a skimpy maple, and locked it. She tied the scarf more securely around her face.

Alice's license plate number, and her name, would be in every police and rental-car databank by now. The medical banks were slower; often they uploaded from local precincts only once a day, resenting the governmental interference in what was still, despite a half century of battle, a private-sector enterprise. Alice and Stella would probably be all right in the hospital. Probably. But Alice could not rent another car.

Leisha could.

But the data file that would flash to rental agencies on Alice Camden Watrous might or might not include that she was Leisha Camden's twin.

Leisha looked at the rows of cars in the lot. A flashy luxury Chrysler, an Ikeda van, a row of middle-class Toyotas and Mercedes, a vintage '99 Cadillac—she could imagine the owner's face if that were missing—ten or twelve cheap runabouts, a hovercar with the uniformed driver asleep at the wheel. And a battered farm truck.

Leisha walked over to the truck. A man sat at the wheel, smoking. She thought of her father.

"Hello," Leisha said.

The man rolled down his window but didn't answer. He had greasy brown hair.

"See that hovercar over there?" Leisha said. She made her voice sound young, high. The man glanced at it indifferently; from this angle you couldn't see that the driver was asleep. "That's my bodyguard. He thinks I'm in the hospital, the way my father told me to, getting this lip looked at." She could feel her mouth swollen from Alice's blow.

"So?"

Leisha stamped her foot. "So I don't want to be inside. He's a shit and so's Daddy. I want *out*. I'll give you four thousand bank credits for your truck. Cash."

The man's eyes widened. He tossed away his cigarette, looked again at the hovercar. The driver's shoulders were broad, and the car was within easy screaming distance.

"All nice and legal," Leisha said, and tried to smirk. Her knees felt watery.

"Let me see the cash."

Leisha backed away from the truck, to where he could not reach her. She took the money from her arm clip. She was used to carrying a lot of cash; there had always been Bruce, or someone like Bruce. There had always been safety.

"Get out of the truck on the other side," Leisha said, "and lock the door behind you. Leave the keys on the seat, where I can see them from here. Then I'll put the money on the roof where you can see it."

The man laughed, a sound like gravel pouring. "Regular little Dabney Engh, aren't you? Is that what they teach you society debs at your fancy schools?"

Leisha had no idea who Dabney Engh was. She waited, watching the man try to think of a way to cheat her, and tried to hide her contempt. She thought of Tony.

"All right," he said, and slid out of the truck.

"Lock the door!"

He grinned, opened the door again, locked it. Leisha put the money on the roof, yanked open the driver's door, clambered in, locked the door, and powered up the window. The man laughed. She put the key into the ignition, started the truck, and drove toward the street. Her hands trembled.

She drove slowly around the block twice. When she came back, the man was gone, and the driver of the hovercar was still asleep. She had wondered if the man would wake him, out of sheer malice, but he had not. She parked the truck and waited.

An hour and a half later Alice and a nurse wheeled Stella out of the emergency entrance. Leisha leaped out of the truck and yelled, "Coming, Alice!" waving both her arms. It was too dark to see Alice's expression; Leisha could only hope that Alice showed no dismay at the battered truck, that she had not told the nurse to expect a red car.

Alice said, "This is Julie Bergadon, a friend that I called while you were setting Jordan's arm." The nurse nodded, uninterested. The two women helped Stella into the high truck cab; there was no backseat. Stella had a cast on her arm and looked drugged.

"How?" Alice said as they drove off.

Leisha didn't answer. She was watching a police hovercar land at the other end of the parking lot. Two officers got out and strode purposefully toward Alice's locked car under the skimpy maple.

"My God," Alice said. For the first time she sounded frightened.

"They won't trace us," Leisha said. "Not to this truck. Count on it."

"Leisha." Alice's voice spiked with fear. "Stella's *asleep*."

Leisha glanced at the child, slumped against Alice's shoulder. "No, she's not. She's unconscious from painkillers."

"Is that all right? Normal? For . . . her?"

"We can black out. We can even experience substance-induced sleep." Tony and she and Richard and Jeanine in the midnight woods. . . . "Didn't you know that, Alice?"

"No."

"We don't know very much about each other, do we?"

They drove south in silence. Finally Alice said, "Where are we going to take her, Leisha?"

"I don't know. Any one of the Sleepless would be the first place the police would check—"

"You can't risk it. Not the way things are," Alice said. She sounded weary. "But all my friends are in California. I don't think we could drive this rust bucket that far before getting stopped."

"It wouldn't make it anyway."

"What should we do?"

"Let me think."

At an expressway exit stood a pay phone. It wouldn't be data shielded, as Groupnet was. Would Kevin's open line be tapped? Probably.

There was no doubt the Sanctuary line would be.

Sanctuary. All of them going there or already there, Kevin had said. Holed up, trying to pull the worn Allegheny Mountains around them like a safe little den. Except for the children like Stella, who could not.

Where? With whom?

Leisha closed her eyes. The Sleepless were out; the police would find Stella within hours. Susan Melling? But she had been Alice's all-too-visible stepmother and was cobeneficiary of Camden's will; they would question her almost immediately. It couldn't be anyone traceable to Alice. It could only be a Sleeper that Leisha knew, and trusted, and why should anyone at all fit that description? Why should she risk so much on anyone who did? She stood a long time in the dark phone kiosk. Then she walked to the truck. Alice was asleep, her head thrown back against the seat. A tiny line of drool ran down her chin. Her face was white and drained in the bad light from the kiosk. Leisha walked back to the phone.

"Stewart? Stewart Sutter?"

"Yes?"

"This is Leisha Camden. Something has happened." She told the story tersely, in bald sentences. Stewart did not interrupt.

"Leisha—" Stewart said, and stopped.

"I need help, Stewart." "*I'll help you, Alice*." "*I don't need your help*." A wind whistled over the dark field beside the kiosk, and Leisha shivered. She heard in the wind the thin keen of a beggar. In the wind, in her own voice.

"All right," Stewart said, "this is what we'll do. I have a cousin in Ripley, New York, just over the state line from Pennsylvania on the route you'll be driving east. It has to be in New York; I'm licensed in New York. Take the little girl there. I'll call my cousin and tell her you're coming. She's an elderly woman, was quite an activist in her youth; her name is Janet Patterson. The town is—"

"What makes you so sure she'll get involved? She could go to jail. And so could you."

"She's been in jail so many times you wouldn't believe it. Political protests going all the way back to Vietnam. But no one's going to jail. I'm now your attorney of record, I'm privileged. I'm going to get Stella declared a ward of the state. That shouldn't be too hard with the hospital records you established in Skokie. Then she can be transferred to a foster home in New York; I know just the place, people who are fair and kind. Then Alice—"

"She's resident in Illinois. You can't—"

"Yes, I can. Since those research findings about the Sleepless life span have come out, legislators have been railroaded by stupid constituents scared or jealous or just plain angry. The result is a body of so-called 'law' riddled with contradictions, absurdities, and loopholes. None of it will stand in the long run— or at least I hope not—but in the meantime it can all be exploited. I can use it to create the most goddamn convoluted case for Stella that anybody ever saw, and in the meantime she won't be returned home. But that won't work for Alice—she'll need an attorney licensed in Illinois."

"We have one," Leisha said. "Candace Holt."

"No, not a Sleepless. Trust me on this, Leisha. I'll find somebody good. There's a man in—are you crying?"

"No," Leisha said, crying.

"Ah, God," Stewart said. "Bastards. I'm sorry all this happened, Leisha."

"Don't be," Leisha said.

When she had directions to Stewart's cousin, she walked back to the truck. Alice was still asleep, Stella still unconscious. Leisha closed the truck door as quietly as possible. The engine balked and roared, but Alice didn't wake. There was a crowd of people with them in the narrow and darkened cab: Stewart Sutter, Tony Indivino, Susan Melling, Kenzo Yagai, Roger Camden.

To Stewart Sutter she said, You called to inform me about the situation at Morehouse, Kennedy. You are risking your career and your cousin for Stella. And you stand to gain nothing. Like Susan telling me in advance about Bernie Kuhn's brain. Susan, who lost her life to Daddy's dream and regained it by her own strength. A contract without consideration for each side is not a contract: every first-year student knows that.

To Kenzo Yagai she said, Trade isn't always linear. You missed that. If Stewart gives me something, and I give Stella something, and ten years from now Stella is a different person because of that and gives something to someone else as yet unknown—it's an ecology. An *ecology* of trade, yes, each niche needed, even if they're not contractually bound. Does a horse need a fish? *Yes.*

To Tony she said, Yes, there are beggars in Spain who trade nothing, give nothing, do nothing. But there are *more* than beggars in Spain. Withdraw from the beggars, you withdraw from the whole damn country. And you withdraw from the possibility of the ecology of help. That's what Alice wanted, all those years ago in her bedroom. Pregnant, scared, angry, jealous, she wanted to help *me*, and I wouldn't let her because I didn't need it. But I do now. And she did then. Beggars need to help as well as be helped.

And, finally, there was only Daddy left. She could *see* him, bright-eyed, holding thick-leaved exotic flowers in his strong hands. To Camden she said, You were wrong. Alice *is* special. Oh, Daddy—the specialness of Alice! You were *wrong*.

As soon as she thought this, lightness filled her. Not the buoyant bubble of joy, not the hard clarity of examination, but something else: sunshine, soft through the conservatory glass, where two children ran in and out. She suddenly felt light herself, not buoyant but translucent, a medium for the sunshine to pass clear through, on its way to somewhere else.

She drove the sleeping woman and the wounded child through the night, east, toward the state line.

William Gibson

William Gibson (1948–   ) is the avatar of cyberpunk, whose novel *Neuromancer* (1984) took the SF field by storm and made him one of the big names of science fiction. He occupies a central position in that decade as J. G. Ballard did in the 1960s, as a nexus of controversy and attention. One can readily see why postmodern writers such as Kathy Acker and publications from *The Village Voice* to *Vogue* have picked up the banner of cyberpunk. *Neuromancer,* and the stories collected in *Burning Chrome* (1986), are the pure essence of the Movement. With his cohort Bruce Sterling, Gibson remains the spokesman for the attitudes and images of cyberpunk, although they have declared the Movement dead. Yet the imagery and the name as a marketing term survive as a major influence on the science fiction of the 1990s.

Gibson's immense popularity among SF readers is rooted in his ability to intuit and portray intimate connections of mind and technology in a plausible fashion. This was especially powerful in a decade where many SF readers for the first time were using home computers and connecting directly by modem to the computers of others through vast networks, and playing sophisticated video games with characters with whom they might identify on the screen—as in the films *Tron* (1982) and *Bladerunner* (1982), the twin sources whose imagery has perhaps overwhelmed Gibson's works as the prime influence on later cyberpunk fictions.

The conventional setting of cyberpunk fiction is a future world dominated by computer technology, massive cartels and cyberspace, an artificial universe created through the link-up of tens of millions of machines. This is the world of "Johnny Mnemonic." It is in this story that William Gibson introduced the word "cyberspace" into the English language and invented a new setting, as well as a metaphor that has aided in the transformation of communications technology by giving a name to the place you metaphorically inhabit when you are connected to a network of personal and other computers.

JOHNNY MNEMONIC

I put the shotgun in an Adidas bag and padded it out with four pairs of tennis socks, not my style at all, but that was what I was aiming for: If they think you're crude, go technical; if they think you're technical, go crude. I'm a very technical boy. So I decided to get as crude as possible. These days, though, you have to be pretty technical before you can even aspire to crudeness. I'd had to turn both those twelve-gauge shells from brass stock, on a lathe, and then load them myself; I'd had to dig up an old microfiche with instructions for hand-loading cartridges; I'd had to build a lever-action press to seat the primers—all very tricky. But I knew they'd work.

The meet was set for the Drome at 2300, but I rode the tube three stops past the closest platform and walked back. Immaculate procedure.

I checked myself out in the chrome-siding of a coffee kiosk, your basic sharp-faced Caucasoid with a ruff of stiff, dark hair. The girls at Under the Knife were big on Sony Mao, and it was getting harder to keep them from adding the chic suggestion of epicanthic folds. It probably wouldn't fool Ralfi Face, but it might get me next to his table.

The Drome is a single narrow space with a bar down one side and tables along the other, thick with pimps and handlers and an arcane array of dealers. The Magnetic Dog Sisters were on the door that night, and I didn't relish trying to get out past them if things didn't work out. They were two meters tall and thin as greyhounds. One was black and the other white, but aside from that they were as nearly identical as cosmetic surgery could make them. They'd been lovers for years and were bad news in a tussle. I was never quite sure which one had originally been male.

Ralfi was sitting at his usual table. Owing me a lot of money. I had hundreds of megabytes stashed in my head on an idiot/savant basis, information I had no conscious access to. Ralfi had left it there. He hadn't, however, come back for it. Only Ralfi could retrieve the data, with a code phrase of his own invention. I'm not cheap to begin with, but my overtime on storage is astronomical. And Ralfi had been very scarce.

Then I'd heard that Ralfi Face wanted to put out a contract on me. So I'd arranged to meet him in the Drome, but I'd arranged it as Edward Bax, clandestine importer, late of Rio and Peking.

The Drome stank of biz, a metallic tang of nervous tension. Muscle-boys scattered through the crowd were flexing stock parts of one another and trying on thin, cold grins, some of them so lost under superstructures of muscle graft that their outlines weren't really human.

Pardon me. Pardon me, friends. Just Eddie Bax here, Fast Eddie the Importer, with his professionally nondescript gym bag, and please ignore this slit, just wide enough to admit his right hand.

Ralfi wasn't alone. Eighty kilos of blond California beef perched alertly in the chair next to his, martial arts written all over him.

Fast Eddie Bax was in the chair opposite them before the beef's hands were off the table. "You black belt?" I asked eagerly. He nodded, blue eyes running an automatic scanning pattern between my eyes and my hands. "Me, too," I said. "Got mine here in the bag." And I shoved my hand through the slit and thumbed the safety off. Click. "Double twelve-gauge with the triggers wired together."

"That's a gun," Ralfi said, putting a plump, restraining hand on his boy's taut blue nylon chest. "Johnny has an antique firearm in his bag." So much for Edward Bax.

I guess he'd always been Ralfi Something or Other, but he owed his acquired surname to a singular vanity. Built something like an overripe pear, he'd worn the once-famous face of Christian White for twenty years—Christian White of the Aryan Reggae Band, Sony Mao to his generation, and final champion of race rock. I'm a whiz at trivia.

Christian White: classic pop face with a singer's high-definition muscles, chiseled cheekbones. Angelic in one light, handsomely depraved in another. But Ralfi's eyes lived behind that face, and they were small and cold and black.

"Please," he said, "let's work this out like businessmen." His voice was marked by a horrible prehensile sincerity, and the corners of his beautiful Christian White mouth were always wet. "Lewis here," nodding in the beefboy's direction, "is a meatball." Lewis took this impassively, looking like something built from a kit. "You aren't a meatball, Johnny."

"Sure I am, Ralfi, a nice meatball chock-full of implants where you can store your dirty laundry while you go off shopping for people to kill me. From my end of this bag, Ralfi, it looks like you've got some explaining to do."

"It's this last batch of product, Johnny." He sighed deeply. "In my role as broker—"

"Fence," I corrected.

"As broker, I'm usually very careful as to sources."

"You buy only from those who steal the best. Got it."

He sighed again. "I try," he said wearily, "not to buy from fools. This time, I'm afraid, I've done that." Third sigh was the cue for Lewis to trigger the neural disruptor they'd taped under my side of the table.

I put everything I had into curling the index finger of my right hand, but I no longer seemed to be connected to it. I could feel the metal of the gun and the foam-padded tape I'd wrapped around the stubby grip, but my hands were cool wax, distant and inert. I was hoping Lewis was a true meatball, thick enough to go for the gym bag and snag my rigid trigger finger, but he wasn't.

"We've been very worried about you, Johnny. Very worried. You see, that's Yakuza property you have there. A fool took it from them. Johnny. A dead fool."

Lewis giggled.

It all made sense then, an ugly kind of sense, like bags of wet sand settling around my head. Killing wasn't Ralfi's style. Lewis wasn't even Ralfi's style. But he'd got himself stuck between the Sons of the Neon Chrysanthemum and something that belonged to them—or, more likely, something of theirs that belonged to someone else. Ralfi, of course, could use the code phrase to throw me into idiot savant, and I'd spill their hot program without remembering a single quarter tone. For a fence like Ralfi, that would ordinarily have been enough. But not for the Yakuza. The Yakuza would know about Squids, for one thing, and they wouldn't want to worry about one lifting those dim and permanent traces of their program out of my head. I didn't know very much about Squids, but I'd heard stories, and I made it a point never to repeat them to my clients. No, the Yakuza wouldn't like that; it looked too much like evidence. They hadn't got where they were by leaving evidence around. Or alive.

Lewis was grinning. I think he was visualizing a point just behind my forehead and imagining how he could get there the hard way.

"Hey," said a low voice, feminine, from somewhere behind my right shoulder, "you cowboys sure aren't having too lively a time."

"Pack it, bitch," Lewis said, his tanned face very still. Ralfi looked blank.

"Lighten up. You want to buy some good freebase?" She pulled up a chair and quickly sat before either of them could stop her. She was barely inside my fixed field of vision, a thin girl with mirrored glasses, her dark hair cut in a rough shag. She wore black leather, open over a T-shirt slashed diagonally with stripes of red and black. "Eight thou a gram weight."

Lewis snorted his exasperation and tried to slap her out of the chair. Somehow he didn't quite connect, and her hand came up and seemed to brush his wrist as it passed. Bright blood sprayed the table. He was clutching his wrist white-knuckle tight, blood trickling from between his fingers.

But hadn't her hand been empty?

He was going to need a tendon stapler. He stood up carefully, without bothering to push his chair back. The chair toppled backward, and he stepped out of my line of sight without a word.

"He better get a medic to look at that," she said. "That's a nasty cut."

"You have no idea," said Ralfi, suddenly sounding very tired, "the depths of shit you have just gotten yourself into."

"No kidding? Mystery. I get real excited by mysteries. Like why your friend here's so quiet. Frozen, like. Or what this thing here is for," and she held up the little control unit that she'd somehow taken from Lewis. Ralfi looked ill.

"You, ah, want maybe a quarter-million to give me that and take a walk?" A fat hand came up to stroke his pale, lean face nervously.

"What I want," she said, snapping her fingers so that the unit spun and glittered, "is work. A job. Your boy hurt his wrist. But a quarter'll do for a retainer."

Ralfi let his breath out explosively and began to laugh, exposing teeth that hadn't been kept up to the Christian White standard. Then she turned the disruptor off.

"Two million," I said.

"My kind of man," she said, and laughed. "What's in the bag?"

"A shotgun."

"Crude." It might have been a compliment.

Ralfi said nothing at all.

"Name's Millions. Molly Millions. You want to get out of here, boss? People are starting to stare." She stood up. She was wearing leather jeans the color of dried blood.

And I saw for the first time that the mirrored lenses were surgical inlays, the silver rising smoothly from her high cheekbones, sealing her eyes in their sockets. I saw my new face twinned there.

"I'm Johnny," I said. "We're taking Mr. Face with us."

He was outside, waiting. Looking like your standard tourist tech, in plastic zoris and a silly Hawaiian shirt printed with blowups of his firm's most popular microprocessor; a mild little guy, the kind most likely to wind up drunk on sake in a bar that puts out miniature rice crackers with seaweed garnish. He looked like the kind who sings the corporate anthem and cries, who shake hands endlessly with the bartender. And the pimps and the dealers would leave him alone, pegging him as innately conservative. Not up for much, and careful with his credit when he was.

The way I figured it later, they must have amputated part of his left thumb, somewhere behind the first joint, replacing it with a prosthetic tip, and cored the stump, fitting it with a spool and socket molded from one of the Ono-Sendai diamond analogs. Then they'd carefully wound the spool with three meters of monomolecular filament.

Molly got into some kind of exchange with the Magnetic Dog Sisters, giving me a chance to usher Ralfi through the door with the gym bag pressed lightly against the base of his spine. She seemed to know them. I heard the black one laugh.

I glanced up, out of some passing reflex, maybe because I've never got used to it, to the soaring arcs of light and the shadows of the geodesics above them. Maybe that saved me.

Ralfi kept walking, but I don't think he was trying to escape. I think he'd already given up. Probably he already had an idea of what we were up against.

I looked back down in time to see him explode.

Playback on full recall shows Ralfi stepping forward as the little tech sidles out of nowhere, smiling. Just a suggestion of a bow, and his left thumb falls off. It's a conjuring trick. The thumb hangs suspended. Mirrors? Wires? And Ralfi stops, his back to us, dark crescents of sweat under the armpits of his pale summer suit. He knows. He must have known. And then the joke-shop thumb-tip, heavy as lead, arcs out in a lightning yo-yo trick, and the invisible thread connecting it to the killer's hand passes laterally through Ralfi's skull, just above his eyebrows, whips up, and descends, slicing the pear-shaped torso diagonally from shoulder to rib cage. Cuts so fine that no blood flows until synapses misfire and the first tremors surrender the body to gravity.

Ralfi tumbled apart in a pink cloud of fluids, the three mismatched sections rolling forward onto the tiled pavement. In total silence.

I brought the gym bag up, and my hand convulsed. The recoil nearly broke my wrist.

It must have been raining; ribbons of water cascaded from a ruptured geodesic and spattered on the tile behind us. We crouched in the narrow gap between a surgical boutique and an antique shop. She'd just edged one mirrored eye around the corner to report a single Volks module in front of the Drome, red lights flashing. They were sweeping Ralfi up. Asking questions.

I was covered in scorched white fluff. The tennis socks. The gym bag was a ragged plastic cuff around my wrist. "I don't see how the hell I missed him."

"'Cause he's fast, so fast." She hugged her knees and rocked back and forth on her bootheels. "His nervous system's jacked up. He's factory custom." She grinned and gave a little squeal of delight. "I'm gonna get that boy. Tonight. He's the best, number one, top dollar, state of the art."

"What you're going to get, for this boy's two million, is my ass out of here. Your boyfriend back there was mostly grown in a vat in Chiba City. He's a Yakuza assassin."

"Chiba. Yeah. See, Molly's been Chiba, too." And she showed me her hands, fingers slightly spread. Her fingers were slender, tapered, very white against the polished burgundy nails. Ten blades snicked straight out from their recesses beneath her nails, each one a narrow, double-edged scalpel in pale blue steel.

I'd never spent much time in Nighttown. Nobody there had anything to pay me to remember, and most of them had a lot they paid regularly to forget. Generations of sharpshooters had chipped away at the neon until the maintenance crews gave up. Even at noon the arcs were soot-black against faintest pearl.

Where do you go when the world's wealthiest criminal order is feeling for you with calm, distant fingers? Where do you hide from the Yakuza, so powerful that it owns comsats and at least three shuttles? The Yakuza is a true multi-national, like ITT and Ono-Sendai. Fifty years before I was born the Yakuza had already absorbed the Triads, the Mafia, the Union Corse.

Molly had an answer: You hide in the Pit, in the lowest circle, where any outside influence generates swift, concentric ripples of raw menace. You hide in Nighttown. Better yet, you hide *above* Nighttown, because the Pit's inverted, and the bottom of its bowl touches the sky, the sky that Nighttown never sees, sweating under its own firmament of acrylic resin, up where the Lo

Teks crouch in the dark like gargoyles, black-market cigarettes dangling from their lips.

She had another answer, too.

"So you're locked up good and tight, Johnny-san? No way to get that program without the password?" She led me into the shadows that waited beyond the bright tube platform. The concrete walls were overlaid with graffiti, years of them twisting into a single metascrawl of rage and frustration.

"The stored data are fed in through a modified series of microsurgical contraautism prostheses." I reeled off a numb version of my standard sales pitch. "Client's code is stored in a special chip; barring Squids, which we in the trade don't like to talk about, there's no way to recover your phrase. Can't drug it out, cut it out, torture it. I don't *know* it, never did."

"Squids? Crawly things with arms?" We emerged into a deserted street market. Shadowy figures watched us from across a makeshift square littered with fish heads and rotting fruit.

"Superconducting quantum interference detectors. Used them in the war to find submarines, suss out enemy cyber sytems."

"Yeah? Navy stuff? From the war? Squid'll read that chip of yours?" She'd stopped walking, and I felt her eyes on me behind those twin mirrors.

"Even the primitive models could measure a magnetic field a billionth the strength of geomagnetic force; it's like pulling a whisper out of a cheering stadium."

"Cops can do that already, with parabolic microphones and lasers."

"But your data's still secure." Pride in profession. "No government'll let their cops have Squids, not even the security heavies. Too much chance of interdepartmental funnies; they're too likely to watergate you."

"Navy stuff," she said, and her grin gleamed in the shadows. "Navy stuff. I got a friend down here who was in the navy, name's Jones. I think you'd better meet him. He's a junkie, though. So we'll have to take him something."

"A junkie?"

"A dolphin."

He was more than a dolphin, but from another dolphin's point of view he might have seemed like something less. I watched him swirling sluggishly in his galvanized tank. Water slopped over the side, wetting my shoes. He was surplus from the last war. A cyborg.

He rose out of the water, showing us the crusted plates along his sides, a kind of visual pun, his grace nearly lost under articulated armor, clumsy and prehistoric. Twin deformities on either side of his skull had been engineered to house sensor units. Silver lesions gleamed on exposed sections of his gray-white hide.

Molly whistled. Jones thrashed his tail, and more water cascaded down the side of the tank.

"What is this place?" I peered at vague shapes in the dark, rusting chain link and things under tarps. Above the tank hung a clumsy wooden framework, crossed and recrossed by rows of dusty Christmas lights.

"Funland. Zoo and carnival rides. 'Talk with the War Whale.' All that. Some whale Jones is. . . ."

Jones reared again and fixed me with a sad and ancient eye.

"How's he talk?" Suddenly I was anxious to go.

"That's the catch. Say 'hi,' Jones."

And all the bulbs lit simultaneously. They were flashing red, white, and blue.

```
RWBRWBRWB
RWBRWBRWB
RWBRWBRWB
RWBRWBRWB
RWBRWBRWB
```

"Good with symbols, see, but the code's restricted. In the navy they had him wired into an audiovisual display." She drew the narrow package from a jacket pocket. "Pure shit, Jones. Want it?" He froze in the water and started to sink. I felt a strange panic, remembering that he wasn't a fish, that he could drown. "We want the key to Johnny's bank, Jones. We want it fast."

The lights flickered, died.

"Go for it, Jones!"

```
        B
BBBBBBBBB
        B
        B
        B
```

Blue bulbs, cruciform.
Darkness.
"Pure! It's *clean*. Come on, Jones."

```
WWWWWWWWW
WWWWWWWWW
WWWWWWWWW
WWWWWWWWW
WWWWWWWWW
```

White sodium glare washed her features, stark monochrome, shadows cleaving from her cheekbones.

```
R    RRRRR
R    R
RRRRRRRRR
     R    R
RRRRR     R
```

The arms of the red swastika were twisted in her silver glasses. "Give it to him," I said. "We've got it."

Ralfi Face. No imagination.

Jones heaved half his armored bulk over the edge of his tank, and I thought the metal would give way. Molly stabbed him overhand with the Syrette, driving the needle between two plates. Propellant hissed. Patterns of light exploded, spasming across the frame and then fading to black.

We left him drifting, rolling languorously in the dark water. Maybe he was dreaming of his war in the Pacific, of the cyber mines he'd swept, nosing gently into their circuitry with the Squid he'd used to pick Ralfi's pathetic password from the chip buried in my head.

"I can see them slipping up when he was demobbed, letting him out of the navy with that gear intact, but how does a cybernetic dolphin get wired to smack?"

"The war," she said. "They all were. Navy did it. How else you get 'em working for you?"

"I'm not sure this profiles as good business," the pirate said, angling for better money. "Target specs on a comsat that isn't in the book—"

"Waste my time and you won't profile at all," said Molly, leaning across his scarred plastic desk to prod him with her forefinger.

"So maybe you want to buy your microwaves somewhere else?" He was a tough kid, behind his Mao-job. A Nighttowner by birth, probably.

Her hand blurred down the front of his jacket, completely severing a lapel without even rumpling the fabric.

"So we got a deal or not?"

"Deal," he said, staring at his ruined lapel with what he must have hoped was only polite interest. "Deal."

While I checked the two recorders we'd bought, she extracted the slip of paper I'd given her from the zippered wrist pocket of her jacket. She unfolded it and read silently, moving her lips. She shrugged. "This is it?"

"Shoot," I said, punching the RECORD studs of the two decks simultaneously.

"Christian White," she recited, "and his Aryan Reggae Band."

Faithful Ralfi, a fan to his dying day.

Transition to idiot-savant mode is always less abrupt than I expect it to be. The pirate broadcaster's front was a failing travel agency in a pastel cube that boasted a desk, three chairs, and a faded poster of a Swiss orbital spa. A pair of toy birds with blown-glass bodies and tin legs were sipping monotonously from a Styrofoam cup of water on a ledge beside Molly's shoulder. As I phased into mode, they accelerated gradually until their Day-Glo-feathered crowns became solid arcs of color. The LEDs that told seconds on the plastic wall clock had become meaningless pulsing grids, and Molly and the Mao-faced boy grew hazy, their arms blurring occasionally in insect-quick ghosts of gesture. And then it all faded to cool gray static and an endless tone poem in an artificial language.

I sat and sang dead Ralfi's stolen program for three hours.

The mall runs forty kilometers from end to end, a ragged overlap of Fuller domes roofing what was once a suburban artery. If they turn off the arcs on a clear day, a gray approximation of sunlight filters through layers of acrylic, a view like the prison sketches of Giovanni Piranesi. The three southernmost kilometers roof Nighttown. Nighttown pays no taxes, no utilities. The neon arcs are dead, and the geodesics have been smoked black by decades of cooking fires. In the nearly total darkness of a Nighttown noon, who notices a few dozen mad children lost in the rafters?

We'd been climbing for two hours, up concrete stairs and steel ladders with perforated rungs, past abandoned gantries and dust-covered tools. We'd started in what looked like a disused maintenance yard, stacked with triangular roofing segments. Everything there had been covered with that same uniform layer of spraybomb graffiti: gang names, initials, dates back to the turn of the century. The graffiti followed us up, gradually thinning until a single name was repeated at intervals. LO TEK. In dripping black capitals.

"Who's Lo Tek?"

"Not us, boss." She climbed a shivering aluminum ladder and vanished through a hole in a sheet of corrugated plastic. " 'Low technique, low technology.' " The plastic muffled her voice. I followed her up, nursing my aching wrist. "Lo Teks, they'd think that shotgun trick of yours was effete."

An hour later I dragged myself up through another hole, this one sawed crookedly in a sagging sheet of plywood, and met my first Lo Tek.

" 'S okay," Molly said, her hand brushing my shoulder. "It's just Dog. Hey, Dog."

In the narrow beam of her taped flash, he regarded us with one eye and slowly extruded a thick length of grayish tongue, licking huge canines. I wondered how they wrote off tooth-bud transplants from Dobermans as low technology. Immunosuppressives don't exactly grow on trees.

"Moll." Dental augmentation impeded his speech. A string of saliva dangled from his twisted lower lip. "Heard ya comin'. Long time." He might have been fifteen, but the fangs and a bright mosaic of scars combined with the gaping socket to present a mask of total bestiality. It had taken time and a certain kind of creativity to assemble that face, and his posture told me he enjoyed living behind it. He wore a pair of decaying jeans, black with grime and shiny along the creases. His chest and feet were bare. He did something with his mouth that approximated a grin. "Bein' followed, you."

Far off, down in Nighttown, a water vendor cried his trade.

"Strings jumping, Dog?" She swung her flash to the side, and I saw thin cords tied to eyebolts, cords that ran to the edge and vanished.

"Kill the fuckin' light!"

She snapped it off.

"How come the one who's followin' you's got no light?"

"Doesn't need it. That one's bad news, Dog. Your sentries give him a tumble, they'll come home in easy-to-carry sections."

"This a *friend* friend, Moll?" He sounded uneasy. I heard his feet shift on the worn plywood.

"No. But he's mine. And this one," slapping my shoulder, "he's a friend. Got that?"

"Sure," he said, without much enthusiasm, padding to the platform's edge, where the eyebolts were. He began to pluck out some kind of message on the taut cords.

Nighttown spread beneath us like a toy village for rats; tiny windows showed candlelight, with only a few harsh, bright squares lit by battery lanterns and carbide lamps. I imagined the old men at their endless games of dominoes, under warm, fat drops of water that fell from wet wash hung out on poles between the plywood shanties. Then I tried to imagine him climbing patiently up through the darkness in his zoris and ugly tourist shirt, bland and unhurried. How was he tracking us?

"Good," said Molly. "He smells us."

"Smoke?" Dog dragged a crumpled pack from his pocket and pried out a flattened cigarette. I squinted at the trademark while he lit it for me with a kitchen match. Yiheyuan filters. Beijing Cigarette Factory. I decided that the Lo Teks were black marketeers. Dog and Molly went back to their argument, which seemed to revolve around Molly's desire to use some particular piece of Lo Tek real estate.

"I've done you a lot of favors, man. I want that floor. And I want the music."

"You're not Lo Tek. . . ."

This must have been going on for the better part of a twisted kilometer, Dog leading us along swaying catwalks and up rope ladders. The Lo Teks leech their webs and huddling places to the city's fabric with thick gobs of epoxy and sleep above the abyss in mesh hammocks. Their country is so attenuated that in places it consists of little more than holds for hands and feet, sawed into geodesic struts.

The Killing Floor, she called it. Scrambling after her, my new Eddie Bax shoes slipping on worn metal and damp plywood, I wondered how it could be any more lethal than the rest of the territory. At the same time I sensed that Dog's protests were ritual and that she already expected to get whatever it was she wanted.

Somewhere beneath us, Jones would be circling his tank, feeling the first twinges of junk sickness. The police would be boring the Drome regulars with questions about Ralfi. What did he do? Who was he with before he stepped outside? And the Yakuza would be settling its ghostly bulk over the city's data banks, probing for faint images of me reflected in numbered accounts, securities transactions, bills for utilities. We're an information economy. They teach you that in school. What they don't tell you is that it's impossible to move, to live, to operate at any level without leaving traces, bits, seemingly meaningless fragments of personal information. Fragments that can be retrieved, amplified . . .

But by now the pirate would have shuttled our message into line for blackbox transmission to the Yakuza comsat. A simple message: Call off the dogs or we wideband your program.

The program. I had no idea what it contained. I still don't. I only sing the song, with zero comprehension. It was probably research data, the Yakuza being given to advanced forms of industrial espionage. A genteel business, stealing from Ono-Sendai as a matter of course and politely holding their data for ransom, threatening to blunt the conglomerate's research edge by making the product public.

But why couldn't any number play? Wouldn't they be happier with something to sell back to Ono-Sendai, happier than they'd be with one dead Johnny from Memory Lane?

Their program was on its way to an address in Sydney, to a place that held letters for clients and didn't ask questions once you'd paid a small retainer. Fourth-class surface mail. I'd erased most of the other copy and recorded our message in the resulting gap, leaving just enough of the program to identify it as the real thing.

My wrist hurt. I wanted to stop, to lie down, to sleep. I knew that I'd lose my grip and fall soon, knew that the sharp black shoes I'd bought for my evening as Eddie Bax would lose their purchase and carry me down to Nighttown. But he rose in my mind like a cheap religious hologram, glowing, the enlarged chip on his Hawaiian shirt looming like a reconnaissance shot of some doomed urban nucleus.

So I followed Dog and Molly through Lo Tek heaven, jury-rigged and jerry-built from scraps that even Nighttown didn't want.

The Killing Floor was eight meters on a side. A giant had threaded steel cable back and forth through a junkyard and drawn it all taut. It creaked when it moved, and it moved constantly, swaying and bucking as the gathering Lo Teks arranged themselves on the shelf of plywood surrounding it. The wood was silver with age, polished with long use and deeply etched with initials, threats, declarations of passion. This was suspended from a separate set of cables, which lost themselves in darkness beyond the raw white glare of the two ancient floods suspended above the Floor.

A girl with teeth like Dog's hit the Floor on all fours. Her breasts were tattooed with indigo spirals. Then she was across the Floor, laughing, grappling with a boy who was drinking dark liquid from a liter flask.

Lo Tek fashion ran to scars and tattoos. And teeth. The electricity they were tapping to light the Killing Floor seemed to be an exception to their overall aesthetic, made in the name of . . . ritual, sport, art? I didn't know, but I could see that the Floor was something special. It had the look of having been assembled over generations.

I held the useless shotgun under my jacket. Its hardness and heft were comforting, even though I had no more shells. And it came to me that I had no idea at all of what was really happening, or of what was supposed to happen. And that was the nature of my game, because I'd spent most of my life as a blind receptacle to be filled with other people's knowledge and then drained, spouting synthetic languages I'd never understand. A very technical boy. Sure.

And then I noticed just how quiet the Lo Teks had become.

He was there, at the edge of the light, taking in the Killing Floor and the gallery of silent Lo Teks with a tourist's calm. And as our eyes met for the first time with mutual recognition, a memory clicked into place for me, of Paris, and the long Mercedes electrics gliding through the rain to Notre Dame; mobile greenhouses, Japanese faces behind the glass, and a hundred Nikons rising in blind phototropism, flowers of steel and crystal. Behind his eyes, as they found me, those same shutters whirring.

I looked for Molly Millions, but she was gone.

The Lo Teks parted to let him step up onto the bench. He bowed, smiling, and stepped smoothly out of his sandals, leaving them side by side, perfectly aligned, and then he stepped down onto the Killing Floor. He came for me, across that shifting trampoline of scrap, as easily as any tourist padding across synthetic pile in any featureless hotel.

Molly hit the Floor, moving.

The Floor screamed.

It was miked and amplified, with pickups riding the four fat coil springs at the corners and contact mikes taped at random to rusting machine fragments. Somewhere the Lo Teks had an amp and a synthesizer, and now I made out the shapes of speakers overhead, above the cruel white floods.

A drumbeat began, electronic, like an amplified heart, steady as a metronome.

She'd removed her leather jacket and boots; her T-shirt was sleeveless, faint telltales of Chiba City circuitry traced along her thin arms. Her leather jeans gleamed under the floods. She began to dance.

She flexed her knees, white feet tensed on a flattened gas tank, and the Killing Floor began to heave in response. The sound it made was like a world ending, like the wires that hold heaven snapping and coiling across the sky.

He rode with it, for a few heartbeats, and then he moved, judging the movement of the Floor perfectly, like a man stepping from one flat stone to another in an ornamental garden.

He pulled the tip from his thumb with the grace of a man at ease with social gesture and flung it at her. Under the floods, the filament was a refracting thread of rainbow. She threw herself flat and rolled, jackknifing up as the molecule whipped past, steel claws snapping into the light in what must have been an automatic rictus of defense.

The drum pulse quickened, and she bounced with it, her dark hair wild around the blank silver lenses, her mouth thin, lips taut with concentration. The Killing Floor boomed and roared, and the Lo Teks were screaming their excitement.

He retracted the filament to a whirling meter-wide circle of ghostly polychrome and spun it in front of him, thumbless hand held level with his sternum. A shield.

And Molly seemed to let something go, something inside, and that was the real start of her mad-dog dance. She jumped, twisting, lunging sideways, landing with both feet on an alloy engine block wire directly to one of the coil springs. I cupped my hands over my ears and knelt in a vertigo of sound, thinking Floor and benches were on their way down, down to Nighttown, and I saw us tearing through the shanties, the wet wash, exploding on the tiles like rotten fruit. But the cables held, and the Killing Floor rose and fell like a crazy metal sea. And Molly danced on it.

And at the end, just before he made his final cast with the filament, I saw something in his face, an expression that didn't seem to belong there. It wasn't fear and it wasn't anger. I think it was disbelief, stunned incomprehension mingled with pure aesthetic revulsion at what he was seeing, hearing—at what was happening to him. He retracted the whirling filament, the ghost disk shrinking to the size of a dinner plate as he whipped his arm above his head and brought it down, the thumbtip curving out for Molly like a live thing.

The Floor carried her down, the molecule passing just above her head; the Floor whiplashed, lifting him into the path of the taut molecule. It should have passed harmlessly over his head and been withdrawn into its diamond-hard socket. It took his hand off just behind the wrist. There was a gap in the Floor in front of him, and he went through it like a diver, with a strange deliberate grace, a defeated kamikaze on his way down to Nighttown. Partly, I think, he took that dive to buy himself a few seconds of the dignity of silence. She'd killed him with culture shock.

The Lo Teks roared, but someone shut the amplifier off, and Molly rode the Killing Floor into silence, hanging on now, her face white and blank, until the pitching slowed and there was only a faint pinging of tortured metal and the grating of rust on rust.

We searched the Floor for the severed hand, but we never found it. All we found was a graceful curve in one piece of rusted steel, where the molecule went through. Its edge was bright as new chrome.

We never learned whether the Yakuza had accepted our terms, or even whether they got our message. As far as I know, their program is still waiting for Eddie Bax on a shelf in the backroom of a gift shop on the third level of Sydney Central-5. Probably they sold the original back to Ono-Sendai months ago. But maybe they did get the pirate's broadcast, because nobody's come looking for me yet, and it's been nearly a year. If they do come, they'll have a long climb up through the dark, past Dog's sentries, and I don't look much like Eddie Bax these days. I let Molly take care of that, with a local anesthetic. And my new teeth have almost grown in.

I decided to stay up here. When I looked out across the Killing Floor, before he came, I saw how hollow I was. And I knew I was sick of being a bucket. So now I climb down and visit Jones, almost every night.

We're partners now, Jones and I, and Molly Millions, too. Molly handles our business in the Drome. Jones is still in Funland, but he has a bigger tank, with fresh seawater trucked in once a week. And he has his junk, when he needs it. He still talks to the kids with his frame of lights, but he talks to me on a new display unit in a shed that I rent there, a better unit than the one he used in the navy.

And we're all making good money, better money than I made before, because Jones's Squid can read the traces of anything that anyone ever stored in me, and he gives it to me on the display unit in languages I can understand. So we're learning a lot about all my former clients. And one day I'll have a surgeon dig all the silicon out of my amygdalae, and I'll live with my own memories and nobody else's, the way other people do. But not for a while.

In the meantime it's really okay up here, way up in the dark, smoking a Chinese filtertip and listening to the condensation that drips from the geodesics. Real quiet up here—unless a pair of Lo Teks decide to dance on the Killing Floor.

It's educational, too. With Jones to help me figure things out, I'm getting to be the most technical boy in town.

Harlan Ellison

Harlan Ellison (1934–   ) is the author of nearly a thousand short stories, essays, screen-plays, and novels. Starting out as a teenager writing science fiction, by his early twenties he was widely published. His fame grew, and in the 1960s Ellison flowered into one of the leading, and cutting-edge, writers of *speculative fiction*—the term in fashion in the 1960s for science fiction with literary ambition and without central dependence on sci-ence. He won many awards in that decade and the next, and edited two hugely influential anthologies of original fiction, *Dangerous Visions* and *Again, Dangerous Visions*—and collected stories for a third, *The Last Dangerous Visions,* that remains to date, legendary and unpublished. *The Essential Ellison: a Thirty-five Year Retrospective* (1987) is a gen-erous sampling of his short fiction.

Ellison is a powerful public figure in the SF field. In recent years he has cut back on his convention appearances, but in the 1990s he has his own show on The Sci-Fi Channel on cable television. He is a man of boundless energy and ambition, passionate, outspo-ken, peripatetic. In the words of Pogo artist Walt Kelly, he never retreats, though some-times he advances backwards.

This story is one of the award-winning works upon which his literary reputation was built in the 1960s. It is perhaps reminiscent of Kurt Vonnegut, Jr.'s "Harrison Bergeron," and certainly grows out of the whole tradition of revolt against social and political re-pression in literature. Its central character is the cocky young rebel artist whom Ellison represented to SF in the 1960s, Harlan the Harlequin.

"REPENT, HARLEQUIN!" SAID THE TICKTOCKMAN

There are always those who ask, what is it all about? For those who need to ask, for those who need points sharply made, who need to know "where it's at," this:

The mass of men serve the state thus, not as men mainly, but as machines, with their bodies. They are the standing army, and the militia, jailors, constables, posse comitatus, etc. In most cases there is no free exercise whatever of the judgment or of the moral sense; but they put themselves on a level with wood and earth and stones; and wooden men can perhaps be manufactured that will serve the purposes as well. Such command no more respect than men of straw or a lump of dirt. They have the same sort of worth only as horses and dogs. Yet such as these even are commonly esteemed good citizens. Others—as most legislators, politicians, lawyers, ministers, and office-holders—serve the state chiefly with their heads; and, as they rarely make any moral distinctions, they are as likely to serve the Devil, without intending it, as God. A very few, as heroes, patriots, martyrs, reformers in the great sense, and men, serve

the state with their consciences also, and so necessarily resist it for the most part; and they
are commonly treated as enemies by it.

—Henry David Thoreau,
"Civil Disobedience"

That is the heart of it. Now begin in the middle, and later learn the beginning; the end will take care of itself.

But because it was the very world it was, the very world they had allowed it to *become*, for months his activities did not come to the alarmed attention of The Ones Who Keep the Machine Functioning Smoothly, the ones who poured the very best butter over the cams and mainsprings of the culture. Not until it had become obvious that somehow, someway, he had become a notoriety, a celebrity, perhaps even a hero for (what Officialdom inescapably tagged) "an emotionally disturbed segment of the populace," did they turn it over to the Ticktockman and his legal machinery. But by then, because it was the very world it was, and they had no way to predict he would happen—possibly a strain of disease long-defunct, now, suddenly, reborn in a system where immunity had been forgotten, had lapsed—he had been allowed to become too real. Now he had form and substance.

He had become a *personality*, something they had filtered out of the system many decades ago. But there it was, and there *he* was, a very definitely imposing personality. In certain circles—middle-class circles—it was thought disgusting. Vulgar ostentation. Anarchistic. Shameful. In others, there was only sniggering, those strata where thought is subjugated to form and ritual, niceties, proprieties. But down below, ah, down below, where the people always needed their saints and sinners, their bread and circuses, their heroes and villains, he was considered a Bolivar; a Napoleon; a Robin Hood; a Dick Bong (Ace of Aces); a Jesus; a Jomo Kenyatta.

And at the top—where, like socially attuned Shipwreck Kellys, even tremor and vibration threatens to dislodge the wealthy, powerful, and titled from their flagpoles—he was considered a menace; a heretic; a rebel; a disgrace; a peril. He was known down the line, to the very heartmeat core, but the important reactions were high above and far below. At the very top, at the very bottom.

So his file was turned over, along with his time-card and his cardioplate, to the office of the Ticktockman.

The Ticktockman: very much over six feet tall, often silent, a soft purring man when things went timewise. The Ticktockman.

Even in the cubicles of the hierarchy, where fear was generated, seldom suffered, he was called the Ticktockman. But no one called him that to his mask.

You don't call a man a hated name, not when that man, behind his mask, is capable of revoking the minutes, the hours, the days and nights, the years of your life. He was called the Master Timekeeper to his mask. It was safer that way.

"This is *what* he is," said the Ticktockman with genuine softness, "but not *who* he is? This time-card I'm holding in my left hand has a name on it, but it is the name of *what* he is, not *who* he is. This cardioplate here in my right hand is also named, but not whom named, merely what named. Before I can exercise proper revocation, I have to know who this what is."

To his staff, all the ferrets, all the loggers, all the finks, all the commex, even the mineez, he said, "Who is this Harlequin?"

He was not purring smoothly. Timewise, it was jangle.

However, it *was* the longest speech they had ever heard him utter at one time, the staff, the ferrets, the loggers, the finks, the commex, but not the mineez, who usually weren't around to know, in any case. But even they scurried to find out.

Who is the Harlequin?

High above the third level of the city, he crouched on the humming aluminum-frame platform of the air-boat (foof! air-boat, indeed! swizzleskid is what it was, with a tow-rack jerry-rigged) and stared down at the neat Mondrian arrangement of the buildings.

Somewhere nearby, he could hear the metronomic left-right-left of the 2:47 P.M. shift, entering the Timkin roller-bearing plant in their sneakers. A minute later, precisely, he heard the softer right-left-right of the 5:00 A.M. formation, going home.

An elfish grin spread across his tanned features, and his dimples appeared for a moment. Then, scratching at his thatch of auburn hair, he shrugged within his motley, as though girding himself for what came next, and threw the joystick forward, and bent into the wind as the air-boat dropped. He skimmed over a slidewalk, purposely dropping a few feet to crease the tassels of the ladies of fashion, and—inserting thumbs in large ears—he stuck out his tongue, rolled his eyes and went wugga-wugga-wugga. It was a minor diversion. One pedestrian skittered and tumbled, sending parcels everywhichway, another wet herself, a third keeled slantwise and the walk was stopped automatically by the servitors till she could be resuscitated. It was a minor diversion.

Then he swirled away on a vagrant breeze, and was gone. Hi-ho.

As he rounded the cornice of the Time-Motion Study Building, he saw the shift, just boarding the slidewalk. With practiced motion and an absolute con-servation of movement, they sidestepped up onto the slowstrip and (in a chorus line reminiscent of a Busby Berkeley film of the antediluvian 1930s) advanced across the strips ostrich-walking till they were lined up on the expresstrip.

Once more, in anticipation, the elfin grin spread, and there was a tooth miss-ing back there on the left side. He dipped, skimmed, and swooped over them; and then, scrunching about on the air-boat, he released the holding pins that fastened shut the ends of the homemade pouring troughs that kept his cargo from dumping prematurely. And as he pulled the trough-pins, the air-boat slid over the factory workers and one hundred and fifty thousand dollars' worth of jelly beans cascaded down on the expresstrip.

Jelly beans! Millions and billions of purples and yellows and greens and licorice and grape and raspberry and mint and round and smooth and crunchy outside and soft-mealy inside and sugary and bouncing jouncing tumbling clittering clat-tering skittering fell on the heads and shoulders and hard-hats and carapaces of the Timkin workers, tinkling on the slidewalk and bouncing away and rolling about underfoot and filling the sky on their way down with all the colors of joy and childhood and holidays, coming down in a steady rain, a solid wash, a torrent of color and sweetness out of the sky from above, and entering a universe of sanity and metronomic order with quite-mad coocoo newness. Jelly beans!

The shift workers howled and laughed and were pelted, and broke ranks, and the jelly beans managed to work their way into the mechanism of the slidewalks after which there was a hideous scraping as the sound of a million fingernails rasped down a quarter of a million blackboards, followed by a coughing and a sputtering, and then the slidewalks all stopped and everyone was dumped this-awayandthataway in a jackstraw tumble, and still laughing and popping little jelly bean eggs of childish color into their mouths. It was a holiday, and a jollity, an absolute insanity, a giggle. But . . .

The shift was delayed seven minutes.

They did not get home for seven minutes.

The master schedule was thrown off by seven minutes.

Quotas were delayed by inoperative slidewalks for seven minutes.

He had tapped the first domino in the line, and one after another, like chik chik chik, the others had fallen.

The System had been seven minutes' worth of disrupted. It was a tiny matter, one hardly worthy of note, but in a society where the single driving force was order and unity and promptness and clocklike precision and attention to the clock, reverence of the gods of the passage of time, it was a disaster of major importance.

So he was ordered to appear before the Ticktockman. It was broadcast across every channel of the communications web. He was ordered to be *there* at 7:00 P.M. dammit on time. And they waited, and they waited, but he didn't show up till almost ten-thirty, at which time he merely sang a little song about moonlight in a place no one had ever heard of, called Vermont, and vanished again. But they had all been waiting since seven, and it wrecked *hell* with their schedules. So the question remained: Who is the Harlequin?

But the *unasked* question (more important of the two) was: how did we get *into* this position, where a laughing, irresponsible japer of jabberwocky and jive could disrupt our entire economic and cultural life with a hundred and fifty thousand dollars' worth of jelly beans . . .

Jelly for God's sake beans! This is madness! Where did he get the money to buy a hundred and fifty thousand dollars' worth of jelly beans? (They knew it would have cost that much, because they had a team of Situation Analysts pulled off another assignment, and rushed to the slidewalk scene to sweep up and count the candies, and produce findings, which disrupted *their* schedules and threw their entire branch at least a day behind.) Jelly beans! Jelly . . . *beans?* Now wait a second—a second accounted for—no one has manufactured jelly beans for over a hundred years. Where did he get jelly beans?

That's another good question. More than likely it will never be answered to your complete satisfaction. But then, how many questions ever are?

The middle you know. Here is the beginning. How it starts:

A desk pad. Day for day, and turn each day, 9:00—open the mail. 9:45—appointment with planning commission board. 10:30—discuss installation progress charts with J.L. 11:45—pray for rain. 12:00—lunch. *And so it goes.*

"I'm sorry, Miss Grant, but the time for interviews was set at 2:30, and it's almost five now. I'm sorry you're late, but those are the rules. You'll have to wait till next year to submit application for this college again." *And so it goes.*

The 10:10 local stops at Cresthaven, Galesville, Tonawanda Junction, Selby and Farnhurst, but not at Indiana City, Lucasville and Colton, except on Sunday. The 10:35 express stops at Galesville, Selby and Indiana City, except on Sundays & Holidays, at which time it stops at . . . *And so it goes.*

"I couldn't wait, Fred. I had to be at Pierre Cartain's by 3:00, and you said you'd meet me under the clock in the terminal at 2:45, and you weren't there, so I had to go on. You're always late, Fred. If you'd been there, we could have sewed it up together, but as it was, well I took the order alone . . ." *And so it goes.*

Dear Mr. and Mrs. Atterley: in reference to your son Gerold's constant tardiness, I am afraid we will have to suspend him from school unless some more reliable method can be instituted guaranteeing he will arrive at his classes on time. Granted he is an exemplary student, and his marks are high, his constant flouting of the schedules of this school makes it impractical to maintain him in a system where the other children seem capable of getting where they are supposed to be on time. *And so it goes.*

YOU CANNOT VOTE UNLESS YOU APPEAR AT 8:45 A.M.

"I don't care if the script is *good,* I need it Thursday!"

CHECK-OUT TIME IS 2:00 P.M.

"You got here late. The job's taken. Sorry."

YOUR SALARY HAS BEEN DOCKED FOR TWENTY MINUTES TIME LOST.

"God, what time is it, I've gotta run!"

And so it goes. And so it goes. And so it goes. And so it goes goes goes goes goes tick tock tick tock tick tock and one day we no longer let time serve us, we serve time and we are slaves of the schedule, worshippers of the sun's passing, bound into a life predicted on restrictions because the system will not function if we don't keep the schedule tight.

Until it becomes more than a minor inconvenience to be late. It becomes a sin. Then a crime. Then a crime punishable by this:

EFFECTIVE 15 JULY 2389, 12:00:00 midnight, the office of the Master Timekeeper will require all citizens to submit their time-cards and cardioplates for processing. In accordance with Statute 555-7-SGH-999 governing the revocation of time per capita, all cardioplates will be keyed to the individual holder and—

What they had done was devise a method of curtailing the amount of life a person could have. If he was ten minutes late, he lost ten minutes of his life. An hour was proportionately worth more revocation. If someone was consistently tardy, he might find himself, on a Sunday night, receiving a communique from the Master Timekeeper that his time had run out, and he would be "turned off" at high noon on Monday, please straighten your affairs, sir.

And so, by this simple scientific expedient (utilizing a scientific process held dearly secret by the Ticktockman's office) the System was maintained. It was the only expedient thing to do. It was, after all, patriotic. The schedules had to be met. After all, there *was* a war on!

But wasn't there always?

"Now that is really disgusting," the Harlequin said, when pretty Alice showed him the wanted poster. "Disgusting and *highly* improbable. After all, this isn't the days of desperadoes. A *wanted* poster!"

"You know," Alice noted, "you speak with a great deal of inflection."

"I'm sorry," said the Harlequin, humbly.

"No need to be sorry. You're always saying, 'I'm sorry.' You have such massive guilt, Everett, it's really very sad."

"I'm sorry," he repeated, then pursed his lips so the dimples appeared momentarily. He hadn't wanted to say that at all. "I have to go out again. I have to *do* something."

Alice slammed her coffee-bulb down on the counter. "Oh for God's *sake,*

Everett, can't you stay home just *one* night! Must you always be out in that ghastly clown suit, running around *annoying* people?"

"I'm—" He stopped, and clapped the jester's hat onto his auburn thatch with a tiny tingling of bells. He rose, rinsed out his coffee-bulb at the tap, and put it into the drier for a moment. "I have to go."

She didn't answer. The faxbox was purring, and she pulled a sheet out, read it, threw it toward him on the counter. "It's about you. Of course. You're ridiculous."

He read it quickly. It said the Ticktockman was trying to locate him. He didn't care, he was going out to be late again. At the door, dredging for an exit line, he hurled back petulantly, "Well, *you* speak with inflection, *too!*"

Alice rolled her pretty eyes heavenward. "You're ridiculous." The Harlequin stalked out, slamming the door, which sighed shut softly, and locked itself.

There was a gentle knock, and Alice got up with an exhalation of exasperated breath, and opened the door. He stood there. "I'll be back about ten-thirty, okay?"

She pulled a rueful face. "Why do you tell me that? Why? You *know* you'll be late! You *know* it! You're *always* late, so why do you tell me these dumb things?" She closed the door.

On the other side, the Harlequin nodded to himself. *She's right. She's always right. I'll be late. I'm always late. Why do I tell her these dumb things?*

He shrugged again, and went off to be late once more.

He had fired off the firecracker rockets that said: I will attend the 115th annual International Medical Association Invocation at 8:00 P.M. precisely. I do hope you will all be able to join me.

The words had burned in the sky, and of course the authorities were there, lying in wait for him. They assumed, naturally, that he would be late. He arrived twenty minutes early, while they were setting up the spiderwebs to trap and hold him, and blowing a large bullhorn, he frightened and unnerved them so, their own moisturized encirclement webs sucked closed, and they were hauled up, kicking and shrieking, high above the amphitheater's floor. The Harlequin laughed and laughed, and apologized profusely. The physicians, gathered in solemn conclave, roared with laughter, and accepted the Harlequin's apologies with exaggerated bowing and posturing, and a merry time was had by all, who thought the Harlequin was a regular foofaraw in fancy pants; all, that is, but the authorities, who had been sent out by the office of the Ticktockman, who hung there like so much dockside cargo, hauled up above the floor of the amphitheater in a most unseemly fashion.

(In another part of the same city where the Harlequin carried on his "activities," totally unrelated in every way to what concerns here, save that it illustrates the Ticktockman's power and import, a man named Marshall Delahanty received his turn-off notice from the Ticktockman's office. His wife received the notification from the grey-suited minee who delivered it, with the traditional "look of sorrow" plastered hideously across his face. She knew what it was, even without unsealing it. It was a billet-doux of immediate recognition to everyone these days. She gasped, and held it as though it were a glass slide tinged with botulism, and prayed it was not for her. Let it be for Marsh, she thought, brutally, realistically, or one of the kids, but not for me, please dear God, not for me. And then she opened it, and it *was* for Marsh, and she was at one and the same time horrified and relieved. The next trooper in the line had caught the bullet. "Marshall," she screamed, "Marshall! Termination, Marshall ohmigod, Marshall, whattl we do, whattl we do, Marshall omigodmarshall . . ." and in their home that night was the sound of tearing paper and fear, and the stink of madness went up the flue and there was nothing, absolutely nothing they could do about it.)

(But Marshall Delahanty tried to run. And early the next day, when turn-off time came, he was deep in the forest two hundred miles away, and the office of the Ticktockman blanked his cardioplate, and Marshall Delahanty keeled over, running, and his heart stopped, and the blood dried up on its way to his brain, and he was dead that's all. One light went out on his sector map in the office of the Master Timekeeper, while notification was entered for fax reproduction, and Georgette Delahanty's name was entered on the dole roles till she could re-marry. Which is the end of the footnote, and all the point that need be made, except don't laugh, because that is what would happen to the Harlequin if ever the Ticktockman found out his real name. It isn't funny.)

The shopping level of the city was thronged with the Thursday-colors of the buyers. Women in canary yellow chitons and men in pseudo-Tyrolean outfits that were jade and leather and fit very tightly, save for the balloon pants.

When the Harlequin appeared on the still-being-constructed shell of new Ef-ficiency Shopping Center, his bullhorn to his elfishly laughing lips, everyone pointed and stared, and he berated them:

"Why let them order you about? Why let them tell you to hurry and scurry like ants or maggots? Take your time! Saunter a while! Enjoy the sunshine, enjoy the breeze, let life carry you at your own pace! Don't be slaves of time, it's a helluva way to die, slowly, by degrees . . . down with the Ticktockman!"

Who's the nut? most of the shoppers wanted to know. Who's the nut oh wow I'm gonna be late. I gotta run . . .

And the construction gang on the Shopping Center received an urgent order from the office of the Master Timekeeper that the dangerous criminal known as the Harlequin was atop their spire, and their aid was urgently needed in appre-hending him. The work crew said no, they would lose time on their construction schedule, but the Ticktockman managed to pull the proper threads of govern-mental webbing, and they were told to cease work and catch that nitwit up there on the spire with the bullhorn. So a dozen and more burly workers began climb-ing into their construction platforms, releasing the a-grav plates, and rising to-ward the Harlequin.

After the debacle (in which, through the Harlequin's attention to personal safety, no one was seriously injured), the workers tried to reassemble, and assault him again, but it was too late. He had vanished. It had attracted quite a crowd, however, and the shopping cycle was thrown off by hours, simply hours. The purchasing needs of the system were therefore falling behind, and so measures were taken to accelerate the cycle for the rest of the day, but it got bogged down and speeded up and they sold too many float-valves and not nearly enough wegglers, which meant that the popli ratio was off, which made it necessary to rush cases and cases of spoiling Smash-O to stores that usually needed a case only every three or four hours. The shipments were bollixed, the trans-shipments were misrouted, and in the end, even the swizzleskid industries felt it.

"Don't come back till you have him!" the Ticktockman said, very quietly, very sincerely, extremely dangerously.

They used dogs. They used probes. They used cardioplate crossoffs. They used teepers. They used bribery. They used stiktytes. They used intimidation. They

used torment. They used torture. They used finks. They used cops. They used
search&seizure. They used fallaron. They used betterment incentive. They used
fingerprints. They used Bertillon. They used cunning. They used guile. They
used treachery. They used Raoul Mitgong, but he didn't help much. They used
applied physics. They used techniques of criminology.

And what the hell: they caught him.

After all, his name was Everett C. Marm, and he wasn't much to begin with,
except a man who had no sense of time.

"Repent, Harlequin!" said the Ticktockman.

"Get stuffed!" the Harlequin replied, sneering.

"You've been late a total of sixty-three years, five months, three weeks, two
days, twelve hours, forty-one minutes, fifty-nine seconds, point oh three six one
one one microseconds. You've used up everything you can, and more. I'm going
to turn you off."

"Scare someone else. I'd rather be dead than live in a dumb world with a
bogeyman like you."

"It's my job."

"You're full of it. You're a tyrant. You have no right to order people around
and kill them if they show up late."

"You can't adjust. You can't fit in."

"Unstrap me, and I'll fit my fist into your mouth."

"You're a non-conformist."

"That didn't used to be a felony."

"It is now. Live in the world around you."

"I hate it. It's a terrible world."

"Not everyone thinks so. Most people enjoy order."

"I don't, and most of the people I know don't."

"That's not true. How do you think we caught you?"

"I'm not interested."

"A girl named pretty Alice told us who you were."

"That's a lie."

"It's true. You unnerve her. She wants to belong, she wants to conform, I'm
going to turn you off."

"Then do it already, and stop arguing with me."

"I'm not going to turn you off."

"You're an idiot!"

"Repent, Harlequin!" said the Ticktockman.

"Get stuffed."

So they sent him to Coventry. And in Coventry they worked him over. It was
just like what they did to Winston Smith in *1984*, which was a book none of
them knew about, but the techniques are really quite ancient, and so they did
it to Everett C. Marm, and one day quite a long time later, the Harlequin
appeared on the communications web, appearing elfish and dimpled and bright-
eyed, and not at all brainwashed, and he said he had been wrong, that it was a
good, a very good thing indeed, to belong, and be right on time hip-ho and away
we go, and everyone stared up at him on the public screens that covered an
entire city block, and they said to themselves, well, you see, he was just a nut
after all, and if that's the way the system is run, then let's do it that way, because
it doesn't pay to fight city hall, or in this case, the Ticktockman. So Everett C.
Marm was destroyed, which was a loss, because of what Thoreau said earlier,

but you can't make an omelet without breaking a few eggs, and in every revolution, a few die who shouldn't, but they have to, because that's the way it
happens, and if you make only a little change, then it seems to be worthwhile.
Or, to make the point lucidly:

"Uh, excuse me, sir, I, uh, don't know how to uh, to uh, tell you this, but
you were three minutes late. The schedule is a little, uh, bit off."

He grinned sheepishly.

"That's ridiculous!" murmured the Ticktockman behind his mask. "Check
your watch." And then he went into his office, going mrmee, mrmee, mrmee,
mrmee.

1967
25th Convention
New York

Chad Oliver

Chad Oliver (1928–93) was the man who brought the science of anthropology into the arena of sciences used in science fiction. In his novel *Shadows in the Sun* (1954) and in the stories collected in *Another Kind* (1955) and *The Edge of Forever* (1971), Oliver introduced and popularized the concepts of his discipline. "Our field's most fascinating and comprehensive collection of anthropological science fiction," said Damon Knight in 1956, and praised him for his "ability to touch the human heart of the problem."

Until the 1950s, when Oliver entered the field and experienced his most productive decade as a writer of SF, there was a great deal of prejudice against the "soft" or life sciences, especially against the areas of psychology, the social sciences, and economics. They were second class sciences because they were not mathematically predictive, not reliable, therefore not real knowledge, so the argument went. Real science fiction, before Oliver, could use them only by making them into predictive sciences in the future (see, for instance, Katherine MacLean's "The Snowball Effect" [1952]). Oliver's easy, pleasant exposition of anthropological ideas and attitudes in his fiction throughout the 1950s paved the way for later writers such as Ursula K. Le Guin and Michael Bishop to write sophisticated anthropological science fiction in the following decades. Oliver himself continued to write novels in and out of the SF genre in the 1960s,'70s, and '80s while a professor of anthropology at the University of Texas in Austin, but no notable short fiction.

Oliver tends to focus on motivations and values, rather than violence or action, in his fiction. "I was strongly influenced by writers outside the science fiction field, notably Hemingway and Steinbeck," he said. As in this story, he usually rewards a connection to the natural world.

BLOOD'S A ROVER

Clay lies still, but blood's a rover;
  Breath's a ware that will not keep.
Up, lad: when the journey's over
  There'll be time enough to sleep.
        —A. E. *Housman*

I

Night sifted through the city like flakes of soft black snow drifting down from the stars. It whispered along the tree-lined canyons between the clean shafts of white buildings and pressed darkly against windows filled with warm light.

Conan Lang watched the illumination in his office increase subtly in adjusting to the growing darkness outside and then looked again at the directive he held in his hand.

It still read the same way.

"Another day, another world," he said aloud. And then, paraphrasing: "The worlds are too much with us—"

Conan Lang fired up his pipe and puffed carefully on it to get it going properly. Then he concentrated on blowing neat cloudy smoke rings that wobbled across the room and impaled themselves on the nose of the three-dimensional portrait of the President. It wasn't that he had anything against President Austin, he assured himself. It was simply that Austin represented that nebulous being, Authority, and at the moment it happened that Authority was singularly unwelcome in the office of Conan Lang.

He looked back at the directive. The wording was friendly and informal enough, but the meaning was clear:

> Headquarters, Gal. Administration.
> Office of Admiral Nelson White,
> Commander, Process Planning Division.
> 15 April, 2701. Confidential.

One Agent Conan Lang
Applied Process Corps
G.A. Department Seven
Conan:

We got another directive from the Buzzard yesterday. Seems that the powers that be have decided that a change in Sirius Ten is in order—a shift from Four to Five. You're it. Make a prelim check and report to me at your convenience. Cheer up— maybe you'll get another bag of medals out of it.

> Nelson.

Conan Lang left the directive on his desk and got to his feet. He walked over to the window and looked out at the lights sprinkled over the city. There weren't many. Most people were long ago home in the country, sitting around the living room, playing with the kids. He puffed slowly on his pipe.

Another bag of medals. Nelson wasn't kidding anybody—wasn't even trying to, really. He knew how Conan felt because he felt the same way. They all did, sooner or later. It was fascinating at first, even fun, this tampering with the lives of other people. But the novelty wore off in a hurry—shriveled like flesh in acid under a million eyes of hate, a million talks with your soul at three in the morning, a million shattered lives. Sure, it was necessary. You could always tell yourself that; that was the charm, the magic word that was supposed to make everything fine and dandy. Necessary—but for *you*, not for them. Or perhaps for them too, in the long run.

Conan Lang returned to his desk and flipped on the intercom. "I want out," he said. "The Administration Library, Division of Extraterrestrial Anthropology. I'd like to speak to Bailey if he's there."

He had to wait thirty seconds.

"Bailey here," the intercom said.

"This is Lang. What've you got on Sirius Ten?"

"Just like that, huh? Hang on a second."

There was a short silence. Conan Lang smoked his pipe slowly and smiled as he visualized Bailey punching enough buttons to control a space fleet.

"Let's see," Bailey's voice came through the speaker. "We've got a good bit. There's McAllister's *Kinship Systems of Sirius Ten*; Jenkins'—that's B. J. Jenkins, the one who worked with Holden—*Sirius Ten Social Organization*; Bartheim's *Economic Life of Sirius Ten*; Robert Patterson's *Basic Personality Types of the Sirius Group*; *Preliminary and Supplementary Ethnological Surveys of the Galactic Advance Fleet*—the works."

Conan Lang sighed. "O.K.," he said. "Shoot them out to my place, will you?"

"Check—be there before you are. One thing more, Cone."

"Yes?"

"Been reading a splendid eight-volume historical novel of the Twentieth Century. Hot stuff, I'll tell you. You want me to send it along in case you run out of reading material?"

"Very funny. See you around."

"So long."

Conan Lang switched off the intercom and destroyed the directive. He tapped out his pipe in the waster and left the office, locking the door behind him. The empty hallway was sterile and impersonal. It seemed dead at night, somehow, and it was difficult to believe that living, breathing human beings walked through it all day long. It was like a tunnel to nowhere. He had the odd feeling that there was nothing around it at all, just space and less than space—no building, no air, no city. Just a white antiseptic tunnel to nowhere.

He shook off the feeling and caught the lift to the roof. The cool night air was crisp and clean and there was a whisper of a breeze out of the north. A half moon hung in the night, framed by stars. He looked up at it and wondered how Johnny was getting along up there, and whether perhaps Johnny was even then looking down on Earth.

Conan Lang climbed into his bullet and set the controls. The little ship rose vertically on her copter blades for two thousand feet, hovered a moment over the silent city, and then flashed off on her jets into the west.

Conan Lang sat back in his cushioned seat, looking at the stars, trying not to think, letting the ship carry him home.

Conan Lang relaxed in his armchair, his eyes closed, an icy bourbon and soda in his hand. The books he had requested—neat, white, uniform microfilm blow-ups from the Administration Library—were stacked neatly on the floor by his side, waiting. Waiting, he thought, sipping his drink. They were always waiting. No matter how much a man knew, there was always more—waiting.

The room closed in around him. He could feel it—warm, friendly, personal. It was a good room. It was a room filled with life, his life and Kit's. It was almost as if he could see the room better with his eyes closed, for then he saw the past as well as the present. There was the silver and black tapestry on the wall, given to him by old Maharani so long ago, on a world so far away that the very light given off by its sun when he was there had yet to reach the Earth as the twinkle of a star in the night sky. There were his books, there were Kit's paintings. There was the smudge—the current one—on the carpet where Rob had tracked dirt into the house before supper.

He opened his eyes and looked at his wife.

"I must be getting old, Kit," he said. "Right at the moment, it all looks pretty pointless."

Kit raised her eyebrows and said nothing.

"We tear around over the galaxy like a bunch of kids playing Spacemen and Pirates," he said, downing his drink. "Push here, pull there, shove here, reverse there. It's like some kind of half-wit game where one side doesn't even know it's playing, or on which side of the field. Sometimes—"

"Want another drink?" Kit asked softly.

"Yes. Kit—"

"I know," she said, touching his shoulder with her hand. "Go ahead and talk; you'll feel better. We go through this every time there's a new one, remember? I know you don't really mean things the way you say them, and I know why you say them that way anyhow." She kissed him lightly on the forehead and her lips were cool and patient. "I understand."

Conan Lang watched her leave the room with his empty glass. "Yes," he whispered to himself. "Yes, I guess you do."

It *was* necessary, of course. Terribly, urgently necessary. But it got to you sometimes. All those people out there, living their lives, laughing and crying, raising children. It hurt you to think about them. And it wasn't necessary for them, not for him, not for Kit. Or was it? You couldn't tell; there was always a chance. But if only they could just forget it all, just live, there was so much to enjoy—

Kit handed him a fresh bourbon and soda, icy and with just a trace of lemon in it the way he liked it, and then curled up again on the couch, smiling at him.

"I'm sorry, angel," he said. "You must get pretty sick of hearing the same sad song over and over again."

"Not when you sing it, Cone."

"It's just that sometimes I chuck my mind out the nearest window and wonder why—"

There was a thump and a bang from the rear of the house. Conan Lang tasted his drink. That meant Rob was home. He listened, waiting. There was the hollow crack—that was the bat going into the corner. There was the heavy thud—that was the fielder's glove.

"That's why," Kit said.

Conan Lang nodded and picked up the first book off the floor.

Three days later, Conan Lang went up the white steps, presented his credentials, and walked into the Buzzard's Cage. The place made him nervous. Irritated with himself, he paused deliberately and lit his pipe before going on. The Cage seemed cold, inhuman. And the Buzzard—

He shouldn't feel that way, he told himself, again offering his identification before entering the lift to the Nest. Intellectually, he understood cybernetics; there was nothing supernatural about it. The Cage was just a machine, for all its powers, even if the Buzzard did sometimes seem more—or perhaps less— than a man. Still, the place gave him the creeps. A vast thinking machine, filling a huge building, a brain beside which his own was as nothing. Of course, men had built it. Men made guns, too, but the knowledge was scant comfort when you looked into a metallic muzzle and someone pulled the trigger.

"Lang," he said to himself, "you're headed for the giggle ward."

He smiled then, knowing it wasn't so. Imagination was a prime requisite for his job, and he just had more than his share. It got in the way sometimes, but it was a part of him and that was that.

Conan Lang waded through a battery of attendants and security personnel and finally reached the Nest. He opened the door and stepped into the small, dark room. There, behind the desk where he always was, perched the Buzzard.

"Hello, Dr. Gottleib," said Conan Lang.

The man behind the desk eyed him silently. His name was Fritz Gottleib, but he had been tagged the Buzzard long ago. No one used the name to his face, and it was impossible to tell whether or not the name amused him. He spoke but seldom, and his appearance, even after you got used to it, was startling. Fritz Gottleib was squat and completely bald. He always dressed in black and his heavy eyebrows were like horizontal splashes of ink against the whiteness of his face. The Buzzard analogy, thought Conan Lang, was more than understandable; it was inevitable. The man sat high in his tower, in his Nest of controls, brooding over a machine that perhaps he alone fully understood. Alone. He always seemed alone, no matter how many people surrounded him. His was a life apart, a life whose vital force pulsed in the shifting lights of the tubes of a great machine.

"Dr. Lang," he acknowledged, unmoving, his voice sibilant, almost a hiss.

Conan Lang puffed on his pipe and dropped into the chair across from Gottleib. He had dealt with the Buzzard before and most of the shock had worn off. You could get used to anything, he supposed. Man was a very adaptable animal.

"The smoke doesn't bother you, I hope?"

Gottleib did not comment. He simply stared at him, his dark eyes unblinking. Like looking at a piece of meat, thought Conan Lang.

"Well," he said, trying again, "I guess you know what I'm here for."

"You waste words," Fritz Gottleib hissed.

"I hadn't realized they were in short supply," Lang replied, smiling. The Buzzard was irritating, but he could see the justice in the man's remark. It *was* curious the number of useless things that were said all the time—useless, at any rate, from a purely communicative point of view. It would have been sheerly incredible for Gottleib—who after all had been checking his results in the computer—*not* to have known the nature of his mission.

"O.K.," said Lang, "what's the verdict?"

Fritz Gottleib fingered a square card in his surprisingly long-fingered hands, seeming to hover over it like a bird of prey.

"It checks out," he said sibilantly, his voice low and hard to hear. "Your plan will achieve the desired transfer in Sirius Ten, and the transfer integrates positively with the Plan."

"Anything else? Anything I should know?"

"We should all know many more things than we do, Dr. Lang."

"Um-m-m. But that was all the machine said with respect to my proposed plan of operations?"

"That was all."

Conan Lang sat back, watching Gottleib. A strange man. But he commanded respect.

"I'd like to get hold of that baby sometime," he said easily. "I've got a question or two of my own."

"Sometimes it is best not to know the answers to one's questions, Dr. Lang."

"No. But I'd like to have a shot at it all the same. Don't tell the security boys I said that; they'd string me up by the toes."

"Perhaps one day, Dr. Lang. When you are old like me."

Conan Lang stood up, cupping his pipe in his hand. "I guess that's all," he said.

"Yes," said Fritz Gottleib.

"See you around."

No answer. Cold shadows seemed to fill the room.

Conan Lang turned and left the way he had come. Behind him, drilling into his back, he could feel the eyes of Fritz Gottleib following him, cold and deep like the frozen waters of an arctic sea.

The ship stood on Earth but she was not of Earth. She was poised, a mighty lance of silver, a creature of the deeps. She waited, impatient, while Conan Lang slowly walked across the vast duralloy tarmac of Space One, Admiral White at his side. The sun was bright in a clean blue sky. It touched the ship with lambent flame and warmed Conan Lang's shoulders under his uniform. A slight puff of breeze rustled across the spaceport, pushing along a stray scrap of white paper ahead of it.

"Here we go again," said Conan Lang.

"That's what you get for being good," the admiral said with a smile. "You get good enough and you'll get my job—which ought to be a grim enough prospect even for you. If you're smart, you'll botch this job six ways from Sunday and then we'll have to give you a rest."

"Yeah—play a little joke, strictly for laughs, and give 'em an atom bomb or two to stick on the ends of their hatchets. Or take 'em back to the caves. There are plenty of delicious possibilities."

The two men walked on, toward the silver ship.

"Everything's set, I suppose?" asked Conan Lang.

"Yep. Your staff is already on board and the stuff is loaded."

"Any further instructions?"

"No—you know your business or you wouldn't be going. Just try to make it as quick as you can, Cone. They're getting warm over at Research on that integration-acceleration principle for correlating data—it's going to be big and I'll want you around when it breaks."

Conan Lang grinned. "What happens if I just up and disappear one day, Nels? Does the galaxy moan and lie down and quit?"

"Search me," said Admiral Nelson White. "But don't take any more risks than you absolutely have to. Don't get the idea that you're indispensable, either. It's just that it's tiresome to break in new men."

"I'll try to stay alive if you're positive that's what you want."

They approached the ship. Kit and Rob were waiting. The admiral touched his cap and moved on, leaving Conan Lang alone with his family. Kit was lovely—she always was, Conan Lang thought. He couldn't imagine a life without her.

"Bye, darlin'," he whispered, taking her in his arms. "One of these days I'm coming back and I'm never going to leave you again."

"This is till then," Kit said softly and kissed him for keeps.

Much later, Conan Lang released her and shook hands with his son.

"So long, old-timer," he said.

"Hurry back, Dad," Rob said, trying not to cry.

Conan Lang turned and joined Admiral White at the star cruiser. He did not look back.

"Good luck, Cone," the admiral said, patting him on the back. "I'll keep the medals warm and a light in the cabin window."

"OK, Nels," said Conan Lang.

He swung aboard the great ship and stepped into the lift. There was a muted

hum of machinery as the car whispered up through the pneumatic tube, up into
the hollowness of the ship. Already it seemed to Conan Lang that he had left
Earth far behind him. The endless loneliness of the star trails rode up with him
in the humming lift.

The ship rested, quiescent, on Earth. Ahead of her, calling to her, the stars
flamed coldly in an infinite sea of night.

II

Conan Lang walked down the long white corridor to the afterhold, his footsteps
muffled and almost inaudible in the murmur of the atomics. It *would* be a long
white corridor, he thought to himself. Wherever man went, there went the long
white corridors—offices, hospitals, command posts. It was almost as if he had
spent half a lifetime walking through long white corridors, and now here was yet
another one—cold and antiseptic, hanging in space eight light-years from Earth.

"Halt."

"Lang here," he told the Fleetman. "Kindly point that thing the other way."

"Identification, please."

Lang sighed and handed it over. The man should know him by now; after all,
the ship was on his mission, and he was hardly a subversive character. Still, orders
were orders—a principle that covered a multitude of sins. And they couldn't
afford to take chances, not *any* chances.

"All right, sir," the Fleetman said, returning the identification. "Sorry to
bother you."

"Forget it," said Conan Lang. "Keep your eyes peeled for space pirates."

The guard smiled. "Who'd want to steal space, sir?" he asked. "It's free and
I reckon there's enough to go around."

"Your inning," acknowledged Conan Lang, moving into the afterhold. The
kid was already there.

"Hello, sir," said Andrew Irvin.

"Hi, Andy—and cut the 'sir,' what do you say? You make me feel like I should
be extinct or embalmed or something."

The kid smiled almost shyly. Conan Lang had half expected to find him there
in the hold; Andy was always poking around, asking questions, trying to learn.
His quick brown eyes and alert carriage reminded Conan of a young hunting
dog, frisking through the brush, perpetually on the verge of flushing the grandfather of all jack rabbits.

"It doesn't seem possible, does it?" asked the kid.

Conan Lang raised his eyebrows.

"All this, I mean," Andy Irvin said, gesturing at the neat brown sacks stacked
row upon row in the brightly lighted hold. "To think that a couple of sacks of
that stuff can remold a planet, change the lives of millions of people—"

"It's not just the sacks, Andy. It took man a good many hundreds of thousands
of years to learn what to *do* with those sacks."

"Yes, sir," the kid said, hanging on every word.

"No 'sir,' remember? I'm not giving you a lecture, and you don't have to look
attentive. I'm sure that elementary anthropology isn't *too* dumbfounding to a
guy who took honors at the Academy."

"Well—"

"Never mind." Conan Lang eyed him speculatively. The kid reminded him, almost too much, of someone else—a kid named Conan Lang who had started out on a great adventure himself too many years ago. "I . . . um-m-m . . . guess you know you're going to work with me on Ten."

Andy looked like Conan had just handed him a harem on a silver platter. "No, sir," he said. "I didn't know. Thank you, sir."

"The name is Conan."

"Yes, sir."

"Hellfire," said Conan Lang. How did you go about telling a kid that you were happy to have someone around with stars in his eyes again? Without sounding like a fool? The answer was simple—you didn't.

"I can't wait," Andy said. "To really *do* something at last—it's a great feeling. I hope I'll do OK."

"It won't be long now, Andy. Twenty-four hours from now you and I go to work. The buggy ride is about over."

The two men fell silent then, looking at the neat brown rows of sacks, feeling the star ship tremble slightly under them with the thunder of her great atomics.

It was night on Sirius Ten—a hot, humid night with a single moon hanging like frozen fire in the darkness. A small patrol craft from the cruiser floated motionless in the night sky, her batteries pouring down a protective screen around the newly cleared field. Conan Lang wiped the sweat from his forehead and washed his hands off in the clean river water that gurgled through the trench at his feet.

"That about does it, Andy," he said wearily. "Toss 'em a Four signal."

Andy Irvin turned the rheostat on his small control board to Four and flipped the switch. They waited, listening to the faint murmur of the night breeze off the river. There was no change, nothing that they could see, but they could almost feel the intense radiation pounding into the field from the patrol ship, seeping into the ground, accelerating by thousands of times the growth factor in the seeds.

"That's got it," said Conan Lang. "Give 'em release."

Andy shot the patrol craft the release signal and shut off his control board. The little ship seemed to hover uncertainly. There was a humming sound and a spot of intense white light in the sky. That was all. The ship was gone and they were alone.

"It's been a long night, kid," yawned Conan Lang. "We'd better get some sack time—we're liable to need it before morning."

"You go ahead," Andy Irvin said. "I'm not sleepy; the sunrise here ought to be something."

"Yeah," said Conan Lang. "The sunrise ought to be something."

He walked across the field and entered a structure that closely resembled a native hut in appearance but was actually quite, quite different. Too tired even to undress, he piled into bed with his clothes on and rested quietly in the darkness.

The strange, haunting, familiar-with-a-difference sounds of an alien world whispered around the hut on the soft, moist breeze from the sluggish river. Far away, an animal screamed hoarsely in the clogging brush. Conan Lang kept his eyes closed and tried not to think, but his mind ignored him. It went right on working, asking questions, demanding answers, bringing up into the light many memories that were good and some that were better forgotten.

"Kit," he said, very softly.

Tired as he was, he knew there would be no sleep for him that night.

The sunrise was a glory. The blue-white inferno of Sirius hung in the treetops across the field and then climbed into the morning sky, her white dwarf companion a smaller sun by her side. The low cumulus clouds were edged with flame—fiery red, pale blue, cool green. The fresh morning winds washed the field with air and already the young plants were out of the ground, thirsty for the sun. The chuckling water in the trenches sparkled in the light.

With the morning, the natives came.

"They're all around us," Conan Lang said quietly.

"I can't see them," whispered Andy Irvin, looking at the brush.

"They're there."

"Do you . . . expect trouble, sir?"

"Not yet, assuming we've got this deal figured right. They're more afraid of us than we are of them."

"What if we *don't* have it figured right?"

Conan Lang smiled. "Three guesses," he said.

The kid managed a wry grin. He was taking it well, Lang thought. He remembered how he'd felt the first time. It didn't really hit you until that first day, and then it upped and kicked you in the teeth. Quite suddenly, it was all a very different proposition from the manuals and the viewers and the classrooms of the Academy. *Just you, all alone,* the alien breeze sighed in your ear. *You're all alone in the middle of nowhere,* the wind whispered through the trees. *Our eyes are watching you, our world is pressing you back, waiting. What do you know of us really? What good is your knowledge now?*

"What next?" Andy asked.

"Just tend the field, kid. And try to act like a ghost. You're an ancestor of those people watching us from the brush, remember. If we've got this figured wrong—if those survey reports were haywire somewhere, or if someone's been through here who didn't belong—you should have a little warning at least. They don't use blowguns or anything—just spears, and they'd prefer a hatchet. If there's trouble, you hightail it back to the hut *at once* and man the projector. That's all."

"I'm not so sure I care to be an ancestor," Andy Irvin muttered, picking up his hoe. "Not yet, anyhow." He moved off along a water trench, checking on the plants.

Conan Lang picked up his own hoe and set to work. He could feel the natives watching him, wondering, whispering to themselves. But he was careful not to look around him. He kept his head down and dug at the plants with his hoe, clearing the water channels. The plants were growing with astonishing rapidity, thanks to the dose of radiation. They should be mature in a week. And then—

The sun blazed down on his treated skin and the sweat rolled off his body in tiny rivulets. The field was strangely silent around him; there was only the gurgle of the water and the soft sigh of the humid breeze. His hoe chopped and slushed at the mud and his back was tired from bending over so long. It was too still, unnaturally still.

Behind that brush, back in the trees—a thousand eyes.

He did not look around. Step by step, he moved down the trench, under the hellish sun, working with his hoe.

•　　•　　•

The fire-burned days and the still, hushed nights alternated rapidly. On the morning of the third day, Andy Irvin found what they had been waiting for.

In the far corner of the field, placed on a rude wood platform about four feet high, there were three objects. There was a five-foot-square bark mat, neatly woven. There was a small animal that closely resembled a terrestrial pig, face down, its throat neatly slashed. And there was a child. It was a female baby, evidently not over a week old. It had been strangled to death.

"It's . . . different . . . when you see it for yourself," Andy said quietly, visibly shaken.

"You'll get used to it," said Conan Lang, his voice purposely flat and matter-of-fact. "Get the pig and the mat—and stop looking like a prohibitionist who just found a jug of joy water in the freezer. This is old stuff to ancestors."

"Old stuff," repeated Andy without conviction.

They carried the contents of the platform back to their hut and Conan Lang wrapped the body of the child in a cloth.

"We'll bury her tonight after dark," he said. "The pig we eat. It won't do any harm to sit on the mat where they can see us while we're eating it, either."

"Well," Andy muttered. "Glad to see you're not going to eat the baby, too."

"You never can tell," smiled Conan Lang. "We anthropologists are all crazy, or hadn't you heard?"

"I've heard," agreed Andy Irvin, getting his nerves under control again. "Where's the hot sauce?"

Conan Lang stepped back outside and picked up his hoe. The blazing double sun had already produced shimmering heat waves that danced like live things in the still air over the green field. The kid was going to be all right. He'd known it all along, of course—but you could never be *sure* of a man until you worked with him under field conditions. And a misfit, an unstable personality, was anything but a joke on an alien planet where unknowable forces hung in the balance.

"Let's see if I've got this thing figured straight," Andy said, puffing away on one of Conan's pipes. "The natives are afraid of us, and still they feel that they must make us an offering because we, as their supposed ancestors, control their lives. So they pick a system of dumb barter rather than sending out the usual contact man to ferret out kinship connections."

"You're OK so far," Conan Lang said. "I guess you've studied about the dumb barter systems used on Earth in the old days; it was used whenever trade took place between groups of markedly unequal strength, such as the African pygmies and trading vessels from the west. There's a fear factor involved."

"Yes, sir."

"Forget the 'sir.' I didn't mean to lecture. I think I'll start calling you Junior."

"Sorry. The bark mat is a unit in a reciprocal trade system and the pig is a sacred animal—I get that part of it. But the baby—that's terrible, Conan. After all, we caused that death in a way—"

"Afraid not," Conan Lang corrected him. "These people practice infanticide; it's part of their religion. If the preliminary reports were correct—and they've checked out so far—they kill all the female children born on the last three days of alternate months. There's an economic reason, too—not enough food to go around, and that's a pretty effective method of birth control. The baby would have been killed regardless—we had nothing to do with it."

"Still—"

"I know. But maybe she was the lucky one after all."

"I don't quite follow you there."

"Skip it—you'll find out soon enough."

"What are you going to leave them tonight?"

"Not sure yet," Conan Lang said. "We'll have to integrate with their value system, of course. We brought some mats, and I guess a good steel knife won't hurt things any. We'll worry about that later. Come on, farmer—back to work."

Andy Irvin picked up his hoe and followed Conan Lang into the field. The clear water bubbled softly as it flowed through the trenches. The growing plants sent their roots thirstily into the ground and the fresh green shoots stretched up like tentacles into the humid air of Sirius Ten.

That night, under the great yellow moon that swam far away and lonesome among the stars, they placed exchange gifts of their own on the platform. Next morning, the invisible traders had replaced them with four mats and another dead pig.

"No babies, anyhow," Andy Irvin said, puffing industriously on one of Conan's pipes. They had decided that cigarettes, as an unfamiliar cultural trait to the natives, were out. Now, with Andy taking with unholy enthusiasm to pipe smoking, Conan Lang was threatened with a shortage of tobacco. He watched the smoke from the kid's pipe with something less than ecstasy.

"We can have smoked ham," he observed.

"It was your idea," Andy grinned.

"Call me 'sir.' "

Andy laughed, relaxed now, and picked up the pig. Conan gathered up the somewhat cumbersome mats and followed him back into the hut. The hot, close sun was already burning his shoulders. The plants were green and healthy-looking, and the air was a trifle fresher in the growing field.

"Now what?" Andy asked, standing outside the hut and letting the faint breeze cool him off as best it could.

"I figure we're about ready for an overt contact," Conan Lang said. "Everything has checked out beautifully so far, and the natives don't seem to be suspicious or hostile. We might as well get the ball rolling."

"The green branch, isn't it?"

"That's right."

They still did not get a glimpse of the natives throughout the steaming day, and that night they placed a single mat on the platform. On top of the mat they put a slim branch of green leaves, twisted around back on itself and tied loosely to form a circle. The green branch was by no means a universal symbol of peace, but, in this particular form, it chanced to be so on Sirius Ten. Conan Lang smiled a little. Man had found many curious things among the stars, and most of them were of just this unsensational but very useful sort.

By dawn, the mat and the circle branch were gone and the natives had left them nothing in return.

"Today's the day," Conan Lang said, rubbing the sleep out of his eyes. "They'll either give us the works or accept our offer. Nothing to do now but wait."

They picked up their hoes and went back into the field. Waiting can be the most difficult of all things, and the long, hot morning passed without incident. The two men ate their lunch in silence, thankful for the odorless injection that kept the swarming insects away from them. Late in the afternoon when the long blue shadows of evening were already touching the green plants and the clean, flowing water, the natives came.

There were five of them and they appeared to be unarmed. One man walked slightly in advance of the others, a circular branch of green leaves in his hand. Conan Lang waited for them, with Andy standing by at his side. It was moments like this, he thought, that made you suddenly realize that you were all alone and a long, long way from friends. The natives came on steadily. Conan felt a surge of admiration for the young man who led them. From his point of view, he was walking into a situation filled with the terror of the supernatural, which was a very real part of his life. His steps did not falter. He would, Conan supposed, be the eldest son of the most powerful chief.

The natives stopped when they were three paces away. Their leader extended the circular green branch. "We would serve you, fathers from the mountains," the native said in his own tongue.

Conan Lang stepped forward and received the branch. "We are brothers," he replied in the same language, "and we would be your friends."

The native smiled, his teeth very white. "I am Ren," he said. "I am your brother."

Conan Lang kept his face expressionless, but deep within him a dark regret and sadness coursed like ice through his veins.

It had begun again.

III

For many days, Conan Lang listened to the Oripesh natives preparing for the feast. Their small village, only a quarter of a mile from the field, was alive with excitement. The women prepared great piles of the staple ricefruit and broiled river fish in great green leaves on hot coals. The men chanted and danced interminably, cleansing the village by ritual for the coming visitation, while the children, forgotten for once, played on the banks of the river. On the appointed day, Conan Lang walked into the village with Andy Irvin at his side.

It was a crude village, necessarily so because of its transient nature. But it was not dirty. The natives watched the two men with awe, but they did not seem unfriendly. The supernatural was for them always just on the other side of the hill, hidden in the night, and now it was among them, in the open. That was all. And what, after all, thought Conan Lang, could have seemed more supernatural to them than a silver ship that dropped out of the stars? What was supernatural depended on one's point of view—and on how much one happened to know about what was *natural*.

The box he carried was heavy, and it took both arms to handle it. He watched Andy puffing at his side and smiled.

"Stick with it, kid," he said, walking steadily through the watching natives. "You may earn your pay yet."

Andy muttered something under his breath and blinked to get the sweat out of his eyes.

When they reached the clearing in the center of the village, they stopped and put their boxes down. Ren, the eldest son of the chief Ra Renne, approached them at once and offered them a drink from a large wooden bowl. Conan drank and passed the container on to Andy, who grinned broadly and took a long swallow of the warm fluid. It was sweet, although not too sweet, and it burned pleasantly on the way down. It was, Conan decided instantly, a great improvement over some native fermented horrors he had been subjected to in times past.

The natives gathered around them in a great circle. There must have been nearly five hundred of them—far more than the small village could accommodate for any length of time.

"We're celebrities," Conan Lang whispered out of the side of his mouth as he waited to be presented ceremonially to the chiefs.

"You want my autograph?" hissed Andy, his face just a trifle flushed from the drink he had taken. "I make a real fine X."

The feast followed a pattern familiar to Conan Lang. They were presented ceremonially to the tribe, having identified themselves as ancestors of four generations ago, thus making themselves kin to virtually all the tribe with their complicated lineage system, and also making refutation impossible since no one remembered that far back. They were seated with the chiefs, and ate the ritual feast rapidly. The food was good, and Conan Lang was interested in getting a good taste of the ricefruit plant, which was the basic food staple of the Oripesh.

After the eating came the drinking, and after the drinking the dancing. The Oripesh were not a musical people, and they had no drums. The men and the women danced apart from one another, each one doing an individual dance—which he owned, just as the men from Earth owned material property—to his own rhythm pattern. Conan Lang and Andy Irvin contented themselves with watching, not trusting themselves to improvise an authentic dance. They were aware that their conduct was at variance with the somewhat impulsive conduct usually attributed to ancestors in native folklore, but that was a chance they had to take. Conan was very conscious of one old chief who watched him closely with narrowed eyes.

Conan ignored him, enjoying the dancers. The Oripesh seemed to be a happy people, although short on material wealth. Conan Lang almost envied them as they danced—envied them for their simple lives and envied them their ability to enjoy it, an ability that civilized man had left by the wayside in his climb up the ladder. Climb—or descent? Conan Lang sometimes wondered.

Ren came over, his color high with the excitement of the dance. Great fires were burning now, and Conan noticed with surprise that it was night.

"That is Loe," Ren said, pointing. "My *am-ren*, my bride-to-be." His voice was filled with pride.

Conan Lang followed his gesture and saw the girl. Her name was a native word roughly translatable as *fawn*, and she was well named. Loe was a slim, very shy girl of really striking beauty. She danced with diffidence, looking into Ren's eyes. The two were obviously, almost painfully, in love—love being a part of the culture of the Oripesh. It was difficult to realize, sometimes, even after years of personal experience, that there were whole worlds of basically humanoid peoples where the very concept of romantic love did not exist. Conan Lang smiled. Loe was, if anything, a trifle *too* beautiful for his taste. Dancing there, with the yellow moon in her hair, moving gracefully with the leaping shadows from the crackling fires, she was ethereal, a fantasy, like a painting of a woman from another, unattainable century.

"We would give gifts to the chiefs," Conan Lang said finally. "Your Loe—she is very beautiful."

Ren smiled, quickly grateful, and summoned the chiefs. Conan Lang rose to greet them, signaling to Andy to break open the boxes. The chiefs watched intently. Conan Lang did not speak. He waited until Andy had opened both boxes and then pointed to them.

"They are yours, my brothers," he said.

The natives pressed forward. A chief picked the first object out of the box and stared at it in disbelief. The shadows flickered eerily and the night wind sighed through the village. He held the object up to the light and there was a gasp of astonishment.

The object was a ricefruit—a ricefruit the likes of which had never before been seen on Sirius Ten. It was round, fully a foot in diameter, and of a lush, ripe consistency. It made the potato-sized ricefruits of the Oripesh seem puny by comparison.

It was then that Conan Lang exploded his bombshell.

"We have come back to show you, our brothers, how to grow the great rice-fruit," he said. "You can grow them over and over again, *in the same field.* You will never have to move your village again."

The natives stared at him in wonder, moving back a little in fear.

"It cannot be done," a chief whispered. "The ricefruit devours the land—every year we must move or perish."

"That is over now," Conan Lang said. "We have come to show you the way."

The dancing had stopped. The natives waited, nervous, suddenly uncertain. The yellow moon watched through the trees. As though someone had flipped a switch, sound disappeared. There was silence. The great ricefruit was magic. They looked at the two men as though seeing them for the first time. This was not the way of the past, not the way of the ancestors. This was something completely *new* and they found themselves lost, without precedent for action. Ren alone smiled at them, and even he had fear in his eyes.

Conan Lang waited tensely. He must make no move; this was the crisis point. Andy stood at his side, very still, hardly breathing.

A native walked solemnly into the silence, carrying a young pig under his arm. Conan Lang watched him narrowly. The man was obviously a shaman, a witch doctor, and his trembling body and too-bright eyes were all too clear an indication of why he had been chosen for his role in the society.

With a swiftness of motion that was numbing, the shaman slit the pig's throat with a stone knife. At once he cut the body open. The blood stained his body with crimson. His long, thin hands poked into the entrails. He looked up, his eyes wild.

"They are not ancestors," he screamed, his voice high like an hysterical woman's. "They have come to do us evil!"

The very air was taut with tension.

"No," Conan Lang said loudly, keeping his voice clear and confident. "The *barath-tui*, the shaman, has been bewitched by sorcerers! Take care that you do not offend our ancestors!"

Conan Lang stood very still, fighting to keep the alarm off his face. He and Andy were helpless here, and he knew it. They were without weapons of any sort—the native loincloth being a poor place to conceal firearms. There was nothing they could do—they had miscalculated, moved too swiftly, and now they were paying the price.

"We are your brothers," he said into the ominous silence. "We are your fathers and your father's fathers. There are others who watch."

The flames leaped and danced in the stillness. An old man stepped forward. It was the chief that Conan had noticed watching him before.

"You say you are our brothers who have taken the long journey," the old chief said. "That is good. We would see you walk through the fire."

The wind sighed in the trees. Without a moment's hesitation, Conan Lang turned and walked swiftly toward the flames that crackled and hissed in the great stone fire pits.

There was nothing else in all the world except the flickering tongues of orange flame that licked nearer and nearer to his face. He saw the red, pulsing coals waiting beneath the twisted black branches in the fire and he closed his eyes. The heat singed his eyebrows and he could feel his hair shrivel and start to burn.

Conan Lang kept moving, and moved fast. He twisted a rigid clamp on his mind and refused to feel pain. He wrenched his mind out of his body, thinking as he had been trained to think, until it was as if his mind floated a thing apart, free in the air, looking down upon the body of Conan Lang walking through hell.

He knew that one of the attributes of the Oripesh ancestor gods was that they could walk through flame without injury—a fairly common myth pattern. He had known it before he left Earth. He should have been prepared, he knew that. But man was not perfect, which would have been a dangerous flaw had it not been his most valuable characteristic.

He saw that his legs were black and blistered and he smelled the suffocating smell of burning flesh. The smoke was in his head, in his lungs, everywhere, choking him. Some of the pain was coming through—

He was out. He felt Andy's hands beating out the rivulets of flame that clung to his body and he forced the clean, pure air of night into his sick lungs. The pain, the pain—

"Stick with it, Cone," Andy whispered in his ear. "Stick with it."

Conan Lang managed to open his eyes and stared blankly into a hot-red haze. The haze cleared and he was faintly surprised to find that he could still see. The natives were awestruck with fear—they had angered their gods and death was in the air. Conan Lang knew that the shaman who had denounced him would quite probably be dead of fear before the night was over—if he did not die before then of some less subtle malady. He had endangered the tribe without reason, and he would pay with his life.

Conan Lang kept his face expressionless. Inside, he was on fire. Water, he had to have water, cold water—

Ren came to him, his eyes filled with pain. "I am sorry, my brother," he whispered. "For my people, I am sorry."

"It is all right, Ren," Conan Lang heard his voice say steadily. "I am, of course, unharmed."

Conan Lang touched Andy's arm and moved across to the chiefs. He felt Andy standing behind him, ready to catch him, just in case. He could feel nothing in his feet—quite suddenly, he was convinced that he was standing on the charred stumps of his legs and he fought to keep from looking down to make sure he still had feet.

"You have doubted your brothers who have come far to help their people," he said quietly, looking directly into the eyes of the old chief who had sent him into the flames. "We are disappointed in our people—there are sorcerers at work among you, and they must be destroyed. We leave you now. If you anger your brothers again, the Oripesh shall cease to be."

He did not wait for an answer but turned and started away from the clearing, back through the village. Andy was at his side. Conan Lang set his teeth and moved at a steady pace. He must have no help until they were beyond the village; the natives must not suspect—

He walked on. The great yellow moon was high in the night sky, and there was the face of Loe with stars in her hair. The moon shuddered and burst into flame and he heard himself laughing. He bit his lips until the blood came and kept going, into the darkness, into nothing. The pain clawed at his body.

They were through the village. Something snapped in Conan Lang—the steel clamp that had carried him through a nightmare parted with a clean *ping*. There was emptiness, space. Conan Lang collapsed. He felt Andy's arm around him, holding him up.

"You'll have to carry me, kid," he whispered. "I can't walk at all."

Andy Irvin picked him up in his arms and set out through the night.

"It should have been me," he said in bitter self-reproach. "It should have been me."

Conan Lang closed his eyes and, at last, nothing mattered anymore, and there was only darkness.

A week later, Conan Lang stood in the dawn of Sirius Ten, watching the great double sun lift above the horizon and chase the shadows from the green field that they had carved out of the wilderness. He was still a very sick man, but Andy had pulled him through as best he could and now the star cruiser was coming in to pick him up and leave a replacement with the kid.

The fresh leaves of the ricefruit plants were shoulder high and the water in the irrigation trenches chuckled cleanly, waiting for the full fury of the sun. The tenuous, almost hesitant breeze crawled through the still air.

Conan Lang watched the green plants silently. The words of the dead *barath-tui*, the shaman, echoed in his brain. *They are not ancestors*, the man had screamed. *They have come to do us evil!*

They have come to do us evil. . . .

How could he have known—with only a pig and a stone knife? A crazy shaman working the discredited magic of divination—and he had been *right*. Coincidence? Yes, of course. There was no other way to look at it, no other *sane* way. Conan Lang smiled weakly. He remembered reading about the Snake Dance of the Hopi, long ago back on Earth. The Snake Dance had been a rain-making ceremonial, and invariably when the very early anthropologists had attended the dance they had gotten drenched on the way home. It was only coincidence and good timing, of course, but it was difficult to tell yourself that when the rain began to pour.

"Here she comes," said Andy Irvin.

There was a splitting whistle and then a soft hum as a small patrol ship settled down toward the field on her anti-gravs. She hung there in the dawn like a little silver fish seen through the glassite walls of a great aquarium, and Conan Lang could sense what he could not see—the massive bulk of the sleek star cruiser waiting out in space.

The patrol ship came down out of the sky and hovered a few feet off the ground. A man swung down out of the outlift and waved. Conan Lang recognized him as Julio Medina, who had been lifted out of another sector of Sirius Ten to come in and replace him with Andy. The ricefruit was green and fresh in the field and it hurt Conan to leave his job unfinished. There wasn't a great deal to do now until the check, of course, and Julio was a very competent and experienced man, but there was still so much that could go wrong, so much that you could never anticipate—

And he didn't want anything to happen to the kid.

"So long, Cone," Andy said, his voice very quiet. "And—thanks. I won't forget what you did."

Conan Lang leaned on Andy's arm and moved toward the ship. "I'll be back, Andy," he said, trying to keep the weight off his feet. "Hold the fort—I know it'll be in good hands."

Conan Lang shook hands with Julio and then Julio and Andy helped him into the outlift. He had time for a brief wave and a final glimpse of the green field under the fiery sun, and then he was inside the patrol ship. They had somehow rigged up a bunk for him in the cramped quarters, and he collapsed into it gratefully.

"Home, James," he whispered, trying not to think about what would happen if they could not save his legs.

Conan Lang closed his eyes and lay very still, feeling the ship pulse and surge as it carried him out into the dark sea from which he had come.

IV

The doctors saved his legs, but years were to pass before Conan Lang again set foot upon Earth. Space was vast and star cruisers comparatively few. In addition, star ships were fabulously expensive to operate—it was out of the question for a ship on a mission to make the long run from Sirius to Sol for the sake of one man. Conan Lang became the prize patient of the ship medics and he stayed with the star cruiser as it operated in the Sirius area.

A star cruiser on operations was never dull and there were books to read and reports to write. Conan Lang curbed his impatience and made the best of the situation. The local treatments applied by Andy had been effective enough so that the ship medics were able to regenerate his burned tissue, and it was only a question of time before he would be strong again.

The star cruiser worked efficiently and effectively in support of Administration units in the Sirius area, sliding through the blackness of space like some leviathan of the deep, and Conan Lang rested and made himself as useful as he could. He often went up into the control room and stood watching the visiplate that looked out upon the great emptiness of space. Somewhere, on a far shore of that mighty sea, was a tiny planet called Earth. There, the air was cool and fresh under the pines and the beauty of the world, once you got away from it and could see it in perspective, was fantastic. There were Rob and Kit, friendship and tears and laughter.

There was home.

While his body healed, Conan Lang lived on the star cruiser. There was plenty of time to think. Even for a race with a life span of almost two hundred years, the days and the weeks and the months can seem interminable. He asked himself all the old questions, examined all the old answers. Here he was, on a star ship light-years from home, his body burned, waiting to go back to Sirius Ten to change the life of a planet. What thin shreds of chance, what strange webs of history, had put him there? When you added up the life of Conan Lang, of all the Conan Langs, what did you get? Where was Earth going, that pebble that hurled its puny challenge at the infinite?

Sometimes, it was all hard to believe.

It had all started, he supposed, with cybernetics. Of course, cybernetics itself was but the logical outgrowth of a long cultural and technological trend. For centuries, man's ally, the machine, had helped him physically in his adjustment to his environment. What more natural than that it should one day help him mentally as well? There was really nothing sinister about thinking machines, except to a certain breed of perpetually gloomy poets who were unable to realize that values were never destroyed but were simply molded into new patterns in the evolution of culture. No, thinking machines were fine and comforting—for a while.

But with the dawn of space travel, man's comfortable, complacent progress toward a vague somewhere was suddenly knocked into a cocked hat. Man's horizons exploded to the rims of the universe with the perfection of the star drive— he was no longer living *on* a world but *in* an inhabited universe. His bickerings and absurdities and wars were seen as the petty things they were—and man in a few tremendous years emerged at last from adolescence.

Science gave to men a life span of nearly two hundred active years and gave him the key to forever. But there was a catch, a fearful catch. Man, who had had all he could do to survive the conflicts of local groups of his own species, was suddenly faced with the staggering prospect of living in an inhabited *universe*. He had known, of course, about the millions and millions of stars, about the infinity of planets, about the distant galaxies that swam like island universes through the dark seas of space. But he had known about them as figures on a page, as photographs, as dots of unwinking light in a telescope. They had been curiosities, a stimulus to the imagination. Now they were vital parts of his life, factors to be reckoned with in the struggle for existence. In the universe were incredible numbers of integers to be equated in the problem of survival—*and the mind of man could not even learn them all, much less form intelligent conclusions about future actions.*

And so, inevitably, man turned again to the machine. But this time there was a difference. The machine was the only instrument capable of handling the data—and man, in a million years, could not even check its most elementary conclusions. Man fed in the facts, the machine reached the conclusions, and man acted upon them—not through choice, but simply because he had no other guide he could trust.

Men operated the machines—but the machines operated men.

The science of cybernetics expanded by leaps and bounds. Men made machines to develop new machines. The great mechanical brains grew so complex that only a few men could even pretend to understand them. Looking at them, it was virtually impossible to believe that they had been born in the minds of men.

The machines did not interfere in the everyday routine of living—man would never submit to that, and in problems which he could understand he was still the best judge of his own happiness. It was in the larger problems, the problems of man's destiny in the universe in which he found himself, that the great brains were beyond value. For the machines could integrate trends, patterns, and complexes of the known worlds and go on from there to extrapolate into the unknown. The machines could, in very general terms, predict the outcome of any given set of circumstances. They could, in a very real sense, see into the future. They could see where Earth was headed.

And Earth was headed for disaster.

The machines were infallible. They dealt not with short-term probabilities, but with long-range certainties. And they stated flatly that, given the equation of the known universe, Earth would be destroyed in a matter of centuries. There was only one thing to do—man must change the equation.

It was difficult for man, so recently Earthbound, to really *think* and *act* in terms of an inhabited universe. But the machines showed conclusively that in as yet inaccessible galaxies life had evolved that was physically and mentally hostile to that of Earth. A collision of the two life-forms would come about within a thousand years, and a life-and-death struggle was inevitable. The facts were all too plain—Earth would lose and the human race would be exterminated.

Unless the equation could be changed.

It was a question of preparing the galaxy for combat. The struggle would be a long one, and factors of reserves, replacements, different cultural approaches to common problems, planets in varying stages of development, would be important. It was like a cosmic chess game, with worlds aligning themselves on a monstrous board. In battles of galactic dimensions, the outcome would be determined by centuries of preparation before contact was even made; it was not a romantic question of heroic spaceships and iron-jawed men of action, but rather one of the cultural, psychological, technological, and individual patterns which each side could bring to bear—patterns which were the outgrowths of millennia of slow evolution and development.

Earth was ready, or would be by the time contact came. But the rest of the galaxy—or at any rate as much of it as they had managed to explore—was not, and would not be. The human race was found somewhere on most of the star systems within the galaxy, but not one of them was as far advanced as were the men from Earth. That was why Earth had never been contacted from space—indeed, it was the only possible explanation, at least in retrospect. And the other galaxies, with their totally alien and forever nonunderstandable principles, were not interested in undeveloped cultures.

The problem thus became one of accelerating the cultural evolution of Earth's sister planets by means of diffusion, in order to build them up into an effective totality to combat the coming challenge. And it had to be done in such a manner that the natives of the planets were completely unaware that they were not the masters of their own destiny, since such a concept produced cultural stagnation and introduced corrupting elements into the planetary configurations. It had often been argued that Earth herself was in such a position, being controlled by the machines, but such was not the case—their choice had been a rational one, and they could abandon the machines at any time at their own risk.

Or so, at any rate, argued the thinkers of Earth.

The long months lengthened into years and, inactive though he was, Conan Lang spent his time well. It was good to have a chance to relax and think things through; it was good for the soul to stop midway in life and take stock. Almost, it was possible to make sense out of things, and the frantic rush to nowhere lost some of its shrieking senselessness.

Conan Lang smiled without humor. That was all very well for him, but what about the natives whose lives they were uprooting? Of course, they were human beings, too, and stood to lose as much as anyone in the long run—but they did not understand the problem, *could* not understand it. The plain truth was that they were being used—used for their own benefit as well as that of others, but used nonetheless.

It was true that primitive life was no bed of roses—it was not as if, Conan Lang assured himself, the men from Earth were slithering, serpent-like, into an idyllic Garden of Eden. All they were doing was accelerating the normal rate of change for a given planet. But this caused far-reaching changes in the culture as it existed—it threw some people to the dogs and elevated others to commanding positions. This was perhaps no more than was done by life itself, and possibly with better reason, but you couldn't tell yourself that when you had to face the eyes of a man who had gone from ruler to slave because of what you had done.

The real difficulty was that you couldn't *see* the threat. It was there all right—a menace besides which all the conflicts of the human race were as nothing. But it had always been difficult for men to work before the last possible moment, to prepare rather than just sit back and hope for the best. That man was working now as he had never worked before, in the face of an unseen threat from out of the stars, even to save his own existence, was a monument to his hard-won maturity. It would have been so easy, so pleasant, just to take it easy and enjoy a safe and comfortable life—and beyond question it would have meant the end of the human race.

Of one thing, Conan Lang was sure—whenever man stopped trying, stopped working and dreaming and reaching for impossible heights, whenever he settled back in complacency, on that day he shrunk to atrophied insignificance.

Sirius Ten had been a relatively easy project because of the planet-wide nature of its culture. Sirius Ten had only one huge land mass, and one great sea. The natives all shared basically the same life pattern, built around the cultivation of dry ricefruit, and the teams of the Applied Process Corps were faced with only one major problem rather than hundreds of them as was more often the case. It was true that certain peoples who lived on the shores of the sea, together with one island group, had a variant culture based on fishing, but these were insignificant numerically and could for practical purposes be ignored.

The dry ricefruit was grown by a cutting and burning method, under which a field gave a good yield only once before the land was exhausted and the people had to move on. Under these conditions, individual ownership of land never developed, and there were no inequalities of wealth to speak of. The joint families worked different fields every year, and since there was no market for a surplus there was no effort made to cultivate more land than was really needed.

The Oripesh natives of Sirius Ten had a well-developed cult of ancestor worship, thinking of their dead as always watching over them and guiding their steps. Since whatever the ancestors did automatically had the sanction of tradition behind it, it was through them that the Corps had decided to work—it being simply a question of palming off Corps Agents as ancestors come back from their dwelling place in the mountains to help their people. With careful preparations and experienced men, this had not proved overly difficult—but there were always miscalculations, accidents. Men were not like chemicals, and they did not always react as they were supposed to react. There was always an individual variable to be considered. That was why if a Corps Agent lived long enough to retire you knew both that he knew his stuff and that he had had more than his share of plain old-fashioned luck.

Sirius Ten had to be shifted from Stage Four to Stage Five. This was a staggering change in economics, social structure, and technology—one that had taken men on Earth many centuries to accomplish. The men of the Applied Process Corps had to do it in a matter of a few years. And so they set out, armed with a variety of ricefruit that grew well in marshy land and a sound knowledge of irrigation.

With such a lever they could move a world.

It was three years to the day when Conan Lang returned to Sirius Ten. The patrol ship came in on her anti-gravs and he waited eagerly for the outlift shaft to open. His heart was pounding in his chest and his lips were dry—it was almost like coming home again.

He swung his newly strong body into the outlift and came out of it in the green field he had planted so long ago. He took a deep breath of the familiar humid air and grinned broadly at the hot, burning sun over his head. It *was* good to be back—back at a place like so many other places he had known, places that were as close to a home as any he could ever have without Kit. The breeze whispered softly through the green ricefruit and he waved at Julio who came running across the field to meet him. These were, he knew, his kind of people—and he had missed Andy all these years.

"Hey there, Julio!" he laughed, shaking Medina's hand. "How goes it?"

"Pretty good, Conan," Julio said quietly. "Pretty good."

"The kid—how's the kid?"

"Andy is dead," said Julio Medina.

Conan Lang stood stock-still while an iron fist smacked into his stomach with cold, monotonous precision. Andy dead. It could not be, *could not be*. There had been no word, nothing. He clenched his fists. It couldn't be true.

But it was. He knew that with ice cold certainty.

"It just happened the other day, Conan," Julio said. "He was a fine boy."

Conan Lang couldn't speak. *The whole planet*, his mind tortured him. *The whole stinking planet isn't worth Andy's life.*

"It was an accident," Julio said, his voice carefully matter-of-fact. "Warfare has sprung up between the rival villages like we figured. Andy was out after information and he got between them—he was hit by mistake with a spear. He never had a chance, but he managed to walk away and get back here before he died. The Oripesh don't suspect that he wasn't a god and could die just like anyone else. He saved the rest of us by coming back here—that's something."

"Yeah," Conan Lang said bitterly, "that's something."

"I buried him here in the field," Julio Medina went on. "I thought he'd like that. He . . . said good-bye to you, Conan."

It had been a long time since Conan Lang had had tears in his eyes. He turned without a word and walked away, across the green field and into the hut where he could be alone.

V

From that time on, by unspoken mutual consent, the two men never again mentioned the kid's name. They gave him the best possible write-up in their reports, and that was all that they could ever do for Andy Irvin.

"I think we've about done it here, Conan," Julio told him. "I'd like to have you make your own check and see if you come up with the same stuff I did. There's a lull in the raiding right now—the natives are worried because that spear hit an ancestor by mistake and they're pretty well occupied with rituals designed to make us feel better about the whole thing. You shouldn't have any trouble, and that ought to about wind things up."

Conan Lang nodded. "It'll be good to get home again, eh Julio?"

"Yes, you know that—and for you it should be for keeps."

Conan Lang raised his eyebrows.

"It's no secret that you're due to be kicked upstairs," Julio said. "I rather think this is your last field job."

"Well, it's a nice theory anyhow."

"You remember all us old men out here in the stars, the slave labor of the Process Corps. Bring us all home, Conan, and we'll sit around in the shade and drink cold wine and fish and tell lies to each other."

"Consider it done," said Conan Lang. "And I'll give you all some more medals."

"I've got medals."

"Can't have too many medals, Julio. They're good for what ails you."

"They're not good for what ails *me*," said Julio Medina.

Conan Lang smiled and fired up his pipe. *The kid*, his mind whispered. *The kid liked that pipe.* He thrust the thought from his mind. A man had to take death in his stride out here, he told himself. Even when it was a kid who reminded you of yourself a million years ago—

A million years ago.

"I'll start in tomorrow," Conan Lang said, puffing on his pipe. "Do you know Ren, Julio?"

"The chief's son? Yes."

"How did he come out?"

"Not well, Conan. He lost his woman, Loe, to one of the men we made wealthy; he has not been the same since."

"We're great people, Julio."

"Yes."

Conan Lang was silent then and the two men stood together in the warm evening air, watching the great double sun float slowly down below the horizon as the long black shadows came marching up from the far edge of the world.

Next morning, Conan Lang was off with the dawn on his final check. He pretty well knew what he would find—Julio Medina was an experienced hand and his information was reliable. But it was always a shock when you saw it for yourself. You never got used to it. To think that such a tiny, seemingly insignificant thing could change a planet beyond recognition. A ricefruit—

It was already hot when he passed the native fields. Their ricefruit plants were tall and healthy, and their irrigation channels well constructed. He shook his head and walked on to the native village.

Where the open, crude, friendly village had stood there was a great log wall.

In front of the wall was a series of deep and ugly-looking moats. Behind the wall, he could see the tops of sturdy wooden buildings, a far cry from the huts of only a few short years ago. Conan Lang made no attempt at concealment but walked openly up to the moats and crossed them on a log bridge. He stopped outside the closed gate.

"You will remember me who walked through the flames," he said loudly in the Oripesh tongue. "You will open the gate for your brother as he would visit you."

For a moment nothing happened, and then the gate swung open. Conan Lang entered the village.

The native guard eyed him with suspicion, but he kept his distance. Conan Lang noticed that he had a bow by the log wall. There was nothing like constant warfare for the production of new weapons, he reflected. Civilization was bringing its blessings to the Oripesh with leaps and bounds.

Conan Lang walked through the village unmolested, taking rapid mental notes. He saw storehouses for ricefruit and observed slaves being marched off to work in the fields. The houses in the village were strong and comfortable, but there was a tense air in the village, a feeling of strain. Conan Lang approached a native and stopped him.

"Brother," he said, "I would see your chiefs. Where are they?"

The native looked at him warily. "The Oripesh have no chiefs," he said. "Our king is in council."

Conan Lang nodded, a sick feeling inside him. "It is well," he said. "Ren—I would see him."

The native jerked his thumb contemptuously toward the back of the village. "He is there," he said. "Outside."

Conan Lang moved through the village, watching, missing nothing. He went all the way through and came out through the back wall. There, the old-style native huts baked in squalor under the blazing sun. There was no log wall around them, although they were inside the moat system. A pig rooted around for garbage between the huts.

"Slums," Conan Lang said to himself.

He walked among the huts, ignoring the fearful, suspicious eyes of the natives. He found Ren preparing to go out into the fields. The chief's son was thin. He looked tired and his eyes were dull. He saw Conan and said nothing.

"Hello, Ren," said Conan Lang.

The native just looked at him.

Conan Lang tried to think of something to say. He knew what had happened—the chiefs and their sons had been so busy with ritual work for the tribe that they had lagged behind in the cultivation of the new ricefruit. They had stuck to the old ways too long and their people had passed them by.

"I can help you, my brother," Conan Lang said softly. "It is not too late."

Ren said nothing.

"I will help you with a field of your own," said Conan Lang. "Will you let me help you?"

The native looked at him and there was naked hate in his eyes. "You said you were my friend," he said. Without another word, he turned and left. He did not look back.

Conan Lang wiped the sweat from his forehead and went on with his work. The sensitive part of his mind retreated back into a dark, insulated corner and he let his training take over. He moved along, asking questions, watching, taking mental notes.

A little thing, he thought.

A new kind of plant.

A week later, Conan Lang had completed his check. He sat by the evening cook fire with Julio, smoking his pipe, watching the shadows in the field.

"Well, we did a good job," he said. "It's awful."

"It would have come without us," Julio reminded him. "It does no good to brood about it. It is tough, sometimes, but it is a small price to pay for survival."

"Yes," said Conan Lang. "Sure."

"Your results check out with mine?"

"Mostly. It's the same old story, Julio."

Conan Lang puffed slowly on his pipe, reconstructing what had happened. The new ricefruit had made it valuable for a family to hang on to one piece of land that could be used over and over again. But only a limited amount of the land could be used, because of natural factors like the presence or absence of available water. The families that had not taken the plunge right away were virtually excluded, and the society was divided into the landed and the landless. The landless gradually had to move farther and farther from the main village to find land upon which to grow the older type of ricefruit—sometimes their fields were so far away that they could not make the round trip in a single day. And they could not get too far away and start over, because of the tribal warfare that had broken out between villages now that valuable stores of ricefruit were there for the taking. The old joint family co-operation broke down, and slaves became economically feasible.

Now that the village need not be periodically moved, it too became valuable and so was strongly fortified for defense. One old chief, grown powerful with fields of the staple ricefruit, set himself up as a king and the other chiefs went to work in his fields.

Of course, Sirius Ten was still in transition. While the old patterns were being destroyed, new ones, less obvious to the untrained eye, were taking their place. Disintegration and reintegration marched hand in hand, but it would be tough on the natives for a while. Process Corps techniques had speeded up the action almost beyond belief, but from here on in the Oripesh were on their own. They would go on and on in their individual development—although no two peoples ever went through exactly the same stages at the same time, it was possible to predict a general planet-wide trend. The Oripesh would one day learn to write, since they already had a crude pictographic system for ritual use. When the contact finally came from the hostile stars in the future, what histories would they have written? Who would they remember, what would they forget? Would there be any twisted legend or myth left that recalled the long-ago time when the gods had come out of the mountains to change the lives of their people?

That was the way to look at it. Conan Lang tapped out his pipe on a rock. Just look at it like a problem, a textbook example. Forget about the people, the individuals you could not help, the lives you had made and the lives you had destroyed. Turn off that part of your mind and think in terms of the long-range good.

Or try to.

"We're all through here, Julio," Conan Lang said. "We can head for home now."

"Yes," said Julio Medina. "It has been a long time."

The two men sat silently in the darkness, each thinking his own thoughts, watching the yellow moon sail through silver stars.

After the patrol ship had been signaled, there was nothing to do but wait until their pickup could be coordinated with the time schedules of the other Corps men and the operational schedule of the star cruiser. Conan Lang busied himself with his reports while Julio sprawled in the shade and devised intricate and impossible card games with a battered deck that was old enough to be in itself of anthropological interest.

Conan Lang was playing a game, too. He played it with his mind and he was a somewhat unwilling participant. His mind had played the game before and he was tired of it, but there was nothing he could do about it. There wasn't any button that would turn his mind off, and while it was on it played games.

It was engaged in putting two and two together.

This was not in itself uncommon, although it was not as widespread as some people fondly imagined it to be. But Conan Lang played the game where others did not even see one, much less a set of twos with a relationship between them. There is nothing so hard to see as what is termed obvious after the fact. Conan Lang's mind had played with the obvious all his life; it would not let well enough alone. He didn't like it, there were times when he would have preferred to junk it all and go fishing without a thought in his head, but he was stuck with it. When his mind wanted to play the game, it played and that was that.

While he waited for the patrol ship, his mind was playing with a set of factors. There was the history of Earth, taken as a vast overall sequence. There were thinking machines, atomic power, and the field techniques of the Process Corps. There was the fact that Earth had no record of ever having been contacted by another world—they had always done the contacting themselves. There was the new principle that Admiral White had spoken to him about, the integration-acceleration factor for correlating data. There was the incredible, explosive energy of man that had hurled him light-years into space. There was his defiant heart that could tackle the prodigious job of reshaping a galaxy when the chips were down.

Conan Lang put two and two together, and he did not get four. He got five.

He didn't know the answers yet, but he knew enough to formulate the right questions. From past experience, he knew that that was the toughest part of the game. Incorrect answers were usually the products of off-center questions. Once you had the right question, the rest was a matter of time.

The patrol ship came for them finally, and Conan Lang and Julio Medina walked across the soil of Sirius Ten for the last time. They crossed the field where the green plants grew, and neither tried to say what was in his heart. Three had come and only two could leave. Andy Irvin had lived and worked and dreamed only to fall on an alien planet light-years away from earth that could have been his. He was part of the price that was exacted for survival—and he was also a kid with stars in his eyes who had gotten a rotten, senseless break.

After the patrol ship had gone, the green leaves of the ricefruit plants stretched hungrily up toward the flaming sun. The clean water chuckled along the irrigation trenches, feeding the roots in the field. Softly, as though sad with all the memories it carried, the lonesome breeze whispered through the empty hut that had housed the men from Earth.

VI

Through the trackless depths of interstellar space the star cruiser rode on the power from her atomics. The hum that filled the ship was a good sound, and she seemed to quiver with pride and impatience. It did make a difference which way you were going in space, and the ship was going home.

Conan Lang paced through the long white corridors and walked around the afterhold where the brown sacks of ricefruit had been. He read in the library and joked with the medics who had salvaged his burned body. And, always ahead of him, swimming in the great emptiness of space, were the faces of Kit and of his son, waiting for him, calling him home again.

Rob must have grown a lot, he thought. Soon, he wouldn't be a boy any longer—he would be a man, taking his place in the world. Conan remembered his son's voice from a thousand quiet talks in the cool air of evening, his quick, eager eyes—

Like Andy's.

"*Dad, when I grow up can I be like you? Can I be an Agent and ride on the ships to other worlds and have a uniform and everything?*"

What could you tell your son now that you had lived so long and were supposed to know so much? That life in the Process Corps filled a man with things that were perhaps better unknown? That the star trails were cold and lonely? That there were easier, more comfortable lives? All that was true; all the men who rode the ships knew it. But they knew, too, that for them this was the only life worth living.

The time passed slowly. Conan Lang was impatient to see his family again, anxious to get home. But his mind gave him no rest. There were things he had to know, things he *would* know before he went home to stay.

Conan Lang had the right questions now. He had the right questions, and he knew where the answers were hidden.

Fritz Gottleib.

The star cruiser had hardly touched Earth again at Space One before Conan Lang was outside on the duralloy tarmac. Since the movements of the star ships were at all times top-secret matters, there was no one at the port to greet him and for once Conan was glad to have a few extra hours to himself. Admiral White wouldn't expect him to check in until tomorrow anyway, and before he saw Kit he wanted to get things straight once and for all.

The friendly sun of Earth warmed him gently as he hurried across the tarmac and the air felt cool and fresh. He helped himself to an official bullet, rose into the blue sky, and jetted eastward over the city. His brain was seething and he felt cold sweat in the palms of his hands. What was it that Gottleib had said to him on that long-ago day?

"*Sometimes it is best not to know the answers to one's questions, Dr. Lang.*"

Well, he was going to know the answers anyhow. All of them. He landed the bullet in the space adjoining the cybernetics building and hurried inside, flashing his identification as he went. He stopped at a switchboard and showed his priority credentials.

"Call the Nest, please," he told the operator. "Tell Dr. Gottleib that Conan Lang is down here and would like to see him."

The operator nodded and spoke into the intercom. There was a moment's delay, and then he took his earphones off and smiled at Conan Lang.

"Go right on up, Dr. Lang," the operator said. "Dr. Gottleib is expecting you."

Conan Lang controlled his astonishment and went up the lift and down the long white corridors. *Expecting* him? But that was impossible. No one even knew the star cruiser was coming back, much less that he was coming here to the Nest. Impossible—

All around him in the great building he felt the gigantic mechanical brain with its millions of circuits and flashing tubes. The brain crowded him, pressed him down until he felt tiny and insignificant. It hummed and buzzed through the great shielded walls.

Laughing at him.

Conan Lang pushed past the attendants and security men and opened the door of the Nest. He moved into the small, dark room and paused to allow his eyes to become accustomed to the dim light. The room was silent. Gradually, the shadow behind the desk took form and he found himself looking into the arctic eyes of Fritz Gottleib.

"Dr. Lang," he hissed softly. "Welcome to the Buzzard's Nest."

The man had not changed; he was timeless, eternal. He was still dressed in black and it might have been minutes ago instead of years when Conan Lang had last seen him. His black eyebrows slashed across his white face and his long-fingered hands were bent slightly like claws upon his desk.

"How did you know I was coming here?" Now that he was face-to-face with Gottleib, Conan Lang felt suddenly uncertain, unsure of himself.

"I know many things, Dr. Lang," Fritz Gottleib said sibilantly. "Had I cared to, I could have told you ten years ago the exact date, within a day or so, upon which we would have this meeting. I could even have told you what you would say when you came through the door, and what you are going to say five minutes from now."

Conan Lang just stared at him, feeling like an absurd little child who had presumed to wrestle a gorilla. His mind recoiled from the strange man before him and he knew at last that he knew nothing.

"I do not waste words, Dr. Lang," Gottleib said, his eyes cold and unmoving in his head. "You will remember that when we last met you said you wanted to ask some questions of the machine. Do you remember what I said, Dr. Lang?"

Conan Lang thought back across the years. *"Perhaps one day, Dr. Lang,"* Gottleib had said. *"When you are old like me."*

"Yes," said Conan Lang. "Yes, I remember."

"You were not ready then," Dr. Gottleib said, his white face ghostly in the dim light. "You could not even have framed the right questions, at least not all of them."

Conan Lang was silent. How much *did* Gottleib know? Was there anything he *didn't* know?

"You are old enough now," said Fritz Gottleib.

He turned a switch and the surface of his desk glowed with dull red light. His face, reflected in the flamelike glow, was unearthly. His cold eyes looked out of hell. He rose to his feet, seeming to loom larger than life, filling the room. Moving without a sound, he left the room, and the door clicked shut behind him.

Conan Lang was alone in the red room. His heart hammered in his throat and his lips were dry. He clenched his fists and swallowed hard. Alone—

Alone with the great machine.

Conan Lang steadied himself. Purposefully, he made himself go through the prosaic, regular motions of lighting up his pipe. The tobacco was healthily full-bodied and fragrant and it helped to relax him. He smoked slowly, taking his time.

The red glow from the desk filled the room with the color of unreality. Crimson shadows seemed to crouch in the corners with an impossible life of their own. But was anything impossible, here? Conan Lang felt the pulse of the great machine around him and wondered.

Trying to shake off a persistent feeling of dreamlike unreality, Conan Lang moved around and sat down behind Gottleib's desk. The red panel was a maze of switches which were used to integrate it with technical panels in other sections of the building. In the center of the panel was a keyboard on an open circuit to the machine and set into the desk was a clear square like a very fine telescreen. Conan Lang noticed that there was nothing on Gottleib's desk that was not directly connected with the machine—no curios, no pictures, no paperweights, not a single one of the many odds and ends most men picked up for their desks during a long lifetime. The whole room was frightening in its very impersonality, as though every human emotion had been beaten out of it long ago and the room had been insulated against its return.

The machines never slept and the circuits were open. Conan Lang had only to ask and any question that could be answered would be answered. The red glow in the room reminded him of the fire and he shuddered a little in spite of himself. Had that really been over three years ago? How much had he learned in those three years when he had seen the Oripesh change before his eyes and had had time for once to really think his life through? How much did he still have to learn?

Conan Lang took a long pull on his pipe and set the desk panel for manual type questioning and visual screen reception. He hesitated a moment, almost afraid of the machine at his disposal. He didn't *want* to know, he suddenly realized. It wasn't like that. It was rather that he *had* to know.

Framing his words carefully, Conan Lang typed out the question that had been haunting him for years:

IS THE EARTH ITSELF THE SUBJECT OF PROCESS MANIPULATION?

He waited nervously, sure of the answer, but fearful of it nevertheless. There was a faint, all but inaudible, hum from the machine and Conan Lang could almost feel the circuits closing in the great walls around him. The air was filled with tension. There was a brief click and one word etched itself blackly on the clear screen:

YES.

Conan Lang leaned forward, sure of himself now, and typed out another question:

HOW LONG HAS THE EARTH BEEN MANIPULATED AND HAS THIS CONTROL BEEN FOR GOOD OR EVIL?

The machine hummed and answered at once:

THE EARTH HAS BEEN GUIDED SINCE EARTH YEAR NINETEEN HUN-DRED A.D. *THE SECOND PART OF YOUR QUESTION IS MEANINGLESS.*

Conan Lang hesitated, staggered in spite of himself by the information he was getting. Then he typed rapidly:
WITH REFERENCE TO GOOD, EQUATE SURVIVAL OF THE HUMAN RACE.
The screen clouded, cleared, and the words formed:
THE CONTROL HAS BEEN FOR GOOD.
Conan Lang's breathing was shallow now. He typed tensely:
HAS THIS CONTROL COME FROM WITHIN THIS GALAXY? IF SO, WHERE? IS THERE USUALLY AN AGENT OTHER THAN EARTH'S IN CHARGE OF THIS MACHINE?
The hum of the machine filled the bloodred room and the screen framed the answers:
THE CONTROL HAS COME FROM WITHIN THE GALAXY. THE SOURCE IS A WORLD KNOWN AS RERMA, CIRCLING A STAR ON THE EDGE OF THE GALAXY WHICH IS UNKNOWN TO EARTH. THE MAN KNOWN AS GOTTLEIB IS A RERMAN AGENT.
Conan Lang's pipe had been forgotten and gone out. He put it down and licked his dry lips. So far so good. But the one prime, all-important question had not yet been asked. He asked it:
IF THE PLAN IS FOLLOWED, WHAT WILL BE THE FINAL OUTCOME WITH RESPECT TO RERMA AND THE EARTH?
The machine hummed again in the red glow and the answer came swiftly, with a glorious, mute tragedy untold between its naked lines:
RERMA WILL BE DESTROYED. THE EARTH WILL SURVIVE IF THE PLAN IS CAREFULLY FOLLOWED.
Conan Lang felt tears in his eyes and he was unashamed. With time forgotten now, he leaned forward, asking questions, reading replies, as the terrible, wonderful story unfolded.

Far out on the edge of the galaxy, the ancient planet of Rerma circled her yellow sun. Life had evolved early on Rerma—had evolved early and developed fast. While the other humanoid peoples of the galaxy were living in caves, the Rerma were building a great civilization. When Earth forged its first metal sword, the Rerma split the atom.
Rerma was a world of science—true science. Science had eliminated war and turned the planet into a paradise. Literature and the arts flourished hand in hand with scientific progress, and scientists worked surrounded by cool gardens in which graceful fountains splashed and chuckled in the sun. Every man was free to develop himself as an individual and no man bent his head to any other man.
The Rerma were the human race in full flower.
But the Rerma were few, and they were not a warlike people. It was not that they would not fight in an emergency, but simply that they could not possibly win an extended encounter. Their minds didn't work that way. The Rerma had evolved to a point where they were too specialized, too well-adjusted to their environment.
And their environment changed.
It was only a question of time until the Rerma asked the right questions of their thinking machines and came up with the knowledge that their world, situated on the edge of the galaxy, was directly in the path of a coming cultural collision between two star systems. The Rerma fed in the data over and over again, and each time the great machines came up with the same answer.

Rerma would be destroyed.

It was too late for the equation to be changed with respect to Rerma—she had gone too far and was unfortunately located. But for the rest of the human race, scattered on the far-flung worlds that marched along the star trails, there was a chance. There was time for the equation to be changed for them—if only someone could be found to change it! For the Rerma had the knowledge, but they had neither the manpower nor the driving, defiant spirit to do the job themselves. They were capable of making heroic decisions and sticking by them, but the task of remolding a star system was not for them. That was a job for a young race, a proud and unconquerable race. That was a job for the men of Earth.

The ships of the Rerma found Earth in the earth year 1900. They knew that in order for their plan to succeed the Rerma must stand and fight on that distant day when galaxies collided, for their power was not negligible despite their lack of know-how for a long-range combat. They must stand and fight and be destroyed—the plan, the equation, was that finely balanced. Earth was the only other planet they found that was sufficiently advanced to work with, and it was imperative that Earth should not know that she was being manipulated. She must not suspect that her plans were not her own, for a young race with its pride wounded is a dubious ally and an ineffective fighting mechanism.

The Rerma set to work—willing even to die for a future they had already lived. The scientists of Rerma came secretly to Earth, and behind them, light-years away, their crystal fountains still sparkled sadly in the sun.

Rerma would be destroyed—but humanity would not die.

Conan Lang sat alone in the red room, talking to a machine. It was all clear enough, even obvious, once you knew the facts. Either there were no advanced races in the galaxy, which would account for Earth having no record of any contact—or else the Earth *had* been contacted secretly, been manipulated by the very techniques that she herself was later to use on undeveloped worlds.

He looked back on history. Such profound and important changes as the Neolithic food revolution and the steam engine had been produced by Earth alone, making her the most advanced planet in the galaxy except for the Rerma. Earth had a tradition of technological skill behind her, and she was young and pliable. The Rerma came—and the so-called world wars had followed. Why? Not to avenge the honor of insulted royalty, not because of fanatics, not because of conflicting creeds—but in a very real sense to save the world. The world wars had been fought to produce atomic power.

After 1900, the development of Earth had snowballed in a fantastic manner. The atom was liberated and man flashed upward to other planets of the solar system. Just as Conan Lang himself had worked through the ancestor gods of the Oripesh to bring about sweeping changes on Sirius Ten, the Rerma had worked through one of the gods of the Earthmen—the machine.

Cybernetics.

Man swept out to the stars, and the great thinking machines inevitably confronted them with the menace from beyond that drew nearer with each passing year. Young and proud, the men of Earth accepted the most astounding challenge ever hurled—they set out to reshape a galaxy to give their children and their children's children a chance for life.

And always, behind the scenes, beneath the headlines, were the ancient Rerma. They subtly directed and hinted and helped. With a selflessness unmatched in the universe, these representatives of a human race that had matured too far prepared Earth for galactic leadership—and themselves for death on the edge of the galaxy. They had unified Earth and pushed and prodded her along the road to survival.

When the Rerma could have fled and purchased extra time for themselves, they chose instead—these peace-loving people—to fight for another chance for man.

Conan Lang looked up, startled, to find the black figure of Fritz Gottleib standing by his side. He looked old, very old, in the bloodred light and Conan Lang looked at him with new understanding. Gottleib's impatience with others and the vast, empty loneliness in those strange eyes—all that was meaningful now. What a life that man had led on Earth, Conan Lang thought with wonder. Alone, wanting friendship and understanding—and having always to discourage close personal contacts, having always to fight his lonely battle alone in a sterile little room, knowing that the very men he had dedicated his life to help laughed behind his back and compared him to a bird of prey.

"I've been a fool, sir," Conan Lang said, getting to his feet. "We've all been fools."

Fritz Gottleib sat down again behind his desk and turned the machine off. The red glow vanished and they were left in the semidarkness.

"Not fools, Dr. Lang," he said. "It was necessary for you to feel as you did. The feelings of one old man—what are they worth in this game we are playing? We must set our sights high, Dr. Lang."

Conan Lang waited in the shadows, thinking, watching the man who sat across from him as though seeing him for the first time. His mind was still groping, trying to assimilate all he had learned. It was a lot to swallow in a few short hours, even when you were prepared for it beforehand by guesswork and conjecture. There were still questions, of course, many questions. He knew that he still had much to learn.

"Why me?" Conan Lang asked finally. "Why have I been told all this? Am I the only one who knows?"

Fritz Gottleib shook his head, his face ghost-white in the darkened room. "There are others who know," he said sibilantly. "Your superior officer, Nelson White, has known for years of course. You were told because you have been selected to take over his command when he retires. If you are willing, you will work very closely with him here on Earth for the next five years, and then you will be in charge."

"Will I . . . leave Earth again?"

"Not for a long time, Dr. Lang. The integration-acceleration principle will keep you busy—we are in effect lifting Earth another stage and the results will be far-reaching. But you will be home, Dr. Lang—home with your family and your people.

"That is all, Dr. Lang," Gottleib hissed.

Conan Lang hesitated. "I'll do my level best," he said finally. "Good-bye, sir . . . I'll see you again."

Conan Lang put out his hand to the man he had called the Buzzard and Gottleib shook it with a firm, powerful grip.

"Good-bye, Conan," Fritz Gottleib said softly.

Conan Lang turned and walked from the dark room, leaving the man from Rerma sitting alone in the shadows of the Nest.

The little bullet rose vertically on her copter blades through the evening sky, hovered a moment in the cool air under the frosty stars, and then flashed off on her jets into the west. Conan Lang set the controls and leaned back in the seat, at peace with himself at last. There *was* meaning to it all, there was a purpose—and Andy and all the others like him on the far trails had not sacrificed their lives for nothing.

Conan Lang breathed the clean air of Earth and smiled happily. Ahead of him, waiting for him, were Kit and Rob, and he would never have to leave them again. He opened the lateral ports and let the wind hurl itself at his face.

Richard A. Lupoff

Richard A. Lupoff (1935–) is an editor, critic, historian of popular culture, and writer—the author of twenty SF and fantasy novels and more than a hundred short stories. The extraordinary scope of his career encompasses novels and stories in every sub-genre of science fiction and fantasy, as well as a series of mystery novels. Notable works include *Sword of the Demon* (1977), a fantastic novel based on Japanese mythology; *Space War Blues* (1978), his experimental SF novel of race war in space, of which "Sail the Tide of Mourning" became a segment; and *Lovecraft's Book* (1985), a fiction adventure featuring H. P. Lovecraft, detective. Indeed, one of the hallmarks of his career is that no two Lupoff works are alike. The result is, as *The Encyclopedia of Science Fiction* says, "it is at times difficult, in spite of his clear and abundant intelligence, to identify a unique Richard A. Lupoff voice."

This story has resonances with the work of Cordwainer Smith, interesting echoes that give some evidence of the inner conversations among texts that are the very nature of a literary genre. The link between mysteries of the psyche and space travel is an enduring one in genre science fiction.

SAIL THE TIDE OF MOURNING

Nurundere, captain, ordered his lighter to be hauled from the storage deck of *Djanggawul* and fitted for use of Jiritzu. Sky heroes bent their efforts, sweat glistening on black skin, dirt of labor staining white duck trousers and grip-soled shoes.

Much thought was given to their work and the reasons for it although little was said of the matter. The people of Yurakosi were not given greatly to speech: a taciturnity, self-containment, was part of the heritage of their race, from the days of their desert isolation in the heartland of Australia, O'Earth.

They alone of the scattered children of Sol carried the gene that let them sail the membrane ships. They alone carried in their skin the pigment that filtered out the deadly radiation of the tracks between the stars, that permitted them to clamber up masts and through rigging as had their ancestors on the pacific waters of O'Earth centuries before, while spacemen of other breeds clumped and heaved about in their massive vacuum armor.

The brilliant light of the multiple star Yirrkalla wheeled overhead; *Djanggawul* had completed her great tack and pointed her figureheaded prow toward home, toward Yurakosi, bearing the melancholy tale of her voyage to N'Jaja and N'Ala and the death of a passenger, Ham Tamdje of N'Jaja, at the hands of the sky hero Jiritzu.

Djanggawul bore yet the scars of the attempt by surner meat to seize control of the membrane ship and force from her crew the secret of their ability to live unsuited in space. At N'Ala she had shuttled the surviving surners to the orbiting Port Corley, along with the bodies of those killed in the mutiny.

And now, passing the great tack at Yirrkalla, *Djanggawul* heeled beneath the titanic solar wind that would fill all sails that bellied out from the rows of masts on her three flat decks. With each moment the ship gained momentum. Under the careful piloting of her first officer Uraroju she would sail to Yurakosi on this momentum and on the force of the interstellar winds she encountered on her great arcing course. There would be no need to start her auxiliary engines, to annihilate any of the precious rod of collapsed matter that hung suspended through the long axis of *Djanggawul*, where it provided the artificial gravity for the ship.

Sky heroes swarmed the storage deck of the ship, readying Nurundere's lighter for Jiritzu. They fitted the tiny ship with food concentrate, tested her recyclers, tried her hinged mast fittings, and clamped the masts to the hull of the lighter in anticipation of her catapulting from the deck of *Djanggawul*.

When the lighter was fully prepared, the sky hero Baime went to *Djanggawul*'s bridge to inform Nurundere and Uraroju. Others in the work party hauled the lighter from its place in the storage deck, refixed the now vacant moorings that had held the lighter, and worked the tiny ship through a great cargo hatch onto the main deck of *Djanggawul*.

High above the deck Jiritzu stood balanced lightly on a spar near the top of a mainmast. He was dressed like any sky hero of the crew of *Djanggawul*, in white trousers and canvas shoes, black knitted cap and turtleneck sweater, the costume declared by Yurakosi tradition to have been the costume of the sky heroes' ancestors on O'Earth.

A tiny radio had been implanted behind one ear, and strapped to his thigh was a close-air generator. The oxygen-rich mixture that it slowly emitted clung to Jiritzu, providing him with the air he needed for breath, insulating him from the extreme temperatures of space, providing an invisible pressure suit that protected him from the vacuum all around.

He watched the cargo hatch roll slowly back onto the deck beneath him, the one of *Djanggawul*'s three identical outer decks most easily accessible from the lighter's storage place, and watched his fellow sky heroes haul the lighter onto the deck. He kept his radio turned off, and by tacit agreement no man or woman of *Djanggawul*'s crew, not even Jiritzu's kunapi half Dua, approached the mast he had climbed or made any sign of knowing of his presence.

Nurundere himself strode from the bridge of his ship to inspect the lighter, now standing empty on the deck. Jiritzu could tell him easily, not merely by his distinctive cap of white with its wide black band, but by his pale skin, the protective pigmentation of the Yurakosi almost totally faded now, whited out by the passing years and long exposure to the radiation of the naked stars.

Soon Nurundere would have to return to Yurakosi himself, give himself over to the life of a ground squirmer, crawl with the small children and the old men and women of Yurakosi, the only inhabitants of the planet whose able sons and daughters were desperately needed to sail the membrane ships between the stars.

Not so Jiritzu.

Again and again his mind flashed to the terrible scene inside the passenger tank of *Djanggawul*, the moments when the surner meat, the passengers whose payments financed the flights of the membrane ships and filled the coffers of the sky heroes' home planet, had shown firearms—an act unknown on the peaceful, neutral ships—and had briefly imprisoned much of the crew.

Again Jiritzu relived the horror of finding his betrothed, Miralaidj, daughter of Wuluwaid and Bunbulama, dead at the hand of Ham Tamdje.

Again Jiritzu relived the pleasure, the terrible pleasure of killing Ham Tamdje himself, with his bare hands. At the thought he felt sweat burst from his face and hands. His legs, where a bullet fired by Ham Tamdje had torn the flesh, throbbed with pain.

He closed his eyes tightly, turned his face from the deck below him to the blackness above, reopened his eyes.

Above him gleamed the constellation Yirrkalla, beneath which *Djanggawul* had made her great tack. The colored stars formed the facial features of the Rainbow Serpent: the pale, yellow-green eyes, the angry white nostrils, the bloodred venomous fangs. And beyond Yirrkalla, fading, fading across the immensity of the heavens, the body of the Rainbow Serpent himself, writhing and curving across the void that separated galaxies.

A drop of sweat fell from Jiritzu's forehead, rolled to the edge of one eye where it stung like a tiny insect, then rolled on, enlarged by a tear.

He looked downward, saw that the work on the deck was completed, the lighter ready for his use. With heavy heart he lowered himself slowly to the deck of *Djanggawul*, avoiding the acrobatic tumbles that had been his great joy since his earliest days on the membrane ships.

He walked slowly across the deck of the great ship, halted before the captain's lighter. A party of sky heroes had assembled at the lighter. Jiritzu examined their faces, found in them a mixture of sadness at the loss of a friend and fellow and resignation at what they knew would follow.

Nurundere was there himself. The captain of *Djanggawul* opened his arms, facing directly toward Jiritzu. He moved his lips in speech, but Jiritzu left his implanted radio turned off. The meaning of Nurundere was clear without words.

Jiritzu came to his captain. They embraced. Jiritzu felt the strong arms of the older man clasp about his shoulders. Then he was released, stepped back.

Beside Nurundere stood Uraroju, first officer of *Djanggawul*. Some junior officer, then, had been left upon the bridge. Uraroju was a younger person than Nurundere, her protective pigmentation still strong, barely beginning to white out; she would have many years before her as a sky hero, would surely become captain of *Djanggawul* with Nurundere's retirement to Yurakosi.

They embraced, Jiritzu for a moment closing his eyes, permitting himself to pretend that Uraroju was his own mother, that he was visiting his old people in their town of Kaitjouga on Yurakosi. The warmth of Uraroju, the feel of her womanhood, comforted Jiritzu. Then they released each other, and he turned to other men and women he would never again see, men and women who must return to Yurakosi with the tale of the tragic things that had transpired between Port Upatoi and Yirrkalla on the outward leg of their sail, and with the tale of the end of Jiritzu.

Watilun he embraced, Watilun the machinist and hero of the battle against the mutineers.

Baime he embraced, a common sailor, Jiritzu's messmate.

Kutjara he embraced, Kutjara with whom he had often swarmed the lines of *Djanggawul*.

Only Dua, kunapi half to Jiritzu of the aranda, spoke in their parting embrace.

Radios mute, Dua spoke in the moments when his close-air envelope and that of Jiritzu were merged, when common speech could be carried without electronic aid.

"Bidjiwara is not here," Dua said. None but Jiritzu could hear this. "The loss of her aranda half Miralaidj is too great for little Bidjiwara to bear. The loss of yourself, Jiritzu, is too great for Bidjiwara. She remains below, weeping alone.

"I too have wept for you, my aranda half, but I could not remain below. I could not forego our parting time."

He kissed Jiritzu on the cheek, his lips brushing the *maraiin*, the swirling scarifications born by all kunapi and aranda, whose meaning he, Dua alone of all Jiritzu's shipmates, understood.

Jiritzu clasped both Dua's hands in his own, saying nothing. Then he turned away and went to inspect the lighter given him by Nurundere. He found all in order, climbed upon the deck of the tiny membrane craft, signaled to the sky heroes on *Djanggawul's* deck.

Watilun himself operated the catapult.

Jiritzu found himself cast from *Djanggawul*, forward and upward from her deck, the distance between the great membrane ship and tiny lighter growing with each moment. He sighed only once, then turned to the task of sailing his new ship.

Above him lay the writhing length of the Rainbow Serpent. By conference with Nurundere and Uraroju over many days it had been settled that Jiritzu would not return with *Djanggawul* to Yurakosi. His act in killing Ham Tamdje was understood. There was no question of trial, no accusation, or even suggestion of crime.

But the tradition of the sky-hero peoples held sacred any passenger on the membrane ships.

Death of meat, membrane-ship passengers, ground squirmers traveling between the stars in the tanks of sky-hero craft instead of sealed in the bellies of massive conventional spacecraft, was almost unknown. There was the half-legendary story of Elyun El-Kumarbis, traveler from the pan-semite empire of O'Earth sailing aboard *Makarata* to Al-ghoul Phi, who had passed as a sky hero and died of space radiation, his body later launched into deep space at his dying request.

And there was the new tragedy of Ham Tamdje and his killer Jiritzu, who could never again be permitted to ride the membrane ships as a sky hero.

Beneath Jiritzu and the lighter, *Djanggawul* dwindled, her great membrane ships bellied out with starwinds, her golden skin reflecting the multicolored lights of the Yirrkalla constellation.

And above Jiritzu, Yirrkalla itself, the serpent face, leering and glowing its brightness.

He erected the masts of the lighter, fixed their bases on the three equilaterally mounted decks of the lighter, climbed each mast in turn, rotating gimbaled spars into position and locking them perpendicular to the masts. The sails, the fine, almost monomolecular membranes that would catch the starwinds and carry the lighter onward, he left furled for the time being.

From the top of a mast he pushed himself gently, parallel with the deck of the lighter. He floated softly to the deck, landing with bent knees to absorb the light impact of his lean frame on the lighter's deck.

He opened the hatch and crawled into the cramped interior of the lighter to check the instruments and supplies he knew were there—the compact rations, the lighter's multiradiational telescope that he would bring with him to the deck and mount for use, the lighter's miniature guidance computer.

Instead, before even switching on the cabin light, he saw two brief reflections of the colored illumination of Yirrkalla—what he knew must be two eyes.

He flicked on his implanted radio and demanded to know the identity of the stowaway.

"Don't be angry, Jiritzu," her voice quivered, "I had to come along."

"Bidjiwara!" he cried.

She launched herself across the cabin, crossing it in an easy, gliding trajectory. She caught his hand in her two, brought it to her face, pressed his palm to the *maraiin*, the graceful scarifications on her cheek.

"Don't be angry with me," she repeated.

He felt himself slump to the deck of the cabin, sitting with his back to the bulkhead, the hatchway leading to the outer deck overhead, light pouring in. He shook himself, turned to look into the face of Bidjiwara, young Bidjiwara, she who was barely entering womanhood, whose voyage on *Djanggawul* was her first as a sky hero, her first offplanet, her first away from Yurakosi.

"Angry? Angry?" Jiritzu repeated stupidly. "No, Bidjiwara, my—my dear Bidjiwara." He brought his face close to hers, felt as she cupped his cheeks in the palms of her hands.

He shook his head. "I couldn't be angry with you. But do you understand? Do you know where this little ship is bound?"

Suddenly he pulled away from her grasp, sprang back to the deck of the lighter, sighted back in the direction of *Djanggawul*. Could he see her as a distant speck? Was that the great membrane ship—or a faint, remote star?

His radio was still on. He stood on the lighter's deck, shouted after *Djanggawul* and her crew. "Dua! Nurundere! Uraroju!"

There was no answer, only a faint, random crackling in his skull, the signals of cosmic radio emanations broadcast by colliding clouds of interstellar gas.

He dropped back through the hatch, into the cabin of the lighter.

He reached for Bidjiwara, took her extended hand, drew her with him back onto the deck of the lighter.

"You know why I am here," he said, half in question, half assertion.

She nodded, spoke softly a word in confirmation.

Still, he said, "I will die. I am here to die."

She made no answer, stood with her face to his sweater, her hands resting lightly against his shoulders. He looked down at her, saw how thin her body was, the contours of womanhood but barely emergent from the skinny, sticklike figure of the boisterous child his dead Miralaidj had loved as a little sister.

Jiritzu felt tears in his eyes.

"I could not go back to Yurakosi," he said. "I am a young man, my skin still fine and black, protecting me from the poison of the stars. I could not become a squirmer, alone in a world of children and ancients.

"I would have thrown myself with all my strength from the top of *Djanggawul*'s highest mast. I would have escaped the ship, fallen forever through space like the corpse of El-Kumarbis.

"Nurundere said no." Jiritzu stopped, looked down at Bidjiwara, at her glossy, midnight hair spilling from beneath her knitted cap, her black, rounded forehead. For a moment he bent and pressed his cheek against the top of her head, then raised his eyes again to the Rainbow Serpent and spoke.

"Nurundere gave me his own ship, his captain's lighter. 'Take the lighter, Jiritzu,' he said. 'I can unload at Port Bralku with the others, by shuttle. I need no glorious captain's barge. Sail on forever,' Nurundere said, 'a better fate than the one awaiting me.'

"You understand, Bidjiwara? I mean to sail the Rainbow Serpent, the tide that flows between the galaxies. I will sail as long as the rations aboard last. I will die on this little ship, my soul will return to the Dreamtime, my body will continue onward, borne by the Rainbow Serpent.

"I will never become a ground crawler. I will never return to Yurakosi. No world will know my tread—ever."

Bidjiwara turned her face, raising her eyes from Jiritzu's ribbed sweater to look directly into his eyes.

"Very well, Jiritzu. I will sail the Rainbow Serpent with you. Where else was there for me to go?"

Jiritzu laughed bitterly. "You are a child. You should have remained aboard *Djanggawul.* You had many years before you as a sky hero. Look at your skin," he said, raising her hand to hold it before them both. No power lights were burning on the little ship, but the colors of Yirrkalla glowed white, green-yellow, bloodred.

"Black, Bidjiwara, black with the precious shield that only our people claim."

"And your own?" she responded.

"My own pigment—yes, I too would have had many more years to play at sky hero. But I killed Ham Tamdje. I broke the sacred trust. I could sail the great membrane ships no longer."

He dropped her hand and walked a few paces away. He stood, his back half-turned to her, and his words were carried to her by the tiny radios implanted in both their skulls.

"And Miralaidj," he almost whispered, "Miralaidj—in the Dreamtime. And her father Wuluwaid in the Dreamtime. No."

He turned and looked upward through naked spars to the glowing stars of Yirrkalla and the Rainbow Serpent. "We should set to work rigging sails," he said.

"I *will* stay with you then," she said. "You will not send me away, send me back."

"Dua knew you were hidden?"

She nodded yes.

"My closest friend, my half, kunapi to my aranda. Dua told me a lie."

"I begged him, Jiritzu."

For a moment he almost glared at her, anger filling his face. "Why do you wish to die?"

She shook her head. "I wish to be with you."

"You will die with me."

"I will return to the Dreamtime with you."

"You believe the old stories."

She shrugged. "We should set to work rigging sails." And scurried away, flung open lockers, drew out furled sheets of nearly monomolecular membrane, scampered up a mast and began fixing the sail to spars.

Jiritzu stood on the deck, watching. Then he crossed to another of the lighter's three equilateral decks and followed the example of Bidjiwara.

He worked until he had completed the rigging of the masts of the deck, then crossed again, to the third of the lighter's decks, opened a locker, drew membrane and clambered to the top of a mast. There he clung, knees gripping the vertical shaft, arms flung over the topmost spar, rigging the sail.

He completed the work, looked across to the farthermost mast, near the stern of the lighter. The Rainbow Serpent drew a gleaming polychromatic backdrop. The mast was silhouetted against the Serpent, and standing on the highest spar, one hand outstretched clinging to the mast, the other arm and leg extended parallel to the spar, was Bidjiwara.

Her envelope of close air shimmered with refraction of the colors of Yirrkalla. Jiritzu clung to the rigging where he had worked, struck still and silent by the beauty of the child. He wondered why she did not see him, then gradually realized, aided by the misty sidereal light of the region, that she stood with her back to him, her face raised to the great tide that flowed between the galaxies, her mind wholly unconcerned with her surroundings and unaware of his presence.

Jiritzu lowered himself silently through the spars and rigging of the lighter, through a hatchway and into the tiny cabin of the lighter. There he prepared a light meal and set it aside, lay down to rest and waited for the return of Bidjiwara.

He may have dozed and seen into the Dreamtime, for he saw the figures of Miralaidj and her father Wuluwaid floating in a vague jumble of shapes and slow, wavering movement. He opened his eyes and saw Bidjiwara lower herself through the hatchway into the cabin, white rope-soled shoes first, white duck trousers clinging close to her long skinny legs and narrow hips, then her black ribbed sweater.

"Our ship has no name," she said.

He pondered for a moment, shrugged, said, "Does it need one?"

"It would be—somehow I think we would be more with our people," Bidjiwara replied.

"Well, if you wish. What shall we make her name?"

"You have no choice?"

"None."

"We will truly sail on the great tide? On the Rainbow Serpent?"

"We are already."

"Then I would call our ship after the sacred fish. Let it bear us to the Dreamtime."

"*Baramundi.*"

"Yes."

"As you wish."

She came and sat by him, her hands folded in her lap. She sat silently.

"Food is ready," he said.

She looked at the tiny table that served in the lighter as work space, desk, and dining table. Jiritzu saw her smile, wondered at the mixture in her face of little child and wise woman. She looked somehow as he thought the Great Mother must look, if only he believed in the Great Mother.

Bidjiwara crossed the small distance and brought two thin slices of hot biscuit. She held them both to Jiritzu. He took one, pressed the other back upon her.

Silently they ate the biscuit.

Afterward she said, "Jiritzu, is there more to do now?"

He said, "We should check our position." He undogged the ship's telescope and carried it to the deck of *Baramundi.*

Bidjiwara helped him to mount it on the gimbaled base that stood waiting for it. Jiritzu sighted on the brightest star in Yirrkalla for reference—it was a gleaming crimson star that marked the end of a fang in the serpent face, that Yurakosi tradition called Blood of Hero.

On the barrel of the telescope where control squares were mounted he tapped all of the radiational senors into life, to cycle through filters and permit the eyepiece to observe the Rainbow Serpent by turns under optical, radio, x-ray, gamma radiation.

He put his eye to the eyepiece and watched the Serpent as it seemed to move with life, its regions responding to the cycling sensitivity of the telescope.

He drew away and Bidjiwara put her eye to the telescope, standing transfixed for minutes until at last she too drew away and turned to Jiritzu.

"The Serpent truly lives," she said. "Is it—a real creature?"

Jiritzu shook his head. "The tides of the galaxies draw each other. The Serpent is a flow of matter. Stars, dust, gas. To ride with it would mean a journey of billions of years to reach the next of its kind. To sail the starwinds that fill the Rainbow Serpent, we will reach marvelous speed. As long as we can sail our craft, we can tack from wind to wind.

"And once we have gone to the Dreamtime, *Baramundi* will float on, on the tide, along the Rainbow Serpent. Someday she may beach on some distant shore."

He looked at Bidjiwara, smiled, repeated his statement.

Bidjiwara replied, "And if she does not?"

"Then she may be destroyed in some way, or simply—drift forever. Forever."

Jiritzu saw the girl stretch and yawn. She crossed the cabin and drew him down alongside the bulkhead, nestled up to him and went to sleep.

He lay with her in his arms, wondering at her trust, watching the play of sidereal light that reflected through the hatchway and illuminated her face dimly.

He extended one finger and gently, gently traced the *maraiin* on her cheek, wondering at its meaning. He pressed his face to her head again, pulled away her knitted cap and let her hair tumble loose, feeling its softness with his own face, smelling the odor of her hair.

He too slept.

They awoke together, stirring and stretching and looked into each other's face and laughed. They used the lighter's sanitary gear and nibbled a little breakfast and went on deck. Together they checked *Baramundi*'s rigging, took sightings with her multiradiational telescope, and fed information into her little computer.

The computer offered course settings in tiny, glowing display lights and Jiritzu and Bidjiwara reset *Baramundi*'s sails.

They sat on deck, bathed in the perpetual twilight of the Rainbow Serpent's softly glowing colors.

They spoke of their childhoods on Yurakosi, of their old people, their skins whited out by years of sailing the membrane ships, retired to the home planet to raise the children while all the race's vigorous adults crewed the great ships, sailed between the stars carrying freight and occasional passengers sealed inside their hulls, laughing at the clumsy craft and clumsy crews of all others than the aranda and the kunapi.

They climbed through the rigging of *Baramundi*, shinnying up masts lightly, balancing on spars, occasionally falling—or leaping—from the ship's heights, to drop gently, gently back onto her deck.

They ate and drank the smallest amounts they could of the lighter's provisions, tacitly stretching the supplies as far as they could be stretched, carefully recycling to add still more to the time they could continue.

They lay on *Baramundi*'s deck sometimes, when the rest time they had agreed upon came, Bidjiwara nestling against the taller Jiritzu, falling asleep as untroubledly as a young child, Jiritzu wondering over and over at this girl who had come to die with him, who asked few questions, who lived each hour as if it were the beginning of a long and joyous life rather than the final act of a tragedy.

Jiritzu felt very old.

He was nearly twenty by the ancient, arbitrary scale of age carried to the star worlds from O'Earth, the scale of the seasons and the years in old Arnhem Land in the great desert of their ancestral home. Six years older than Bidjiwara, he had traveled the star routes for five, had sailed the membrane ships across tens of billions of miles in that time.

And Bidjiwara asked little of him. They were more playmates than—than anything else, he thought.

"Tell me of El-Kumarbis," she said one day, perched high on a spar above *Baramundi*'s deck.

"You know all about him," Jiritzu replied.

"Where is he now?"

Jiritzu shrugged, exasperated. "Somewhere beyond Al-ghoul, no one knows where. He was buried in space."

"What if we find his body?" Bidjiwara shivered.

"Impossible."

"Why?"

"In infinite space? What chance that two objects moving at random will collide?"

"No?"

He shook his head.

"Could the computer find him?"

He shrugged. "If we knew exactly when he was buried, and where, and his trajectory and speed and momentum . . . No, it's still impossible."

"Dinnertime," she said. "You wait here, I'll fix it."

She came back with the customary biscuits and a jar filled with dark fluid. Jiritzu took the jar, held it high against the ambient light—they seldom used any of *Baramundi*'s power lights.

"Wine," Bidjiwara said.

He looked amazed.

"I found a few capsules in the ship's supplies. You just put one in some water."

They ate and drank. The wine was warm, its flavor soft. They sprawled on the deck of *Baramundi* after the biscuits were gone, passing the jar back and forth, slowly drinking the wine.

When it was gone Bidjiwara nestled against Jiritzu; for once, instead of sleeping she lay looking into his face, holding her hands to the sides of his head.

She said his name softly, then flicked off her radio and pressed her lips close to his neck so their air envelopes were one, the sound carried directly from her lips to his ear, and whispered his name again.

"Bidjiwara," he said, "you never answered why you came on board *Baramundi*."

"To be with you, Jiritzu," she said.

"Yes, but why? Why come to die with me?"

"Tall Jiritzu," she said, "strong Jiritzu. You saw me aboard *Djanggawul*, you were kind to me but as you are kind to children. Men never know, only women know love."

He laughed, not cruelly. "You're only—"

"A woman," she said.

"And you want—?"

Now she laughed at him. "You man, you mighty man. You don't understand that all men are the children of women."

She drew away from him, slid her black ribbed sweater over her head and dropped it to the deck. He put his hands onto her naked back, trembling, then slowly slid them around her, touching her little, half-developed breasts, fondling her soft nipples with his hands.

She buried her forehead in the side of his neck, whispered against his throat, "For this, Jiritzu, I came aboard *Baramundi* for this."

He ran his thumbs down her breastbone, to her navel, to her white duck trousers, and peeled them down, and took her.

And the next day they were nearly out of biscuit and they went on half rations to make their supplies last longer.

They played children's games, shouting and chasing each other up and down the lighter's masts.

They leaped and sailed from the decks, past the membrane sails, into the emptiness, then hung for a moment and fell back, gently, to *Baramundi*.

Jiritzu leaped too hard, too high, and feared that he had broken from the ship. He looked up—down—into the coils of the Rainbow Serpent. He felt himself revolving slowly, helplessly hanging in the emptiness, alone and unshielded except by the close air his generator made and the protection of the pigment he carried in his skin.

He thought to cry for help, then held back. If he was afloat, Bidjiwara could not help him. He turned slowly, facing toward *Baramundi*, her membranes bellied with stellar wind, her deck reflecting the lights of the Serpent; he could not see Bidjiwara.

He turned slowly, facing toward the Rainbow Serpent, feeling as if he could fall forever into its colored bands, its long coils stretching no lesser distance than the span between galaxies.

He turned slowly, revolving on the axis of his own body, feeling no motion himself but watching the stars and the Serpent and *Baramundi* the sacred fish revolve slowly around him, wheeling, wheeling, when his out-flung arm struck an object as hard and cold as the ultimate ice of a deadstar world.

He recoiled, spun involuntarily, stared.

It was—yes.

He looked back toward *Baramundi*, revolved using his own limbs as counterweights, placed himself between the corpse and the lighter, and pressed gently with the soles of his rope-soled shoes against the hard, frigid corpse.

Slowly he drifted back toward *Baramundi*—and, wheeling again as he drifted, saw the corpse drifting away, upward or downward into the lights of the Rainbow Serpent.

As he approached *Baramundi* he pondered whether or not to tell Bidjiwara of his find. Finally he told her—the incredible happenstance had occurred.

Later they crept to the farthermost deck for their loving, then back into the tiny cabin to sleep.

And soon *Baramundi*'s supplies were exhausted, and still Jiritzu and Bidjiwara continued. Their water remained, and a few of the capsules. They had wine from time to time. They gave less effort to running the ship, ceased to play in the rigging, ceased to leap.

The wound in Jiritzu's leg resumed its throbbing intermittently. He would rub it, or Bidjiwara would rub it for him, and the pain would ease.

They made love, it seemed, with increasing frequency. The sensations of their couplings seemed to increase as lack of nourishment drew their bodies ever tighter, ever more acutely into awareness of each other.

They lay together most of the time, seldom dressing fully.

They drank water only, their wine capsules exhausted.

They slept increasingly.

In *Baramundi*'s cabin Jiritzu fed telescopic data into the lighter's computer, read the responses displayed on its little illuminated screen. After the acclimatization of his eyes to none but sidereal light, even the miniature display lights were dazzling: his eyes pulsed with after-images for minutes following the exercise.

It was difficult to climb from the cabin back onto the deck.

Bidjiwara waited for him there, barefoot, sitting on the deck with her wrists clasped around her knees, wearing only her white trousers and black knitted cap. She smiled a welcome to him, asked a question wordlessly.

"Here," he said with a shrug. "Here is where we are. As we have been. Riding the Rainbow Serpent. Riding the tide. Sailing the starwinds."

He felt dizzy for a moment, reached out with one hand to steady himself against the telescope mount, then sank to a squat beside Bidjiwara.

She put her arms around him and he lay on the deck, his head in her lap. He looked up into her face. She was Bidjiwara the lovely child, Miralaidj her aranda half, she was Jiritzu's own mother on Yurakosi, the Great Mother.

He opened and closed his eyes, unable to tell which woman this was.

He reached and traced the *maraiin* on her cheek.

She nodded, began speaking softly, telling him the meaning of the scarifications.

When she had finished he took her hand, held it against his chest, and slowly told her the meaning of his own *maraiin*. He spoke with closed eyes, opened them when he felt a drop of wetness, saw her weeping softly, drew her face down to his own to kiss.

She lay down beside him and they embraced gently, then both slept.

After that they paid less attention to *Baramundi*'s needs. Jiritzu and Bidjiwara grew weaker. They slept more, confined their activity to occasional short walks on *Baramundi*'s decks. Both of them grew thinner, lighter. Their growing weakness seemed almost to be offset by the decreasing demands of the ship's artificial gravity.

They lay on deck for hours, watching the glow of the Rainbow Serpent. They were far beyond the Serpent's head now, the stars of Yirrkalla clustered now into a meaningless sparkler jumble far, far astern of *Baramundi*.

Jiritzu was awake, had taken a sparse sip of their little remaining water, left Bidjiwara to doze where she lay, her hair a mourning wreath circling her emaciated features. Jiritzu made his way unsteadily to the prow of *Baramundi*, bracing himself against masts and small stanchions as he walked.

He sighted through the ship's telescope, enjoying in a faint, detached manner the endless, kaleidoscopic changes of the Rainbow Serpent's multiradiational forms. At length he turned away from the scope and looked back toward Bidji-wara. He could not tell if she was breathing. He could not tell for a certainty who she was.

He returned to the telescope, tapped its power squares to cause it to super-impose its multiple images rather than run them in sequence. He gazed, rapt, at the Serpent for a time, then swung the scope overhead, sweeping back and forth across the sky above *Baramundi*.

He settled on a black speck that floated silhouetted against the glow of the Serpent. For a while he watched it grow larger.

He turned from the telescope back to the deck of the lighter. Bidjiwara had wakened and risen; she was walking slowly, slowly toward him.

In the glow of the Rainbow Serpent her emaciation was transformed to a fine perception that etched every line, every muscle beneath her skin. She wore sweater and trousers; Jiritzu could see her high breasts, the ribbed sweater con-forming to their sharp grace, her nipples standing as points of reference for the beauty of her torso.

Her white trousers managed to retain their fit despite her starvation; Jiritzu discerned the lines of her thighs, the pubic swell over her crotch.

Her face, always thin, seemed all vertical planes now, forehead and temple, nostril and cheek. The ridges of her brows, the lines of her mouth were as if drawn on her face.

Her eyes seemed to have gained an intense brightness.

As she crossed the deck to Jiritzu she gained in strength and steadiness.

She held her hands toward him, smiling, and he felt his own strength returning to him. He took the steps needed to come to her, reached and took her two hands, clasped them in his. They embraced, calling each other's name.

The dark figure of Elyun El-Kumarbis dropped onto the deck of *Baramundi*. He strode to Jiritzu and Bidjiwara.

"Lovers!" he said. "Sky heroes!"

They turned to him, arms still around each other. Each extended a hand to him, felt his: cold, cold.

"All my years," the O'Earther said, "I wanted no thing but to sail a membrane ship. To be a sky hero."

"Yes," Jiritzu said, "you are known to all sky heroes, Elyun El-Kumarbis. Your fame spans the galaxy."

"And where do you sail, sky heroes?"

"We sail the tide, we sail the Rainbow Serpent."

"Aboard your ship?"

"*Baramundi* has brought us this far, but no farther. It is fit now for us to return to the Dreamtime."

Elyun El-Kumarbis nodded. "May I—may I greet you as brother and sister sky heroes?" he asked.

"Yes," answered Jiritzu.

"Yes," answered Bidjiwara.

Elyun El-Kumarbis kissed them each on the cheek, on the *maraiin* scarifica-tions of each. And his kiss was cold, cold.

Full of strength Jiritzu and Bidjiwara sprang to the spars of *Baramundi*'s high-est mast, scrambled up lines to the topmost spar of the lighter.

They looked back at Elyun El-Kumarbis, who stood wondering beside the ship's telescope.

They took each other's hands, dropped into place on the topmost spar, and together sprang with the full strength of their sky heroes' legs, toughened and muscled by years of training in the rigging of membrane ships.

They flew up from the spar, up from *Baramundi* the sacred fish, and, looking back, saw the fish flip his tail once in farewell.

They peered ahead of themselves, into the Rainbow Serpent, saw it writhe toward the far galaxies, heard its hissing voice urging, welcoming them.

They laughed loudly, loudly, feeling strength, warmth, and joy. They plunged on and on, skimming the tide of the Rainbow Serpent, feeling the strength of the aranda, of all Yurakosi, of all sky heroes, mighty in their blood.

They threw their arms around each other, laughing for joy, and sped to the Rainbow Serpent, to the galaxies beyond the galaxies, to the Dreamtime forever.